Louis sieur de Pontis, Charles Cotton

Memoirs of the Sieur de Pontis

Who served in the army six and fifty years, under King Henry IV. Lewis the XIII. and

Lewis the XIV. Containing many remarkable passages relating to the war, the court,

and the government of those princes.

Louis sieur de Pontis, Charles Cotton

Memoirs of the Sieur de Pontis
Who served in the army six and fifty years, under King Henry IV. Lewis the XIII. and Lewis the XIV. Containing many remarkable passages relating to the war, the court, and the government of those princes.

ISBN/EAN: 9783337175436

Printed in Europe, USA, Canada, Australia, Japan

Cover: Foto ©Raphael Reischuk / pixelio.de

More available books at **www.hansebooks.com**

MEMOIRS

OF THE

Sieur De PONTIS;

Who ſerved in the Army Six and fifty Years,

UNDER

King *Henry* IV. *Lewis* the XIII. and *Lewis* the XIV.

CONTAINING

Many remarkable paſſages relating to the WAR, the COURT, and the GOVERNMENT of thoſe Princes.

Faithfully Engliſhed

By *CHARLES COTTON*, Eſq;

IMPRIMATUR,

July 7. 1693.   *Charnock Heron.*

LONDON,

Printed by *F. Leach*, for *James Knapton*, at the *Crown* in St. *Paul's* Church-yard,   MDCXCIV.

To His GRACE

THE

Duke of ORMOND.

May it please your Grace,

IF a Present so mean as this Book, were worth a Dispute of Title, none could pretend to so good a one, as YOUR GRACE. The Subject, and Character of the Person, are suitable in some, though a much inferiour degree, to that Generous Gallantry and Exemplary Courage, by which you have attracted the Esteem and Admiration of all Mankind; and so Eminently and Early signaliz'd your self; as not only to Answer, but Exceed what the World expected from a Person so descended. For it is an Honour peculiar to YOUR GRACE, that as No Man ever received more Lustre from Noble Ancestors, so None ever reflected it back again upon them, with greater Advantage.

But that, MY LORD, which gives YOU an Inherent Right to these *Memoirs*, is, that they were put into our own Language, by the particular Choice, and Recommendation of Your Illustrious Grandfather; And therefore the Heir of His Honours and His Virtues may so justly challenge this Address, that it were a Rudeness at least, if not a Robbery, to appropriate it to any other Person. The Sieur *de Pontis* therefore

for

for himself, and **I** for the Translator (my deceased Father) beg leave to plead Succession and Descent. And I am very sensible, that after the Approbation of one such great Person already, there remains no farther possible Addition of Honour to these Writings, but only to have that Judgment confirm'd, by YOUR GRACES Acceptance and Protection.

These Considerations, My LORD, give me the Confidence to hope, that YOUR GRACE will pardon a Man, who presumes to lay at Your Feet, what is upon so many accounts your own; and who, in so doing, is proud to tell the World, that he is

My LORD,

YOUR GRACE's most Obedient

and most Devoted Servant,

Beresford Cotton.

THE

THE
Publiſhers Preface.

THat the Reader may have no ſcruple left upon him, con-cerning the following Papers, I ſhall beg his leave to remove two Objections, which it is not improbable may be raiſed againſt them.

The firſt relates to the ſubject of the Book it ſelf, which perhaps may ſuffer in ſome peoples eſteem, becauſe the Perſon whoſe Life is deſcribed, attained to no higher a Poſt, than that of a Captain in the Guards, and Commiſſary General of the Swiſſe Troops. This, tho it may ſeem a reaſonable diſadvantage, yet, when well exa-min'd, is what men ſhould rather be aſham'd to pretend: For the bottom of it all is that vulgar Error, that Titles and Preferments are the only marks of Merit; as if a mans Accompliſhments and his Valour, were not to be meaſured by any inſtances of Wiſdom and Gallantry in his actions; but by the Rewards and Advancements he hath met with, in conſideration of them. Which is in effect to make unſucceſsful Vertue none at all; and to ſet up Chance and Partiality, a lucky Hit, or a powerful Intereſt, for the only Standard to judge men by. Upon theſe terms indeed, the Sieur de Pontis is like to find but little reſpect; but if True Courage and Conduct, inviolable Fidelity, and generous Friendſhip, be ſtill Characters of any figure in Story, theſe Memoirs may have the advantage of many more pompous Writers. And it would be a double hardſhip, that not only his Fortunes, while he was living, but his Memory now too, ſhould ſuffer for thoſe diſappointments, which were chiefly owing to his Vertue and Conſtancy, and the

a

Spightful

Spightful Resentments of an Arbitrary and Intriguing Statesman.

I own that Persons of the first Quality are more entertaining subjects, as their Vertues and their Vices commonly bear proportion to their high station. They have it most in their power to be eminently Good or Bad; and consequently such relations fill our minds with greater and more surprizing Ideas. But since the principal Benefit of History is to present us with Examples, proper to be imitated, or to be declined, those of a middle size must needs be exceeding useful, because they fall more within the compass of mankind. The actions of persons a great deal above us, are matter of Contemplation rather than Practice; for when we have done all we can, mens Virtues are suited and peculiar to their Conditions in this World. We must be content with the things in our own Sphere, and consequently are best instructed by Examples that come within our Imitation. We may admire and gaze at those that stand higher, and shall do well to make their good Qualities our Patterns, because there is no such inequality in Souls; but if we hope to exert them in the same manner, and make their way of Living and Management a Rule for our own behaviour, while we want their Fortunes and their Advantages, we may as well pretend to fly without Wings. Our Ruine in this case will be as certain, and our Folly as ridiculous, as the Frogs in the Fable, which swell'd, and would fain have come up to the bigness of the Ox, but burst in the vain attempt. There must go something more than Nature to the making a very great man; Just worth is therefore to be duly regarded where-ever we find it; and a noble Soul is not the less, but really the more so, when it shines by its own light, without any of that borrowed lustre, which is so often owing to Greatness and Fortune.

These,

The Publishers PREFACE.

These, and possibly some other and better Considerations, might incline some persons of Great Quality, and particularly One, whose Judgment all the World knew, and whose Memory they will ever honour, to propose the putting this Book into our own Language: and it were unreasonable to doubt the good acceptance of a Work, recommended by so Judicious a person, and performed by so known, and so faithful a hand.

But because this performance too may be called in some question, I will here give a very brief account of the Translation it self; which is the other Objection I suppose these Papers liable too.

Mr. Cotton began it some six Months before his Death, and at his leisure hours had made so considerable a progress, that some of the first Part was transcribed fair for the Press. The Papers, left in the Hands of one of his Children, lay neglected for some Years; till at last, a Relation happening to read some of them, undertook to see them corrected, and perfected for the World, as you now have them. Had the Author himself been living, they had appeared long ago; or had Good Fortune directed to the perusing them sooner, there had been no place for an objection, of coming out five Years after the Author's Decease. I know what injuries Men receive sometimes from Posthumous Pieces, and were not this genuine, the most part now by me, under his own hand, and such as I know to have been certainly intended for the Publick, I durst not have made bold with his Memory and his Name. I would not have done it with any Man's, but especially not with his; which hath suffered too much already, by the indirect Publication of another Piece.

The only thing I shall say, (though not the only one that deserves to be said) on this occasion, is, that if the Person, who disposed of those Poems to the Booksellers, had consulted Mr. Cotton's Relations, as he ought to have done, both his Memory and

the

the World had been much more obliged to him. For by theſe un-
generous Proceedings, he hath obſtructed the publiſhing of a Col-
lection very different from that; and well choſen by the Author,
with a Preface, prepared by himſelf, and all copied out for the
Preſs. This digreſſion I thought due to the Character of a Perſon,
whoſe other Performances have been ſo well received, who knew
how to diſtinguiſh between writing for his own Diverſion, and
the Entertainment of others, and had a better Judgment, than to
thruſt any thing abroad, unworthy himſelf or his Readers. I only
beg pardon for being in one ſenſe very unſeaſonable; for in truth,
the World ought to have been undeceived in this point a great deal
ſooner, and by an Advertiſement very different from this.

MEMOIRS

OF THE
Sieur De PONTIS.

PART I.

BOOK I.

Containing what paſt during the time that the Sieur De
Pontis *was a Cadet in the Regiment of Guards. He
is forc'd to retire into* Holland, *from whence he
returns, after having run a great hazard of his life.
He comes back into* France, *and ſuſtains a Siege in
the Caſtle of* Savigny.

I. BEing grown up to fourteen years of age, and my Father and
Mother being both dead, I found in my ſelf an extraordinary
inclination to a Souldiers life, and preſently reſolved to begin
to learn the Trade. I accordingly ſerv'd a year in the Regiment of
Bonne, where I carried a Carabine, the Musket being as yet not there
in uſe. After which I returned back to *Pontis*, to try if my elder Brother, who (according to the cuſtom of the Country, had the whole
eſtate of the Family) would be diſpoſed to do ſomething for me, and
ſtay'd ſome months with him; where, finding that he would only employ me in the care of Husbandry, a thing that I found my ſelf very averſe to, and unfit for, I took up a reſolution to go to *Paris*,
there my ſelf to labour my own Advancement in the World, as well
as I could. I therefore entreated of my Brother ſo much as was neceſſary for me in order to this deſign: but his coldneſs compell'd me to
ſeek out to my other Relations, and particularly to addreſs my ſelf to
an Aunt I had, who had a great affection for me. From her I received
all I could deſire for my Journey; and from an Unkle, who alſo lov'd
me very well, a little Horſe; and with this younger Brothers equipage,
after having taken leave of my friends, I ſet forward for *Paris*. Going
by *Grenoble*, which is two days Journey from *Pontis*, I thought
B   my

my felf oblig'd to go wait upon Monfieur *de L'Ediguieres*, to whom I had the honour to be a-kin; I was by him receiv'd with great demonftrations of bounty and favour; and he was pleas'd to ask me what was my defign in the Journey I had in hand; I made anfwer, That I had a defire to learn to become an honeft man, and to render my felf fit to make him a tender of my fervice. He was pleas'd with my anfwer, and being willing to ferve me in my defign, gave me a Letter of Recommendation to Monfieur *de Crequy*, his Son-in-law, who was then in treaty about the Regiment of Guards, to receive me into them, as a Kinfman of his, and a young Gentleman for whom he had a particular efteem. But Monfieur *de Crequy* did not fo foon conclude his bargain, which hindred him from executing the order he had receiv'd. In the mean time, the violent defire I had to enter into the Regiment of Guards, as the beft School wherein to learn the Trade I had fo great a paffion for, pufht me on to go and prefent my felf to Monfieur *de Grillon*, who was Camp-mafter of it; of him to entreat the favour, that I might be there receiv'd. But Monfieur *de Grillon*, who would not allow that any one fhould enter fo young, told me that he could not admit me; he accompanied his denyal neverthelefs with the greateft teftimony of friendfhip that it was poffible for him ever to give; promifing that he would entertain me a year in his own houfe, till I fhould be ftrong enough to enter the body. And accordingly he fail'd not fome time after to receive me into it, with a particular affection, which he alfo continued to me ever fince, as in the progrefs of thefe Memoirs I fhall make appear.

II. Seeing that Acts of Generofity ought to be recorded for example to other, I think my felf oblig'd in this place, to give an account of one, which Monfieur *de Vitry*, Captain of the *Guards du Corps*, practic'd in my favour, at the time when I was a Cadet in the Regiment of Guards under King *Henry* IV. Being one day at *Melun*, I went a hunting, with three of my Comrades in the Forreft of *Fontain-bleau*. At the entring into the Forreft we were aware of a great Stag, that came running directly towards us. The ardour of the Chafe tranfported me fo far on the fudden, that without demur, or giving my felf the leifure to confider whether this Beaft was priviledg'd or no, I prefently difcharg'd my Fufee upon him, and laid him dead upon the place. I prefently charg'd again for fear of furprize, and immediately we heard the Hounds that were in chafe of him, and faw a Cavalier, who was Monfieur *de Vitry*, galloping towards us, who began to cry out to us, So-ho, Cadets, down with your Arms: but feeing we were not difpos'd to obey him, he drew his Piftol, and I prefenting my Fufee againft him at the fame time, call'd out to him to approach no nearer, and not to compel me to fire upon him. It had been a great rafhnefs in him to have advanc'd, and he took the wifeft courfe, which was to turn about, and go make his complaint to the King. In the mean time, as it was not fafe for us to ftay any longer there, we retired as privately as we could to *Melun*; and very well believing that this affair might have fome ill confequences, I askt leave of my Captain, Monfieur *de Brifac*, to make a little Journey to *Paris*, where I pretended to have fome bufinefs. My three other Comrades alfo found out one way or other to abfent themfelves from the Company. So that the King having given order to the Officers of the Regiment, to make a review in the prefence of Monfieur *de Vitry,*

Vitry, that he might take notice of the Offenders, he could never dif-cover any one of us. Yet was I, for all that, under some suspicion, by reason that I was known to be a little eager of the Chace; but having obtain'd my leave in due form, they could not well conclude me absolutely guilty : and so at last this affair past over, without much more talk of it.

About three months after it fell out, that I being upon Duty before the Gate of the *Louvre*, Monsieur *de Vitry* passing by, knew me again, and immediately applying himself to me, O ho! Cadet, said he, you are my man! Do you remember the Stag at *Fontain-bleau*? In good earnest I was very much surpriz'd at his Complement, especially in the post I then was, which I was by no means to quit; so that having no other way left me but that of entreaty and submission, I said to him, in the most humble and moving Accent that I could form my voice to, Ah Sir, would you ruine me ? Have compassion upon a poor Cadet as I am. He answer'd me after the most obliging manner in the world ; 'Tis enough that I know you, said he, and I am so far from being the cause of your ruine, that I resolve to serve you : Come see me, I give you my word, upon the faith of a Gentleman, no harm shall befall you. In the mean time, so soon as he was gone from me, I not yet having the honour to know him, and the apprehension wherein I was, not permitting me to repose too much confidence upon his word, I made my Corporal believe that I had some inconvenience upon me, that would not suffer me to continue any longer upon my Post; and withal intreated, he would put some other in my place, which he did, without suspecting any thing, and I kept my self afterwards upon my guard. I deferr'd three or four days going to wait upon Monsieur *de Vitry*, fearing always, and not being able, after the fault I had committed, to present my self before him ; but at last I resolv'd to go one morning, and took two or three of my Comrades along with me ; we found him abed, and being enter'd the Room, I made him my Complement with a thousand excuses, for the misfortune that had befaln me ; assuring him that I was extreamly troubled, that I had carried my self so like a Beast, towards a person of his quality, and one to whose generosity I stood obliged for my life. He was pleased to receive me with great testimonies of affection, and embracing me, told me, with the greatest civility in the world, that he was extreamly glad to be acquainted with me, and that he would make use of me upon occasions ; and supposing rightly, that I might stand in need of Money, he presented me with some Pistols, and compell'd me to receive them, telling me that a Souldier ought to refuse nothing.

III. About the same time, I had a Contest of an extraordinary kind, with a friend of mine, and was very near bringing my self into a scurvy circumstance, by insisting upon the punctilio's of generosity and friendship, in his behalf. His name was *Esperance*, and he was the natural Son of the famous Monsieur *de Grillon*. This Gentleman having fought a Duel, after a very severe Edict of the King, that expresly Interdicted all Duels, he was seiz'd, and condemn'd to be shot to death. He, according to the custom, conjur'd me, being his intimate friend, to be his Godfather, (as they call it) and to give him his first shot : but I, who could not suffer my friendship to be govern'd by this cruel, and false Custom, plainly told him, That for the very reason, that I was his

int?

intimate Friend, I would not be his Executioner ; and that absolutely I could not kill the man I lov'd. He still urg'd me to do it with great earnestness and importunity, and gave me several instances to induce me to give him that last testimony of friendship ; telling me, that it was a Custom, and practic'd by the most faithful friends : I resolutely reply'd, that I did not follow the fashion in my Friendship ; and that it was in vain to press me to do an act, I could not think on without horrour, and that I would never do it. Our Lieutenant-Collonel, Monsieur *de Sainte Colombe*, and Monsieur *de Brisac*, my Captain, did both of them command me to do what my friend requir'd ; but I roundly answer'd them, That the friendship I had for him would not suffer me to do it : They then proceeded to threats, telling me, That if I did not obey Justice, I should be executed in the Criminals stead. I made answer with the same constancy, That I could not obey in this particular, and that I was ready to dye in my friends stead, rather than set my hand to his death ; and thereupon was presently committed to Prison, and went without regret, for so good a cause. But they were satisfied in the end, that my refusal in this affair, did not proceed from humour, or obstinacy, but a true foundation of friendship, which will not permit a generous man to take away the life of his friend, in obedience to a false and ridiculous custom ; so that I was soon set at liberty ; and tho the rules of military discipline oblig'd the Officers to reprimand me for my disobedience, they made it notwithstanding appear, that they had me not in less esteem upon this account, but commended the resolution I had manifested in this affair.

IV. I had after this an opportunity to be known of the King, and some of the greatest men of the Court, by an accident, which though very inconsiderable in it self, was not however disadvantageous to such a younger Brother as I. King *Henry* IV. being at *Fontain-bleau*, had some jealousie of one of the principal Lords of his Court, about a Lady then in the Castle, and suspected that he went privately to her. But he making those visits with so much circumspection that he could never be discovered, after the King had contriv'd the means by which he might be surprized, he concluded at last to choose out a person that was faithful, subtle, and bold, to execute his design, and to deliver him from the disquiet he was in upon that subject. He gave order therefore to Monsieur *Belingan*, one of the principal Gentlemen of his Bed-chamber, and the great Confident of all his Intrigues, to find him out two such as he design'd, to plant upon two Avenues, where they might stand as Spies upon him, of whom his Majesty had the suspicion. Monsieur *de Belingan* having accordingly spoke to Monsieur *de Sainte Colombe*, Lieutenant Collonel of the Regiment of Guards, he immediately commanded the eldest Corporal of his own Company, to choose him out two Souldiers, such as were capable of executing the Kings design. The lot fell upon me, and the Corporal having chosen me for one that was to be presented to his Majesty, he carried me to his Lieutenant Collonel, who brought me to Monsieur *Belingan*, who told me, that an occasion presented it self very advantageous for me, such as was likely to make my fortune, and bring me to the knowledge of the King, in doing him a considerable service. 'Tis believ'd, said he to me, that you neither want Courage nor Conduct to carry on this affair ; and it very much concerns you to make it appear that we are not deceived in our choice.

How

How well difposed a young man as I was muft be, when I heard talk of the Kings fervice, and my own fortune, I leave every one to judge. I return'd Monfieur *de Belingan* my moft humble thanks, affuring him, that I fhould never forget the favour he did me in procuring me fo advantageous an occafion of making my fortunes; affuring him in the mean time, that I would faithfully acquit my felf of the commands he fhould pleafe to give me. He thereupon acquainted me with the Kings pleafure, which was, that I fhould at night poft my felf Centinel in fome part of the Gallery, where I could not be feen, and from whence I might fee him, who his Majefty fufpected, about eleven of the Clock would go into a certain Chamber of the Caftle: That I fhould dog him every where, till he came back to the Chamber where he lay, to the end one might be certain who he was; and becaufe he might open and fhut feveral Doors, to hinder me from following him, he deliver'd me a Key that would open them all; adding to his Inftructions, That I fhould fatisfie my felf with following him, without faying any thing to him; but be fure never to lofe fight of him, till he was return'd into his own Chamber: I again affur'd Monfieur *de Belingan*, that he might wholly rely upon me for this affair, and that I foon hop'd to give him the fatisfaction he defired.

I went upon that inftant to look out the poft moft proper for my defign, and having chofen it, return'd, expecting the hour that I was to go thither, which was, when the King went into his Bed-chamber, where I was told this Gentleman ufually was. I return'd then about eleven of the Clock into the Gallery, and pofted my felf in an obfcure place, where I could not be perceiv'd. About an hour after, I heard my Gentleman come, but being there was no light, one could not know him. I gave him not time to enter into the Chamber, whither he was going, becaufe I follow'd him, and he hearing me, turn'd off into another Gallery, into which he flipt fo foftly, and fo quick, that I had very near loft him in the dark. This oblig'd me to mend my pace, that I might follow him clofer, and made him doubt that he was dogg'd; fo that entring into the Stagge Gallery, he fhut the door after him, hoping there to give me a ftop. But he was very much aftonifht to hear the door prefently open again behind him, and to fee himfelf follow'd, as before. To difengage himfelf then from him by whom he was fo clofely purfu'd, he took a hundred turns in the Courts and bafe Courts, and at laft whipt on a fudden into the Garden; the door of which he clapt hard to, thinking by this means to efcape from me, and to hide himfelf in fome place or other from my fight. His defign fucceeded well enough at firft, for having convey'd himfelf into a great and thick Pallifade that caft a great fhade, and conceal'd him from the light of the Moon, I faw no creature when I came into the Garden. I began to fall into great fears, and ran up and down the Garden like mad, without being able to difcover any thing at all: but when I was almoft in defpair, and enrag'd at my felf, that I fhould let him efcape fo, returning towards the Garden-door, and prying into the thickeft of the neareft Pallifadoes, I there efpied him; and refolv'd, that I might lofe him no more, to follow him clofe at the heels. He perceiving himfelf to be thus difcover'd, in a great rage came out of his corner, making as though he would walk a great pace, but on a fudden turn'd about, faying aloud; *Ha! this is too much!* and at the fame time made an offer to draw his Sword. I ftopt, and ftood my ground without fpeaking a word, as I had been commanded.

C   And

And withal gave him to underſtand by my poſture, that I was reſolv'd to defend my ſelf, if urg'd to it. This Lord judging by my countenance, that I was not of a humour to ſuffer my ſelf to be ill us'd, took ſome few turns more in the Garden, after which he came into the Gallery again, and from thence retir'd into his Chamber ; at the door of which I remain'd, as if upon Duty. But I was not long alone in this place, for about two hours after midnight, Monſieur *de Belingan* came to ſeek me out, to know what diſcovery I had made : I began to give him a relation of all that had paſt, when the King himſelf appeared at the end of the Gallery, in his Night-gown, with a little Lanthorn in his hand. We immediately advanc'd towards him, when, though I had never before had the honour to ſpeak to the King, I endeavour'd to give him the beſt account of my Commiſſion I could, and related to him, without any confuſion, all the walks I had had, and all the turns and returns that I had caus'd this Lord to make ; and when I repreſented to him in downright terms, the fury with which he ſally'd out from the Palliſade, and had made a ſhew of drawing his Sword, the King interrupting me askt, But what wouldſt thou have done, Cadet, if he had ſaln upon thee ? I ſhould have defended my ſelf, Sir, ſaid I, for your Majeſty had commanded me not to ſpeak, 'tis true, but not that I ſhould not defend my ſelf ; at which his Majeſty burſting out a laughing, ſaid I believe thou wouldſt, by what I ſee in thee. After which he would have me more particularly act before him both the poſture and action of this Lord ; which I alſo attempted to do, after the moſt lively and pleaſant manner that I poſſibly could ; and that I thought would beſt pleaſe him. Which little Farce being ended, he told me that he was perfectly ſatisfied with my ſervice, and promis'd me that he would bear it in mind. From thenceforward Monſieur *de Belingan* had a particular affection for me, by reaſon of the manner after which I had receiv'd, and executed the propoſition he had made to me ; and that he might have more room to ſerve me with the King, he askt me if I had not had Relations, that had done his Majeſty ſome conſiderable ſervice. To which I nam'd to him, amongſt others, an Unkle I had, call'd *d'Eſtoublou*, who had bravely ſignaliz'd himſelf in the Wars of *Provence* ; from whence he afterwards took occaſion to tell the King, ſpeaking of me, that this Cadet began to follow the ſteps of his Unkle, who had done his Majeſty very particular ſervices, and whoſe name was *d'Eſtoublou*. The King ſaid he remembred him very well, adding, that he was a very brave man, and had done him great ſervices ; and gave Monſieur *Belingan* order at the ſame time to give me a hundred Crowns. Monſieur *de Belingan* took the liberty to tell him that I deſerved ſo much every year, upon the account of the good ſervices of my friends, and that which I had done his Majeſty in my own perſon ; which the King with great bounty immediately conſented to : and thus was I on a ſudden provided for by the State, having a penſion from the King. Going the next day to Monſieur *de Belingan*, I there found the hundred Crowns ready told out ; and he promis'd me withal to ſollicit the Patent for the penſion, which alſo in few days he obtain'd. I found my ſelf ſo ſenſibly oblig'd by the generous faſhion, wherewith he ſerv'd me upon this occaſion, that I have all my life ſince ſought opportunities of manifeſting my acknowledgment, as well towards his own perſon as his Sons. For, though what he had procur'd for me was very inconſiderable in it ſelf, I rather valued it from the heart, wherewith he had done it, than from the value of the thing ; and I can

truly

truly fay, that I had even then a great averfion for interefted friend-
fhips, which are proportion'd according to the fervice a man hopes to
receive from his friends, and not by the mutual confidence and union
of hearts. I thought, having receiv'd this money I fpeak of, that I
could not better gratifie the choice my Corporal had made of me, than
by giving him a fhare with me. And being willing others fhould alfo
fhare in the Kings bounty, I lent fome to fome of my Comrades, who
ftood in need enough.

V. I continued yet fome years in the Guards, till I was forc'd to leave
them by a wretched affair, which I fhould be afham'd to fpeak of in
this place, were it not to fhow, with how great wifdom the King hath
caft a fcandal upon Duels, which paft before for honourable, though fo
contrary to all, both Divine and Humane Laws, and that they were
the ruine of the *French* Gentry.

A young Cadet, like my felf, call'd *Vernetel*, receiv'd a box of the
ear from another Gentlemen, whofe name was *Du Mas*, who was of the
fame Company, and who, having fell'd him with the blow, fpurn'd him
under foot, and went over his belly. This outrage put him out of all
temper, and in the unhappy neceffity, wherein he thought himfelf engag'd, by the falfe honour of the world, either to revenge himfelf or
to perifh, being deaf to all propofals of accommodation upon this account, he addreft himfelf to me, who was his particular friend, and entreated me to affift him in the recovery of his honour. I, who at that
time was corrupted with the fame Maximes, thought I could not deny
him that fervice, and confequently embrac'd the motion. I had much
ado to fpeak in private to *Du Mas*, by reafon that his action having
made a great noife, he had many eyes upon him. But at laft, about fifteen days after, all the Regiment being at *Argenteuil*, and the Officers
being all at a Council of War, to fentence a Souldier who had robb'd,
I came up to him, and told him that *Vernetel* ftay'd for him about the
thing he knew of: He made anfwer, that he had two friends, from
which he could not difengage himfelf; I thereupon entreated him to
content himfelf with only expofing one of them in his fervice, becaufe
there was none but I with my friend. But, feeing I could not perfwade him, I went away, only telling him, that I would prefently bring
him more news. A Cadet that overheard us, came and told me, that
he faw very well what we were about, and threatned withal to difcover me, if he might not make one; fo much the fury of thefe fenfe-
lefs Duels paft in thefe days for an Heroick action. I then did all that
in me lay to undeceive him from this fufpicion: but not being able,
with all I could fay to perfwade him, I faw my felf conftrain'd to confefs to him the true ftate of the cafe: to which he coldly anfwer'd, The
caufe is too good, a man cannot perifh in it. The bargain being thus
agreed on both fides, we went over by Boat into an Ifland, which was
the appointed place, and bound the Water-man, that no body might
get over to us, as alfo that we might get back again after the Combat:
which was fo bloody, that of fix, five were very much wounded,
whereof one was left upon the place, and within four and twenty hours
died, and another about three weeks after.

It happen'd that we were perceiv'd at laft by the Officers of the Regiment, who were all along by the water fide: Thefe immediately took
Boats to come over to us; but we having had fo much leifure as to recover

cover our own, we got over to the shore before they could reach us, from whence every one made the best that he could to save himself. I for my part, being very much wounded, by him of whom I had had the advantage, I was taken before I could get to the place where I hop'd to secure my self, and carried to prison in the *Fauxbourg St. Jacques*, the very same place where now stands the Abby-Royal of *Val de Grace*, which was then the prison for the Souldiers of the Regiment. There were also some others of us taken, but I was the only man committed to prison, not having found so much favour as they. A few days after, they prepared to bring me to my Tryal, of which the issue could not doubtless have been advantageous to me : but upon *Whitsunday*, by all good tokens, whilst the Jaylor and his Wife were at Church at their devotions, some of my Comrades undertaking some means to save my Life, as well of their own good will, as that of Monsieur *de Grillon*, who had hinted to them, that he should be glad it could be done, found means to let me down a Rope by a Chimney, by which I got up to the top, and escap'd over the Tiles ; I was discover'd and pursu'd, but I got into a Cellar of the Castle of *Bissetre*, where I lay conceal'd. Thus was God pleas'd doubly to save my life, as well from him against whom I had fought, as from Justice, which I could not otherwise have escap'd. I then made a very serious reflexion upon the action wherein I had been so lately engag'd, and indeed it appear'd to me so bloody and inhumane, that, tho I could not as yet absolutely wean my self from those they call the Rules of Honour, I did nevertheless from that very instant make a firm resolution, to try all arts imaginable never to be again engag'd in so unhappy a necessity.

Seeing my self then no more in a condition to appear, and enforc'd to withdraw till this affair should be husht up ; I resolv'd in the year 1602 to accompany several Gentlemen, who were going into *Holland*, and there to pass away all the time of my disgrace. And accordingly thither we went all together, and continued there some ten months.

VI. At the expiration of these, we resolv'd to pass into *Germany*, and thence into *Muscovia* ; but our Journey was cut short, for about three days Journey from the *Hague*, we were taken by some Light Horse belonging to the Prince of *Orange* ; who, looking upon us as Run-aways from the Army, carried us to the next Town, where we were all clapt up in prison. The Justice that usually passes upon Deserters being very quick, they did not long deliberate upon our Sentence ; but they consider'd the number of us, and thereupon order'd that we should be decimated, and that every tenth man, upon whom the lot fell, should be hang'd. In the mean time, chance being uncertain, every one was equally in fear for himself, and all of us interested our selves in a misfortune, that nevertheless could only fall upon a part. A Priest came to visit us in the prison to comfort us, and to prepare us for death, which induc'd some of us to confess our selves to this good father : but I for my part must acknowledge that I was in so great an astonishment, and so affrighted at such a kind of death, that I could not take any care of my Conscience.

At last the immediate danger wherein we saw our selves involv'd, open'd our understandings, so that we entreated one of our Companions, who had a great deal of art, and was a good Scholar, and that above all was very perfect in the *Latin* Tongue, to write a Letter to the

Prince

Prince of *Orange*, by way of Apology, to try if that might not so move him, that we might obtain our pardon. He did it with marvellous facility, representing to his Highness, That we were several Gentlemen, who after that our curiosity and ardour for War had made us leave our own Country, to come and bear Arms in a foreign State, to learn the military exercises there, by practice; we were in some measure excusable, if the same curiosity had prompted us to go on further into other Provinces, that we might the better know the different customes of diverse Nations, and so of every one to cull out the best. That this inclination was more natural to *French-men* than to all other people; and if we had committed a fault upon this occasion, in not first obtaining leave, we hop'd his Highness would have the goodness to pardon us, and to excuse the hot humour of the *French* youth: that there had been no malice in the proceeding, but only a little of the levity natural to the Nation; that it was becoming his Grandeur to make a difference betwixt offenders, and to distinguish the quality of offences, by the natural disposition of those who did commit them. In fine, he couch'd this short Apology in so elegant *Latin*, and did illustrate it with so many Reasons, borrow'd from a Military Rhetorick, which the fear of present death did very much animate, that it was impossible for the Prince of *Orange* to resist so just, and so soft a violence; so that he immediately granted our pardon: but upon condition nevertheless, that we should yet serve some time in his Army. And thus, contrary to all expectation, we escap'd from so great a peril.

VII. After we had stay'd some months longer with the Prince of *Orange*, according to the injunction he had laid upon us in granting our pardon, we resolv'd to return into *France*; and accordingly came all together to a Kinsmans house of one of the company call'd *L'Anglise*, who was of *Picardy*; where I was entertain'd by a pure effect of the generosity of Monsieur, and Madame *L'Anglise*, as if I had been one of their own Sons. After having staid a month there, I resolved to return to the Guards, there being no Wars abroad at that time; and that Regiment being the ordinary School for young Gentlemen who follow'd the exercise of Arms. But, being the occasion upon which I had gone out, could not permit me to re-enter into it, and that nothing had been said about that business all the time of my absence, it was necessary that I should keep my self private for some days, during which Monsieur *de Grillon*, who exprest the affection of a Father to me, obtain'd my Pardon, but upon condition notwithstanding, that I should give my self up Prisoner for two or three hours only, in observation of the ordinary forms. I did so, but being the Court of the *Provoste de l'Hotell*, where I was to be quitted, could not sit that day, I was very much surpriz'd to see my self shut up four and twenty hours without hearing a word. I believ'd that they play'd foul play with me, and fearing scurvy consequences of this delay, I began to fall into one of the greatest anxieties I had ever been in the whole time of my life; looking upon my self every moment as a man condemn'd to dye. I made thenceforward a firm resolution, never again so to commit my self to a voluntary Prison, from whence a man cannot go out when he would; and where a man is continually in fear of being taken out, to go whither he would not. I was nevertheless soon after deliver'd from this fear, being the next morning released out of Prison, and at the same time admitted

D   into

into the Guards, according to my own defire. I here continued fome years, where beginning to be weary of doing nothing in *France*, by reafon there was no War there, I refolv'd to go into *Savoy*, with one of my Comrades, an intimate friend of mine, whofe name was *St. Maury*.

VIII. The War began in that Country about the year 1604, and I underftood that *Rofe*, the Duke of *Savoy*'s Embaffador, levied under-hand fome Souldiers at *Paris*: I went to wait upon him, and promis'd him that my Comrade and I would raife him 40 men, provided he would affure us of the Commands of Captain and Lieutenant, and fur-nifh us with fo much Money as was neceffary for the raifing, and con-ducting them to the confines of *Savoy*. He granted what I defir'd, and I was as good as my word. But, not daring to march our Souldiers together, becaufe the King would not allow that any one fhould make levies of his Subjects to go ferve another Prince, I fent them feveral ways, being very well affur'd they would not fail me, becaufe moft of them were Souldiers of the Regiment of Guards whom I knew, and in whom I did abfolutely confide. Some of which went by the way of the *Swiffe* Country, and others which way they could; as for me, and my Lieutenant, who would needs ferve in that condition, we took the way of *Lyons*, where a Guard was kept to ftop fuch kind of people, that they might not pafs. The Guard having ftopt us at the Gate, I told them that it was a Gentleman who was travelling that way; and that I belong'd to him: for I being more known than *Sainte Maury*, I rather chofe to pafs for his Servant, that I might be the lefs taken no-tice of. But for all that, we were carried before the Governour, which was Monfieur *d'Alincourt*, that we might have his Pafs; we there met with feveral of the Court, one of which remembring my face, askt me if he had not feen me in the Guards? whom I anfwered after fuch a manner, that he thought himfelf miftaken. We were however a little watcht; but they by whom I had been known, being bufie about a quarrel, thought no more of us, and fo we got away, and went to meet our Souldiers, who attended us at the Rendezvous. There we found them increafed in number, having pickt up fome others by the way, which made our Company fifty men; who were receiv'd by the Com-miffary of Monfieur *d'Albigny*, who was our Camp-mafter. They had fome Money diftributed amongft them, and quarters affign'd to refrefh themfelves in, till they fhould have Orders fent to march away to the Army.

But thefe Orders were fo long in coming, that the Countrey where we lay had time to be weary of us, and fent us word that we fhould prefently retire, or that otherwife they would fall upon us; fo that we faw our felves on a fudden oblig'd either to disband our Company, or to ftand our ground, and ftiffly to defend our felves, by all the ways we fairly could. We refolv'd upon the laft as the moft honourable, and began to make War for our felves, till we fhould be call'd to do it for his Highnefs of *Savoy*. In this defign we judg'd it neceffary to have fome Cavalry to fuftain our Foot; and in order to it, accommodated our felves with fome Horfes of a Town, the Inhabitants whereof made fhew to fall upon us. With this fmall number of Souldiers, confifting of forty Mufqueteers, and twenty Horfe, or thereabout, we kept the field, and found we were in a condition to defend our felves againft all thofe that intended to attack us. Of which Monfieur *De Bois-pardaillan*, Gover-nour

nour of *Bourg* in *Bresse*, upon the Confines of *France* and *Savoy*, was the first, who fore'd us to withdraw from his territories, to re-enter those of *Geneva*; where we liv'd a good while, and got some booties, till the news of us being carried to *Geneva*, the Republick sent so many Troops against us, that we were compell'd to retire to the Confines of *Bresse*.

Monsieur *de Saint Chaumont*, who was Governour of the Country, having notice of our march, would keep the Pass against us; and to that purpose drew together above five hundred Gentlemen, with whom he set out to meet us. I had intelligence of it, and found my self in a great perplexity, with so few people as I had, having not above fourscore at the most, and of them the Cavalry very poorly mounted. Seeing my self then in no condition to make head against so great a body, I conceiv'd it requisite to think of retreating, and that with the soonest. There was no Country for us so safe as *Savoy*, by reason that we march'd under his Standard. But the difficulty was how to get thither : For we were to pass the *Rhone*, which was two long leagues march from us, which appear'd to be impossible, no Boats being there. So that, not daring to show our selves, in the assurance we had of being charg'd, I bethought me of concealing my men in a Wood, and in the mean time to send out to seek a Boat upon the River, to be brought to the place where I design'd to pass. But this requiring a great deal of time, I thought it requisite to amuse Monsieur *de Saint Chaumont*, in laying him an Ambuscade with our Horse only, to the end that we might in the interim file off our Infantry towards the River, and have them all ready to pass; and the more to fortifie this Ambuscade, I kept the Drums with the Trumpets to make the greater noise. The knowledge I had of the Map of the Country made me guess, that Monsieur *de Saint Chaumont*, who fear'd nothing, would certainly pass through a little Wood, that lay betwixt him and us; and accordingly posted my self there, with my Horse, my two Trumpets, and my two Drums; I lay still till the Enemies Forlorn should advance. About midnight they fail'd not to fall directly into our Ambuscade, when we sallying out upon them, with a great rattling of Drums and Trumpets, when they least expected any such thing, put them into so great a fright, that they all run away, without firing so much as one Pistol; and went to carry news to Monsieur *de Saint Chaumont*, that the Enemy was in the Wood, and had so many Trumpets and Drums, that they must of necessity be much stronger than had been reported to him. This news did a little startle him, as well as the rest, and put them upon a long deliberation of what course they should take : where it was at last resolv'd, that they should stay till it was day, that they might not rashly engage, without first discovering the Enemies post and number.

This was just as much as I expected, or desir'd; for by this means we had time sufficient to recover the River, where we found the Boat coming back from passing over our men, in which I shipt our Cavalry, that were to pass over first, and stay'd my self the return of our Boat, into which at last I went, with the rest of our people. We were scarce got to the middle of the River, when we discover'd all Monsieur *de Saint Chaumont*'s Cavalry, and himself at the head of them, marching a soft trot, for fear of engaging himself too far : I leave every one to judge of the satisfaction he had to see us in so little number, and himself not able to get to us, especially after having been stopt by so ordinary a stratagem, put upon him by such a company of young fellows as we were;

were, and that he was asham'd he had not the judgment to discover. So soon as we were landed, I saluted him at distance, and took my leave, being careful to keep the Water-man on our side, lest he should carry over his Boat; and went to post our selves upon the first little Eminence of the State of the Duke of *Savoy*.

From thence I sent to give an account of all these transactions to our Camp-master, and to demand his Orders; which I expected with great impatience, finding my self no longer in a condition of making War at my own expence: But was very much astonisht at his answer, which was, That the Peace being already concluded, he stood no longer in need of our Troops. For having got all the advantage he pretended to, which was, by his authority to render himself considerable with the Duke, he easily consented to the order the Duke gave him to disband his Regiment; and coming after to see me, to acknowledge the great obligation he had to me, he told me, to give me a more particular testimony of his gratitude, that if I did not think of returning into *France*, I should oblige him in staying with him, and depending upon the same fortune with his own. I receiv'd his offer with the respect I ought to do, assuring him that I was sorry no occasion had presented it self, wherein I might have made it appear, that I was not altogether unworthy of the honour he had done me; and so took my leave. I gave the Souldiers Money, that they might return to *Paris*, after the same manner they had come from thence; and *Sainte Maury* and I took post to return thither also. Our way was to go back again by *Lyons*, where we had an affair of considerable importance; which was, there to receive the remainder of our Pay, upon the account of our Company. But though two Treasurers of the City had jointly engag'd to see us paid, we had much ado to get the Money, being at the first demand roundly answer'd, That we were come too late, and that they had order to pay no more, because all the Troops were disbanded. Yet, when I gave our Money for gone, I was happier than I thought; and by the mediation of a Commissary, obtain'd that which I could not do by applying my self to the Treasurers. We continued our Journey, and being arriv'd at *Paris*, from a Captain as I was lately, I saw my self reduc'd once more to the condition of a private Souldier.

IX. I had a kinsman, Monsieur *de Boulogne* by name, who was of *Provence*, and that had the Government of *Nogent* in *Bassigny*, together with a Company in the Regiment of *Champagne*. He had a great desire to provide me some command in his Company, or in his Government; but there being none at that time vacant in either, I could not prevail with my self to stay and lye idle, but chose rather, as I said before, to enter again for some months into the Guards, into which Monsieur *de Crequy*, who was Collonel, receiv'd me with great kindness.

I was scarce entred into them, when he employ'd me in a very dangerous affair, and from which I had much ado to disengage my self. Monsieur *de Monravel* had married a Sister of Monsieur *de Crequy*, who for her fortune was to have an Estate call'd *Savigny*, near unto *Juoisy*, which Monsieur *de Crequy* disputed with him, and whereof he was in actual possession. Monsieur *de Monravel* attempted to surprize the House-keeper, and did effectually, though with much ado, put him out of the place. To keep this Castle, which he had thus got the possession of, he made choice of three Souldiers, who had serv'd under his command;

giving

giving them charge to keep this House, as a Fort of War, and not to suffer any persons whatever to come in, without first very well knowing who they were. Monsieur *de Crequy* being very much vexed at this affront, resolv'd at any rate to recover the possession of his Castle. He thought he might employ me in this enterprize, and accordingly entreated me to serve him in it, to the best of my power. He said nothing to me of the means of executing it, but wholly relied upon my conduct; assuring me, that he would furnish me with all things necessary, and which was of much greater importance; that he would powerfully justifie and sustain me in all things, as he was oblig'd to do. I told him, that he did me a great deal of honour in choosing me to do him this service, but that the business appear'd to me something hard to perform, seeing that, being very well acquainted with the situation of the house, I knew it to be environ'd with a deep Moat, full of Water, that could not be past but over a Draw-bridge, which could not be let down, being guarded by Souldiers: but that however I would attempt the enterprize; that being he would not have me lay a formal Siege to it, I had no need of many people, but of two or three men only, which I would choose out of the Regiment; and that I begg'd the favour of him to bear me out in the consequence, as he had done me the honour to promise he would. He again assur'd me that he would, and with this assurance, taking three good Souldiers along with me, I went about my business.

Being come to *Savigny*, I made a shew of shooting with one of my Comrades, and being acquainted with the chiefest of the three Souldiers that were in the Castle, I call'd to him from the end of the Bridge; which was down. As he was coming to me, I told him that my sport had brought me thither, and then speaking to him of a Mall, that was hard by the house, askt him if he were not in the humour to play a Game with us. He then askt me on the other side, if I would not come in; and I answer'd him with such indifferency, as took from him all cause of suspicion. One of his two Comrades was already out of the Castle, and as he also was coming out, whilst he was yet upon the Plank, which had no Rails, I took him by the hand, and pull'd him a little roughly to me, which he resisting, his foot slipt, and he fell into the Moat. I presently threw him a pole, to help him out of the Water, and at the same instant, my two Souldiers, who had conceal'd themselves at some distance, to see how matters would go, came running, and with us made themselves Masters of the Bridge. We then pull'd up the Bridge, and I bid him who had faln into the water, Go, and dry himself; and that as he had entred this place by surprize on the behalf of Monsieur *de Monravel*, he ought not to take it ill that I should enter by the same way for Monsieur *de Crequy*, who was the true proprietor. The third Souldier, who had remain'd in the Castle, seeing us four against him alone, made no manner of resistance, but suffer'd himself to be turn'd quietly out, as well as several women, who were in the place. I immediately gave Monsieur *de Crequy* an account of all that had past, and he presently sent us two Horses laden with provision; writing to me withal, That we should maintain what we had got against all the world; assuring us anew, That he would uphold us to the last, and would therein rather engage his whole authority and estate, than that this difference should not end to his honour. I thought my self with this Letter, in an absolute assurance, but I did not yet know the ordinary course of

E   the

the affairs of the world, nor the ways of proceeding of great men, as I have done since.

X. A few days after, they came and told me, that there was at the end of the Bridge an Usher of the Parliament, who commanded me, by virtue of an Arrest, immediately to open the Gates, and restore the Castle into the hands of Monsieur *de Monravel*; or otherwise there would be a Decree against us, and the neighbouring Provosts and Commoners would be order'd to bring us alive or dead. I confess I was surpriz'd at such a Complement, not having dreamt that I should have the Parliament to dispute against; I believ'd the solemn promise that Monsieur *de Crequy* had made to uphold us against all pretenders, did absolutely secure us. In the mean time I imagin'd that he might know nothing of this proceeding, and that till he could be inform'd of it, I might return the Usher this answer, That I knew him not; and that he must bring me a Letter, under Monsieur *de Crequy's* own hand, who had put me into this Castle. The Usher return'd to carry back my answer to Madam *de Monravel*, who had sent him, and who sollicited this affair with the Parliament, with so much heat, that immediately she went to demand of them, that since the Garrison had not thought fit to obey their Arrest, they would please to send a Councellour, for whom doubtless we should have more respect. Her request was granted, and the Court appointed a Commissary to come presently to us.

Now I having taken a resolution to stay for Monsieur *de Crequy's* order before I would deliver up the Castle, return'd the same answer to the Councellor that I had done to the Usher; telling him withal, That I was infinitely sorry I could not obey him, in the extreme necessity wherein I found my self of executing my Collonels commands. The Councellour was offended to the last degree, to see that we should thus refuse to obey him, and in that heat presently commanded a Boat to be brought from *Juvisy* to set over men to scale the Walls. This Order was immediately executed, by reason that Madam *de Monravel*, who had provided for all things, had made ready for it before-hand. The first Provost who came to the place, commanded one of his Archers to mount the Ladder; but this Archer having made a little too much haste, had no sooner clapt his hand upon the top of the Wall, but that he was made to quit his hold, and tumble headlong into the Water. This accident put all the party into a very great fury; and another, who would be braver than the rest, having said, that give him but a Pistol, and he would take order that they should not serve him so, mounted resolutely, with his Pistol in his hand; but when he thought himself already Master of the Castle, one of my Comrades and I, who lay conceal'd behind the Wall, so soon as ever he put up his head, caught him by the collar of his doublet, strongly pull'd him in to us, and having held him down below, bound him and clapt him in prison.

After this second adventure, none of the Assailants had the courage to mount the Wall, so that Madam *de Monravel*, conceiving it was necessary to have more company, call'd in yet another Provost, with all the Rabble of four or five neighbouring Villages; and of all these people gather'd together, made several *Corps de Guard*, which blockt up the Castle. She caus'd the Draw-bridge to be under-propt, that the besieged might not let it down and escape, when they found themselves too nearly prest; and sent to *Paris* for Cannon to force us, resolv'd to

take

take us alive or dead : For she was perswaded that we were above fifty, by reason that every night we set out above fifty light Matches upon forkt sticks, that held ten or twelve apiece, every one plac'd at the due distance of Musketeers. We moreover plac'd others at the corners of the house, and mov'd them from time to time, to make them believe that we reliev'd the Centinels. In the mean time, seeing our selves thus destitute, and hearing no news of Monsieur *de Crequy*, we found means to let him know the condition we were in, and the night following he commanded two hundred men of the Regiment of Guards, under the command of some Serjeants, to go betimes in the morning to *Savigny*, to charge all the besiegers, and afterwards to enter into the Castle. But this Order could not be so private, but that Madam *de Monravel*, who was return'd to *Paris*, had notice of it, which made her come away in an instant ; and she made so great haste, that she kill'd two of her Coach-horses. She came but just before the relief, and having plac'd her Coach just before the Bridge, she being on foot, told the Serjeants of the Guards, who commanded the two hundred men, that they should not pass but over her ; and therefore they were to consider whether they would destroy her or no, for she was resolv'd not to stir from the place. This discourse did so confound the Commanders, that they alter'd their design, having respect to a Lady of her quality, and the Sister of him for whom they had undertaken the Journey. So that they only try'd to put some men into the Castle by a little Bridge on the backside of the House ; but it was so rotten that it broke under ten or twelve that were upon it, and there were but two that could recover the door ; of which one was the *Valet de Chambre* of Monsieur *de Crequy*. All this relief ended there, and the rest retir'd, without having done any other thing, than to give us at least some little comfort in the reiterated word of Monsieur *de Crequy*, who assur'd us afresh, that he would bring us off with honour whatever came on't.

XI. But a whole day being past, and we seeing all the Machines making ready, and every one preparing himself to come on to the Assault, we began with good reason to apprehend, that in longer expecting the effect of our Collonels promises, we should be forc'd, and reduc'd to the necessity, either of dying with our Swords in our hands, or to undergo the severity of an offended Parliament. Yet before we would resolve in this strange extremity wherein we saw our selves, I plac'd a Centinel, to look if he could not discover any Troops coming to our relief : but instead of Troops, he saw only one man appear on the top of a little eminence close by, who making a sign to him with his hand, threw him a stone wrapt about with paper, wherein I read these words :

I am at my wits end : Save your selves as well as you can ; for it is not in my power without perishing my self to disengage you ; but if you can get out, come forthwith to Juvisy, *where you will find in the Inn Horses ready, and all things necessary.*   De Crequy.

This Ticket put us into no less despair than our Collonel, to see our selves so far engag'd upon his word, so oft reiterated, and yet that he would not keep it with us. Nevertheless we were to think of getting out one way or another ; and seeing we must of necessity perish if we should suffer our selves to be forc'd, we resolv'd to prevent an Assault, not

not despairing but that we should be able to open our selves some way to escape. I contriv'd then the night following to cause a great noise to be made behind the Castle, to draw the besiegers to that part, and I was busie in the mean time, as softly as I could, in unnailing the plank of the Draw-bridge, to make us way. Having at last drawn it to me, I let down from the top of the Wall a Ladder by a Rope, and made the lower end rest upon the frame of the Bridge : I stay'd that end from slipping back, and with a Rope that was fastened to the upper end of the Ladder, I let it fall gently upon the other end that supported the Draw-bridge, when it was let down. This Ladder thus resting the two ends upon the two firm parts of the Bridge, that we might walk upon it, I laid over the plank I had taken out of the Bridge, and having thus made a Bridge of the Ladder, we all six sally'd out with our Swords in our hands, and immediately fell upon the first *Corps de Guard*, where, by making a mighty noise, and crying out Kill, Kill, we put them into such a fright, that they gave way and let us pass, as if we had been a great number.

But all was not yet done, and we were to make wonderful great haste to gain the River, before the Archers of this Guard had recover'd their wits, and could mount to Horse, to come and fall upon u.. Also having recover'd *Juvisy*, where I knew that Horses were ready for us at the inn. I would not enter into it, for fear lest staying to go take these Horses, we should be all on a sudden surpriz'd ; but we ran to get into a Boat, where we got over the River. We immediately perceiv'd on the other side of the River that we had quitted, the Archers that pursu'd us, and who attempted not to pass, by reason that the Forest of *Senac* came down to the River on our side. We entred into it to repose our selves, and there remain'd all day, having sent a Country fellow for something to eat, as if we had been Hunters.

XII. The night following we went on our Journey, and came to Monsieur *de Crequy* to *Paris*, who receiv'd us as persons whom it went to his Soul to have engag'd, and that he saw had escap'd beyond all manner of hope. But though his house was our refuge for the space of six weeks, that we lay conceal'd there, because they had decreed against us ; yet was it no great satisfaction to see our selves depriv'd of our Liberty, and that he upon whose account we had lost it, was not able to restore us to it. I then found that I was to work for my self in an affair that so nearly concern'd me, and to disengage my self from the hands of Justice, after having escap'd from those of the Besiegers. Which also I effected happily enough, in making use of a little foresight I had had, at my first entring into the Castle. I had taken an Inventory of all I found there, being unwilling any one should accuse me of failing in the least punctilio of my duty. The chiefest member of this concern was a Chamber, in which there was a great quantity of Plate, I had taken care to lock the Chamber up, after having brought into it whatever was most considerable from the other rooms of the Castle, and had taken the Key, so that not a Soul entred into it of all the time that I was there, neither could any the least thing be imbezled. I took occasion from this exact care of mine to preserve what appertain'd to Madam *de Monravel*, to make my peace with her ; and I thought it best to address my self immediately to her, without employing any Mediator, hoping that out of generosity she would be just to herself, in pardoning a man, whose

good

good conduct would make it appear to her, that the sole command of his Collonel had forc'd him to maintain the Castle against her.

I ventur'd therefore to write to her with all possible civility and submission, *That I was extremely concern'd it had so faln out, that the duty of my place had compel'd me to appear against her : But I assur'd her Ladyship withal, that if I had been faithful to her Brother, I had also been so in her concerns, in preserving with a particular care all I had found in the House, of which I had taken an exact Inventory, which I took the boldness to send her. I humbly besought her to consider that the sole duty of obedience having made me undertake this action, and not the prospect of any interest, which I was infinitely far from, it would redound to her own honour, to pardon a fault she herself would have justified in another, that had committed it on her behalf : that had I had the honour to have belonged to her, as I did to Monsieur de Crequy her Brother, I should have serv'd her with the same zeal, and by a like service should have thought to have merited her esteem ; which gave me reason to hope, knowing her generosity, that she would less consider her self upon this occasion, than the obligation of my Duty : and in this assurance I durst make her Ladyship, who was my Party, my Judge, and commit my Cause absolutely into her hands, thence to expect the Grace which she only had the power to grant.*

This Letter, together with the truth of the fact, prevail'd so far with Madam *de Monravel*, that instead of prosecuting any further against me, she spoke in my favour; and having first pacified her Husband, who was irritated to the last degree, and after that, having easily obtain'd the Abolition that I desir'd. Thus she, who had depriv'd me of my Liberty, restor'd it to me again ; and that which had so cruelly incens'd her against me at first, became a favourable occasion to me in the Issue of receiving from her all the testimonies of a most sincere Friendship.

The End of the First Book.

F   BOOK

BOOK II.

The Sieur de Pontis *enters into a Regiment of* Champaigne. *A great Accident that befell him in the Forreſt of* Beaumont. *He is made the King's Lieutenant in the City of* Nogent, *during the War of the Princes. He goes to force a Captain of Light Horſe in a Caſtle, and brings him as a publick Incendiary to his Trial, notwithſtanding the Oppoſition of all the Gentlemen of the Country. How he made an end of all the Quarrels he had with the Gentry there. He makes Head in the open Field with* 200 *Foot, againſt* 600 *Horſe commanded by the Cardinal of* Guiſe. *And goes to the Seige of* St. John d'Angely.

I. SOme months after this affair I had had with the Parliament, about Monſieur *d' Crequi's* concerns, Monſieur *de Boulogne*, that I mentioned before, procured me the Enſigns place of his own Company, which was to me the firſt ſtep by which I began to enter into Command; not reckoning the ſhort employment I had had in *Savoy*, for any thing at all: But in the time that I ſerv'd in this Commiſſion, there hapned to me a rencounter, which well deſerves to be mention'd in this place.

About the Year 1611, our Regiment, which was that of *Champaigne*, finding it ſelf very much ſtreightned in *Verdun*, where we lay in Garriſon, entreated leave of the King, that they might quarter in *Mont-Faucon* too, which is a very pretty Town, ſome Leagues diſtant from *Verdun*. Monſieur *de Ville*, at that time Governour of *Verdun*, writ about it to Court, and obtained of the Queen Regent the favour we deſired, ſo that his Majeſty writ to Monſieur *de Nevers*, who was Governour of the Province, that it was his pleaſure it ſhould be ſo; and ſo ſoon as the Letter was writ, I was choſen out to carry it to *Caſſine*, the ordinary place of Monſieur *de Nevers* his reſidence, and ſo to bring back his Orders for the Quarters. I accordingly went, and finding that Monſieur *de Nevers* was gone to *Montaigu* in *Flanders*, I went after him thither, and had from him all the ſatisfaction I could deſire. But I was not ſo happy in my return.

II. When I was ſome ten leagues off *Verdun*, at a Bourg called *Raucourt*, about three or four in the afternoon, and I was preparing to continue my Journey through a Forreſt, which I muſt of neceſſity go over, I had warning given me at the Inn, that they would by no means adviſe me to travel alone through this Forreſt, becauſe there were a great many High-way men there, and that it was better for me to ſtay till the morning, that they might provide a good Guide, and that there might peradventure be ſome body in Town with whom I might paſs with more ſafety. I thought it convenient to take this Councel, and
not

not to stand upon the punctilio of Bravery, and so rashly to expose my self, where there was no Duty to engage me. I sent therefore to the Inns to enquire whither there was any body that was to go over the Forrest. It hapned luckily that a Canon who was returning to *Verdun*, being in the same concern that I was, sent at the same time to my Lodgings to make the same enquiry. About eight a clock in the morning we set out with a Guide, of whom they gave us a very good character. Being advanc'd into the Forrest we met a man a foot in red Breeches, and a blew Doublet, with a Fusee upon his Shoulder; I askt the Guide the meaning of that odd kind of habit, who made answer, that it was a Countryman that was shooting. The way we rid was very troublesom, by reason the branches of the Trees hung down so low, as forc'd us continually to stoop, which made me tell the Canon, that we were better to alight, and lead our Horses in our hands; and this little foresight serv'd not only to, ease us, but moreover to save our lives, seeing that we could very hardly have escap'd in the rencounter that presently after befel us, had we not been alighted from our Horses. Being then a little further advanc'd in the Forrest, we met with three men laid down by the road side, with Fusees lying by them. As we past by they rose up and complimenting us, God protect you Gentlemen, said they, whether are you travelling after that manner? and we had need indeed that God should protect us from the consequence of such a Compliment. We replied that we were going to *Verdun*. We will bear you company, said they, very civilly, if you please, for we are going thither too. I, who thought it not convenient to tye our selves to such Company, and that absolutely concluded them to be Rogues, made answer, though civilly enough too, That it appear'd a little hard we should travel far together, and that they could not well keep pace a foot with us who had Horses. They, who desir'd nothing more but to begin a quarrel, presently made what I had said an affront of honour, and brutishly replying, What! Gentlemen, said they, because we are a foot, are we less men of honour, and less honest men? I reply'd again very civilly to this huffing return, That I was very far from undervaluing them, and that it was not my humour so to do. Upon this, instead of taking notice of what I said, they grew hotter, and proceeded to rage, when three or four more at the instant rusht out of the Wood, asking their Comrades what was the matter? and almost before they could give them an answer, were all upon us with fury, crying out, Kill, Kill. I had no more time at the instant, but to seize on our Guides Quarter-staff, who ran away in a moment, with all the good testimony had been given us of him; we let go our Horses, and clapping my self back to back to the Canon, who I spoke to not to forsake me, but to defend himself on his side as well as he could, I began to lay about me with my Quarter-staff with all my force and art; and I stood in need of it all in this rencounter. The great blows and thrusts I made at them kept them at a distance, and hindred them from approaching too near: They presently made some shots at us, with which the Canon was only wounded in the Thigh; but the heat of the Combat made him that he did not feel it: for he defended himself on his side with incredible ardour, having about him a girdle of 300 Pistols, which made him fight like a Tyger.

After this manner we defended our selves above a quarter of an hour without intermission, against all these fellows, arm'd with a Halbert, Fire-

Fire-arms, and Swords. They made but little ufe of their Fufees, he that had the Halbert made mighty attempts to get in to us; but being I had a continual eye upon him, and that the furious blows I every moment dealt amongft them with my Staff kept them in awe, they could do us no harm, and durft not venture too far. The braveft, or the moft furious amongft them, was a young red-headed Rogue, who preft very hard upon me, and that I found always upon the attack. But beginning to feel my felf weary with fo long and fo rough a Combat, I made a final effort, and having as it were mufter'd all my forces together, and made a kind of a *falfifie*, I reacht this young Rogue fuch a rap, as made him immediately retire forty paces, and fit down upon the ground. Never were people fo aftonifht, to fee us fo obftinate, not to yield our felves to fo many as they were; and I affure my felf that could they have forefeen fuch a confequence of their firft Compliment, they would have fav'd both themfelves and us fo much fruitlefs labour. In the end, feeing the ftouteft of their company hurt, they began by little and little to flacken their ardour, and to talk amongft themfelves: which made us judge that it was time to think of a retreat, and accordingly we threw our felves back together into the Wood, and got away in the ftrangeft equipage that ever eye beheld, having neither Cloak, nor Hat, nor my Sword, which was alfo loft from my fide: and being out of breath, and almoft quite fpent, we refted our felves a little in the Bufhes. Our Horfes, which at the firft firing of a Fufee had ran away, ftay'd for us about a league off, as much out of breath as we; we found them too in fo ill equipage, that their Bridles and Girts were broken, and the Piftols batter'd; but however we made fhift after the beft manner we could to get to a Bourg call'd *Beaumont*.

The noife of our adventure being fpread abroad, the Judges of the place came to feek us out, and compell'd us againft our wills, to ftay a day or two, by reafon that they had orders the next day to raife the Country, and fearch in the Forreft, to fee if they could find out thefe Robbers, of whom fo many perfons made every day publick complaints; and they hop'd that peradventure we might know fome of them. It hapned indeed the next day that the young Rogue that I had hurt was taken, not being able to get away: I knew him as foon as ever I faw him, and he was himfelf conftrain'd to confefs the truth. In the mean time we took our leaves, and departed, leaving the miferable wretch upon the point to be hang'd, and came to *Verdun*, with the Orders from Monfieur *de Nevers* for the Quarters at *Mont-Faucon*.

III. The Lieutenant of our Company having been kill'd, I fome time after had his command, and return'd the Colours into the hands of Monfieur *de Boulogne*. I remain'd in Garrifon in *Nogent* upon *Marne* at the time when the Princes rebell'd againft King *Lewis* XIII, and began to raife Forces, having many of the Gentry of *Baffigny* on their fide, which was the reafon that *Nogent* was befet round with enemies. Monfieur *de Boulogne*, who at that time had bufinefs at *Paris*, entrufted the place to me, with the quality of the Kings Lieutenant, which he procured for me.

IV. Some time before this War, a Gentleman within two leagues of *Nogent*, call'd *Guyonnel*, was fo out of order in his affairs, that there was a Decree granted for the fale of his Houfe of *Bonnecourt*; which
Mon-

Monsieur *de Boulogne* having bought, this man was so enrag'd to see himself turn'd out of his House, that he lookt upon this War as a happy opportunity to revenge himself, and by siding with the Princes, by force to get into possession again; but Monsieur *de Boulogne* having as it were foreseen his ill design, had plac'd some good men for the guard of the Castle.

Guyonnel had also a kinsman call'd *Avrillot*, who was in the Princes party, and had rais'd a Troop of Light Horse, with which he resolv'd to force and pillage *Bonnecourt*. He came therefore demanding to Quarter there, and seeing himself deny'd, fell to plundring the Village, saying that he would presently do as much by the Castle. He accordingly advanc'd towards the Castle, as if to enter by force, but the Souldiers that kept it, shewing a resolution still to defend it, and beginning to fire upon him, he was fain to retire. The spite of this disappointment made him set fire to the *Basse-Court*, and animated him to such an excess of barbarity, as there to burn the Farmer, his Wife, and Children; whom he cruelly repulst when they attempted to save themselves through the flames. *Bonnecourt* being near to *Nogent*, the news of this was presently brought thither to us; for besides, that we had heard shooting, and seen the flame, some of the Inhabitants came crying out that they put all to Fire and Sword. I was surpriz'd, and afflicted to the last degree at hearing the least violences; but I found my in a sad perplexity, having but a very few men in the Garrison, and fearing to expose the place, should I go out with my Souldiers.

I contriv'd notwithstanding to cause the young people of the Town to mount to Horse, and with them to command fifty Musqueteers of the Garrison. Having drawn them together ready to march, I aloud laid before them the cruelty that had been exercis'd upon the Inhabitants of *Bonnecourt*, and gave them to understand that they were to revenge it; assuring them upon my word, that I would post them so, as that they might charge the enemy without danger: whereupon they all promis'd me to do wonders, and they kept their words as I did mine. I plac'd them in an Ambuscade, where they had all manner of advantage without peril; for having caus'd a false Alarm to be given at one end of the Village, which made the Country go out at the other, they there met with our young people, who had march'd all night without their knowledge; and who on a sudden gave them so brisk, and so unexpected a Charge, that they all fled without any manner of resistance, leaving their prey behind, with some of their own men, who were all either kill'd or taken. I restor'd to every one of the Inhabitants what was properly his own, caus'd the fire to be put out, and put courage and life into these poor people again.

After this I return'd to *Nogent*, to put the Inhabitants of the Town out of the pain they were in about their Sons, whom they thought dangerously engag'd with the Enemy. The joy they were in to see them all safe return'd, with the glory of having so bravely reliev'd their Neighbours, made them forget the fear they had been in of losing them; and as oftentimes there needs but a very light occasion to acquire either the affection, or the hatred of a people; this little Action procur'd me so absolute a credit with the whole Town, that I needed but to say the least word to be obeyed in a moment, and they call'd me the Conservator of their Country.

V. *Aurillot*, vext to the foul to fee himfelf thus baffled and put to flight, refolv'd to be reveng'd at any rate, and having feveral Perfons of Quality of his Kindred, as the Marquefs *de Creance*, *de Clermont*, and others, who were of the Princes Party, as well as himfelf; he affembled them all together, to acquaint them of the affront he had receiv'd from me, and the refolution he had taken to recover his reputation; entreating them to joyn with him to this end, and all together to fwear a mortal War againft the *Gafcon*, for fo it was that in contempt they were pleas'd to call me. Thefe Gentlemen made no great difficulty of confenting to his requeft, and confequently openly declar'd a War againft the King's Lieutenant of *Nogent*.

Having intelligence of this practice I gather'd together fome Horfe, and put my felf into a condition, not only of defending my felf, but of attacking them upon feveral occafions, wherein my chiefeft aim was to take *Aurillot* Prifoner, to make him repair the horrible crime he had committed in *Bonnecourt*, not being able to forget fo great a barbarity. To this end I fent out feveral Spies on all fides, to bring me certain intelligence of the feveral places to which he went, and where he ftayed, that of them I might make choice of that which was moft proper for the executing my defign. One of thefe Spies one day brought me word, that *Aurillot* was that night to lye within three Leagues of *Nogent*, at a Caftle call'd *Perfe*, or elfe in another call'd *Perfigny*, which was but half a League from the firft, in order to a defign he had to go out with a party the next morning towards *Langues*, which held out for the King. Upon this intelligence I immediately fent in all poft hafte to tell Monfieur *de Franciere*, who was Governor of *Langues*; to Monfieur *de Rhefnel*, Governor of *Chaumont*; and to Monfieur *de Saint Aubin*, Governor of *Montigny*; which were three places united to *Nogent*, and which had all promifed mutual affiftance againft thefe Invaders, that if they would fend me fome Troops, I did affure them the next morning to take *Aurillot* Prifoner; that it was of moment to the publick quiet, fince it was he almoft that difturbed the whole Country.

Monfieur *de Rhefnel*, and Monfieur *de St. Aubin*, fent me forthwith fome Horfe, and Monfieur *de Franciere* would come himfelf in perfon; but he came a little too late: for the very moment that the men from the two others arriv'd, having no time to lofe, I made thofe men I had, which were about 60 Horfe, and as many Foot, ready to march; and with them fet out about midnight, and came to inveft the Village of *Perfigny*, into which *Aurillot* was retir'd. I plac'd *Corps de Guard* on all the Avenues, and with the reft of my men without any noife went to ftorm the Houfe; yet could I not do it fo foftly, but that thofe within heard us, and did what they could to oppofe us: but we made our felves Mafters of it, and having forc'd the doors, we ftruck fo great a terror into all thofe within, that they made little or no refiftance. *Aurillot*, feeing no poffible way to efcape, barricado'd himfelf in a Chamber, and having a Piftol in his hand, cry'd out, that he would kill the firft man that advanc'd, and that he would dye before he would furrender himfelf to me, being confcious without doubt that he was guilty enough, to know that he was not to have any very good compofition from me. He enquir'd at the fame time, whither there was no other Commander; to which he was anfwer'd, that Monfieur *de Franciere* was juft arriv'd, and that if he had a defire to furrender himfelf into his hands, I was

willing

willing to consent to it. *Aurillot* took the course, and so became a Prisoner; as also were all the rest of his men, some few excepted, who by the favour of the night escap'd into the neighb'ring Houses, and there conceal'd themselves.

VI. Monsieur *de Franciere* and I, were of opinion, that we ought to carry our Prisoners to *Langues*: and being accordingly about to enter the Town, we were very much surpriz'd to see all the Citizens come out of the Gates to meet us. The joy wherein they were, to hear that we were bringing in *Aurillot* Prisoner, would not give them leave to stay till he came within the Walls of their City; and one of them, more foreseeing and zealous than the rest, fearing lest he should compound for his Ransome, as he might have done, had he not committed that barbarity at *Bonnecourt*, thought it best, in good time to prevent it, and fir'd a Musquet at him; but was so ill a Marks-man, that instead of his Head, he hit mine, the ball cutting my Hat-band in two, and graz'd upon my Hat, yet without any other harm to me at all. This heat did a little surprize us, and made me tell Monsieur *de Franciere*, that there was no safety there for *Aurillot*, and that it was better to carry him to *Nogent*; but he made answer, that he would go and speak to the people, and going immediately up to them, he there gave them to understand, that if they would permit Justice to have its course against this publick Enemy, they should have all satisfaction; but if they would make use of violence, he should be constrain'd to convey him to some other place. This remonstrance stopt their fury, and they past their words, that they would do him no harm, wishing much rather to see him dye upon a Scaffold; and so they brought him into the Town, and clapt him up in Prison.

VII. This news of taking *Aurillot* made a mighty noise in the Country; all the Gentry mounted to Horse, and sent to Monsieur *de Franciere* that he might be ransom'd, as being a Prisoner of War. Monsieur *de Franciere* return'd them answer, that it was I who had taken him, and that he being my right, they were to apply themselves to me; but that if he was absolutely at his disposal, he could not treat him as a Prisoner of War, having been taken not only as an Enemy to the King, but as a Destroyer of the Country, and a publick Incendiary; who had burnt Men and Villages, and committed Outrages that were not according to the ordinary Rules of War. To which the Noblesse return'd answer again, that all this could be no other but an occasion of inhancing his ransom, that due satisfaction might be made; and therefore did humbly beseech him to set his rate, and to consent, that every Gentleman amongst them might have a particular obligation to him for the favour. Monsieur *de Franciere* found himself in a very great straight, being unwilling to fall out with all the Gentlemen of the Country, and very well foreseeing all the consequences of this affair, told me, that he thought he should not be able to detain this Prisoner any longer; and that therefore I was to consider whither or no I would take him into my own Custody, for that otherwise he should be compell'd to deliver him upon Ransom. I for my part, who thought I ought not to prefer any consideration to my duty, made answer, that I would take the charge of him upon me, and would keep him safe enough; and accordingly two hours before day in the morning, I took him, and with

my

my Horse convey'd him to *Chaumont*, where I secur'd him in a good strong Prison.

Monsieur *de Franciere* at the same time sent to acquaint the Nobless, that he had him no longer in his power, not having been able to deny him to him by whom he had been taken, and to whom he did of right appertain. This news troubled them very much, not doubting but that I was resolv'd to proceed to the last, as I had begun. The only remaining comfort they had, was that being condemned at *Chaumont*, he might appeal to *Paris*, and that in so long a way, they might find some means or other to rescue him. They sent nevertheless to demand him of me, and upon my refusal said, that I should make haste then to bring him to his Trial, hoping for the forementioned reason, to procure his deliverance so much the sooner. They had the satisfaction they desir'd; for in a few days he was condemned to have his Head cut off; and to make restitution to all those he had undone.

He appeal'd from this Sentence to *Paris*, demanding to be carried thither, and withal gave notice to all his Friends, that if they would rescue him now was the time to do it: His Relations hereupon drew all their Friends together, and mounting to Horse, came to place themselves in Ambuscade upon the way by which they thought he was to pass: but I easily put the change upon them, for having sent to take up an Inn at *Bar-sur-Aube*, which was the great road to *Paris*, for the next night; all these Gentlemen who had had intelligence of it, made themselves sure upon the orders I had given, and not doubting of any thing else, posted themselves in the place I named before. In the mean time I sent *Aurillot* away the same day by eight of the clock in the morning, in the sight of the whole Town; having put him into a close Waggon, and order'd Thirty good Souldiers for his Guard, of which Twenty four, after having conveyed him three Leagues return'd; and the six others under the command of a Serjeant carried him, not by the way of *Bar-sur-Aube*, which I had commanded them to quit, but by another which was all wood, and the concealing them there kept them in absolute safety. And thus all this rout of Gentlemen were deceiv'd; not imagining that any one would have taken a way that was 30 Leagues about; and after having continued four days on Horseback retir'd, and gave over their design. The Convoy convey'd their Prisoner to *Paris*, where Monsieur *de Boulogne* expected him with great anxiety and impatience, knowing that so many Gentlemen had taken the Field to rescue him. He caus'd him to be put into Prison, and pursu'd his process with might and main.

In the interim the Peace of *Lodun* was concluded, and an Act of Oblivion was past without exceptions; which Monsieur *de Boulogne* having notice of, he presently took Post and went to Court, where he mov'd, that Incendiaries at least might not be comprehended in the Pardon, as having committed actions too black, and too cruel to be forgiven. His request was granted; and there was a particular Article inserted in the Treaty to that effect.

VIII. Whilst Monsieur *de Boulogne* was busie at *Paris* in pursuit of his Process, I had no less to do at *Nogent*, to maintain my self against all this NoblesS, who were furiously enrag'd against me for the affront they conceiv'd I had put upon them. Of which some proceeded so far as out of bravado to send me word, that if I durst come out of the

Gates,

Gates, they might fee what I was in the Field, where a better Judgment might be made than within the Walls of a Town. Thus it fell out, that in doing my beft for the King's intereft and the publick peace, I brought a hundred inconveniencies upon my felf, from which I fhould have had very much ado to difengage my felf, had I inconfiderately abandon'd my felf to the heat of youth : But as I conceiv'd, that I ought not to recede in affairs that preft upon me, fo I thought it indifcreet to make too precipitous advances : and alfo having created my felf fo many enemies all at once, I muft either have been forced to engage all my friends in the quarrel, which I have ever evaded as much as poffiblyI could, or I muft have render'd my felf ridiculous, as the common mark of all the Bravo's in the Country. I therefore upon neceffity chofe that way of proceeding which appeared to me the wifeft and moft fafe, which was as much as I could do to joyn prudence with conftancy in the whole management of this affair, and I fucceeded fo well in it, that I put an end to feventeen quarrels I had upon my hands at once, without being oblig'd to draw my Sword : which I purpofely fet down, as conceiving that true honour does not confift in a blind and brutifh courage, and that all my life have been of opinion, that nothing was more worthy a truly generous man, than to conftrain himfelf to gain his enemies by civil ways, and to overcome them by his moderation and wifdom. Every one may make of it what judgment he pleafes; but I can boldly fay, that even they, of thofe Gentlemen of whom I fpeak, who thought themfelves the moft offended by me, have fince confeft that they efteem'd me the more for that manner of proceeding with them, and for having as it were compell'd them to be my friends ; and it will not peradventure be unfeafonable to give here one example, that what I fay may be better underftood.

IX. The King had order'd Monfieur *de Boulogne* to bring fifty Villages about *Nogent* under contribution for the fubfiftence of the Garrifon ; which was no very new thing, but had been a great while in practice. I who acted for him in his abfence, fent to thefe Villages to fignifie to them the Kings order ; but was a little furpriz'd when I was told that feveral of thefe Parifhes belonging to one Lord, which was the Baron of *Clermont*, had made anfwer that they would pay nothing, and that their Lord had commanded them the contrary. I had moreover word brought me, that this Lord himfelf had faid, that if *de Pontis* found fault, and was not fatisfied, it would be eafie to fatisfie him after another manner. To which I made no other anfwer, excepting, that I fhould fee that.

But though I felt my felf very fenfibly toucht with fuch a complement, I confider'd neverthelefs that I ought not to mix my particular interefts with thofe of the King ; and that I was oblig'd firft to try all civil ways to acquit my felf of my Commiffion, and to make the fault lye at this Lord's door, that nothing might be laid to my charge. Some days after therefore I went to his Houfe, and fent him word, that I was come to have the honour to fee him; he was furpriz'd at the news, not expecting to fee me there, and came to receive me ; I told him at the firft meeting that I was come to pay him my refpects, and after fome difcourfe of indifferent things, it being dinner time, he invited me after fo obliging a fafhion, that I could not refufe to ftay, and there was no body at Table but us two, and Madam *de Clermont*. Being rifen from dinner, I told him, that befides the honour I was ambitious of, of kiffing his

hands,

hands, I was come to speak with him about the Order I had received
from the King, to put fifty Villages under contributions, of which several belonged to him, and that I did beseech him, he would please to
command them to obey this Order, which withal I presented to him.
He return'd me answer, that this affair being of Monsieur *de Boulogne's*
business, and not mine, and he being upon no good terms with him,
he could not consent to it, but that had it been my own particular
concern, he would have granted it with all his Heart. I reply'd, that
having the Honour to be the King's Lieutenant in the Government of
Monsieur *de Boulogne*, his interest was mine, and that I hop'd he would
not separate them; that on the other side it was the King's business, and
not Monsieur *de Boulogne's*; and that in short, if he would not make his
Villages contribute, I entreated he would sign his refusal under the King's
Order, that it might serve me for a discharge. Being much surpriz'd at
this, he answer'd me with heat, that he would not do it; neither would
he make his Parishes pay contribution; and fairly added, turning towards his Page, give me my Sword; and to me, Sir, we had better go
walk in the Garden. I understood his meaning well enough: but I
fear'd nothing in performing my duty, and obeying the orders of the
King.

He led me quite round the Garden, all the while discoursing of indifferent things, and after carried me into a great Park that was much more
remote, and walk'd me quite round about it, all the while looking me
in the face, and observing my countenance, which was still that of a men
that fear'd nothing in maintaining the interest of the King, and my own
duty. At last, seeing that I was always equally firm and civil, he final-
ly told me, that he had so much esteem for me, that for my sake, seeing
I desir'd to have it so, he would make his Tenants pay, but that it was
not out of any respect to Monsieur *de Boulogne*. I replied, that I stood
oblig'd to him for his civility, and that, provided he caused his Majesties Order to be obey'd, it was all one to me in favour of whom it was
granted: but that nevertheless I was oblig'd to tell him, that he ought
to remember who Monsieur *de Boulogne* was, and not to forget the
Friendship that had ever been betwixt their two Families; which also
he ought not to break, when there was as much reason as ever to preserve it, and that the advantageous qualities they were both Masters of,
seem'd to be a kind of new tye to unite them faster: That as to the rest,
I did once more beseech him to beleive, that Monsieur *de Boulogne's*
interests were mine, and ought not to be separated: I further intreated
him to give me the order he was pleas'd to send to his Villages in writing,
that they might not doubt of what I should tell them, nor have any
excuse if I compell'd them to obey. He granted every thing I desir'd,
setting down in the writing that he commanded all his Villages to pay
contribution, and entreated Monsieur *de Pontis* to compel them to it, in
case they should refuse; and so at last we took leave of one another with
mutual assurances of a true and sincere Friendship, such as in effect it
has been ever since. And this example, that may peradventure be of
some use to others, to retain them within the bounds of a temperate
conduct and a regular courage, was also very serviceable even to me
my self, to put an end to a great number of other disputes. For the
issue of this affair made so great a noise in the Country, that all who
were upon ill terms with me, began to consider me after another kind
of manner than they had done before: and even seeking means of accommodation

commodation with me, became most of them my Friends; prudently judging, that it was no dishonour to live in amity with a person who had thus engag'd one of the chiefest amongst them, from an enemy that he had been before, to become his Friend. I can also say, that this civil way of proceeding, which I practised as much as possibly I could upon all occasions, did not only acquire me the Friendship of the Noblesse, who at first were so violent against me, but moreover the affection of all the Inhabitants of *Nogent*, who in acknowledgment of the Friendship I manifested to them in all the Wars, ever after maintain'd the custom of presenting me with Wine, when ever I past through the Town, as if I had been still the Kings Lieutenant there; which I say, not out of any vanity to my self, but only to let such as are in employment see, how much moderation in all sorts of Government is preferable to insolence, especially when supported by steadiness and constancy.

To conclude this affair, which has put me upon saying all that I have said, and the cause of most of the quarrels of which I have spoken; Monsieur *de Boulogne* so vigorously pursu'd his prosecution against *Aurillot*, that he soon caus'd the Sentence of *Chaumont* to be confirm'd by an Arrest, that condemn'd him to have his Head cut off in the open Market-place, and to carry a Writing upon his back, that set out the cause of his condemnation in these terms; *For burning Houses:* which gave great satisfaction to all the Country, where he was lookt upon as a common enemy.

X. Two Years after the first War of the Princes they began a second; when Monsieur *de Boulogne*, having sent to me to come to him with a recruit of 200 men, that I had raised about *Nogent*; I prepar'd my self to march them up to the Army, commanded by the Mareschal *de Bassompierre*, where our Regiment of *Champagne* was already arriv'd, and set out with my Recruit, having only a young Ensign with me called *Saint Aubin*. After two days march we had intelligence, that the Cardinal of *Guise* was at hand with 600 Horse, that he had rais'd about *Metz*, which he brought up to join with the Army of the Princes towards *Pont de Sè*. The Match being unequal, I thought presently to recover *Sezanne*, a little Town that held out for the King; but being I was to pass a great Plain, I fear'd a surprizal there, and would have been very glad to have found some means to shelter my self.

It fell out by good luck, that I met a great many Waggons of *Bar-sur-Aube* laden with Wine, which I thought very proper to serve me for a retrenchment in case I should be surpriz'd upon the Plain. I therefore told these Carters, that they must help to cover us if they expected that we should defend them, promising them that they should run no other hazard but what we would first be expos'd to our selves. The danger wherein they saw themselves engag'd, together with the necessity of obeying me, prevail'd with them immediately to unlade their Wine, because I would have them in a condition to make more haste; and so of all these Waggons link'd to one another I made two Files, which I caus'd to march on the right and left of my Souldiers, of whom I form'd a Battalion, and gave order to those at the Head and the Rear of these two Files, to draw up near one another so soon as they should see the Enemy, that so they might wholly shut up the Battalion.

XI. We

XI. We had not march'd far in this order, but that being yet a League from *Sezame*, in the open Field, we saw the Avant-Couriers of the Enemy appear upon the top of a little Hill that bounded one side of the Plain, and presently after discovered the whole body, which consisted of six Squadrons, making full drive toward us. I caus'd my men to halt, who were at the same instant enclos'd by the Waggons, according to the order I had given; I there endeavoured to encourage them to the fight, assuring them, that if they would faithfully obey my orders, I would disengage them from the danger wherein they were, but that if they would not do it their ruine was inevitable. I also gave them my word, that if it should so fall out, as I despair'd not but it would, that they should get any prize by the spoils of such as they should kill, it should be entirely their own; and that I would pretend to no other share, but only that of procuring them the Glory of the Victory, and in saving their lives, to enrich them at the Enemies expence. The pressing danger in which they were, and the hopes that I gave them made them presently obedient, and they all assur'd me that they would faithfully acquit themselves of their duty. Having, as I said before, form'd one sole Battalion of all my men, I made them make a Front every way, to the end that on which side soever the Enemy should fall they might be in a posture to receive him. I only drew out twenty, which I plac'd some six paces without the Waggons in two ranks, consisting each of ten, that they might fire at greater liberty than if enclos'd; giving them order to kneel on one knee that they might be more sure of their execution, and not to do it till they came very near, and when I should give the word.

XII. The Cardinal of *Guise*, who was himself in person at the Head of these six Squadrons of Horse, sent a Trumpet to bid us throw down our Arms, being of so unequal force as not to be able to resist him; assuring us at the same time of fair Quarter if we did so: but that if we refused to yeild, he would kill us every man, and cut us all to pieces. I made answer to the Trumpet, that I return'd the Cardinal of *Guise* thanks for the favour he offer'd us; but that we demanded no other Quarter, than what we could procure our selves by a good defence, for which we were all very well prepar'd; and that he should return no more on the same errand, because we should no longer consider him as any thing but an Enemy. So resolute an answer made the Cardinal a while deliberate what he should do, where he resolv'd to send the Trumpet a second time to try if he could fright us by new threats, but I made my men cry out that they would fire upon him if he approacht any nearer; and the better to shew him his danger, order'd them to present their Muskets against him. So resolute a proceeding made him think better on't, and the Cardinal seeing we were resolv'd to stand upon our defence, detach'd fifty Light Horse with a command to discover our posture. These Cavaliers rid round about us at so great a distance, that I did not think fit to fire upon them, and returning to make their report, were immediately order'd to come and charge the Head of our Retrenchment; the Cardinal assuring them, that so soon as they had routed the first, he would come and fall on with all the rest. They came up accordingly at a good round trot, and being come on within twice Pistol shot, spur'd on to a Gallop, as if with design to break into our twenty
Musqueteers.

Mufqueteers. I let them approach till they were advanc'd within Piftol fhot, and then commanded thofe of the firft rank to give fire;
which they did fo refolutely and difcreetly, that they laid feveral of
them dead upon the place, and the reft wheel'd off, not daring to advance, by reafon that the other ten Mufqueteers having immediately
taken the place of the firft ten that had given fire, were ready to have
done as much. Being thus return'd fewer than they came to their main
body, I fent in the mean time to rifle their dead, about whom they
found near a Hundred Piftols, which I put into a Hat fhaking them,
and faying, Here my Boys, thefe are all your own, I pretend to no
other fhare but only to divide them amongft you; this happy beginning prefages Victory; Courage! let us ftand firm, and expect till they
bring us as many more.

These words, together with the fight of the firft advantage they had
had, encouraged them to that degree, that they wifh'd with impatience
the Enemy would attack them again, in hopes of a greater booty. And
they were not long before they had that fatisfaction; for we prefently
faw one of the fix Squadrons advance a trot, till they came within Carabine fhot, and there on a fudden they feparated themfelves into two
bodies, to fall upon both fides of our Battalion; but the firft rank
making a front every way, they gave them from behind the Waggons
fo brisk a Volley at the Muzzel of the Mufquet, that feveral Men and
Horfes lay dead upon the place, and fome that were difmounted were
forc'd to get up behind the others to get off. After this they retreated
towards their main body, and went to fee if they fhould receive a new
order to come back to be knock'd o'th' head. I made thefe dead be
rifl'd too, about whom we found fome twenty Piftols more, which
encourag'd our Souldiers anew.

XIII. In the mean time the Cardinal of *Guife*, feeing the night draw
on, and very well judging that he fhould lofe a great many men, fhould
he attack two hundred defperate men that were retrench'd, refolv'd to
encamp in a little Wood that was near at hand, and fo to keep us as it
were befieged, till he could fend for fome more affiftance. And, being he ftood in need of Foot, without which he believ'd he fhould not
be able to force us, he fent to fome neighbouring Garrifons to fupply
him. But fo foon as I had intelligence of his defign, I thought it not
good for me to ftay till the morning, and that it would be neceffary to
attempt to efcape away by the favour of the night. But the bufinefs
was, how to decamp that the Enemy's Sentinels and Guards fhould not
perceive it; and to this end I thought fit to make a fhew of encamping
as well as they, and that I had no defign of drawing off no more than
they. I therefore caus'd a great fire to be made in our Camp, and order'd the Souldiers to make a great noife, as if they were merry and
diverting themfelves; but gave them notice withal, that when they
fhould fee another fire kindled at midnight, that fhould be their fignal
to decamp, and they were then every man to follow his Leader in File
without fpeaking a word. I commanded the Waggons alfo not to ftir
from the place till we had recover'd the Wood, fearing the noife of
the Horfes and the Wheels; and being affur'd by the knowledge I had
of the Map of the Country, that we fhould find a little Wood, in which
we might march all the way under cover till we came to *Sezanne*.

I This

This refolution taken, the orders given, and midnight come, I caus'd the Fire to be lighted which was the fignal, which every one was careful to obey, and in a very little time we recover'd the Wood I fpoke of, without any fign that the Enemy had in the leaft difcover'd our march, and at break of day found our felves under the Walls of Sezanne; where we were in abfolute fafety. I then kept my word with the Souldiers, and divided amongft them the Spoil of the Enemy, by which means the joy of feeing themfelves efcap'd contrary to all appearance, was encreas'd by the fight of the booty they had got, but much more, when within a few hours after we had intelligence that the Enemy had purfu'd us as far as to the Wood, but no further; being told that we were already arrived at *Sezanne*.

This action mightily pleas'd the Cardinal of *Guife*, who openly commended the valour of thofe who had fo dar'd to refift him, and particularly enquir'd who was the Commander. It made alfo a great noife in the Country, in the Army, and as far as the Court by reafon of the great number of thofe who had attacked us, and of the quality of him that was Chief. For the firft rumour went, that two hundred Foot having been met with in the open Field by fix Hundred Horfe, under the command of the Cardinal of *Guife*, had been all cut to pieces: but the truth was foon known, and they heard the whole thing as it paft, with great joy.

XIV. Sometime after that we had join'd with the Army at *Pont de Sé*, the Peace was concluded; where the King having a mind to take a review of his Troops, commanded them to be drawn up in battaille, and fo Regiment by Regiment to march off before him. Here it was that the Cardinal of *Guife* manifefted an extraordinary bounty and generofity in my favour; for being return'd to his obedience, and reconcil'd to the King, and at that time about his Perfon, he defired Monfieur *de Villedonné*, a Captain of the Regiment of *Champagne*, to fhow him when the Regiment paft by, an Officer called *de Pontis*, who was of that body. When I came to pafs, and that Monfieur *de Villedonné* had fhew'd me to him, he came to me, and in the prefence of the King himfelf embrac'd me, and faid to me thefe very words, *That he would have me to be his Friend, having known me by that which paft near Sezanne; that he thought himfelf oblig'd to love me after fo particular a proof of my conduct, that he affur'd me no occafion fhould offer it felf wherein he might do me fervice, but that he would do it with all his heart, and that he conjur'd me to employ him in whatever fhould lye in his power, whether in himfelf, or towards the King, to ferve me.* The extraordinary aftonifhment and furprize, wherein I was at fo great a generofity, did not hinder me from making anfwer with all acknowledgment and due fubmiffion; and from telling him that he highly reveng'd himfelf on me, in putting me into fo great a confufion before the King and the whole Army.

The King in the mean time was in pain to know the fubject of this conference, and Monfieur *de Villedonné* having told him his thought, which was, that the Cardinal was doubtlefs talking to me, about what had paft betwixt us near *Sezanne*; his Majefty expreft a defire to fee that Officer, to hear a particular account out of the Cardinal's own mouth, after what manner I had efcap'd from his hands. The relation he then made gave me occafion of being known to the King, and was,

as

as it were, the foundation and beginning of the great favour and
bounty his Majesty has manifested towards me ever since; as shall be
made appear in the progress of these *Memoirs*. He very much commended the generosity of Monsieur *de Guise* his proceeding with me in
this affair, as indeed it was highly commendable, especially in a person
of his great quality and merit : and this Cardinal was always mindful
of the promise he had done me the honour to make me, having exprest
so much kindness to me even to the end of his Life; as in the sickness
whereof he died at *Xaintes*, to send for me, and tell me with extraordinary favour and goodness, that I ought to regret his death, since I in
him lost one of the best Friends I had in the world, of which he would
have given me proof, had he lived longer.

XV. The Army was after this sent away to several Quarters upon
the confines of the Kingdom; and we of the Regiment of *Champagne*
had the little Town of *Oleron* in Bearn assign'd for ours. Our Company and another was lodg'd in a Suburb call'd *Mercadet* : and the two
Captains being retir'd to their own Houses, had left their Companies
to their Lieutenants, of which I was the eldest, and consequently
commanded the Quarters. About a Year after the *Hugonots* began the
War again, and to rise in Arms. The Marquess *de la Force* was Governour
of the Country, but being one of the greatest zealots of the *Hugonot* Party,
he abandon'd the King's service, and laboured to raise all the men he could.
Having one day sent a Trumpet into the Suburb of *Mercadet*, to proclaim that all the Captains of the Religion were suddenly to repair to
Pau, the Capital City of *Bearn*, where he made his ordinary abode, to
receive his orders : I was surpriz'd at the noise, and stept to the Trumpet to demand of him what it was that he proclaim'd, and why he was so
bold as to dare to sound in my Quarter without my leave, seeing he knew,
what was but too well known throughout the Country, that his Master
had already manifested himself to be less affected to the King's service,
than that of his Enemies; and therewithal commanded him immediately
to be gone, threatning him if he did not do it, to make him know,
that I very well understood how to maintain his Majesty's interests.
Upon this he left the place where he had begun to sound; but being
got a little further off, fell to sounding again. This so manifest contempt of the interdiction I had given him, in order to the maintaining
the King's right, so far incens'd me, that coming up to him, and seeing
that, relying upon the authority of his Master, he, to this first contempt
of my orders added an insolent reply; I snatcht his Trumpet from him,
broke it over his shoulders, and beat him out of my Quarters; assuring
my self, that the King would not disapprove my defending thus his
interests against an Enemy of his Crown.

Nevertheless I went immediately to wait upon Monsieur *de Poyenne*
the King's Lieutenant in *Bearn*, who was very affectionate to his Majesties service, and consequently little belov'd by the Governour, and
gave him an account of what I had done; who told me I had done
well, and no more than my duty : But foreseeing the consequence of
this affair, being well assur'd that Monsieur *de la Force* would never pardon this affront; and being moreover afraid, that should the King
come to hear of it before he was inform'd of the truth, his Majesty
might perhaps accuse my zeal of some excess; I entreated Monsieur *de*
Poyenne that when he writ to Court, as he frequently did, he would

put

put in a word in my behalf, to prevent all the ill reports by which my enemies might have decry'd my conduct. He did accordingly, and so effectually withal, that the King to assure me he was satisfied with my service, gave me the Government of the Tower of *Oleron*, a little Fortrefs that commanded the Town; which, though a little thing in it self, and that no great revenue belong'd to it, yet was it of consequence that this Tower should be in the hands of a faithful person to keep the Town in its duty; and it was no less advantageous to me after the Act I had committed, that had made a great noise in the Country, that the King should publickly manifest his being satisfied with it, in giving me this Government; whilst Monsieur *de la Force* was making my procefs at *Pau*. For though it was not hard for him to cause me to be condemn'd there, to have my Head cut off, he did not find it so easie to execute the Sentence, seeing I was of his Majesty's Party, and under his protection.

XVI. The War breaking out still more fiercely, our Regiment of *Champagne* was commanded to the Rendezvous of the Army, which oblig'd me to think of divesting my self of my Government, being unwilling to be stinted to so small a preferment; I thought fit therefore to resign it into the hands of Monsieur *de Poyenne*, who had procur'd it for me: who, after having been very importunate with me to stay there, and giving me many assurances to procure for me something more considerable for the future; seeing me absolutely resolv'd to leave it, compell'd me however, whether I would or no, to name another in my stead. I therefore presented him a Gentleman call'd *Domvidaut*, who was indeed a *Higmot*, but who had always manifested so great a zeal for the Kings service, that I thought it impossible for him ever to fail in his duty. And because I would tye him yet faster to Monsieur *de Poyenne*, I gave him to understand, that he was oblig'd to him only for this Government. He on his part thought he could not better exprefs his acknowledgment, than by entrusting me with his Son, whom he entreated me to receive in the quality of a Cadet, into the Company of which I was Lieutenant.

XVII. We went presently after to the Siege of *Saint John d' Angely*, which the King in person came to besiege, in the year 1620, of which Siege I shall only make report of one action, wherein I with several others underwent a very great peril, from which it appears we were only deliver'd by a kind of miracle.

Being upon the point to spring a Mine, I was commanded with 40 Men to charge into the breach so soon as ever it should be open, by that means to deprive the Enemy of the means to repair it. We were therefore of necessity to approach very near, and to have something to cover us, in case we should be forc'd to retrench our selves. I therefore desired Baskets instead of Sacks, which were commonly made use of upon such occasions, arguing that it would be much more easie to fill them that stood open, and stiff of themselves, than Sacks that did not so; and accordingly we had forty deliver'd to us, which serv'd us very much, but after another manner than we propos'd to our selves. We then advanc'd as near as we could to the Mine, which in playing had an effect quite contrary to what was expected: for instead of throwing the Earth into the Town, it threw it back upon us, the soil being lighter on our
side,

fide, and buried us under its ruines.   But by the greateſt good fortune imaginable, having made all our Souldiers by my example carry all their Baskets upon their heads, that our hands might be at liberty to handle all our arms, they not only broke part of the force of the Earth, and Stones, and preſerv'd us from having our brains beaten out, but moreover ſerv'd to give us a little breath, in leaving us a little vacuity, that preſerv'd us from being ſtifled before we could be reliev'd.   Monſieur *de Cominges*, who was at the end of the Trench, having ſeen ſome Souldiers hurt with the Stones that the Mine had blown about, and judging in what extremity we were likely to be, came running to aſſiſt us, and diſengag'd us from under the Rubbiſh, whilſt the Enemy were buſie in repairing the breach, without thinking of us.

In the mean time, that which by accident ſav'd our lives on this occaſion, was afterwards put into practice in other Sieges ; and they have ſince often made uſe of theſe Baskets, as very proper to make quick lodgments, and ſpeedily to cover themſelves; which alſo made the King himſelf to confeſs, that I had herein done him a very conſiderable ſervice, which was almoſt all the recompence I had for having ran ſo great a hazard.   My inclination for War, and the averſion I have ever had for all remedies, hindred me from cauſing my ſelf to be let blood , as I had been advis'd: but I found my ſelf ſo ill by having been ſo bruis'd and overwhelm'd by theſe ruines, and by having been more led by my own inconſiderate heat than the counſel of my Friends, that I had the Jaundice for a month together, to that degree that I was hardly to be known.   But my better parts being ſtill in their vigour, and my heart always whole and good, I never excus'd my ſelf from my ordinary duty upon the Guard, in one of which I receiv'd a Carabine ſhot in the body, which entring but a little way, kept me but a very ſhort time in bed.

The End of the Second Book.

K   BOOK

BOOK III.

What past at the Siege of Montaubon. *The great and strict Friendship that was* contracted *betwixt the Sieur* de Pontis *and Monsieur* Zamet, *Camp-master of the Regiment of Picardy, who makes him his own Lieutenant of his Majesty's Armies. The Sieur* de Pontis *withdraws all the Army from a very great Danger. The Siege is rais'd from before Montaubon. An* excellent Discourse *of Monsieur* de Zamet *upon that Subject.*

1. THE City of *St. John d' Angely* having surrendred it self to the King, his Majesty went before *Montaubon* with an Army of four and twenty Thousand men, or thereabouts, commanded by Monsieur *le Connestable de Luines*; and invested it the 17th of *August*, in the year 1621. The Constable had for Lieutenant Generals, his Brothers, Messieurs *du Maine, de Chevreuse*, and *de Lesdiguieres*: Monsieur *de Schomberg* was grand Master of the Artillery, and Surintendant *de Finances*, and executed also in part the command of a Lieutenant General. Of these Forces, and of these Chiefs, the King made three Attacks, of which the first was his own, wherein the Constable and his Brothers commanded; the second was commanded by Monsieur *du Maine*; and the third by Messieurs *de Chevreuse*, and *de Lesdiguieres*. Monsieur *du Maine* attackt the *Fauxbourg de Ville-bourbon*, which was very strongly fortified, and very commodious to the Enemy, both for the passage of Victuals into the Town, and a Commerce with their Neighbours; by which means this attack, though the most important, was of the greatest difficulty and danger. That of Monsieur *de Chevreuse* was call'd that of *Dumontier*, and was weaker than the other, which made Monsieur *de Schomberg*, Grand-master of the Artillery, plant his principal Batteries there, compos'd of four and twenty pieces of Cannon, and the best serv'd that ever any were, by reason that he himself was Overseer of the Treasury. The Regiments of *Picardy* and *Champagne*, of which he had a particular esteem were encampt at this attack. He having a design to advance fourteen pieces of Cannon much nearer than they had been planted when we first sate down before the place, had a mind first to know what this *Fauxbourg* of *Dumontier* was, which at distance appear'd ruinous and uninhabited; but he fear'd they might have posted some Ambuscade there, that might sally out and nail his Cannon, should he approach so near. He propos'd this doubt to the Generals, who presently gave order that two Officers should be commanded to discover these places; and Monsieur *de Cominges* and I, were appointed for this service. The order being given us, I leap'd up behind Monsieur *de Cominge*, my own Horse not being there, and we went in open day to ford a current of water call'd the *Tescou*. So soon as we were over I alighted, and entred not only into the *Fauxbourg*, but into the ruinous houses that remain'd standing, and search'd them one after another. Monsieur *de Cominge* on

his

his side did the same, and when we thought we had seen all, we bethought us to examine some by-corners, where we conceiv'd we might make some new discovery, and found that in truth it was one of the most important places, and that men cannot be too exact upon such occasions. We return'd to make our report to the Generals, amongst whom Monsieur *de Lesdiguieres* was he who judg'd the best of our exactness, by reason that he had particular knowledge of this place.

The Enemy having had notice, that some had been sent to discover this Suburb, fear'd we would post our selves there to straighten them the more; which prompted them to defend it by a lodgment, that they made in a little Island, which was at the head of this Suburb, and that was encompassed with the *Tescon*, a Rivulet that was but narrow, but very deep. There was no Bridge over this Current, and to pass over it they had laid a Tree across, over which it was not easy to pass upright on ones feet, but only by getting astride, and shifting forward by the help of ones arms, which made the Enemy not fear to be that way surpriz'd by the Foot: As to the Horse they could pass no way but over the same Ford where we had past in going to this *Fauxbourg*; and which being very open, was moreover so straight that they could march but very few in a front. All these advantages prevail'd with them to place two Out-Guards at the end of this Island, one of fifty men nearest to the Town, and the other of ten, which was almost half way betwixt the advanc'd Battery and the Town.

II. The Generals, and particularly Monsieur *de Schomberg*, were a little perplext, fearing very much for the Cannon, which might easily be all nai'd in a night; it was therefore resolv'd in the Council of War to fall upon the first *Corps de Guard*, though it was a very dangerous thing to attempt, by reason the passage was so straight and difficult, by which they were to go and come : but the great importance of driving off that *Corps de Guard* so much advanc'd, made the Generals resolve to hazard some men. For this service the Officer of *Champagne* was nam'd, for so it was, that the King and Lieutenant Generals were pleas'd to call me, knowing me much better by that name than that of *de Pontis*; and I had orders to take with me fifty men to charge this *Corps de Guard*. Being that I came off the Guard that very day, and that according to rule I ought not to be commanded, Monsieur *de Schomberg* thought fit to make me some excuses, and to them added, that this attack being of the last importance to him, he entreated me for his sake to do as if it had been my turn. These occasions being as every one knows honourable, I told him that I found my self very sensibly oblig'd in the choice he made of my person to perform this service for him, assuring him withal, that if the thing was to be done, it should not stick at us to procure him all manner of satisfaction. I chose out fifty brave Souldiers, who all followed me with great joy, knowing me for a man who would not expose their lives, but when I expos'd my own, who always gave them their due praises upon all occasions, and was ever as sparing of them as possibly I could. With their men I came to the little Bridge of which I spoke before, which took us up some time to pass over, by reason of the difficulty already observ'd, and afterwards falling all together upon the first *Corps de Guard*, without giving them so much leisure as to observe how many we were, we gave them so brisk a charge, as forc'd them to retire with fewer of their number to the other *Corps de Guard*, which sallied not out of its Post, for fear of laying them-

selves

felves open, thinking that we had been more than we were. Their retrenchments were of Trees laid upon one another, and we were preparing our felves to affault them, when on a fudden we heard a great noife of confus'd voices from the King's Army, who cry'd out to us to retire: but the diftance hindring us from hearing diftinctly what they faid, we were as much induced to believe that they encourag'd us to charge the Enemy, as that they admonifh'd us to retire.

In the mean time Monfieur *du Maine*, who had planted himfelf upon a little eminence to fee the fuccefs of our enterprize, difcover'd, when he leaft dreamt of any fuch thing, a great number of the Enemy, who being fallied out of the Town, behind the *Fauxbourg*, march'd along by the *Tefcon*, and were coming to enclofe us. He prefently caus'd two little Field-pieces to be drawn by ftrength of hand down to the Banks of the River, and to be levell'd to fire upon them; which fucceeded fo well, that their Battallion was fhot through and through, and a great many of their men were laid dead upon the place. The reft frighted at this execution, ftood fome time ftill without advancing, or retreating, by which means, before they could come to themfelves, and take new meafures, we had time, after having feen from whence thefe Cannon fhot came, and perceiv'd the inevitable danger we were in, fpeedily to return, and to recover the Bridge, as by thofe great outcries our own people had given us warning to do. The Enemy had no ftomach to purfue us, but return'd the fame way they came, very much difpleas'd that they had fail'd of their defign. I loft in this action but two men, and had but three wounded. For my own part I had no hurt at all, and had only my Hat ftruck off by a Mufquet fhot. Monfieur *de Schomberg* who was extreamly generous, thinking himfelf very much oblig'd by this fervice I had done him, made me a very particular acknowledgment, and promis'd to ferve me to the King. He effectually did fo, and fpoke fo advantageoufly of me, that I was in the extreameft confufion at the praifes he gave me for only acquitting my felf of my duty.

III. In the mean time I can fay this, that by this publick teftimony of his efteem, he procur'd me the greateft treafure that I could ever have had; which was the Friendfhip of the worthieft, moft vertuous, and moft generous man, that in my life I ever knew, I mean Monfieur *de Zamet*, at that time Camp-mafter to the Regiment of *Picardy*, who was prefent when Monfieur *de Schomberg* fpoke publickly in my favour before the whole Army. What he heard him then fay, join'd with what he already knew of me on feveral occafions, made him refolve to chufe me for his Friend, and from that inftant he wifh'd, as he told me afterwards, to have me for his Lieutenant. He began to exprefs a very particular affection for me, and entreated me to come often to fee him. It was by this then that the ftrict Friendfhip which was contracted between us began, of which I can fay the foundation was on one part built upon the knowledge I had of the merit and wifdom of this great man, and the other on his own bounty to look upon me, as a man whom he thought not altogether unworthy of his Friendfhip.

The very particular obligation that I had to Monfieur *du Maine*, for having fo feafonably reliev'd me in fo perilous an occafion, prompted me for the future to feek out all ways whereby I might manifeft my acknowledgment. For though he in this only follow'd the ordinary Rules of War, which oblige every one to fuccour the King's Forces, when they fee

them

them expos'd as we were, neverthelefs the manner after which he did it, gave me fufficiently to underftand, that it had been a particular effect of his own bounty. And I confefs I was a little mortified; when thinking I had found a favourable occafion wherein to return part of what I ought him, I was hindred from doing it, by him from whom I was to receive my Orders. Monfieur *du Maine* having a defign to carry the *Fauxbourg de Villebourbon* by affault, commanded almoft all his Foot to fall on, who pufh'd the Guards with fo great fury and vigour, that three hundred men were already mounted upon the Wall, and held themfelves affur'd to remain Mafters of it. The Enemy feeing themfelves fo forc'd, call'd in above two Thoufand Men to their releif, who being behind good retrenchments, beat our men off, and made them defcend much fafter than they had mounted, but in lefs number, by reafon of thofe who were left upon the place. Being this fight could not be made, but that it muft be heard to the other Quarters, where we had fufficient notice both by the firing, and the noife that was made both on the one fide and the other, I thought that Monfieur *du Maine* might very well be in a condition to admit of fome relief, and therefore at the inftant went to ask leave of our Lieutenant Collonel call'd *Pyolet*, that he would permit me to go manifeft to Monfieur *du Maine*, to whom I was fo much oblig'd, a part of my acknowledgment, in offering my fervice to him, with fifty or threefcore men of our body. Monfieur *de Pyolet* commended my defign, but told me withal, that being but Lieutenant Collonel, he could not fuffer what the King had forbid, which was, that no one fhould go from one quarter to another. Thus was I afflicted to the laft degree to lofe this occafion, and might fay methinks, that had I had but a part of that gratitude for the infinite favours I have receiv'd from Almighty God, that I had for Men; I had been as good a Chriftian, as I was then remote from God, and all true Piety.

Monfieur *de Pyolet* having afterwards fpoke to the Lieutenant Generals about this affair, had permiffion upon the like occafion to grant what I had defir'd of him, provided the detachment fhould confift but of fifty or threefcore men at moft. Wherefore feeing one day a great fire at Monfieur *du Maine*'s Quarter, I ran thither with threefcore men, in hopes that I might do him fome fervice, but I found it was only fire that had caught in the Huts. He, very much furpriz'd to fee me there with my men, askt me the reafon of it, which I told him; expreffing withal, that I thought my felf extreamly unhappy in that I could not meet with an occafion wherein to acknowledge the favour, for which I fhould be eternally oblig'd to him. He thereupon took me in his arms, telling me publickly, that he was fo much the more oblig'd to me, in that having done nothing for me but what was his duty, I did that for him which I was no way oblig'd to do; that he would never forget it, and that he entreated me to come often to fee him, and to employ him as one of the beft friends I had. But the protection of this Prince, that in all appearance might have been fo advantageous, continued not long; for a few days after, Monfieur *du Maine* was kill'd with a Mufquet fhot, which paffing betwixt two Barrels, went firft through Monfieur *de Schomberg*'s Hat, and thence into the Eye of Monfieur *du Maine*, by which he was laid dead upon the place. This confiderable lofs made me remember the other I had fuffer'd in the perfon of the Cardinal of *Guife*: but all this could not work fo upon me, to think of any thing more ferious and folid.

L

IV. To continue what befell me during this Siege; being upon the Guard at the Trenches, I was one day commanded by Monfieur *de Pyolet* to fuftain the Miner, who was at work under the Wall; and being of a little unquiet nature, I fancied, I know not for what reafon, that the Enemy might very well countermine againft our Work. I faid as much to fome of our Officers, and to the Miner, who all laught at me; but judging neverthelefs that the Enemy might very well do, what I fhould have done had I been in their place, I thought to aſſure my felf further of the truth of the thing: I therefore call'd for a Drum into the Mine, of which I fet one end upon the ground, and laid a Mufquet bullet upon the other, that at every blow the Counterminers gave, it might found upon the Drum, by the means of the Ball. This defign took effect, and made us hear what I defir'd. The Miner, a little aftonifht, laugh'd no more as before, but told us that we muft immediately retire; whereupon I prefently made ready our men, and fent to acquaint them at the tail of the Trench, with what we had difcover'd. The Miner having afterwards examin'd the bufinefs a little nearer, affur'd me that there was but little Earth betwixt us and the Enemy; and that they would prefently ftrike through into his Mine, and accordingly we prefently faw light, by which hole they fir'd upon us fome Piftol-fhot, to which I made anfwer with one I had in my hand; commanding my Souldiers to beat back thefe Counterminers with their Halberts; which doubtlefs had been no hard matter to do, but that at the fame time a great many men being fallied by another way came directly towards the Trench, with a defign to cut it off; and oblig'd me to retire fighting, and making good our Retreat, till the reſt of our Regiment fhould advance to our relief. I found my felf much more perplext, when I faw at leaſt thirty Granadoes fly in the air, which the Enemy threw into the Trench. There were a great many Souldiers hurt, and all fo daunted, that I was forc'd to withdraw, to make way for the whole Regiment, who came in freſh, and repell'd the Enemy. I was wounded in the Thigh with a fplinter of one of thefe Granadoes, of which I was neverthelefs prefently cur'd.

V. The fecond time I mounted the Guard after this, my poſt was again to fuftain the Miner, upon whom, as he was at work at the Baftion, they continually from above threw down Stones, and a thoufand other things to brain him; which made us contrive to cover this place with Beams, that he might work in fafety. Dinner time being come, we withdrew from the Trench, and plac'd our felves in the mouth of the Mine, to be yet in greater fecurity. This forefight fav'd all our Lives; for immediately after the Enemy threw down from above Pipes filled with the drofs of Iron that comes from the Forges, and which is fo ponderous a thing, that thefe Hogfheads falling upon the forementioned Beams, broke them all, and fo fill'd the Trench, that no body could pafs, fo that had they made ufe of their advantage, they had certainly had a good bargain of us: but not knowing what had hapned, they gave us time to difengage our felves, though with much ado. We did not get off fo well afterwards, for as I was engag'd in feveral dangerous occafions, and that my too much forwardnefs was the caufe that I too frankly expos'd my life, one day as I was again fet to guard the fame Miner, the Enemy made a Sally upon the head of the Trench, which
we

we at firſt ſuſtained vigorouſly enough, but by reaſon that, to make a better reſiſtance, and to ſtand more firm, we had drawn our ſelves up cloſe together, the Enemy, who came on another open ſide on the top of the Trench, having thrown down on a ſudden twenty great pots of boyling Pitch, put us in the moſt miſerable condition that ever poor men were in, being reduc'd almoſt to be burnt alive in our cloaths. Many of us died, and others eſcap'd by tearing off their cloaths ; I for my part having rowl'd my ſelf to no purpoſe upon the earth to cool me, and finding my ſelf ſtill extreamly afflicted with the pain, I could think of no better remedy than to throw my ſelf into the River, where I began a little to breathe; and from whence neverthelefs I came not out quite cur'd, for I had my Shoulders ſufficiently broil'd, as well as ſeveral others, which gave the Enemy occaſion to jeer us, in crying, *To the Grill, To the Grill*; and to ask us if we had not been pepper'd and ſalted enough. Adding, That they would take care we ſhould be better handled the next time.

VI. Monſieur *de Schomberg*, who has ever done me the honour to love me, and to make it appear he had ſome confidence in me in theſe affairs, ſent for me a few days after, and told me that he had a great mind to force a Half-Moon, that had kept it ſelf but too long; that he believ'd with Fire-works it might be brought to paſs; and that he remembred he had ſeen certain Fire-pots that plaid with great effect, but that he did not know any one in the Army, that either knew how to make them, or to make uſe of them. It hapned by good luck that I not only knew this ſort of Pots, but alſo how to make and uſe them; which made me tell Monſieur *de Schomberg* that I would be reſponſible to him for theſe Fire-works, and that he might rely upon me for the proviſion. But being there was great danger in the throwing them, he would not ſuffer me to throw them my ſelf; but only told me, that after I had made them ready, I ſhould make choice of ſome good Souldier, whom I ſhould inſtruct after what manner they were to be thrown. I prepared then theſe Pots, which were of Clay, and fill'd them as they ſhould be with Gunpowder, covering them very well, and tying them with good Pack-thread, about which were ſeveral ends of lighted Matches; to the end that the Pots being thrown, and breaking with the fall, ſome one of the bits of Match ſhould fall into the Powder, and fire it, which would break the Pot into a thouſand pieces, and make a terrible havock by reaſon of the broken pieces that flew on every ſide, and which in wounding and killing ſeveral people would ſtrike a terrour into the reſt, who were not accuſtom'd to that ſort of fire.

I then began to conſider of chooſing a perſon capable of throwing theſe Pots, and of doing it ſo dexterouſly, as to be ſerviceable to us; and at laſt bethought me of a Souldier that was very brave, and very handy, call'd *Montably*, who had long importun'd me to put him upon ſome ſervice, wherein he might ſignalize himſelf, and who every time he met me urged me to that effect; which made me think of propoſing this to him, that he might make himſelf be taken notice of by Monſieur *de Schomberg*. Having therefore ſent for him, I open'd to him my whole deſign, and made him withal ſenſible of the danger, that I might not deceive him : Which having done, I demanded his reſolution. He immediately with great joy embraced an occaſion he had ſo long wiſht for, telling me withal, that it would be the means either to puſh his fortune, or to

put

put him out of need on't. I then instructed him more than he desir'd, in all things, designing at once to make our enterprize succeed, and to precaution him against the danger, and for my last order commanded him positively after he had thrown these Pots to retire, and let them fall on who were commanded to give the Assault. Had he taken my advice, I had been entirely satisfied in this affair; but this young man more generous than obedient, after the happy execution of what had been commanded him, could not forbear proceeding to what he was forbid, and to go with his Sword in his hand upon the Enemy, where he received a Musquet shot that laid him dead upon the place; which gave me a sensible displeasure in the midst of the joy we had to see our Enterprize perfectly succeed. For the Pots I have spoken of, wrought so great an effect, and the Besiegers push'd the Enemy with so great vigour, that without any considerable loss, saving that of this brave young man, the Half-moon was forc'd and won.

VII. Some days after, as I was mounting the Guard, the Enemy made a great Sally, and they had already begun to nail two pieces of Cannon, when I was commanded to repel them with a body that I had rally'd together, in which there was a very brave *Swiss*. The Enemy having at this time also thrown some Granadoes which made a sufficient havock amongst us, one that fell into a Barrel of Powder gave fire to't, and cut off both the poor *Swisse*'s Legs, blew the Heads of one of the barrels against my stomach with much force, that I thought my self cut in two, and was ready to swoon; it put me to the greatest pain that ever I had felt in all my life, but being come to my self, and having examined my body all over, feeling no blood, and discovering no wound, I confess I was extreamly glad, because I thought my self a dead man; and though I ventur'd my life as freely as another, I had no mind at all to dye. That which sav'd me was a Cuirasse I had put on that day, which resisted the blow, and which by the reverberation caus'd my pain.

VIII. Eight or ten days after this, mounting the Guard in a Trench, whilst Monsieur *de Zamet* mounted another on the right hand which belong'd to his Regiment, as the first of *France*, it hapned, that as he was advancing his work very far, the Enemy sallied in so great number, and with so much resolution, that they overturn'd the head of the Trench upon the tail, which also gave way. Monsieur *Zamet* having rallied some Souldiers stood firm for some time, and made good his ground with his own person, till being wounded in the Arm with a Musquet shot, and out of condition of fighting, he was taken Prisoner, and led into a corner at distance, with several others of his Officers, where he was under Guard, whilst the Enemy still pusht the rest of his Regiment.

In the mean time that of *Champagne* not being commanded, we had our own Trench to guard, and I seeing that of *Picardy* so handled and broken, and perceiving the gross of the Enemy at distance drawn up in the corner, who there kept these Prisoners, without thinking that Monsieur *de Zamet* was of the number; I ask'd leave of Monsieur *de Pyolet*, to go and relieve our Companions, before they were carried away, assuring him that I would have but fifty chosen men to deliver them, and to drive away the Guard that kept them. He granted my request, and immediately chose out fifty men, that I knew to be very brave; but above twenty Serjeants out of generosity took the places of so many Souldiers, I

sent

sent them back, and all the Regiment (the occasion appear'd so honorable) would have been of the Party. I made them all take no other Arms but Halberts only, and took one my self, being I had ever found it the best Weapon when men come to blows. After having concluded how we should attack the Enemy, we march'd through a little cover'd way that wholly conceal'd us, till we were just upon them; and charging all together into the middle of this body that kept our people enclos'd, we so astonish'd them with this surprize, and unexpected attack, that thinking they had all the Army upon them, they made very little resistance, but ran away, leaving some of their men behind them.

IX. But I was very much astonish'd to see Monsieur *Zamet* amongst these Prisoners, which also made my joy the greater, though it was not without some mixture of fear, when I saw him cover'd all over with blood. I ask'd him where he was hurt, and he gave me comfort, by telling me it was only in his Arm. I conducted him back to his Regiment, where he embrac'd me several times, telling me, he would never forget this service I had done him, of which, that he might give me further assurance, he entreated me to come see him the next day, so soon as I should be reliev'd from the Guard, and I fail'd not to come according to his desire. As soon as he saw me, he made me lean down upon his Bed, that he might embrace me, and told me with infinite kindness, that he would not only love me so long as he liv'd, but would publickly acknowledge that he stood indebted to me for his life and liberty; that he could not better manifest his gratitude, than by assuring me that I should be Master both of the one and the other, as things that belonged to me, and to which I had acquir'd an absolute right in preserving them; that he would for the future divide with me both his goods and fortune; that he would have me from this time forward, look upon him as my Brother; and that being he could not confer upon me any command that could tye me nearer to him, than that of his own Lieutenant, he entreated I would accept the offer he made me, that I might begin to enter upon my share of whatever belonged to him, that he might hereafter advance me, and change my Command according as he should rise himself, and advance his own fortune. To conclude, he said all this to me after so tender and affectionate a manner, adding withal that he promis'd in the presence of God to make all this good to me, that I cannot express the disposition I found my self in, after such an obliging discourse.

I told him, to do Monsieur *de Pyolet* a good Office, who had entreated me to lay part of this obligation upon him, that I had not only done what I was commanded, and that it was in executing the commands of another, I had been so happy as to do him this service; but that I stuck not from that moment to a man so worthy to be belov'd, to engage both my person and my life; so that from that very day there was so strict an Union contracted betwixt us, as death it self could not dissolve, being I still find it so firmly engraven in my heart, four and thirty years after the loss of this Friend, that I cannot think or speak of it without being mov'd to a degree that I cannot express.

I began then from this moment to live with this incomparable Friend, not only as with a Brother, but as with my own Father, having for him the same respect, and paying him with all possible assiduity the same duty, and the same deference, as if I had really been his Son. For all my Duties upon the Guard, and the occasions upon which I was commanded

M   excepted,

excepted, I was continually by his Bed fide; lying with my hand in the ftateliest Union that can poffibly be imagin'd; which alfo was much augmented upon a new accident, which I think my felf oblig'd to relate.

X. The Enemy having made another furious Sally, came and fet fire to our Powder, lam'd the Carriages of two pieces of Cannon, to which they fet fire alfo, and were endeavouring to nail the reft, when I was commanded out with a body of threefcore men to repel them; where I once more thought I fhould have been fcorch'd to death by a Barrel of Powder they gave fire to in their retreat. After having beaten them from the Battery, I retir'd with the reft of our Regiment, which with great vigour beat the Enemy back even into their own Fort, though it could not be done without great lofs on our part. Amongft the Officers that were kill'd in this action, there was one very brave man call'd Captain Robert; of whofe death the King being inform'd, he prefently thought of the Officer of *Champagne*, to confer the command upon: for, befides other occafions wherein I had been particularly taken notice of by his Majefty, he had heard of the fervice I had done Monfieur *Zamet*, and the other Prifoners, in refcuing them out of the Enemies hands. Calling therefore for Monfieur *de Puiffeux*, he told him that he gave me the Company of Captain *Robert*, commanding him to difpatch my Commiffion, and to fend it to me before I knew any thing of it. Monfieur *de Puiffeux*, who thought himfelf highly oblig'd to me, for having without fpeaking to him, or his having entreated me, preferv'd a Country Houfe of his, that was near the Army, from being plundred by the Souldiers, by putting into it a Gurrd of fix Mufqueteers, was exceeding glad of this opportunity of ferving me to the King; and therefore taking the liberty to tell him his opinion concerning the choice his Majefty had made, he fpoke of me to him the moft advantageoufly that he poffibly could, fo much as, unknown to me, to acknowledge the little fervice I had endeavoured to do him. The Commiffion therefore was difpatch'd that night, and being deliver'd to me in the morning, without my having had the leaft intimation of it, I confefs I more valued the King's remembring me of his own accord, than I did my preferment to the Command; tho I did pretty much covet that too, not believing that the Lieutenancy of Monfieur *Zamet* could be conferr'd upon me fo foon.

I went forthwith to carry my Commiffion to Monfieur *Zamet*, who look'd a little coldly upon it, and ask'd me if I had rather have the Company than to be his Lieutenant; adding withal, that he very well knew, that in order and pay, a Company was worth more, but that he believ'd it was much more advantageous to me to be Lieutenant to a perfon who was fo abfolutely my own, as he was, who affur'd me no lefs than his goods and fortune, and therefore entreated me to think on't before I accepted the Command. To this I made anfwer, that he very well knew, that I had already affur'd him, that I was entirely his, and that accordingly he fhould be the abfolute Mafter in this affair; that as I had hitherto no hand at all in it, being meerly oblig'd to the King's bounty, who had thought of me of himfelf; and to the kind remembrance of Monfieur *de Puiffeux* who had difpatch'd the Commiffion before I had heard a fyllable of it, I could not better let him fee how much I was at his difpofal, than by bringing him the Commiffion to do with it as he himfelf thought fit. He then told me, that he had a great mind to inform the King of the particulars that paft in that Sally of the Enemy I have mention'd before, where I reftor'd him his liberty, and

that

that being there was no one who had had so great a share in it as my self, I was able to give a better account than any one of that action, and therefore he should be glad I would go wait upon his Majesty in the afternoon and present him a Letter that he would write. I did so, where after I had presented Monsieur *Zamet*'s Letter, and given an account of his health, which his Majesty enquir'd after, he immediately fell to speaking of the occasion, wherein I had rescu'd him out of the Enemies hands, commanding me to tell him the whole story, which I accordingly did as well as I could: I then took my opportunity to return my most humble thanks for the honour his Majesty had done me, in remembring me after a manner so much to my advantage, and of which I should retain a profound acknowledgment all the days of my life. But the King seeing I took no notice of Monsieur *Zamet*'s design, said to me, But you have not told me all this while that *Zamet* would have you for his Lieutenant? to which I made answer, That I was in the first place bound to let his Majesty know my sense of this very particular favour he had been pleas'd to shew me, when I least thought of any such thing; and as to the other, which Monsieur *Zamet* sollicited in my behalf, it was not for me to mention it to his Majesty, and that I should seem not to value the favour he had conferr'd upon me as I ought, should I at the same time I came to return my thanks for the one, make suit for another: But since your Majesty, said I, obliges me to answer to that affair, I can assure you, that I am ready with great chearfulness to do whatever your Majesty shall please to command, whether in accepting, or surrendring the Company in the Regiment of *Champagne*, for the Lieutenancy of Monsieur *Zamet*; which I confess to be to me much more considerable and desireable than many Companies, by reason of the tender Friendship I am happy in from a person of his merit, which is to your Majesty sufficiently known. Being then, Sir, to receive the one or the other from your Majesties hand, I with all my heart resign the Commission your Majesty did me the honour to send me, with an humble request, that your Majesty would be graciously pleas'd to make for me a choice, that I protest, I know not how to make for my self. At the same time I presented my Commission to the King, who very much surpriz'd at my complement, and the free manner wherewith I had referr'd my self into his hands for the choice of one of these two Commands, left me on a sudden to go to the other end of the room, where the Constable *de Luines* was, to whom he told all that I had said to him, and shew'd him the Commission I had return'd into his hands.

The Constable had not been very well satisfied with me in the beginning of the War, by reason of a little occasion wherein I had not manifested so great a complacency as is expected by great men, but notwithstanding he had alter'd his opinion of me upon further knowledge; so that what the King had then told him, having given him yet a better character of my conduct, he answer'd his Majesty, that it was not just to leave so generous an act without recompence; to which he added, Your Majesty expresses an intention to grant Monsieur *Zamet* the favour he desires of you, in giving him Monsieur *de Pontis* for his Lieutenant; but this Command being less advantageous both in respect of pay, and of the honour of Captain, which you have already conferr'd upon him; your Majesty may find a way if you please, to recompence both the one and the other, in ordering him Captains pay, and in adding to the Command of Lieutenant to the Camp-master of the Regiment of *Picardy*, which is the first Regiment of *France*, the new Title of Honour of eldest Lieutenant

in

in your Majesty's Army. Nothing could have been more obliging, than what the Constable spoke to the King in my favour, and he needed to say no more to prevail with him to consent to all things; for immediately Monsieur *de Puisseux* had order to deliver me the dispatches, which accordingly were brought me the same day.

After having return'd my most humble thanks to the King and the Constable, I went back to Monsieur *Zamet*, to whom I deliver'd a Letter from the King, wherein he left it to the bearer to give him an account how he had order'd his affairs; adding only, that he gave him to understand before hand, that the Officer of *Champagne* was now that of *Picardy*, as he had so much wish'd to be; and that he had been easily perswaded to make him so, having found in him a perfect submission, and all possible esteem and friendship for him. Monsieur *Zamet* having read this Letter embrac'd me with all his soul, telling me that it was only to manifest to me, the strict union he was resolv'd henceforward to have with me; after which with a particular tenderness, he repeated to me what he had already protested; namely, that he desired I should now begin to share with him both estate and fortune, as his Brother. I reply'd with the best expressions I could give him of my perfect acknowledgment, and of the passion I had to let him see by my future actions, that I was not altogether unworthy of the choice he had made of me.

XI. The next day having sent for all the Captains of the Regiment, he told them, that he would acquaint them with a piece of news, that he knew would please them very well, which was that the King had given him for his Lieutenant, a man to whom he had before granted a Company in the Regiment of *Champagne*, and who had been so generous, and had so great an esteem for the Regiment of *Picardy*, as to surrender it into his Majesty's hands, that he might be his Lieutenant; that they all knew him particularly well, having often been with him in action, and that they could not choose but remember him, when they saw their Collonel wounded and abed, seeing that without the assistance of the person of whom he was speaking, he had not now been with them; but in the hands of the Enemy: that therefore he assur'd himself they would receive me into their body with great joy, which had the rather mov'd him to ask me of the King; that he conjur'd them to unite in the acknowledgment of the honour I did the Regiment, in preferring a Lieutenancy there, before a Company in that of *Champagne*, my ordinary Regiment. To which all the Officers gave a very obliging answer in my favour.

I presently after came into the Chamber, not having been by when he had thus spoken to them, where, after having receiv'd extraordinary civility on their parts, I told them that I thought my self very happy, that the King had receiv'd my resignation of the Company he had given me, to honour me with that of the Lieutenancy of their Regiment. That though men did not usually love to change a Company for the place of a Lieutenant; yet a man might do it with reason, when it was to enter into a body wherein were so many brave Officers; that I entreated them all to consider me as a person absolutely devoted to them, seeing that for the honour of serving in their Regiment, I quitted another with all its advantages. Monsieur *Zamet* had the satisfaction of seeing, that the jealousy which ordinarily mixes in such occasions, had nothing to do here; for the Captains made me a thousand kind expressions in his presence, with several protestations of the joy they were in to see me united to their body.

And

And the next day the Regiment being drawn up, I took poſſeſſion of my Command of Captain Lieutenant to the Collonel's Company. Nevertheleſs two days after there hapned an occaſion of honour, which had like to have ſet me at odds with the whole Regiment.

XII. One of the Lieutenants diſpoſing himſelf to command in turn, I told him that as Lieutenant to the Collonel, I ought to paſs for youngeſt Captain ; that in this quality I had right to chooſe occaſions of honour at my own pleaſure, and that I made choice of this. This Lieutenant took what I had ſaid to him very ill, and told all the other Lieutenants of the Regiment, who all together came to me, telling me that I had but my turn, no more than they, and that I ſhould not be Maſter of theirs.

To this replying a little roughly, that I very well underſtood my Command, that it gave me the ſame right it did the Collonel Lieutenants of all the old Bodies, and that I could not endure it ſhould be diminiſht in my hands ; they anſwer'd me very briskly, that they were not afraid of my words, by reaſon there were a great many brave men in the Body ; had I not believ'd ſo, Gentlemen, ſaid I, I had not enter'd into it, and 'tis that it may not be ſaid there are any Cowards, that I will maintain my right ; ſeeing I ſhould be look'd upon as ſuch a one, ſhould I fail therein. This ſmart reply, no leſs civil than reſolute, made theſe Gentlemen at laſt to ſeek out ſome way of accommodation, which made them propoſe to me this condition ; that ſince I would have the choice of all occaſions of honour, they askt, that they might rely upon me when they could not go to ſome Guards, where the fatigue was too great. The eaſineſs with which I conſented to their demand, ſaying aloud, that I promis'd it them with all my heart, by reaſon of the experience I had, that there is often more honour to be acquir'd in theſe perillous occaſions, put them into a new confuſion: but they could not go back, having engag'd themſelves into it of their own accord.

XIII. To return to what concerns the Siege of *Montauban*, the Artillery being admirably well ſerv'd by the care of the Grand Maiſtre, who alſo was ſuperintendant of the Treaſury, the Battery of Meſſieurs *de Chevreuſe*, and *de Leſdiguieres*, which a man might alſo call that of Monſieur *de Schomberg*, he being almoſt continually there, wrought a great effect upon the Baſtion of *Dumontier*, ſo that the breach was thought reaſonable for an aſſault. But being they would firſt be very ſure of the true condition of the place, an Officer was appointed to go and diſcover. He did ſo, but with very little exactneſs, having ſeen almoſt nothing, either peradventure becauſe he was afraid, or that he did not advance ſo far as was neceſſary to make a full diſcovery. The diſtruſt they had of his report, made them ſend another, who at his return gave no better account than the firſt. The King then reſolv'd upon an Aſſault: he commanded that the Army ſhould be drawn up in Battaile, and ſhould go on to the attack, when upon the Hill of *Pillis*, which was his Majeſty's Quarter, they ſhould ſee him wave a Handkerchief upon the end of his Cane, which was to be the Signal.

All things were ready, and they only ſtaid expecting the Sign ; when Monſieur *de Schomberg*, prompted by I know not what inſtinct, and ſuſpecting every thing, told the King, that he did not know, whether it would not be proper upon this occaſion, where his Majeſty's honour and the ſafety of his Army were in queſtion, to ſend a third time to diſcover

N   the

the Baftion by fome exact perfon, and of whofe report they could have no reafon to doubt, at the fame time naming me; thinking he did me a great deal of honour in expofing me to the utmoft peril: The King approv'd of the motion, being of opinion, that in fuch occafions, a great many people fee things but by halves, by reafon of the extream danger, and of the little time they have to look about them. I was call'd for inftantly, and Monfieur *de Schomberg* having acquainted me with the anxiety the King was in, and the little certainty they had of the true eftate of the place, told me withal, that he had thought fit to name me to his Majefty, and to propofe that I might be fent to difcover again, by reafon they could not think themfelves fure, till I had made my report. Neverthelefs having a particular affection for me, and knowing very well, that to perform this with the exactnefs requir'd, I could not choofe but expofe my felf to very great danger, he thought fit to tell me farther, that though this affair was of the laft importance to the whole Army, he did not neverthelefs pretend to engage me in it contrary to my own liking. I return'd him the fame anfwer that any other man would have done upon the fame occafion, which was, That he did me wrong to doubt of the joy I was full of upon fuch occafions, to fee my felf honour'd with his efteem, and the good opinion he had of me; that I would go prepare my felf, and that I hop'd to return, and to bring fo good an account, that nothing fhould be found in my report that was not exactly true.

Having then put on a Cuirafs, and a Cask, with a Piftol hanging at my girdle, I eat a bit or two, and then fet out in the fight of his Majefty, and the whole Army, who had their eyes attentively fixt upon me. Being come to the foot of the breach, I there kneel'd down, and pray'd behind fome Stones that were tumbled down, and afterwards began to mount, creeping as well as I could upon my belly. Being got to the top, I had a mind to difcover the place in the fame pofture I had got up, that is to fay lying upon my belly, that I might not be too open, nor too much expos'd to the Mufquet fhot, that whisk'd round about me on every fide: but this pofture affording me but little advantage of feeing what might be beyond the Eaftion, I ftarted up on a fudden, and expofing my felf to a danger, from which God alone was able to protect me, I ran to the very brink of it, from whence I difcover'd the bottom, which was a dreadful retrenchment, and in it a Battalion that feem'd to be of above two thoufand men, of which the firft ranks were all Pikes, and the reft Mufqueteers. At the very inftant that I difcover'd my felf, and lookt down, they made fo furious a difcharge upon me, that I have ever fince lookt upon it as a Miracle that I could efcape; and yet of all thefe great number of fhots, I only reciev'd two upon my arms, which made but flight impreffions, and of which I was not fo much as fenfible at that time.

Affuring my felf then that I had feen all, I return'd with all the hafte I could make, only obferving an eminence near the Kings Quarter, from whence I thought I might poffibly fhew his Majefty himfelf the retrenchment of the Enemy. After which I let my felf fall, on purpofe that I might rowl down to the bottom, and be more out of danger of the fhot; which made all the Army believe I was kill'd; and Monfieur *de Schomberg* turn'd his back, that he might not fee a thing which gave him a great and real affliction, accufing himfelf of being the caufe of my death. But I came off at the expence of a great giddinefs only, out of which being prefently recover'd, I gave God thanks upon my knees for having pre-

ferv'd

serv'd me from so great a danger. After which I presently call'd to mind what I had seen, and writ it down in my Table book, being secure behind the same Stones I mention'd before, and presently appear'd again, when every one thought I was dead.

There may be peradventure some Bravo's, and especially young men, who will look upon it as a weakness, that in so perilous an occasion I should rather have recourse to God, than to give my self up to a foolish confidence, that makes a man run brutishly, and as it were blindfold every where, where death is most terrible: but in my opinion in occasions of this kind, where a man hardly discovers any possible means to save both his honour and his life at once, though he should forget that he was a Christian; to be a man only is sufficient to make him think of him, who can take away not only his Life, but even Courage too, from the man that fancies he has the most. And having been for fifty years together in as many hazardous occasions as any man perhaps of my time, I can witness this, that I have seen very many who have made a vanity of no Religion, as if their impiety ought to pass for a mark of their Valour, whom I have often found to be rather great Braggadochio's than really brave, and that if the danger was on the right hand, would turn to the left; and that would make use of dexterity, where they ought to have staked down their persons, and by their actions to have made good their **vaunting words**.

XIV. After having in this manner escap'd so great a danger, Monsieur *de Schomberg*, as much surpriz'd as overjoy'd to see me, made me drink a glass of Wine, by reason I was almost quite spent, having taken extraordinary pains; I then made my report to him, which put him into a very great astonishment; and when he askt me over again, if I was very sure of what I had told him; I made answer, that I would undertake to shew it him, and to assure both the King and himself by his own sight, having taken notice of an eminence from whence one might discover what I had seen nearer at hand. The King being very impatient to know what I had discover'd, I got on Horseback, and went with Monsieur *de Schomberg* to wait upon him at *Piccis*. Being there, and they having much ado to beleive me, the King would be satisfied by his own eyes, which made me guide him to the same place I had observ'd, and from thence with the help of a Perspective, his Majesty plainly discover'd the Retrenchment, and behind it the Battalion of which I had given him account. He was very much surpriz'd at it, and could not forbear declaring aloud the extream peril to which his Souldiers had been expos'd, without this foresight of Monsieur *de Schomberg*, which had sav'd the lives of a great many men. After which his Majesty had the goodness to tell me, that I had that day done him a very great service, and that he would remember it upon occasion; I did not nevertheless percieve at that time that I was much remembred, and was accustomed to serve without any other interest than that of honour, which also sometimes cost me very dear.

I then return'd to find out Monsieur *Zamet*, who having believ'd me to be dead, cry'd out so soon as he saw me, I protest you shall go no more upon such designs, and I will take very good order for the future, that you shall receive no more Commissions of this kind. For in truth, the thing which nettled him the most, and made him speak after that manner was, that whether I was upon the Guard or no, they thus us'd to make me as it were the publick Victim in all perilous occasions. He ask'd me

me whether I was not hurt, and I aſſur'd him I was not, but only that Monſieur *de Schomberg* had ſhew'd me two ſhots upon my Arms.

XV. The Army upon this was drawn off, and they thought no more of an aſſault. Some days after, Monſieur *de Roban* who kept the Field with a little body of an Army for the *Hugonots*, was reſolv'd to come and relieve *Montauban*. In order to this deſign, he gave fifteen hundred men to a very brave Gentleman call'd *de Beaufort*, to try if he could put part of them into the place. Upon the intelligence his Majeſty had of their March, he caus'd the Guards to be doubled, and reinforc'd in his Camp, which notwithſtanding could not hinder *Beaufort*, being come up to his Quarter, from forcing the Guard, and getting into the Town with eight hundred men, the reſt having been either kill'd or fled : Upon the arrival of theſe ſuccours they two days after made ſuch furious Sallies, as very much diſcourag'd our men, and gave his Majeſty occaſion to conſider, that Winter drawing on, it was better to retire and preſerve his Army for the next Campaign, by reaſon he would have loſt too many men after this relief. Thus at the expiration of fifteen days, namely the firſt of *November*, 1621, we raiſed the Siege; order having been given throughout the Quarters, that upon hearing the firſt Cannon ſhot that ſhould be fir'd that night, every one ſhould be ready with his Arms to march where their Officers ſhould lead them; and before they went, to make extraordinary Fires throughout the Camp. This order thus executed, made the Enemy expect ſome new thing, and rather a general aſſault than the raiſing of the Siege. Wherefore contenting themſelves with cauſing their Poſts to be well guarded, they never thought of commanding out any Troops to fall upon the Rear of our Army, that began to file off, about the dawning of the day.

Monſieur *Zamet* who had been cur'd a few days before, was order'd to make good the retreat, wherein he was not a little aſtoniſh'd to ſee the precipitation, not to ſay the flight, wherewith our Troops march'd away. I being with him, he made me obſerve this haſty retreat, that favour'd indeed of a pannick fear, for they made off as if they had ſeen the Enemy at their heels. And being ſo good a Chriſtian, and a man of ſo much judgment as he was, he began to ſpeak to me a language I had never heard before. *I aſſure you* (ſaid he) *that reflecting upon the Order of Providence in the management of affairs here below, I manifeſtly diſcern, that the God of Juſtice is the God of Battels; that he gives the Victory to whom he pleaſes, and oftentimes to thoſe that are againſt him, by reaſon that they who defend his cauſe do it ſo very ill, and ſo juſtly draw upon themſelves his indignation by their own Crimes; that he puniſhes them by caſting the diſadvantage on their ſide, and filling their Armies with unreaſonable terrors. Thus much is plain upon the preſent occaſion, where our Forces run away without knowing any reaſon why. 'Tis viſibly a ſtroke from the hand of our good God, that contrary to all humane appearances, we have not been able to take this place, which according to the ordinary courſe of Arms muſt have fallen into the Kings Poſſeſſion. His judgments are very different from thoſe of men which ſtop at the outſide of events, without penetrating into the ſecret ſprings of them. Our Enemies no doubt will be as much deceived as we; for they will magnify themſelves for this advantage, without ever conſidering, that the Victory that God gives them will at length but render them the more unhappy, by a falſe aſſurance, that it is a mark of the Juſtice of their Cauſe; and he will at one time or other find means to make them ſenſible what loſs they ſuſtain, while they flatter them-*

selves with a thought of winning all.   Let us admire then and adore the Chastisements he inflicts after so different a way, both upon the one and the other.

I confess I was marvellously surprized at this discourse, having never, as I said, been used to hear the like, and acknowledged the obligations I had to him, for the insight he gave me into so great a truth.   And I must also say, that I did not reckon this favour among the least I received from him, and have since been sensible, that it was one of the first, God was pleased to confer upon me, in order to the giving me some sense of Christianity. The virtue and pious conduct that I observed in this great man, did in some sort contribute to laying the first seeds in the bottom of my heart, and 'tis that which hath infinitely increased my acknowledgments to him, and value of his memory; especially, since after abundance of mistakes and wandrings I had the Grace to know how little to value the world, and absolutely to renounce it.

The End of the Third Book.

The Sieur de Pontis *defends the Town of* Moutefche, *which is attack'd by the Enemy. His Conduct towards an Officer of the Collonel, and of Monfieur* le Duc d' Efpernon, *in a great Difpute they had about the concern of his Command. The Siege of* Tonins. *The great Wound which the Sieur* de Pontis *receives, which reduces him to extremity. The Sack of* Negrepelice. *The Sieur* de Pontis *makes himfelf Mafter of a Fort poffeft by the* Hugonots, *and razes it ; which begets him a great deal of trouble.*

I. THe Siege of *Montauban* being rais'd, the King return'd to *Paris*, and difmift all his forces into their winter quarters. The Regiment of *Picardy* had a little Town of *Guyenne* affign'd for theirs, call'd *Moutefche*, fome feven or eight leagues from *Montauban*. Monfieur *Le Marefchal de Saint Geran*, who ftay'd to give the Orders, feeing that all the Captains of *Picardy* were gone home to their own houfes, gave me the Regiment in charge, and the government of the place, as the order was ; telling me, that being fo near to the Enemy, I ought to keep good guard, and that he rely'd upon my care. I told him he might do fo, and that I would be refponfible to him. Five or fix hours after that the Marefchal *de Saint Geran* had left us, he met a man upon the Road, who was coming to give him notice, that the Enemy were preparing themfelves to attack our Town the night following, intending to take it by affault ; and that it was the Garrifon of *Montauban* that was to execute the defign. Upon this intelligence, Monfieur *de Saint Geran* writ me immediately a Ticket, in which he gave me notice of what he had heard, and advis'd me to take very great care that I might not be furpriz'd. I hereupon prefently affembled all the Officers of the Garrifon, whom I acquainted with the news Monfieur *de Saint Geran* had fent me, and the Orders he had given ; entreating them that we might all together fee which way we fhould beft prepare our felves to receive the Enemy ; telling them withal, that for my part I thought it beft that we fhould prefently take a review of all our Men, of all the Arms, and of all the Ammunition, of the Gates of the Town, of all without, and to confider of the means to fortifie the weakeft places. They all approv'd my advice, and we went prefently about it.

II. Towards the evening one of them call'd *Raftillat*, who was an *Aide Major*, thought fit to come and tell me that I very well knew he was my Servant and my Friend, and that therefore he was forry he was oblig'd to declare that he could not ftay with me upon this occafion, feeing that being *Aide Major*, he was an Officer of Monfieur *d' Efpernon*, who was Collonel of the Infantry, and that therefore in this quality he could not obey me, being that I was but Lieutenant to the *Maiftre de Camp*, of whom Monfieur *d' Efpernon* would not in the

per-

person of his Officers receive Orders.   Adding withal, that he was sorry
to find himself constrain'd to leave me in so brave an occasion; but that
rather chusing to retire betimes, than to occasion any trouble, by reason
he could not obey me, he came to take his leave of me, and to bid me
good night.   I return'd him answer, That as his Servant and his Friend,
I was also oblig'd to tell him that he was not now at liberty to retire;
neither was it in my power to let him go, after he had receiv'd orders
from Monsieur *de Saint Geran*, as well as the rest; and that he had consented to it as well as they in not going out then : That it was not to
decide the pre-eminence betwixt the Collonels Officers and those of the
Maistre de Camp, to obey me upon this occasion, seeing that in this there
was no other thing in question, but to follow the Orders of our General the Mareschal *de Saint Geran*, who had at his going away committed
to me the care of the Regiment, and the defence of the place, and yet
more particularly by the Letter he had sent me; and that I had shew'd
him : And that therefore I entreated him to consider that this was not
a time for punctilio's of Honour between Officers, but that here the question was purely the interest and service of the King, to whom alone
the Town did appertain; and who would be the only loser if we did
not unite in its defence, and make it appear to the whole Kingdom that
we were not unworthy of the commands his Majesty had been pleas'd to
honour us with.   This remonstrance, tho very civil and very rational
too, did not however satisfie this Officer, who could not prevail with
himself to hearken to what he was resolv'd he would not do; so that
seeing the stiffness wherewith I oppos'd my self to his design, he again
urg'd the same thing in an accent civil enough; but perceiving me still
to persist in my opposition with the same obstinacy, he resolutely resolv'd to go, and told me with some vehemence flatly, that he would do
it; which oblig'd me to answer him with some heat too, that he should
not do it; and that he ought to believe that I knew very well how to
make my self obey'd, where I was my self to obey the orders of the
King and the General : To which he reply'd in a great fury, that he
could have wisht I had spoke to him after that manner in a place where
I had not been the Master; to which I made answer, that the business
now in question was to look to the defence of the place, and that it
was not fit to mix personal interest with those of the King; and it was
my part in this occasion to command him, and his to obey me.   Upon
which he turn'd very angrily from me, and went to his Quarters to
make ready his equipage to be gone.

In the mean time I went to find out the Officers who commanded the
guards of the Gates, and gave them express order not to suffer any one
to go out, though it were an Officer; adding, that it was just that every one should partake both the danger and the honour of the service
the King expected from us on so important an occasion.   The two Officers, who were two Lieutenants, answer'd me after such a manner as assur'd me I might rely upon them, and I return'd home.   A little after,
Bastillat, follow'd by his man, rode to the Gate of the Town, where
being stopt by the Centinel, he call'd the Lieutenant Captain of the
Guard, who told him that he had receiv'd Orders to let no one pass.
What do you not know me ? reply'd *Bastillat*. Yes Sir, said he, but my
Orders extend to Officers as well as others, and therefore I beseech you
urge me no more to a thing I cannot grant you.   *Bastillat* nettled to
the quick at this repulse, rode back to his Quarters, and from thence
came

came to speak to me again; but I prevented him, by saying aloud at the head of the Regiment, Sir, 'tis a thing concluded for this time, another time we will talk of it if you please, but for the present 'tis the order you must obey. Seeing then himself in an inevitable necessity that he must submit, he told me, that I had a whole Garrison on my side, and so was the Master, and therefore he would obey me; but that he would find another time when I should not be so well accompanied. To which I gave him only this answer, that in the first place we were to serve the King.

III. At the same time I commanded him to draw up the Regiment in Battaile to see if the Companies were compleat; to visit all the Army, to give out Ammunition to those that wanted, and to acquit himself of all other duties of his command of Major, and he punctually obey'd. I then came to view all these things in general, and taking all the principal Officers along with me, of which he also was one, we went all together to visit the advantageous posts we were to defend, and to give out the necessary Orders, that there might be no confusion nor trouble in the night. I divided the Regiment into three Bodies, the first and greatest to be upon the Parade, and thence to send out relief to those who should stand in need; the second, which was less, was commanded to guard the Gate of the Town, which I thought was likely to be attackt; and I again divided that into three, one of thirty men, which I posted upon a little Van-guard, some fifty paces without the Town; the second, consisting of a hundred men, were posted in the Town-ditch, to sustain the first; and the third, which consisted of about as many, were planted upon the Walls, to defend the second *Corps de Guard:* The third body, which was the least, was appointed for the guard of the other Gate, which was not easie to be attackt, and therefore did not require so great a defence. After I had plac'd all these Guards my self, I sent some hours after to have them again visited by *Bastillat,* who obey'd without any manner of reply, taking great pains, and shewing himself very zealous in the execution of all the Orders he receiv'd.

Night being come, I gave the Word and the Orders to *Bastillat,* to carry to the Serjeant upon the Parade, telling him that at ten a clock I would give another, and that therefore he must come to receive it. Whereupon he told me that it was not an ordinary thing, and that this gave him occasion to believe that it was peradventure to justle and provoke him to the utmost, that I proceeded after this manner. I made answer, that I was not capable of doing so ill a thing : that it was only for the greater security, and that men could not take too much care when they expected an Assault; that I was so far from any thought or intention of disobliging him, that on the contrary I entreated he would come and sup with me; adding that we must make provision of strength and vigour for the labour of the night. He thankt me, and said he would return at ten a clock to receive new Orders. He accordingly came at the hour, and being very weary with the great pains he had taken, I desir'd him to lye down and repose himself a little till further news. For my own part, I went a third time to visit all things, not thinking it seasonable to sleep, and be at rest, when I had so much reason to expect an Enemy.

IV. I

IV. I had caused a Horse to be held ready, that I might ride up and down to every place at the first Alarm, which was not long before it came; for about two of the Clock after midnight, the advanc'd Centinel at the Gate which I had foreseen would be attackt, heard a noise, and gave fire. I had notice of it instantly, and having rous'd *Bastillat*, we went together to the Gate where the Alarm was. I found at my arrival that the first *Corps de Guard* had made their discharge, and that they were vigorously attackt by the Enemy. I enter'd into the second, to which the thirty men of which the first was compos'd came to retire, fighting all the way they retreated, with very great bravery. I then caus'd a discharge to be made by thirty Musquets of that *Corps de Guard* where I was, which a little astonisht the Enemy, who did not expect to meet any other but the first; yet did they for all that continue to charge the second *Corps de Guard*, when I commanded thirty more Musqueteers of the same body to give them another Volley. I sent *Bastillat* at the same time to the other Gate of the Town, for fear the Enemy should attack them both at once; and put a Lieutenant in his place, to carry the Orders, and to bring relief when there should be need.

This choice that I made of *Bastillat*, in giving him a place of honour which did not belong to his command, and supplying his by another, pleas'd him very much, and inspir'd him with other sentiments than he had entertain'd before of my disposition towards him.

In the mean time the Enemy still continu'd their attack, which was equally sustained by our men; but they were soon out of heart, when I commanded all the Musqueteers upon the Walls to fire continually; for being very well inform'd by this that we were too well prepar'd to receive them, and knowing that it would be something hard to force men well resolv'd to defend themselves, they took the wisest course to retire with the loss of some of their men. The attack being over, I encourag'd, and highly prais'd the valour of all our men, who had shew'd themselves equally zealous and obedient in this occasion of honour, wherein they had fought so generously for the service of their Prince.

V. The next day *Bastillat* came to tell me, that he hop'd I would not deny him the liberty of going out of the Town, now that he had satisfied all I could demand of him. I made answer, that I consented to it with all my heart, and that I would bear him testimony, as I had already made it appear, in placing him in the honourable post he knew I had done; that he had behav'd himself with all the vigour and resolution of a man of honour; and that so I left it to his own disposal to go out when he pleas'd, after he had done the King the service, from which he could not honourably have excused himself. After this manner he took his leave, without the least sign of discontent; but going immediately thence to *Cadillac*, to make his complaint to the Duke of *Espernon*, where he told him that I had usurpt upon his command, having compell'd him by force, as Governour and Master of a Town, to obey me, though he had declar'd to me that he could not do it, having the honour to be one of the Collonels Officers, who were not to receive Orders from the Officers of the *Maistre de Camp*; and that I had detain'd him by force in the place, which was to be attackt the next day; that being he could not help obeying me in this occasion, where his Majesties service was in question, and where he had not the liberty to do as he

would

would otherwife have done, he was come fo foon as he could get out, to acquit himfelf of his duty in making his complaint to him, whofe honour alone was therein engag'd, by reafon of the priviledges of his command. Monfieur *d' Efpernon* having only made anfwer that he would talk with me about it, fent an exprefs meffenger to me to come to him to *Cadillac*.

Really I was very much perplext and furpriz'd at this order, fufpecting what the occafion was, and knowing the feverity with which Monfieur *d' Efpernon* maintain'd the honourable priviledges of his command. I thought it would be convenient that I fhould firft fee Monfieur *le Marefchal de Saint Geran*, by whofe order I had acted, to have his advice what I ought to do ; and therefore went to wait upon him at *Caftel-Sarafiu* where he then was, and told him the occafion of my coming. In good earneft, faid he, this is a very fcurvy bufinefs for you ; for though your action was perfectly right and good, and though therein you have exactly obferv'd the rules of military difcipline, yet you will have much ado to defend your felf, being to give an account to Monfieur *d' Efpernon*, who is not eafie to be fatisfy'd in things that refpect the leaft punctilio of his command. He faid moreover, that he apprehended they would put upon me fome affront, and therefore doubted whether or no I ought to go to *Cadillac*. But Sir, faid I, if I do not go, can I fecure my felf from his authority ? Can I find any way to excufe my felf from giving him an account of what I have done ? for if that may be, I do not ftick at not going thither, but being oblig'd in fpite of my teeth to fubmit to his order ; and that he can, by vertue of the authority his command gives him, caufe me to be laid by the heels ; I think I fhould make my caufe worfe, or rather of a good caufe I fhould make a very ill one, fhould I fail to obey him : for doubtlefs he would never pardon me a thing, that he would have fome reafon to look upon as a great affront done to him by fuch a fimple Officer as I. But if he will hear my reafons, and when he fees the Order I receiv'd from you, Sir, as my General, I hope he may be fatisfy'd, if any thing can fatisfie him. Monfieur *le Marefchal de Saint Geran* having heard me fpeak after this manner, feem'd to approve of my opinion, and offer'd me to write to the Duke of *Efpernon*, to affure him that he himfelf had given me the Order to command in the Town ; but I would not engage him in an affair, that I was much more willing to end alone ; and therefore returning my thanks after the moft civil manner I could, I told him that I had kept his Letter, which being the Order I had receiv'd from my General, would amply juftifie me in what I had done.

I took my leave, and went to *Cadillac* about the time that the Duke of *Efpernon* was going to dinner ; when having fent him word, that I defir'd to kifs his hands, he gave order to have me brought into the Parlor, where he was with above thirty Gentlemen with him. So foon as he faw me make him a profound reverence, he prefently turn'd his back towards me, and talking to a Gentleman, left me, without giving me one word. He askt all the reft that were prefent to wafh, and fit down to Table with him ; but as for me, he was not pleas'd to fhew me the leaft civility, and us'd me no otherwife than he would have done a Serving-man. 'Tis true, I found my felf wounded to the laft degree with this affront, which I receiv'd fo publickly, for having ferv'd the King, and perform'd the duty of my command ; but I faw no remedy, having to do with a man that has been known throughout the Kingdom for the

moft

moſt imperious that ever came into the world ; and knowing of old, that it had been his cuſtom to uſe all Officers at this rate, by whom he conceived he had been any ways injur'd. Wherefore thinking of nothing at that time but how I might juſtifie my ſelf, which was the only end of my Journey, and not ſeeing how I could do it without ſpeaking to him, I addreſt my ſelf to one of my friends, who had great acceſs to him, which was *le Commandeur de la Hiliere*, and having acquainted him with the occaſion of my coming, entreated him to aſſiſt me to get out of this ſcurvy affair, in obtaining me the audience that was neceſſary for my juſtification : And thus matters ſtood for that day.

VI. In the mean time the Commander ſpoke to the Duke of *Eſper-non*, as he had promis'd me he would, and did it with ſo much zeal and friendſhip, that he obtain'd his requeſt. So that the next day Monſieur *d' Eſpernon* bid him go fetch his friend, telling him that he would hear what I had to ſay. So ſoon as I was enter'd the room, and had ſaluted him, I told him that I was come in obedience to his command ; that I very well perceiv'd Monſieur *de Baſtillat* had done me an ill office to him, and that I could not doubt but he had ſent for me upon the com-plaint that this Officer might have made of me, about ſomething had paſt at *Mouteſche* ; but that I hop'd, that after his Lordſhip had done me the favour to hear me, and that I had given him a true and ſincere account of the affair, he would not condemn me ; that I aſſur'd him at leaſt be-forehand, that I was come reſolv'd to ſubmit to whatever it ſhould pleaſe him as my Judge to impoſe upon me, if I did not make my innocence appear. I then gave him an account of the command the *Mareſchal de Saint Geran* had given me by word of mouth, to give all the Orders in the place, and in the Regiment. I ſhew'd him the Order in writing he had afterwards ſent me, wherein he gave me warning to prepare my ſelf well to defend the Town againſt the Enemy, who were reſolv'd to attack it. He took and read it, and ſeeming ſatisfy'd, gave me very well to underſtand that he had already chang'd his humour as concerning me. I continu'd my juſtification in telling him, that I had read the order to all the Officers, that Monſieur *de Baſtillat* had heard it, and ſubmitted to it, as well as the reſt, without any manner of oppoſition ; that it was true he after-wards came to me in the evening, and made ſome difficulty, telling me that he was afraid of doing a prejudice to the authority of the Collonel, ſhould he obey an Officer of the *Maiſtre de Camp* ; but that I had made him anſwer, that I did not pretend to violate it in any ſort, ſeeing it was not in the quality of an Officer to the *Maiſtre de Camp*, that I pre-tended to command an Officer of the Collonel ; but in the quality of Governour, and as appointed by the General to command in that place ; and that I had declar'd to him at the head of the Regiment, that nei-ther did I pretend that this occaſion ſhould be drawn into a precedent upon the account of this diſpute, nor that I ought to draw from thence any particular advantage to my ſelf. That having thus ſecur'd the Ho-nour of the Colonel, I thought my ſelf oblig'd at the ſame time to look after the Kings Intereſt, in making thoſe obey me receiv'd his Pay, in an occaſion where the defence of one of his Majeſties Forts was in queſtion : that I had given a very ill example to all the Garriſon, in ſuffering an Officer to go out, who askt leave to do it, upon a falſe pretence, in a time when it could not be ; that it manifeſted that I underſtood little of my buſineſs, had render'd me unworthy of my command, to

have

have suffer'd my self to have been surpriz'd by so poor an argument: that therefore, seeing the Kings service and my own duty only concern'd in the thing, without the Collonels honour being any way engaged in it, I believ'd that I could not do less: That his Lordship himself would without doubt have been the first to have blam'd me if I had done it; and therefore I was bold to beg of him the justice that was my due, of protecting my innocence against so ill grounded an accusation; and that I consented with all my heart, to call all the Officers of the Regiment, and even Monsieur *de Bastillat* himself, to witness the truth of what I said; who knew very well, that after the provoking language he had given me, I forbore not for all that to give him a post of honour which was not his due, in intrusting him with the guard of one of the Gates of the City. The Duke of *Espernon*, very much surpriz'd at this discourse, made answer that things had been much otherwise represented to him; that having carry'd my self after this manner, instead of blaming, he very much commended me, for having acquitted my self of my duty: that he saw by that, I understood my command much better than *Bastillat* did his: That it was want of understanding to bring the honour and authority of a Collonel in question, in a thing where they were no way concern'd; and that he would rattle him, to teach him to instruct himself better in the right of his command, and not to fall any more into such mistakes.

This answer, so differing from the ordinary language of the Duke of *Espernon*, was follow'd by the effect; for having bid me go and take a turn in the Garden, he sent for Monsieur *Bastillat*, with whom he talkt so much more roughly about this affair, as he was sensibly nettled, to see himself by his fault thus to blame to a simple Officer. And after having been assur'd from his own mouth of the truth of all things, which he durst not deny, and having reproacht him, that he by his ill conduct had been the cause that his Collonel had receiv'd an affront upon account of the first Regiment of *France*. He would not let him stay dinner, whereas he made me sit down with great kindness, using me with as great civility then, as he had roughly repulst me the day before. So soon as we were risen from Table, he sent for him up, where he told him before all the company, that he ought to have taken the action which he would have made a crime, after another manner than he had done; that the knowledge I had of the rights of the Collonel, and of my own command, had taught me to distinguish the truth from appearance, and how to maintain my own right, without intrenching upon that of others; that the very obliging manner which he himself confest I had proceeded in respect to him, ought to have made him judge more favourably of my intentions; that he could not possibly take any thing ill at my hands, and that he charg'd him to be my friend as before, entreating us to embrace, which we immediately did. This being done, having begg'd Monsieur *d'Espernon*'s order to return to the Regiment, that I had much ado to leave, being intrusted with the care of it as I was, I took my leave, after having receiv'd particular marks of his being very well satisfy'd with me, as he himself openly declar'd.

VII. The year following, which was the year 1622, the King did not go into *Guyenne*, and only sent thither Messieurs *d'Elbeuf* and *de Themines* to command the Army, which consisted of about twelve thousand men; the Prince who commanded the rest of the forces, staying about the person of the King. The Rendezvous for the Army was the Plain

C.

of *Marmande*, from whence we went to fit down before *Tonnis*, which was a little, but ftrong place, held by the *Hugonots*, and of which Monfieur *de Monpouillan*, Son to the Marquis *de la Force*, and a very gallant man, was Governour. The Generals order'd three Attacks, of which each of them commanded one, and the third, which was on that fide by the River, was commanded by Monfieur *de Pontagne*, who was *Maiftre de Camp*. The Regiment of *Picardy* was of the Attack of Monfieur *le Duc d'Elbeuf*, who had the brave *Vignoles* for his *Marefchal de Camp*. The Trench being open'd, the Enemy began every day to make great Sallies, particularly on that fide where they had a Half-Moon of great advantage to them, by reafon that it very much favour'd their retreat; and thefe frequent Sallies thus made with fo much advantage, extreamly incommoded the Befiegers, and made us lofe a great many men. The Generals therefore refolv'd to attack this Half-Moon at any rate, tho they knew it could not be done but with great lofs : and only ftay'd till the next day, when the Regiments of *Picardy* and *Navarre*, that always marcht together, were to mount the Guard.

Monfieur *de Vignoles*, to whom I had the honour to be particularly known, had a defign to make ufe of me in this occafion; and not having found me where he came to give order about this attack, he came to feek me in my Tent, where I had ftay'd behind fick. He askt me what was the matter with me ? when having told him my indifpofition, he knew fo well how to excite me in point of honour, and engag'd me after fo obliging a manner to fhare in the glory of the attack they were refolv'd to make upon this Half-moon the night following, that I could not handfomly excufe my felf. For he affur'd me that the Duke *d'Elbeuf* had made choice of me to lead on the men to this affault, and abfolutely rely'd upon me; to which he added, that this enterprize being of the greateft importance, he hop'd I would do all I poffibly could to be there; and that in the mean time he would fend me a Quilt into the Trench, whereon to take fome repofe till the hour of execution. I made anfwer that I was very ill of an Ague, but that, fince Monfieur *d'Elbeuf* and he commanded me, I would do the utmoft I was able to come. Night being come, Orders were given for the attack, which was to begin on both fides at once. The firft, which was on the right hand, fell to my fhare; and the other, which was on the left, to an Officer of the Regiment of *Navarre*.

This Half-moon being not fortify'd as fuch places us'd to be, and the Parapet which was wont to be made with Earth, being only of Cask, which the Cannon had feveral times beaten down, but that had been ftill repair'd, I faw very well that we could not gain it, but by entring by force of arms. Wherefore, having taken my meafures about this affair, after that I had lined the Trench with good Mufqueteers, that fir'd very thick, I went with fifty Halberdeers to hook the Casks towards us, and pull them down. The Enemy at the fame inftant making ufe of the fame artifice, hookt them alfo on their fide with other Halberts, by which means each fide pulling thus towards them, we could not pull them down; when I bethought me, feeing the Enemy pull with all their force, to hinder us from overturning thefe Barrels; to make ufe of them themfelves, and of their own refiftance, to make them do that which they did by no means intend. I therefore made all our Halberdeers on a fudden leave pulling againft them, and inftead of drawing the Casks towards us as before, they on the contrary pufht them the other way,

and

and did it with so much violence, that they were immediately over-turn'd upon the Enemy, of which some were overwhelm'd with them: So soon as we had by this means made a breach, we mounted, and by dint of Halberts, made our selves Masters of the Half-moon, and also of the person of Monsieur *de Monpouillan*, who being come into this place, without knowing any thing of the attack, found himself engag'd in the Fight; and trapt under one of the Barrels that fell upon him, and from which he cou'd not disengage himself, till I got to him, and took him Prisoner.

But our first good fortune was soon follow'd by a misfortune, and a strange reverse; for as we all held our selves very well assur'd of the success of our Enterprize, above six hundred men being sally'd out of the Town, came all on a sudden to fall upon us, and gave us so brisk a charge, that we were constrained to abandon what we had already taken, and to retreat with all the speed we could, without being able so much as to take our Priso-ner along with us: for the Officer of *Navarre* who commanded the other attack, having fail'd to enter on his side, as we had done on ours, we found our selves too few to withstand so great a number of men. And yet the advantage we had got so far astonish'd the Enemy, that after ha-ving seen themselves thus forc'd, fearing they might be so again, them-selves overthrew all that remained of the Half-moon, that might have done them a great deal of mischief if taken from them; and absolutely quitted that Post.

VIII. I was commanded a few days after, to go discover a kind of ad-vanc'd Bastion, and separate from the Town, that had been very much batter'd by our Cannon, and that did us a great deal of mischief. No body at that time appear'd in it, and we thought we might have possest it with great ease, which made me go to it, as to a post that was as good as quitted: but so soon as ever I was got up, and that I went to look in-to the place, I felt my self struck with a great blow of a Scyth that was laid upon me, and that gave me a cut on the left shoulder of half a foot long. I was as much surpriz'd as stun'd with so unexpected a blow: but by good luck having a very good Buff-Coat, the Coat was only cut, and having born all the force of the blow it sav'd my life, and my shoul-der from being cut off, since so much force had not been requir'd to the cutting off that, as to the cutting of the Buff; and this blow I re-ciev'd from a little *Corps de Guard* of Eighteen or Twenty men, that were cover'd and retrench'd in this post. Upon the report I made to the Generals, they concluded to force the Bastion, but the frequent Sallies the Enemy made almost every night, gave them not leisure to do it; and they reciev'd in the mean time a dispatch from Court, wherein they had word sent, that the King was very impatient of the length of the Siege, of which he laid the whole fault upon them; and that he would send the Prince to command there. This news nettled them all to the quick, so that from that time forward they resolv'd no more to observe any mea-sures, nor to make the best of any thing; but either to perish, together with the whole Army, or to carry the place before the Prince should come up to them. They accordingly assaulted the Bastion, which they took: but when they thought to lodge themselves in the ditch, they had word brought, that the Enemy had that very night shipt six hundred men in Boats, which were slipt down the River without being perceiv'd by the *Corps de Guard*, which had been posted to stop their way. Thus were

they

they forc'd to content themselves, with keeping what they had already got, till the succours that Monsieur *de Parabelle*, Governour of *Poitou*, had promis'd, upon the news of the Enemies approach, who were marching under the conduct of Monsieur *de la Force*, should come up to them.

IX. The Generals having had notice, that the besieged were preparing to make a great Sally, and to make use of the advantage they had recieved, by the relief of six hundred men that were got into the Town; redoubled their Guards, and made ready to receive them; I crawl'd as well as I was able to my post, though some days before I had received a Musket-shot in my Thigh, and was not yet cur'd; for it was not fit, when every body else prepar'd to fight, to lye at ease at home, and a man easily forgets his infirmities in these occasions, wherein one finds one's self, as it were, animated with a new vigour. Being then advanc'd towards a quitted Half-moon, that look'd into the Town, I got up to it, and there saw by the light of the Moon, a great many men hurrying up and down in great haste, by which I was assur'd that they were preparing for a Sally : Some Officers of my Companions, who had follow'd me saw the same, which made us return in all diligence to give notice of it to the Generals, and to all the *Corps de Guard*. About two hours after midnight they gave a Faulcon shot from the Town, for the signal; and the Enemy at the instant sallied out of the Town in so great numbers, that instead of attacking the head of the Trench, as men commonly do; they assaulted it by the Flanks and the Tail, and struck so great a terror into all the Guards, though prepar'd, that they overturn'd all our people one upon another. The Regiment of *Bourdeaux*, which lay a little on one side behind us, having given way, was beaten back upon my *Corps de Guard*; and forc'd me to retire after the best manner I could with part of my men, not being able no more than others, to stand firm against so many victorious People. I had a mind to have rallied with a Captain of our Regiment, a very brave man, called *Bonneuil*, whose lodgment was advanc'd even to the Graffe of the Town, and that had made a little pair of steps of Wood, by which he might easily recover the top; but being he had neglected to take the advice I had given him, to keep a Centinel always there, to watch the Souldiers from stealing away the steps to burn, I found him dead, together with most of his men; that having befallen him which I had foretold, he not having been able to retire when he wou'd, by those steps which he found pull'd to pieces, by reason that the Souldiers had carried away most of the Wood to make fires; which by the way may make it appear, that though it be commonly said, that some men are more fortunate than others; it may nevertheless often be attributed to the little foresight of the unfortunate sort, that sometimes neglect means as easie as important to their preservation.

The Enemy after having thus clear'd the Trench with all the lodgments, there posted themselves, with a design to ruin it; at which the Duke d'*Elbeuf* being enraged, resolv'd to perish or to drive them thence, and indeavouring to inspire the Regiments with the same resolution, who had thus lost their Posts, What Gentleman, said he, has the Enemy thus beaten us from our Posts, and taken from us in one night what we have been so long in gaining; and cannot we do in open day, as much as they have done by night? For my own part I am resolv'd to drive them out, as quickly as they have driven us, or to lose my life; and will take no longer time than 'tis to noon to do it in; and I doubt not but every one will

follow

follow me, since every one is engaged in honor as well as I, and ought to be asham'd to outlive such an affront. Therefore Gentlemen, I have no other Order to give but this, that noon being come every one make to his Post, either to regain it or there to die. This short Speech did so rouze their Spirits, and animated every one to that degree, that seeing themselves inevitably dishonour'd if they did not follow their General, and bravely second his design; they effectually did it with so extraordinary vigour and resolution; that in spite of the Enemies resistance which was very great, they recover'd all their Posts, and before night restor'd the Trenches and Works into the same condition that they were before.

X. During these vigorous attacks and defences, Monsieur *de Parabelle* with six hundred Gentlemen arriv'd in the Camp, and Monsieur *de la Force* approach d also within two or three Leagues of the Town with four thousand men. A Souldier returning late from forrage, discover'd the Enemy within half a league of the Camp. He gave notice of it, and immediately the body of the Army was commanded to that side; part of the Guard of the Trench was drawn off, and there was only left the old Regiments in which most confidence was repos d. The Enemy, either advertiz'd of the thing, or having foreseen it, took this time to attack the guard of the Trench, with so much more advantage as it was so much weaker, and withal made the most furious Sally, that ever had been made till then. I was attackt at the post where I was, by an Officer who commanded about fifty men, all arm'd from head to foot; he came directly up to me with a Tuck he had in his hand, with which he gave me a thrust, that he run me through and through; and did it at the same moment that I fir'd a Pistol, which taking the default of his Arms, broke his Thigh, and made him fall backwards, without leaving his Sword nevertheless, which he drew out of my body. The Souldiers that accompany'd this Officer were so frighted to see him fall, that, victorious as they were, they retir'd above fifty paces; which gave me leisure, not falling with the thrust, as great as it was, to crawl along as well as I could, supported by a brave Souldier call'd *Mutonis*, to try to get to the bank of the River, which being of difficult access, by reason of a very steep descent, that I must go down to arrive at, as it might secure me and save me from being taken; creeping thus and leaning upon my poor Souldier, a new misfortune befel us, that had like to have put us both into despair; which was a Musket shot, that *Mutonis* receiv'd in his arm. He had then almost as much need of help as I, and really it was a very sad sight, to see two men so cover'd over with their own blood, and both maim'd to have no other help, but that of one another. For my own part, sustaining my self with one hand upon that arm of this Souldier, that was not broken, I with the other stopt the fore part of my wound, from whence issued a great deal of blood.

It will doubtless appear incredible, how, in the condition we then were, we could attempt to recover the bank of the River, to which I have described the access to be so difficult, even to sound and vigorous persons. But what will not the love of liberty and life make men do? And why should it be a wonder, that God, who determin'd to do us both, without comparison, much greater graces, should bring us off from this, as well as several other dangers, to guide us to the place he had predestin'd, after long wandrings and very crooked ways; For he at last withdrew this poor Fellow, as well as my self from the Army, and inspir'd

him

him to embrace a private and altogether christian life, where he meditated nothing but his Salvation; in the prospect whereof he desired to
become a *Chartreux*, tho they would not admit him by reason of his arm,
that he remain'd lame of his Musquet shot.

Being then reduc'd to the inevitable necessity, either to be knockt
o'th' head by the Enemy, or beaten to pieces by the fall we were to
have in rowling from the top of the hill to the bottom, because we
could not go down upright in the condition we were, after having disputed which of the two we should choose, we resolv'd at last rather to
give our selves up into the hands of God, than to fall into those of men.
Thus having recommended our selves to his holy protection, we let our
selves tumble from the top of this Hill to the bottom (and (God visi-
bly assisting us) the thing being humanely impossible, we got up, and by
the help of one another march'd as before to recover our Quarters. In
the way, which was all along by the River side , we found an Officer
of our Regiment very much wounded, called *L'Anglade*; and presently
another called *Miranne* of the same Regiment, who seeing me cry'd out,
Monsieur *de Pontis* I am dying, have pity on me.   To whom I made answer, I am dying my self too, my poor Friend, and stand in as much
need of help as any one; but where are you hurt ?   To which having
reply'd, that he knew not where, but that he was about to expire; I
thought that being arm'd it might peradventure be his arms, that stifled
him; so taking his Sword from his side, as well as I cou'd, I cut the lea-
thers of his arms, and let them fall off him, which I had no sooner done,
but that he began to breathe at liberty, and to come to himself; for he
was so squeez'd in these arms, being fall'n upon them in coming down the
Hill, that they stifled him; and thus God gave me yet strength enough
to save this Officer's life, when I was in as much danger of losing my own.

Being at last arrived at the Camp, we were carried to *Marmande*,
where some of the Enemies Souldiers that had been taken Prisoners, and
who belike had been present at the occasion where I had been wounded,
told me that the Officer with whom I had had to do, was at least as ill as I,
having his Thigh-bone broke, and that his name was *Feron*.   This news
did surprize and afflict me at once, because he was my intimate Friend,
and that we had formerly been Comrades together in the Guards.   I had
not known him in the fight, but immediately sent a Drum to inquire how
he did, and to let him know how sorry I was to have encounter'd him.
Feron was no less surpriz'd than I, to understand that I was the man to
whom he had given so desperate a thrust; and having return'd an answer
with the same sentiments of civility and grief, concerning what had befallen me, he sent the next day also to enquire how I did; and we continu'd the same kindness on both sides, so long as we were near another,
which linck'd us faster than before, and encreas'd our old Friendships,
which we have preserv'd to this day.   From *Marmande* I was afterwards
remov'd to *Toulouse*, where I verily thought I should dye, as well of my
Wound, as of a burning Feaver that was added to it.   I requested and
received all the Sacraments , and being willing to reward two Servants
that I had, I bid them divide my Cabinets betwixt them so soon as I was
dead.   These Fellows were both of them so good natur'd , and had so
great an affection for me , that the prospect of so considerable a gain,
could not comfort them for the much greater loss they conceiv'd they
should undergo in losing me.   And indeed they were overjoy'd, when
the fourth day of my Feaver I had a Crisis, that seem'd at first to threaten

                                    R   my

my death, but that turn'd to my cure; for in few days I was cur'd of my Feaver, but not of my Wound, which was above six months in closing, so as that I could march, and that was not wholly heal'd till some years after.

XI. Being come to *Rabastins*, which was the winter quarters, I receiv'd a Letter from Monsieur *Zamet*, wherein he sent me word, that being it was the Kings pleasure to have him nearer his person, he was oblig'd to put off his Regiment, and was now in treaty with Monsieur *de Liancour* about it; that this news, which peradventure might surprize me, ought not nevertheless to afflict me, seeing that changing his Command, he did not alter his disposition towards me; and that he should be in a better condition to serve me, being nearer the King, from whom I was to expect the reward of my services.

I must confess, that this Letter was to me a more violent and more sensible blow, than that of which I was so lately cur'd. The excess of grief I felt put me in as great danger of death; and I could not see, without being afflicted beyond measure, that the person to whom I had so particularly united my self, and for whom I voluntarily quitted a Company in the Regiment of *Champagne*, and was moreover ready to abandon all I had in the world, should divest himself of the Regiment that united us, and kept us together, during the whole Campaign; for I very well foresaw, that I remaining in this body, and Monsieur *Zamet* being with the King, I could no more have the happiness of possessing him as before. And he also very well foreseeing how averse I would be to this business, would not write me word of it, till first the business was concluded with Monsieur *de Liancour*, into whom he endeavour'd to inspire the same sentiments of esteem and friendship for me, that he himself had. The answer I return'd him in the height of my grief was, that seeing he quitted the Regiment, I entreated that he would give me leave to quit it too, to follow him in all places wherever he went, having devoted to him both my person and my life. But he writ back presently again, with great earnestness to entreat me to continue in my Command, protesting that I should oblige him more, and should manifest my affection to him better if I stay'd in the Regiment, than if I should come to him. Adding withal, that it was not yet time, but when that time should come, he would not fail to advertize me, that this outward separation would not hinder us from being as much united as before; and that he hop'd it would not be long before he should see me again.

This Letter gave me some comfort, tho I was extremely afflicted, when I consider'd that I was no more Lieutenant to him, for whom I had quitted all. In the bargain that Monsieur *Zamet* made with Monsieur *de Liancour*, he made me share, without my dreaming of any such thing; in the quitting of his Command having told him, that he did not part with his Regiment to him for two and twenty thousand Crowns, but upon condition that he should over and above give a thousand more to his Lieutenant. And accordingly I receiv'd the said summ of Monsieur *de Liancour*; who being come to *Rabastins* to take possession of the Regiment, gave me great testimonies of kindness, nay more, of friendship and confidence; assuring me, that if I did not find in him all the qualities of Monsieur *Zamet*, I might at least expect a true and perfect friendship; entreating me to proceed with him upon this promise; and added, that being he could not at present give a more manifest proof of the

trust

trust he reposed in me, he desir'd I would assist him in his initiations ; where he confest he had need by the experience of others to supply the defect of his own. He could not possibly have proceeded after a more civil and obliging fashion, and I reply'd with all the submission and acknowledgment that was due to so obliging a complement.

The first Siege of this Campaign was a little Town call'd *Sainte Foy*, which was carried by assault ; and where Monsieur *de Liancour* did wonders in his own person, having first leapt a great Ditch, where many others were left behind, who could not leap it as he did. This young Lord was extreamly brave, and manifested an extraordinary Courage, but being he had never before commanded at the head of a Regiment, and that I saw him advance too far, I did what I could to restrain him ; but his Courage would carry it against me, and forc'd him on.

After the taking of *Sainte Foy*, the Army marcht directly to *Saint Antonin*, where the King would himself be in person. This Town was attackt without Trenches, and we presently came to handy blows, which occasion'd a furious fight, for the Besieged defended themselves with great vigour. Our Regiment was not commanded on upon the attack, being reserved to attend the Enemies relief, which was said to be near at hand, but that however never appear'd, so the Town was taken : There it was that Monsieur *de Saint Preuil* was receiv'd Collonel Ensign of the Regiment of *Picardy* ; he, whom his fortune and misfortune have since rendred famous enough. I contracted so great a Friendship with him, that we did always eat together, and had but one Bed, and I can honestly say, that I at that time stood him in the stead of a Brother, and a true Friend.

XII. The King came afterward with all his Army before *Negrepelice*, having longingly desired for above a year, to see himself once in a condition to punish, as he did, the barbarous and inhumane treachery, that this Town had exercised upon four hundred men of the Regiment of *Vaillac*, that had been there plac'd in Garrison the Winter before ; all whose Throats the Inhabitants had cut in one night. This Prince, from the first moment that he receiv'd the news, had openly declar'd, that he would chastise them all after the same manner, and would not pardon any one of them whatever. So that the year following, after he had taken the two or three fore-nam'd little places, he came before this, He had, for Lieutenant Generals of his Army, Monsieur *le Prince*, Monsieur *d' Angoulesme*, and Messieurs *de Themines* and *de Saint Geran*. The King himself in person order'd all the Quarters, and the Attacks, which he caus'd to be given to the two extremities of the Town ; it not being his pleasure that they should lose time in discovering it, nor in opening Trenches, but that they should go on directly to the Assault, without giving them leisure to look about them ; both because the Town was not so strong that Trenches were absolutely necessary, and that, on the other side, the impatience he was in to punish them according to their desert, did not permit him to go a longer, tho a safer way to work.

The Army, drawn up in Battaile, was put into two divisions, for the two Attacks ; and all things being in a readiness, the Generals sent me to the King about noon to receive the last Orders, which he had commanded should be taken from his own mouth before the Assault. I found him in a paltry thatcht Cottage, where a man was almost choakt in the smoak, and where he was constrain'd to shut himself up, because he found

himself

himſelf indiſpos'd : Having told him, that the Lieutenant Generals had
ſent me to aſſure his Majeſty that all things were in order, as he had
commanded, and that they waited for his laſt order ; This is it, ſaid he,
that they attack the Town, as I ſaid, at both ends of it ; and that you
are all of you to have ſome white thing ty'd in your Hatbands, leſt meeting in the Town you ſhould kill one another : For I charge you that
you give no quarter to any one whatever, becauſe they have provok'd
me to the laſt degree, and deſerve to be us'd as they have handled others.
I return'd to carry back this Order, and every one having ty'd a Handkerchief in his Hat, the aſſault was given ; which continued ſome hours,
in diſputing the Out-works, and the entrance into the Gate, which they
defended very bravely, fighting with extraordinary valour. But at laſt
they were forc'd on both ſides, and retir'd fighting into a corner of the
City, where they call'd out for Quarter, which being deny'd them, they
cry'd out, Well, we muſt dye, but we will dye like men of honour, and ſell our
lives very dear. In effect, they maintain'd the fight with ſo much obſtinacy,
that they kill'd a great many of our men, and defended themſelves to the
laſt man, not parting with their Arms, till they parted with their Lives. And
this example ought methinks to moderate a little the juſt indignation of
Princes upon theſe occaſions, where tho they might reaſonably incline
to puniſh many guilty perſons, yet they might at leaſt pardon ſome few,
if but to ſpare many faithful Souldiers, who are thus knockt o'th' head
by Rebels.

At the end of this ſlaughter, the Souldiers fell to plundering, and to
catching up all the women they could meet ; when I, being at the head
of the Regiment, ſaw a moſt beautiful Virgin, of about ſeventeen or
eighteen years of age, come running in great haſte out of a houſe that
had not yet been enter'd, and throwing her ſelf at my feet, entreated
that I would ſave her honour and her life : I gave her my word ſo to do,
aſſuring her, that I would ſooner loſe my own life, than to ſuffer that
either the one or the other ſhould be taken from her. To this end I
would have had her guarded by me by four or five Souldiers, but ſhe
thought ſhe was not ſafe unleſs ſhe held me by the ſkirt of the Doublet.
In this poſture I walkt her through the Town, where ſhe was ſeen by
part of the Officers of the Army, of which ſome were ſo inſolent as to
dare to demand her ; others importun'd me to deliver her into
their hands, which inforc'd me to come to high words with them ; chu-
ſing rather to have them for my enemies, than to betray my word, and
the juſtice I conceiv'd was due to a vertuous Maid, who had importun'd
my protection. I conducted her after this manner to my Hutt. Her parents were of the beſt of the Town, whereof her Father was Miniſter ;
and it fell out, by the greateſt good fortune in the world for them, that
they were that day at a houſe they had in the Country, having left their
Daughter in the Town to look to the houſe. Seeing my ſelf importun'd
afreſh by the ſollicitations of ſeveral perſons, ſome whereof boaſted themſelves to be the principal men of the Army, I conſider'd of all poſſible
means to conceal her, till I could reſtore her into her Father and Mo-
thers hands, that both they and I might be deliver'd from the fear of
the continual danger to which ſhe was expos'd. But ſeeing this could
not eaſily be done in a Camp, where there was nothing but Hutts, and
where I knew there was ſo little fidelity, I bethought me at laſt of as odd
a way as can poſſibly be imagin'd, and that may ſeem incredible to many.
The beſt places to hide ones ſelf in being ſometimes not the moſt private

corners, but those which are least suspected by being most in sight; I conceiv'd that a great Heifer, which I had caus'd to be kill'd the day before, and which was yet hanging entire from the top to the bottom of my Hutt, might very well serve my purpose. I therefore turn'd the belly side towards the wall, and put my Prisoner into the body of the Beast, to try if she might there stand unseen. The thing succeeded marvellously well, for the fear of so imminent a danger assisting to make her fit herself to that little room, which was the only place where she could be safe; did there so lessen and contract her self, that she was not to be seen at all. I therefore told this young maid, that so oft as she heard any one knock at the door, she should run and hide her self there, that she might not be too much incommodated by being always there. And it happen'd, almost as soon as I had tryed this invention, that some General Officers, under colour of visiting the Camp, came to knock at my Hutt. So soon as they were come in, they acquainted me with the true reason of their coming, and importun'd me to let them see her, who fell into my hands; but I answer'd them with so great freedom, having given them leave to look round my Hutt, where they saw nothing but the Heifer hanging up by the heels; that they went away very well satisfied that she was no longer in my custody. It would be to no purpose to speak of all the rest, who as confidently swallow'd the banter, and who after having been there, return'd seeing nothing but the Heifer hanging in the roof.

But the affair went further, and being come to the King's ear, he sent for me to him. Being assur'd of my Servants, whose affection and fidelity were sufficiently known to me, I entrusted them with the Guard of my Prisoner, giving them charge to be always without the door of my Hutt, to tell every body, that I was gone abroad, and to hinder any one whoever from entering in. So soon as I came into the King's presence, he askt me if what he had heard, that I had a very beautiful Maid in my custody was true. Whereupon I who had never conceal'd any thing from my Prince, gave him a true account of the whole business, as all things had past, to the very moment that I came from my Hutt. At which the King looking me full in the face, said to me; And hast thou honestly kept thy word? I then swore to him in the presence of God, and his Majesty, that I had: Upon which the King said to me again; I am exceedingly pleas'd with thee for it, and esteem thee a hundred times the more; finish what thou hast so well begun, for it is one of the worthiest actions thou canst ever do whil'st thou liv'st, and that I shall look upon as one of the best services thou hast ever done me. If any one shall by chance discover her, and sollicit thee to have her, tell him the Order thou hast receiv'd from me to preserve her, and that 'tis I my self who have given thee charge of her. I then entreated his Majesty, that he would permit me to send a Drum to her Father, who liv'd four or five Leagues from the Camp, that I might restore her to him so soon as I could. This Request, which justified the sincerity wherewith I acted, mightily pleas'd the King, who told me, that he gave me leave so to do with all his heart; and that I could not do better.

I took my leave of his Majesty, and making haste to return to my Hutt, where I found all things well, I advis'd the Maid to write a Letter to her Father, therein to send him word, that he should come fetch her at a certain place I nam'd to her, and to assure him, that the Drum, who brought him the Letter, should safely conduct him to the place, where she and I would not fail to be. She accordingly writ the Letter, which contain'd

in

in few words, what I had dictated to her, leaving it to her at their meeting, to tell him by word of mouth the whole Story of the state wherein
she had been, and from which I had redeem'd her. The Father and Mother receiv'd this news with such joy, as one may better conceive than
express; and were soon at the appointed place, where I exactly met them
with their Daughter; and where, delivering her into their hands, I
protested to them that I had preserv'd her at the peril of my own life,
as if she had been my own Child; assuring them withal, that I thought
my self very happy, that God had given me the opportunity of rescuing
a young Virgin from so inevitable a danger. They would acknowledge
this favour, and made me an offer of all that ever they had in recompence
of the precious present I made them, in restoring their Daughter, whom
they gave for lost. But I contented my self with their friendship, telling
them that I thought my self over rewarded in having sav'd their daughters honour. But I was not yet got back to my Hutt, when I saw behind two Horses that came after me laden with Fowl and other sorts of
provision. The man that brought them told me that his Master sent them
to me, conjuring me at least to accept of that small present, which he
was almost asham'd to offer me. I could not civilly refuse this present,
for fear of putting him too much out of countenance that sent it, and
only told the Servant that brought it, that I desir'd him to let his Master
know that I had accepted it, that I might not disoblige him, and that I
return'd him my thanks. They have ever since been mindful of the obligation; and travelling five or six months after through the Village
where the Father of the Maid liv'd, and going to give him a visit, the
poor Girl was so transported with joy to see me, that she clung about
my knees, and would not leave me; being then so much the more sensible of the obligation she had to me, as she was now more her self, than
in the other occasion; and saying in the presence of her Father and Mother, that she lookt upon me as another Father and Mother, seeing I had
preserv'd both her life and her honour.

But as I did after this manner save this Maids honour, whose beauty
expos'd her to so great peril; so I ought not to conceal an heroick action
done by one, whose name was *Roger*, first Gentleman of the Bed-chamber to the King in this occasion of the sack of *Negrepelice*. This man,
who was very generous and very honest, seeing the Souldiers carrying
away a great many Women and Virgins, presently ran up to them with
a purse full of Pistoles, and cheapning one for one Pistole, another for
two, and another for three, and going after this manner through all the
streets of the Town, he bought to the number of forty, which he carry'd to the Kings Quarters, where he plac'd them in safety, and from
thence sent them home to their own habitations, so soon as the Army
was withdrawn.

XIII. The King being return'd to *Paris* after the ruin of *Negrepelice*,
the Army blockt up a little Town call'd *Sonniere*, which we resolv'd to
carry by Assault. We therefore attackt the *Fauxbourg*, wherein was the
principal defence; and Monsieur *de Liancour* being at the head of his
Regiment, pusht the first of the Enemy with so much vigour and fury,
as compell'd them to give way, to abandon the defence of the Gate,
and to retire into the corners of the streets, and into the houses. But being they were there under covert, and that firing thence continually
upon us, they kill'd a great many men, where we were in the open street,

I be

I bethought my self of an invention that depriv'd them of part of their advantage, in causing the Souldiers to carry many Counterpains and Blankets hung upon the ends of two Poles, behind which those that march'd were conceal'd from the fight of the Enemy, so that having no aim at us, they hardly shot but at random and in vain. Yet could not this so hinder nevertheless, but that one of my intimate Friends called *Roquelaure*, a very good Souldier, and a very brave man, who had been a General in the *Venetians* Army, was killed, in a place where a man would have thought he had been absolutely secure. He served at this time in the King's Army, in the quality of Mareschal *de Camp*, and commanded the attack, when the Regiment of *Picardy* went on to the assault, having always Monsieur *de Liancour* and me by his side. Being now Masters of the Town, and there only remaining some Runaways that yet made some shots in the Air, he told me he was so thirsty, that he was able to do no more, and that he should certainly dye, unless he had something to drink. I ran presently to fetch a Flagon, that I commonly made a Souldier carry by his side for such extremities; and *Roquelaure* taking the Flagon, enter'd into a house to be more out of danger. But it was there that Fate expected him, and it very well appear'd, that all the foresight of man is vain, against the stroaks of Providence; for when I was in this House close by him, staying till he had drank, that I might drink too; as he had the Flaggon at his mouth there came a Musquet Bullet, which hitting upon the Mullion of the Window, and being resisted by the Stone, by a strange glance struck full into the head of *Roquelaure*, who fell stone dead at my feet, and made me almost fall upon him by endeavouring to hold him up. This accident so little foreseen did doubtless much more sensibly strike me, than if I had seen him fall in the Fight; where a man expects to be kill'd himself, or see those fall whom he most loves. I did intirely love this man, and I can say, that he had an equal love for me, having said to me at the beginning of the Campaign, that if he should chance to be kill'd, he entreated I would accept of his equipage, to put me sometimes in mind of my Friend. I doubtless stood in no need of that to remember him, loving all my Friends from the bottom of my heart, and having not been accustomed to borrow from these exterior testimonies the remembrance I have of their Friendship. I could not nevertheless avoid this present he had made me, being unwilling to disoblige his Kindred, who would by all means perform the Will of the dead, and compell'd me to accept it.

XIV. *Lunet*, which is but a little pitiful weak place, having surrendred upon composition, after the taking of *Sommiere* the Army marcht, without any ones knowing whither it was design'd to go, and past by a little Bourg, wherein there was a kind of Fort into which a great many *Hugonots* had withdrawn themselves, very well resolv'd to defend the place: Monsieur *d'Angoulesme* did not think it worth his while to stay there, despising the place as too inconsiderable, and so continued the march of the Army. The honest men within thought they might make their advantage of our passing thus by, without attacking them, and hoping to get some booty, and elevated with their good fortune, resolv'd to sally, and to fall upon the Rear of the Army. I was at that time in the Van, and being aware of them, and having shew'd them to Monsieur *de Cerillac*, our Lieutenant Collonel, I told him, that if he would give me leave, I thought I could cut off their retreat, and with threescore men make my self Master of their Gate before they could return. The proposal pleas'd him very

very well, and he gave me leave to do what I would; which he had no sooner done, but that with threescore chosen men I slipt along through a Ditch, that conceal'd us from the Skirmishers, when they thought of nothing but the Rear of the Army, and not of the Head, which they knew to be far enough off; and so finding themselves on a sudden surpriz'd, and their Retreat intercepted, from that part whence they least suspected any such thing, they began to run full drive toward their Gate; but they could not get thither before me, so that we enter'd pell-mell with them, and my Souldiers being better acquainted with this kind of work, than this sort of Rabble, we had no great ado to force them to give way, and to make our selves absolute Masters of the Gate. I there left ten Souldiers to guard that, and went with the other fifty to charge the rest of the Bourg, who were so frighted with this surprize, that they made no manner of resistance.

After having disarm'd and turn'd out all the men that were to be fear'd, and let the rest alone without giving my self any trouble with them. I sent to acquaint Monsieur *de Cevillac* with the success of my enterprize, and to entreat him to give Monsieur *d' Angoulesme* an account of the same, that I might know what Order he would please to give about this Bourg. Monsieur *d' Angoulesme* sent a Gentleman to command me from him, to raze the place to the ground before I left it. I receiv'd this Order with all due submission; but fearing lest this affair might one day be laid in my Dish, I entreated the Gentleman not to take it ill, if I desir'd him to tell Monsieur *d' Angoulesme*, that I durst not well raze the place, without first having his Order in Writing. This Gentleman forsooth, standing upon the punctilio of honour, briskly reply'd, that the word he brought me from Monsieur *d' Angoulesme*, was doubtless as good as a Letter. 'Tis true, Sir, said I, in things where the question only is, whither they are true or false, but not in an affair like this, where for my own indemnity it is requisite the word should remain, and subsist, which it cannot do but in writing; and therefore do not take it ill I beseech you, if I entreat you to let Monsieur *d' Angoulesme* know, that I never dismantle nor burn any place, without having first a written Order to do it. I thought I had sufficiently explain'd my self, to give this Gentleman to understand, that I did not doubt of the truth of his report, but that I look'd after my own security for the future; but he took the highest offence imaginable, and would make it a particular quarrel: whereupon I told him, that nothing was farther from my thoughts, than to offend him in the least; but that also he ought not to engage me in an ill business, in making a point of honor of a thing that was nothing so, and that I was very well assur'd if he himself was in my place; he was a man of too much understanding, not to take the same measures and precautions that I did. Being then satisfied with my answer, he went back to Monsieur *d' Angoulesme*, who immediately sent me a Ticket in these words.

This is to give Order to raze and burn the Fortifications and principal Houses of Cabos, *it being a place that serves for a Retirement to the Kings Enemies, and therefore absolutely necessary for his Majesties Service.*

                 D' Angoulesme.

After

After having receiv'd this Order, I commanded the Inhabitants to carry away what they would, and sent to proclaim in the neighbouring Villages, that it was free for every one to come and take what they thought fit, upon condition that they should raze the Fortifications, or burn what could not be pull'd down. This work lasted two whole days, at the end of which I came back to the Army.

XV. This precaution, which I thought fit to make use of, before I pull'd down this Castle, was of great use to me in the consequence; and it well appear'd, that it is good to think of the future in the present time, and to foresee, during the time of War, what may happen in the times of Peace. For some years after, a Receiver General of *Guyenne*, who had a part of his estate in *Cabos*, and to whom the houses appertain'd, that I had demolisht and burnt, came and made his complaint to the Chamber of accounts, that he could not produce his Acquittances and Accounts, being that all his Papers had been burnt by one called *de Pontis*, that during the War had plundred and burnt the Town; and who was at present a Lieutenant in the Guards; requiring that he might be permitted to prosecute him, to compel him to restore all things to the estate they were in before: The affair was carry'd to the Parliament, where I was inform'd against, and where a Decree past against me. But I not appearing, I was summon'd at the sound of Trumpet, and a Process issu'd out against me for Contempt. In this extremity, to which I was on a sudden reduc'd, for serving the King, I went to his Majesty, and having acquainted him with my business, told him, that I was very well assured Monsieur *d' Angoulesme* had given me his Order in writing, and that I had stiffly insisted to have it, but that I could not call to mind where I had laid that Paper. The King then bid me go to Monsieur *d' Angoulesme*, and to entreat from him a note of his hand, that should signifie that it was he who had commanded me to demolish the Castle. But Monsieur *d' Angoulesme* making it a matter of mirth, and turning it into raillery, told me he remember'd nothing of it, and that he would not give me a note of his hand.

With this answer I came back to the King, who seem'd to be very much surpriz'd at Monsieur *d' Angoulesme*'s answer, and told me, that he would order me to have an act of oblivion. I must confess that word struck to my heart, not being able to endure that they should treat what I had done by the express Order of the General, like a crime that deserv'd remission. I most humbly thankt his Majesty, telling him, that I would not make use of what he was pleas'd to offer me, but in the last necessity, and that I would once more search my Papers. But I know not how, it always fell out, that in the precipitation wherein I then was, this Paper being lapt in another, fell divers times into my hands, and never was discover'd by me. Seeing my self then reduc'd to such a condition, that I no more dar'd to shew my head, and being forc'd to walk the streets by night only, I went again to the King, who said that since Monsieur *d' Angoulesme* deny'd me the justice I demanded of him, he would have me take Letters of Abolition. But it is most true, that I could not hear the word Abolition without being quite besides my self; and I confess I had a secret spite in the bottom of my heart, believing that this Prince, who was satisfy'd of my innocency, ought to have done something more for me upon this occasion. I could not therefore yet prevail upon my self to have recourse to these Letters, which in absolving at the same time

T   made

made me appear guilty. I therefore again fell to ranfacking all my Papers, and at laft had the good fortune to find that, which my hafte before had till then made me overlook. And thus, by the Kings order, carry'd to the Parliament that which ferv'd for my juftification. I made my innocency appear, and was at the fame time difcharg'd from all farther profecution. Monfieur *d' Angoulefme* hearing of it, did nothing but laugh, faying only that I had been once frighted in my life; fuch is the conduct, and fuch are the railleries of great perfons, who value themfelves upon looking unconcern'd upon the misfortunes, into which they not only fee the meaner men fall, but into which they make them fall, as if they thought it below them to fhare therein. And this example makes it appear, that a man cannot fail in always dealing cautioufly with them, feeing they eafily engage men in danger, and as eafily leave them in it when they are engaged.

The End of the Fourth Book.

BOOK

Several Circumstances of the Siege of Montpellier. *Monsieur* Zimet, *Mareschal de Camp is wounded to death. An excellent Discourse of his to the Sieur* de Pontis, *upon the Miseries of this Life, and upon an Excess he had committed upon the Enemy, out of love to him. The Sieur* de Pontis *is himself wounded, and like to dye; what past betwixt him, the Surgeons, and some Religious Persons, that came to assist him. The King makes him a Lieutenant in his Guards and makes use of him for the Re-establishment of military Discipline in the Regiment.*

I. To proceed in the course of our History, (which I have digrest from, in the account I have given of the unjust prosecution, that the demolishing the Castle of *Cabor* brought upon me.) The Kings Army, having taken a great many other little places, towards the middle of Summer drew near to *Montpellier*, and sate down before it, which Army at that time consisted of twenty thousand men. The King was there in person, and had for his Lieutenant Generals, Monsieur *le Prince*, and Messieurs *de Montmorency* and *de Schomberg*. Monsieur *de Chevreuse* was there also, but he was not much employ'd, and Monsieur *de Lesdiguieres* came thither towards the end. They made three Attacks, the first whereof was that of the King, commanded by the Prince; the second, that of Monsieur *de Montmorency*; and the third, that of Monsieur *de Schomberg*. The Regiment of *Picardy* was in this last, Monsieur *de Schomberg* always making suit to have it, both because of Monsieur *de Liancour* his Son-in-law, as also out of the esteem he had for that Regiment. Monsieur *de Rohan* was shut up in the place, with a little body of an Army, that was instead of a Garrison. The first Sally they made was on the side of a Half-Moon, that was over against Monsieur *de Schomberg's* Attack, and that was very well cover'd with their Out-works, because they had cover'd the Bulwarks very close, and that the Mounts of Earth which they had rais'd were such, as the Fortification was not to be seen. The Duke of *Fronsac*, who served there in the quality of a Volunteer, was kill'd in this Sally.

II. Monsieur *de Schomberg*, judging that it was of the last importance to force this Half-Moon, propos'd the enterprize to the King, who thereupon call'd a Council, wherein it was resolv'd to cause it to be discover'd. They accordingly sent thither several Officers one after another, who brought word that there was only a Ditch full of Water, and a Pallisado of plain'd Timber beyond the Ditch. Monsieur *de Schomberg* desiring to be yet better satisfy'd, and remembring the service I had done him before *Montauban* in the like occasion, put me upon the employment of going again to discover this Half-Moon; adding to this Order of his, a thousand civilities and complements, to encourage me to go to have my

brains

Brains beaten out. I told him, that not to omit the least thing, or at least that what I had seen might not be useless to him, in case I should be kill'd, I would carry my Tablets along with me, wherein I would write every thing as I advanc'd, and that he should only take care to have them brought off to him.

I arm'd my self as at *Montauban*, with a Cuirass and a Cask; and passing over the Trench about noon, I gave notice to the Guard, which was of the Regiment of *Navarre*, that I had order to go to discover the place, and that therefore they should have a care not to mistake me. After this, I crawl'd up a great Mount the Enemy had cast up, to retrench themselves with; and having seen what the other Officers had discover'd before, namely, the Ditch full of Water, and the Pallisado beyond the Ditch, I would try if I could not discover something more : Wherefore exposing my self to extream peril, I advanc'd and mounted higher, from whence with great astonishment I saw another Pallisado like the first, betwixt the Ditch and me, and which appear'd almost incredible to me my self, a second Half-moon enclos'd within the great one, as strong, and of the same form as that which enclos'd it. I look't upon it over and over again, not being able almost to believe my own Eyes, and set every thing exactly down in my Tablets. But when I was got down again to return, I had not gone a hundred paces before I began to consider, that possibly they might laugh at my report; and fearing, as indeed it fell out, that I should be look'd upon as a Visionary, whom fear had made to see what was not, I resolv'd to go back again, yet nearer hand to assure my self of the truth of things, and to see if I could not observe some place, from whence, as at *Montauban*, I might make the King's own Eyes witnesses of what I should tell him. I return'd then with this design, and went straight to the very top of the retrenchment, where I could not long stay, by reason of a Centinel of the Enemy, who was not above thirty paces distant from me on the other side; and who having let fly at me, gave a great Alarm to the *Corps de Guardes*, who immediately stood to their arms, and all fir'd upon me. But the same instant that I was assur'd of what I desir'd, I threw my self from the top to the bottom, and came to Monsieur *de Schomberg's* Quarter, who had already given all the necessary orders for the Attack.

Monsieur *de Schomberg* took me immediately aside into a corner of his Tent, where I made him my report; and seeing him seem hard to perswade himself to believe me, concerning the second Half-moon of which I have spoke before, after all the assurances I could give him, we went together to the King; who presently began to smile, and fall to rallying me, as I had very well foreseen. *Did ever any one hear of such a thing, and is there any likelihood in it?* I then entreated his Majesty, that he would please to believe his own eyes, assuring him, that I would make him see the truth of what I had said, from a place that was not far off : I carried him to the place, from which both himself, and Monsieur *de Schomberg*, were satisfied of the truth of my report. But what shall we do? said the King then; All the orders are already given, do you believe, said he, that we cannot force the Enemy from their Post? I believe not, Sir, said I, both by reason of these Pallisado's, these Ditches, and the great number of men by which they are guarded; and that it would certainly be too much to attempt to take them all at once, but that it would be much better to take them one after another.

Upon this one of the Generals, came and whisper'd to the King, do

you

you think, Sir, this Officer has not a mind to save his own Regiment,
which has the head of the Attack ? you must keep him back, and employ
others, for when a leading Officer goes on without hoping well, it never
succeeds. I heard every word he said, being near enough ; and heard
the King make answer, that he knew very well it was not that, which
made me to speak after that manner, adding withal, that nevertheless he
might do as he said. But the deference the King had for this General's
advice cost his Army very dear. Being then sensibly wounded to see my
self look'd upon as a Visionary, and a Coward, I entreated his Majesty
with great instances, not to let the all Regiment have this affront put upon
them, to be deprived of the honour they were wont to have, of going
on first upon the Enemy ; adding with some heat, that if I had committed a fault, it was not just that the whole body should be punish'd for it
by the loss of so honourable a priviledge, and that I alone ought to be
chastiz'd, and answer it with my head. The King, who very well difcern'd my emotion, made me this answer ; I do not pretend, said he, to
wrong the Regiment, for on the contrary, I will keep it for a reserve,
neither have I any intention to punish you, seeing that I rather ought to
reward you for the service you have done me : and therefore speak after
another manner, and entertain other sentiments of my justice.

I then retir'd to carry news to my Lieutenant Collonel of the Orders
the King had given, and the reason that had mov'd him to do after that
manner, insisting much, that having done all in me lay to hinder it, it was
now his part to plead our cause anew : Monsieur *de Cerillac* made answer,
without being mov'd, that if the King and his Generals would have it so,
we must resolve to acquiesce, and peradventure they will do us a cour-
tesy ; for they will doubtless save our lives by taking our places ; and yet
I make a very great question, whither they will be able to carry the
place or no : but they will stand in need of us, and we, tho the last, may
possibly have the honour of the fight. He spoke after this manner,
making a virtue of necessity, and conceiving that it was more discretion
to keep there ; but added, that nevertheless for decency's sake, we should
do well to present our selves, lest we should give the world an occasion
to censure and suspect us. Accordingly we went, but were presently
told, that we had not the Attack, and that we should stay till we were
commanded ; whereupon without being very importunate, we return'd
to our Quarters, there to expect a new order.

Monsieur *de Chevreuse* who did not command the Attack, having entreated me to carry him to some eminence from whence he might easily
see the fight, I carried him to an old kind of Battery, where the Cannon
had been plac'd when they first invested the place ; and from whence he
might see all without any manner of danger. The Attack was presently
begun, and succeeded so ill, that *Navarre* and *Piedmont*, who had the
head, with other Regiments that sustain'd them, were almost all cut to
pieces ; and it fell out according to what Monsieur *de Cerillac* had said,
that they would at last have recourse to us, for we were commanded
with all the Regiment to repel the Enemy, who were not content to
have made so brave a resistance, but moreover had sallied out, and thrown
themselves into our Trenches ; and finding them tir'd with so long a fight,
we beat them back with ease enough, and recover'd what we had lost
of our Trenches and Lodgment, but not our dead men, which were
not to be restor'd to life ; and thus the ill grounded conjecture of the
General succeeded. Tis strange, that an engagement of honour should

U   some-

sometimes seduce the greatest men to act contrary to their own reason, and to precipitate themselves and whole Armies into inevitable danger. Tho they had slighted my report as incredible, yet at last satisfied with their own eyes, and things being known for such as I had represented them, it was to attempt an impossibility to engage in this Attack: In the mean time the Orders were already given, an Officer is suspected for a Coward, and upon this without any other assurance they go on headlong to the Assault; so true it is, that mens Judgments, by an effect of divine Justice, sometimes fail them in the most important occasions.

III. This bloody experience made the Generals alter their resolution; they gave over the Attack of the Half-Moon to fall upon the great Bastion; and this change was of so great importance, that a man may say it was the cause of taking the place: for from that day forward the Enemy despair'd of being able to keep it, as much as they were confident of doing it before, as they themselves have since confest. The new Attack being begun, the Enemy made a great Sally upon our Regiment, which had the Guard; they immediately charg'd the flanks of the Trench, and did it with so great fury, that one part of it gave way, and was totally routed, and the other came to rally themselves to a Lieutenant call'd *La* . . . . and to me, who yet kept our post. The Enemy, who still prest on, and that thought of no less than gaining all that was left, were a little astonisht, when they saw us come on all in a body directly upon them, and charge them so home, that from Assailants as they were before, they saw it concern'd them to look to their defence. This alteration put them to their shifts: they disunited, and the one half retiring into the City, left the other to be shut up in a corner, from whence it was impossible for them to get away. But just as they were going to call out for Quarter, a Souldier came crying out, all in a fright, Monsieur *Zamet* is kill'd, Monsieur *Zamet* is kill'd! I askt him, How dost thou know it? Because I saw it, said he; at which being desperate, and quite out of my wits, I miserably gave my self up to the fury that transported me, in the thought wherewith I was then possest, that I had lost all in losing this intimate friend, without making any manner of use of my Reason, or other reflection, and threw my self with the utmost fury upon these poor people, whom I sacrific'd to my revenge, in causing them to be all cut to pieces.

IV. After this bloody execution, to which I had suffer'd my self to be carried away, I ran, being yet quite out of my sences, to see if I could find Monsieur *Zamet* dead, as I had been told: I was a little comforted when I was told, that they were gone to put him to bed; but when I saw, coming into the room, that his Thigh was taken off with a Faucon-shot, that he had receiv'd, in going from place to place as *Mareschal de Camp*, I lookt upon him as a dead man. I stood by his Bed-side without being able to speak one word, my heart was so opprest; when he himself began to speak to me after so Christian a manner, that I remain'd in the greatest confusion, comparing what he said to me to the condition wherein I found my self. *Must Christians* (said he to me) *as we are, desire any thing contrary to the will of God? If it be by his appointment that all things happen in the world, and if we cannot doubt that this is a stroke of his providence, why should we oppose what he has ordain'd? Is not he master both of Life and Death? And it would be mockery towards Almighty God, to whom we pray*

every

every day that his will may be done, not to submit to his good pleasure, when he thus shews his own immediate arm. 'Tis proper in these great occasions, that a man can throughly prove himself, and found the bottom of his heart, to know whether he be truly his or no. The little ones are more apt to deceive us: but in this Hypocrisie has no place. How happy are we to leave this world, that is only full of sins and miseries, to go unto God! I have, 'tis true, great reason to apprehend his Justice, but he commands us to hope in his Mercy, and it were to offend him to lose this hope. He will have compassion of us, and tho his Judgments are terrible, yet he will shew Mercy. Even this is a great favour, to dye in his quarrel, in defending the true Religion against those that would subvert it. And then looking upon me with eyes full of tenderness, and there fixing them for some time, as if to make me more sensible of the reproach he intended me concerning the action he knew I had so lately committed; *But you,* said he, *who love me as your friend, must that love of yours render you so cruel, that to revenge the death of a man whom Providence will have dye, you should destroy so many others without mercy, and without justice! Where was your generosity and natural humanity, to have deny'd Quarter to these poor men, and to damn them most miserably for my sake, as if my death could be reveng'd by theirs, or that I could approve this transport of so irregular a friendship? Have you been able to restore me to life, in taking it so cruelly away from these wretches? And was it not rather to pull down the anger of God both upon your self and me, to pretend to revenge my death, which he has appointed, by the death you have so unjustly given to so many persons contrary to his order, and contrary to his will? I beseech you repent of this fault, as one of the greatest that peradventure you have ever committed in your whole life. The remedy which you have thought to apply to my misfortune, has been much more painful to me than the mischance it self; and I think my self oblig'd to conjure you from the bottom of my heart, that you never for the death of any friend whatever, or your own being mortally wounded, fall again into the same transport of fury.*

We were alone when he spoke to me after this manner; and I confess, that as I then wanted words to make answer to such a moving discourse, so I want them now to represent the condition wherein I found my self; being compell'd both by Monsieur *Zamet*'s reasons, and my own nature, to pronounce a terrible sentence upon my self for this excess, of which I was so inexcusably guilty. Words then being wanting to me, I made him understand my repentance by the abundance of my tears, which I could not refrain. And I must also confess, that this so Christian discourse of his, together with the condition of him who made it to me, imprinted so lively a sense in the bottom of my heart, that I have ever since retain'd a continual sorrow for that barbarous action. I stay'd with him that night, and all the next day, being I could not find in my heart to leave him; and went not out of the Room, but to perform my duty upon the Guard.

V. But it was not long before I was chastis'd for the criminal fury wherewith I had suffer'd my self to be transported. I was commanded to go attack the Enemy with a hundred men, in a little Half-moon, that they were resolv'd to carry, and from whence they fir'd nightly upon us: where tho they made a brave defence, were yet more vigorously attackt; and we were now upon entring, having nothing but a little Ditch to leap, to make our selves masters of the place; but at the same moment I felt my self wounded with two Musquet shots at once,

one

one in the body which entred not very far, and only past betwixt the flesh and the skin, the other in the ankle, the bone of which it broke into several splinters, making me fall at the same time into the Ditch, from whence attempting to rise, I fell down again. I was therefore fain to satisfie my self with encouraging my Souldiers only, bidding them not to concern themselves about me, but perfect what they had so successfully begun; and that it would by no means be honourable for them, by reason of my being wounded, to lose a Half-moon, which it had cost them so much to gain. The men being all very brave, the sight of the condition I was in, serv'd only the more to excite their Courage, so that before I could be carry'd off, I had the satisfaction to see them lodg'd in the place.

I then entreated a Gentleman, a kinsman of Monsieur *de Valencay*, my intimate friend, that serv'd with us upon this occasion in the quality of a Volunteer, that he would help to conduct, or rather to carry me back to the Camp, which he did with a very particular affection; and so soon as I was arriv'd at my Tent, I sent to acquaint Monsieur *Zamet* with the condition I was reduc'd to; and to let him know that my greatest grief was that I could not pay him my duty in his sickness, and do him those services that I could heartily have wisht, and to be thus depriv'd of the only consolation of being near his person. He was sensible of my misfortune, as of a new wound he had receiv'd, believing me to be worse hurt than I was, and nearer death than he. He sent to me immediately to let me know his sence of my condition; which it was no hard matter for me to understand, by reason of the union, and perfect openness of our hearts. We sent afterwards daily every hour reciprocally to know how one another did, having this only way left of conversing in some sort with one another, and of giving one another a mutual consolation.

VI. Finding my self in very great danger, and that the Kings chief Physician, and the Chyrurgions assur'd me, that there was no other way left to save my life, but by cutting off my Leg, which began to gangreen, I had a mind to acknowledge the obligation I had to the Gentleman, my friend, of whom I spoke before, who brought me back to my Tent: I therefore told him, that God being pleas'd otherwise to dispose of me, I entreated him to permit me to surrender my Command into his hands; and that he would go in my name to request it of the King, and to tell his Majesty, that I did humbly beseech him, in consideration of my services, to give it him. This Gentleman with great generosity deny'd me, telling me flatly, that he would not do it. But after this first denial I renew'd my importunity, and importun'd him with so great instance, assuring him that he could not disoblige me more than by such a refusal, that he saw himself compell'd, as it were, to gratifie my desire. He went then, tho very unwillingly, to attend the King, and acquainted him with the humble request I had oblig'd him to deliver in my name. The King a little surpriz'd, ask'd him, what is he dead then? to which the Gentleman made answer, that I was not; but that I would not be satisfied except he would come to his Majesty, to acquaint him, that his first Physician Monsieur *Eronard*, who had apply'd, and taken off the first dressing, had found my Leg in such a condition, the Gangreen being got into it, that he saw no hopes of saving my life, but by cutting it off. that I could not consent to it, being not well assur'd to out-live so violent a remedy, and choosing almost as soon to dye, as to see my self
miserable,

miferable all the remainder of my life, and out of condition of ferving
his Majefty, having thus loft one of my Legs. Tell him, anfwer'd the
King, that I will have him do whatever the Phyficians and Chyrurgions appoint, that he muft not fuffer himfelf to be thus transported by defpair;
and that I will not forfake him: that, as to what concerns his Command,
I will not difpofe of it, till he fhall be totally incapable of ever exercizing
it again, and that I am very forry to fee him reduc'd to fuch a condition,
as to make me fuch a requeft. The Gentleman came back to me, and
brought me the King's anfwer, at which I was really very much afflicted,
having a great mind to procure this favour for my Friend, and feeing
almoft no hopes of my felf, after all that the Chyrurgions had told me of
my condition.

In the mean time I could by no means refolve to have my Leg cut off,
and I had almoft as willingly have died; when being thus agitated betwixt fear and defire, and the profpect of a prefent and inevitable death
preffing hard upon me, I on a fudden remembred, I had heard a Chy-
ruryion, who had cur'd me of fome wound or other, boaft, that he had
an infallible remedy to ftop a Gangreen, and one who liv'd not above
fifteen Leagues off at a Town call'd *Tournon*. The affair being preffing,
I fent my man in poft hafte to tell him what condition I was in, and to
conjure him to come with all fpeed to fave my life, by reafon that I was
refolv'd rather to dye, than to have my Leg cut off. This Chyrurgion,
who remembred that I had paid him very well the firft time he had had
me in his hands, mounted to Horfe in a trice, and made all the hafte he
could to come to me. In the mean time the King's Chyrurgions, not believing that a Country Chyrurgion could know any particular fecret that
they were ignorant of, and looking upon this hope of mine as a pure allu-
fion, that might occafion my death, refolv'd to ufe violence, to do me, as
they thought, a very great piece of fervice, and to fave my life by cutting off my Leg, whether I would or no. So that after they had laid before me the inevitable neceffity of doing it, and that all my Friends had
jointly pray'd, and conjur'd me to fuffer it; feeing me ftill remain inflexible, and obftinate not to fuffer it to be done; they plainly told me,
that feeing I would be the caufe of my own death, they fhould peradventure be forc'd to proceed after another manner with me. Accordingly
they came the next day into my Tent with all their preparations of
Lints, Salves, Ligatures, and Inftruments to make their operation. I
perceiv'd them through the Curtains of my Bed, and was in fo great a
fright, that my Hair ftood on end, choofing infinitely rather to lofe both
Arms and Legs in an affault, or a battel, than to fee any of them cut off
in cold blood in my Bed, efpecially whilft I was in hopes to preferve them
by another way.

Two *Francifcan* Fryers prefented themfelves at the fame time, to ex-
hort me by a very Chriftian difcourfe to fuffer this operation with patience, giving me to underftand that for an hour or two of pain, I fhould
preferve my felf many years; and that though I did not care for this life,
yet that I ought to do it in confideration of the other, feeing that God
did as much forbid us to be Murtherers of our felves, as of others, and
that here this perifhable life was not only concerned, but life eternal, to
which I was going, and where I fhould foon be obliged to render an account of my life; and fhould be guilty of cafting it away, if I refus'd the
methods proper for preferving it. I anfwered, that it was not certain
the cutting off my Leg would fave my life, and that I had much greater

X   hopes

hopes from an able Chyrurgion, who had a particular secret to stop a Gangreen, and would be with me presently. The two Fathers regarding more what the Chyrurgions pretended, that such a Medicine was impossible, than any thing I could say, concluded out of an honest but indiscreet zeal, that force must be used, and I must be held during the operation; so that both falling upon me on the sudden, they told me, they saw they must save my life by violence. This proceeding I confess strangely disordered me, so that in rage and transport of passion, I cry'd out, What! will you rob me, both of this and the next life too? Are you resolv'd to damn me? Let me go, except you resolve to throw me into a condition more dreadful, than the loss of ten thousand lives. These amazing expressions so startled and confounded them, that they straightway let me go, and were much concern'd to find their zeal so unseasonably employ'd. They chang'd their note, and spoke afterwards to me with great charity and tenderness; letting all expressions alone, that might any way discompose me, and appeasing my mind by all the soft ways they could. This return quite won my heart, and convinc'd me, that what they had done imprudently proceeded from friendship and kindness; and I exprest as much gratitude for this last, as I had done aversion for their former behaviour to me; entreating them, that they would visit me often in my illness; which they readily engag'd to do; and then we contracted such a Friendship, as continu'd between us ever after; and they have come to see me in the place where I now dwell retir'd, a great many years after this accident.

At last the man I expected with so much impatience, and upon whom I depended for my Cure arrived, and extraordinary haste he made. Assoon as ever I saw him enter the room, I cry'd out, Oh! how much am I oblig'd to you for coming so quickly, and answering all the confidence I reposed in you! I have told every hour, and every minute, and am sensible you could not possibly have come sooner to my relief. You see here one, who is a lost man in the opinion of all the world, unless you relieve him. The Chyrurgion reply'd, that he hoped he should be able to stop the Gangreen, provided it were not gone too far, and that my case were not absolutely desperate; and that his remedy did not use to fail. I sent away to beg Monsieur *Erouard*, and the other Chyrurgions to come, and take off their applications, it not being allowable that it should be taken off without them. Assoon as the dressing was remov'd, the Chyrurgion was a little surpriz'd to see the Gangreen got so high, and said it was gone so far, that he durst give me no assurance till after once or twice dressing: The others said, he spoke very reasonably; and it would be very happy if there were any hopes then. He apply'd his remedy, and next day they met again at the same hour to see the effect. The thing appear'd still doubtful, and he would warrant nothing yet; tho this first application had prevented the Gangreen from rising any higher. So he reserv'd the giving any positive Judgment till the next time; and then at taking off the second dressing, and duly examining the wound, he declar'd boldly, that now he would be answerable for my Cure, and that his remedy had been successful. Monsieur *Erouard* and the rest looking upon it, were a little astonish'd, and confest this was a secret they did not understand. It is easie to judge whether I repented of my obstinacy, in not submitting either to the pleasure of the King, the ignorance of my Chyrurgions, and the zeal of my Ghostly Fathers; and whether I did not think my want of Courage upon this occasion a

happi-

happiness, which would not let me throw away a Leg to no purpose, that hath serv'd me so long, and so well since that time.

A few days after, Monsieur *Schomberg* sent to see me by his Steward, who found me better of my wounds, but ill enough of my purse, my pay not being sufficient for so great an expence, as the condition I was then in expos'd me to, above the ordinary charge of the Army: Which Monsieur *Schomberg* having intimation of from the person he had sent to me, procured me some money of the King. Part of this I employ'd in rewarding *Mutonis*, the Souldier that helpt me to escape into our Camp, and whom I kept in my own Tent as my Brother, ever after he had receiv'd that Musquet-shot in his Arm; till at last I got him a place in an Hospital, where he subsisted very comfortably without my help. But the summ Monsieur *Schomberg* procur'd for me being not very considerable, by reason that a greater would have made it necessary to get a Ratification from the Chamber of Accounts, he was so generous to send me some of his own; and did it after so pressing and so obliging a manner, that I thought my self bound to accept, what a better man than I would have made no scruple to receive from a Superintendant; and what indeed I could not have told how to refuse, from a person that hath all along done me the honour to love me so tenderly; for to have declin'd it must needs have given him great offence.

VII. In the mean while Monsieur *Zamet* was dead of his wound, but they conceal'd his death from me, and durst not be too hasty in letting me know what were enough to have kill'd me, in that condition. The City of *Montpellier* being at last surrendred upon terms, and the general Peace concluded with the *Hugonots*, the Regiment of *Picardy* was plac'd there in Garrison, where I was lodg'd rarely well; and my Chyrurgion in six weeks had put me in a way of doing without him, and letting my self be drest by one in the Town, till my Cure was perfected. I return'd him the best acknowledgment I could, and gave him a reward, which tho but inconsiderable if compar'd with the service he had done me, yet proportionable to my present ability. What was wanting that way I endeavour'd to make up by the tenderest testimonies of friendship, and of the gratitude I should ever retain while that life lasted, which he had preserv'd, when every body else thought me sure to lose it.

The death of Monsieur *Zamet* was kept from me, as I said, for some time, but the great impatience I was in to know how he did, would not suffer it to be long conceal'd, for I was every hour enquiring after him with extraordinary concern. So that after they had prepar'd me by degrees for the afflicting news, I receiv'd it at last with a grief not possible to be exprest; and except people knew both our hearts, and the strict union of them, they can never judge what disorder I was in upon the thought of our being separated for ever, and that I should no more enjoy the blessing of his Conversation, whose friendship I valu'd above all things in the world. But this first grief was follow'd by another; for having made me his Executor, and deliver'd his Will into my hands the day after he was hurt, I could not but be sensibly afflicted to see that some of his Relations should quarrel with me, in opposing the intention of the Dead, and the care I took to have his Will perform'd. Yet afterwards they all acquiesc'd but one, who still retain'd a coldness toward me upon this account; as if the last Will of the Dead ought not to be respected by the Living; or that he whom they make choice of to see

it

it executed, could be to blame for acquitting himself faithfully of this duty.

VIII. After lying seven or eight months under Cure, when I began to walk a little, and get on Horseback, Monsieur *Valencay*, Governour of *Montpellier*, gave me a Commission to go see what the Inhabitants of *Sevennes* were doing. These were little Bourgs and Villages scituated in the Mountains, and possest by the *Hugonots*. They were all gallant Souldiers, having past most part of their youth in the *Low-Country* Wars, from whence they return'd expert and brave, which gave some occasion to suspect them, and oblig'd Monsieur *Valencay* to order this enquiry, that he might be secure they were not contriving some new disturbances. I found them all very quiet as oft as I came among them: and this visit that I made into their Country was not unprofitable to me, because by this means I was capable of informing the King, who afterwards examin'd me about it, as shall be told in due place.

IX. I had not been at *Paris* of a long time, and indeed had some business there. The Regiment deputed me to go sollicit for payment of their Musters that were in arrear. Monsieur *Valencay* contributed to this Deputation too, and I almost fancy'd he was not sorry of so fair an occasion to put me at some distance from him, knowing the particular friendship Monsieur *Schomberg* honour'd me with; who being now in disgrace, he might fear my raising a faction in the place, for a person to whose Interests I had ever shewn my self so much devoted. But in this he betray'd his ignorance of me, if he thought me capable of a thing so contrary to my temper: For I ever knew very well how to distinguish between the duty of acknowledgment to private persons, and that of fidelity to my Prince. I took post with one single Servant, and just after I had past *Nevers*, fell into a good pleasant adventure. I met very late in the Evening with a Courier, who past me, and went up to my man; he being very weary, and not turning his Horse out of the way, the Courier justled him so roughly, that both of them were dismounted, and came down together. A quarrel ensu'd, and to cuffs they fell, and when they had box'd one another pretty tightly, and saw no body come to part them, they began to cool themselves, and fell to parleying. The Courier askt my man whom he belong'd to? and who that was that rode before? and hearing my name, How! said he, that is the very person whom I am sent to: How lucky an accident is this that hath brought me to the man I look for. Come on, let us mount presently, and spur on till we overtake him. Thus they gallop'd away together, shouting after me at a great distance; at last I heard them, and stopt; but not knowing the meaning of this, nor who I had to deal with, I drew a Pistol. The Courier coming up, told me of the good fortune he had in meeting my man, and how he came to discover that I was the person, upon whose account purely it was that he was going to *Montpellier*; at the same time drawing out of his pocket an Order from the King, which contain'd these words: *Upon receipt of this Order, you are without fail to repair to My Person, with all speed.* This put me into a confusion betwixt hope and fear, not being able to guess upon what account I should be sent for; though I could not find any great reason to fear, as not being conscious of any fault I had been guilty of: So I told the Courier he might go on his journey about his other dispatches. But he

re-

reply'd, that he had none of importance, or that requir'd haste but mine, and therefore as to the rest he would put them into the common Post. I urg'd him again, and would fain have got rid of him, telling him he might pay him for his whole Journey, and I would satisfie him for his pains; but he answered it would be so much Money thrown away, and besides he must go back with me. Thus we rode Post day and night, and repos'd our selves for two or three hours only at *Essone*; from whence setting out three hours before day, we came betimes in the morning to *Paris*.

X. Monsieur *Valencay's* dispatches, of which I was the Bearer, were for the King, and Monsieur *Puisyeux*; but I thought it my best way to light at Monsieur *P.'s* Gates, hoping he might give me some light into the occasion of my being sent for by the King. He was not a little surpriz'd to see me, believing I had left the Army by the King's Order; but when he had open'd his Letters, and seen the purport of them, he told me, I must needs go carry the King that directed to him, and present his too seal'd up again, because his Majesty would be the better pleas'd: I very well perceiv'd by the manner of Monsieur *Puisyeux's* speaking to me, that the business upon which the King had sent for me, had no harm in it; and in that thought went straight to the *Louvre*, in the habit of a man that rides Post in the Winter, that is, all dirt from head to foot. Being come to Court, I spoke to the Usher of the Chamber, who very roughly told me, I must wait, for the King was not drest yet, and that I was not in so great haste. As we were talking, Count *Nogent* came out of the Chamber, and I knowing his obliging temper, went to salute him; telling him, upon a supposal that he might not know me, That not having the honour to be known to him, I begg'd leave to beseech him, that he would please to order that the King might be told, that the Officer of *Picardy*, for whom his Majesty had sent, was there to attend his pleasure. And thereupon, as I was about to tell him my name, he interrupted me, saying, Are not you Monsieur *de Pontis*? Come, come, the King will be surpriz'd to see you, for he did not expect you so soon. Then he took me in, and immediately shewing me to the King said, Look you, Sir, is not this the most diligent man, and one of the best dispatch in your whole Kingdom? And can any but he, come from *Montpellier* in so short a time, as that since he was sent for? To which the King made answer, it was incredible I should come so soon. I let the King alone in his wonder for a while, which seem'd to divert, and at last clear'd up the matter, and deliver'd the Dispatches from Monsieur *Valencay*. After he had read it, he commanded me to carry it to Monsieur *Puisyeux*, telling me, I had done well, in bringing it to him first. Monsieur *Valencay* (said the King) sends me word that you are the person he sent to visit the *Savennes*; you shall give me an account of that matter by and by, for I will call my Council, and then send for you in; be ready at the time, and in the mean while go, and refresh your self.

I came accordingly when the Council was set, and was call'd in before a great many of the Court, who were then in the Antichamber, and who begun to look upon me after another manner than they had done before. For in this world those are respected who are look'd upon by the Prince, and People have a regard for them in proportion to the share they have in their Soveraigns favour. The King then commanded me to make a report to the Council, of what I knew concerning the state of the Country I had

Y   seen, feen, and from whence I came, and particularly of the *Savennes*. In order whereunto I began firft to fpeak of the City of *Montpellier*, of which I gave an account, that the Inhabitants were very well fatisfied with Monfieur *Valencay*, and feem'd pleafed with his Government ; from thence I proceeded to the concern of the whole Country, and affured his Majefty of the good difpofition the People were in, which gave very good reafon to judge, that they had no averfion to living under his Government, and the direction of thofe he appointed to command there. At laft I came to the *Savennes*, telling him, that after having vifited all thofe Mountains in order, I could difcover nothing but an abfolute fubmiffion in all the Inhabitants, and as great a zeal to his Majefty's fervice now, as there had been want of it before; that I had gone thither feveral times, and found it always the fame; and therefore as far as I was able to judge, durft be refponfible to his Majefty, that there was not any reafon to fufpect their fidelity, which was all I had to fay, according to the prefent condition I left them in. To which the King made anfwer, that it was enough, and as much as he defir'd, bidding me ftay without, and attend him at Dinner.

XI. I took care to be there accordingly, but there was fo much Company the King could not fpeak to me, and therefore deferr'd it till Supper; where there happening to be but a few, I had a convenient Audience. After Supper the King took me into his Clofet, and Marquis *Grimant* only being by, faid thus to me; I have fent for you, to let you fee I am mindful of you, and willing to acknowledge the fervices you have done me; and therefore I give you your choice, either of a Company in the old Body, or a Lieutenancy in my Guards; choofe which you had rather have, I leave you at full liberty. I confefs this propofal a little furpriz'd me, for to fpeak truth I expected fomething more, and was of opinion, that the fervices I had done, after having refufed a Company in the Regiment of *Champagne*, deferved a higher recompence, than that of a Command no better, than what I had formerly refufed. However I was forc'd to fet a good face upon the matter, and acknowledge it a great thing, that his Majefty had done me the honour to think of me. Wherefore I made anfwer with all imaginable humility, that fince his Majefty was pleafed to do fo much in my favour, I humbly begg'd he would make it compleat by pointing out to me himfelf the choice I ought to make; protefting at the fame time, that what pleas'd his Majefty would by moft acceptable to me, fo great was the paffion I had to ferve him in any Poft, he thought fit to affign me. I thought (faid the King) how I fhould find you affected, and had a mind to try, which of the two Commands you had a greater inclination to. Whereupon Monfieur *Griment*, who pretty well knew the King's intention, took the liberty to fay to him, methinks, Sir, you had better give him a Lieutenancy in the Guards, for by that means, you will be fure to have him conftantly near your perfon. That is what I defire, reply'd the King, and do you do fo too? (faid he) fpeaking to me. I have already told your Majefty (faid I) that I have no other choice to make, than what your Majefty directs me to; and I am fixt in that refolution as I ought to be. But I know your Majefty's goodnefs is fo great, that you will not be difpleas'd, if I put you in mind, that you did me the favour to promife me a Company. This was modeftly to afk a Company in the Guards; and the King, who underftood my meaning well enough, prefently interrupted me, and faid, True; but it was in an

old

old Body, and I am now ready to do it; though I give you my word, that if the Company of which I now make you Lieutenant, comes to be vacant, either by the death of the Captain, or any other accident, you fhall have it. I am willing too to acquaint you at firft, that I am defirous to reftore one thing in my Guards, and to begin to do it by you; which is that you neither practife, nor give any Orders in the Company, but what come firft from me : In extraordinary cafes I mean, and not in things of courfe and common ufe; and that you never go off your Guard, nor out of your Quarters, when 'tis your turn to command. This I refolve to have done, that I may reftore difcipline in the body, which at prefent is quite loft among them; and alfo with a defign to have you always near my Perfon. I anfwer'd, That as he was my Mafter and my Prince, and had done me the particular favour to command me nearer to him, I hop'd by my conduct to let his Majefty fee, that my greateft defire was to obey and ferve him all my life. Then he ordered Monfieur *Grimant* to fee my Commiffion difpatch'd prefently, by which I was to be made Lieutenant to Count *Saligny's* Company.

XII. But though I fet a good face upon the matter, as I thought my felf oblig'd to do; yet I return'd very little fatisfy'd with my fortune, and thinking very ferioufly of the conditions propos'd to me, which appear'd very burdenfom and difficult ; I look'd upon my felf from this time forward, as entring into a dreadful flavery; fo that I confefs I could have wifh'd, had I dar'd to deny the King, that I had not been fo unfeafonably complemental, and had made choice rather of a Company in an old Body. But I was now engag'd over head and ears, and had no retreat left, nor any remedy, but to fee my miftake, and make it an ufeful example to other people.

Monfieur *Saligny's* Company was one of the firft in the Regiment, and his younger Brother was Enfign of it, which I knew nothing of before. Cuftom and Order feem'd to require, that he fhould fucceed as Lieutenant, efpecially in his own Brother's Company. I found my felf a little perplex'd fo foon as I was inform'd of this : But ftill that inconvenience muft be encounter'd too, and fo I refolv'd to pay all imaginable civility to Monfieur *Saligny*; and going to wait upon him, I faid, That had I underftood fooner, that his Brother was Enfign in that Company, I fhould have begg'd the King's excufe for accepting the Lieutenancy, and being plac'd between two Brothers, who by Order of War, as well as Birth, ought not to have been feparated upon this occafion. But that I but juft then had come to the knowledge of it, and all left in my power to do, having already accepted the Commiffion, was to exprefs my concern. This complement fucceeded very well, and I can fay, that the two Brothers did me the honour to teftify fo particular a Friendfhip for me, that as oft as any little coldnefs happened between them, I was always the Mediator, and chofen for the Umpire of their differences.

After having been received at the head of the Regiment, it being neceffary to have my felf admitted by the Duke of *Efpernon* too, who was Collonel of the Infantry, I refolv'd to incline his favour to me by a complement that I knew would pleafe him very well, and gratify the ambition fo natural to all great men. The day that I was to mount the Guard, I marched at the head of the Company without a Corflet directly to his Houfe, where caufing my men to halt in a corner, fome twenty paces from it, fo that they kept out of fight, and going by my felf, I defir'd to speak with him. As soon as I came into his presence, after the first salutes, I told him, that the King having honoured me with the Command of Lieutenant to Monsieur *Saligny*, and sealed my Commission, I had been the day before receiv'd at the head of the Company, drawn up in Battalia, by which I was obliged this day to mount the Guard ; but that I would not take upon me the last mark of that Authority his Majesty had given me, till I had first received it from his hand, and presenting him the Corslet at the same time ; I added, that I tendered that to him, to whom it belonged to give it me ; and that having brought the Company near his house, I would not march it by the Gate, till his Lordship had first given me right to walk at the head of it in the quality of the Kings Lieutenant.

Monsieur *Espernon*, a little surpriz'd, but much pleas'd, made so obliging an answer, as plainly shewed he had lik'd the surprize. He assur'd me of his service upon all occasions, and putting on my Corslet very gracefully, would in some sort hint to me, that he still remembred what past between Monsieur *Bastillat* and me, about the attack of *Montefche* ; telling me, there were but few persons that so well deserv'd , or that could acquit themselves better in this Command. I then askt him, if he would please to see my Company, and he accordingly going presently down stairs, I went to put my self at the head of them, and marcht by, saluting him with my Pike after the most graceful manner that I could. I marcht them on to the *Louvre*, where Monsieur *Saligny* took the head of them. The King, as a particular mark of favour, and in pursuance of his design to use me in restoring discipline among his Guards, would needs see me this first time in my new Post, and to that purpose made us pass and repass before him. Our Arms being set down in the Guard-room, Monsieur *Saligny* told me , he would carry me to wait on the King in the quality of his Lieutenant : I followed him. But though I had the satisfaction to see, that this Command gave me easie access to his Majesty's person, yet I had as much trouble to find my self made a better sort of Slave, by the burdensom engagement I was entring into, and which the King spoke to me of now again, repeating what he had said before, That I was not to stir from my Quarters, nor give any new Orders in the Company, without first consulting him.

His Majesty being pleas'd to give the Orders , Monsieur *Saligny* advanc'd to receive them ; but I being then near the King, and standing still as he advanc'd, his Majesty stept in between us, leaning upon me, as if he would give the Orders to us both. This immediately gave great jealousy to Monsieur *Saligny*, and had doubtless created an unlucky misunderstanding betwixt us, had not I at the same time prevented the ill consequence. My experience in the profession had taught me, that a Lieutenant never takes Orders from a General, when his Captain is present, and that he ought to receive them from his own Captain. So that turning aside my head, and seeming not to hear what the King said, as soon as ever his Majesty had done speaking, and was retir'd a little from us, I stept to Monsieur *Saligny*, and entreated his Orders, as if I knew nothing. He was so surpriz'd at this, by reason of the ill impression he had taken before, that he presently thought with himself after this trial, he should never have the least occasion to be offended with my conduct ; since contrary to all appearance, I had kept my self so strictly to the severest Rules, even then when it seem'd that the King himself had given me an occasion to lay it aside. His Majesty taking notice of this passage, as I

had

had a mind he fhould, had the goodnefs in fome meafure to condemn himfelf, by approving and commending what I had done.

XIII. Some time after the King requiring of me an account of the ftate of theCompany,which was then wholly under my care,theCaptain and Enfign being both abfent, I thought good to take this opportunity of informing my felf more particularly, what his Majefty expected from me; and would at the fame time, for my own fecurity, beg a Copy of the Orders I was to obferve in writing. Having entreated his leave to fpeak freely, I told him, I was very much afraid, I fhould not be able to give his Majefty all the fatisfaction he expected, and left the too favourable opinion he might have of my conduct might turn to my prejudice at laft, when I was found lefs capable than he took me to be; therefore I thought my felf oblig'd honeftly to acquaint his Majefty, that I was by no means a man of that active and fprightly parts, that was requifite in one, who was to give an account of fo many things, and to execute fo many orders; but a heavy and flow Fellow, and of a very treacherous memory: And therefore not being able fometimes to do things by my felf as others do, I ftood in need of affiftance. But as I had reafon to fear I might not always have thofe helps ready at hand, I very much apprehended I fhould not pleafe; and therefore had I dared to take the liberty of begging a favour, I fhould moft humbly have befought him, that for the relief of my memory and underftanding, his Majefty would pleafe to give me the Order I was to execute in writing; that by this means I might the better difcharge my duty. I perceive plainly, reply'd the King, you would have me think you a Blockhead, but it concerns my honour not to have been miftaken in the choice I have made of you. I have not given you this command, without a perfect knowledge of you; neverthelefs I will grant you your requeft, as well becaufe you defire it, as becaufe it will be an eafe to me too. And accordingly his Majefty caus'd inftructions to be drawn up for me in writing, upon which I afterwards gave him an account upon all occafions.

XIV. The Souldiers were at this time very great Libertines, and little or no difcipline was obferv'd among them: They did not fo much as re-pair to their Colours to march in order, when they went to mount the Guard at *St. Germains*, where the King was: fome came before, and others ftraggling behind, or on one fide, fo that oftentimes there were not fo much as a dozen together with the Officers that led them. My humour would not endure fuch diforder, which vexed me, fince it was fure to draw the hatred of all the Souldiers upon me, befides the flavery I found my felf reduc'd too; and I was perfectly weary of my life, and lamented the lofs of my Lieutenancy in the Regiment of *Picardy*, which I had quitted for this. Another greater vexation ftill was, that I had not one acquaintance in the Regiment, into which I was now taken, and fo had no body to open my griefs to. When I began to confider how to difengage my felf from all this perplexity, and get out of this condition which I faw was fure to be attended with fo many uneafineffes, I faw very well, there was no poffible way of doing it, without abfo-lutely renouncing my fortune, and lofing my felf for ever with the King. At laft therefore I took up my refolution, conceiving it much better to make a virtue of neceffity, and place all my delight in doing what the King required of me, and trying at the fame time to gain the good will

Z

of

of the Officers, who were then in a manner all Strangers to me; and acquiring authority with the Souldiers, among whom I was a new man, and not yet very much regarded by them. And after having thus settled my defign to execute the King's commands cheerfully, I found by experience, that the will overcomes the greateft difficulties, and felt a great deal more eafe in the performance of my duty, than I could have imagin'd, or had ever propos'd to my felf.

In order to contract an acquaintance with the Officers at firft, I invited all the principal of them to a Dinner, which was reafonably fplendid, there I began my Friendfhip with fome of them, which afterwards I took great care to improve. This entertainment pafs'd off with fo many teftimonies of affection and efteem on both fides, that it look'd like an acquaintance of twenty years ftanding. I intermixt a fmall piece of Gallantry with the Feaft, which contributed much to the diverfion of the Company; for Monfieur *Bouteville*, with ten or a dozen more Captains of Horfe being at the fame Eating-houfe, in another Room, I fent for all the Drums of the Regiment, and with them we went all together to drink thofe Gentlemens Healths, faluting them the mean while with a Point of War upon all our Drums. They thought they could not return our Civility better, than by fending for their Trumpets unknown to us, and taking their turn of drinking our Healths too, founding all the while. Thus from a trifle, I produced fomething confiderable for my felf. For this Dinner made a great noife, and acquired me the efteem of feveral that did not know me before.

The End of the Fifth Book.

BOOK

BOOK VI.

The Sieur de Pontis *his Management of a young Gentleman, called* du Buisson; *and how, after having been forc'd to fight him, he himself obtain'd his Pardon of the King. His Severity towards another dissolute and obstinate Cadet, whom he reduces to his Duty. The Jealousy of the Officers of the Guards, who endeavour to no purpose to do him ill Offices with the King. He is sent by the King to* Fort-Louis, *to learn the Exercises, and Military Discipline practic'd there, under the Conduct of the Sieur* Arnaud. *The excellent Qualities of this Governour. The great Suit between the Sieur* de Pontis, *and an eminent Commissioner, about a Donation from the King.*

I. IT was doubtless of no small consequence for such an Officer as my self, at my entring into the Regiment of Guards, and designing, as I did, to cause Martial Discipline to be exactly observed by the Souldiers, in obedience to the King's pleasure, to gain at first the good will of the Officers, that I might be upheld by them in the execution of his Majesty's Orders. But that which was to be done afterwards, as it was of much greater importance, so was it beyond all comparison the more difficult undertaking. For the business was to attempt the re-establishing of good Discipline among the Souldiers, who had in a great measure shaken off the Yoke; and to reduce a great many wild young Gentlemen to the duty they owed their Officers. I conceived therefore, that in the first place I was obliged to acquaint them, what the King expected both from them and me; that they might not be surpriz'd when I should compel them to it. So I ordered the Company to be drawn up, and at the head of it told them; That the King having commanded me to make it my business, to restore that Discipline which was entirely lost among them, I thought it my duty to let them know it, before I took the thing in hand; to the intent that such as were not dispofed to obey what should be commanded, in conformity to his Majesty's pleasure, might have liberty to withdraw; which I entreated them to do betimes, since after I had advertiz'd them of their duty, as I was about to do, they could afterwards have no pretence to exempt them from an absolute obedience: That I requir'd nothing of them but the ordinary duties of a Souldier; which were, to be discreet; to have a care of their Arms; not to depart from their Quarters; to repair punctually to their Colours when they were to mount the Guard; to march thither in order with their Arms shoulder'd, every one in File following his Leader; and not to quit the Company without leave of their Officer; not to go off the Guard; to perform the Centinels duty exactly; not to quarrel; to obey even the meanest Officers; not to wrong, or purloin from any one; and lastly, not to swear. To which I added, that if I found any reluctancy in observing all these things (though it was with great concern, that I found my self obliged to represent to them, what it was fit they all should know) I

should

should have the first trouble, being constrain'd by the King's order, both to see them observed by others, and to practice them my self, in giving the first example: That I advis'd every one to consider how far his fortunes were concern'd in this case, since the pleasing or displeasing the King was the consequence of it: That being bound to give his Majesty an account of such as should not discharge their duty, I was my self oblig'd to do it too, of those who should faithfully perform it; which would be a certain means for them, either to obtain some command in the Army, or to exclude themselves for ever; and that I did now promise all them that behave themselves honourably, to set a just value upon their services, and to sollicit the King that they might be well rewarded.

To this remonstrance they reply'd, that they were all as willing and ready to obey as I could desire. But the licentious part of them did not speak their hearts: For, as shame would not suffer them to quit the service, so the glory they affected, to continue independent, made them resolve to shake off a yoke, which they thought below them to submit to. They intended to live on, as they had us'd to do; that is, without being subject to any command: These for the most part were such as serv'd in the quality of Cadets, who look'd upon themselves as priviledg'd by their birth to be above these Rules, which they fancy'd were not made for them; as they show'd by all their Extravagances, and particularly the expence in their Cloaths, which were very near as rich as their Officers.

II. The first time it came to our turn to mount the Guard, being all repair'd to their Colours, I acquainted them with the Order they were to observe in their March; which was, to go four and four abreast through the City; and that when we went to *St. Germains*, such as had Horses were not to mount them, till we were out of *Paris*; adding, that they ought not to scruple the doing what I would do first my self to give them an example, and that they were free to quit their Arms, and take their Horses, when I should give them away my Pike, and mount mine. After having given this order, I made them take their ranks four abreast, and marched my self at the head of them on foot, with my Pike in my hand: They observ'd this order a pretty while. But these young Gentlemen, I spoke of before, thinking their honour concern'd to distinguish themselves from common Souldiers, began to take greater liberty, to give their Arms to their men to carry, and march out of their Ranks: I made them return to their Arms, and their Ranks again, by touching them in point of honour, upon the word they had pass'd punctually to obey me. But three or four of them, thinking this a fit occasion to make themselves taken notice of by all the Company, neglected these orders as before; I then proceeded to menaces, declaring aloud, that I would have them punished, upon which they return'd to their duty.

One of these young Cadets named *du Buisson*, a man of birth and courage, but withal a little proud too, having again laid aside his Musquet, I commanded the Serjeant to correct him, but he not daring to do it, and the Cadet taking his Arms again, and putting himself into his Rank, laid them aside a fourth time. I went, and took the Serjeant's Halbert, who had not dared to do as I commanded him, and with it gave this Cadet four or five good bangs; who told me, that he was a Gentleman: Whereupon, not very well considering what I did, I drew my Sword, and gave him some blows with the flat of it; which the Gentleman took very patiently,

tiently, without daring to give a word more; and from this time forward not a man ever offer'd to go out of his Rank, and every one obey'd me with a perfect submission. Insomuch that the King himself soon took notice of a great alteration in the Company, and took himself so particular a care of it, that I having told him there was amongst our men one Cadet of ill example, and he having thereupon commanded me to cashier him, when I made some difficulty of it, and told him that he was related to some of our Officers, said, he would cashier him himself then, and would tell his friends of it.

In the mean while every body was buzzing me in the Ear, that *Buisson* was likely to resent so publick a correction; and yet I had no reason to believe it, for he made no outward shew of any such thing; and from a very disorderly man, was grown the soberest and most regular of the whole Company: nay, he gave me a visit about three weeks after, to ask my pardon, and acknowledge the favour I had done him in that chastisement; telling me withal, that if ever he made a good man, he should think himself oblig'd to me for his reformation. These words surpriz'd me, and gave me great hopes of him; and indeed his whole behaviour was agreeable to them: which made me tell him, how glad I was to find him of so generous a temper; and I assur'd him, that he should find an equal change in my respect for him, as he was changed with regard to his duty; promising withal, to do him the best service I could to the King. He repeated the same thing to me two months after, and for eight months that he continu'd in the Regiment, behav'd himself after the same manner. Which gave me all the reason in the world to believe, that all resentments of what had past between us were quite laid aside. So well had he studied to dissemble his design, by an evenness of humour, and fair comportment; such as might seem incredible in a *French* Gentleman, which Nation are usually of a temper more open, and less capable of disguise. But at length, he came to me with a Letter from his Father, who had sent for him, and entreated his dismission, which I easily granted, and thereupon he again made a publick acknowledgment of the favours he had receiv'd from me; as I on my side assur'd him I would neglect no opportunity of doing him service: And then he told me he was to take Post next morning for *Touraine*, which was his native Country.

III. About two days after, some that had been present at this parting, came to tell me, that they feared *Buisson* had mischief in his heart, because he was not yet gone out of Town, as he said he would. I then began to suspect as well as they, but since I could do nothing to prevent him, and considering how distant from any kind of resentment his whole behaviour had appear'd, made as though I did not believe it, and carry'd my self so that no body could suppose I did. In the mean while, he knowing I was to be upon the Guard at *St. Germains*, took the time when I was to return, which that he might be more certainly informed of, he went to enquire for me at my Lodging, upon pretence of making me a parting visit: And there being told, that I was to come back at night, he went to wait for me upon the Road betwixt *Montmartre*, and *le Roullo*. Seeing me at some distance coming alone, he put on to a gentle trot, and made directly up to me. Assoon as ever I perceiv'd him, I said within my self; Is it possible, that Dissimulation should be so discreetly carry'd, and that so violent a passion as Revenge, can lye thus long smother'd in a *French-mans* bosom?

A a   Coming

Coming up near to one another, I gave him the time of the day, and askt him whither he was going? He boggled a little in his answer, and told me he was taking the air; at the same time turning his Horse, as if he would go back with me, and rode at least a hundred paces without speaking one word of his design. At last out it came : and then he told me, he was very sorry to find himself oblig'd to demand a thing of me, which seem'd so contrary to his duty; but that the extremity to which he was reduc'd, and the necessity that lay upon him of passing otherwise for a man utterly dishonour'd, forc'd him to it. That the affair which had been betwixt us about eight months ago was so publick, as not to be repair'd except by another as publick, which was the satisfaction he requir'd for that affront. That it was with great reluctancy he made me this request, knowing with how little rancour I had acted; but since my intention could no way secure his honour, he knew I was too generous to refuse him so just a demand.

I reply'd, That his Complement surpriz'd me much after what he had so often said , and the obligations he had formerly profest that he had, and should as long as he liv'd, have to me, for having both done my own duty, and reduc d him to a regular way of living, and such as was becoming an honest man, and a Gentleman; and askt him, whether he could have forgot all these things, or whether they had really never been his real sense? He made answer, that at the time when he said them they were; and would be so still, did he not see himself absolutely dishonour'd, and under a necessity of demanding this satisfaction. I told him, that according to Rule I ow'd him none, having done nothing but what was my duty to do; and that it was not customary for Officers to give this sort of satisfaction to their private Souldiers. But I saw he was resolv'd to have what he ask'd, and was constrain'd in spight of my heart to do a thing that was against all order and discipline. He oblig'd me then to alight, as he did; and it was my good fortune to have the advantage, of which nevertheless, tho I was wounded, I made no other use, than to preserve that to him, which he had so brutishly resolv'd to take from me , contrary to all Justice in the world. I then told him, that a great many other men would not have done as I did, after so many testimonies of acknowledgment formerly made me; all which he had now given the lye to, after a manner most unbecoming a Gentleman of his quality. He confest what I said to be true, which made me assoon as he got up, offer him his Sword; but for all the rage he was in, he directly told me, that having already been so great a Beast as to use it against me, he could not promise but he might be brutish enough still to turn upon me a second time, and therefore entreated I would keep it, and carry it away with me.

Monsieur *Rambures*, who at that time was hunting about *Montmartre*, having seen naked Swords at some distance, and guessing easily what the matter was, came riding full speed up to us, and found us in the condition I have related, both of us wounded, and one with two Swords. He exprest a great concern, that he could not come sooner to prevent this misfortune; but would however needs do that now, that he could have wisht done before, which was, to make us embrace, and to prevail upon us to forget all that had past. I then begg'd him to give Monsieur *Buisson* his Sword again, which he did , and went along with us both to *Paris*, where each of us having caus'd our selves to dress, were soon cur'd, for neither was much hurt.

IV. But

IV. But this unlucky bufinefs, which I could have wifh'd might have been kept fecret, was fhortly after made publick. For fome people, who envied my fortune, made ufe of this occafion to reprefent me ill to the King; who was ftrangely furpriz'd to hear fuch news, and extremely difpleas'd at me upon it. Monfieur *Saligny*, who was acquainted with the whole truth of the Story, endeavoured to excufe me, by telling the King, that I could not poffibly have done otherwife, and that I was to defend my own life. Monfieur *Rambures* too, who had been an Eyewitnefs of the action, fpoke to his Majefty, and told the thing as much in my favour as he could. But all this would not fatisfy the King, who ftill fhewed himfelf very angry, by reafon of the ill impreffions fome back-friends of mine had made upon him. In the mean while, though I had intimation given me, that ill offices had been done me to the King, yet I kept on mounting the Guard, as I us'd to do, being refolv'd to lay the naked truth before his Majefty, if he fhould think fit to fpeak to me about it. And having one day prefented my felf before him, he gave me a look full of indignation, and when the reft of the company went out of the room, he commanded me to ftay. Then he afk'd me, how I had the confidence to appear in his prefence, after the fault I had committed, and if this was the order I intended to reftore in the Regiment by my example; that the leaft Cadet might challenge an Officer, and that a man fhould be thought wanting to his own honour, if he refufe to anfwer him? Whether I had not forefeen all the confequences of this action, which being of fo pernicious example to all the Officers and Soldiers, particularly offended him in his own perfon, and made it plain to all the world, that he was miftaken in the judgment he had made of me; for whereas he took me for a fober difcreet perfon, I had now forfeited all that good opinion, by fo irregular, fo unworthy a management of my felf. To this he added threats too, telling me, he was very near letting all the world know, in my perfon, that no Officer can never be allow'd to fight a private Souldier; but if, as a mark of particular favour, he forbore to punifh me as I deferv'd, yet I was unworthy to approach his perfon any more; and as for *Buiffon*, he would make him a publick example, for he fhould be fhot to death.

The King had no fooner ended thefe words but he turn'd about, and was leaving me; but feeling my felf cut to the very heart, I threw my felf at his feet, humbly begging his pardon, and telling him how infinitely I was afflicted, that I had incurr'd his difpleafure: I told him I acknowledg'd his Juftice, and the truth of every thing he had faid to me; but if his Majefty would grant me this further favour to hear me, I hop'd, that tho the action I had done was criminal in it felf, yet the particular circumftances of it might make me appear lefs guilty; but neverthelefs, that I durft not attempt to juftifie my felf, unlefs his Majefty would firft affure me, that he would have the goodnefs to bear me. The King, mov'd with the paffion I was in, anfwer'd in a milder tone, that he gave me leave to fpeak. I began then to do it, in the manner I thought moft proper to qualifie his opinion of that which he thought moft criminal in the action, and fo as might tend to juftifie both of us, rather than to vindicate my felf fingly, to the prejudice of *Buiffon*. Your Majefty may pleafe to remember (faid I) what condition I found the Company in, when you did me the honour to give me the Licutenancy of it, and the ftrict Orders I receiv'd to reftore the ancient difcipline there. Having a young Gentleman to deal with, whom the general diforder had made ungovernable, and who by a falfe punctilio of honour, valued himfelf upon being independent on the Officers, I proceeded againft him with all the feverity, that to me feem'd neceffary, for the reducing him to his duty, and reftraining the reft by his example. 'Tis true, the method I took was a little violent, and if I may prefume to fay fo, a little inconfiftent with the honour of a young Gentleman, who had lived at large, and who thought it his glory to be under no Government. But yet, as hot and wilful as he was, he came to himfelf, acknowledged the juftice of his correction, and the good I had done in chaftizing him after that manner, he became a patern of fubmiffion and difcretion to the whole Company; fo that every body return'd to their former order, and your Majefty was very well fatisfied with the regulation. But, Sir, there are a fort of men, who becaufe they can do no good themfelves, are impatient that any body elfe fhould; and fome of thefe afterwards perverted this young Gentleman, perfwading him, that his honour was loft, and he had no courage, if he did not require fatisfaction for this affront; and that a Gentleman of his birth and quality ought to efteem his honour dearer than his life. Thefe ftrange impreffions, Sir, and ill counfels of rafh people, that are falfly jealous of anothers honor, was the thing that pufh'd on Monfieur *Briffon* to this extremity; who, knowing well enough, that I was a man ftrict in the obfervance of my duty, and one that would never confent to an action fo contrary to the Rules of military difcipline; becaufe he would unavoidably engage me, to give him, what he was put upon requiring of me, laid wait for my coming back from *St. Germains*, watch'd me upon the Road, and after he had put himfelf out of my Company, and received his difmiffion from me, compell'd me to that fatisfaction, which he never would have dared to demand in any other place, where I could have refufed him. In this circumftance, Sir, faid I, there was no courfe could be taken, but either to run away, or to do as I did : So that having upon this occafion only obey'd the indifpenfable Laws of Nature, which command us to defend our felves when we are affaulted; I dare promife my felf thus much from your Majefty's Juftice, that you will pronounce me as innocent, as I had been criminal, and worthy of death, had what has been reprefented to your Majefty been true, that I had voluntarily fought with a Cadet of my own Company. I do therefore, Sir, moft humbly befeech your Majefty to give judgment upon the cafe, and rather to believe what I fay, and fwear in the prefence of God, than what may have been told you, by fuch as are not fo well inform'd of the truth of the bufinefs; or that perhaps have proceeded upon fome private fpleen againft us both.

This difcourfe of mine fo wrought upon the King, that he was almoft perfectly overcome by it, fo that his Majefty reply'd, That indeed he did not underftand the bufinefs before, to be as I had now related it to him; nor had he heard any thing of this laft circumftance, which very much alter'd the quality of the action : but though he might fee fome reafon to excufe me, and pardon this fault, which he look'd upon as done againft my will, yet *Briffon* was abfolutely inexcufable; fince having at firft been fo difcreet as to receive his chaftifement as became him, he was but the more guilty in hearkning to the counfels of rafh, giddy young Fellows, and by fo ill an action giving the lye to all the good conduct he had fhew'd before : That to way-lay his Lieutenant upon a common road, to affault him, and drive him to a neceffity of defending himfelf, himself, was a crime not only against him who was attackt, but all the Officers of the Regiment were concern'd, and all injur'd in this action; which being an example of so pernicious consequence, he would have it punish'd accordingly, and that Justice should be done upon him.

V. Finding the King's countenance change, and clearing up towards me, I thought I might take the liberty to move him still farther in favour of him, whom he had condemn'd to dye; and from a suppliant in my own case, to become intercessor for another: And I had that hope in his Majesty's goodness, to believe that he would rather incline to my humble request, in regard I interested my self for the person that had injur'd me. I then humbly besought him not to be angry, if after the pardon he had been graciously pleased to grant me for my self, I had the boldness to presume upon begging this young Gentleman's, upon whom his Justice intended the whole weight of the punishment should fall. I told him, that his action, though criminal, yet seeming rather to have been the effect of ill counsel, than ill nature, it might deserve some allowance to be made for it; that if he should receive his life, after having so well deserv'd to lose it, he must needs think himself oblig'd ever after to devote it to his Prince's service; that it would be the greatest affliction in the world to me, to have been the occasion of the dishonour of a whole Family: And therefore I was bold to conjure his Majesty, that he would extend his clemency to two Criminals, who were in effect but one, seeing I should think my self punish'd in the person of him, for whom I presum'd to speak, and that I could not rise from his Majesty's Feet, till he had granted my request.

The King, though inwardly touch'd with what I had said to him, made answer, What! You are not content with your own pardon then, and take upon you to move me for another! Are not you afraid of making your self more guilty, and by that in some sort to betray, that you have the greatest share in the fault of him, for whom you intercede, when you ought to be the first man that should desire to have it punish'd! But nevertheless, I know your temper, and forgive the excess of your friendship. I give him the life you beg of me, and I give it as the greatest testimony of my acknowledging your services. But for examples sake, and the publick satisfaction, I will have him brought to Tryal, and process entred against him: that in the mean time he may retire into *Holland*, and not return, till there be no more talk of this business, and I have granted him a formal Pardon.

It is impossible for me to express the joy and grateful acknowledgments, that these words raised in my breast, I embrac'd the King's knees, and having return'd my thanks more by sighs and tears, than words, I withdrew out of the Chamber.

When the Lords of the Court were come into the room, the King told them all, after what manner he had humbled me, and how he had conceiv'd he ought to chastise me for the fault I had committed, declaring at the same time, that, though he had forborn to punish me with greater severity, in regard of the services I had done him, he would yet make *Buisson* an example, and have him condemn'd in a Council of War to be shot to death; which made the whole Court believe, that he really intended to have him executed, not any one knowing the extraordinary grace his Majesty had promis'd me in his favour.

In the mean time I went to look out Monsieur *Buisson*, and told him all that had past, and gave him assurance, that during his absence in *Holland*,

I would omit no occasion of ufing my utmoft endeavour for his return, and putting him into a condition to expofe that life for the King's Service, which he now ow'd to his Mercy. The poor young man was fo aftonifh'd to fee the ftrange way I had taken to revenge my felf upon him, that he was able to fay no more than this, that he was extremely confounded, and that now I had repaid his brutal paffion with the greateft generofity I could poffibly exprefs, he had nothing more to offer in return, but his life, which fhould ever be as much mine as his own; that he fhould from thence forward look upon me as a fecond Father, and was refolv'd abfolutely to depend upon me, and my conduct. Whereupon we embrac'd, and he went to make himfelf ready for his Journey into *Holland*. His affair was fhortly after debated in a Council of War, where he was condemn'd, but being got out of the way, they lookt no farther after him.

VI. The King for a good while after put on fome coldnefs to me before company, tho in private he was as kind to me as ever. I underftood the meaning of it well enough, and behav'd my felf the beft I could to fecond his Majefty's defign. But I was ftill wanting for fome occafion to procure Monfieur *Buiſſon*'s return, and a whole year efcap'd me without ever difcovering any hopes of it. At laft I refolv'd to be bold once again, and obferve meafures lefs than ever, in an affair where I thought my interceffion not unlikely to prevail. A Lieutenant of the Regiment of *Normandy* was at that time very fick at *Paris*, the moment I heard of his death, I conceiv'd I ought to take this opportunity to ferve the man; whofe being at a diftance was a great affliction to me; and accordingly I went forthwith to the King. I told him at firft, without laying open my defign, that I was come humbly to entreat a favour of his Majefty, which was the Command of fuch a Lieutenant juft now dead. The King, as far as I could guefs, prefently fufpected for whom I made this fuit, but not willing to let me know that he penetrated into my thoughts, he fatisfy'd himfelf with telling me, that he muft firft know what I would do with it, and whom I intended it for. I anfwer'd, that it was for a friend of mine, whom I would take the liberty to name, as foon as his Majefty fhould have done me the honour to affure me of the place. Is it not for *Buiſſon*? (reply'd the King) for I know your temper, and do almoft read it in your heart. Ah! Sir, (faid I) thus to penetrate into ones thoughts is to be truly a Prophet; and doubtlefs I ought to be careful to have none but good ones, fince your Majefty hath fuch piercing eyes. 'Tis true, Sir, I am heartily forry to fee this young Gentleman, who is capable of doing your Majefty good fervice, fo long out of a condition to fhew it; and I take the confidence to hope your Majefty will compleat the favour you have fo generoufly begun, in giving him, who holds his life from your goodnefs, an opportunity of employing it all in your fervice. The King, mov'd with this preffing importunity in behalf of one who had fo highly difoblig'd me, was moft gracioufly pleas'd to fay, that it was not in his power to deny me any thing, and that the generofity of this requeft engag'd him to grant that, which regularly ought not to be granted.

With this promife of the King, which filled me with great joy, I went home, and immediately difpatch'd away an exprefs Meffenger into *Holland* to Monfieur *Buiſſon*, to bid him prefently come away to me, about fome bufinefs of very great confequence. Accordingly he was foon at *Paris*, where having told me, that he very well underftood he was afrefh oblig'd to me for the favour of his liberty, feeing that I brought him to

a place,

a place, from which his ill behaviour had constrain'd him to fly: I made answer, that it was the King to whom he was oblig'd for all; and now especially for a favour he did not expect, which was a Lieutenant's place in the Regiment of *Northway*, for that his Majesty had conferr'd upon him, and upon this account to was that I sent for him: To which I added; that I would carry him to kiss the King's hand, that he might in person pay his acknowledgments for so very exceeding a favour, which engag'd him to lay out the rest of his life upon his Majesty's service, and that therefore he should be in a readiness to go along with me that Evening to the *Louvre*. This poor Gentleman, very well understanding from what hand his Lieutenancy came, was so confounded, that he had not one word at command to return me thanks in, and therefore did it only in dumb shew. I carried him at night to the *Louvre*, and having first askt his Majesty's leave to present him, I brought him in. As soon as he came into his presence, he threw himself at the King's feet, without speaking otherwise than by his posture, and profound humiliation. The King then told him, he was happy in having such a man as I to deal with, who after such an injury, had made it my business to obtain the pardon of him who wrong'd me to that degree; a thing that he could not have granted to any other, and that very few besides me would have dar'd to ask it. That therefore he would let him know, that he was oblig'd to me both for his Life and his Command, which he gave him upon my account; that all these things laid together oblig'd him to look upon me for the future as his Benefactor, and to repair the wrong, and the fault he had been guilty of against the whole body of the Army, by a life and behaviour proportionable to the sense he ought to have of so extraordinary a favour. Respect, Joy, and Grief all at once made so strong an impression upon the mind of Monsieur *Buisson*, that he could not return one syllable of answer to the King; but as he came into the room without daring to speak, so he went out again without being able to do it. Which also pleas'd his Majesty more, than if he had made a long Complement, for he judged better of the sentiments of his heart, by this respectful silence, than he could have done by any studied harrangue.

I afterwards sued out his Pardon, and procured the Commission for his Command, and got him admitted into the Regiment; where I am able to say, that he acquir'd a great deal of esteem, having perfectly made good what was expected from him, and passing for one of he bravest men in the Army. He also very faithfully obey'd the command his Majesty laid on him, always to consider me as his faithful friend. For both from an effect of his natural inclination, and the deep sense he had of the service I had done him, he ever after lived with me, as with his Father, by which name also he us'd to call me. And I shall take notice in the following part of these Memoirs, that having heard I was embroil'd in a business of such consequence that my head was in danger, he came post from a very remote place to *Rochel*, where I then was, to make me a tender of his life and fortune.

VII. The course I took with another Cadet, was yet more severe than this with Monsieur *Buisson*, and had an effect no less successful, to the making him a good man, and winning his heart absolutely. Having receiv'd into my Company a young Gentleman, a Relation of our Captain's, the Count *de Saligny*, that so I might train him up, as I did several others, in the Art of War; I told him at first, that as he had the honour
to

to be Monfieur *Saligny*'s Kinfman, fo it would be neceffary that he fhould
become an example to the whole Company. I then commanded a Serjeant to lodge him with another Cadet; but this young man was fo ill con-
ditioned, and fo perverfe, that he with whom I had quarter'd him, foon
begg'd of me to part them, for he could not live any longer with fuch a
Mad-man. I had alfo complaints from all hands of his violences and extravagancies; nay he was of fo devilifh a difpofition, and fo unbecoming
his quality, to go at nights and ftand in corners of ftreets to watch for
peoples paffing, taking fingular pleafure to give them private thrufts
with his Sword, and all this upon no provocation, but out of meer ill
nature, and to do mifchief. Hereupon I fent for him one day to my
Chamber, where with great feverity I told him, that I had complaints
of him made me every day, and fome of mifdemeanours fo foul and black, as
I durft fcarce believe of a Gentleman, being unworthy even of a Porter;
that could I have perfwaded my felf he had been guilty of fuch things, I
fhould have done him the favour to clap him up in a Dungeon; and that
I advifed him to let me hear no more fuch matters of him.

This however could not prevail with him, but within four or five days
he fell back to his old villanies, and news was brought me, that he had
wounded a woman, an Advocate, and another man, and was fled upon
it. This news put me into a great paffion, feeing all my remonftrances
fo foon followed by frefh and greater extravagancies, than he had been
guilty of before. So that I immediately cried out to a Serjeant, and two
of my Servants, to take my Horfes and purfue the Wretch, and bring him
to me (faid I) bound hand and foot; I'll make him fmart for it. Whereupon they prefently took the way they knew he was gone, and having
overtaken him within three leagues of the City, brought him back. I
would neither fee him, nor fpeak to him, but immediately clapt him in a
Dungeon, charging that nothing fhould be given him but bread and
water. It is not to be believed to what a degree he was enraged, and
how many impertinencies his fury prompted him to utter againft me: I
fhall only repeat one inftance of his rage, which was, that in the tran-
fports of his paffion he would fay, that if the five fingers of his hands
were five pieces of Cannon, he would level them all at *Pontis*, to beat
out his brains, and pound him to powder. In the mean while I thought
my felf oblig'd to acquaint the King with what had paft, both in regard he
was a perfon of quality, and Monfieur *Saligny*'s Kinfman, and alfo becaufe I had fome reafon to apprehend the confequences of this affair. The
King approved what I had done, and according to his cuftom, recommended to me the feverity of difcipline.

After I had let this Cadet lye a month or fix weeks in the Dungeon, I
had a mind to try whether it had wrought any alteration in his temper,
and to this purpofe fent a Monk to found him, and put him under fome
terrours. The Father going down into the Dungeon told him, the Captains were upon meeting; and there was fome reafon to apprehend, it
was for bringing him to his Trial; that therefore he advifed him to take
fome care of his Confcience, and not fuffer himfelf to be furpriz'd, and
that the leaft he could do was to manifeft his repentance by a confeffion
of his faults. At this heavy news the poor young man began to quake
every bone of him, and conjur'd the Father to intercede for him to me,
faying, that he acknowledged his paft offences, and that they would make
him wifer for the time to come. The Father told him he durft not fpeak
to me of it, I was fo incens'd againft him; and that he had no other commiffion

miſſion but only to prevail with him to think upon his ſoul. This anſwer troubled him yet more, and he conjur'd the Monk not to forſake him. The Monk reply'd, that he durſt not ſo much as come frequently to viſit him, for fear he ſhould be ſuſpected of ſome ſecret intelligence with him, and by that means loſe the opportunity of ever ſeeing him at all. This put the Gentleman into great anxiety, to think what would become of him. The Monk came and told me what a change he found, and how ſucceſsful a viſit he had made, of which I alſo preſently gave an account to the King, who made me this remarkable anſwer : I adviſe you not to depend too much upon this haſty repentance. This looks like a falſe penitence, and he being of ſo wicked a nature, may kill you in a fit of his paſſion : It will be convenient firſt to try whether his converſion be real, or not. Oh Sir, (ſaid I) I fear him not, and know very well he is ſo afraid of me, that I am very confident, he will always tremble but at the ſight of me.

The King gave me leave to do what I thought fit, and I ſent the ſame Prieſt to my Priſoner again, to whom he confeſt himſelf with great teſtimonies of repentance, and afterwards receiv'd in the Chappel, as to prepare himſelf for death. When he had ſcarce any hopes left, I ſent for him by a Serjeant into my Chamber. There I told him, that his Trial being pretty far advanc'd, I thought fit to ſend for him, that I might know from his own mouth, whether he was ſtill the ſame man he had been, and if he ſtill perſiſted in not acknowledging his fault. Then he threw himſelf at my knees, and begg'd of me to ſpare his life. He told me, that he confeſs'd his crimes deſerv'd death, but if I would have compaſſion on him, he did proteſt and ſolemnly engage, that his life ſhould for the future be wholly employed in the King's ſervice, and that he would never again commit the like diſorders, confirming what he ſaid, by taking God to witneſs of the ſincerity of his heart. Whereupon I told him, that as to the ſaving his life, that was not wholly in my power, but I promis'd to do what I could in order to it; and that he ſhould only have a care to keep his word faithfully. Then I ſent him back to Priſon again, and let him lye there a little longer ſtill, till his buſineſs had been examin'd, and his Pardon obtain'd. The acknowledgment of this favour I had procur'd for him, when he look'd upon himſelf to be no better than a dead man, made him love me ever after as his Father. He grew from this time forward a very civil honeſt man, and was advanc'd to a Command, in which he loſt his life honourably. I was willing to ſhew by this inſtance, that there is ſcarcely any diſpoſition ſo preverſe, but it may be reclaim'd, and that there are ſome ſeaſons, when we muſt not be afraid to oppoſe the rougheſt Chaſtiſements to the torrent of corrupted habits, and brutiſh paſſions, when they are not to be dealt with by leſs violent methods.

VIII. The Captains of the Regiment of Guards, and one eſpecially above all the reſt, that ſhall be nameleſs, had a long time been incens'd againſt me, and born me a private grudge, becauſe the King out of particular favour, appointed my Quarters before all the other Lieutenants, when he went into the Field; but yet the greater part durſt not make any open diſcoveries of there hatred me, only one there was, who out of ſpight, ſeiz'd upon the lodging his Majeſty had aſſign'd me, and lay in my very bed, where I found him at my return from the King. But being not yet aſſur'd with what intention he had done it, I would make no buſtle, but went and lay all night upon the Straw. The next day, in-

ſtead

ftead of excufing himfelf, he told me plainly, that I muft go feek out fome other Lodging. This was more than enough to fet us together by the ears; but age and experience having taught me a little to moderate my paffion, I only told him, that it was my humour to content my felf with what belonged to me, and for that matter, fince it was the King's favour to me, is was not for him to oppofe it, and the King himfelf was the perfon to whom he was to make his complaint.

The King being inform'd of the bufinefs, declar'd himfelf very much diffatisfy'd with it, and faid, He was free to do what he pleas'd in his own Kingdom, and that it was not for Captains to King it with him, and controul what he did in favour to any particular Officer, who always attended his perfon : Declaring at the fame time, that the Captains fhould not have their lodgings markt out any more, but they fhould lye where they pleas'd in the Quarters that fhould be affigned them. This nettled them to the quick, and they waited only for fome fair occafion to be reveng'd on me. My Company was at that time the firft of the Regiment, by reafon of the great number of Cadets of Quality, whom their Parents did me the honour to commit to my care, that I might bring them up in the firft exercifes of War; and I had there among the reft, the Marefchal *de St. Geran's* Son, of whom I fhall have occafion to fay more by and by.

IX. One day, being upon the Guard at *Fontainbleau*, as another Company was coming on to relieve us, and I had thoughts, according to my cuftom, to go back with mine to *Montereau*, which was our Quarters, the King call'd me out of his Window, where he ftood to fee the Tilting, and running at the Ring, which were then doing in the Court below. I prefently went up, and being come into his Chamber, orders were given me to fend away my Company, and to ftay my felf about his perfon. I went then prefently to look out the Serjeants, and gave them order, as his Majefty had exprefsly commanded, that they fhould be very careful to prevent all quarrels, efpecially among the Cadets, (who ftood mightily upon their honour, not to put up any thing from one another) and alfo not to let any one ftay and drink by the way, by reafon of the difputes which are often occafioned by Wine. I had once a mind, by a fort of prophetic fear of the misfortune that happened, to detain the Marefchal of *St. Geran's* Son with me, whofe forward humour, and too generous Soul made me eternally uneafy for him. But at laft, I know not how, I let him go back with the reft.

That very day in the month of *May*, 1624. the King had refolv'd upon caufing Collonel *Ornano* to be apprehended, who in the Evening came into his Chamber, and was entertained by his Majefty as formerly, with all the kindnefs imaginable. The King talked with him a great while about a Chafe the Duke of *Orleans* was to make next morning in the Forreft of *Fontainbleau*, asking him very familiarly, what ways they had beft to hunt, becaufe he was well experienc'd in the Forreft, and knew all the leaft, and blindeft paths of it. At laft the hour defign'd for his Arreft being come, Monfieur *Hallier*, Captain of the Guard at that time, and feveral other Officers came into the Chamber. Now it is the cuftom, when the Captain of the Guard is upon entring, for the Ufher to give three blows upon the threfhold of the door, which was alfo the fignal the King had given for his own retiring. So then his Majefty hearing the three ftroaks, bid Collonel *Ornano* good night, and withdrew into

another

another room, whither I also followed him, according to the order he had given me. Immediately Monfieur *Hallier* came in, and making up to Monfieur *Ornano*, gave him a very furprizing Complement; which was, that he was forry to tell him he had orders to fecure his perfon. How! (faid the Collonel in great amazement) I am but juft now come from the King, and he receiv'd me with all the kindnefs in the world; let me fpeak to him however. Monfieur *Hallier* told him, he had no order to fuffer that, and he entreated him to give leave, that he might execute what orders he had; that as for any other matters, his own innocency ought to fupport him with a good affurance, and put him out of fear. Monfieur *Ornano* then feeing himfelf under a neceffity of obeying, follow'd the Captain of the Guards, who led him into the chamber of *Saint Louis*, which was appointed to ferve him for a Prifon.

At the very moment he was arrefted, the King, fuppofing that fome of his Family would not fail to make all poffible fpeed to *Paris*, that they might fecure his Papers, gave me and three Officers more orders to go into the Forreft, that we might lye upon the great Road, and ftop all that fhould attempt to pafs that way. So we divided our felves into two and two, and about eleven at night took our feparate pofts, upon each of the Roads; where we waited a great while before any body appear'd. At laft we faw at fome diftance a man mounted upon a *Spanifh* Gennet, that came galloping full fpeed toward us. Our orders were not to fhoot, and fo the other Officer and I refolv'd to turn our Horfes head to head acrofs the way, when he came up near us, that fo we might ftop his paffage. But this man, who was admirably well mounted, fhew'd us a trick for our trick, and without any manner of concern, riding full drive upon us, he gave us fuch a brufh, as threw my Companion and his Horfe above ten paces off : We never thought of purfuing him, for indeed it had been to no purpofe, he being fo much better mounted; and I for my part was not forry we had been thus broke through, for the refpect I bore to Collonel *Ornano*. I went back to give the King an account of what had paft, who only laught heartily at the ftory.

X. But that very morning I had moft afflicting news brought me : For the Serjeants of my Company not having executed my commands as they ought, fome Cadets ftopt at *Moret*, and the Wine being got into their Heads, they quarrell'd, and fought three to three, fo defperately, that two of them were kill'd upon the fpot, one of which was Marefchal *St. Geran's* Son; and two more very dangeroufly wounded. When this news came to *Fontainbleau* it put me almoft out of my wits : I went immediately to wait on the King, and tell him of it firft, humbly befeeching him to remember the order he had given me, that I fhould ftay that night about his perfon. Whereupon his Majefty commanded me to go and tell the Marefchal *de St. Geran* my felf, and promis'd to make my peace with him. I went, but very unwillingly God knows, having fo fad news to carry; and I had fcarce began to fpeak, but he underftood me at half a word, and askt prefently if his Son was kill'd? I did my beft to comfort him by confiderations meerly humane, thinking more of what concern'd his Honour, than his Salvation; and at laft entreated him to do me the juftice upon this occafion, not to impute this misfortune to me, whom a pofitive order from the King had put out of a capacity to prevent it. He anfwer'd me with all the goodnefs I could expect, and immediately lockt himfelf up in his Clofet. The King fent fhortly after to

let

let him know that he bore a part of his grief with him; and when he came to return his thanks, his Majesty, after comforting him with all the expressions of a particular tenderness, did me the honour to justifie me to him, and to assure him that I was in no fault at all; to which the Mareschal reply'd, with all the Civility imaginable, that he was very far from accusing me, that he knew me too well to lay the misfortune to my charge, and that he should always love me, at the same rate he had ever done.

But the Captains of the Regiment, who were all of them very angry at me, for the reason I gave before, thought this a favourable opportunity to do me an ill office with the King. For not knowing that I stay'd behind at *Fontainbleau* by his express command, they came all in a body, and entreated leave of his Majesty, to proceed against me in the ordinary methods of Justice; giving him to understand, that some Lieutenants thought it below them to do their duty, and to attend their Companies, and lov'd to be at Court, and by that means were the cause of infinite disorders. The King, who very well knew their malice against me, and the private jealousie that animated them to it, would not however take any notice to them, but let them go on, and prefer their informations. But as soon as they were perfected, and they came to present them to his Majesty, he took them, and told him, he would take care to have them examin'd. But afterwards he threw them into the fire, and gave the Provost order to stop all farther prosecutions. This made them understand too late, that they had committed an errour, in attacking a person, whom the King honour'd with his particular protection, and in whose favour he so openly declar'd himself.

XI. Some years after the King had given me a Lieutenancy in the Guards, he sent me to *Fort-Louis* with a private Commission, and upon an occasion, that he would have no body know, but me only. Monsieur *Arnauld*, Camp-master to the Regiment of *Champagne*, and Governour of this Fort, was at that time in great repute for his knowledge and experience in War, and in all the arts of Military Discipline. He was equally prudent and bold in his undertakings, and no less successful in the execution of them. The prudence of his conduct made him admir'd, even by those who were above him in birth and command, and there seem'd nothing wanting, to restore the old *Roman* Discipline in *France*, but his being made General of the King's Forces. One may truly say too, that *France* owes part of the glory of destroying *Rochel*, that Citadel of the *Hugonots*, to him, for he first began by *Fort-Louis* of which he was Governour, to block up the City, and cut the Inhabitants off from ravaging the Country, till the King afterwards came to make himself Master of this important place. This great reputation that Monsieur *Arnauld* had, both in the Armies and at Court, was the cause, why the King, who hath ever had a natural inclination to all the concerns of War, desired to learn his methods of drawing up men, and exercise, and discipline. Resolving therefore to employ some one of his Officers, in a thing impossible for him to learn in his own person; he cast his eyes on me, as one proper to keep the secret, and likely to inform him of what he had a mind to know. He intrusted me with his design, and told me, that to make the matter more private, I should first take a Journey into *Provence*, and go from thence to *Fort-Louis*, to pass some time in the quality of a Volunteer with this Governour, as if more particularly to instruct my self in a trade, for which all the world knew I had a great paſſion. He gave me order to ſtay there, till he ſent for me, and till I had exactly obſerv'd all the particulars he had a mind to learn, but he expreſly forbad me to tell any man alive, that I went thither by his command.

With theſe inſtructions away I went, not ſo far as *Provence*, but from *Lions* turn'd toward *Rochel*, and ſo directly to *Fort-Louis*, to lye at a Gentleman's quarter, with whom I had been acquainted when I was in the Regiment of *Champagne*. He receiv'd me with ſeveral teſtimonies of friendſhip, telling me, that I muſt of neceſſity go wait upon the Governour, who was very exact in his Diſcipline, and expected an account of every one that came into the Garriſon. This was juſt as I would have it, and accordingly he carried me to him two days after. Being not known to Monſieur *Arnauld*, or at leaſt believing my ſelf not to be ſo, I told him, his great reputation had drawn me thither, and that having ever from my youth been ſtrongly inclin'd to make my ſelf expert in martial matters, I was come with a deſign to be inſtructed under him, and to ſerve ſome time in his Garriſons a Volunteer, that I might try to improve by his judgment, in obſerving what he made to be practis'd by his Troops in their exerciſes, and in practiſing the ſame my ſelf the beſt that poſſibly I could, under his command. He reply'd, that he had indeed made it his particular buſineſs and ſtudy, to underſtand his profeſſion, and thought he might ſay, that he had made ſome little progreſs in it by his pains and experience; and that he hop'd, if he liv'd any time, to ſettle part of the antient diſcipline once again among his Souldiers. The openneſs he us'd in the end of his diſcourſe, gave me ſome ſuſpicion, that I might poſſibly be known to him, though he were not to me. And he being one of a piercing wit, might perhaps think, that I came to paſs ſome time there by private orders from the King, for he added at laſt in a very obliging way, that I did him honour in coming to learn under him, what he himſelf had acquir'd with great pains; that he promis'd to conceal no part of his knowledge from me, and that he would keep me there, and ſhew me every thing. I return'd his civility the beſt I could, but entreated him to conſent, that I might perform all the exerciſes as a Volunteer, ſo to learn things more exactly, and be able to do them with the better grace·

Thus I ſtaid with him about three months, eating almoſt every day at his own Table, and keeping near his perſon as much as I could, and ſtudying what I came to learn with extraordinary application of mind. And I can truly ſay, that though I had ſome knowledge and experience before, having been bred up from a Child in War, yet I learnt a great deal in a little time under ſo good a Maſter, and knew ſeveral things which were not practis'd by others. For being happy in his inclination for me, and I having one too for the Art he excell'd in, I improv'd both by practice and exerciſe, and by the private conferences he was pleas'd to honour me withal, and learnt a great deal of that, which made him ſo great a Souldier, and gave him ſuch eſteem in the world, I took great care to ſet down whatever I learnt that was new, and drew out upon Paper ſeveral ſchemes of Exerciſes, Battalions, Encampments, Marches and Defiles, pretty well gueſſing what would beſt pleaſe the King.

XII. At this very time one of the Captains was upon ill terms with his *Maiſtre de Camp*, who complained of him, that he ſcarce ever came at his Company, and when any command in it fell, he ſtill procur'd it for ſome of his own Relations, without regarding merit, as he ought to have done.

It

It was no wonder, that one so exact for discipline, should blame an Officer who observ'd it so little; and who having more respect to fitness and services, than to affinity, should condemn a conduct so unlike his own. For whenever he observ'd any brave Souldier, who had serv'd the King well in his Armies, he would without any notice taken of his quality, procure him the recompence of some command in the Regiment, which was a great encouragement to others, who saw, that under such a Governour honourable employments were made the reward of doing well. This different conduct then produc'd a misunderstanding; which was increas'd upon a particular occasion. The Ensign of this Captain's Company being dead, Monsieur *Arnauld* desir'd the Colours might be given to a very brave Serjeant, who had signaliz'd himself in several actions that merited reward. The Captain on the contrary would give it to one of his own Kinsmen, who seem'd to have no other Title to this command, but that of being related to him; and Monsieur *Arnauld* having sent him a very civil Letter, took it ill to be deny'd, of which he complain'd highly, and spoke of him, as a person that sought all opportunities to disoblige him. I, who had the honour to be this Captain's near Relation, and intimate Friend, and who had so many engagements to Monsieur *Arnauld* too, thought my self concern'd to manage this business, and to do a piece of service to both of them at once. I told Monsieur *Arnauld*, that having the honour to be particularly acquainted with this Officer, I knew him in his own temper very far from this disobliging carriage, which he seem'd not without some reason to resent upon this occasion; that I could not impute this refusal to any thing but pure misfortune, and some misunderstanding; that he had Enemies, and that a man when absent easily passes for more guilty, than he really is. I engag'd my self at the same time to write to him, and it was my good fortune to manage the matter with so good success, as to bring them to a very fair understanding of one another.

XIII. A few days after this difference was compos'd, I receiv'd a private Order from the King to return to Court. I knew very well that the Governour, who was grown kinder to me, by reason of my great assiduity and constant application, would be much troubled at my going away, so that I was fain to prepare him for it, lest a sudden departure should give him any reason to accuse me of being less grateful than his obliging entertainment of me deserv'd. So I signify'd to him the indispensable necessity of my returning to *Paris*, upon business of great consequence. He was very importunate for my stay, and offer'd me any thing in the Regiment, that was in his power; but he found at last I could not help going, and perhaps suspected too (as I hinted before) the true reason of my coming thither, and so left me at full liberty to follow my own inclinations. After which I staid with him a few days longer, and in that time was witness of a very generous act of his, which deserves a room in these *Memoirs*. As we were going the Round with him one night, he stept alone a little before to hearken what the Souldiers said, who were very loud in their Hutt; where he heard one of them begin his health, and the rest took him up, cursing and railing in very insolent and injurious terms. At first indeed he was a little surpriz'd, to find the Governor's health so odly receiv'd, but knowing how naturally men are inclin'd to licentiousness, and how far this inclination works with some sort of people, and how great a violence it is upon them to be reduc'd to so exact a

discipline

discipline as that he made them observe; he was not angry, but turn'd all into raillery, and calling me to him, These are rare Fellows (said he) they drink my health after a strange fashion, and make fine Panegyricks in my praise. Then he continu'd his Round, and visited all the streets, and at last coming again to the door of these precious Health-drinkers he knock'd. They within, whom the Wine had a little elevated, answer'd briskly, Who comes there? The Governor reply'd with Authority, Open the door; which they, being a little astonish'd to hear his voice, presently did. He only ask'd them, why they were not in bed so long after the Tat-too, to which they made answer, that they humbly begg'd his pardon, but having by his leave been out to forrage, and got something, they were merry together, drinking the King's health, and his. Whereupon throwing them some Gold, and giving them caution to behave themselves more discreetly for the future, that they should drink his health after a more decent manner; they transported with joy, fell down and embrac'd his knees. Thus instead of punishing the insolence of these Souldiers, who had dared to give him such language for the severity of his discipline, he rather chose to win them by gentle ways, and vanquish them by his bounty.

Nor can I forbear in this place to report another action yet more generous than the former, as indeed the occasion was more important. He was very punctual in keeping his Regiment always full, and in this method consulted both the Kings advantage, and his own inclination; whereupon orders were given that no Skip-jacks or intruders should appear upon the review of the Companies. One of the Captains of his Regiment fail'd in this point, and upon being reproved, took such offence, that he broke out into a passion, openly declar'd he would not obey the order, and was so far transported at last, as even to draw his Sword upon his Collonel. This revolt needed the Kings authority to suppress it, which made Monsieur *Arnauld* write to Court, and represent the dangerous consequences of so rash an action, if it past unpunisht. Whereupon the King commanded that the Captain should be broken; and this great example wrought its due effect upon the Garrison. In the mean while, the Officer humbled to the last degree by this disgrace, was sensible of his fault, when it seem'd irreparable. Monsieur *Arnauld* had notice of it, and resenting what was past no farther than was necessary to promote the Kings real Interests, he writ to Court a second time, and conjur'd the Ministers to procure this Captains restauration; entreating them to consider, that it was of more consequence to a Governour to make himself lov'd than fear'd; and therefore this extraordinary grace which he entreated of them, would be of no less service to the King, than their Justice had been. His reasons prevail'd; and all the Officers of the Regiment were so mov'd with this generosity, and the consideration they found their Governour in at Court, that they ever after took a delight to please and obey him.

XIV. I took my leave of Monsieur *Arnauld*, and went from *Fort-Louis* to the King, whom I found at *Compeigne*; and when I presented my self, his Majesty, the better to disguise the matter, took no notice of me at first, and rather seem'd to be angry, asking me why I had stay'd so long? I, who very well understood this language, readily answer'd that I had scarce had time to obey his Majesty's orders, and had made all the haste I could away upon his Letter. The next morning he took me alone with
him

him into his Closet, and there lockt himself up, demanding an account
of what I had learnt in my Journey. I gave it him as exactly as possibly
I could; shewing him the Observations, and the Draughts I had taken.
This Prince, who took a singular delight in this noble Diversion, spent
an hour alone with me in his Closet almost every day for a month together; making me set out all that I had done in Companies of Souldiers,
by knotted Threads, or little figures of Lead. And after he had learnt
all that I my self could learn of Monsieur *Arnauld*, he would command,
and be commanded in turn, as well as I, so that we did as it were perform our exercises one after another, by the ranging of these figures,
according to the different methods that I had observ'd.

XV. This very particular confidence of the King's put several at Court
to a stand, who knew not what to make of my being shut up with him so
often alone. Among others the Serjeant Major of the Regiment of
Guards, grew so extremely jealous, as to tell me one day, that I had an
ill reputation among the Souldiers, and many of them began to suspect
I inform'd the King of all they did, not being able to guess from what
other cause this exceeding familiarity between his Majesty and me should
proceed. I must confess so rude a complement nettled me much, so
that I reply'd briskly, I thought till then he had known me, but what
he had said, being very distant from my nature, and constant course of
life, he made it plain that he was little read in men; that those who understood me better than he, could have no such jealousy concerning me,
and all my acquaintance (himself exeepted) were satisfy'd I'd rather
dye than do a thing so base, and unbecoming a man of honour. Must
people wonder (said I) that the King should sometimes talk to me in
private, and after having sent me into so remote a Province about several affairs, require of me an exact account of all I have done there? does
not all the world know this is his humour, and that he delights to discourse over his business very particularly? But that which disgusted this
Officer, was, that the King had shew'd him my draught of Battalions,
without telling him whose it was, only he gave him to understand, that
he liked this method better than his, which he had caus'd to be printed.
He had some suspicion however that I might be the man that had drawn
it, and question'd me about it; but the King having forbidden me to tell,
or give it to any body, I answer'd him so as was likely to take off his
jealousies of that kind.

XVI. My life was so cheequer'd and mixt, that it was one continu'd
succession of good and ill adventures. I had about this time a great contest with a famous Commissioner concern'd in the Salt-Customes, grounded upon a Donation from the King. For the Duke of *St. Simon* and I
having obtain'd a considerable Grant, assign'd us upon this Commissioner;
and I having need enough to make the best of his Majesty's favour, prest
upon him for payment; and upon his refusal, thought my self oblig'd
to prosecute him in the Kings Council, and obtain'd a Decree against
him. But he was a Master in his Trade, a cruel litigious fellow, that
car'd not a rush for a Decree, and carry'd his pockets always full of Ap-
peals and Injunctions. I soon saw he was too cunning for one so ignorant in Law-suits as I, and that the safest way was to think of an accommodation. To this purpose I apply'd my self to his younger Brother,
who was my very good friend, telling him I was so well perswaded of the
                                                                    Justice

Justice of my Cause, that I should not scruple the referring the matter between his Brother and me, to him. He promis'd me to speak about it. But the Commissioner little regarding his Brothers recommendation, and thinking a Souldier as I was would soon be weary of those dilatory proceedings, and that he might save his money by this means, was deaf to all propositions made in my behalf, and absolutely refus'd any terms of accommodation.

One day, as I and some other friends were walking in Monsieur *Deffiat* the Superintendant of the Treasury's Hall, I saw my adversary come in; and without employing any other Mediators, went to discourse him my self; where I told him freely thus: Sir, I know you do not love me, but for my part I bear no ill will to you: I ask you nothing but what the King has given me; and is it not a shame for a rich man, as you are, to refuse that little you owe me; and slight the Rules of Court obtain'd against you? I am naturally so averse to Suits, that I had rather submit peaceably to the Judgment of any Arbitrator you will name, so we may but put an end to this business. Since you open your heart to me (reply'd he) it is but fair that I deal as openly with you: I have only one thing to say, which is, that I have at this very time seven and twenty Causes depending, and I have Money enough to maintain them seven and twenty years: So that you had best consider whether it will be for your purpose to engage in a Suit with me. This knavish answer, and ridiculous boast, was what I least expected, and made me really angry. Give me your hand (said I to him) I promise you upon the faith of a Gentleman, and a man of Honour, that since you resolve to stand Suit, I will ply you so close, that the Kingdom shall be too hot for one of us. From that time forward I began to sollicit my Judges with all my might and main, and sparing neither pains nor money, obtain'd at length another Decree against him, and a Writ to seize his Body. This forc'd him to leave *Paris*, and flee to *Lions*; I pursu'd him thither, but he seeing himself prest, stopt the proceedings by a fresh Injunction; so that we were to begin all again. Both of us return'd to *Paris*; and about this time I found a way to humble the insolence of a Serjeant after a very pleasant manner.

I had some new Citation brought me every day, either to command my appearance, or the producing some paper or other; and the Serjeants took a pride to serve these Citations, because they were under protection. At last, growing weary of this sort of Officers, who are not very acceptable Guests to men of our way in ones own house, I resolv'd to make use not of force, but cunning, to rid my self fairly of the inconvenience I suffer'd by them. To this purpose I invented a Trap at the entrance into my Chamber, as wide as the door, so that when the Bolt was drawn, none could go in or out, but they must needs fall into it. Then I had a great Sack nailed to the roof of the room below, wide open, just under the Trap, that whoever slipt into the hole might fall into the Sack, and hang in the air. In regard I had often company with me, they thought fit to choose out one of the stoutest Serjeants to serve these Citations. One of which having boasted that he fear'd me not, and being very jolly upon the account of some Pistoles that were promis'd as his reward, came to my House, and enter'd my Chamber, with a Citation in his hand. As bold as he pretended to be, he appear'd to me not much assur'd; and told me that being oblig'd to bring me a Citation, yet he would ask my leave, and not serve it unless I were willing he should. I answer'd, that he very little understood how to be civil to men of ho-

nour,

nour, and that he ought not to mock me, by asking my consent to bring what I saw him hold in his hand. He seeing me angry, had recourse to submissions and excuses; but at last I began to raise my voice, and then fearing if he did not get out of the Room, that I should reward him with a Cudgel, he began to retire, and shift towards the door. In the mean while my man had drawn back the Bolt that staid the Trap, and so my brave Serjeant, that thought of nothing but making his escape, vanisht in an instant, being fallen through the Trap-door into the Sack, which clos'd at the top with the weight of his body, as did the Trap also, returning in a moment to its former posture. There was my Gentleman dangling between Heaven and Earth, in an astonishment so great, that he scarce knew whither he was dead or alive. I gave him leisure to come to himself, and let him hang about a quarter of an hour. After I had order'd him to be drawn out, he begg'd of me, as the greatest favour I could do him, not to divulge a thing which would disgrace him for ever; which I promis'd, being sufficiently satisfied, that I had so innocently humbled the pride of a Serjeant. But he would ever after put me in mind of the Sack, and laugh heartily at the jest.

In the mean while I prest my Commissioner as close and vigorously as I could, and made him know, that, if he had better knowledge in Craft and Quirks of Law, yet I had the better Cause, and credit enough to defend it. At last seeing his business in an ill condition, he resolv'd to gain the Judges by great Presents, and found a way to surprize the Superintendant, entreating the assistance of his credit, against a Gentleman of *Provence* that perplex'd him with a Suit of Law. Monsieur *Deffiat* being thus caught, sent the Marquess his Son to sollicite all the Judges in his name against me, without knowing all this while that I was the party concern'd. My Advocate gave me notice of it, and tho I had much ado to believe this of a person who had always giv'n me great testimonies of his good will, yet I entreated the King to speak to him about it. Next morning putting on my Corslet, and taking three or four of the bravest Cadets of my Company along with me, I went to wait on the Superintendant just as he was at Dinner: I stay'd till he rose from Table, and coming up to him while he was washing his mouth, I told him in his Ear, I am come hither, Sir, to present you a Request, whether it be a civil one or no, I can't tell, but I'm sure however it is just. Am not I very unhappy, Sir, I who have ever had the honour to be your Servant, to pass all on the sudden for a Criminal in your opinion, and to draw your displeasure upon me, without knowing how I have done it? You must needs think me guilty of some great fault sure, Sir, since after having honour'd me with your favour and affection, you now sollicit against me in so just a cause, and where the execution of the King's pleasure is the only thing in dispute. Monsieur *Deffiat* much surpriz'd at such a complement, said, interrupting me, I sollicit against you! I protest I do not know what you mean, pray unfold the mystery, and make me understand you. Here is Monsieur *F.* (replied I) who is present in the room, hath commenc'd a Suit against me, and maliciously trifles off the Duke of *St. Simon* and my self, about a Donation the King hath been pleas'd to bestow upon us. I have obtain'd several Decrees against him both in Parliament and Council, but he is an Eel, that always slips through my hands, when I think to grasp him. If you undertake to defend him, Sir, as it appears you do, by the sollicitations the Marquis your Son has lately made in his behalf against me; I know too well that it is in vain for a poor Officer as I am,

to

to stand it out, and think to carry his point against a Superintendent; and if the case be so, I had better give up my cause to my Adversay, and be quiet. I protest to you (reply'd Monsieur *Deffiat*) that I did not know it was you, that was at Law with Monsieur F. he has surpriz'd me, but I will make him know, that there is nothing to be got by surprizing men of honour. At the same time he call'd him, and made but few words, but in short took my Gentleman down; you have abus'd me, (said he) and surpriz'd me, in making me ignorantly sollicit against Monsieur *Pontis*. You owe me Five hundred thousand Livres, I declare if you do not pay me within a week, I will lay you by the heels. He was offering to justify himself, but the Gentleman commanded him to withdraw, and think of what he had said to him. All the Company were extremely pleas'd to see an Excise-man so humbled. At the same time he order'd his Son, the Marquis, to go along with me and undeceive the Judges, and to tell them, he was sorry he had suffer'd himself to be so surpriz'd, and that he had sollicited against a man he lov'd. Several of them had receiv'd great Presents, and some whole Cart-loads of Orange-trees; which when I saw in their Gardens, I could not forbear saying in jest to these Gentlemen: Oh! what corruption! Oh how do I suspect my Cause! For God's sake, Sir, when my concern comes before you, do not look upon these Trees, for they will be very ominous to me if you do.

I was advis'd by my Friends to except against one of these Judges, because having been my Adversary's Advocate in this very Suit against me, he had since by his means obtain'd to be Master of Requests, and so all on the sudden from his Council, was preferr'd to be his Judge. The thing appear'd odious enough of it self, and a man of any equity at all, would never have staid to be excepted against for such a reason. But two thousand Crowns pension, which he receiv'd from this Commissioner, made him proceed against the ordinary Rules of Justice. Before I would except against him, I had a mind to try what civility would do; and accordingly went to see him, where I complemented him to this effect: I am come, Sir, (said I) upon a business that is very just, and I think you a man of more equity than not to grant it. You know you have formerly pleaded for Monsieur *F.* with whom I have a Suit now depending, and I do not wonder you have serv'd him the best you could, for it is the business of an Advocate so to do. Nay, I have several times commended the Wit, Learning and Wisdom, that you have shewn upon this occasion. You are since made a Master of Requests, which, Sir, is the Reward of your Merit; and we must believe, that having been so good an Advocate, you will prove as good a Judge; but pray, Sir, give me leave to tell you, that I conceive the first testimony of your Justice, ought to be the refusing to sit as Judge, in a Cause where you have been Councel. For though I do not doubt your probity, yet it would reflect upon your honour to judge him, as a Master of Requests, whom you have already so severely condemn'd as a Pleader. To which he reply'd, that if he should wave all the Causes he had been concern'd in, he might even as well throw up his place, for most of the business had gone through his hands. After a long debate, finding him resolute, and that he would not decline sitting upon this Cause, I took my leave: And going immediately to the King, I told his Majesty the whole story. Just as I had done, in came Monsieur *Seguier*, Chancellor of *France*, and the King taking him by the Arm, said, Hark you my Lord Chancellor, I have a Question to ask you: May an Advocate, who hath pleaded against a man, and after-

wards

wards bought a Judges place, be Judge in a Cause of his own pleading?
The Chancellor look'd a little surpriz'd, and answer'd, that he did not
believe any body would say he might; that it was a thing contrary to
all Law, and all Reason. But yet, said the King, it is what ...... pretends to do in *Pontis*'s case here. This was enough to engage the Chancellor to promise me Justice, and next day he was as good as his word,
in granting me a Decree, forbidding Monsieur *De la* .... to be present at the Judgment not only of this, but of any other Suit that I might
hereafter have with the Commissioner aforesaid. I deliver'd this Decree to
an Usher of the Court, to signifie it to this Master of Requests; but he had
notice of it, and being at his wits end, to see his design publickly condemn'd by King and Council, he immediately apply'd to my best friends,
to interpose with me, that this business might go no farther. I gave
them a true account of my behaviour in it, which they approv'd, and
told them it was meer necessity made me proceed after that manner;
so that upon any other account I should be ready to serve him. But this
business having made a noise, and Monsieur *De la* .... fearing, that
my access to the King might give me opportunity to do him ill offices,
as it had been no hard matter to have done indeed, had I been of so mean
a Spirit, he came to me himself not long after, and after a great deal of talk,
which is not necessary to be repeated here, he desir'd me at last to go
with him to the King, and speak in his behalf. I went with him in his
Coach to *St. Germains* at the Kings rising, and presenting my Judge, said,
Sir, Monsieur *De la* .... upon consideration that I belong to your
Majesty, will needs be formally reconcil'd to me, tho indeed we have
never been Enemies; but he knowing that your Majesty is pleas'd to do
me the honour to allow me about your person, will out of an extraordinary generosity use my mediation to beseech your Majest, to forget what
has past between us, seeing I have forgot it with all my heart. Had I
known him for the generous person he is, I should have proceeded in a-
nother way, as I believe he would have done with me, had he known
me for such as I am; and therefore I most humbly beseech your Majesty
ever to look upon him, as one of your good and faithful Servants. The
King was pleas'd to take this address well, and Monsieur *De la* ....
and I went out, very well satisfy'd with one another.

But I was not rid of my Suit for all this; but forc'd to continue my
prosecution against him, who had held me in hand so long about the
Donation from the King. I obtain'd at last another Attachment against
him, which forc'd him to leave *Paris* a second time, and flee to *Lions*.
I pursu'd him so close, that he was fain to take Sanctuary in the Popes
territories at *Avignon*. Then I writ to the Kings Ambassador at *Rome*,
which was the Marquis *d'Estree*; and having obtain'd leave of his Holi-
ness, I was about to arrest him, and he escap'd from me again to *Orange*.
I was not discourag'd for all this, but writ to the Prince of *Orange* at the
Hague; to demand Justice against this litigious Knave. He had notice of
it, and seeing no refuge left, but either flying into *Germany*, or *Spain*,
and hazarding the being taken in his flight too, he writ to the Duke of
St. Simon, to desire an accommodation; and chose at last to pay, though
against his will, what at first he resolv'd never to give us, rather than
to banish himself the Kingdom. So he paid the Duke twenty thousand
Crowns, and me about forty thousand Livres. But this Suit, tho upon
a summ so trivial to so rich a man, was the cause of his utter ruine. For
he spent above four hundred thousand Livres in it, and was made a perfect

fect Bankrupt. So truly was the promise I made him kept, that the Kingdom should grow too hot for one of us. And I thought it not amiss by this remarkable instance, to shew the world how very apt the false trust a man puts in his Credit, and cunning in Law, is to betray and undo him. Yet for all this, I did his Brother a very good office to the King; for he having a mind to buy a Lieutenants place in the Guards, and the King asking me what I thought of him, I gave the best Character I could, both of his valour and deserts: Adding withal, that since he had Money, it was fit he should spend it in his Majesty's service, who had an original right to it.

XVII. It was near about this time that Monsieur *Bouteville*'s misfortune happen'd; who having fought (as 'tis well known) contrary to the Kings express prohibition, was seized, just as he was upon the point to escape into *Lorrain* with the Count *de Chapelles*. The Marquis *de Buffy*'s Servant, knowing his Master was kill'd, follow'd them close, and made so good haste, that he overtook them at *Vitry-le-Brushe*. It had been the easiest thing in the world for them to ride on, till they had got into a place of safety, for they wanted but two Post-stages, and the Count *de Chapelles* did all he could to perswade Monsieur *Bouteville* to it: But providence so order'd it, that himself should be the cause of his own ruine, by pretending an unseasonable bravery, and reproaching the Count with want of Courage, for the necessary caution he advis'd him to. In the mean while this Servant had time to go to *Vitry-le-Francois*, of which the late Marquis *de Buffy* was Governour, where he gave notice to the Provost Marshal of the place, where the men that kill'd him were; and this Provost with his Archers beset the house, took them, and carry'd them to *Vitry-le-Francois*. The King heard of it, and immediately order'd Monsieur *de Gordes*, Captain of the Guards, and me, to go with two hundred men to *Vitry*, and bring Monsieur *Bouteville* and *des Chapelles* to *Paris*. I, who had the honour to be particularly acquainted with Monsieur *Bouteville*, was employed in such a Commission sore against my will, and it went to my heart to do so sad a piece of service to one who had always exprest a great deal of favour and affection for me. Tho on the other side, I could not choose but disapprove and condemn so criminal a thing, in them whose death I lamented before-hand. As soon as we were arrived, he exprest great joy for my coming, and in complement said, I was exceeding welcome; for he knew now I was of the party, there would be no foul play. I answer'd, that indeed he had reason to think so, for Monsieur *Gordes* was a man of too much honour to suffer any such thing. He was very pleasant all the Journey, and shew'd little or no trouble, depending no doubt upon his great relations, and the Interest of his friends. When we came to the Inn, he would needs have me to play with him, as being undisturb'd in his thoughts, and perfectly master of himself. There was a rumour abroad, that the Duke of *Orleans* had put seven or eight hundred men into the field to rescue Monsieur *Bouteville* out of our hands. The King was made acquainted with it, and sent us a reinforcement of five hundred men a league beyond *Logny*, with positive order to defend our selves very well, if any attempt were made upon us. I observed Monsieur *Bouteville* was a little surpriz'd at the arrival of this great Convoy, and said to me, by way of confidence; What's the meaning of all this Company? What are they afraid of?

F f   Have

Have I not given you my word? and having given it, can any body imagine I will break it? But I, who thought I might eafily difengage a man from his promife, who was fo well guarded, and had no great reafon to hope well in this bufinefs, told him again with the fame freedom, Look you, Sir, this is not a time to ftand upon generofity, and punctilio's of honour, I releafe you of your promife, and if you can make your efcape, do not fcruple to do it. In good earneft I could heartily have wifht it done, provided it might have been without any fault of mine. When we drew near *Paris* he began to be apprehenfive, and told me, that if we carry'd him to the *Conciergene*, he was a gone man: But when he found he was to be convey'd to the *Baftille*, he expreft great joy, and affur'd himfelf he fhould not dye. In the mean time, we knew well enough his hopes would deceive him, and that the King would make him an example; the rather by reafon of the Holy-days, which he had profan'd by his bloody Duels. And not being to be prevail'd upon by the interceffions of the moft eminent perfons in this Kingdom, he gave all his Nobility to underftand, by this inftance of feverity, that it was their duty to referve their valour for his fervice, and the publick Interefts of the Crown.

The End of the Sixth Book.

BOOK

BOOK VII.

Several considerable particulars of the Siege of Rochelle. *Cardinal* Richlieu *tries to draw the Sieur* de Pontis *into his Service. Father* Joseph's *Conference with him, to that effect. He is out of Favour with the King. upon the account of Monsieur* Saligny's *Command, which he had a mind of, and that was bought by* St. Preuil. *The great Difference between him and Monsieur* Canaples, *Maistre de Camp of the Regiment of Guards. He is tried in a Council of War, he justifies his Innocence to the King in private, and afterwards before the whole Court. The Mareschal* de Bassompiere *obtains his Pardon. The Generosity of Mareschal* Crequi, *Monsieur* Canaples *his Father. The City of* Rochelle *is surrendred to the King. The great Qualifications of* Guiton Mayor *of* Rochelle.

I. IN the year 1627, the King resolv'd to go lay Siege to *Rochelle*, intending by that means to deprive the *Hugonots* of the strongest Rampart they had in *France*. It is not my design here to give an account of all the passages of this famous Siege, the publick events whereof are recorded in History; but I shall only take notice of some circumstances wherein I my self was concern'd, and shew how providence was pleas'd to order my affairs, whether in putting me by the present fortunes I might reasonably have aspir'd to; or in preserving me from those great dangers, in which, according to all humane appearance, I must otherwise have perish'd. Having staid at *Paris*, by the Kings order, to gather some Troops that were left behind, and bring them to the body of the Army; after I had discharg'd that Commission, I went to wait upon the King at *Fontainbleau*, from whence after a few days he mov'd towards *Rochelle*. Assoon as he came near, he lay the first night at *Surgeres*, about three or four leagues off from the City; and afterwards came up to *Etray*, which was but a mile from the Camp. One day Monsieur *Marillac*, who was then but Mareschal *de Camp*, but afterwards Mareschal of *France*, was commanded to attack a Fort, that was far advanc'd, by night; and being he was first to discover the Ditches, and all without, he chose two Serjeants, who were very brave Souldiers, for that purpose. But before he sent them, he went to the Kings Quarters at *Etray*, to give him an account of what he intended to do. The King, who knew the gallantest men of his Army, askt the two Serjeants names; which being told him, after a little pause turning to Monsieur *Marillac*, As for *Cadet*, said he, (which was the name of one of them) I know him to be a very brave fellow; but I have not so good an opinion of the other. I know a man, (said the King) who would acquit himself well of this Commission, and bring us an exact account of every thing : I have made tryal of him upon many such occasions : I mean *Pontis*, the Lieutenant of my Guards : tell him I desire him to go, and bring me an account of what he can discover.

The

The defign had been taken to attack the Fort about two hours after midnight; fo that I was to go by eleven of the Clock at fartheft, for it requir'd at leaft an hour to go thither, and as much to get back again. I went in the dark of the night, accompany'd with two Serjeants, whom I fent two feveral ways, and went my felf a third. Inftead of going directly to the Ditches, where I fhould have had much ado to get down, I fetcht a compafs, and put my felf into *Rochelle* road. When I came near the Draw-bridge, I went all along by the fides of the Ditches, as if I had come out of the City, that fo if any one fhould chance to meet me, he might think I belong'd to the Town. After I had gone a little way, I found a great Gate, that they were building to come down into the Ditches by, but it was not yet finifh'd. I went down by this Gate as foftly as I could, but yet I could not do it fo as to efcape being heard by the Centinels, who cry'd out, Who goes there? and made feveral fhots at me, which whiskt on every fide of me. I kept on my way in the Ditches, and found in one corner a pair of winding ftairs, that led up to the top of the Ditch: Up I went, but when I was got almoft to the top, I met a man coming down the fame fteps. I fixt my felf inftantly, and without betraying any furprize, made as though I was peeping through one of the Skit-gates, that was upon the ftairs, that lookt down into the Ditch. The man that was coming down, finding my back toward him, and taking me for one of their own fide, askt what I was doing? to which I anfwer'd, that having heard fhooting, and a great noife, I was looking to fee what was the matter. Whereupon, without having the leaft fufpicion of me, he reply'd, It is nothing but thefe rafcally Centinels, that are afraid of their own fhadows; and having faid fo, he went down, and I went up to the top, where I met a Serjeant, who was come from pofting and relieving the Centries. He askt me whither I was going? and I anfwer'd coldly, that I was order'd to come and fee what was the meaning of thofe fhots that had been made. Whereupon the Serjeant, who was an honeft old fellow, without giving himfelf any further trouble to examine who I was, told me it was nothing but a falfe alarm; and askt me, if I had nothing elfe to fay to him? I told him, No; and in truth I was a little impatient to be gone out of his company. After this manner I paft, and efcap'd fo great a danger, by a vifible effect of the protection of Almighty God.

I return'd the fame way I came; and found *Cadet*, who waited for me, and when he heard me ftruck two ftones one againft another, which was the fignal agreed upon betwixt us. He had a Bottle of Wine, of which he made me drink two or three draughts, which refrefht me very much; and I had great need of it, having taken a great deal of pains, and ftumbled a long time up and down in very uneven way. As foon as we were return'd to the Camp, I made a report of all I could obferve of this Gate I had found into the Ditches, the depth and breadth of the Ditches themfelves, the little Winding Stairs, and all the reft I had difcoverd. But there being fome conteft upon a report made by one of the two Serjeants, which made it neceffary to call a Council of War, and a great deal of time being fpent that way, as the Troops were marching along the fhore to gain that Gate, day broke upon them, and the Enemy difcerning our men at a diftance, made fuch a furious fire upon them with their Cannon, that feveral of our Souldiers were killed and wounded. This conteft, which was in part the caufe of our misfortune, made the King after the taking of *Rochelle* declare, that he would fee himfelf whether my report were true.   II. I

II. I shall only take notice of one example more upon this occasion, to shew of what importance it is in these enterprizes not to expose an Army rashly, upon the reports of silly People, or the vain projects of such as do not understand the profession. Father *Joseph*, a famous Capuchin, who had a rambling kind of Wit, and employed himself principally in War, and State affairs, had intimation given him, that there was a large Common-shore by which all the nastiness of the Town was carried off, and that it would be an easy thing to make our selves Masters of the place, by sending men up this Shore by night. Immediately he resolv'd upon this attempt, and proceeded so far as to propose a terrible Engine to serve for the effecting it. But first we must know, whether the Passage were good, for it was a Citizen who had told Father *Joseph* of it, and we were not secure, that the information was to be depended upon. They straight began to talk of sending me thither, and the King made great enquiry after me, but I kept my self out of the way, as growing weary of being perpetually employed upon such discoveries, which got me but little honour, for my report was not always credited, and yet expos'd me to abundance of danger. However, found out I was at last, at a friends quarter, where I was at Supper; and not knowing how to excuse my self, I went presently to wait upon the King, who told me; he had sent for me upon a business of consequence, which Father *Joseph*, who was then by, could give me an account of.

The good Father, acting the part of a General, represented to me his whole design, and told me afterwards, with a grave and discreet zeal, that the King having singled me out from ten thousand for this important service, I ought to think of answering the good opinion his Majesty had of me; and that if I did not find my self so much dispos'd to it, as the matter requir'd, I had better fairly desist, than undertake it unwillingly. This discourse displeas'd me much, and I knew not well how to relish it, that a Capuchin should take upon him to read Lectures of Courage and Resolution to me. Which made me reply with some resentment, tho in the Kings presence, that he did me wrong, and it did not become him to talk at that rate; that his Majesty had never commanded me any thing, wherein I had not behav'd my self like a man of honour; and that had the occasion been less perillous, where there could have been no ground to suspect me of fear, I would have begg'd his Majesty to excuse me from undertaking it, after such an affront put upon me in his presence. The King, who saw me a little mov'd, appeas'd me, by turning to Father *Joseph*, and telling him that he knew me very well, and durst answer for me. So away I went with an Ensign, in a dreadful windy night, which favour'd our design. There were Souldiers plac'd at every fifty paces to sustain us, in case we should be attack'd, as also to shew us where the Ditches were, lest we should lose our selves in the dark. Being come to the Drain, we sounded the Ouze with a long pole, and found the Mud cruel deep on all sides; and after having searcht every passage, concluded there was no possibility of getting thorough. We return'd, and made our report, that forty thousand would perish there as well as two, and nothing was to be hop'd for from this project. Upon this Father *Joseph* began to fret, and said, it could not be; that he had been otherwise inform'd by a Citizen of *Rochelle*. To which I boldly reply'd, that if he could take that man, he would do well to hang him for a Liar, and a Rogue; adding withal, that had the passage been good, it were impossible to do

G g   any

any thing that night, because there was no Bridge over the Graffe, but a Plank, over which one man had much ado to pass. At this the Father grew louder, saying, he had ordered Bridges to be made, and he believ'd they were ready. The conclusion came to this, that there being no Bridges, and his great Machine being broken, all this project fell to nothing. The King, after the surrender of *Rochelle*, would needs view this Drain, and there shew'd Father *Joseph* the danger to which he would fain have expos'd the Army. Which puts me in mind of what past between the Father and Collonel *Hebron*, who hath been so well known both in *Germany* and *France*. For as he was forming mighty projects, and laying wise designs, above any mans comprehension, he shew'd him three or four Towns in a Map, which he would have observ'd to be taken; the Collonel, who was not us'd to receive such orders from a *Capuchin*, answer'd with a smile, Hark you, Master *Joseph*, 'tis an easie thing to talk, but Towns are not taken with ones fingers ends.

III. Being now engag'd in discourse upon this good Father, I think it may not be amiss to take notice of what past between him and me much about the same time, with regard to Cardinal *Richelieu*. This Cardinal is well enough known to have many eminent qualities, and such as gain'd him great respect, both at home among the Kings Subjects, and abroad with Foreign Princes, and a Great Minister he was, and a most celebrated Politician. But as the greatest men never are without some defects, every body doubtless must have observ'd this mighty fault in him; That in the services he did the State, he did not manifest all that zeal for his Prince that became him, but made it his business to entice away his faithfullest Servants, and decoy them out of his Majesty's service into his own. He knowing me to be a person most inviolably devoted to the person of the King, and having either observ'd himself, or been told by others of something in me, that was not displeasing to him, so as to incline him to wish me about his person, he had the goodness to look upon me, and discover his inclination chiefly upon the following occasion.

Being one day remov'd nearer the King's Quarter, from which he lay very remote before, he desir'd his Majesty, that some Companies might be sent to keep Guard at his Lodgings, by reason that now he lay more expos'd to the Sallies of the *Rochellers*. The King order'd him some Companies of his own Guards, and I was the first that kept Guard before his Quarter with my Company. In pursuit of his design to win me over to his service, he gave order that a very fine Chamber should be got ready for me, where nothing was wanting: but I would not so much as lye down all night, that I might look to what I had in charge, and observe my duty the better. He found means even from hence to take an occasion of courting me, and industriously spoke in my commendation before some persons at Court, that they might tell me again. At last he would have me tried in good earnest, and made choice of Father *Joseph* for this purpose. A man very fit to execute his designs, being entirely in his Interests, and one of no less cunning and dexterity than himself. He made sure of my hearkening to his proposals, because Monsieur *Beauplan*, Captain of his Guards, was at that time dangerously sick, and he design'd in case he should dye, to give me that Command if I would accept it so, as to give my self up to him wholly, and without reserve; For so much I was in plain terms given to understand, that he expected all his Officers should look upon him as their Soveraign, and that in all the disturbances and

revolutions

revolutions at Court, they should stand by him against all opposition, and without all exception. This was the principal condition, upon which he gave them to understand, that he admitted them into his service; and it was what I confess raised great indignation in me to see, that they were thus made by a kind of new Oath, to renounce the engagements they had made to the King, whom I have ever consider'd as my Master, and could never dispose of my self to any other to his prejudice.

Father *Joseph* passing by my Lodging one day, or at least pretending to make that in his way, that I might not think he came on purpose, askt pretty loud, whether I was within. They presently came and told me, and I as soon coming down to meet him, we went up together into the Chamber. Every body in Company straight withdrew, to give way to this Minister of the Cardinal, who was fear'd almost as much as he. The Father before he open'd himself upon the chief occasion of his visit, ask'd me, if I had made trial of a certain invention he had learnt from a Souldier, who had frequently discours'd about some Engines, that might be proper to incommode the *Rochellers*; which was, to fire a Ship at a great distance by a Musquet shot. Having desir'd to know my opinion of it, I told him, since he did me the honour to consult me, I was oblig'd to tell him, that I thought it a very casual thing; that this Souldier, upon a tryal he made in my Garden of three or four shots, there succeeded but one, and therefore I conceiv'd no great stress ought to be laid upon so great an uncertainty. He then entreated me, that I would bring the Souldier with me to his house next day, that we might make the experiment in his Garden, and there (said he) we will regale you, and I will engage you shall be very well receiv'd. Father (said I) I shall be much better receiv'd than I deserve, 'tis too great an honour for me, that you are pleas'd to think of me. Oh (replied he) I am sure I have good reason to think of you, we are old acquaintance. Do you remember the time, when you offer'd me your Horse? I am asham'd Father (said I) to think of so poor a thing, and it shews your generous temper to remember it so long.

The business he spoke of was, that going one day to *St. Germains* in very hot weather, I overtook this Father *Joseph* upon the road, and a Frier, who were likewise both going thither; it was about the time he first ingratiated himself with Monsieur *Luines*, and to creep into Court. I very civilly desir'd he would ease himself and ride my Horse. He, who at that time did not think it decent for a Capuchin to ride on Horseback (though he hath been of another mind since, and discover'd that he might travel in a Coach for the service of the State) return'd me many thanks, but told me withal, that since I was so obliging, he entreated I would ease them in taking their great Cloaks, and a Wallet that the Frier carried, which I very readily did. So that it was as pleasant a sight to see a Captain carrying a Wallet before him then, as afterwards it was to see a Capuchin turn'd Courtier, and Minister to the prime Minister of State. This was the thing the Father referr'd to, who continu'd his discourse to me after this manner. I have ever since bore in mind (said he) the Charity you shew'd to us then, and I could not forget you when I remembred that. I have taken several occasions to speak to the Cardinal in your behalf; and have found, that he hath a very great esteem for you. He is much dispos'd to serve you, and is never deceiv'd in his choice of men. Really he hath a marvellous talent in judging of merit, and a liberal hand in rewarding it wherever he finds it. Father (said I) I am extremely oblig'd to you, for fo great an acknowledgment of fo fmall a piece of fervice. I did not deferve thus much from you, that you fhould recommend me to the Cardinal, and am fearful, that what you have had the goodnefs to fay to him in my favour, may turn to my difadvantage; for fince fo great a Soul as his can fet a value upon nothing that is not very eminent, and I have nothing in me but what is very common, it is in fome fort to wrong his Judgment to poffefs him with an opinion of a perfon that does no way deferve it. I have only one thing to boaft of, which is the inviolable fidelity I have ever born to the King, and in that I can fay without vanity, I give place to none. The Father, perceiving I was aware of his defign, and that his Mine was fprung, was not at a lofs however, but took occafion from my own words to return me this anfwer. Why this, faid he, is the very thing that the Cardinal values moft in you, 'tis that ftrict fidelity fo known to all the world that he chiefly looks after. He would have Officers that fhould be faithful to him, and be only his without exception or referve; he cares not for them who ferve two Mafters, (thefe were his very words) knowing very well no good is to be expected from fuch people. This is it that hath made him fix upon you, becaufe he knows when you have once devoted your felf to a Mafter, you look upon him only, and after God will ferve him only. And it is fo rare in thefe times to find men of that temper, that were they to be bought, the Cardinal would purchafe them at the price of their weight in Gold.

A man could hardly pufh a thing more home, or declare himfelf more openly, and truly I, believing I ought then to come out of the Clouds, made no fcruple to declare my felf as openly as he had done. I know Father (faid I) that it is too great an honour for me, that his Eminence looks upon me, and am very well fatisfy'd, that in being about his perfon, I fhould fecure my fortune; but fince the Cardinal himfelf declares, that fidelity is fo valuable a qualification in his Servants, would not he be the firft that fhould condemn me of unfaithfulnefs, if after the King has done me honour in placing me near his perfon, and giving me a Command in the Guards of his own accord, I fhould fo foon quit his fervice, and difpofe of my felf to another. This would betray a moft inexcufable levity and ingratitude, and every body muft conclude, that after having ferved a King of *France* fo ill, I were very unworthy to ferve the greateft Cardinal in *Chriftendom*. Doubtlefs, Father, I have all the reafon in the world to believe, that the Cardinal intends only to try me upon this occafion, and hope you will have the goodnefs to reprefent it to him, and add this favour to fo many others, for which I am already oblig'd to you. The Father then taking the opportunity I gave him of coming fairly off, feem'd to be very highly fatisfy'd with me, and having commended me for the due fenfe I had of his Majefty's favours, he went away, appearing outwardly as well content, as he was inwardly difturbed to fee his complement fo ill return'd.

IV. The Cardinal feem'd no lefs fatisfy'd with my anfwer, highly commending the fidelity I had expreft in it, and though he could not choofe but be vext, that fo poor an Officer durft refufe entring into his fervice, it is not to be believ'd how many fubtle contrivances the ambition of not being defeated in what he had once attempted, put him upon to win me ever. If he fpoke of any of the Officers, he always preferr'd me above the reft, and affected to commend me in the prefence of the King, and the great men at Court: Infomuch that feveral of my Friends told me,

me, I was highly oblig'd to the Cardinal for the advantageous characters
he constantly gave of my conduct. These complements I receiv'd with
seeming submission and acknowledgment, but inwardly I had no relish for
the affected speeches of a man whose pretences I so well knew. One day the
King having granted me a favour for one of my Kinsmen, bad me go
complement the Cardinal upon that account. Accordingly I went and
told him, that since his Majesty had put all things into his disposal, he
had sent me to ask his consent to a gift he had done me the honour to
confer upon me; at which I perceiv'd he was mightily pleas'd, and said
with a smiling countenance, that he was very glad of the King's kindness to me, that he knew my merit, and instead of repining at any thing
his Majesty should do for me, would with all his heart contribute to it
whatsoever lay in his power. But the kindness he was pleas'd to shew
me did not continue very long; for I shall shew before I have done, that
after having try'd promises and entreaties, and all the gentle ways that a
Minister so subtle as he could contrive, he proceeded at last to methods
of severity and violence. But now I must proceed to give an account
of what past during the Siege of *Rochelle*, and relate the most troublesom
business that ever I was engag'd in in my whole life; which I dare affirm
to have been just at the beginning, however several circumstances of
time and place, and persons rendred it criminal to the last degree.

V. Before I give an account of the great difference I had with Monsieur
Canaples, my *Maistre de Camp*, and the Son of Mareschal *Crequi*, it will not
be improper to set down in short the cause of a little coldness toward me
formerly. It happen'd that being one day at play with Count *Saligny*, the
Captain of that Company where I was Lieutenant, he had the better,
and won of my Captain six hundred Pistoles. The Count *Saligny* not
knowing what to lay his ill fortune to, would needs examine the Dice, and
finding them false ones, he said a Cheat was put upon him, and he was
robb'd of his Money. Monsieur *Canaples* vindicated himself by saying,
that he plaid fair, that he could not answer for the Dice, they were what
he bought for true ones, and since both plaid with the same Dice, whatever advantage there was both had it equally. Count *Saligny* went presently out of the house, and finding me out, told me what had past, and
that he was resolv'd to be reveng'd, not being able to be so cullied by
his *Maistre de Camp*. I return'd such an answer, as the false honour of
the world inspires men with upon such occasions, and assur'd him of my
service; but letting him know withal, that I had rather make them
friends if that might be, and so, both preserve his Honour, and keep my
own Command. The Quarrel was soon compos'd, but as nothing can be
a secret in this world, what I had said was told Monsieur *Canaples*, who
was furiously incens'd against me; yet he always dissembled his displeasure,
and no resentment appeared outwardly, till the occasion of which I shall
presently give an account.

VI. But still notwithstanding the accommodation there remain'd some
bitterness in the heart of Count *Saligny*, so that being no longer able to
endure to be commanded by one who he thought had affronted him, he
resolv'd to sell his command. He spoke of it to me, and promis'd, if I
would buy it, to make me a better bargain than any other man by two
thousand Crowns. I answer'd, I desir'd it of all things in the world,
but I wanted Money; yet that should not hinder my acknowledgment

H h   of

of the obligation I had to him, and that I could not hope for any thing but from the Kings bounty, who had promis'd to give me a Company, as he had already made me a Lieutenant. Monſieur *Bologne*, whom I have often mention'd, hearing what had paſt between us, was very urgent with me to buy this Command, promiſing to help me to Money, and to ſtand bound for it. But I, who never car'd to trouble my friends, except there was an abſolute neceſſity for it, told him, the difficulty did not lye in procuring the Money, but in paying it again : that if he ſtood bound with me, he would run a great hazard, and I was not of a humour to make my own fortunes at my friends expence. Monſieur *St. Preuil* coming to ſee me a little after that Count *Saligny* had ſpoke to him about ſelling his Command, but for his part he would never think of it, till he knew firſt whether I had not ſome proſpect of the Commiſſion my ſelf. I made anſwer as I had done to Count *Saligny*, that I could be glad to have it, but I would not buy it. That is not the thing, ſaid he, there are enough of your mind, all that I have to ſay to you is, that while you have any thoughts of it, I will never have any ; I know very well what juſt pretenſions you have to it, and if you'll buy it, I have four thouſand Crowns at your ſervice, of which I now make you an offer. I then very ſeriouſly made anſwer, that I was very much oblig'd to him, and had much rather he ſhould buy it than any body elſe, becauſe I heartily lov'd him, and wiſht him as well as I did my ſelf : but added withal, that ſince my hopes of a Command were thus loſt, which I had ſome right to expect from the Kings bounty, as Count *Saligny* himſelf had it given freely, I begg'd at leaſt he would give me leave to complain, and not take it ill if I laid hold on this opportunity to draw ſome advantage from my misfortune ; for I ſtand in need (ſaid I ſmiling) of a little ſweetneſs to moderate the ſharpneſs of my Choler, and ſoften my Melancholy. Monſieur *St. Preuil* promis'd to aſſiſt me with all his heart, in getting ſome Money from the King, and told me, I might ſafely impart to him any contrivance I could make uſe of to that purpoſe.

Neceſſity quickens a man's invention, and I was not long in forming the expedient I ſtood in need of ; but preſently told him, that being he was to go to *Taillebourg*, where the King then was, he muſt take the pains to write me a Letter from thence, and there acquaint me with his reſolution to buy this Company, and that I would return an anſwer to it, full of grievous complaints of the injuſtice done me. That afterwards he might ſpeak to the Duke of *St. Simon* in my favour, and ſhew him my Letter, that he might ſhew it to the King, and by making him underſtand the juſtice of my complaints, might at leaſt procure me a recompence for the cauſe that was given me to complain. Monſieur *St. Preuil* engag'd to do ſo, and to ſerve me the beſt he could. And accordingly he writ to me from *Taillebourg*, as we had agreed before ; which I anſwer'd by another complaining one, writing him word, that I ſhould be the moſt unhappy man in the world, if this Company went ſo out of the hands of one, who had receiv'd it from the King's meer bounty ; that I ſhould have nothing left to hope for, ſince it would be always ſold at this rate ; that I was not concern'd he ſhould be the Buyer, but that it was ſuffer'd to be bought at all ; that the grief to ſee all my pretenſions ruined was ſo violent and ſo juſt, that I could not quickly overcome it, nor lay aſide the reſentment I ought to have ; that he ſhut the door of his Majeſty's liberality againſt me ; but that when I had ſuffer'd this injuſtice for the love I bore him, I might perhaps at one time or other declare my
reſentment

resentment more openly. Monsieur *St. Preuil* shew'd my Letter to the
Duke of *St. Simon*, and spoke to him in my behalf according to the agreement betwixt us. The Duke shew'd it to the King, and seeing his Majesty begin to be angry, he told him, that really there was a great deal to
be said in my excuse, if I did complain, finding my self thus disappoint-
ed; that he did beseech his Majesty to surprize me with some unexpected
favour; that complaints being the natural effects of grief, they were
allowable when the cause of that grief was just; that I was one of his
Majesty's most faithful Servants, one that had expos'd my life in a hundred engagements, that carry'd many honourable scars about me, and
deserv'd a Company in his Guards as well as any Gentleman in *France*.
The King a little calm'd with this discourse, reply'd, 'Tis true, he is a
brave man, and it is but just to consider him a little upon this occasion.
After which he sent an Order to Monsieur *Deffiat* to pay me four thousand Franks.

But still he was not satisfy'd with my Letter. And when I came to
him at *Surgeres* a little after, he gave me to understand by his silence and
coldness, that he was displeased with me. Not knowing then, whither
I ought to speak, or hold my tongue, fearing on one side, that if I spoke
I should be thought insolent, and if I said nothing it might look like guilt;
at last however I chose the latter, and resolv'd to try if by silence and
submission I could overcome the good nature of the King. At Supper
the Count of *Soissons*, who was upon no very good terms with his Majesty,
came to wait on him, and after a little discourse took his leave, and all
the rest of the great Lords one after another went away. Still I staid,
hoping by my perseverance to oblige the King to speak to me, and knowing that he took it well to have people assiduous about his person. But
my patience at last was quite worn out, and being inwardly vext to see
the King keep on a coldness toward me so long, as soon as he rose
from the Table I fell at his knees, and told him, that my fear to displease
his Majesty, and the confusion which the remembrance of my fault gave
me, had oblig'd me till then to keep silence, but I hop'd he would permit me now to ask his pardon most humbly for my passions and complaints.
Ho ho! (said the King roundly to me) who then put you upon writing
such a huffing Letter? I reply'd, that his Majesty having given me hopes
of the Company he had bestow'd on Count *Saligny*, and Monsieur *St.
Preuil* having since bought it, I knew very well, that he would not do
him an injury, in giving me what another had bought. Whereupon
the King ask'd me, what I complain'd of then. It had been easy to tell
his Majesty, that this was the very reason of my complaint, that having
given his word to gratify me with that Command; he had suffer'd it to
be sold; but this was no time to insist upon the justice of my cause, and it
was better to take a more submissive course; and therefore laying all the
fault at my own door, I made answer, I had no body to complain of but
my self, and I most humbly begg'd his Majesty's Pardon for having offended him. The King who pretended to be more angry than he really
was, suffering himself to be easily overcome, said to me, Be more temperate another time, and do not complain thus of having injustice done
you. I have commanded *Deffiat* to give you four thousand Livres.

VII. I was well satisfy'd with this gentle reproof, having great reason
to apprehend very scurvy consequences of this affair. But going to get
my self paid this gift of the King's, I had like to have spoil'd all by a
false

falfe piece of Gallantry. Meeting with a Commiffioner of Monfieur *Deffiat* who told me, the Superintendent would fpeak with me, I prefently went, believing it was to pay me the four thoufand Livres; and accordingly he told me, I was much oblig'd to the King's bounty, who had remembred my fervices, and order'd him to give me four thoufand Livres. I anfwer'd, that I acknowledg'd my obligations to his Majefty with all due refpect, but if he would give me leave to fpeak my thoughts, though four thoufand Livres might appear fomething confiderable for me to receive, yet it was but a fmall matter for fo great a Prince to give. I thought Monfieur *Deffiat* would have taken my meaning right in what I faid fo freely, and prefently have offer'd me his fervice, to perfwade the King to fomething more, and the kindnefs he had all along profeft for me, was what might juftify my expecting this from him; but I was much furpriz'd to find all my hopes and my policy baffled. For he fell on a fudden into a violent paffion, reproaching me in very harfh language, with ingratitude, and the unbecoming returns I made for his Majefty's bounty. Then I faw my fault too late, and thinking of nothing more but how to repair it, inftead of folliciting a new grant, I begg'd him to excufe me, if the neceffity I was in of being at great expence to fubfift honourably upon my Command, had put me upon taking this liberty with him; affuring him it was only the confidence I had in his goodnefs and favour, that had encourag'd me to fpeak after that manner, and that, as to any thing elfe, I had all my life, and ever fhould retain, a due and grateful fenfe of his Majefty's liberality to me.

The Commiffioner I mention'd, who was a very good friend of mine, began then to take my part, and endeavour'd to appeafe Monfieur *Deffiat*; telling him in confirmation of what I had faid before, that the ftation I was in about the King expos'd me to great charges above my fortune, that I was forc'd to run in debt continually, and fo it was rather for my Creditors than my felf that I was urgent for Money; that I was indebted to himfelf four thoufand Franks, and he had an Intereft in the Kings gift to me. This laft however was faid only in kindnefs to me, that by making his Mafter his own debtor, he might preferve what the King had already given at leaft, which was in fome danger of being loft too. But with all that both of us could fay, we had much ado to appeafe the Superintendant, who appear'd perhaps a little more fevere towards others, than he was to himfelf; for 'tis fure he was not of a difpofition apt to think the Kings bounty guilty of any exceffes, when his own fervices were rewarded. At laft however, being intreated, and follicited by feveral confiderable perfons, he promis'd to do me no ill office to the King, but to ferve me as far as it lay in his power.

Some days after, being upon Guard with my Company at Sea on board one of his Majefty's Ships, the *Rochellers* fent out four Fire-fhips to burn our Veffels. When I faw them bearing down upon us, I order'd all my men to put out Hand-fpikes, and fet them like a Hedge to keep them off. This was immediately done, and fo the Fire-fhips were ftopt, and not able to get within us, or do us any harm, and all their artificial fires play'd inwards, without flying out upon us. The King at a diftance faw all that paft, as he was going to walk upon the Beach; and fending Count *Nogent* for me, would know from my own mouth what method I had taken for our defence againft thofe Fire-fhips: And being a Prince of a noble nature, he was glad of this occafion to tell me that he abfolutely forgave my laft fault. And when I had given him an account of our behaviour

viour

viour in this action, he said with a smiling countenance, that he was satisfy'd with me, and my services pleas'd him well. The Duke of *St. Simon*, who was by, immediately after gave me to understand what the King meant by saying so; telling me that I must live in good understanding with Monsieur *St. Preuil*, and that he would serve me to the King upon any occasion.

VIII. Having given an account before of Monsieur *Canaples* his displeasure against me, and the cause of it, with some other particulars that happen'd since, I am now oblig'd to speak of the great falling out we had some months after, and during the same Siege of *Rochelle*. Going one day to view a place proper to set a Guard in, about four hundred paces distant from the Sea-shore, I saw from that eminence Masts of Ships a great way off, that lookt like Spires of Steeples. I was a little surpriz'd at first, to think what it might be, but after considering a little, and counting to fourteen, I concluded it must be the *English* Fleet, commanded by the Lord . . . . . whom all the world hath heard of. Therefore riding full speed to the Kings Quarter, to make a report of what I had seen, I said it could be nothing else but the *English* Navy. The King having discover'd the whole Fleet from the Garret of his Lodgings, (the bravest and stoutest Fleet for both the number and prodigious bulk of Ships, that had ever been known) commanded me to go and give notice to the Officers, to come and receive his Orders, that all the Army might be in a readiness to engage this Fleet, in case it should make any attempt; and at the same time he bid me afterwards go and chuse out a fit place, wherein to draw up the Regiments in Battaille. Being come to Monsieur *Canaples* Quarter, who was my *Maistre de Camp*, I told him the King had commanded me to give him notice to draw up his Regiment, by reason of the arrival of the *English* Fleet. But the Major of the Regiment being very sick, and his Deputy that day a little out of order too, besides that he understood but little of the business, Monsieur *Canaples* desir'd me to go and put the Regiment in Battaille my self. I told him, that as soon as ever I had executed the Kings Orders, who had commanded me to go view the field, I would not fail to obey his; but entreated him withal to remember, that it was my turn to command the Forlorn-hope that day; for since my entring into the Regiment of Guards, there had no occasion offer'd it self for me to command them; and 'tis well enough known, that those employments, tho full of danger, are lookt upon as posts of honour, and such as a man never gives up to any body whatsoever. Monsieur *Canaples* promis'd me to remember, and not dispose of that Command to any other. Upon this promise I left my *Maistre de Camp*, not apprehending that a man of honour would fail me in a thing that was my due, and especially upon so important an occasion. I went afterwards to chuse the ground, whither all the Companies both of the Regiment of Guards, and *Swisses*, repair'd in a trice. There I form'd all the Battalions, plac'd every Company in its post, every Souldier in his rank, and the Officers at the head of them, to encourage the Souldiers by their example, and have the first and greatest share, both of the hazzard, and of the Conquest.

IX. After having thus with my utmost diligence obey'd the Kings Orders, I return'd to Monsieur *Canaples*, to give an account of what I had done; and hard by his Lodging met my intimate friend Monsieur *Savig-*

nac, Lieutenant to Monfieur *Rhoderick*'s Company, who told me for good news, that he was going to his Poft, and had receiv'd Monfieur *Canaples* his Order to command the Forlorn-hope. You may guefs what a furprize I was in to fee fuch a flight put upon me, in failing of the promife that had been made me in this bufinefs; and I fancy my paffion will appear excufable, fince fuch an affront requir'd a very fteady vertue to fupport it with patience, in a man of Courage: Efpecially fince it was that time my opinion that Heaven always declared for him, who when his honour was injur'd, repell'd the offence by force of arms. Monfieur *Savignac* had no fooner faid fo, but I anfwer'd in heat, How! hath Monfieur *Canaples* given you that Order? He cannot do it, he hath promis'd it me, and befides it is my right: This were to act contrary to his own Word, and to Juftice. I askt it not of him, reply'd he, fpeak to Monfieur *Canaples*, perhaps he will give you fome other employment; I pray be not angry till you have heard his reafons. No, no, faid I in great fury, a man can have no reafon for acting contrary to Juftice, and his own Word; I will have no other employment but that which belongs to me, and that cannot be given you juftly, which cannot without injuftice be taken from me. Monfieur *Savignac*, who lov'd me very well, but did not think he ought to yield to me upon fuch an occafion, faid to me, Look you Sir, I made no fuit for it, it was given me voluntarily, and without a particular Order I cannot leave it.

Thereupon taking it for granted that Monfieur *Canaples* had put this affront upon me defignedly, fince it was not poffible he fhould have forgot in fo fhort a time what he promis'd me but juft before; I went to feek him out, fmothering my refentment, and taking no notice that I knew any thing. I told him the Regiment was in Battaille, and when he pleas'd to come to it, he would find all in order according to the Kings command. And now Sir, faid I, I doubt not but you have remembred me. About what? faid he. The command of the Forlornhope, that you promis'd, and which of right belongs to me to day, faid I. At which putting on great furprize, Oh! truly I have given it to Monfieur *Savignac*, I am very forry for't, but in earneft I forgot. I, who had a mind to fhew him that I was more angry than he was forry, made anfwer a little roughly, How Sir, forgot! Is it poffible a man of honour fhould fo foon forget his promife? I know not how to help it, faid he, I did not remember it. Seeing him dally thus with me, I raifing my voice, reply'd, You perhaps forgot it Sir, becaufe you would forget it; but it fhall not pafs fo, for if you have forgot your promife, I very well remember that it is my place, and am refolv'd not to lofe it. What would you have me do? faid he, the Orders are already given. Change the Orders Sir, faid I, if you pleafe. Would you have me (reply'd he) be unjuft to another, in taking away a poft that I have given him? How! Sir, faid I, louder than before, you have been unjuft to me before, in taking from me what was my right, and what you promis'd I fhould have. Why, what would you have me do? faid he, very angrily; I cannot change the Orders, get you gone to the Regiment. Yes Sir, faid I, I will go, and go to the head of the Forlorn-hope; you have given me your word, the faith of a Gentleman, and a man of honour. I have done what you commanded me, and you have not been juft to your word. I declare to you Sir, that I am refolv'd to dye rather than part with what is my due; you fhall fee ftrange work. I have not eaten the Kings bread fo long, not to fhew him in fuch an occafion of danger as this, that he has not been miftaken

in

in the choice he has made of me to be near his person. All that troubles me is, that I have spoke to you of a thing I should not have spoke to you about. Monsieur, Monsieur *de Pontis*, said he, consider who 'tis you speak to. At which, raising my voice yet higher, I know very well Sir, said I to him, that I speak to a person, who engag'd his faith and his word to me, and hath fail'd in both. Whereupon Monsieur *Canaples*, enrag'd to the last degree, to see himself so us'd by an Officer of his own Regiment, reply'd, Get you gone, you are an insolent fellow. Sir, said I, the respect I owe you, with-holds me from saying a thing, that would very much displease you ; but, said I, drawing my Sword a little way, and clapping it down again, Here is that shall one day do me right. Monsieur *Canaples*, extremely surpriz'd at this menace, said to me, I suspend you from your Command. But I, knowing he pretended to a thing out of his power, reply'd calmly, Sir, you usurp an authority that does not belong to you, while the King is present, none but he can suspend me.

X. Thereupon I left him, and seeing this affair was like to be of dangerous consequence, if I did not prevent it, thought it my best course to make haste, and acquaint the King with it. Accordingly I went and told him, that while I was executing his Majesty's command, Monsieur *Canaples* had given away my post to another. The King, who was then very busie in giving all the necessary Orders for the Army, had not leisure to hear me, and therefore referr'd me to the Duke of *Espernon*, as Collonel of the *French* Infantry. I lost no time, and had none to lose, in the great bustle and hurry every one was in, and therefore went immediately to the Duke, to whom I gave an account of my dispute with Monsieur *Canaples*, for having executed the Kings Orders, and his own : Telling him, that having addrest my self to the King, his Majesty had referr'd me to him to do me Justice, being himself so busie in giving out Orders, that he had no leisure to hear me ; and therefore I humbly begg'd his Lordship to give me the post that belong'd to me. Monsieur *Espernon* made answer, that this was no fit time to decide such controversies, the Enemy being in sight ; and publick busines being always to be preferr'd before private : that when the fight was over, they should be at leisure to consider my case, and to do both of us Justice. But, my Lord, said I, what will become of me, he hath interdicted me my Command. Oh, said Monsieur *Espernon*, that is what he cannot do, while the King is present, that belongs only to him ; and when I am present, and the King away, it belongs only to me. Go tell Monsieur *Canaples* from me, that he must permit you to exercise your Command, and this difference shall be decided, when that we have now in hand with the Enemy is decided. This word of the Duke's put me in some heart again, but considering that it would not be proper to carry it to Monsieur *Canaples* my self, for fear of making things worse, and quarrelling afresh, I presented my Table-book, and entreated his Lordship that he would please to write in them himself, the message he would have delivered to Monsieur *Canaples* ; telling him, I was afraid if I should go back to acquaint him with his Lordships pleasure, that he might fall into a passion with me ; and then I might perhaps forget the respect that was due to him. Monsieur *Espernon* then writ in my Table-book, and sent to Monsieur *Canaples*, to permit me quietly to exercize my Command ; and thus being very well content to see my self supported by the Collonel, I went away to the Regiment.

Meet-

Meeting my Captain *St. Preuil* by the way, I gave him a short account
of the matter, according to the short time I had to do it in, deliver'd
him Monfieur *Efpernon*'s Order, and entreated him to carry it to Monfieur *Canaples*, with all the fpeed he could. After which I went to take
my poft that had been deny'd me; and by great good fortune, Monfieur
Savignac, to whom this poft had been given in my wrong, was not there
when I came : For tho we were very good friends, I was refolv'd not
to lofe my place, and Moufieur *Savignac* would have been as refolute as
I, to keep what had been given to him.

XI. But it happen'd unluckily, that Monfieur *Canaples*, who was making the round of the Regiment of Guards. juft as I took my poft, faw
me at a diftance, before he had receiv'd the Duke of *Efpernon*'s Letter.
He made up to me inftantly upon a round gallop, with his Cane in his
hand, and thinking to fright me with threats, cry'd out as he came, I
fhall remove you with a vengeance, I'll make you quit that poft. I being not of a humour to be eafily affrighted with big words, let him come
within thirty or forty paces, and then call'd out to him to advance no
nearer : Do not go about to offer me an affront Sir, faid I, for I am abfolutely refolv'd not to endure it : What right have you to take that
from me, which the King has given me ? Upon this, leaping out of his
Saddle, and drawing his Sword, he came up to me, as if it had been my
duty to fuffer my felf to be beaten and abus'd; but being willing to fave
him that trouble, I drew mine too, and advanc'd half way to meet him,
with a refolution not to attack him, but only to defend my felf. I confefs
this was an extraordinary proceeding, and fuch as might appear a capital offence, for a Lieutenant to draw upon his *Maiftre de Camp*, at the
head of the whole Army : But thinking my felf backt by the authority
of the King, and the Collonel, and being like to be aflaulted, and for
ever difhonoured, without having committed any other fault than obeying the Kings Orders, I thought of nothing but getting quit of this
fcurvy bufinefs, tho it fhould coft me my head.

The Duke of *Angoulefme* and fome other great Lords, being come in
to us, when we had made two or three paffes at one another, parted us;
and there the matter refted, till we faw the *Englifh* Fleet come to an An-
chor in the Road, without preparing for any manner of Engagement.
But then Monfieur *Canaples*, enrag'd to the laft degree, at the affront he
thought he had receiv'd in the fight of the whole Army, refolv'd to go
immediately to the King, that he might prepoffefs him about this bufinefs. I faw him take Horfe, and prefently guefs his defign, and knowing
of what confequence it was to prevent him, mounted the beft Horfe I
had inftantly, refolving, if I could, to get thither before Monfieur *Canaples*. But he, knowing me to be a little hot, and fufpecting I would
follow him, took a by-way, and left the direct one to me; by which
means he arriv'd firft, and related the whole matter to his Majefty, wholly to his own advantage, telling him that I attempted to affaffinate him,
and drew upon him at the head of the Regiment. But he did not tell
him that he himfelf had firft attempted to take away my Honour, and
perhaps my Life too, in the prefence of fo many honourable witneffes.
He aggravated my fault all that poffibly he could, and told his Majefty,
that if Juftice were not done upon it, all Military difcipline would be
utterly confounded, and loft; that there could be no more fafety to be
expected, either for the Officer from private Souldiers, or for the *Maiftre*
                                                                    de

de Camp and Generals from the meaneſt Officers in the Army. The King made anſwer, that he wovld not obſtruct Juſtice; but that he would have him go to Monſieur *Eſpernon*, and let him inform himſelf of the buſineſs.

I came into the room juſt as Monſieur *Canaples* went out, but found the King ſtrongly prejudic'd againſt me; for I no ſooner open'd my mouth, but he told me with great ſeverity, *Canaples* hath told it me already, 'tis a ſcurvy buſineſs for you, if it be as he informs me. Sir, replies I, your Majeſty knows that better than any body. If you have a mind to inform your ſelf, and will be pleas'd to hear me, your Majeſty will then ſee that I have done nothing but for your ſervice, and by your Order : I moſt humbly beſeech you Sir, to call to mind the Order you gave me. Well, well, ſaid the King, go to Monſieur d' *Eſpernon*, and tell him I ſent you, and will talk with him about it. I went accordingly as faſt as I could, hoping to find ſome acceſs with the Duke, becauſe of the Order he had given me for Monſieur *Canaples*, but was ſtrangely ſurpriz'd to find him yet leſs diſpos'd to hear me than the King. Aſſoon as ever I came in, he ſaid, O Monſieur *Pontis*, Monſieur *Canaples* hath ſpoke to me about your affair, there is now a ſtrange confuſion among the Officers of the Army : There is no ſuch thing as ſubmiſſion or dependance left among them : The Enſigns will turn Lieutenants, the Lieutenants Captains, the Captains are *Maiſtres de Camp*, and the *Maiſtres de Camp* will be Collonels : I ſhall take good care to hinder theſe diſorders : I wonder how you dare appear before me. I come hither, my Lord, ſaid I, under the King's protection; he hath ſent me to tell you, that he will diſcourſe you upon this buſineſs. You have done wiſely, reply'd the Duke, to come to me from the King, for otherwiſe I ſhould have laid you by the heels, to have given you leiſure to think of what you could ſay in juſtification of your crime. Seeing then no defence left me but that of humility and ſubmiſſion, I humbly begg'd of him, not to condemn me upon the ſingle report of my Adverſary, and without firſt hearing what I had to ſay for my ſelf. I conjur'd him to conſider, that the innocent are often oppreſt by the authority of their Enemies, who will have every thing paſs for a fault, that oppoſes their injuſtice; and all men Criminals, who defend themſelves from their oppreſſions. I hope, my Lord, ſaid I, if you will pleaſe to hear the truth of the whole matter from unprejudic'd perſons, you will excuſe my misfortune, and your ſelf undertake my defence, and think me more worthy of your compaſſion, than your anger. I beſeech you, my Lord, to remember the Letter you did me the favour to write in my behalf to Monſieur *Canaples*, wherein you blam'd him for preſuming to ſuſpend me, when the King and you were preſent in the Army; and commanded him from the King to let me alone in the free diſcharge of my Command. When after this he went about to diſhonour me, againſt the Kings, and your Lordſhips expreſs Order, I conceiv'd that both the King, and you your ſelf, my Lord, had put the Sword in my hand, to repell the injury that was offer'd to the Kings authority, and at the ſame time to defend my ſelf from the affront they would have put upon me.

Theſe reaſons were of force to work upon Monſieur *Eſpernon*, whoſe honour and authority ſeem'd to be engaged in my quarrel; but he not being then at leiſure to conſider of it, and poſſeſt too by what Monſieur *Canaples* had told him, and in regard my action appear'd really very foul and odious in it ſelf, when all the circumſtances were laid aſide, that

might

might make it appear more excufable, I plainly perceiv'd that he was very ill difpos'd toward me, and that I ought to take my leave. And withal, thinking my felf not very fafe, I refolv'd to withdraw to Marefchal *Schomberg,* who hath ever done me the honour to love me, and to protect me with extraordinary kindnefs and favour.

XII. Then it was that I began to reflect on the inconftancy of mens fortune : I figh'd heartily to fee, that after ferving the world fo faithfully fo many years, I fhould be fo ill rewarded by it, that after expofing my life a thoufand times in the fervice of my Prince, I was now like to lofe it ignominioufly by the rigour of publick Juftice; or at leaft to pafs the remainder of it in exile and oblivion. I reprefented to my felf the mifery of a fugitive, and a vagabond, who fears every thing, hath nothing to hope, looks upon all Creatures as combin'd againft him to render him unhappy, and one that can only expect from death the end of all his miferies and misfortunes. And indeed I never wifht to dye but that day, for then I thought death the greateft good fortune that could have befallen me, fearing above all things the hand of Juftice, and almoft as much as that, to live wretchedly, out of the Court, and my native Country. Such were the thoughts meerly humane, and the low confiderations that wholly poffeft my mind. I was not then fenfible, that it is a happinefs for a man who hath liv'd long in Courts and Armies, to be oblig'd to leave them, and driven to think of fomething more ferious, to dedicate the remainder of his life at leaft to God, when the World will have no more to do with him. But God was pleafed thus at a diftance, and by degrees, to prepare me for renouncing the world, by giving me a tafte of its bitternefs; and tho I did not then apprehend it, yet the various afflictions he try'd me with were fo many earnefts of his mercy to me. While I was thus intent upon my felf, with regard to the outward confequences of this extremity, to which I was then reduc'd, God was pleafed to look upon me, and infpire me with a thought of begging his affiftance. This made me with deep fighs fay, Lord thou knoweft my mifery, and I know thy mercy, take upon thee my defence, for I have no defender. My prayer was fhort, but my devotion was ardent and fincere. But my grief and difquiet were fo exceffive, that within a few days I was fo chang'd, as hardly to be known; my very hair turn'd grey in that fhort time; and I am fure none who have not experimentally known what it is for a man of Honour and Courage to fee himfelf reduc'd to fear the hand of a common Executioner, can be a competent Judge of the condition I was in.

XIII. When I had withdrawn to Marefchal *Schomberg*'s houfe, they began to examine my bufinefs. The ufual informations were made, and the Drum beat throughout all the Quarters to cite me to a perfonal appearance; but I, chufing rather to pafs for a Criminal when at Liberty, than to furrender my felf up a Prifoner, and be expos'd to all the violent defigns of my Enemies, was interdicted and cafhiered, and all Souldies and Officers of the Regiment were forbid to own me for an Officer.

The Proceedings when concluded were carry'd to Monfieur *Efpernou,* as Collonel of the Infantry, and fo the principal Judge. He fpoke of it to the King, who not being able utterly to caft off the extraordinary goodnefs he had ever had for me, and defigning to fave my Life, had a mind not to oppofe Juftice publickly, but to fpin the Caufe out as long as he could, that so when time had qualify'd mens Spirits, he might the more easily grant my Pardon, without being blamed by the principal Officers of the Army, whose authority seem'd to be concern'd for my punishment. The King therefore answer'd the Duke of *Espernon*, that they were to have the opinion of the Mareschals of *France*, and the principal Officers of the Army; and so the business was ended.

But that which made very much for my Justification, was the extraordinary generosity of Mareschal *Crequy*, Monsieur *Canaples* his Father, who as soon as ever he heard of our quarrel, declar'd highly in my favour against his own Son. He condemn'd Monsieur *Canaples* publickly, as a person that broke his word, and commended what I had done, as an argument of my Courage, and repelling an extraordinary injury by an extraordinary action. This declaration from Mareschal *Crequy*, who thus renounc'd his natural inclination for the sake of Justice, was of very great weight in my Cause; for it could not easily be imagin'd, that a Father would pronounce against his own Son, if he could have found any Justice on his side. Nevertheless my business was examin'd in the Council.

In the mean while Mareschal *Schomberg* wrought privately with the King, to have compassion upon an Officer, who had serv'd him all along with so great fidelity and zeal; and to incline him to order it so that all things might be compos'd. The King, as I said, was pretty well inclined to this of his own accord, and had often spoken of it to several people; but every body answer'd cautiously, fearing on one side to offend his Majesty, and doubting on the other lest they should offend Monsieur *Canaples*, who was a person of great Interest and Power. There was one however that spoke his thoughts freely to the King upon this subject: But this mans opinion was as base and unworthy, as Mareschal *Crequy's*, my adversary's Father, was generous. He had formerly been my Captain, under *Henry* the Great, when I was a young Cadet in the Regiment of Guards. And the King being pleas'd one day to do him the honor to unbosom himself to him upon my concern, said, You have known *Pontis* longer than any body: He seems to me to be patient, tho he be a little hot and provencal; doubtless he must have been highly provok'd, what think you? This was plainly to declare himself for me, and to engage this Officer to speak favourably of a man, whose cause the King himself had taken upon him to defend; but he, contrary to all people's expectation, had the ill nature to answer the King, that though it had been his own Son, that had committed such an action, he would condemn it as criminal even in his Son. The King, who look'd for another kind of answer, and that his own opinion ought to have met with more respect, gave some significations of his being much surpriz'd at so rude a return, and went off toward the Window, without saying any thing at all: This was in effect to condemn a man severely, whom his Majesty had by his own question absolv'd; and there's no great doubt to be made, but his Vote had been sold against me, or he would never have exprest himself at that rate upon such an occasion. And indeed after the matter was absolutely determin'd, and my Pardon obtain'd, he several times made me great excuses, which serv'd really only to aggravate his own Condemnation.

XIV. While my affair lay before the Council, Monsieur *Hallier*, then a Captain in the Guards of the Body, who hath since been made Mareschal of *France*, and Governour of *Paris*, under the name of *de l'Hospital*; and

Monsieur

Monsieur _d'Eſtiſſac_, _Maiſtre de Camp_ of a Regiment of Infantry, either came, or ſent to me every day, to give me notice of all that was ſaid in Council, or in the King's ordinary Diſcourſe concerning my buſineſs; ſhewing by this good office the particular kindneſs they had for me, even in the time of my greateſt diſgrace. And by this means too, I knew who were my true, and who my falſe friends; and who my declar'd enemies. I knew there were in the Council eight and forty Judges againſt me, Princes and Mareſchals of _France_, Dukes and Peers, Collonels, Mareſchals _de Camp_, and _Maiſtres de Camp_; the reaſon of which was, that theſe great Officers were willing by favouring Monſieur _Canaples_, to raiſe the authority of their own Commands, and to render themſelves more formidable to the Captains, Lieutenants and Enſigns. Thus were they in ſome ſort both Judges and Parties, and had a mind to make me an example, for fear, if this boldneſs of drawing upon a _Maiſtre de Camp_ were authoriz'd by eſcaping unpuniſhed, that they ſhould hereafter find more reſiſtance than ſubmiſſion among the inferior Officers; and ſo be often engag'd to fight like private Gentlemen, inſtead of making themſelves obey'd by vertue of the King's authority.

And I muſt confeſs their fear had been juſt, if the circumſtances of my action had not abſolutely ſecur'd me from this reproach, and made it plain to all the world, that if an inferiour Officer is never permitted to draw his Sword upon the perſon that commands him, a _Maiſtre de Camp_ is no more allowed to break his word with one that is commanded by him, and without any manner of Juſtice, contrary to the King's, and the Collonel General's Order, to take from him that rank which belongs to him by his Command.

But at the ſame time that ſo great a number of perſons declared themſelves for my death, I had the comfort to ſee a great many others take my part to the laſt, and make my cauſe their own. Beſides thoſe I have named, Count _Soiſſons_ a Prince of the Blood, ſent to invite me to retire at his Lodgings, aſſuring me of his protection, and that as long as he had life he would preſerve mine. Monſieur _Thoyras_, Governour of Fort _St. Martin_ in the Iſle of _Rhé_, ſent me a tender of his ſervice, and begg'd of me to come into that Iſland, where he promis'd me all imaginable ſecurity. But Mareſchal _Schomberg_ advis'd me not to ſtir out of his houſe, by reaſon of the favour the King ſhewed in my concern. So that returning my thanks to thoſe Gentlemen, with all the reſpect and acknowledgment due for ſuch honourable and advantagious offers, I ſtill continued where I was.

At laſt the King being eternally importun'd by Monſieur _Schomberg_, and put forward by his own inclination too, ſent me word by Monſieur _Schomberg_ that I might retire into his Quarter, which he gave me for my refuge. But fearing every thing in the condition I was then in, and apprehending above all, leſt I ſhould fall into the hands of Juſtice, I contented my ſelf with ſtaying in the King's Quarter in the day time, and retir'd my ſelf at night in the Mareſchal's.

XV. One day as I was walking in the _Baſſe-Court_ of the King's Lodgings, with Monſieur _Montigny_ and _Marſillac_, both Captains in the Guards, theſe two Officers told me, they would not adviſe me to ſtay any longer in the Camp, for as long as I paſt for criminal, I was always in danger, and if ever I came to be arreſted, there would be an end of me. Nay, Monſieur _Marſillac_ offer'd me an hundred Piſtoles, and Monſieur _Montigny_ fifty,

fifty, entreating me, as I lov'd them, to accept the offer. I told them I had two hundred left, and that their kindness was what I valu'd much more, than the Gold they made me a tender of just then; the King putting his Head out at Window perceiv'd me, and becken'd me to come to him, but as unhappy people see every thing by the fear that possesses them, and my mind was full of the fright these Officers had put me into, I took this sign from the King in the worst sense, and believing it to be a manace, was perfectly confounded; Did you see the King threaten me? said I. You told me as much. I am a dead man. I must flee for it. You'll never see me more. At that instant, without any farther deliberation, I embrac'd them, and out I went, betook my self to my Heels, and fled, as if all had been lost. I look'd all about for my Man and my Horse, but could find neither, which made me quite mad, and I concluded now that I was deliver'd up into the hands of Justice. I repented my self of going into the King's Quarters at all; and not knowing at last whom to blame, I discharg'd all my anger upon my man who was missing, resolving with my self to be very liberal of my Cudgel, as soon as ever I could set my eyes on him. But while all things seem'd to conspire to trouble me more, as I was thus running up and down among the Sutlers, like a Mad-man, to seek my Servant, and could not find him, I was frighted more than ever to see a man come running and calling after me: It was a young fellow call'd *Cadet*, that belong'd to the Kings Chamber, whom his Majesty had sent to assure me all was well, and to fetch me to him. I thought he pursu'd me with an ill intent, and therefore fell to running faster than I had done before. At last however coming a little to my self, and beginning to fancy I might have taken a false alarm, I stopt. The man came up and told me, The King had sent for me to him. I askt what people said of me? at which he fell a laughing, and answer'd merrily, Why they say that you have taken a fright, and have led me a fine course: But what are you afraid of? The King would only speak with you. I have had this day the satisfaction of seeing Monsieur *Pontis* run away from me. Then I presently resolv'd to go wait upon the King, tho the trouble and agitation both of my mind and my body had been so excessive, that I had sweat to that degree, that it appear'd on the outside of my Doublet.

I had no great need of consideration what I should say to the King. My retirement had given me but too much leisure for revolving in my mind every thing that might serve to prove my innocency. And having always hoped that at one time or other the King would give me liberty to justifie my self before him, I had meditated and prepared an exact narration; wherein following only common sense, I had put together, all that a Souldier (who had liv'd thirty years about Court, and had no other Eloquence than what Nature gave him) could say, that was plausible to render such an action less odious; and to cloath it with all those circumstances, that could make the Justice of his Cause appear.

XVI. So soon as I came into the Court of the Kings Lodgings, the Duke of *St. Simon*, who was looking out at window, made a sign to me to come up the stairs by the Wardrobe; and when I was there he told me, the King had sent for me to learn the truth of the whole matter from my own mouth. The King was laid down, by reason of some little physick he had taken. Being come to the Bed-side I fell upon my knees, and in my countenance plainly discover'd the remorse I had for

L l   having

having offended my Prince, who had ever been so gracious to me. His Majesty then told me, he would have me declare the whole truth without any disguise; and that he had sent for me purely for the same purpose.

There was all that time no body present in the room but the King, the Duke of *St. Simon*, and my self; so that having an opportunity of speaking freely to him, I did it after this manner:

Sir, I can never sufficiently thank your Majesty, for the grace and honour you are pleased to do me, in permitting me to render you an account of my actions; for I have ever hoped from your Majesty's goodness, that would you vouchsafe to hear me, you would judge me rather unfortunate than faulty. I dare boldly say, that if my Conscience could reproach me with having failed in my duty, or ever disobeying your Majesty's orders, I should never have had the boldness to present my self before you; and that I should voluntarily have banish'd my self both from your Court and Army; and have sought death out of your Kingdom, for in it I could not have liv'd after I had lost my Honour. So that tho those in the Council of War, who are either friends to Monsieur Canaples, or have not been rightly informed of the truth of the matter, have declared against me; yet I hope your Majesty being so equitable as all the world knows you to be, will judge things as they are, and as I shall lay them before you; That it was Monsieur Canaples only, who acted contrary to your Majesty's orders, to the Rules of War, and his own Honour; and that, whereas he complains of my having done him an injury, 'tis he on the contrary who hath injured me. Your Majesty knows I have always told you the truth, but I protest afresh, that upon this occasion I will not utter one syllable, not only that is not true, but nothing except what your whole Regiment of Guards know to be so, as well as I, and what Monsieur Canaples himself cannot but acknowledge for such.

Your Majesty may please to call to mind, that having brought you the news of the English Fleet's arrival, you commanded me to go give notice to the Officers to go and receive your Majesty's Orders, and afterwards to make choice of a fit place to draw up the Army in Battaille. Thereupon I went immediately to carry this Order to the Officers, and acquainted Monsieur Canaples with it among the rest. He entreated me to go draw up our Regiment my self, because our Major was sick. I told him I would first execute your Majesty's Orders, and when that was done, I would not fail to obey his. But it being my turn to command the Forlorn-hope that day, having never yet done it, since I had the honour to be received into the Regiment, I entreated him to remember it, telling him the passionate desire I had, by some considerable piece of service, to acknowledge the singular favour your Majesty had done me, in commanding me to be near your person, and in preferring me of your own accord to be a Lieutenant in your Guards. He promis'd me he would, and upon that assurance I left him. When I had obeyed your Majesty's Orders first, and then his, I return'd to give him an account of the whole, and at the same time to beg the effect of his promise, asking him if he had remembred me? But he at first made as if he did not understand what I meant; and after I had explained my self to him, he shew'd me as plainly that he had forgotten me. I beseech your Majesty to consider, whether it was possible for a man of honour, as Monsieur Canaples is, to forget in so short a time the promise he had made me but just before; and whether this was not plainly to tell me, he had forgot me, only because he would forget me.

I confess, Sir, I was sensibly touch't with this injury, and found my self nettled to see that Monsieur Canaples had not only used me like a pitiful fellow, and a Foot-man, in breaking his word with me; but besides that he usurp'd a power which no way belong'd to him, to take from me the rank your Majesty had given me; and meerly out of a design to affront me, to change the general and establish'd order of your Army. I thought, Sir, that Monsieur Canaples was not allowed to set himself above your Majesty, nor by his own private authority to take from me that right, which my Command and my Rank made mine, and which I have endeavour'd to deserve. This affront, Sir, wounded me more than all the injurious words he could give me in the heat of passion; and I humbly beg your Majesty's pardon, if I told him, that he toucht me in the tenderest part, and made me mad: For I saw very well, that he used me so in cold blood, and that the affront he put upon me was a premeditated one. I do also Sir confess, for I dare conceal nothing from your Majesty, who command me to speak freely, that in the heat of my passion, I could not forbear giving him some language that was a little rude, the better to represent the injury he did me; but if I failed something in the respect due from me to him, as my Maistre de Camp, he first failed in that which he owes to your Majesty, and his own word. And therefore I think I may say, that his fault was greater, and less excuseable than mine; because, Sir, it was upon your own authority that he attempted; and how much soever I am his inferiour, yet there is more proportion between a Maistre de Camp as he is, and a Lieutenant as I am, than between your Majesty and Monsieur Canaples. Besides Sir, he was the first offender, without any provocation from me, and contrary to his own word, so that if I said some disrespectful things to him, it was himself that drove me to that extremity. Your Majesty knows, I am, I thank God, patient enough, but Sir, he provokt me to the last degree; and had a mind I think to try whether there was any spark of Honour in me, after he had endeavoured to take it all away by this affront. Thus your Majesty sees plainly enough, he was not only guilty of his own fault, but of mine too; nor can he justly complain of my being loud with him, after he had so sensibly injured me.

He was not content, Sir, to deprive me of the rank that was my due, and in that to go against your authority, but he proceeded yet farther; for upon my letting him see that I had the resentments of a man of Honour upon this occasion, and told him roundly, I could not quickly forget so great an affront, he took my sense of this offence for an injury, and flew into such a passion, that forgetting the order of War, which forbids every Maistre de Camp to suspend an Officer, when your Majesty, or Monsieur Espernon is in the Army, he would needs take upon him the power of interdicting me the exercise of my Command. But I knowing this was more than he could do, contented my self with telling him so, and left him as ill satisfy'd with me, as I had reason to be with him, to come throw my self at your Majesty's feet, and beg justice for the affront that had been done me.

The great affairs with which your Majesty was taken up at that time not affording you leisure to hear me, your Majesty sent me to Monsieur Espernon, who after having heard our difference, made answer, that I should go tell Monsieur Canaples from him, that it was your Majesty's pleasure he should permit me to execute my Command. I entreated he would give himself the trouble of writing to him himself, that I might not be ingaged in some new Contest with him, which he accordingly did upon my Tablets presently, and this I deliver'd to Monsieur St. Preuil, who promis'd me to carry it immediately to him.

Upon this confidence I went and took my place at the Head of the Army, assuring my self, that Monsieur Canaples would make no scruple of obeying the D. of Espernon's, which indeed was your Majesties Orders; but was very much astonish'd to see him oppose them throughout, meerly to dishonour and ruin me:

me. For as soon as ever he spy'd me at a distance in my Post, he immediately gallop'd up to me with his Cane in his hand, threatning all the way what he would do. I, Sir, who knew my self supported by your authority, and the Collonels, seeing my self like to be used like a Rogue in the presence of the whole Army, thought fit to caution him both for his honour and my own, while he was a good way off, not to come near me in that posture, nor offer me an Affront, which I was not prepared to suffer; telling him, Your Majesty had given me that place, and Monsieur Espernon maintain'd me in it, and therefore I could not quit it without an express Order from your Majesty, or the Collonel. Monsieur Canaples guessing then by my countenance, and my words, that I was not dispos'd to receive a Caneing, thought to deal better with me, and leapt from his Horse, advancing toward me with his Sword in his hand. I confess, Sir, when I saw my self prest after this manner, and perfectly constrained to defend my life, which I had reason to believe he had a mind to take away, as well as my honour, I made a Virtue of Necessity, and put my self in a posture to defend both the one and the other.

I dare not declare more particularly to your Majesty what I did afterwards, nor how I found my self dispos'd. I know the respect I owe, and the confusion the remembrance of my fault ought to put me in, while your Majesty is so gracious to hear me. At that the King interrupting me, said, Speak boldly, and fear nothing, you know I charged you to conceal nothing from me, and I would know all. This answer, and the change I observ'd in the King's countenance, made me think he took some pleasure in hearing me, and that what I had to say would not be disagreeable to him. So continuing the discourse with a more free and Souldier-like air, Since your Majesty (said I) will have me speak out, I confess, that when Monsieur Canaples did me an honour, I durst not have hoped for from his generosity, I accepted it, being pretty well dispos'd to defend my life, which it was more honourable to preserve for your Majesty's Service, than to give it up cowardly to the passion of a man that would have destroy'd me. So that when he came up hotly with his Sword drawn and blustring words, I was not dismaied at it, and only thought of acknowledging the honour he did me, in saving him part of the way, and putting my self in a posture for returning his civility. And I may boldly tell your Majesty, since 'tis your pleasure I should dissemble nothing, that if the Duke of Angoulesme had not come in seasonably to part us, Monsieur Canaples might perhaps have found, that it was an easier matter to threaten, than to kill me; and to interdict me my Command without any Authority to do so, than to drive me from my Post by force of Arms.

The King well pleased with so sincere and natural a narration, and seeing that the Circumstances did really render what I had done very excusable, was so moved at these last words, which I had pronounced in a Military and kind of Provencal tone, that he said to me with a smiling countenance, What then drew'st too? I did indeed Sir, reply'd I, and dare not deny it to your Majesty, but 'twas Monsieur Canaples that forced me to it; and I think your Majesty would not have been pleased with having me killed like a Rogue that had neither Courage nor Honour. And how didst thou do then? said the King. Sir, Your Majesty will pardon me if I tell you, that I began to measure my Sword with his, and was defending my self the best I could when they came in to us. But that was not what the King would have, for perceiving me a little warm'd with the recital, he would have the diversion of seeing me represent my action with something of that heat which was but too natural to me. So that the Duke of St. Simon, who had withdrawn toward the Window, to leave me at greater

liberty

liberty with the King, comprehending what he meant, gave me to understand it. At which animating my self as much as the presence of the King would allow, throwing my Cloak upon my left shoulder, and standing upon my Guard, I did that with my Hand and Arm, which respect would not suffer me to do with my Sword. The King, who saw the sprightliness of my gesture, and observ'd the fire that sparkled in my Eyes, cover'd his face a little with the Sheet, that he might laugh without being discover'd, which made me presently conclude the Cause was won, and all my own.

As soon as this little Farce was over, the King bad me be sure to remember all the particulars I had told him, and let no body living know of my having been with him: And withal he commanded me to be ready at his Chamber-door when he went to Council, there to throw my self at his Feet, and give him an account of my whole business, as if I had never spoke to him of it before. Upon which I immediately withdrew, and went down the Stairs by the Wardrobe as privately as ever I could.

XVII. Then I plainly saw, that Providence, instead of forsaking me, (as I imagin'd at first) had assisted me after a visible and extraordinary manner, and that two ways: First by inclining the King to be favourable to my Cause; and then in not permitting me to find either my Horse or my Man, in order to the making my escape, for had I fled, I had been utterly lost.

At eleven of the Clock I presented my self at the King's Chamber door, and at his coming out with a great deal of Company that attended him, and among others the Cardinals *Richelieu* and *la Vallette*, I threw my self at his Majesty's Feet, and began to speak and beg his audience after this manner.

Sir, I am come to lay my self at your Majesty's Feet, to implore your mercy. I put my life into your Majesty's hands, for I had better lose it by the Sword of your Justice, if I have deserv'd to lose it, than live miserable, a Fugitive, and under your Majesty's displeasure. But I most humbly beseech you, Sir, that you will first do me the favour to hear me, that if I shall have the good fortune to make my Innocence appear, I may have the consolation of being absolv'd by your Majesty's own Judgment; and on the contrary, if I cannot justify my own conduct, I may be condemn'd out of my own mouth.

The King, who seem'd very cold to me, on purpose to conceal his secret intelligence betwixt us, heard me with a fierce countenance, his hand on his side, and standing between the two Cardinals. Then with a fierce look he said, *Rise, that I may the better hear you, and if you have any thing to say in your own justification, speak it, but be sure you speak truth.* All the Court was present at this extraordinary Audience, and I pleaded my cause for half a quarter of an hour, after the same manner I had done it in private, in the King's Chamber, but much more seriously, as speaking now in publick before the Cardinals, Princes, and Lords of the Court.

While I was harranguing thus, the King said softly to Cardinal *Richelieu*, as I have been since told by a Lord that overheard him, *You see Canaples provoked him to the last degree, for my part I do not think him so much in fault;* and when I had done speaking he said aloud, *'Tis true, he ought not to deprive him of the Post due to him by his Command, when he did nothing but only execute my Orders.*

Upon

Upon this they went prefently into Council, and Cardinal *Richelieu* having underftood from the King, that he would have the judgment upon this bufinefs put off, by reafon of the *Englifh* Fleets lying there, in expectation of a fair Wind to affault the Mole, his Eminence declared it to the Council.

Thus the matter was deferr'd, that is, the King referv'd the judgment of it to himfelf, and at his coming from Council he very gracioufly told me fo; I humbly begg'd of his Majefty to do me the favour, not to let me lye idle, but to employ me fome way in his fervice, which he promis'd me to do, but withal ordered me in the mean time to ftay in his Quarters, without going to the Regiment of Guards, or executing any part of my Command.

XVIII. The King accordingly did remember me as he had promifed, and a few days after made me Captain of a Galliot, to go out to Sea, and difcover the Enemy. I then began to think of reconciling my felf to the King, by fome fignal action in this new Command his Majefty had conferr'd upon me. I bought a great many Ells of Taffata, and made Streamers of them with the Arms of *France*: Thefe I plac'd round about my Veffel, and made it look fo fine, that feveral Lords were eager to come aboard, and would needs go with me to Sea. Finding my felf thus crowded in the time of my difgrace, and fearing it might do me fome new mifchief with the King; or at leaft, that I might not be able to execute his orders faithfully, if I were not abfolutely Mafter of the Veffel, and had her to my felf; I thought fit to acquaint him with it, and did fo. His Majefty was well pleafed to fee that I rejected the favour of others, and fought after his only, and that I would apply my felf to no body elfe, but him, as in truth, I had more occafion to do now than ever. Therefore forbidding the Lords and all others to go aboard me, and having told them for a blind, that he would have them all keep about his perfon, except fuch as had Commands, I was left to my felf, and my Ship at my own difpofal. Then I fell to cruifing, to try if I could difcover the Enemies defigns, paffionately defiring to do the King fome confiderable fervice, that I might have a little merit to intercede for my peace, and gain an abfolute Pardon.

I was once at open Sea in the night, when my Pilot, who was a Mafter in Navigation, came about an hour before day, and told me, a frefh gale was rifing, and both Wind and Tide ftood fair for the Enemy; and therefore he was afraid, if they had any mind to attempt the Mole, they would not lofe this opportunity. The Pilot was in the right, and fpoke like a man of wifdom and experience; for a little after we heard a Cannon fhot from that part where the *Englifh* Fleet rid, which the Pilot told me was the firft fignal for the fight, and if we fhould hear a fecond we might depend upon it that it was fo. Having a great confidence in this man, I immediately raifed all my People, both Souldiers and Slaves, commanding them to be ready, and at the firft touch of the Boatfwain's Whiftle, fall to their Oars amain. The fecond Cannon fhot came to our Ears prefently after, and then I made them row toward the fhore as faft as they could, and faw the Enemy fpreading their Sails, to prepare for attacking the Mole. Being landed, I immediately went to the King, and acquainted him, that the Enemy were hoifting Sail, and that the Weather, Wind and Tide were fo favourable, that they could not lofe fo fair an occafion.

At this news the King gave his orders throughout, and afterwards went with part of the Nobility to the Battery, which was at the Head of the Bay, commanding me to lye under the shelter of this Battery.

There was nothing very remarkable in this fight, except the Cannon shot, of which a prodigious number was fir'd on both sides. There was nothing to be heard but Peals of Thunder, nor to be seen but Lightning, in the midst of a dark Smoke, that cover'd the whole Sea. It was a fine sight to see those monstrous Vessels too, that resembled great floating Castles; and advancing one after another in very graceful order, gave Broad-sides at our Mound, of fifty or threescore Cannon shot at a time.

But as the *English* attack'd briskly, they were as warmly receiv'd. The Battery where the King was did wonders. He made several shot himself, delighting extremely in every thing that related to War, and never was more liberal, either of Lead to the Enemies, or Gold and Silver to his Souldiers and Gunners. During the whole fight, I kept my self close under the Cannon of his Battery, according to the orders I had receiv'd, venturing out only a little now and then, to pursue a Vessel when it retir'd from the Charge, but being fore'd to return very quickly, for fear of being snapt by some other that came on. There was only one Cannon Ball fell into my Galliot, with which she was much damag'd, and two Slaves kill'd.

XIX. At length the Enemy seeing Heaven declare on our side, and that all their attempts were vain, made a retreat, fatal to *Rochelle*, and advantageous to the King and his Arms. Then I fell to cruising again, and was so happy as to meet with a favourable accident, which was of great advantage towards restoring me to the King's favour. Seeing a very beautiful guilded Prow floating upon the water, and the Arms of *England* in it, I made up, and found it was a considerable Prize, and a Present worthy the King. With much ado I haled it up into my Galliot, and return'd a proud man toward the Beach, where after I had got it ashore, I went straight to the King's Quarter. As I was going, Monsieur *Bassompiere* met me, and told me, Monsieur *Canaples* had entreated him, to beg my Pardon of the King in his name, by reason that his Father Mareschal *Cremi* did, as I said formerly, very much condemn his behaviour, and besides he knew well enough how the King stood affected, which made him speak first, to get the merit of a thing which he hop'd might turn to his honour. I told him of the good luck I had met with, and he gave me all the hopes imaginable, advising me to make use of this advantage to ingratiate my self with the King. I then declared my design, which was to let the King know, that the Shot which took off this Prow, came from his Battery, as indeed it did, and so by degrees insensibly to persuade him, that his Majesty himself had made the shot. He approv'd of my design, telling me, he thought the true way to go to work for my own interests, was to advance the King's honour.

On I went, and at my entring the King's Lodgings, I compos'd my countenance the best I could, without discovering the least gayety, but looking very modest and dejected, as became a man, who had reason to apprehend the consequences of so unlucky an affair as mine, I told his Majesty, that one of the *English* Vessels was much disabled, and I had found a great piece of her Prow, which I thought it my duty to bring away, that his Majesty, if he pleased, might see it. I would not say any thing more at first, thinking he would be apt enough of his own accord to

attribute

attribute the glory of this shot to himself. He told me he would go view it, and askt me by the way whereabouts I had found it. I answered very innocently, and without spurring on too fast, in such a place, on the right hand, which was the part expos'd to his own Battery. The King, who passionately desir'd it might be thought his own doing, but durst not yet take it to himself without some ground, was pleas'd with my answer, and reply'd, 'twas I that made that shot at such a time, I saw the Vessel fall off as soon as ever I had discharg'd, and did then believe she had receiv'd some damage, Upon this I began to confirm his opinion by several circumstances, which was matter of great Joy to this Prince, who stood much upon his being a good Marks-man, and did really excel in all military matters; there being perhaps scarce a man in his Kingdom, that could draw up the greatest Army in Battalia so soon, or so advantageously as himself. He took great pride in showing this Prow, and telling every one that came, that I could testify it fell upon a shot of his; which was as much for my satisfaction as his own, for thus I was made a Judge in the case, and did not question, but having determined favourably for him, he would not fail to do as much for me.

Mareschal *Bassompiere*, loth to lose so fair an opportunity, when the King was in so good a humour, got his Majesty to do that at his request, and for his sake, which he was inclin'd enough to do of himself, but that he would have seem'd to proceed more upon favour than justice. I humbly beseech your Majesty (said he) to grant me one humble request which I have to make you. The King who probably guest what he would be at, he seem'd a little shy, telling him, he could not engage his word till he knew for what. Sir, reply'd Monsieur *Bassompiere*, I can assure your Majesty the cause is good, and you will have no reason to repent of the favour. But tell me what it is (said the King) if the cause be good, why are you so nice in declaring it? Is it something that concerns your self, or some of your Relations? Sir, said he, the favour I would obtain neither concerns my self, nor any Relation of mine, but another that hath more need. Oh! you are too subtile for me, reply'd the King, I am no Diviner to know your thoughts. At last Monsieur *Bassompiere* told him that it was my Pardon, he took the boldness to beg, and did it from Monsieur *Canaples* too, who was infinitely troubled for the misfortune he had brought upon me. The King seeming mightily surpriz'd, stood some time silent, as if he had much ado to grant his request, and yet at the very moment that Monsieur *Bassompiere* spoke, he prest a little upon my shoulder, as it were to signify his secret consent. Monsieur *Bassompiere* repeated it again with more than ordinary importunity, and the King, who only held off to disguise his own inclination, made a shew at last of being vanquisht, and said to me, Thank *Bassompiere*. I, who all this while had kept my eyes down, without speaking a word, as soon as I heard the King's Command, went to thank Monsieur *Bassompiere*, and, then fell down to embrace the King's knees with these words, Sir, 'Tis to your Majesty that I owe every thing, I hold both my fortune and life from you, which I hope one day to lay down for your service, and with my blood to seal my acknowledgments for your bounty. The King after a short whisper with Monsieur *Bassompiere*, bad me go along with him, and do as he should direct me.

XX. We went immediately to Monsieur *Canaples*, who having had notice by a Gentleman whom Monsieur *Bassompiere* had sent before, came out to the top of the Stairs to receive him. As soon as we were come into the

the Chamber, Monsieur *Baſſompiere*, ſaid to Monſieur *Canaples*, Here is
Monſieur *Pontis*, Sir, whom I bring to you by the King's Command.
I will be the Mediator of a perfect reconciliation betwixt you two ; You
muſt either utterly forget all that is paſt, or otherwiſe I declare my ſelf an
Enemy to you both.   Monſieur *Canaples* whoſe deſire it was, that this
buſineſs might be huſht up, for the reaſons I mentioned before, came immediately to embrace me, and willing to prevent me, in civility, ſaid
pleaſantly ; Sir, I entreat you let us no more remember any thing that
hath happen'd, for it will not be for our advantage, for either of us to
have ſuch an Enemy as Monſieur *Baſſompiere*. We have both of us been a
little too obſtinate ; there hath been heat on both ſides, and exceſs of
paſſion, and ſo both ought to excuſe it, becauſe both are to blame ; and I
hope that this will produce a great good, and that we ſhall love one another the better for it hereafter.   Finding my ſelf highly oblig'd by ſo generous a complement, I made anſwer with great ſincerity and freedom,
that I now eſteem'd my ſelf happy in my misfortune, ſince it procured
me the honour of his friendſhip ; that I hoped to let him ſee how ſenſibly
I was oblig'd by this generoſity, that he very well knew the air and humour of my Country ; but could aſſure him, that tho I were a little rough
ſometimes, yet I had a great deal more and better heat for thoſe who honour'd me with their friendſhip.   I make you no excuſes, Sir, becauſe
you have been pleaſed to prevent me in firſt excuſing me your ſelf ; and
it is beſt, that neither of us think of a thing, which both wiſh had never
happen'd.   With that we fell to embracing afreſh, and Monſieur *Baſſom-*
piere made us do it a third time, the better to confirm the Union, which
was ever after ſo ſincere, that Monſieur *Canaples* could not forbear expreſ-
ſing a coldneſs toward thoſe who had ſollicited him to proſecute this affair
againſt me, for he ſeveral times declared, that he had not done it of himſelf, ſo much as by the ill advice of ſome falſe friends.

Then Monſieur *Baſſompiere* carried me to Mareſchal *Creqni*, who had
ſhewn himſelf ſo generous upon this occaſion.   And being I could never
ſufficiently acknowledge the particular teſtimonies he had given me of
his noble nature ; after the firſt complements I told him, that I was much
concern'd it was not in my power, to ſhew by my actions the ſenſe I had
of his generoſity to me in this buſineſs ; that I ſhould moſt impatiently
long for ſome occaſion of aſſuring him by my ſervices, how much I thought
my ſelf obliged by his extraordinary goodneſs in vindicating me, when
almoſt all the world beſides had deſerted me ; and that this had been one
of the principal arguments, that convinc'd me I had not been altogether
ſo guilty, as ſome others would repreſent, for I knew him too good a
Father, and too juſt a perſon, to declare himſelf without good reaſon
againſt his own Son in favour of a Stranger, whom nothing but the merits
of the cauſe could render worth his conſideration.   Mareſchal *Creqni* anſwered me with all imaginable civility, that I did him wrong in magnify-
ing what he had done ; as if for being a Father he was to deveſt himſelf
of all humanity and juſtice toward thoſe who might have ſome difference
with his Children ; and that having done no more than his duty, he deſerved to be commended ſo much leſs, as he ought to have been
condemn'd if he failed in it.   And turning to Monſieur *Baſſompiere*, Is it
not fit (ſaid he) that every one ſhould have their due? Why ſhould my
Son be allowed to affront a Gentleman, and a man of honour? Let us not
take ſo much upon us. My Son, though a *Maiſtre de Camp* in the Regiment
of Guards, hath no right to offer violence to Monſieur *Pontis*, who is

but

but a Lieutenant. Perhaps my Sons Command is an honour to him, whereas other perhaps are an honour to their Commands. In short, I have only this to say, that in case Monsieur *Pontis* had been condemn'd, I would have carry'd my Son my self to have made him ask him pardon, for the affront he had put upon him.

After this I went to pay my respects to the Duke of *Espernon* and some other Lords, that had done me service in my affair: but it happen'd I know not how, that I failed of acquitting my self to Cardinal *Richelieu* of what I was indebted to him upon this account. The conference I had with Father *Joseph*, and the design I knew he had to draw me from the Kings service, together with my refusal of entring into his, made me unwilling to appear before him. In the mean while, being a little jealous of the good offices he did to those who sought his favour, he was much offended, that after he had himself sought to gain me by his chief Minister, I had failed of thanking him upon this occasion, for what he said from the King to the Council, about deferring to give Judgment in my Cause. I knew too, that he had not conceal'd his disgust, for some days after, the Bishop of *Manda* asking me if I had been to pay my thanks to the Cardinal? and I innocently answering, That my little access to his Eminence had hindred me from doing it; he said I was much to blame, and that the Cardinal would certainly resent it. Then I saw my fault too late, and desiring to redeem it, I begg'd Monsieur *Cominges Guitaut* to introduce me to him. But the Cardinal, who never cared for late homages, and liked only the first incense, receiv'd me very coldly, and by his set countenance gave me to understand, that my civilities were not at all acceptable to him. The Bishop of *Manda* too, being willing to make my excuse, his Eminence could not conceal his indignation from him, but said these words, which were told me again; He did come indeed to return me thanks, but it was after he had been with every body else; I had nothing but the leavings of his Complements: He allowed me only the last place in his memory and respects, though I had the first in the defence of his cause; and then too, he did not come so much of his own accord, as he was brought by Monsieur *Cominges*. So that this fault, which he took for a slight, joyn'd with my refusal of his service to Father *Joseph*, was the principal ground of that obstinate aversion he hath had to me ever since. I was afterwards restor'd to my Command as formerly, and all the informations preferr'd against me were torn to pieces.

XXI. The excess of trouble and fear this unhappy business brought upon me threw me into a violent Feavor. The distemper was suspended till the affair was over, and then as excessive a joy succeeding, Nature found herself overpowred by so sudden and so different a change; so that after having escaped death by the hand of Justice, I found my self in a new danger, both from my Disease and my Physicians, who were very near dispatching me, tho without any ill intention. During this illness, I was somewhat disturbed with the remembrance of my past life, and particularly for having upon some occasions caused a great many of the Enemy to be knockt on the head, more out of passion, than for the service of the State: I fancy'd I saw all those men remonstrating against me, and demanding justice of God for their deaths. This imagination afflicted me much, and I resolved to make some amends for this fault: But upon my recovery I soon found that the resolutions of sick and dying men seldom are sincere; for when I was well I scarce ever remembred what I promis'd when I lay sick.

Upon

Upon my growing better, the Kings Physicians, Monsieur *Bouvart* and Monsieur *Privos*, having order'd me a purging potion, a wretch that I forbear to name, took this occasion to get rid of me, and procure my Command : He corrupted the Apothecary, who sold him my Life, and instead of the Apozem, mixt me the most mortal poyson he could think of. But I can never sufficiently acknowledge the good Providence that took care of me ; for the night before I was to have taken this deadly draught, I had a very great Crisis, and sweat to that degree from ten a clock to one, that I found my self perfectly well. The aversion I ever had to Physick made me order the Vial to be set by in my Closet, and leave Nature to finish what she had so well begun. The Physicians coming to visit me, and see the operation of their Medicine, I told them Sparkishly, Look you Gentlemen, here is a Miracle, is not this a prodigious effect, and a plain proof of the vertue of your Physick? They believing it in earnest, began presently to magnifie their prescription, not seeming so much surpriz'd at it, but to expect all this from a remedy so well chosen ; adding, that since the first dose had succeeded so well, I must needs take another, to carry off what that might have left behind ; and so went away highly pleas'd with the success of their Physick. I thought however it was not fit to conceal it from Monsieur *Privos*, who was my particular friend ; and when the company was gone, told him, I had a great Crisis in the night, and finding my self better upon sweating, had forbore my Physick : And to confirm what I had said, bid my man bring the Potion. Assoon as he saw it he cry'd out, Ah Sir! what did they intend to do with you? They would have destroy'd you, this is rank poyson. God hath had a particular care of you, for if you had taken this you had been a dead man. Then he fell to exclaiming and swearing to vindicate his own reputation, and sent away immediately for the Grand Provost. They went presently to the Apothecary's, but he was run away, which made me conclude it was a design, and no mischance, or mistake. I had a suspicion of the person that thus attempted upon my Life and my Command, but it was enough for me that I got off so. I would not bring any information upon it, and was glad the Apothecary was not taken, lest the Author of this Crime should have been discovered.

XXII. And here I must not omit the generosity of Monsieur *Buisson*, that Gentleman that was a Cadet in my Company, and afterwards quarrell'd with me, for whom as a testimony of my forgiveness and friendship, I procur'd first a Pardon, and then a Lieutenants place : For he hearing, tho very late, of this unfortunate business of mine, which was the chief cause of my sickness, came purposely from *Italy* to the Camp before *Rochelle*, some months after I was restored to my Command, to make me a proffer of his person, and all he had in his power ; assuring me, that both himself and his fortune was absolutely at my service and disposal. By this extraordinary acknowledgment he had a mind to vye friendships with me, and let me see, that no misfortune could cool his affection, nor any distance of place stop the zeal he had for the safety of a person, to whom he thought himself oblig'd for his life and preferment.

XXIII. The King, resolving to relieve the Isle of *Rhe*, commanded by Monsieur *Thoiras*, and invested by the *English* Navy, gave Mareschal *Schomberg* orders to pass over into it, with the best of our Forces. His Majesty was then at *Etray*, within a mile of the Trenches. As I was one night

night upon the Guard, I saw on a sudden a great flame and thick smoak over *Rochelle*; and at the same time heard a great noise. I dispatched two or three Souldiers to know the cause of this uproar, and none of them returning back, I thought the Enemy might have taken this opportunity of our Forces being separated, to make some attempt upon the King's own Quarters. So I drew up our men, and after acquainting Mareschal *Brezay* with what past, with him and Monsieur de l'*Isteroy* I went to the King's Bedchamber. The Mareschal waked him, and I told his Majesty what I had seen and heard, which continu'd still. The King presently got up, and went into a Garret to satisfy himself of the truth of it, and having been an Eye-witness of my report, lookt upon us, and said, This is no jesting matter. Then he askt me if I had sent to the Trenches, and order'd the Guards to stand to their Arms; and when he was satisfy'd I had, he commanded them to dress him, and bring him his Arms. At that time a considerable Officer, and otherwise a brave man, but perhaps a little too rash in his zeal upon this occasion, said to the King, Save your Servants, Sir, save your people; if the Eneme attack us here your person may be in danger, since part of your Army is gone to the Isle of *Rhe*, and we are but a few left here; I conjure your Majesty retire to *Surgeres*. The King answered without any concern, I will not stir from this place, but will fight at the head of my Foot in person. Bring me my Arms presently. In earnest this generous stout answer from the King, gave me a joy not to be exprest, which made me fall down at his feet, and in a great transport say to him; Sir, when we have our King at the head of us, every single man will be as good as twenty, and each Company as good as a Regiment; no body will presume to spare himself upon such an occasion, but we will all serve you with the last drop of blood, in our veins. The King then armed and gave out necessary orders for sustaining an Assault, in case the Enemy should attack him in his Quarter. But while every one was preparing to engage, the Souldiers I had sent to the Trenches came and assured us, that instead of making a Sally, the *Rochellers* had been terribly frighted with a mischance that had befallen them, by their Magazine of Powder taking fire, which caused that great noise we heard. The King received this news, as he had done the other, without any great concern, or discovering any more joy to see himself in safety, than he had done fear at the expectation of danger. Then Mareschal *Brezay* made this reflection to me, Look you, said he, if the King had followed the advice that was given him, to retreat to *Surgeres*, he would have had us all three tost into the Sea, when once he found a false Alarm had made him run away. I was of the same opinion too, and whatever might have happened, I could never have prevailed upon my self to have given him counsel, which though it might be for his safety, could never have been for the honour of so great a Prince. But unexpected accidents do not always leave us the liberty of thinking, and the wisest men in such cases may sometimes be mistaken. I remember too, while every one was in trouble about the King's person, which we thought too much expos'd, an Officer, consulting perhaps his Majesty's safety more than his own, after debate what might be the cause of this great noise, let this word slip by chance, I hope 'tis nothing in grace of God. Whereupon all that were by, and little used to such language, fell to rallying him, as one who betraid his fear by that expression. And tho I was no better than the rest, yet I could not choose but be offended at those kinds of Jests, which

seem'd

seem'd to me so ill grounded. For is it not brutish to imagine, that to appear brave a man must forget that he is a Christian? and doubtless if that Officer had called upon the Devil instead of God, they would have thought better of him, and not have reproved him. So little do we know what a man of courage is, when men think being impious is enough to make them thought brave. In the mean while the affronts there were perpetually put upon this Officer, were so severe, that not enduring to be the constant jest of all the Hectors and young Bullies, he was forc'd a little after to beg a dismission, and withdraw from out of the Army.

Next morning all the General Officers came to pay the King their respects, accompanied with great praises; his Majesty had ordered me to be about his person, and indeed I made my Court that day after a very pleasant manner. For the King did me the honour to call upon me every now and then, and said, Ask *Pontis* how it was, choosing rather to have it told by another than himself. And accordingly I represented this action of his Majesty's with all imaginable advantage and zeal; nor was it any hard matter to succeed that way, for upon this occasion a man might be a good Courtier without any flattery, and there needed only a relation of what I had seen to give the King his due commendation.

XXIV. One day going to relieve the Guard, and being to pass through a little Valley that lay expos'd, and commanded by a Hill, where four or five pieces of the Enemy's Cannon were planted; as I rode at the Head of four hundred men, marching very leisurely, and talking with a Corporal called *de la Croix*, I laid my Leg upon my Horse-neck, as men do sometimes to ease themselves, though indeed it was no proper time to do it, but rather to mend my pace: Just then came a Cannon Bullet, which exactly took off the Stirrup out of which I had taken my Foot, and battered it to pieces. The force of the blow beat down my Horse, but he got up again presently, and attempting to recover my Stirrup, I found it was clear gone. Then I acknowledged the good providence of God, that had thus saved my Leg, and probably my Life too, fearing nothing more than to be maim'd, and out of a capacity to serve the King. They made a jest of it to the King, and told him I had one of my Legs taken off by a Cannon ball, but his Majesty hearing afterward that I had only lost my Stirrup, turn'd it into mirth, and laught at the oddness of the accident.

The *English* had blockt up the passes by Sea so effectually, that we could put no provisions into the Isle of *Rhe*. But the King resolv'd to thrust in twenty light flat-bottom'd Boats, and order'd me to go along with Monsieur *d'Esplandes*, who was to conduct them, that I might bring him back an account of the expedition. When all things were ready, and the Wind favourable, we embark'd by night, and in a short time came very happily ashore in the Island, through all the fire and ball that was liberally bestow'd upon us, and in spight of six great *English* Ships, that made after us, but could not come up to us for want of Water. The Bullets lighting upon the Grabel of the Beach, beat great heaps of Stones into our Skiffs, and kill'd us a great many men; and sometimes one of them would take off a Sack of Flour from a Souldiers shoulder, as they were unlading. Monsieur *d'Esplandes* and I sat down to rest our selves, and a Cannon Bullet hit a Portmantua upon which I sat, carried away part of the things within it, without doing me any other harm, than throwing me some fifteen paces off. And as Monsieur *d'Esplandes* urged me to sit down again, upon a Free Stone hard by him, divining as it were, that this was no safe place, and better to stand up; just in that nick of time (which is almost incredible) a shot struck this Stone, and shatter'd it to pieces. There was but little pleasure in being so familiar with great Guns, which made me think of hastening back with my report to the King. And so going aboard a small Boat with only one Waterman, I got over this Arm of the Sea, through above four hundred Cannon shot that were made at us in our passage: but that which was a greater difficulty, was several long chains of beams of wood laid in the Sea at every quarter of a League, and these linkt together with great rings of Iron, so that at each of these we were forc'd to wait for some great wave to lift the Bark over the beams. The King, who scarce expected to see me any more, believing we had all been sunk, by reason of the great firing that continu'd all night, was very much surpriz'd at my return, and the successfulness of our passage.

XXV. At last the time was come for the City, which was the main hope and support of the *Hugonot* party, to fall into the hands of its lawful Prince. It was reduced to such extremity by famine, that a great many people died for want of Bread; and I will here relate what I had from my Landlords own mouth, when we were got into *Rochelle*. Describing the necessities they were in, he protested to me, that for eight days together, he made himself be let blood, and made it be fry'd to nourish his poor Child, so by degrees taking away his own life to preserve his Son's. The Eloquence of one *Salbert*, a Minister of great consideration among them, contributed much to the perswading them to endure great extremities; their religious zeal made them insensible of every thing, together with the authority and heroick conduct of *Guiton*, Mayor of the City, who got great renown in this Siege, seem'd to inspire them with new vigour and courage. To give you some Idea of his resolution, I need only say, that one of his Friends shewing him an acquaintance of theirs languishing and dying of hunger, he answered coldly, Is this so strange? 'Tis what we must all come to. And when another came, and told him they were all dying of hunger, he reply'd as coldly, Provided there be one left to shut the Gates it's well enough. But Heaven seem'd in favour of the King's Arms; the *Rochellers* themselves were aware of it, and confest it very surprizing, to see the weather so fair in that season, when the Storms and the Sea were used to make all *Rochelle* tremble, and overflow all the Streets of the Town. But that which made it yet more astonishing, and which might be very well thought a miraculous Providence in this great undertaking, was, that tho the Plague then raged with great fury in two thirds of the Kingdom, this Canton continu'd entirely free from it, in the midst of the dreadful necessities of a City reduc'd to this miserable condition, and of the infection used to attend great Armies, especially after so long a Siege.

The *Rochellers*, having no hopes left of fresh succours from *England*, and the Fleet having several times in vain attempted to relieve them, began to treat about a Capitulation. One Article of which was, that the Mayor *Guiton* should still enjoy the honours of his dignity, and its priviledges entire. The 29th of *October*, 1628. ten Deputies came with the ratification to lay themselves at his Majesty's feet in his Chamber, where, he was attended with Count *Soissons*, the Cardinals *Richelieu* and *la Vallette*, Monsieur *Cheverense*, and *Bassompiere*, *Schomberg*, *Deffiat*, and others, where

where they implored his Majesty's mercy afresh; and the Sieur *de la Gou-fre*, the King's Advocate in the Presidial Court, spoke for them. At the same time the Citizens from the Rampiers and Counterscarps, crying out, God save the King. Four hundred men were appointed to go take possession of the Town, and prepare the King's Lodgings, to clean the Streets and Houses, and make all things ready for his Entry. He made choice of four Captains and four Lieutenants, of which I was one, to command them, under the Duke of *Angoulesme*, whom we were to obey, and had express charge not to make the least disorder in the City, with threatnings of exemplary punishment in case of any complaints against us. Among other things, the King ordered particularly, that we should not suffer the Souldiers to sell bread to these hunger-starv'd Wretches, and only to let them receive some little presents in case people offer'd them of their own accord. Thus we entred *Rochelle*, possest our selves of the Gates, and posted Guards in several places. We found the Town in a most horrid and deplorable condition; the Streets and Houses tainted with dead bodies, which lay about very thick, without being so much as covered: For toward the end of the Siege the *Rochellers* were meer Skeletons, and not men; they were so feeble, that they had not strength enough to dig Graves, or carry the dead out of their Houses. The greatest present a man could make to them that remained alive, was Bread, which they preferr'd as their only remedy that could save them; and yet this remedy too prov'd mortal to some, who eat it so greedily as to choak themselves.

I had like to have been ruined by a quarrel with a *Rocheller*, which happen'd thus. Having given some Loaves of Bread to one in great want, I had a mind to a Gun of his, which was a very neat one; I ask'd him if he would sell it, and finding him a little unwilling, I prest him, till at last he was content I should have it for eleven Cardecu's. But as soon as I had paid him, and was carrying off the Gun, he repented of his sale, or rather that he had not so much Bread as he desir'd, and fell into a rage, speaking so loud as I heard him, I wish (says he) the silver of those eleven Cardecu's were melted in his Heart, and the lead of the Gun in his Brains; he takes my Gun, and makes me sell it him, whether I will or no. I was surpriz'd at so brutish a complement, and presently turning back toward him said, Why what's the matter Friend? Have I done you any wrong in paying the price we agreed upon for the Gun? I thought you had been an honest man till now, but now you have undeceiv'd me. The other presently gave me the lye; and then my patience escaping me, without regard to the King's charge, or the poor fellow's extremity, I gave him a good swinging Cuff upon his lean Cheek, telling him he ought to know whom he spoke to, and not give the lye to a man of honour. With that he began to chafe and storm, crying out, that he wou' complain to the King, that he had violence done him, contrary to his Majesty's promise.

I quickly saw where this would end, if it were not taken up in time, and was pretty sure to lose my head, if it came to the King's ear; and therefore did all I could, both by my self and friends, and this man's relations to pacify him; I offer'd him eighteen Cardecu's more, which he refused, and resolv'd to be reveng'd whatever came on't. But at last he was follow'd so close with the entreaties of his best friends, that he grew calm, and for the pains he had been at to make himself so very angry, I gave him about a dozen loaves over and above what he had received before. Afterwards he came and excused himself to me, and said, his extremity had thrown him into that violent passion. I made him a friendly remonstrance,

strance, which he took kindly, and gave him to understand, that one of the greatest points of conversation, was to know whom a man spoke to, and not to offend men of honour by rudely giving them the lye, as he had done. At the same time I proffer'd him my service, and as much bread for himself, or his friends, as he wanted; and thus this difference was compos'd.

When the King had made his Entry into *Rochelle,* the Duke of *Angoulesme* would needs visit the famous *Guiton,* who had held out so long against the greatest Prince of *Europe;* and some Officers, of which I was one, attended him thither. He was a little man, but of a vast understanding, and a great Soul; and I was really extremely pleas'd to see in him all the marks of a gallant person. His House was magnificently furnisht, and his Hall adorn'd with a vast number of Ensigns, which he shew'd one after another, naming the Princes from whom he had taken them, and the Seas he had sailed. He had a great many Arms in his House, and amongst the rest one very fine Partisan, taken from a Captain in fight. I had no sooner commended it, but being exceedingly generous, he would needs present me with it, and forced me to accept that and a hundred Pikes besides. He made Cardinal *Richelieu* a handsom answer, when he went to pay him the civility of a visit, speaking to him of the King of *France,* and the King of *England.* He was afterwards very much dissatisfy'd with the Cardinal; for not having surrendred the City to the King, till after a promise of having all the Ensigns of his Dignity continued to him, and one of his Priviledges being, to go attended with a dozen Halberdeers in his Livery, whenever he appeared in the Streets of *Rochelle:* His Eminence one day sent him word, That the King being present in the City, it was contrary to rule that he should retain these marks of a Dignity, that did not now belong to him, and that the King was then the only Master and Mayor of *Rochelle:* This new order strangely offended *Guiton,* who saw himself thus deceived, and fallen from his honours, contrary to the assurance that had been given him. Insomuch that he told me, Had he believed they would have broken their word with him, the King should not have found one living creature at his entring into *Rochelle,* for he would have held it out to the very last man. And probably the King would have been forc'd to raise the Siege, by reason of the Winter, and Storms that came on immediately upon the surrender of the City; for the fair weather ended the very same day the Town was reduc'd; and the seventh of *November* following, the Sea was so boisterous in the night, that it broke down above forty fathom of the Mound on *Marillac* side. The Chevalier *de la Fojett's* Vessel was driven by a gust of wind into the Port, and broke three or four Machines without any damage to it self; and five or six *English* Ships ran ashore upon the Coast of *Angoulia:* So that a man may say, had *Guiton* taken a resolution to hold out but one month longer, as he might have done, we had been in great danger of losing in one day all the fruit of so many labours, and so long a Siege. For the ill weather, together with the breaking of the Bank, would infallibly have relieved the besieged, and there was nothing but a visible and eminent Providence, that oblig'd them to yield in a time so favourable to the King's Arms.

After his Majesty had made some stay in *Rochelle,* to give necessary orders, and prevent any new revolts, he returned triumphant to *Paris,* with the Glory of having in a great measure disarm'd the Protestant Religion in his Kingdom, by the taking of this City.

The Duke of Rohan *makes a great Attempt upon the City of* Montpellier, *and is betray'd by the person who was to give up the City to him. The Sieur* de Pontis *is sent to visit the* Alpes, *for the Passage of the King's Forces. His Moderation towards a Man that would have kill'd him for another. His behaviour toward the Cadets and Souldiers of his Company. His Quarrel with a Captain who quarter'd by force upon his Estate at* Pontis. *The King goes with all his Army into* Savoy, *and forces the Pass of* Suza. *The Sieur* de Pontis *obtains an Escheat of the King, which only gets him a great Suit at Law. The Duke of* Orleans *attempts to force the Guard at the* Louvre, *when the Sieur* de Pontis *was upon the Guard.*

I. DUring the Siege of *Rochelle*, they of the same Party with the *Rochellers*, under the Command of the Duke of *Rohan*, made a great attempt upon the City of *Montpellier*, and had a mind to draw in one of my intimate Friends, the Baron *de M.* second Captain in the Regiment of *Normandy*; the event whereof was so considerable, as to deserve a mention in this place, before I go on to the rest of my *Memoirs*. This Baron *de M.* had married a Wife of the *Hugonot* perswasion, and being one day at a house of hers, the Baron *Bretigny* propos'd to him to favour the Duke of *Rohan* in his design upon *Montpellier*, and in reward they promis'd to make him Governour of the place, and Lieutenant General of Monsieur *Rohan*'s Army, or to give him two hundred thousand Crowns, which the Duke himself engaged to pay him. The Baron *de M.* was a person of greater fidelity than to consent to so base an action; but by avoiding one mischief he engaged himself in another, and resolved for the Kings service to betray the man, who pretended to engage him in betraying the King. The answer he return'd to the Baron *de Bretigny* was, that an affair of such consequence deserved some consideration; that he would go back to *Montpellier*, where his Company was in Garrison, and from thence would acquaint them with his resolution, by a very brave Souldier, one *Cadet*, whom he had bred up from a Foot-boy, and in whom he reposed great confidence.

He lost no time, but gave notice immediately to Monsieur *des Fosses*, Governour of *Montpellier*, what proposals had been made him. These two conspired in the same design, which was to betray them, who dar'd to propose the betraying of their Prince. Monsieur sends *Cadet* away presently, to strike up the bargain with Monsieur *Bretigny*; and the Duke of *Rohan* was made acquainted with it, who said, he would not engage in the attempt, except the Walls were laid open on that side by the Cittadel. Monsieur *Fosses* accordingly caused them by little and little to be laid open, in several places, and upon different pretences. Upon which the Duke, to make sure work, sends an Engineer in the habit of a Souldier,

P p   dier,

dier, who was received into the Governours own Company, that he might see all without any manner of suspicion. The Guard in the mean while was kept but negligently both in the Cittadel, and the lines of Communication, by which the Duke of *Rohan* with four hundred men was to storm the Wall, and the Ditches which were but of a moderate height, and so make himself Master of the *Esplanade*, which lay between the Cittadel and the City. When all things were ready, Baron *M.* gave notice it was time to execute their design. The Duke of *Rohan*, to prevent all jealousies from the drawing his Forces together, gave out, as if he intended to besiege the Castle of *Courconne*, three leagues from *Montpellier*, to which place he came with seven thousand Foot, and three hundred Horse. The night appointed came, and Baron *M.* and *Guitaut* a Captain of the Regiment of *Normandy*, to whom the Governour had entrusted the secret, mounted the Guard in the Cittadel. The Engineer, disguised in the habit of a Souldier, saw all that past, so that he could not have the least jealousy of foul play. Monsieur *M.* after this opened all the Gates, Draw-bridges and Posterns, and the Engineer went out with *Cadet*, to go fetch the Duke of *Rohan*. They agreed before, that when the Duke should be near with his Army, two Officers should be sent to know, whether any alteration had happened. As soon as ever the Engineer was gone, the Governour understanding it from Monsieur *M.* call'd all the Captains together, and made the Regiments of *Picardy* and *Normandy* stand to their arms, which might all make up two thousand eight hundred men. Of these eight hundred were posted in the principal places and avenues of the City, with order to kill all the Citizens that should stir out of their houses, or that attempted to throw themselves over the Walls, by reason four thousand *Hugonot* Inhabitants were to take arms. He posted twelve hundred at the breaches of the Wall of the City, that looked into the *Esplanade*, going to the Cittadel; and there threw up in haste great retrenchments with very good barricadoes behind, and openings to give way for the twelve hundred men, who had order to sally out upon the Enemy, as they entred the *Esplanade* by the Lines of Communication. He set eight hundred men in the Cittadel, of which five hundred were likewise to sally at the same time, and the other three, who were all chosen men, to remain with him in the Cittadel. He caused besides all this twenty pieces of Cannon to be planted upon the *Esplanade*, and loaded them with Musquet Bullets, and placed a certain number of good Souldiers with Halberts behind the inner door, within the Cittadel. On the top of the Draw-bridge, which was made like a Trap-door, he set *Beine* the Engineer of the place, with a Hatchet in his hand, and express order not to cut the Rope of the Bridge, till Monsieur *Goustonville* should cry out to him, *Harle la main*. All things being thus disposed with incredible diligence, Baron *M.* told the Governour, that if the two men they were to send would have him go back with them to Monsieur *de Rohan*, he was absolutely resolv'd to go, rather than give them any suspicion, tho he were very well assur'd they would give him a thousand stabs after he was dead, when they saw themselves so cheated; but he valued not death, provided he could do the King service, in revenging himself upon those who thought him capable of failing in his duty.

II. All things being hush't, at last two Officers according to agreement, came to the Postern to meet Baron *M.* He told them things were in a

very

very good condition, and that if they pleased, he would bring them into the place. But they made anfwer, that knowing him to be a man of bravery, they had an abfolute confidence in him ; that Monfieur *de Rohan* was hard by, and would give his orders out, and be with them in half a quarter of an hour. The Baron reply'd, he would go in then, and keep himfelf behind the door within the Cittadel, to open it for them when they came. Thus they return'd back, and immediately all the Enemies Forces drew near. Monfieur *de Rohan* in coming altered his firft defign of falling on by the lines of Communication, hoping that if he could get into the Cittadel at firft, he fhould in three hours be mafter of the Town. He had with him feven thoufand Foot, and three hundred Horfe, and the next morning came three thoufand more of *Vevarets*. The order was, that two hundred chofen men, among which were a great many Gentlemen and Officers, were to fall on firft ; that they fhould be backt with a thoufand more, and the reft according as need fhould require. The Baron of *Bretigny*, author of the Enterprize, who marcht foremoft of all, came and knockt very foftly at the outward Gate of the Cittadel, and addreffing himfelf to Baron M. ask'd, Coufin, are you there? To which a Serjeant, who was well inftructed what to fay, made anfwer, Sir, He is gone to take a turn at the Guard, but he hath left me to affure you, that he will come again immediately to receive you ; in the mean time draw your men up clofe into order of Battel. With that Baron *Bretigny* gave the word from hand to hand, Clofe, clofe. One and fifty of thefe firft two hundred being advanced with him, *Beine*, who was afraid to fee fo many let in, cut the Rope with his Hatchet, without ftaying for the word, and immediately the Bridge fell down behind, and one part being inclofed between the Gate of the Cittadel and the Bridge, the reft fell into the Ditch. Thofe of the Cittadel immediately threw a great many Fire-works, both into the Ditch, and all about it, that they might the better fee what they did, and fhot at the main body without, of which a great many were kill'd and wounded. As for thofe that were trapt between the Gate and the Bridge, there were nine and thirty kill'd, and twelve taken prifoners, of whom moft part were very much wounded. *Cadet* who guided them, naming himfelf, and our men having let down a Rope to pull him up to them, they who were near him drew him back, and detain'd him by force, faying, They would never fuffer him to efcape, unlefs the Governor, or fome body in his name would promife them their lives. And accordingly when they faw that they fhot at them without proffering them any thing at all, they gave him above twenty wounds, of which however he did not dye: Monfieur *Rohan* withdrew, full of concern and paffion, and ordering his Ammunition-bread to be thrown away, he loaded his Carriages, with as many of his dead and wounded, as he could recover.

What judgment others may pafs upon this action I cannot tell, but for my own part, though fome perhaps may excufe it by reafon of the indignation a man of honour may conceive, to fee himfelf thought capable of being falfe to his Prince ; yet I own it troubled me very much, and I could look upon it as no better than a piece of treachery: Nor could my inviolable devotion to the King's fervice and intereft, prevail with me to approve that in my friend, which I muft have condemned in my felf. The treachery they would have drawn him into, ought not to have engag'd him in another treachery; nor was it in my opinion an argument he underftood the rules of honour and fidelity, to pretend to

merit

merit frmo his King, by betraying thofe that tempted him to betray him. Treachery does not change its nature, when it changes its objeƈt, and it is always infidelity to break a promife; and to forfeit faith once given, though it were for the intereft of the greateft Prince upon Earth.   This Officer was doubtlefs highly to be commended for rejeƈting the advantageous offers made him by the Duke of *Rohan*, that he might ftand firm in his duty; but that it was not confiftent with that duty to furprize the Duke with fair promifes; and that word ought not to have been given, which ought not, nor ever was intended, to be made good.   There was a way open, and the Duke of *Rohan* muft have efteemed him the more, if he had flatly refus'd to ferve him againft the King; but he drew upon himfelf the cenfure of his beft friends, in quitting the way of honour, and taking double and indireƈt methods; and I confefs I could never look upon a man guilty of fo foul and unfaithful an aƈtion, as my friend.

III. A little while after, upon our return from *Rochelle* to *Paris*, the King commanded me to go into *Dauphine, Savoy* and *Piedmont*, to difcover all the paffes of *Italy*, defigning to march his Army into thofe parts, againft the Duke of *Savoy*. I went accordingly, and having examined with all the care I could, all the ways by which an Army could poffibly pafs the Mountains, I took an exaƈt account of them, and after two or three months return'd to *Paris*.   The King fent for Monfieur *de Efcures*, who made the Charts, and was Quarter-mafter General of the Army, and fhewed him the account I had prefented; ordering him to examine it carefully, and compare it with his Charts; and found after by his report, that my account was exaƈtly true as to the leagues, which was all he would undertake to anfwer, not being acquainted with the paffes, fo well as I, who was of the Country.   Whereupon his Majefty was gracioufly pleas'd to fay, he was fatisfied very well with my fervice, and that he would remember it.   And he gave prefent order for all things, for the expedition of *Piedmont*, whither he intended to go in perfon with his whole Army.

IV. About this there happened to me a very unlucky accident at *Paris*, from which it was a great providence that I efcaped.   Coming one night late from the *Louvre* on Horfeback, and going to carry my Captain, Monfieur *St. Previl*, fome orders, that I had juft receiv'd from his Majefty, found him at play in a houfe beyond the *Hoftel de Bellegarde*. As foon as I was paft this *Hoftel*, and got over againft the Chappel of the *Hoftel de Soiffons*, my Footman going before me fome twenty paces with a Flambeau, a man at the corner of a ftreet made a thruft at me with all his might, enough to have run me through and through, and kill'd me upon the fpot; but God guided both the Hand and the Sword fo happily for me, that inftead of running me into the belly, it hit under the pummel of my Saddle, and there broke.   The thruft was fo violent, that a piece of the Sword, half a foot long, ftuck in the Saddle. Surpriz'd at this pafs, which I heard before I faw it, I leap'd off my Horfe, and drawing, I threw the Fellow down, beat him, and in the heat of my paffion was very near killing him.   He profeft to me, that he was miftaken, that he was *Valet de Chambre* to Monfieur *Bellegarde*, and took me for another Gentleman, by whom he had been cudgell'd.   Such a miftake difpleas'd me very much, but however, taking fome compaffion on him, I turn'd back, and went into the *Hoftel de Bellegarde* and his Mafter being in bed, I contented my felf with committing his *Valet de Chambre* into the cuftody of the Gentle-

man

man of his Horfe. The next morning I thought my felf oblig'd to go, and make my complaint to him, and tho he lov'd the fellow very well, yet to make me fatisfaction, he told me, He was a Rogue, and fhould be hang'd. But that was not the thing I came for, but chiefly to give him notice of this diforder, that he might prevent any thing of that kind for the future; and therefore I told him, That fince it had been my chance, and the man had no malice againft me, nor had I received any harm, I entreated he would pardon him, and only give him warning to be wifer another time. Notwithftanding he ftill infifted upon what he had faid, that he would have him hang'd. But affoon as I was return'd home, he fent him to me by the Gentleman of his Horfe, to tell me, he put him abfolutely into my hands, to do what I would with him. I made an-fwer, that fince Monfieur *Bellegarde* was fo generous to leave him to my difpofal, I freely forgave him. But the King heard of it, and faid he fhould be hang'd; tho he contented himfelf with faying it only, and did not caufe it to be done.

V. Another occafion was given me of acknowledging the Divine pro-tection, which did not only very vifibly fpare my life, but gave me an opportunity of faving another perfon's, which was in danger. Having fupp'd one night with a Courtier, a good friend of mine, and going home on Horfeback about eleven a clock, attended by two Foot-men, one of which carry'd a Flambeau, I faw at a diftance upon *Noftre-Dame* Bridge, three or four Villains affaulting a man, whom they had forc'd up to a Wall, where he was defending himfelf the beft he could. I did not much deliberate upon giving him the relief I my felf fhould have expected from another man upon the like occafion, but fpurring as hard as I could in among thefe Rafcals, I fo amazed them, that immediately they ran: but the man was almoft as much troubled and aftonifh'd, as if he had been ftill among the Rogues. He did not think himfelf fafe with me, and I could fcarcely bring him to his fenfes. I askt him, who he was? to whom he belong'd? and where he liv'd? but could not get one word out of his mouth. In the mean while, I could not find in my heart to leave him in this condition neither, doubting he might be attempted again, and more eafily robb'd. I gave him time to recover, and naming the moft confiderable parts, and Inns of *Paris*, I got it out of him at laft, that he lodged in the Place *Maubert*, and was Steward to the Duke of *Lorrain*, who was then at *Paris*. I try'd to get him up behind me, but not being able, becaufe he was a very big fat man, and not yet cur'd of his fright, I thought it beft to alight my felf; and giving one of the Foot-men my Horfe to lead, I walk'd with him to his Lodging; where he return'd me thanks as well as he could, being not yet perfectly come to himfelf. He ask'd one of the Footmen who I was, and where I liv'd, and came next morning to acknowledge the fervice I had done him, and a few days after invited me to Supper, to which I took fome Perfons of Quality, my Friends along with me, who were no lefs furpriz'd than I, at the Magnificence of this Entertainment.

VI. The King defigning (as I faid) to march his Army againft the Duke of *Savoy*, made them fet out in the depth of Winter, and he himfelf follow'd in *February*, 1629. I ftaid a little after him at *Paris*, to pick up fome Souldiers that were left behind, and went with about two hundred to overtake the King beyond *Fontain-bleau*, according to the

order

order his Majesty has given me. As soon as I was come up, I distributed every Souldier into his own Company, and then took my own place in the head of mine, to march along with the Army to *Lyons*. My Company (that is Monsieur *St. Preuil's*, which I almost always commanded) consisted at that time of two hundred and fifty men, all lusty fellows, and well clad. There were among them about fourscore young Gentlemen, most of them of very good families, and had very handsom equipage. I having the honour to be known by all the persons of the Court, and all the principal Officers in the Army, for one that had always with great industry apply'd my self to my profession, was very exact in my discipline, and had a great care of my Souldiers; this made a great many people of Quality do me the honour to entrust their Sons with me, to learn what the experience and diligence of so many years had taught me. And I think I may say without vanity, that I was beloved, feared and obeyed by my men after a very extraordinary manner. But I try'd by a particular address to win upon the affection of the Cadets; for I gave them the Command of the Company by turns, that while they were learning to be Souldiers, they might learn to be Captains and Officers too at the same time.

The King was much pleas'd to see this Company in so good order, and exprest his satisfaction, by granting it a priviledge which others had not. Forseeing my Company so large, and full of Gentlemen of Quality, I thought it my duty to acquaint his Majesty, that being alone, as I then was, without my Captain, and having so many young Gentlemen, whom their Parents had committed to my care, I should find my self over-burden'd with the charge, unless his Majesty made me some grant in favour of all those young Cadets, that they might be treated with more respect than the common sort of Souldiers; for they not having been inured to hardship, would soon grow discontented, and complain to their Relations, whom I should by that means make my Enemies, and so might make most of them at last disband, and quit the Army. The King very graciously reply'd, That I did him a kindness in giving him this notice, and I am glad (said he) that you have askt me what I grant you most willingly. Thus I had ever after double Quarters for my Company, and by this means had it in my power to make some distinction betwixt the Cadets, and the ordinary sort of Souldiers.

I was also very careful to prevent any disorders in the Quarters, not being able to endure that the Souldiers should wrong poor people in the Villages. To this purpose, when I went out, I always drew up my Company, and made proclamation, that if any Countryman had cause to complain, he might come and do it without any fear. Before I dislodg'd I saw all things restor'd, and never went out of the Town, till I had first got a Certificate from the Lord and the Parish Priest; being resolv'd always to carry my justification in my Pocket, and fearing left I should be accus'd to the King, who was more severe to me than all the rest, because he made me the instrument of reforming the discipline among his Guards. But I had another reason still, which oblig'd me to some exactness in this point, and that was, that having so many Gentlemen in my Company, who were like to be Commanders themselves shortly after, I would not use them to pilfering, left when they came to be Officers, they should suffer their Souldiers to do the same, that they had been formerly allow'd in themselves. And those mean things were not to be indured in men of birth and quality, whose minds ought to be noble and generous above the meaner sort of men.   VII. As

VII. As soon as our Army was arriv'd within some few leagues of *Lyons*, we being to pass the River in Boats, fearing some disorder might happen in the passage, I told Monsieur *Vientais*, a Captain of the Guards, that we must endeavour to pass first, if we would do it safely, and without confusion; and accordingly we embarkt our Companies, and past early without any loss or tumult. It afterwards appear'd that our fear had not been groundless, for there was such a disorder in getting over the Army, that a great deal of Baggage was lost. The King staid a while at *Lyons*, and we refresht our selves in the Country round about, and I and my Company went to a Village about a league beyond *Lyons*; but it happen'd that this Village, which was assign'd for our Quarters, belong'd to a Kinsman of mine, a Captain of a new-rais'd Regiment, who was then in *Dauphine*. His Wife frighted to see so many Souldiers, came and conjur'd me to use my best endeavour for exempting her Estate from Quartering. This was no easy matter to obtain, the Army lying so disperst all over the Country as it did; and I had much ado to prevail with my self to go about it, but told, the orders were given, and it would breed a great confusion. But at last yield I did, to a Woman's, and a Relation's request, and went back to *Lyons*, to see if I could obtain what this Lady desir'd. As soon as I came into the King's presence, I humbly besought him to remember, he was now entring into my Country, and that I came to beg one favour, which was, that he would direct our Quarters to be chang'd, because the Village assign'd us belong'd to a Kinswoman of mine. They press me hard, Sir, said I, to make use of my credit with your Majesty upon this occasion, or at least the credit they imagine I have. The King turning to the Lords about him; 'Tis true (said he laughing) we do now approach his Country, and ought to consider him a little. So he gave order presently to Monsieur *d'Escures* to change the Quarters; and as soon as I had receiv'd the order, I return'd to the Village, and dislodg'd the three Companies the same day, who lost nothing by the bargain, for they were much better provided for in their new Quarters.

VIII. But it fell out by an odd accident, that at the same time I did this good Office for my Kinsman, in clearing his Village of Souldiers already fix'd in their Quarters; he who had raised a recruit of thirty or forty men, must needs, forsooth, go quarter at *Pontis*. In my Mannor-house, I had a good stout Bailiff, one of generosity and wisdom too. This Captain then coming into the Castle, and telling the Bailiff, that he came to quarter in the House, the fellow receiv'd him very civilly, knowing him to be my Relation, and told him, all there was at his service. Accordingly he entertain'd him well, had his Horses set up and drest, and gave Bread and Wine to the Souldiers. But when the Captain declar'd he would stay three or four days, and the Tenants were to receive and lodge the Souldiers at their own charge, this Bailiff a little surpriz'd at that, told him, He receiv'd him as his Master's Kinsman, and not as a Captain, and that it was not reasonable his Master's poor Tenants should be opprest; at which the Officer began to huff, telling him he had his orders to quarter there. The Bailiff, who was no Fool, thinking it best to give way, dispatch'd a Messenger privately to me, and inform'd me of all that past.

This man's ill nature and unworthy carriage vex'd me I confess, and in my ill humour I wrote my Bailiff an angry Letter, wherein I said, I re-

nounc'd

nounc'd his kindred and friendſhip, and could no longer look upon him as a man of honour; and that if his Trunks and Baggage were ſtill in the Caſtle, he ſhould not deliver them, till he was paid for all that had been ſpent. In the mean while thisCaptain after two or three days was upon going, and entreated my Bailiff to ſend him his Trunks to a certain place that he nam'd, which the fellow, having not yet receiv'd any orders from me, promis'd to do; and thus he march'd away with his Company, much pleas'd with having us'd a Kinſman and a Friend, as if he had been the moſt perfect Stranger in the world. My Bailiff, upon the receipt of my Letter, took an honeſt reſolution to execute my pleaſure faithfully, and like a brave fellow; for ſoon after, the Captain troubled that his Trunks were not ſent him, ſent again to demand them, but the Meſſenger was ſurpriz'd at his anſwer, That when the Captain paid for what he, and his Company, and his Horſes had eaten and drunk, the Trunks ſhould be delivered. This news was no ſooner brought him, but he came himſelf in a great fury to demand his Baggage. The Bailiff anſwered, When he would pleaſe to defray what expences he and his Souldiers had put me to, the things were ready for him. How! ſaid he, the expence of my Souldiers; why was it not their due ? Sir, ſaid the Bailiff, I have order to deliver nothing without that : My Maſter hath forbidden me, I know he will be obeyed, and it would not be ſafe for me to fail in it. Here is his Letter, and if you will give your ſelf that trouble, you may read it your ſelf. He read all my angry Letter againſt himſelf, and ſeeing his ill nature and baſeneſs repreſented there to the life, he could not look oh it without abhorring his own deformity; and not knowing which way to diſcharge his paſſion, he ſputtered it out in railing and injurious language, and at laſt went away in a rage, ſeeing his ſtrength too ſmall; for there were in this Village near a hundred good Souldiers, and brave Fire-men, ready to fight, as Provencals uſually are, and theſe were all very well reſolv'd to defend the right and intereſt of their Lord.

But this Captains mind was ſoon changed; His Wife, to whom I had ſo lately done the good office you heard of, writ him a Letter at this very time, of the conſiderable ſervice they had received from me, conjuring him, that where-ever he met me, he ſhould expreſs the acknowledgments they would ever have of my generous proceedings, and the proof I had given of my friendſhip to them, and my credit with the King. It is not eaſie to think the perplexity this news put him into: He ſaw himſelf overpower'd with civilities, when he was loading that very friend with opprobrious language, and ill uſage. Thus he was divided between two contrary paſſions; Anger on one ſide, and Shame on the other; and he could not tell at firſt whether of theſe he ſhould yield to: but at laſt Shame carried it, he confeſſes himſelf to blame, is ſenſible how he had wounded our friendſhip, and reſolves to make amends. Thus full of confuſion he goes back to my Bailiff, makes a thouſand excuſes, pays both for himſelf and his Souldiers, and hath his Baggage delivered to him. Afterward he employ'd all his friends, and among others Monſieur *de Bonne*, who was a Lord of *Dauphine*, to reconcile me to him. But I could never prevail with my ſelf to own a man for my friend, who had betray'd ſuch want of honour and generoſity; and all I could grant thoſe who intereſted themſelves for him upon this occaſion, was only an Interview, where all the Complement I made him was this, That having the honour to know him, I thought my ſelf no leſs happy in being known by him, for the man I was. He excus'd himſelf mightily, but I would

never

never see him more, thinking a man that had been capable of so much baseness, would hardly ever change his Nature, or render himself worthy to be beloved.

IX. When the King had staid some time at *Lyons*, he past on to *Grenoble*, and from thence to *Ambrun*; and being his Majesty was to continue there some days, I askt leave of him to go before, as far as *Pontis*, which was not far off, with fifteen or twenty Officers of the Guards. We stay'd there four or five days, in which time I entertain'd them so magnificently, that it cost me two years Revenue. We thought of nothing but diverting our selves, when all of us had a great combat to undergo. On a sudden we heard a great noise as we were walking, that rattled like a Whirlwind, and looking that way from whence it came, we saw a prodigious large Eagle, which had fallen upon a flock of Turkies. Twelve or thirteen of us that were there, all ran with our Swords drawn to engage this King of the Air; but the Bird, instead of being frighted, came on himself to charge us, not being able to mount, because the Country was low, and he had not air enough to raise himself, being very heavy, and surpriz'd too, before he could take all the advantages for flying away. 'Tis incredible with what fury he made at us, his strength being so great, that with one blow of his Wing, he stunn'd and fell'd one of us to the ground, and had like to have kill'd one of the biggest Mastiffs in the Country, with seizing him in his Talons, as the Dog came out to seize him. To conclude, after all we could do could not hurt him with our Swords, nor ever get the better of him, till we sent for a Fowling-piece, and shot him twice or thrice to get him down. We carry'd this Eagle along with us to *Ambrun*, to shew it to the King, to whom Monsieur *Comminges*, who was one of the company, gave a narration of our Combat; and his Majesty saying he wish'd he had been there, he very pleasantly replyed, that his Majesty's person had been less secure in an engagement with this Eagle, than if he had fought against that of the Empire.

X. I had order'd all the Souldiers of the Village of *Pontis* to give a Volley of all the Shot they could make (which amounted to no more than a few Musquets, and a good many Chambers that I had got ready) to salute the King, when he past by the foot of the Hill on which the Village stands. Thus when nothing less was expected, on a sudden a great noise was heard, and the King standing still upon the Bridge over the *Durance*, which was in the Valley, seem'd pleased with this Rattle that I endeavoured to honour my House with, and said in merriment, He will furnish us with Cannon for a need. After this came the Parish Priest with the Cross, and all the Inhabitants, to salute the King; the Curate harrangued his Majesty in his Provencal language, and the King attempted to reply in the same tone, but could hardly make himself understood, which gave great diversion. After the King had with great goodness lookt upon these poor people, who fell on their knees before him, he made them rise, and dismist them.

I thought this a favourable occasion humbly to entreat his Majesty would determine a great controversie this Village was engaged in, which being scituate upon the Confines of *Dauphine* and *Provence*, was every day by the ears with the Officers of each Province, while both of them equally pretended to it. I represented to his Majesty the Tyranny exercised

ercised every year over his poor Subjects, in making them pay their Taxes twice over; and humbly begg'd his authority would put an end to these unjust persecutions. The King spoke of it to the Council, and I had it left to my choice, which of the two Provinces I would settle it in. Monsieur *Crequi*, who was Governour of *Dauphine*, hearing of it, laid hard at me to fix it there, promising me his service and protection upon all occasions. To whom I answer'd, that he did me great honour, but I humbly begg'd of him, that I might have leave to consult the advantage of the poor people, who found it much more commodious to be seated in *Provence*; and I knew him so generous and kind, that he would continue me the honour of his protection, tho of another Government, since of what Province soever I were, I should still belong to the King, whom he himself was proud to serve. I chose then with his Majesty's good liking to fix it in *Provence*, to which it belonged indeed in Monsieur *d'Esenre's* judgment, rather than to *Dauphine*; and I obtain'd an Order of Council upon the matter. But the King granted me besides, a fair Privilege to the Mannor-house of *Pontis*, which was, that whereas all Affairs and Differences of the Village were to be determin'd by the Judicature of the Province, those that concern the Mannor-house are all referred to the Kings Council. And this hath been observed ever since, as well in respect of the Parish business, as the Lords; the Officers of *Dauphine* make no more pretensions to the one, and the other acknowledges no Judge but the Council.

XI. The King came to *Braincon*, where there is a Mountain not to be past but upon Hurdles, a kind of Carriage, behind which the person that guides it sits, and makes it slide down extreme steep places, with marvellous swiftness. His Majesty told me, I being the Guide must shew the way. The Consul's Daughter of the Country came and offer'd her self to let me down. The King at first was in some concern, to see a young Maid undertake a thing that he thought had so much danger in it. But they assured him this Maid understood the Trade very well, and so he said smiling, Well, we shall grow wise however at his cost. I sat down upon the Hurdle, under the conduct of this Girl, and away we flew down over the Snow, as swift as an Arrow out of a Bow; and having scrambled up again to come tell the King there was no danger, he sat down, and was guided by the Consul himself, and down he went as fast and as safe, as I had done before. He rewarded the man with a Priviledge and some Pistoles; and all that waited on the King had the same passage, but for the Army they were order'd to fetch a compass, that they might pass with greater ease.

When the King was advanc'd with his Army, within a league of the City of *Suza*, he commanded Monsieur *Comminges*, a Captain of his Guards, to go next day to *Suza*, with the Quarter-masters, to take up Lodgings for him and all the Court. He order'd me to bear Monsieur *Comminges* Company, that if Count *Verrue*, who guarded the Pass of *Suza*, should give us free passage, I might bring him back an account; but in case he should deny it, we might observe the places and manner by which it should be attackt. We went away next morning some twelve or fifteen in company, and being come within two hundred paces of the streight, we founded a Trumpet. Upon which Count *Verrue* sent an Officer with ten or twelve Souldiers, to know who we were, and what we would have. Monsieur *Comminges* askt if he were the person that

commanded

commanded there, becuse the King had sent him to speak with him.
The Officer bid us stay where we were, and he would return with an
answer immediately. After he had made his report to Count *Verrue*, who
kept this Pass with about two thousand men, he came again to tell us,
That the Count was coming himself, and that we need not draw forward;
which he said to prevent our discovering the place. Presently after the
Count appeared at the head of two hundred Musqueters, and after a
civil salute, Monsieur *Comminges* said to him; Sir, the King my Master
hath commanded me to go to day to *Suza*, to prepare his Lodgings, because he intends to lye there to morrow night. To which the Count reply'd very civilly, Sir, His Highness would take it for a very great honour
to lodge his Majesty, but since his Majesty comes with so much attendance,
you shall give me leave if you please to acquaint his Highness with it
first. What then, Sir, reply'd Monsieur *Comminges*, will not you let us pass?
Sir, return'd the Count *de Verrue*, You must give me leave, as I told you
before, first to acquaint his Highness. To which Monsieur *Comminges*
made answer, Well, Sir, then I go, and make my report to the King.
You may do as you please for that Sir, reply'd the Count.

Thus we took leave of him, and went back to his Majesty, who declar'd he did not take Count *Verrue*'s answer ill at all, but said, he answer'd like a wise man, and a good Commander; and he would prepare
to act like a great King. So orders were presently given for attacking
the Pass. What was most remarkable upon this occasion, which hath
been so much talkt of since, was, that the Enemy standing firm to expect
us at this streight, which it had been impossible for us to force, was very
much surpriz'd, to see the Count *de Saux*, who had shovell'd away the
Snow, and crawl'd up those high Mountains, come fall on them on a sudden,
and enclose their Rear, upon which they fled immediately, and left all
their Fortifications; so that our Souldiers had leisure to make them feel
the weight of the King of *France*'s Arms, to whom they had the boldness to deny a passage. There were however a great many of our men
kill'd by the Cannon of *Suza*, which scowred all the passage after a strange
manner. Mareschal *Schomberg* was wounded there, but his wound only
serv'd to render him more glorious, and more hardy against the Enemy.
Suza presently surrendred to his Majesty, and a Peace soon after being
concluded, the King was visited there by his Highness; and the King resolving to pay his visit, did all he could to surprize him, but he could not.
For the Duke having notice of his coming, came down stairs to meet the
King, who said, I had a mind to surprize you, and have got into your
Chamber. To which his Highness very pleasantly reply'd, So great a
King as he, could not easily be conceal'd. And as the King and the Duke
were passing with a great crowd over a Gallery, that was not very strong,
the King saying, That they had best make haste, left the Gallery should
fall under them. The Duke return'd this complemental answer, That
one might see, that every thing trembled under so great a King. His
Majesty then shewed him all his Army, and gave him the pleasure of
contemplating the *French* Nobility, after having made him some time
before feel the force of their Courage.

While our Army lay in *Piedmont* before the Peace, they plunder'd by
right of War; and I having three very beautiful *Neapolitan* Coursers
for my share, Count *Soissons* sent to entreat me to sell him one of them,
to restore it to the Duke; I sent him word, that having given thirty
Pistoles for one of them, he should have him for the same price if he
thought

thought fit; but for the other two which coſt me nothing, I would freely ſend them to him, without taking any thing for them, The Count was a little ſurpriz'd at my anſwer, and ſent me a Purſe full of Piſtoles, with this Meſſage; That he would not have my Horſes unleſs he might pay for them; but though I was not ſo rich as many others, yet my Soul was as great, ſo that I ſent him back his Purſe with the Horſes, without ever taking any more but the thirty Piſtoles, that the Horſe I mention'd coſt me.

XII. The King while at *Valence*, after having repaſt the Mountains, underſtood there, that ſeveral Cities had revolted by the inducement of the Religioniſts, and therefore went to beſiege *Privas*, which was one of the ſtrongeſt. Here I loſt a very good friend, a Captain of the Guards, who was unfortunately kill'd by one of our own Centry's, as he was going to diſcover ſome works. And what was moſt deplorable of all in this accident was, that his beſt friend was the cauſe of his death againſt his will. For as he was climbing up the ſide of a little Hill, this Officer taking him for one of the Enemy, commanded the Centinel to fire, which he did, diſcharging a great Muſquet ſhot upon him, by which he was ſlain. I miſs'd but little of ſharing in his misfortune, having offer'd my ſelf to go along with him; but he would go alone, and ſo periſht alone. Who can in ſuch caſes but acknowledge and admire that Providence, that rules and ordains ſo many different events, as beſt pleaſes him, who parts two friends to take away one, and ſave the other; and permits that one who would have given his blood for his friend, ſhould himſelf be innocently the cauſe of his death! But my Eyes at that time were too much fix'd upon the earth, to raiſe me up to this principle, and went along as other people with the ſtream of the age, lamenting the loſs of a perſon whom I lov'd, and improving that thought no farther. I ſhall ſay nothing more of this Siege, nor of the other Towns that ſurrendred to the King; my deſign being not to compile a Hiſtory, which were an undertaking above my abilities, but only as I ſaid, to obſerve the different accidents and circumſtances that occur to my mind; ſuch as may be uſeful to manifeſt the Government of the Almighty in the courſe of this mortal life; or may afford ſome light into a profeſſion that I have addicted my ſelf to ſo many years with more than common aſſiduity and application.

XIII. At the King's return to *Paris*, there befel me what the world would think a great fortune, eſpecially for ſuch a one as I, who ſeem'd to be cut out more for the acquiring Honour than Wealth; while I ſaw ſo many others advance and enrich themſelves in a ſhort time. One day as the King was at *St. Germains*, and coming very nimbly down ſtairs to go a hunting, I happen'd to be there, and his Majeſty leaning upon my arm, that he might go faſter and ſurer, I thought to ſnatch this opportunity of begging a conſiderable Eſcheat of a Sempſtreſs of the Queen's, one *Rachel de Viaga*, a *Spaniard* by birth, one who had not been naturalized; and then lay extremely ſick. I contented my ſelf at that time with giving a very ſhort account of the matter, and beg that his Majeſty would pleaſe to remember me, as he had done me the favour to promiſe he would. His Majeſty aſſur'd me he would not forget it; and accordingly hearing ſome days after that the woman was expiring, and could not live till morning, he promis'd me the Eſcheat. I was ſenſible I ſhould not want

Competitors,

Competitors, and begg d the King's protection, representing to him, that a great many would attempt to deprive me of his bounty, as being more worthy than I. To which the King reply'd, Go, go, take you no care, I'll support you against them all. And his Majesty shewed afterwards, that he had taken me into his protection, preferring me before several Lords, who would fain have been nibbling at this Escheat, which was indeed very confiderable, and what I might very well look upon as a reward his Majesty's bounty intended me for all my past services.

The Sempstress dying that night, next morning by break of day several great persons, as the Duke of *Elbeuf,* the Marquis *de Rambouillat,* Great Master of the Wardrobe, and some others, came to beg this Escheat of the King; but his Majesty, mindful of the promise he had made me, told them all, It was not in his power, for he had dispos'd of it already. He explain'd himself no farther as yet; but presently after told the Duke of *Elbeuf* all, who had a great kindness for me, and declared himself very well satisfied with my having it; protesting that had he known his Majesty's inclination to do me that favour, he would have joyned with me in the request; but the rest were not of his temper, and especially a great Officer in the Houshold, who shew'd himself too importuning and troublesome, when it was too late; and after he knew it was given to me, charged the Usher of the Chamber not to let me in the next day. So that when I thought to prevent the ill offices which I knew very well were design'd me, and came to present my self betimes in the morning at the Chamber-door, to have audience one of the first, the Usher a little roughly bad me stay till the King was up. I guest whence this came, and knew the shutting me out of the Kings Chamber was to shut me out from his bounty too : But I believed that a Prince, when he had declared himself as his Majesty had done, would soon stop his Subjects mouths, and that no one could be so bold to ask, or so successful to obtain a Grace that his Majesty had so frankly bestow'd upon me.

I waited then till the Crowd came, and went with some Lords into the Chamber; as soon as I was in the room I made my reverence to the King, and pray'd him to remember me; to which his Majesty replyed, I have remembred you, I give you what I promised, and what others have tryed in vain to take from you. Go presently to *la Vailliere,* and bid him from me draw up your Bill of Donation for this Escheat. I entreated his Majesty to send some one immediately from himself, telling him, that Monsieur *la Vailliere* might otherwise make some difficulty of the thing. I see, said the King, you are used to take your securities; go you before, and I will send some body after you. I went away immediately, and it fell out as I had foreseen, for Monsieur *la Vailliere* told me, he would speak to the King about it first; that he was going to the *Louvre,* and would discourse him about it. I had a mind to be by, and therefore going into the Coach with him, we went together to the King. There I found Mr *L.* and *St. G.* who not judging so favourably of me, as his Majesty had done, and thinking this gift more fit for them, were so bold as to ask him, If he knew what this Escheat was worth ? The King told them, he thought it might be worth fifty thousand Francks. How, Sir! said they : Yes, above two hundred thousand; whereas if your Majesty had given Monsieur *Pontis* fifty or threescore thousand Livres, would not he be well enough rewarded ? This confident answer very much displeased the King, who not liking to have his actions so controul'd, said with a voice of Authority, Kings govern themselves by their own wills, if this Efcheat were worth a hundred thoufand Crowns, I would give it *Pontis* with a much better will. You think becaufe he has but little, I fhould give him but little; and I quite contrary would give him much more than I do, becaufe I know he hath a great deal of Merit, tho but a fmall Eftate. This anfwer out of the mouth of a King, and pronounced with a more than ordinary Emphafis, ftruck them all dumb, and gave me a joy paft my power to exprefs, to fee his Majefty take my part fo warmly againft the great ones, who thought they had a right to oppofe his favours to me.

My Bill being prefently difpatched, a Courtier who had a confiderable Office, made me this pretty Complement; Sir, You are not acquainted with affairs of this kind, if you will give me one half of this Efcheat, I will quickly put you into fecure poffeffion of the reft, without any trouble or difpute at all. I knowing him a very cunning man, and a little concern'd in the bufinefs, thankt him civilly for his kind proffer, to do me, or rather indeed himfelf that good Office, telling him, the burden was not fo heavy, but that I both would, and could, bear it all my felf. I fent away fome Souldiers of my Company into the Country-houfes that belonged to this Sempftrefs, whofe Heir I was conftituted; and being defirous to acknowledge in fome meafure his Majefty's liberality toward me, I fent him a Prefent of all the Holland and Baptifte which was in her Shop at *Paris*; and among other things a great Point-bed, which the King gave the Queen, valued at ten thoufand Crowns. The Hollands he gave among the Queens Maids of Honour. But I afterwards found I had been too free, thus to give back again a good part of what the King had given me: For after I had cleared my hands of the rich Cloaths and fumptuous Bed, and had taken poffeffion of the Lands and other Eftates of this Sempftrefs, one of her Kinfmen prefented a Requeft to the Parliament, in purfuance of an old Letter, by which he pretended to fhew, that this *Spanifh* woman had been naturalized. I was bafely down in the mouth at this news, and refolved to fend one on purpofe into *Spain* for more particular information; but all the fervice that did me, was only the throwing away five hundred **Crowns** more, which this mans journey coft me. For after the matter had lain a long time before the Parliament, at laft Judgment was given againft me, that all the Land fhould go to the Kinfman, and the Movables fhould be mine. Thus after I had given the beft of the Goods away, I was difpoffeft of the Land; and that which fhould have been worth to me above two hundred thoufand Livres, was not worth above ten thoufand, all charges born. The King not being able to forbear laughing at me, faid one day, Well *Pontis*, thou wert born to be a man of Honour, but not a man of Fortune. Sir, re-reply'd I fmiling, it has depended upon my felf to make me a man of Honour, but it will depend only upon your Majefty to make me a man of Fortune, and that may be done whenever you pleafe. But how comes it to pafs, faid the King, that thou couldft not keep this Efcheat? Sir, faid I, your Majefty gave it me, but your Juftice hath taken it from me; but you have it in your power always to repair this lofs of mine with advantage, by fome other Grant. The King only laugh'd at what I faid, and I remain'd the fame I was before. For moft certainly, God who knew that Riches might have been my ruine, by tying me fafter to the World, always fet thofe great fortunes, to which I might have fome pretenfions, at a diftance from me; and by an effect of his infinite mercy, that I did not then difcern, let me be croft in the defigns of

my

my whole life, because he had another design upon me, much more advantagious, than all I could wish for then. The more diligent I was in my Command, and the more faithful in all parts of my duty, the less I advanced in my fortune. The King, whom I serv'd with incredible zeal, shew'd a particular affection for me, as several passages in these *Memoirs* declare; but then his keeping me always about his own person, hindred him from raising me to considerable Commands, that might have given me greater liberty to retire; and he was not over-hasty in doing any great matters for me in the condition I then was, that so he might keep me to a more absolute dependance upon him alone.

XIV. There happen'd to me about this time, as I was upon the Guard at the *Louvre*, a rencounter pleasant enough in it self, but untoward for the consequence it might have had, and the quality of the person concern'd in it. The King had given me command to lye upon the Guard, contrary to what other Officers used to do; desiring to have me extraordinary obsequious to him, and fixt to his person, knowing me particularly faithful and affectionate in his Service. The Duke of *Orleans*, who then lay in the *Louvre*, coming home on foot one night very late, resolv'd to surprize the Guard in a jest, which had like to have cost both him and us very dear, He being always well attended, some of his Train had got within eight or ten paces of the Centinel; and then threw themselves so nimbly upon him, that they wrapt him up in a Cloak, and stopt his mouth with a handkerchief to hinder his crying out. Then they came all together to the Guard, and began to cry, Kill, kill: I was laid down upon the Mattrice, and most of the Souldiers were asleep; but we were soon rouzed; and I, surpriz'd to see my self so prest on a sudden, ran out of door with my Sword, crying, To me, To me. I call'd the Pikes and Musquets, and began to push our assailants very vigorously; whose shoulders were well cudgell'd with bangs of Pikes distributed very liberally; and finding such warm entertainment, they cry'd out, The Duke of *Orleans*; and he himself cry'd out, *Gascon*, *Gascon*. But the more they cry'd the more I laid on, without hearkning to any thing they said, till at last we enclosed them all in the Guard-room, and were about to use them very scurvily: But knowing the Duke, I cry'd out, Oh, my Lord! what have you done? you have hazarded your own, and all our lives. I got him presently into my Chamber, and with much ado appeas'd the tumult, the Souldiers being heated, and much enrag'd, for having suffer'd themselves to be so surpriz'd.

There were no lives lost, because it was done all on the sudden, and the Souldiers had not time to recollect themselves, or come into a posture for doing mischief. I came afterward to the Duke of *Orleans*, and told him, I was at my wits end for what had happen'd; but his Highness ought to pardon us, since we could not do otherwise than we had done, not knowing who they were, and that we had all been lost, had we suffer'd our selves to be forc'd. To which the Duke answer'd, Go, go, it was only a frolick, and if you say nothing, we have no great reason to brag of it. I could not take this for a jest though, and apprehended some disgrace from it. The Duke of *Orleans* protested that he pardon'd me with all his heart, and gave me the assurance of it by looking graciously upon me. Never was Prince in such a fright, his Jest having succeeded so ill, and seeing himself so vigorously attack'd by his own fault, and ready to be knock't o'th' head by those whose duty it was to defend him. It

was

was very fortunate both for him and us that he came off with life, since otherwise we had all been lost without remedy, though it was but the performance of our duty. It is ill playing such pranks, unworthy not only of a Prince, but of the meanest Gentleman. I attended him to his Apartment, where he caus'd himself immediately to be let blood. I reprov'd the Centinel severely, who was a brave Cadet, and more unfortunate than faulty, though according to the Rules of War, he deserv'd to have been punish'd.

In the morning I was at the King's rising, not daring to conceal this affair from him, which he must needs have heard from others. He took me into his Cabinet, and I gave him an account of all that past. He askt whether his Brother were hurt, and understanding that he was not, he only laught, and said, I perceive they were well beaten, but 'tis no matter, they deserv'd it. But fearing still lest the Duke of *Orleans* might resent this affront, I took the liberty to beseech his Majesty to make my peace with him, which he promis'd to do. He sent one of the Gentlemen of the Chamber to see how he did, without taking notice of any thing. The Duke, who had no great mind to divulge what had befallen him, sent word he was well, but had been let blood for a slight indisposition. And coming a little after to the King, his Majesty took him into into his Cabinet, where, after having intimated that he had heard of the business, and rattled him soundly for his rashness in exposing his person so, he call'd me in, and said to the Duke; Here is *Pontis* in great confusion about your matter. To which the Duke immediately made answer, That he did not take any thing I had done the least ill, but was ready to serve me upon all occasions. And indeed he resented it so little, that when I desir'd a little after a Colours for one of my Souldiers, his Royal Highness gave it me at first word.

The End of the First Volume.

MEMOIRS

Sieur De PONTIS.

PART II.

BOOK I.

The King sends Cardinal Richelieu with a powerful Army to the Relief of the Duke of Mantua. The Death of Monsieur de Canaples. Cazal besieg'd by the Enemies, and the Siege rais'd. An Interview of the French and Spanish Generals when the Peace was concluded. The Cardinal Mazarine saves the French Army, and the Sieur de Pontis afterwards brings them off from a great danger.

I. THE Duke of *Savoy*, seeing the King at a distance, and now gone back to *Paris*, thought his honour concern'd to break that Treaty with him, the making of which had been indeed the effect of necessity more than choice. To this purpose he sought the alliance of the King of *Spain*, and of the Emperour, who had sent the grand *Colalto* with a strong force to invest the Duke of *Mantua* in his Capital City. The King conceiving a just indignation at this breach of Faith in the Duke of *Savoy*, sent Cardinal *Richelieu* in the beginning of the year 1630. to repass the Mountains, that he might relieve his Ally the Duke of *Mantua*, and revenge this false dealing of the *Savoyard*. The Cardinal's March was very splendid and remarkable, when he past through the Plain of *Montobris* to go to *Pignerol*. For he march'd the Army in Battalia, and all the Officers on foot for a whole day, himself in the middle of the Army in his Coach, playing with a very pretty little Boy, that was almost always with his Eminence, and never from him, except when he came as a Spy to make his observations in the Army. He discharged this piece of service notably, though he was but very young, and in this respect proved himself a wonderful Scholar of so great a Master. For he would come and toy and play up and down among the Officers and Souldiers, without ever discovering any thing of

his

his defign, and then all he heard he was fure to tell to the Cardinal. Thus he put a trick upon all the world the more fecurely, becaufe of the innocence that appear'd in his behaviour, and concealing his malice under the ufual fimplicity of that age. I for my part being then in the Army, and particularly obferv'd, by reafon of my refufing to put my felf into his Eminence's fervice, no doubt was no more fpar'd by this youngfter than all the reft; though I kept my felf pretty much upon my guard, fo as to be careful not to fpeak any thing worth telling again. But who would ever have fufpected fo young a Spy, or have thought that the play of a Child fo little, fhould have been made ufe of to cheat, and put a trick upon all the Officers of the Army?

When we were come to a Village near the little River of *Oria*, his Eminence was vifited there by his Highnefs of *Savoy*, to whom, by his orders, we all paid the fame honour as to the King himfelf. After this firft interview, which was to propofe an accommodation, the Cardinal made ready to pafs the River with all the Horfe at the Foord, having fent the Foot another way about to go over the Bridge. That which I thought very obfervable on this occafion, was to fee a Bifhop and a Cardinal with a water-colour'd Cuiraffe on, and a Feuille-mort colour'd Habit, embroiderd with Gold, a curious Feather round his Hat, two Pages marching before him on Horfeback, one of which carried his Gantlet, and the other his Head-piece; and two more Pages on Horfeback, on each fide of him one, with a very fine led Horfe; and after him came the Captain of his Guards. Thus equipp'd he paft the River *Oria*, with his Sword by his fide, and a Cafe of Piftols at his Saddle-bow. And when he was got to the bank on the other fide, he made his Horfe prance and curvett before the Army, fome a hundred times together, as if he took a pride to fhew the world, that he very well underftood that exercife.

II. From thence we remov'd and lay at *Rivoli*, where the Cardinal receiv'd a fecond vifit from his Highnefs of *Savoy*, to whom at his coming we paid the fame refpects as before. But after the Cardinal and the Duke had fome difcourfe together, and the Duke would not comply with fome propofals made to him, we receiv'd orders to take no more notice of him at his going away than if he had been a meer private man. So that prefently laying down our arms, we walk'd and talk'd with one another, and made as though we had not feen him pafs by.

III. The Cardinal refolving from *Rivoli* to go befiege *Pignerol*, made ufe of a common ftratagem to impofe upon the Duke of *Savoy*, by pretending a laying Siege to *Turin*, that fo his Highnefs being wholly taken up with the fortifying himfelf there, might not take any care of putting any fuccours into *Pignerol*. His Eminence therefore having march'd upon the Van-guard and Artillery within a league of *Turin*, gave order that the Rear fhould immediately draw off towards *Pignerol*, and fo changing the Rear of his Army and making it the Van, he gave this City fuch a furprize that they faw themfelves invefted before any fuccours could get into them, which reduc'd them to a neceffity of furrendring in very few days. Poor Monfieur *de Comminges*, a Captain of the Guards, and my very particular friend, loft his life at this Siege through his own fault. For I having been two or three times to make my obfervation of an advanc'd work, and fee if it could be carried on ftill further, fo as to make

a Lodg-a Lodgment nearer the Town. He would needs go to view it too, and ask'd the Marefchal *Crequi's* leave to do fo : Who told him at firft, that he advis'd him not to put himfelf upon any unnecefary hazard of his life, fince I had feen all that there was to be feen already. This however did not prevail with him, but he urg'd the Marefchal on, till at laft he got leave to go have his brains knockt out; not confidering that God often punifhes the rafhnefs and oftentation of fuch as court danger. He begg'd of me to fhew him the way, which I knew not how to deny; and he went on farther than I did. As we were coming back again, it happen'd I know not how, that I ftay'd a little behind, and as he walk'd on before me very foftly in a place that was much expofed, I defir'd him to mend his pace, and not value himfelf upon his Courage, becaufe I faw a fellow levelling directly at him.

He, without queftion loth to difcover any fear, went on at his old rate, defying the death that threatned him, and in that very inftant was fhot quite through the body, with a Mufquet-bullet, with which he fell to the ground. He did not dye however upon the fpot, but was carry'd into the Camp, and liv'd fome days; and then, tho too late, he confeft himfelf to blame, for not having taken Monfieur *de Crequi's*, and my advice. I was fenfibly afflicted to fee him in this condition, but there is no preventing a mans misfortune, that will run upon his own death; and I never faw a plainer inftance of the Divine Juftice, in punifhing thofe that prefume to tempt Providence, and caft themfelves into danger, when there is no occafion for it. For tho he was really a gallant man, and my very good friend, yet I cannot but condemn fuch imprudent carriage as this was. It is fit, nay it is necefary not to be afraid of death, when the difcharge of one's duty is concerned, but to brave it unfeafonably is the very extremity of folly. I own I always difdain'd that ridiculous fool-hardinefs, and never could value my felf upon expofing my perfon to a Gun, without being called to it. Nothing is more idle than to dye at this rate; 'tis to draw upon ones felf the fcorn and the cenfure of all mankind, for the fake of a miftaken notion of Gallantry. Indeed I cannot inveigh too feverely againft this vain imagination of Courage, that takes off a world of young perfons; and they would do well to learn from the examples of thofe that have gone before them, that fuch a fort of death cannot be reputed honourable, either by God or Man.

After the furrender of *Piguerol*, I was one of them that were commanded to fee the Town fortify'd, and there I built a large Baftion, that went afterwards by the name of *Pontis.*

IV. While the Kings Arms met with fo good fuccefs in *Piedmont*, under the command of Cardinal *Richelieu*, his Majefty made preparations for removing with the whole Court to *Lyons*, about the middle of *May*, 1630. And in regard the Duke of *Savoy* ftill perfifted in maintaining what he had begun, the King went and befieged *Chamberry*; which yielded prefently, with very little oppofition. But as little as it was, Monfieur *de Canaples* received a Mufquet-fhot before it, of which he dyed a little while after. Upon the furrender of the place, he was carry'd in thither. It is impoffible for me to exprefs the friendfhip and tendernefs which he did me the honour to profefs for me during his illnefs: Perhaps there never was a more perfect reconciliation feen. He defired me not to ftir from his Bed-fide; and once mentioning the difference that happen'd between us at the Siege of *Rochelle*, he said, with a most extraordinary goodness, *Really, poor* Pontis, *I did not know thee, and it seems a quarrel was necessary to bring us to a right understanding of one another, and make us good friends.* I had much ado to steal from him to discharge the duty of my Post; and unless he was told that the King or some of the Generals had sent to speak with me, he complained that I had a mind to desert him, in a condition, when he profest to repose the greatest confidence in me. I did all in my power to return so sincere a kindness: I comforted him the best I could, I encourag'd him, and gave him good hopes; and I may say, that if Providence had not otherwise disposed of him, I might have expected to find a second *Zamet*, for friendship and open-heartedness. But his hour was come, and so will ours at one time or other; and I must do him the Justice to say, being by when he expired, that he dy'd with a great sense of Piety.

V. Several other places followed the example of *Chamberry*, and every thing yielded to his Majesty's Arms. But one remarkable accident befell me at *Montmelian*; which the Mareschal *de Chatillon* was ordered to besiege, or rather indeed to carry on the Siege begun by the Sieur *de Vignoles*. Our men having one day raised a Battery against two low Flankers, and distressing them pretty much, the Enemies cast up another against ours, consisting of five or six of their biggest pieces of Ordnance, which fired so terribly, that all the Carriages of our Guns were broke to pieces, and the Gunners either kill'd or beat off from their Post. I was upon the Guard about fifty paces off, and apprehending that the Enemy, exalted with this good success, might make a Sally; I immediately went to the Centinel, and directed him to keep close upon his Guard, for fear of any surprize, which I very much suspected; and then repaired to my own Post. Assoon as ever I came there, a Cannon-bullet grazed along a Wall, against which the Souldiers of the Guard had set their Musquets an end, and taking them in a row, cut them all off in the middle, and at the same time made them all go off. This great noise, and the surprize of so odd an accident, made me retreat some few steps backward, as men commonly do in the first fright: But Providence so ordered it, that the consternation I was in at this sudden and prodigious Crack, was the occasion of saving my life. For in the very instant, came one or two Cannon-bullets more, that took the top of the Wall, and overturn'd it just in the place, from whence the first had made me retire. God however design'd to make me sensible that my preservation was owing to him, by suffering me to be overtaken by a great Stone, which falling upon me, broke my Gorget, and bruised my Shoulder.

VI. In *September* the same year 1630, the King was taken very ill at *Lyons:* And in the time of this sickness Cardinal *Richelieu* had very ill offices done him to his Majesty. The Cardinal having notice of it, thought his presence at Court necessary, to scatter this great storm that was gathering against him, by the secret practice of some very powerful Enemies. He left the Army therefore under the command of the Mareschals *la Force, Schemberg,* and *Marillac*; giving nevertheless all the private instructions to Monsieur *Schemberg,* who was his particular Friend and Confident; and so went straight to *Lyons.* The King, afterwards being recovered, return'd to *Paris,* whither the Cardinal attended him, that his fortune might not run a second risque by his absence. While

While our Army were refreshing themselves in quarters, I was appointed by the Generals and Controllers, to fit up all the Mills on the River *Mante*; and the Commissioner for Victualling being fallen sick at the same time, i receiv'd a Commission to provide the Army with Bread. Going one day to view the mills that wanted repairing, I saw at some distance a Chapel, which I went up to, not out of devotion, but curiosity. Finding the doors barricado'd, I had a mind to know what was within; so I made a Souldier get up, who having broke a piece of Glass, discover'd a great many Sacks of Corn heaped one upon another. After this so fortunate discovery, and so beneficial to our Army, who were then in want of Bread, I waited on the Generals, and promised to furnish them with a great supply of Corn, provided they would but find me a good many Waggons, and a sufficient Convoy. The next day all the Waggons of the Artillery, and about a hundred and fifty belonging to the Army, were sent me in, and with them as many Souldiers as I desired. We loaded, and carry'd off this Corn, all except some fifty Sacks, which we could not bring away, because the Country was alarmed, and some Troops fell upon our Convoy, which charging the rear of the Baggage, had done us a great deal of mischief, if we had not made a timely retreat. The Generals order'd me for my recompence the fourth part of a Crown for every Sack: But I can safely say, that in the trust committed to me of providing Bread for the Army, I could easily have made my self a very great gainer, had I not declin'd industriously all other advantage, but what I thought fair, and strictly agreeable to the rules of honesty and honour.

VII. Thus our Army refresh'd themselves in the County of *Mante*, when the King was importun'd by Monsieur *de Thoiras*, who held out the Cittadel of *Cazal*, to relieve him against the *Spanish* Troops, that were set down before it. Hereupon he sent orders to the Generals, that the Army should march with all possible speed to the relief of *Cazal*. When this resolution was taken and made publick, Monsieur *de Schomberg* order'd me to provide Bisket-bread sufficient for the whole Army for eleven days march; which accordingly I did. And besides this provision, I presented Monsieur *de Schomberg* with two thousand Aniseed Biskets, Monsieur *de la Force* with eight hundred, and Monsieur *de Marillac* as many; and to the Mareschals *de Camp*, Controllers, and Treasurers of the Army proportionably.

The whole Army, with all their equipage, being come to the plain of *Raconis*, was drawn into form of Battel, and divided into three bodies, the Van-guard, Main body, and Rear. Thus they continued to march, till we advanced within fourteen or fifteen leagues of *Cazal*; when notice was given, that the Duke of *Savoy* had joyn'd the *Spaniard* to fall upon our Flank. This obliged us to alter the method of our march. The Army was then ranged in three Columns; the Van-guard composed the right, the Battalion the middle, and the Rear the left Column. Between the middle and the right Column marcht all the Cannon, Carriages and Ammunition; between the left and the middle, went the Baggage of the Generals and all the Army; so that all was hemm'd in. The Horse went upon the wings, in front and flank, by Squadrons, and in form of Battel. Marching in this manner through all the plains, our Army was continually in a posture for fighting, either for the *Savoyards*, who were upon our Rear; or the *Spaniards*, that were in Front of us.

But the *Spaniards* would not ftir out of their Trenches, making themfelves fure of the Fort of *Cazal*, which they kept clofe blockt up. When we came to the Village of *Oximeane*, about four fmall leagues diftant from *Cazal*, we halted there three days, in expectation of news from Monfieur *de Thoiras*; to whom fix men had been fent to give him intelligence of our approach, and to affure him of relief, as alfo to agree upon a time, when our Troops fhould be drawn on, to attack the Trenches. But only one of thofe fix that were fent came back to us again. All meafures being duly adjufted, orders were given to lead on ftrait to *Cazal*. About a league from the Town we halted, to ftay for the fignal from the Cittadel, which was to be a great fmoak, to give us notice that all the Garrifon were ready, and in Arms.

As foon as ever the fign was given, all the Troops advanc'd, being diftributed into three bodies: Monfieur *la Force* commanded the right wing, Monfieur *Marillac* the left, and Monfieur *Schomberg* the main battel, becaufe this happened to be his day of commanding in chief. Before we came up to the Trenches, he gave us a fhort fpeech to this effect, but with abundance of warmth, and fuch a lively and warlike eloquence as becomes the mouth of a General, and is moft likely to infpire an Army with courage. Fellow-Souldiers, (faid he) you have now an occafion of the greateft honour, and higheft confequence that our age hath ever feen: I cannot but expect a good event of it, when I obferve both the courage and zeal of fo many brave men, whom the King hath entrufted with the honour of his arms; and the confufion of our Enemies that tremble already, before they engage us. If you have been ftout formerly, to day you muft be Heroes. Danger and Death overtake thofe that fear and fly from them, but the man that can look thefe in the face, and fear nothing, is half a Conqueror already. We have one Army before, and another behind us. They that flee will be killed fhamefully for Cowards, and they only that take their enemies lives while they lofe their own, will dye like men of honour. I pardon that man from this minute that falls upon me, if he fees me behave my felf like a Coward, but I will not pardon him that runs away himfelf. Come on then ftoutly, where honour and duty call, and I engage my word to all them, that fhall fignalize themfelves in the fervice of their Prince, to give his Majefty a true eftimate of their bravery, and to take care, that their fervices fhall be honoured and rewarded as they deferve.

Thefe few words, with the advantage of that vehemence with which they were uttered, and the courage of thofe that heard them, made the whole Army go on, as though they were already fecure of coming off Conquerors. The Forlorn-hope, and thofe appointed to fupport them advanc'd. When they were within half Cannon fhot they went to prayers, as is ufual; and all in deep filence expected the difcharge of a Cannon from the Town, which was to be the fignal when we fhould fall upon the Enemy. In the moment we heard it, our Troops advanc'd with incredible refolution and heat, though we put our felves full upon the mouth of the Cannon, that was planted along the Enemies Trenches, and muft needs make a horrible flaughter among us. The Marefchal *Marillac*, who by his Poft was the forwardeft, had began the attack, and we were all in the beft difpofition that ever Army was feen, to fight for the honour of our Prince and Country; when all on the fudden, to the great diffatisfaction of the whole Army, Monfieur *Mazarin* was difcovered riding from the Enemies Camp, holding a Sheet of white paper in his hand, and

waving

waving it about, for a sign of a Treaty of Peace, crying aloud, Halt, halt: Stand, stand. The Souldiers were so enraged to see themselves checkt in the midst of their Career, that some of them were so extravagant as to discharge several Musquets at him. Our Generals had much ado to stop them. But at last Monsieur *Mazarin* having liberty to draw near, and confer with the Mareschals of *France*, declared to them, that the *Spanish* Generals, had sent him to present them that paper, that they might propose what terms of peace they pleased. Monsieur *Schomberg* reply'd, that this matter was of so great consequence, that it was fit the Generals on both sides should personally confer together, and that as long as they treated by Messengers and Writing only, there would always be some scruples remaining, which would only be the seeds of fresh disturbances.

VIII. Then Monsieur *Mazarin* return'd to the Enemies Camp, to agree upon a place where they might meet together. One between both Armies was chosen, as the best and most secure. All the Generals on both sides repaired thither, and there formed the Articles of Treaty as was agreed between them : that is, *That the Town of* Cazal *should be put into the Duke of* Mantua's *hands ; that the French Souldiers should be commanded out, and* Montferrins, *who were the Duke of* Mantua's *Subjects, sent thither in their room; That the Kings Army should draw off from* Montferrat, *but yet keep the post where they then were, till such time as they had embarked all the Enemies Cannon and Baggage upon the* Po; *and that the Cittadel should be delivered to a Montferrin Officer, such as they should name.* The Articles being mutually signed, the Generals parted, after great Complements on both sides; and our Army retired about a quarter of a league, that they might give the Enemies no Jealousie ; and encamped there that night in their Arms for fear of any surprize. The Enemies also encamp'd that night in their Trenches, and decamp'd next day very early, that they might pass the River the same day, according to our agreement.

That night there fell such abundance of rain, that the Souldiers Arms were all spoyled with it, and they wet to the skin. Wherefore next morning the greatest part dispersed themselves into the Villages all thereabouts to dry themselves, and left their arms at the Camp in much disorder. In the mean while Monsieur *Thoiras* came from the Cittadel to our Camp, to wait on the Mareschals. Monsieur *Schomberg*, who had no great kindness for him, said at first meeting, *So, Sir, this is the second time;* meaning that he had relieved him once before at the Isle of *Rhe*, when he was besieged in St. *Martin*, by *Bouquinquan* the *English* General. Monsieur *Thoiras* return'd him a civil, but cold answer, *Yes, Sir, I am beholden to the King's Arms, and to you, Sir.* Afterwards Monsieur *Schomberg* invited him and the two other Mareschals to dinner.

While they sat at Table in the great Hall, with a great many persons of quality, where I also was, and saw all that past, immediately the *Spanish* Generals, *Picolomini* and *Colalto*, had passed through our Camp, and came into the Hall. Monsieur *Schomberg* being extremely surprized, as well as the rest of the company, said to them, *Really Gentlemen, I am much concerned that I had no notice of your coming, for I would have rode to meet you.* Whereupon *Picolomini*, who was a man of Wit as well as Courage, reply'd, *Sir, we did it on purpose; and since we could not surprize you in War, had a mind to try if we could do it in Peace. But I must confess, that I my self was a little surpriz'd as I came through your Camp: For* whereas I must own, that tho I have commanded several Armies, and in several Countries, I never saw any that lookt better, and more orderly, nor more eager of fighting, than yours was yesterday when drawn up in Battel, and ready to attack our Trenches; yet to day I see no body in your Camp, nor any thing but the Souldiers Arms lying up and down in great confusion and disorder. Monsieur *Schomberg* tipping us the wink, to go and get the Souldiers to their Colours presently, answer'd *Picolomini* with great readiness of wit, *This need be no surprize to you at all Sir, for I who am a German Lord, when I came to settle in France, and put my self into the King's service, was in truth at first at a loss, what this humour of the French should mean. But when I had been a Commander some time, and was used to the Genius of the Country, I presently found, that the French were the briskest Fellows in the world, when there was occasion for fighting; and the most inclined to ease and divert themselves, when there was none. One good quality they have is, that as they quickly lay down their arms, so they quickly stand to them again. And that you your self may bear me witness that I say true, I will immediately shew you an instance of the French temper. I will order the Drum to beat through the Quarters, and dare promise you, that before we have gone through the Camp, you shall see all the Army in good order.*

At the same time all the Officers that were there went out, and getting on Horseback, rode about to get the Souldiers together. In the mean while Monsieur *Schomberg* employed all his dexterity, to hold the *Spanish* Generals in discourse, and detain them insensibly. Afterwards he prevailed with them to take a little walk, and amused them a good while without their suspecting any thing. At last the diligence and address of the Officers was such, that when *Picolomini* and *Colalto* return'd, they found the Army in excellent order. The Officers with their Pikes in their hands, and the Souldiers their Arms made a very graceful appearance; which the *Spanish* Generals were so much surpriz'd at, that they could scarce perswade themselves, this was the same way they came before, fancying it was rather delusion upon their senses, so much was it beyond any thing they had ever seen, either in *Spain*, or any other part of *Europe*. *Picolomini* observing this good order, and the courage of the men, could not forbear expressing his admiration of it in very complaisant terms, saying to *Schomberg*, That it could not be any dishonour to be vanquisht by so many brave Souldiers, and such great Commanders. After this they took leave of one another, and return'd each to their own Army.

IX. But what follow'd was not agreeable to all this civility; and our Generals ill conduct had like to have lost the whole Army. The Treaty of Peace was broken in some of the principal Articles; and whereas it was agreed, that our men should give safe conduct to all the Enemies Baggage, Cannon and Artillery, as far as the River; the *French* behaved themselves very unworthily, and in such a manner as all the world condemned, fell to pillaging the Ropes, Bridles, Horse-collars, and the rest of the Baggage that belonged to the *Spanish* Army. And whereas we had engag'd, as I said before, to draw all the *French* out of the Cittadel, and put *Montserrins* in their Rooms; they set men on work night and day to make *Montserrin* Habits, and so many Taylors were employed on this occasion, that in four and twenty hours time near eight hundred of these Habits were made, in which they drest up as many *French* Souldiers, and after having taught them two or three words of the language of the

Country,

Country, put them into *Cazal*, under pretence of so many *Montferrins.* Thus by means of their Coats with Hanging Sleeves, and the help of these words, *Seignor se, Seignor la!* they possess themselves of the Castle ; and, which helpt to conceal the cheat yet more, they mingled some real *Montferrins*, whom they had bribed, among these *French* Souldiers, that so one part might keep all the rest from being discovered.

Nay, they went farther still, and fail'd in making good the chief Article of all, which was that concerning the Governour, who was appointed (as I said) by the common consent of both parties. For, resolving to remove him from this Post, upon pretence that he was a *Spaniard* in his heart, they chous'd and surpriz'd him as you shall hear. Two days after the Enemy had past the *Po*, with their Baggage and Ordnance , our Army divided it self into two bodies. Eight thousand Foot, and some Squadrons of Horse past the River also, without any Cannon, at *Libourne*; the remainder of the Foot, and all the Horse that staid behind with the Cannon, for greater security, march'd along the River side , without passing it , fearing lest the Enemy should make any attempt upon our Army, that was on the same side with theirs, and not caring to clog it with the whole Train of Ordnance, which would have made their retreat difficult. In the mean time Monsieur *Marillac*, who had resolv'd to surprize the new Governour of the Castle, when our Army, except the Generals and some few Troops, were gone over, contrived to invite the Governour to Supper. When he was come out of the Castle, the Souldiers, disguis'd like *Montferrins*, had orders to change the word, and to deny him entrance at his return from Supper, as not knowing him, and he not knowing the word. The Governour then after having supp'd with Monsieur *Marillac*, who shewed him great civility, took his leave full of satisfaction, to go back to his Castle. But he was astonisht at the complement the Centinel gave him at the Gate. For as soon as he heard him he bid him stand, and ask'd who was there. The Governour, said he. The word, reply'd the Centinel ? The Governour having told him the word, which himself gave before he went out, the Centinel cry'd out, Stand where you are, you *French* Traitor, would you seize the Castle ? if you come here I will shoot you: The Governour was in a strange confusion; he heard himself call'd Traitor, and *French-man*; but he presently perceived it was a *French-man* that betray'd him. He bawls and rages against *France*, calls us treacherous Villains, Knaves, and all that ; but the more he raged, the more the Centinel cryes, that he was a Traitor, and charged him not to come there. He repairs immediately to our Generals, who after they had chous'd him with so much civility, answer'd him as civilly, That they could not be responsible for the treachery of the *Montferrins*, that he must make his complaint to the Duke his Master, since it was into his hands that the King had delivered the Town. But the Governour, who saw through the meaning of this answer, was not mistaken in the matter, and immediately writ after the *Spanish* Generals, who were not above two or three leagues off, to acquaint them how the *French* had kept him out of the Castle.

X. Mean while our Generals having past the River to joyn their Army, which waited for them at a Village about a league off, made great haste, and advanc'd with all their Troops as far as *Libourne*. On the other side, the Enemy understanding the breach of faith we had been guilty of to the Governour of *Cazal*, and being enrag'd besides at the plunder of their

Baggage.

Baggage, resolv'd to fall in upon us, when we were weakned by the division of our Troops, and began their march to this purpose. But Monsieur *Mazarin*, who performed the part of a Mediator, and had procur'd this peace, plaid the *Spaniards* a true *Italian* trick, and came riding full speed to our Camp at *Libourn* about midnight. I happen'd that night to be upon the Guard on that side of the Camp where he came, and the Centinel having stopt him, and hearing the name of *Mazarin*, immediately call'd me to him. I came presently and saw it was Monsieur *Mazarin*, who with great passion cried out, Ah, Sir, you are all lost, the Enemies are within a mile, and are coming to fall upon you with their whole Army. Give orders to sound to arms throughout the whole Camp immediately. I answered him with some kind of indifference; *Sir, we have no Commission to sound to arms without the Generals order, his Tent is but just by, and I will conduct you thither if you think fit.* However I took the advantage of this Intelligence, and sent to give notice in all the quarters, that they should be ready; and in the mean time I waited on Monsieur *Mazarin* to Mareschal *Schomberg*'s Tent. He threw himself about his neck, and made him this Complement, *Ah Sir, must I embrace the man now, that I shall see dead within this hour? How so, Sir,* said Monsieur *Schomberg, methinks you have a mind to try if you can fright us.* Monsieur *Mazarin* reply'd, *I have no design to fright you Sir, but to preserve your life, and the whole Army; for your Enemies are coming to charge you, and are not above a mile off.* They were really however two leagues distant, but he had a mind to alarm us the more, that we might make greater haste. Monsieur *Schomberg* reply'd with the indifference of a great General, *If we can but see them when they come, we shall not fear them; but yet it is fit we should take care to secure our selves as well as we can.* Immediately he ordered to sound an alarm through the whole Camp; and as many of us Officers as were there, ran about to carry his orders; so that in a very little time our Army was ready for the march.

XI. They call'd a Council of War however, to debate what was fit to be done, and it was determin'd that our Army not being in a condition to stand so great a shock, we ought to provide for a retreat. It went against the grain though to see our selves forc'd to flee from the *Spaniard*; but at last it was judg'd that a Retreat is never dishonourable, when opposition is manifestly hazardous. Monsieur *Schomberg* commanded the Van-guard, and the two other Mareschals the Rear. Our whole Army was drawn up in Battalia, and kept this order during the whole Retreat, because we had two leagues of wide Champaign to go over. Monsieur *Marlissy*, Captain of the Guards, commanded the Forlorn-hope, and under him a Lieutenant and my self commanded those of the Forlorn that were nearest the Enemy. This Lieutenant and I had a great quarrel; for I would command alone, as being his ancient, and he would needs command with me in the quality of Lieutenant; telling me besides, that if I happened to be kill'd, there would no body to command, which would occasion much disorder, and might expose those first Troops to great slaughter. Our stiffness in maintaining each his post, flew so high, that we had like to have come to blows, so blind and so furious is ambition, even in the most dangerous circumstances. The Generals coming in to compose this difference, appointed that I should command the Lieutenant; but that the Lieutenant too should command under me, which was the regular way, and put an end to the whole dispute.

When

When we were got a good way in this plain, I fpy'd a great way off four Horfe-men making full fpeed toward us. I fent to acquaint the Generals, who came to the head of the Forlorn-hope to wait for them; who when they were come up within a Trumpet, told the Marefchals of *France*, That the *Spanifh* Generals had fent to tell them, that they were much injured and provoked by our breach of Articles, and that they were coming with the *Spanifh* Army to demand fatisfaction. Our Generals replyed, That fince they thought themfelves wrong'd, and intended to revenge it, they alfo were ready to do them reafon in a fair fight; That for their parts they were fo far from breaking the Agreement, that they were making it good at that very time, by drawing off from *Montferrat*, as one of the Articles enjoyn'd; that their march was not now a running away, but that of gallant Souldiers who return'd Conquerors; that the *Spaniards* themfelves had dealt unfaithfully, who not daring fome few days ago, to ftand the affault of the *French* Army, were now attempting to fall upon their Rear, when they were divided; that this difcover'd their Treachery and Cowardice, fince it was manifeft that they made the Peace before, only becaufe they thought themfelves too weak; and broke it now, only becaufe they thought themfelves too ftrong for us. That notwithftanding our unequal number, would make them know, that a few *French* are able to deal with a great many *Spaniards*; and that Courage, not numbers, made men Conquerors. Thus they drill'd on thefe four Horfe-men with fuch bluftering words as thefe, fitter indeed for a *Spaniard* than a *French-man*, who commonly loves to talk big of what he has done, more than what he fhould do.

All this while our Troops continu'd marching, and made all the fpeed that poffibly they could, notwithftanding all our General's brave words, which might amufe thofe Horfe-men, but could not put a ftop to our Army, that knew it felf too feeble. At length, having had enough of our Generals eloquence, they took leave, and return'd back as faft as they came. At the fame time our Army were order'd to mend their pace; and the Van-guard being come into a dale to a River call'd *Doni-Balta*, over which there was a Bridge, they paft as quick as they could to make way for the Rear againft they fhould come up. On the other fide, the Rear being at fome diftance, began, as they came up a little rifing ground, to difcover by degrees fome five and thirty or forty Squadrons of Horfe, coming on at a great rate. We after faw more and more of the Enemies drawing up to us, who made fure of cutting us in pieces, and lookt upon us as facrifices to their revenge; as indeed it was impoffible, that fo few as we were fhould ftand out againft fo many Troops. But they were mightily difappointed in their expectation, and we gained time enough to leave the River I mention'd between us and them. Which happen'd after a very odd manner, and by a fmall ftratagem that I contriv'd, and which thefe great Generals of *Spain* were not able to difcover.

XII. When our Rear was come into the road by which they muft go down into the dale, at the entrance into which there was an old ruinous houfe: We taking it for granted that we were loft, and efpecially thofe of us that were the hindmoft, and were almoft clofe to the Enemy; I made fome ftout Souldiers and a Serjeant leap all on a fudden into this Cottage, and order'd them, that when the Enemy were about forty or fifty paces from them, they fhould difcharge upon them, fhooting leifurely one after another; which I was in fome hopes might a little ftop, or it may be, be, divert thofe that purfued us, upon a furprize they might have, that the danger was greater than in truth it was. This contrivance fucceeded very well: For the Enemy coming on, and our Mufqueteers making feveral fhot fucceffively, as I had directed them, all that part of the Horfe halted immediately; and fearing that there might be among thofe ruines a great number of men, that might put a ftop to their march, becaufe they were loath to give our Army time to file off, they never attackt this fuppofed Guard, but immediately wheeled away to the left to fall upon us at another place. But the fetching this compafs was a greater hinderance to them than they lookt for, and occafioned all our Rear's getting off fafe, who by this means gained time to pafs the River, fome by the Bridge, and fome at a Mill, where they waded only up to the wafte. The Mufqueteers whom I had pofted in the old houfe, feeing the Enemy's Army gone off, came on to joyn our Rear, and only one young Fellow ftaid behind, who was loaded with a Sheep that he had caught up. Monfieur *Schomberg* made him come over too with the reft, and telling me in raillery, that we had not left fo much as a Sheep behind us, embrac'd me very kindly for the good fervice I had done the Army. He went over the laft of them all, followed by me only, and immediately we broke up the Bridge after us. The Enemies came up almoft the minute we got over, and fhewed themfelves on the other fide of the River. But finding this bar betwixt us, and not being able to come to blows, they reveng'd themfelves upon us with reproaches and hard words. They made one furious difcharge however, which made a terrible noife in the Vale, but did little execution, there not being above five and twenty or thirty of our men killed and wounded, for a monument of fo noble and honourable a retreat.

Our Army then marched on toward *Fouijs*, having left a ftrong guard upon the River to hinder the Enemies croffing it, which they attempted to do that very night, but were fo briskly repulfed both by the Guard, and a Relief fent to them from our Army, which as yet was got but a little way off, that they were forced to give over their defign, and return fhamefully to the place from whence they had pofted fo faft. Our men alfo came up again to joyn the body of the Army, which went into Quarters at *Fouijs* and the Towns thereabouts.

'Twas in the Caftle of this Town, which belongs to three Counts of that Countey, that Marefchal *Marillac* was arrefted fome days after by a ftrange turn of fortune, or to fpeak more like a Chriftian, by the judgment of God, which fhould make thofe men tremble, who look upon their fortune as fixt and fure. There are in this Caftle three or four pretty Bed-chambers, in each of which each Marefchal of *France* took up his Lodging

The End of the Firft Book.

BOOK

BOOK II.

Cardinal Richelieu *in disgrace ;   he is restor'd to favour again.
The* Mareschal *de* Marillac *is confin'd and condemn'd.   The
Battel of* Castelnau-d' Arry.   *The Duke of* Montmorency
*is taken in the Fight.   An Account of his Process and Death.
The Siege of* Nancy.   *Some discourse between the Duke of*
Lorrain , *and the Sieur* de Pontis.   *That Town is reduc'd to
Submission.*

I. **D**Uring this whole War that I have been treating of, *Mary of Medicis,* the
Queen Mother, *Marillac* Keeper of the Seals, and some other Lords, removed to *Paris,* and there by private intrigues form'd a very strong party
against Cardinal *Richelieu,* to remove him from Court. It would require a long dif-
course, to unravel this great mystery, and relate all the particulars of it, which indeed
were a subject for a large History. I need only tell you then in short, that the Cardinals enemies prevailed so far with the King, as to forbid him the Court. The
Keeper of the Seals dispatcht a Courier instantly, to his brother the Mareschal *de Marillac,* to inform him of this disgrace, of the man whom they lookt upon as an Enemy
to them in particular, as well as to the whole Kingdom in general.

This news gave mighty satisfaction to the Mareschal, and fill'd him full of great
expectations. He publickly declared his joy to the two other Mareschals of *France,*
his joynt Brothers in Commission ; one of whom, Monsieur *Schomberg,* who was particularly dear to the Cardinal, was very melancholy, that he had received no Letters
himself, and suspected that his fortune too might be tottering, by the fall of his old
great Patron. I was that very day upon the Guard in *Fonijs* Castle, where I told you
our Generals had taken up their Quarters ; and continuing upon duty the next day
too, and the night after that, was an Eye-witness of all that passed upon this occasion.
Monsieur *Schomberg,* thinking of nothing but his own disfavour, which he judg'd in-
separable from that of the Cardinal, would not sup that day. And the Mareschal *de
Marillac* for his part, fancying now that he should be the greatest man in *France,* fill'd
his imagination with vast preferments, which he promis'd himself shortly, and had
in some measure tasted of already. But we shall see in the person of this Lord, one of
the terriblest instances imaginable, how unstable all humane affairs are, and how
empty the projects of the wise men of this world.

II. Cardinal *Richelieu,* who was lookt upon as one perfectly subdu'd by the party
that hated him, and past all hopes of rising any more, deceiv'd all his Enemies in an
instant, and by one of the strangest turns of policy that ever was known, trod all those
under foot that insulted over him. He turn'd all the effect of their malice upon themselves, and took advantage of the easiness of that very Prince whom they had difposed to ruine him, to get the better of them again. His Friend, the Cardinal *de la
Vallette* being acquainted with his disgrace advised him to take courage, and not let
matters go off so. He perswaded him to go wait upon the King once more, and make
another tryal how far he could prevail upon him ; he argued with him, that Kings
being the images of God, did in this resemble their divine original, that they loved
men should importunately address to them, and that nothing but perseverance could
carry the point. Cardinal *Richelieu* followed this politick advice of his friend, and
couragiously went to the King : and making use of all his cunning upon this occasion,
and arming himself with all his resolution, to do violence as it were to his Prince, he
accosted him to this effect. *I am come, Sir,* (said he) *to make an offer of my head to
your Majesty, that you may dispose of my person as you think good, if I do not prove by undeniable
arguments, nay, by Papers of unquestionable authority, that the Mareschal* de Marillac, *and*

Y y   *his*

his Brother the Keeper, and some others have designs against your person. That the only reason why they are Enemies to me, is because they are so to you, Sir; That they lead me with false accusations, meerly because I support the interest of your Majesty, against their wicked attempts; and that my quarrel is not that of a single or private person, but such as all the State is concern'd in. They know very well, Sir, that I see through all their disguises, and that I make use of your Royal Authority to disappoint their treasonable projects, and therefore would fain take me from about your Person and Court, and drive me out of your Kingdom, that they may more secretly abuse your goodness, while you take them for faithful Servants, but while they are in truth hatching nothing but Treason and Falshood. If your Majesty will give me leave to inform you, what I can do of my own certain knowledge, you will scarcely believe, what really I could very hardly have believed my self, and yet all but too true. You will see that my Enemies are privately contriving to depose you, and that their Cabals strike at nothing less than the securing your Royal Person; that so when they have shut you up in a Monastery, (instances whereof we may find in our own History) they may get the Government into their own hands.

III. These and many other such expressions deliver'd with an air of assurance, and by a person who had gained an absolute mastery of the King's breast, perswaded so strongly, or rather indeed confounded this Prince to so great a degree, who (as all the world knows) was naturally of a very jealous and distrustful temper, that he gave the Cardinal leave, to cause the Mareschal *de Marillac*, and his Brother the Keeper to be apprehended. The latter was imprison'd immediately; and a Courier presently dispatch'd to the Mareschal *de Schomberg*, with orders from the King to secure the Mareschal *de Marillac*. This Courier used such wonderful expedition, that tho he came out two days after the former, which brought the news of Cardinal *Richelieu's* disgrace, yet he reacht the Camp the next day after him. Monsieur *Schomberg* at the reading the order from the King, was infinitely surpriz'd, to see the whole face of affairs at Court so prodigiously chang'd, and in so short a time. He was well pleased to find his own hopes and fortunes so quickly settled again, but much concern'd to see this done by the ruine of his friend, the Mareschal *de Marillac*. He acquainted the Mareschal *de la Force* with the command sent him from the King; and calling me to him, he bad me go fetch Monsieur *de Mixtigny*, the first Captain, and all the other Officers of the Regiment of Guards, to draw up my Company in the Castle-Court, and then to take up the Draw-bridge. I perform'd what he had given me in charge without delay; all the Officers came into the Castle, my Company, which kept guard, into the Court; and the Bridges were all drawn up. All this preparation might have given the Mareschal *de Marillac* some jealousy, had not this been muster-day; and he himself declared his opinion the day before, that all the Officers should be shut up in the Castle to prevent the foisting in of false Musters, so that he had not the least suspicion of any thing at all.

We came all together into the Mareschal *de Schomberg's* Chamber, and Monsieur *Marillac* with us at the same time, who only congratulated him upon the receiving a Courier, and desir'd he would shew him his Letters, that he would go to Dinner, and when that was over, come again to see the news. Monsieur *Schomberg* desir'd him not to give himself that trouble, and assur'd him he would come himself to his Apartment, and communicate his Letters to him, and then waited on him half way to his Lodgings. The Mareschal *de Marillac* seeing my Company below in the Court, said to Mareschal *Schomberg*, without suspecting any thing, I see you have taken care to prevent false Musters, it is very well done indeed. So he went to Dinner, for Monsieur *Schomberg* would not have him apprehended then, because he had no opportunity of imparting his order to the Officers. He came back therefore into his Chamber with us all, and after having observ'd, whether there might not be some body by, who was a particular Confident of Mr. *Marillac's*, he shut the door, and spake to us after this manner. *Gentlemen, the King hath done you the honour to intrust you with the Glory and the Security of his Arms, and now he intrusts you with the Safety of his Person and Kingdom. I am sensible the Order I have received from his Majesty will be a great surprize to you all, but it is no part of our business to pry too curiously into the secrets of a Prince's pleasure; all that we have to do is to respect his Commands, and to execute his Orders. The King hath commanded me to secure Monsieur Marillac's person. It is enough that I let you know what he would have done, and I know you are too loyal not to obey him, especially in a matter of this consequence.* Afterwards that the business might not be suspected, and be the more effectually done, he bad us make some complaints at the going down from his Chamber, as if he always kept back our Musters, and refus'd to pay us.   It's

It's impoſſible for me to expreſs the amazement and concern I was in at this bad
news. For Monſieur *Marillac* being a perſon whom I lov'd and honour'd very particularly, and one who, I may take upon me to ſay, did me the honour to have a
kindneſs for me; my very heart was ready to burſt when I heard this order for apprehending a perſon for whom I had an infinite reſpect, and ſaw that my duty made it
neceſſary for me to have any hand in his ruine. But there was no remedy, I muſt
contain my ſelf, and yield to the powers above me, my poſt obliging me to obey the
King's comand. We went down then all together out of the Mareſchal *de Schomberg's*
Lodgings, every one complaining loudly, that it was a miſerable caſe to have a man
of that temper to deal with, that continually promis'd us pay, and we never could get
any thing but words; That kept men in a diſtant Country, and would not ſuffer them
to come near their King; that after all, there was nothing like being about one's
own Maſter. Theſe complaints they made, and ſeveral ſuch like, which he had ordered them to diſguiſe the ſame buſineſs withal.

IV. When the Mareſchal *de Marillac* had din'd, Monſieur *Schomberg* and *la Force*
went with us all to his Chamber, and he coming to meet us, with a very pleaſant
and gay countenance, askt what news from Court? but alas! he heard very bad
news for him, when Monſieur *Schomberg* preſenting him the Kings Letters that
contained the order for apprehending him, deſired he would give himſelf the trouble
of reading thoſe Letters. One may eaſily imagine what an operation ſo ſtrange and
ſudden a turn of Fortune would have upon a mans mind; but for all that, it is impoſſible to repreſent the violence of his paſſion, which indeed put him quite beſide himſelf, when he read the crimes falſely laid to his charge, and upon which he was commanded to be ſecured. For then forgetting himſelf utterly, and not knowing where
he was, he loſt all fear and reſpect, and fell to railing againſt the Cardinal in a moſt
furious manner, ſaying aloud, tho without naming him, That he that told the King
thoſe things, was a Raſcal, a Traytor, and a Perjur'd Villain.

The Mareſchal *de la Force* ſeeing him ſo enraged, and thinking this paſſion might
turn to his prejudice, if the Cardinal ſhould come to know it, endeavoured to ſoften
him, telling him very wiſely, *Come Sir, matters are not deſperate yet : You know I my ſelf
had once the misfortune to be in Arms againſt my Prince, and yet he was ſo gracious to pardon me,
and ſince that to truſt me with the Command of his Armies. If you are innocent, your Innocence will by this means be render'd more conſpicuous; and if you be guilty, your
Offence cannot be greater than the Clemency of the King, and his diſpoſition to forgive, if you do
but throw your ſelf at his Majeſty's feet, and implore his Mercy, as I did.* But nothing was
able to ſtop the tranſports of his juſt indignation. And tho I cannot approve the exceſs of his paſſion, yet at the ſame time I muſt needs own, that if it were allowable
upon any occaſion, to repel a falſe accuſation with violence, this was ſuch a caſe ;
when a man of Mareſchal *Marillac's* quality and honour, who had always preſerv'd
an untainted Loyalty to his Prince, ſaw himſelf maliciouſly charged with attempts
upon his Liberty, his Crown, and his Life. And theſe accuſations, of which he
knew himſelf perfectly innocent, put him quite paſt his ſenſes, and carry'd him to
ſpeak without any conſideration or regard to perſons, whoſe intereſt and power at
leaſt he ought to have ſtood in fear of.

Mareſchal *Schomberg* ſeeing that there was no bringing him to any temper, and not
being able to ſee him any longer in that exceſs of trouble and deſpair, was about to
withdraw, and took his leave, telling him, that he could not put a better guard about
his perſon, than that the King honoured with the ſecuring of his own. But in regard
he had his Sword on ſtill, Monſieur *de Montigny* told Monſieur *Schomberg*, that it was
neceſſary he ſhould be deſired to take it off, and ſo put himſelf into the condition of
a Priſoner : Then Monſieur *Schomberg* whiſper'd him in his ear, that ſince the Kings
order muſt be ſubmitted to, it were well if he would of his own accord ſtep into a
Wardrobe juſt by, and lay aſide his Sword ; which he did immediately. But if he
had had his wits about him, he might eaſily have made his eſcape out of a Window
in that Room, under which there was a load of Hay, and he need not have leapt
down above ſix or ſeven foot at moſt. But he was ſo full of trouble, and ſo utterly
paſt all ſenſe, that he thought of nothing but the injuſtice they had done, without
ever conſidering how to ſave himſelf from it. I being, as I ſaid, upon the Guard at
that time, guarded him the remaining part of that day, and all the night following.

V. The

V. The Marquis of *Amicky*, who was his relation, having obtain'd leave to come speak with him, after some discourse, the Mareschal desired him to go write to several persons, but not seal his Letters for fear of giving any suspicion. In the mean while he pray'd me to go ask Mareschal *Schomberg*, whether he would please to inclose in his Pacquet a Letter, which he was desirous to write to the King. Monsieur *Schomberg* after having consider'd of it a little while, answer'd, That he would do it with all his heart, but in regard the Courier belonged to the Cardinal, he durst not engage it would come to the King's hand. He said to me afterwards, speaking of Monsieur *Marillac*, *I thought him passionate I confess before, but could never have imagined it to this degree. How poor a thing is man when left to himself! His Judgment always fails him when he stands most in need of it.* But without question any other man in his circumstances would have felt what a shock so heavy and so unexpected a blow as this of Monsieur *Marillac*'s can give to the most resolute man in the world. 'Tis a much easier matter to find faults with those lamentations and complaints, which excess of grief forces from the mouth of others, than to bear up with patience and temper under ones own. But yet this great man, 'tis true, was guilty of a great fault upon this occasion, and did by no means behave himself to his own advantage. For the very Courier hearing part of what he spoke with too much heat against the Cardinal, no question but he helpt to make matters worse with his Eminence, who to be sure was very particularly inform'd of all these things.

Well, I went to return Monsieur *Schomberg*'s answer, about the Letter Monsieur *Marillac* desir'd to write to the King, and he composed a very handsom, and very eloquent one of four pages long; for Grief always expresses it self well. In this Letter he told the King, That his Enemies made it their business to ruine him upon the account of the good service he had done his Majesty, which therefore made them hate him: That it is the very character of Envy, to fall upon the most commendable actions of them that it looks upon with an evil eye; That it endeavours to find evil in good, darkness in light, and turns vertue into vice; That it inspires those that are acted by it, to accuse and murder the innocent with a greater degree of confidence, then these innocent persons themselves can attain to for their own vindication; but that he hoped, the King's wisdom and justice would not suffer him to be prepossest by the malice of his Enemies; and that on the contrary, he would please to take a true estimate of him and his Loyalty, and judge how inviolably he was devoted to his service, from the publick testimonies he had given of it all along, and not by the false prejudices of his Slanderers and Accusers: That therefore he cast himself wholly into the arms of his mercy, who had always been a Protector of the Innocent. That, for his part, he could not believe that his Majesty, after having done him the honour of a most gracious Letter but the day before, should so very quickly change his opinion of him to that degree; that in this he plainly discerned the working of his Enemies, who betrayed themselves, and began already to usurp his Royal Authority, at the very instant that they accused him of attempts against it. Several other passages there were, which I cannot now recollect, and after having given it me to read, as to one whom he was pleased to honour with his particular favour, he desir'd I would carry it to Monsieur *Schomberg*, that he might peruse it too. Monsieur *Schomberg* when he had read it, gave it me again to carry back to Monsieur *Marillac*, and to beg that he would make it short, for fear that the King seeing so much of it should not trouble himself to read it. Monsieur *Marillac* according to his advice shortned it, and then sent it him again. But Monsieur *Schomberg* in civility would not read it, saying, That he was satisfied Monsieur *Marillac* had said nothing, but what was agreeable to the respect due to the King: which pleased him very much, and put him upon extolling Monsieur *Schomberg* for this great civility to him.

VI. All night long he never once shut his eyes, and did nothing but walk about, cry out, bewail himself, write Letters, and then tear them to pieces again; so violent was the disorder of his mind. He reflected perpetually upon the horrid malice of his Enemies, and could scarce perswade himself, that there was, either any Wretches so vile as to put about such calumnies against an innocent person, or any Princes so credulous and easy, as to be possest with them. Sometimes he did not know where to lay the fault, and after many reflections upon the respect he owed the King, the Cardinal's pique against him, and his own innocence, he lookt up at last to the Divine

Providence,

Providence, as the supreme Disposer of all humane events, and humbly besought the Justice and Mercy of God. In short, I cannot express how many, how various, how violent motions, even to a degree of Convulsions appened in his body and mind both, that fatal night next after his disgrace. Then he felt plainly, that his Greatness weighed him down, that his Eminent Post only served to increase his misfortune, and make it more remarkable; and in short, that his innocence had never been accused, if his condition had not made him a mark for Envy.

I confess the seeing a person, for whom I had an exceeding great respect, and had the honour to be beloved by him, in these deplorable circumstances, rent my very heart to pieces that night, when I was present at all he said and did upon this occasion. And, committing great violence upon my self to contain, and not daring in point of precence to give any vent of that which opprest me within, I found my passion grow upon me the more, the more I strove to stifle it. Then sure I had time enough to make many reflections, and to see clearly by several instances, how little the best and most fixed fortunes in this world are to be depended upon. A Cardinal in disgrace one day, and in favour again the next, and the hopes of all his Enemies defeated and overturn'd in an instant, were subjects large enough to furnish me with arguments, to pall my appetite of favour at Court. But the time for effecting this was not yet come, and indeed it very seldom happens, that what we see come upon other people is apply'd home to our own selves. The mind observes the accident, and considers it after a speculative kind of way, and then stops there, and seldom goes any farther. I could dwell for ever on this subject, which yet I cannot to this day so much as once think upon without great concern. All that I need add more of it here is, that this great Mareschal two or three days after he was apprehended, was carry'd almost as far as Turin, and that from thence he was sent under a Guard of five hundred Horse to Paris.

VII. It was now about the end of the year 1630, and an Indictment being prefer'd against him by the King's, or rather by Cardinal Richelieu's order, they set up at Ruel a Chamber of Commissioners chosen out of several Parliaments for this purpose. But the Tryal was not brought to an issue till 1632. I shall not take upon me to relate here the particulars of what past in this important affair. The publick News, and Memoirs, that are in every bodies hands, tell us, that if the opinion of some of his Judges, who till then never were thought incompetent ones, had prevailed, the conclusion of this affair had been as much for his honour, as at last it prov'd fatal; and his Enemies would have had reason to be asham'd for the assault they had made upon his Innocence. But God in his Justice, which Monsieur Marillac himself found reason to adore, permitted him to be over-power'd by the majority of his other Judges.

Near the end of his Tryal, about a fortnight or three weeks before his Condemnation, when he was guarded at Ruel, by Monsieur des Reaux, Lieutenant of the Guards du Corps, whom he had no affection for, the King order'd me to go and guard him. I had much ado to bring my self to comply with this, dreading what might come on't, because I knew the Cardinal hated me, and that he knew I had a particular esteem for Monsieur Marillac. For being to deal with so vigilant and so formidable an Enemy, I knew very well, that if I fail'd in the least punctilio of my duty, he would be sure to take all advantages to ruine me. I resolved therefore to do all that ever I could for declining this Commission, and earnestly entreated his Majesty, that I might not be removed from about his person, to take the charge of guarding a Mareschal of France, who had often commanded me in the Army. I added moreover, that all the world was sensible he had some kindness for me, and therefore my Enemies would be sure to keep a strict eye upon me, and I should be exposed to all the mischief their malice could do me. Why, what are you afraid of, said the King, is it not I that send you? Do you suspect your self, that you shall not be true to me? I answer'd, That I had rather dye a thousand deaths than be false to my duty; that this was no part of my fear, but that I was afraid of what his Majesty knew better than my self I had good grounds to fear; and at the same time I threw my self at his Majesty's feet. The King reply'd mildly, and with a great deal of goodness, Go, go your way man, and be obedient; be true to me, and fear nothing. So I was forc'd to go.

The Mareschal de Marillac profest himself much comforted to see me, and to be under the custody of a man he lov'd. I found him full of all the confidence and resolution, that a good Conscience uses to inspire men with. He would often say to me, What can they convict me of, except having been a most faithful servant to the King? Let

Z z   them

them but do me *Justice, and I am sure they cannot hurt me.* He drew up all his Writings himself, and was so assured of his own Innocence, that he thought it absolutely impossible they should condemn him to death. I declin'd discoursing with him alone as much as I could, that I might give no suspicion of any private correspondence with him. In the mean while, the Commissioners sent for him before them several times, to examine him upon several Articles exhibited against him. One day as I was conducting him into their Chamber, he leaned upon my arm, and with a smiling countenance said to me, *Look you Sir, all that I can accuse my self of, is not fault enough to whip a Page for.* But he was much astonisht, when coming into the Chamber, and finding how his Judges stood inclined, (who made what his Enemy had a mind to have done the measure of their proceedings) he saw that he was to expect nothing better than a Scaffold. From that minute he was so alter'd, that one could scarce know him when he came out of the Chamber. Death was plainly to be seen in his face and eyes: His mind was full of nothing but this horrid Injustice that triumph'd over Innocence; and his body grew so weak from that instant, that he could scarce stand. He lean'd upon me, and cry'd aloud, but alas! in a voice very distant from that at his going in, *Ah! where is the God of truth, that knows my innocence! Lord, where is thy Providence, and thy Justice! make haste my God to help me.* Nothing can be imagin'd more moving, and any one may judge, whether I was not melted with it. But I was oblig'd to put a good face upon the matter, and stifle that grief within me, with which I was ready to burst.

I had used to go and acquaint the King from time to time of all that past, and when I saw the Mareschal sentenc'd to death, I took occasion to beseech his Majesty, that he would please to discharge me from guarding him any longer, for that I could not bring my self to conduct a person to Execution, for whom I could most willingly have laid down my own life. The King very graciously condescended to my request: So that I shall say little of his death, the particulars whereof have been carefully collected and publish'd. I only add, that notwithstanding all the heat and passion of his temper, and all the confidence he had from the knowledge of his own innocence, yet at last he submitted with an entire resignation to the Divine Justice, which knows how to use the injustice of men, when he sees fit, and make that an instrument of bringing about his own decrees. And then being sensible, with all due humility, that God intended this publick death for a mercy to him, thereby to chastise his secret faults; in this sense he suffer'd this last punishment, and all the shame that attended it, having his Head struck off in the common place of Execution, and amidst a vast throng of People. Nay not only that, but he endur'd the barbarous insults of his Enemies too, whose malice seem'd scarce satisfied with his death. For, which is very odd, when Cardinal *Richelieu* was told of the Mareschal's Condemnation, he could not be of opinion, that the matter ought to have gone so far neither; but it was likely the Judges saw further into the case than other people. Thus after having used his utmost endeavours to destroy the man he hated, he would appear to justify himself, by casting upon the Judges all the odium of a Sentence, which every one knew was owing to him alone. And that which must needs seem the greatest, and most intolerable hardship to the Mareschal *de Marillac*, is, that the Cardinal's speaking of his death with all that coldness and indifferency, after having been so eager and warm, both in wishing and procuring it, could not be supposed to come from any thing but a secret bitterness and spight, that made him insult over the barbarous end of an innocent person; whose blood deserved the tears of all good and wise men, much better than the keen jest of an Enemy.

VIII. I shall not now insist on any thing that happened to his Brother Monsieur *Marillac*, Keeper of the Seals, who dyed in Prison upon the same account; nor to the Queen Mother, that illustrious Princess, whose banishment and death gave her yet more lustre than her life. All these were so many Victims devoted to the humours and petts of that great Minister of State, who found, that the only method to secure his own high station, was to ruine all that stood in his way, and that were entirely fixt in the service and true interest of their King.

IX. I proceed now to what concerns another of his Victims, whose person was indeed more eminent than Monsieur *Marillac*, and his death every whit as tragical, tho the cause in which he suffer'd, deserved it more. The great Duke of *Montmorency* I mean;

mean, who, not being able to endure the Tyranny of that arbitrary man, that had got both the foul and person of the King absolutely in his power, combined with the Duke of *Orleans* to rescue *France*, all the Grandees, and even the King himself from the oppression under which they all groaned. The design was highly commendable, if the methods of compassing it had but been as innocent. For knowing, that he could have no sufficient ground to take up arms against his Prince, he thought himself safe enough by engaging the Duke of *Orleans*, the King's only Brother, and that back't by him he might rise, not so much against the King, as against the man that abus'd the King's Authority, to lower all the great Lords, and make Princes truckle under him. In this he was not so wise as he ought to have been, for reason and duty both would have told him, that he should first have considered how unsafe it is to have any great dependance on the obligations of Princes, who are engag'd the more easily, because afterwards they can easily leave them in the lurch that engag'd them, and are sure by the greatness of their quality to secure themselves from punishment at last.

X. Monsieur *Schomberg* being at that time with an Army in *Languedoc*, to oppose the designs of *Monsieur*, and the Duke of *Montmorency*; Monsieur *St. Preuil* and my self were ordered to go joyn him there with some Companies of Guards. When we were come up, the whole Army, which was not above six or seven thousand strong, marched to *Castelnau-d'Arry*, the Capital City of *Auragais*, that held out for the King. Monsieur's and the Duke of *Montmorency*'s Forces, consisting of thirteen thousand men, came up within three leagues of us. But between the two Armies there were great Waters and Bogs, which were a great security to us, and made us amends for the disadvantage of unequal numbers. About a quarter of a league from thence there stood among some Vineyards an empty house, very convenient to put a Guard into, because the situation of it being high, all the Enemies motions might be discovered from it. For this reason Monsieur *Schomberg* sent a Serjeant and some Souldiers thither, but yet with orders to quit it again, if they should find themselves prest by the Enemy. The Duke of *Montmorency* likewise, who with five hundred men advanc'd to make his observation of the posture and condition of our Army, perceiving this house, thought there might possibly be some Guard there. He went therefore immediately up to it and charg'd them, and with great ease beat them from that Post, where he placed a strong Guard of his own afterwards, of a hundred and fifty men.

Our Army never stirr'd all this while, Monsieur *Schomberg* resolving to stay till he was attackt, in regard he was so much weaker, and had the Town of *Castelnau d'Arry* to secure his retreat upon occasion. The Duke of *Montmorency* return'd mighty brisk to Monsieur, and said to him, *Oh, Sir, The day is now come, that will make you Master of your Enemies, and bring the Son and the Mother together again* (meaning the King and the Queen Mother) *but* (says he, drawing his Sword) *we must dye this up to the hilts in blood.* The Duke of *Orleans* fearing what the event of an engagement might be, return'd him a very cold answer, *Ho, Monsieur Montmorency, you will never leave your blustering. You have promis'd me mighty conquests a long time, but still I see nothing but hopes, I would have you know, that I for my part can make my peace, and retreat whenever I please, and make a third man.* Upon this some hot words arose on both sides, and the Duke of *Montmorency* withdrawing to a corner of the Room, to the Counts of *Mores*, and *Rieux*, and Monsieur d'*Aiguebonne*, (one of my particular friends, who related all this to me) said to the two former, *Our young Spark* (meaning the Duke of *Orleans*) *is turn'd Coward he talks of securing himself, and making a third man; but neither you Monsieur de Moret, nor you Monsieur de Rieux, nor I will shew him the way; and we must engage him so far now, that he shall be forc'd to fight to day, whether he will or no.*

In the mean time Monsieur *de Montmorency* put himself in a readiness to come up to us, and Monsieur *Schomberg* put his Army into line of Battel before *Castelnau d'Arry*, into which place he designed to retreat if he were prest to it; a Gentleman of that Country, about seventy years of age, came and told him, that if he would trust him with five hundred Musqueteers, and two or three hundred Horse, he would secure the day to him; and engage to make him master of the Enemies Army, by laying an Ambuscade, which they could not possibly avoid, at a Bridge, by which they must of necessity come, to attack the Kings Army. Monsieur *Schomberg* very gladly received the Gentlemans advice, and seeing that he could not well decline following it, since not above eight or nine hundred were hazarded for a whole Army, he ordered

Monfieur *St. Preuil*, and fome Officers befides, and my felf, to go along with the Gentleman, and take five hundred Mufqueteers of the Guards, we had brought into the Army, and gave us befides three hundred Horfe. The place prov'd very fit for an Ambufcade, for there were feveral bogs, and hollow ways and ditches, by which the Monfieur's Army muft needs come to gain the Bridge. We fet the Mufqueteers in thefe hollow places, where they could not be difcovered, and the Horfe a little higher, for they had orders to make the onfet, and to draw the Enemies into the Ambufh among the Foot; who were fo placed, that they could eafily make five hundred fhot in a very little time.

The Duke of *Montmorency* having prevail'd with Monfieur to come up with the Army, notwithftanding the ruffle that had been betwixt them, marched at the head of the Van-guard, and after him the Counts *Moret* and *Rieux*. Monfieur's poft was the main body, and there was no Rear guard, but a party of Referve. Monfieur *Montmorency* commanding the Van in chief, came firft into the way where the Ambufcade lay, and being attackt by our Horfe, repuls'd them very briskly, and in fome meafure defeated them. But as he was pufhing on his advantage a little too warmly, he and the Van guard fell together into our Ambufcade, who made in an inftant fo violent a fhot, that perhaps there never was a greater flaughter in fo fmall a time. The Counts of *Moret*, *Rieux*, and *la Feuillade* were killed in it. The Duke of *Montmorency* himfelf, after having done all that a great General could poffibly do upon fuch an occafion, and even forc'd feveral ranks of our men, was at laft beaten down under his Horfe; and the news fpreading immediately, that he and all his party were flain, Monfieur threw down his Arms, and faid the fport was too hot for him. So he commanded to found a Retreat immediately.

Mean while one *St. Mary*, a Serjeant in the Guards, came and told me, that he thought he faw Monfieur *Montmorency* lying under his Horfe. But I, who had a particular honour and efteem for this Duke, upon the account of his great worth, was much concern'd at his misfortune, and would not go my felf to make him my Prifoner. I went then and told Monfieur *St. Preuil* of it, being very well fatisfy'd to leave the honour of this to him. He did not care for going alone neither, but urg'd me fo earneftly, that I yielded at laft to go with him. We went then with fome Souldiers and the Sergeant, to the place where he had feen him lye. Monfieur *St. Preuil* perceiving him in this lamentable condition, cry'd, *Ah Mafter!* for fo he always ufed to call him. The Duke, who had formerly had a quarrel with *St. Preuil*, and had no kindnefs for him, thought he was very glad of an occafion to difoblige him, and to take his revenge upon one that he thought his Enemy: And in this apprehenfion cry'd out in a great paffion, *Come not near me, I have life enough left to kill thee ftill.* Monfieur *St. Preuil*, who was very far from having any malicious intentions toward him, and indeed was much affected to fee matters thus with him; protefted to him, that he came thither with no other defign than to do him fervice; and that he would rather dye a thoufand deaths, than do any thing unbecoming the refpect due to his perfon. The Duke, a little better fatisfied, and feeing me with Monfieur *St. Preuil*, told us he was engaged to us, and thought himfelf happy in falling into fuch hands as ours, who had fuch kindnefs for him. Then we came nearer to help him, and had very much ado to get him out of the Ditch, where his Thigh was fec faft under his Horfe, which was dead, and lay very heavy upon him. It was really a very fad fight, to fee him all over blood, and almoft ftrangled with that that came out of his mouth, for he was much hurt. At laft I got him in my Arms, and laid him in a Cloak, which I made four Souldiers carry, at each corner one. We met Monfieur *Brezay* by the way, whom as foon as the Duke perceived, (as indeed he was afraid of every thing, and had not the perfect ufe of his reafon) he was concern'd to fee him, becaufe he was his particular Enemy. He begg'd of Monfieur *St. Preuil* to bring a Confeffor to him, that he might dye like a Chriftian at leaft: But Monfieur *St. Preuil* encourag'd him afrefh, and engag'd to him that no wrong fhould be done him, while he was under his Cuftody. We brought him after this to Monfieur *Schomberg*, who expreft great refentments of tendernefs and compaffion, and that he was extremely concern'd at his misfortune, and could have wifht, rather to have left his own blood, than to fee him in this miferable condition: For in truth all the world lov'd and honour'd this excellent man. He defir'd Monfieur *Schomberg* to let him have a Confeffor, fearing he fhould dye every minute without Confeffion. But the Marefchal bad him fear nothing, for he would fend his own Chyrurgion, or any

other

other he should make choice of, to dress his wounds, and shortly after he was carry'd to *Letoure*.

XI. The King had commanded me, if any action happen'd, to come and bring him the news; so I went with all the expedition I could, and of three Couriers that were dispatcht at the same time, I got first to *Pezenas*, where his Majesty then was. Being come into the Hall, where the King, the Cardinals, and several great Lords of the Court were, I directed my self, not to the Cardinal, as others frequently did, but to the King; and acquainted him, that we had engaged, and his Army had got the day. The King at this news was seized with such fear that Monsieur might be kill'd, that he grew very pale and disordered, and cry'd out in great confusion, *What! and is my Brother dead then?* I reviv'd him presently, by telling him, No, he was not, but very well. Cardinal *Richelieu* was so surprized with this sudden exclamation and the tenderness his Majesty had exprest for his Brother, that he could not forbear saying to some persons that stood by; *Ay, he makes War upon his Brother to fine purpose; you see Nature discovers herself, and commits violence upon him.*

Then I inform'd the King particularly of the several passages in the action, and the taking of Monsieur *Montmorency*; and while I was telling my story, the other Couriers arrived, and these addressing themselves to the Cardinal, and not to the King, told him the same that I had just before told his Majesty.

XII. Some time after this the whole Court remov'd to *Tholouse*; and now the War was ended, I being desirous to take this opportunity of going for a little while to *Pontis*, where I had a great deal of business, asked leave of the King, but he would not give it me, and commanded me to wait on him to *Tholouse*. This design was, to employ me in conducting Monsieur *Montmorency* to *Paris*, where in the right of a Peer of *France*, he ought to be try'd by a Parliament of Peers, which is that of *Paris*. But Cardinal *Richelieu*, who lookt on him as his peculiar Enemy, had no mind to such tedious methods; and fearing that the Quality, the great Alliances, and the Worth of the man he hated, might by gaining of time incline the King to mercy, he went a shorter way to work, and waving the stated forms of Tryal for Peers of *France*, perswaded the King to appoint the Duke's Process before the Parliament of *Tholouse*. Besides, it was some satisfaction to him, to have him try'd in the midst of his own Government, and before the face of a Country, that honour'd him exceedingly.

Then the King commanded me to go to my Company, which was some leagues off, and which I had left, to attend his Majesty's person, under the command of an Ensign only, when Monsieur *St. Prenil* and I were ordered with five hundred Musquets into *Languedoc*. His Majesty directed me to be the next day at *Narbonne*, whither himself intended to come, in his way to *Tholouse*. There had been heard for some days before, terrible noises, like the roaring of Bulls, upon the Sea; which to me seemed to foretell some great raging storm: And thus we quickly found it: For as I and my Servant were upon the Road, we heard of a sudden a loud clap of Thunder, attended with mighty Lightnings, and immediately upon it fell a fearful shower, which continued for four hours with such violence, as if Heaven and Earth would come together. I had a Bridge to pass, over a small Brook, and rid full speed to get over before the Waters rose, but they were so high in a very little time, and there ran so strong a stream over the Bridge just at my going over, that it took my Horse up to the Belly, and had like to have carry'd him away. My Servant, who came after, was in more danger than I. We had like to have been drowned a hundred times, our Horses being forced to swim in many places, and the Roads being all like Rivers. The King, who was then upon the Road too towards *Narbonne*, had much ado to recover the Town; all the Court lost their Baggage, more than three hundred men drowned; several Coaches, and some of the Queens were left behind, and her Maids had much ado to save their lives. A Light-Horse took up two of them, and set one before, and another behind him. I for my own part, after a world of hardship, getting to my Company, saw all sorts of Birds and Beasts, nay, even the very Rabbets run into Houses and Barns before mens faces. I do not at all magnifie the matter, for one would have thought a second flood had been coming, the Rain continuing (as I said) for four hours together without any abatement, and four and twenty hours in all.

I ne-

I never was more put to it in all my life : For being much concern'd to observe my order exactly, which was to be at *Narbonne* next day with my Company, I resolved not to fail. I got them thither at last, but fatigued them beyond what you can imagine ; insomuch that the King chid me, and told me, I play'd the fool in bringing my Company cross the Country such weather as that was. His Majesty went forward to *Tholouse*, and Monsieur *Montmorency* was brought thither by his order : Where he arrived the 7th of *October*, in the year 1632, about noon. They carry'd him to the Town-house, and put him under the Custody of Monsieur *de Louroy*, Lieutenant of the *Guards du Corps*. The streets and publick places, from the Gate where he came in, up to the Common Hall, were lin'd with Souldiers and *Swisses*; and several Guards were set in other places about the Town ; so very loth was the Cardinal, that he man, whom he lookt upon as his Prisoner, should get out of his hands.

XIII. Some three hours after the Duke's arrival, two Commissioners came to the Town-Hall to examine him. The Commission given the Parliament to proceed upon his Tryal was first read to him : Whereupon he said, with a great deal of temper, that tho his Peerage made him accountable to the Parliament of *Paris*, and no other Court, yet he must confess his offence was such, that if the King was not favourable, any Judges had right enough to condemn him ; that he was very well satisfied therefore to be try'd by the Parliament of *Tholouse*, whom he had ever had a respect for, and lookt upon them to be very honest Gentlemen. The Commissioners sat at the end of the Table, and seated him on their left hand. They brought seven Witnesses in against him, that is, four Officers of the Regiment of Guards, two Serjeants, and the Clerk of the States of *Languedoc*. He owned all that the Officers of the Guards evidenc'd against him, concerning the action of *Castelnau-d'Arry*. And one of them being questioned, whether he knew Monsieur *Montmorency* in the battle, answered with tears, that seeing him covered with fire, and blood, and smoak, he had much ado to know him at first ; but when he saw him break six of their ranks, and kill several Souldiers in the seventh, he concluded this could be no body but Monsieur *de Montmorency* ; and that he knew him perfectly well afterwards, when his Horse fell dead under him, and he lay there without being able to get off.

The Commissioners askt him, if he had sign'd the debate of the States of *Languedoc*, of the 22d. of *July*, in which they entreated Monsieur to give them the honour of his protection, and promis'd to supply him with whatever Money he should want, for the support of his Party, and that they would never desert his Interests. He denied that he had subscribed it, and the Clerk being produced against him, and affirming that he had, he fell into a great passion, calling him a forging Knave, and charged him with counterfeiting his hand.

All this while the whole Court was employed in importuning his Majesty for Monsieur de *Montmorency*'s Pardon, and every body pray'd to God in his behalf. For (besides that he was a person extremely to be valu'd) his great alliances with the Royal Family, having the honour to be Brother-in-law to the first Prince of the Blood, and Unkle to two Princes besides, and one Princess, which is my Lady Dutchess of *Longeville* ; and the illustrious reputation of his own Family, the eminent renown of which is as old as Religion in *France*, was the reason that all the Kingdom interess'd themselves in his preservation. The Cardinal *de la Valette* exprest an extraordinary zeal above all the rest, and when he had done all he could with the King, as well as the Pope's Nuntio, and all the Princes, he betook himself to the Prayers of the Church, which he directed to be made every where, assisting in them himself, and several great persons at Court with him, and omitting nothing, that so affectionate and generous a friendship as his could inspire a man with upon such occasions.

The Blue Penitents also made a solemn Procession, among whom walked a great many persons of Quality, and they went to visit the bodies of St. *Simon* and *Jude* on their Feast-day, at the Abby of St. *Cernin*, where they sung Mass, and abundance of people communicated, every one professing those devotions to be perform'd upon Monsieur *Montmorency*'s account, and with an intent to beg his life of God. Nay, Monsieur the Duke of *Orleans*, though a party in that revolt himself, having, as I said before, laid down his arms, and return'd to his obedience, was not unmindful of the Duke of *Montmorency* in this extremity : But sent a Gentleman, who threw himself

thrice

thrice at the Kings feet, and entreated him in his name, with all the earneſtneſs imaginable, to ſpare a perſon, who had ever expreſt an exceeding great zeal for his Majeſty's ſervice, and who had engaged in this unhappy buſineſs (as he himſelf had done) more out of levity and inconſideration, than out of any malicious principle, or ſettled diſaffection to his Majeſty.

Among all theſe perſons of Honour that importun'd for Monſieur *Montmorency's* Pardon, my Captain, Monſieur *St. Previl*,had the weakneſs to preſume to put in his particular interceſſion too,and begg'd his life of theKing inCardinal *Richelieu's* preſence, which was thought ſo very ridiculous,as to be made the Jeſt of the whole Court.The King laught at him for it ; and the Cardinal, when he heard him offer this requeſt to his Majeſty, reply'd to him, with a true *Richelieu* complement, *St. Previl, if the King ſerv'd you right, he would ſet your head where your heels ſtand.* I heard this complement my ſelf, which I confeſs to me ſeem'd ſomething Sparkiſh for a Biſhop to make. But it muſt be own'd, that it ill became a ſmall Officer, to take upon him the asking a favour, which ſo many Princes and Nobles could not obtain. Thus much however may be ſaid in his excuſe, that having not only a very great reſpect, but a particular friendſhip for Monſieur *Montmorency*, and having made him his Priſoner, he thought he had ſome priviledge upon this account to ſue for his Pardon ; and in ſo doing was more guided by his affection, than judgment. For my own part, tho I had it may be as great a reſpect and as tender a concern for him as he, and had as much reaſon to look upon him as my Priſoner, yet I thought it my duty to ſatisfie my ſelf with the ſuppli-cations of the principal perſons of the Kingdom, and by no means proper to joyn my ſelf with them, any farther than by my good wiſhes and my prayers. I was affected more ſenſibly than it is poſſible for me to expreſs, both by my own private concern, and by that general dejection obſervable, not only in the Court, but even among the common people ; which was ſo great, that one day as the King was in his Palace, with abundance of company, we heard all on the ſudden a mighty noiſe, occaſioned by the people, who quite tranſported with grief, came to the Kings Lodgings, and cry'd out, *Mercy, Mercy, Pardon, Pardon.* The King askt what was the meaning of all that noiſe? and Monſieur *de Brezay*, that had been made Mareſchal of *France*, up-on the action of *Caſtelnau d' Arry*, told him, that if his Majeſty would give himſelf the trouble to look out at the window, he would have pity upon thoſe poor men. But the King anſwer'd him very roughly, and without all queſtion, more according to the Cardinals ſenſe than his own, *If I would be guided by the different inclinations of my people, I ſhould not behave my ſelf like a King.*

XIV. While theſe important applications were making for ſaving the Duke of *Montmorency*, and thoſe ſo univerſal and unanimous, that it ſeem'd almoſt one voice of Nobles and People, that begg'd of God and the King, the life of a perſon entire-ly beloved of all the world ; the Duke himſelf ſeem'd the only man that had forgot all concern for the preſervation of his preſent life. The convictions of his own breaſt, that he deſerved death ; and the knowledge he had particularly, what temper his chief Enemy was of, made him very little ſollicitous about his Pardon: and ſo com-mitting himſelf into the hands of God, he employ'd himſelf wholly for the obtaining a favour, much above this life, which he was about to leave. So that we may ſay, tho all that pray'd for him were not heard as to their particular requeſt, yet that they were in another reſpect much more for his advantage; for at the ſame time that the King deny'd him favour, Almighty God was particularly good to him, having wrought him to a lively repentance for his miſcarriages, and a deſire to atone for them by his death. To this therefore he ſeriouſly prepared himſelf by a general Confeſſion, and for that he qualify'd himſelf by a very particular reflection upon all his paſt life, for two days together. And deſiring to ſtrengthen himſelf yet more againſt a tryal ſo ſharp as that he was to undergo, he requeſted, and received the Body of our Lord, as that holy *Viaticum*, from whence he expected his whole ſupport.

The ſame day, being the 29th of *October*, the Courts being met in Parliament, the Keeper of the Seals came thither, attended with ſix Maſters of Requeſts, and there his Tryal was examined. The next night, all the Souldiers quarter'd about *Tholouſe* re-ceiv'd orders to come into the Town, and were poſted in all the ſtreets and avenues, to the number of twelve thouſand men. About ſeven or eight of the clock next morning, the Count *de Charlus* took Monſieur *Montmorency* from the Town-Hall, and brought him to the Palace in his own Coach. He conducted him to the Chamber

where

where the Court were met, and where the Keeper of the Seals had taken the Chair; and after having plac'd him at the Bar upon a Stool, he withdrew. The Judges all cast their eyes down upon the ground at his coming in, and most of them held their handkerchiefs before their faces, as if they were desirous to hide their tears, which they could not with any decency let the world see upon such an occasion. The Stool was set in the middle of the Court, and rais'd higher than ordinary, so as to be almost even with the Benches, where the Judges sat. He sat upon it bare-headed, and unbound, which is not usual with the Parliament of *Tholouse*; before whom none are brought to the Bar unshackled. The Keeper of the Seals, having first askt him the usual questions, which are but matter of form, desir'd to know whether he had sign'd the Deliberation of the States of *Languedoc*? to which he reply'd, that he confest he had ; and that upon second thoughts, he had recollected it, and was to blame for denying it before.

It was then put to him, whether he had not invited Monsieur the Duke of *Orleans* into his Government? he reply'd, No, but that the States of that Province had entreated him to take their priviledges into his protection. Being farther question'd, whether Monsieur had not put him upon taking up arms ? he said, he was not dispos'd to excuse himself by laying the fault upon Monsieur. Being askt, what it was then that put him upon doing what he did? he answer'd, that it was his ill fortune, and his own imprudence. When he was prest to declare the persons that were engag'd with him, he reply'd, that he own'd all that the Witnesses had depos'd against him. They demanded, whether he had kept any correspondence with the foreigners upon the frontier? he deny'd it positively, and affirm'd, that it was never any part of his design to injure the Kingdom at all. He reply'd indeed to every question they put to him so modestly, and like a man of honour, and with so engaging an air, that the Judges had much ado to contain themselves, when they saw this great man in so moving circumstances. When the Interrogatories were over, the Keeper of the Seals askt him, whether he did not acknowledge himself in a great fault, and that he deserv'd to dye ? To which he made this feeling return, that he deserv'd more than could be exprest. Afterwards being order'd to withdraw, he begg'd to be admitted once more, and then before the Court excus'd the Clerk of the States, whom he had accus'd, and used him roughly the day before.

After he was withdrawn, and while they carried him back to the Town Hall, the Parliament proceeded to give their voices. A case so plain would not bear any long debate; and it was impossible but a person taken actually in arms against his Prince, must be condemned. One of the Commissioners therefore first pronounc'd him guilty, and it was observ'd, that in the close of his Sentence the tears stood in his Eyes. All the rest of the company exprest their consent, in dumb show, by taking off their Caps ; and the Keeper of the Seals confirming the same, he drew up the Sentence, and signed it before the Court broke up. Then all the Judges made haste home, that they might at their own houses give free vent to those tears and groans, which Ceremony put a restraint upon in the publick Court of Justice. The Sentence being brought to the King, his Majesty could not bear being a little mollified, and changed two Articles in it. The one, that whereas he was to have been executed in the publick Market place, this should be done privately within the Town Hall; and the other, that Monsieur *Montmorency*'s Estate, which was confiscated, he should have leave to dispose of as he pleas'd. Which accordingly he did by Will, and deliver'd it to Monsieur *St. Prenil* to carry to the King, desiring him to beg his Majesty's Pardon in his Name. Nay, which was an action truly worthy of a good Christian, he had a mind to let his bitterest Enemy see, that he died without any grudge or revengeful thoughts against him ; and therefore gave the same Monsieur *St. Prenil* a Picture of St. *Francis*, with charge to make a Present of it to Cardinal *Richelieu*, as a testimony that he died his humble Servant.

About noon, the same day that Sentence was given, two Commissioners and the Recorder came into the Chappel of the Town Hall, and sent for Monsieur *Montmorency* thither ; who, kneeling down at the foot of the Altar, and fixing his Eyes upon a Crucifix, had his Sentence read to him. Then rising up, and turning to the company, he said, *Gentlemen, I beg your Prayers, that God would enable me to suffer like a Christian, the Execution of what was just now read to me.* The Commissioners leaving him with his Confessor, one of them as he was going said, *Sir, we are going to obey your commands, we will pray to God to strengthen you.* He, continuing in the Chappel, and looking

looking again up to the Crucifix, and afterwards down upon his Clothes, which were very rich, threw away his Night-gown, and said, *Shall such a sinful wretch as I presume to go to dye gaily habited, when I see my innocent Saviour stript naked upon the Cross? No Father* (said he to his Confessor) *I must strip to my Shirt, that I may do some fit penance for the Sins I have committed against God.* Just at this instant the Count *de Charlus* came from the King, to demand the Order of the Holy Ghost, and the Mareschal's Staff of *France.* The remainder of his time was employed in committing himself to God, and strengthning his mind against death, by the Contemplation of his Saviour's Sufferings; and in praying him to pardon his Sins.   When notice was brought him of the hour appointed for his Execution, he begg'd they would do him the favour to let him suffer about the same time of the day that Christ dyed, which was some two hours sooner than the Order; and this was left to his own choice.   Before he went to dye, he wrote a Letter to his Lady, Madam *Montmorency*, conjuring her to be comforted, and to present the concern for his death as an offering to God; to procure rest for his Soul, by moderating her grief in consideration of the Mercy God had shewn him.

XV. He order'd his Hair to be cut short behind, and being stript to his Shirt and Drawers, he went in the middle of the Guards, who saluted him as he past, cross a walk that leads into the Court of the Town-Hall, at the entrance of which he found the Scaffold, which might be some four foot from the ground.   When he was come up upon it, attended with his Confessor and his Chyrurgeon, he saluted the company, which were only the Clerk of the Parliament, the Grand Provost and his Archers, and the Officers of the City Train-bands, who had orders to wait there.   He begg'd of them to acquaint the King, that he dy'd his most humble Subject and Servant; infinitely troubled for having offended him, for which he begg'd his and their pardon. He enquir'd for the Executioner, who had not yet come near him, and, in great humility, would not allow his Chyrurgeon to do any thing about him, but giving himself up entirely to be dispos'd of by the Executioner, as to the binding part, the putting him into a right posture, and the cutting off his hair again, which was not cut close enough before; he said with great significations of remorse, that so great a sinner as he could not dye too ignominiously.   At last he kneel'd down near the Block, upon which he laid his Neck, and after he had recommended his Soul to God, the Executioner immediately cut off his Head; all the company turning away their eyes from the sad sight, all melting into tears; and even the Guards themselves expressing their concern, by deep sighs and groans.

Thus dy'd *Henry* of *Montmorency*, Duke and Peer, Mareschal, and sometime Admiral of *France*, Governour of *Languedoc*, Grandson of four Constables and six Mareschal's, first Christian, and first Baron of *France*, Brother-in-law to the first Prince of the Blood, and Unkle to the renowned Prince of *Conde*; after having won two Battels, one by Sea against the *Hugonots*, by which he made way for the taking of *Rochelle*; and the other by Land, against the Empire, *Italy* and *Spain*, by which he forc'd the *Alpes*, and sav'd *Cazal*: Both which actions contributed much to that Glory which the King of *France* hath.   Those that were present at his death gave him this testimony, That so much Piety and Courage was never seen upon such an occasion, and in a man of that Quality; and indeed it was but fit, that both Nature and Grace should work wonders in the person of the first Christian, and the bravest man in all *France*.   Since our Monarchy began there never was any Nobleman in the Kingdom, with whom both Nature and Fortune had dealt so bountifully.   He was born in the year 1595. the wealthiest, best accomplished, most generous Lord in the whole Kingdom; graceful in his Speech, and charming in all his Conversation: A person of that honour and genteel address, that all the world lov'd and admir'd him.   He exerted all his powers of Wit, Wisdom, Quality, and every other advantage of Honour and Reputation both at home and abroad, in the service of his Majesty; and that to so great a degree, that he sacrific'd his own interests to the good of the King and State, and for ten years together maintained a War against the Rebels in *Languedoc* at his own proper charge.   In short, the King himself was pleased at two several times, to proclaim his praises throughout his whole Realm, in so honourable and advantageous expressions, that it might be truly said of this last design in which he was unhappily engag'd, that it was in some degree excusable, not being able to endure to live, and see the Queen Mother driven out of *France*, the King's only Brother remov'd from Court,

and

and so many persons of Honour, some banish'd, some clapt up in Prison, some publickly put to death, and all this by the Tyranny of one single Minister of State; and that it was his great misfortune to be of opinion, that the taking up arms against that Minister, was the best way of doing a real service to his Master.

XVI. After all that has been said it cannot seem strange, if the people, and the whole Kingdom where so sensibly affected with his death. As an instance of their being so, as soon as ever the Execution was over, and the Grand Provost had ordered the Gates to be opened, they throng'd in prodigious crowds to see the body. Their concern, and the mighty respect they had for the great *Montmorency*'s person were such, that when they could find no other comfort for the loss they sustain'd in him, they almost stifled one another to get near the Scaffold, and to gather up the blood in their Handkerchiefs, and lay it up by them at home. Nay some were so very extravagantly zealous, as to drink of it, and the least that any body did, was to go away again in tears.

In the mean while, two Priests that belong'd to Cardinal *Valette*, came and took the body into the Chapel of the Abby-house of *St. Cernin*, where it was first embalmed, and put into a leaden Coffin, and afterwards, by a very particular favour, bury'd in *St. Cernin*'s Church, a place that no person had been allow'd to lye in, ever since *Charlemayne* brought the bodies of the Apostles thither; and this was so strictly observed, that the very Counts of *Tholouse* could never obtain leave to be laid there themselves. An eminent mark of respect this, for this illustrious man, that he should be esteem'd worthy an interment, where no body else had the priviledge of lying. At four in the morning they began to say a great many Masses, as was usual, and among others, the Bishops of *Pamiez* and *Commenges* said Masses. The greatest part of the Parliament came thither with the common people, to pay their last respects to the person, whose condemnation they could not pronounce without tears and extreme regret. And thus ended this bloody Tragedy, which by presenting the greatest man in the Kingdom beheaded publickly upon a Scaffold, in the very midst of that very Province, and the Capital City of it, which was under his Government, shews us at the same time how much that favour and the grace of heaven, which assisted him so powerfully at his last hour, is a more desirable blessing, than the good Graces of the Court, which forsook him when he stood most in need of them. It may not be amiss to present you here with a Copy of Verses, which may serve for an Epitaph upon him, and with them I shall conclude this story.

How short Man's Glory, and how frail his State,
Learn here from noble Montmorency's *Fate.*
These are the poor remains of that great Name,
Whose Praises fill the loudest Mouth of Fame.
Such were (if any such) fair Thetis' *Son,*
Such the Victorious Youth of Macedon.
In Life scarce equal, equal in their End,
From which nor Force, nor Virtue can defend.
For in rude heaps, the Valiant, Wise and Just,
With Fools, Knaves, Cowards, undistinguish't, must
Lye down at last, and mix one common Dust.
'Midst heaps of slain, lavish of Life, he stood,
And, like a Rock, scatter'd th' invading Flood.
The God of War observ'd th' unequal strife;
Threatned, but would not spill so brave a Life.
But (oh Respect perverse, malicious, vain,)
That generous blood, which could ev'n Mars *restrain,*
Was vilely shed, and did a Scaffold stain.
Thus Heaven consults poor Mortals Innocence,
Just shews, and snatches back such excellence:
Lest by bright Virtue charm'd we prostrate fall,
The Image court, and slight the Great Original.

XVII. Af-

XVII. After the Duke of *Montmorency*'s execution, the King and all the Court went back to *Paris*. And the next year, which was 1633, we met with new disturbances from another Prince, who though he was a Soveraign one, yet was so with dependence upon the King. The Duke of *Lorrain* having violated several Treaties, formerly made with his Majesty, and denying to pay homage to the Crown, upon account of the Dutchy of *Bar*, the King resolved to go do himself reason by force of Arms. He went about the month of *August*, and sat down before the Town of *Nancy*, which was then one of the best Fortifications in *Europe*. I had the honour to attend him constantly, when he gave himself the trouble to go in person, and mark out the lines of our Trenches, which he did with most extraordinary skill, being, as I said, eminently ingenious in all matters relating to War.

XVIII. The Duke of *Lorrain*, perceiving himself in very great hazard to lose his whole Dominions by his own fault, sent his Brother, the Cardinal of *Lorrain* to the King, to propose a Treaty of Peace: He was forc'd at last to truckle under a stronger force, and a more discerning judgment than his own. He resolv'd to come himself at last, and wait on the King in his own Quarters, which were at *Neuville* a league off of *Nancy*, and there made all manner of Submissions. The King receiv'd him with great kindness and respect, and entertain'd him with the same expressions of friendship, as if he had never had reason to take any thing ill from him. He stood for some time bare-headed, and afterwards putting on his own Hat, obliged the Duke to put on his too. But being by several experimental proofs sufficiently convinc'd, of how fickle and crafty a temper he was, he was resolv'd by some contrivance to hinder his return to *Nancy* that day; vilely suspecting that if he let him go back, he might trump up some new device upon him, and shutting himself up in the Town, deny to open the Gates, notwithstanding his word was engaged to the contrary. The Kings Chamber was a very dark room, and therefore pretending he could not see to read some Letters that were brought him, he called for Lights, that so the Duke might not be sensible when night came on. And this was about four of the clock in the afternoon, in the month of *September*.

The Duke of *Lorrain*, who would fain have been going to *Nancy*, seeing the King taken up in reading of Letters, would have taken his leave, and desir'd he would permit him to go home, and give directions for the due performance of what he had promis'd should be done. The King, who was much of opinion, that his going was rather design'd to obstruct, than to further the performance, answer'd him, without taking any notice, *Methinks, Cousin, you are quickly weary of my company ; it is not late yet, you have but a league to* Nancy*, and may go it in less than an hour.* Thus the King manag'd the matter so dextrously, that what between caressing him, reading of Letters, and turning the discourse from one thing to another, night drew on before he was aware of it. At length the Duke of *Lorrain* began to be very uneasie, and made a second offer to take his leave, and be going : The King enquir'd of those about him, what a clock it was ? and being answer'd, that it was seven, he reply'd to the Duke, as in a seeming surprize, *Oh strange, how time runs away ! Nay, it is too late for you to go now, Cousin.* The Duke, who had much rather have travell'd all night, than have staid where he was, in the Kings custody, answer'd, That he knew the Road very well, and as his Majesty had done him the honour to observe, should soon be at his journeys end. The King, who saw him extremely eager to be gone, and had no mind to discover any thing of his own design, brought himself off very handsomely, by asking some Officers that were there, whether the Guard was set? For, upon their informing him that it was, and the Orders all given, he said to the Duke of *Lorrain*, *Cousin, you cannot well leave me to night, it is too late to go ; and if you should, now the Guards are set, it would make a great confusion : You had much better lye here, and to morrow morning you may be going very early.* So after a great many fresh attempts to go, he was under a necessity at last to comply with the Kings invitation, not daring, as matters then stood, to give him any occasion of displeasure.

XIX. The Cardinal of *Valette*'s apartment was appointed for the Duke of *Lorrain*'s Lodging ; and the King commanded my Lord Duke of *St. Simon*, and the Count of *Nogent*, to keep him company at Supper, and some other Officers and my self to wait upon him. But all this honour done him by his Majesty, was only meant to secure him

him the more effectually. And upon the same account twelve *Swisses* were ordered
to keep Guard at his door, which was to pass for respect to him. The Duke of
Lorrain invited the Duke of *St. Simon* and the Count of *Negem* to sup with him, who
staid till eleven at night. In the mean while, ten or twelve Souldiers were privately
posted to secure the house within, and then as many Officers of us as were there withdrew with the Duke of *St. Simon* and Count *Nogent.*

When his Highness of *Lorrain* was gone to bed, I receiv'd orders to keep a strong
guard about his house with my Company, for fear he should make any attempt to
get off under the covert of the night. Therefore considering of what consequence
such a Guard might prove, I set a Centry at every six paces, and posted my self near
one of the Centinels, under a Tree, just over against a Window of the Chamber
where the Duke lay. The jealousie he had that he was caught, and trickt by the
wile of the King, as in truth he was, gave him great disturbance, and not being able
to sleep in his Bed, he had a great mind to try if it were possible for him to make
his escape. Well, about one a clock at midnight he got up, and came to look out at
the Window, that lay directly against the Tree where I sat, and was at least as
wakeful as he. At first he began to sing, as if he intended to divert himself; and
presently after calling to the Centry, he cry'd, *Centry, Centry, I hear a great noise, what
is the matter?* I reply'd instead of the Centry, and told him it was a body of Horse
that were walking the Rounds. *How many of them may there be?* said the Duke; *About
two thousand, Sir,* said I. *How!* said he, *two thousand Horse! this is something more than
ordinary; the Guard does not use to be so great.* Excuse me, Sir, said I, *it is commonly of
this strength. O there must be less,* reply'd he, *you represent it bigger than is;* away,
away: And who commands there? Every one in his turn, Sir, said I; *sometimes the Mareschals de Camp, sometimes the Lieutenant Generals, and so the other Officers in course. On my
word,* said the Duke, *that is a stout Guard, you need fear nothing.* I reply'd, That where-
ever the King in person, the Guard was always thus big. Afterwards having a
mind to pump me, he proceeded thus: *But is not the person I am talking with, an Officer?* I reply'd, That I was a poor Cadet, and his humble Servant. *Say you so?* answer'd he, as if he were surpriz'd at that, *by your discourse I should have taken you for an
Officer. Well then, Fellow Souldier, since thou art but a Souldier, how long hast thou been at
this trade? Some ten or twelve years, Sir,* said I. *And how long hast thou serv'd in the
Guards?* I told him, *About some five or six years. How!* added he, *methinks thou hast serv'd
a great while, to have no reward; prithee how comes it to pass thou art advanc'd no higher?* I
made answer, That some men had better fortune in the world than others; and that
I for my part was one of the unlucky ones; but still I expected every day the same
good fortune, that I saw some of my fellows attain to. He askt me, whether we
receiv'd our pay duly however? I told him I had no reason to complain for that
matter, and that if I was unhappy in other respects, yet in this I was not. After that,
he askt me, how much my pay was? and I answer'd, the [common] pay of Souldi-
ers. *But,* said he, *methinks it is cruel hard for all that, to stick at the mark thou one's whole
life, and never rise to any Command; Couldst not thou be well pleas'd to have some employ?
To be sure, Sir,* said I, *if the King saw fit to give me a Command, I should not refuse it. Very
well,* said he, *and hark you Souldier, if you have a mind to it, there are methods for an honest
man to make his fortune.* I answer'd him, That I had the honour to serve the greatest
Prince in the world, who hath it in his power to reward, if I am but able to do him
service. He return'd very pleasantly, *It seems then thou hast not serv'd him well all this
while, for thou hast been a long time in service, and he hath made thee no amends yet. It is a
sign, Sir, that he hath a mind to try me long and throughly,* said I, *that he may be able to make
a surer Judgment whether I deserve his favour. A man loses nothing by waiting: Therefore I
am in expectation every day, and it may be I shall be rewarded to morrow. This I am sure of,
that I can never be false to my duty, and that this is the only way to raise my fortunes.*

The Duke of *Lorrain* understood very well by my answer, that I knew who I
spoke to, and that he was to expect nothing from me. Upon this account, tho he
was toucht to the quick, and much enrag'd to see himself so put upon, yet he made as
though he valu'd our Centinel, and said, *Go thy way for a brave fellow, I love thee for
this humour. Good night.* And then he withdrew immediately. A Gentleman that
was with him, and who heard this dialogue between us, said to him upon this, *Ah
Master, you are made Prisoner, there is no possibility of getting off.* In the mean while, I
went forthwith to acquaint the Duke of *Espernon* with the discourse that had passed
with his Highness, that he might inform the King. My Lord *Espernon* imagining,

that the Duke might possibly come to attack me a second time, had a mind to divert himself with the hearing it, and came and posted himself with me under my Tree. The Duke accordingly appeared again at the Window presently after, and cry'd, *Comrade, Centry, What's the Clock?* I told him, it wanted something of Two. He askt me, whether it was I that he had spoke to before? I told him I was the person to whom he did that honour. He added, *You are a great while upon duty:* For he was terrible uneasie, and would have been glad to have had some body else to deal with. I answer'd, That I had not been two hours there yet, and that now I should be soon reliev'd. *What's the reason,* said the Duke, *that I hear no more of the noise there was even now? Sir,* said I, *because the Petrole is gone by, and within a little while it will come round again.* *In earnest,* said he, *this is a fine strong Guard, but it must be confest that they have a great Prince to guard.* *Well, thou art happy to serve under such a King, he understands Military Discipline the best of any Prince in* Europe. *Sir,* said I, *I should be the most miserable man alive, were I not sensible of my happiness to serve so great a Master;* and you, Sir, continu'd I, *are as able to judge of his greatness as any body, for you have had some knowledge of it.* *Does not he exercise you himself?* reply'd the Duke. *Yes Sir,* said I, *he exercises his own Regiment of Guards, his Musqueteers, and all the Regiments.* *For ought I perceive* (reply'd he) *he keeps you to hard work, and allows you but little time to rest in.* *Yes indeed, Sir,* said I, *he often makes us sweat soundly, but he favours himself no more than he does us.* Then he askt me, Whereabouts the Cardinals Lodging was there? adding, That he was afraid there was but indifferent Guard kept there; and when I answer'd him, That the Guards were equally set through all the Kings Quarter; he said with a laugh, *Nay, nay, there must be more and less, there is not the same occasion to guard all.* After this he enlarg'd mightily in praise of the King; and when he had try'd and turn'd me every way, and found that I was proof still against all his methods, he said to me at last, *Well, fellow Souldier, whoever you are, your servant: Good night.* And so he went in again.

The Duke of *Espernon* had like utterly to have spoil'd all, for the jest pleas'd him so well, that he had much ado to forbear bursting out into a loud laughter. For besides, that the subject of our discourse was pleasant enough, the manner of our talking together, without ever seeing one another at all; and one lying all the while upon the attack, and the other acting defensively, had something very comical in it. I withdrew too a little after, leaving directions with the Centinel, that if the Duke came again to the window, and had a mind to talk any more, he should answer him a little roughly, *Pray Sir be pleas'd to go in and sleep, this is a very unseasonable time of night.* But he never was put to this trouble: For the Duke perceiving himself caught, came out no more. The King understanding by my Lord *Espernon* at his waking, what pleasant discourse had passed, diverted himself and the company with it, and was very desirous to hear the whole story from me. I made all the haste I could to wait on him, and related the whole matter to him as naturally as I could. When I told him how the Duke had sounded me, by some hints that there were methods for an honest man to make his fortunes; his Majesty told me, that I should have urg'd him a little further, and have pretended to accept his proffer, to see how far he would have gone; whereupon I very readily made the King this reply, That if the thing were to do again, I should do so, having authority from his Majesty for it; but that I could by no means think it safe before, because perhaps it would have been hard to perswade him, that this was only put on; and therefore I chose rather to jest within compass, and keep on the safer side, than to venture upon any thing that would stand in need of a favourable construction. The King laught heartily, and because he would have the diversion of telling this story himself, which indeed he did very pleasantly, charg'd me not to speak of it. But when he told it to any of the Lords at Court, he would send for me to confirm what he had said. Every body was well pleas'd with it, and the conference between the Duke of *Lorrain* and the Lieutenant of *Pontis,* was the constant entertainment of all companies.

XX. The King sent in the morning to enquire how the Duke of *Lorrain* had rested, and to tell him withal, That he was something surpriz'd to find the people of *Nancy* did not open their Gates according to agreement, after the Letter he had written to them; For his Highness had writ once before upon this occasion, but had forbidden them to comply with his Letter, how positive soever the orders were, till they should see a particular token from him, such a one as was agreed on between them beforehand. The King therefore sent him word, That he began to suspect he did not intend

tend

tend to keep his promise with him: That he desir'd he would shew himself a man of honour, and write again to his Subjects of *Nancy* to surrender. The Duke wrote a second time, but still without the token I mention'd; which he did, hoping the King would let him go to *Nancy*, to give his personal orders for opening the Gates. The men of *Nancy* shewing no more obedience to this second Letter, than they had done to the former, the Duke of *Lorrain* was urged afresh by the King to be true to his promise: Whereupon, and upon seeing no hopes of getting leave to go to *Nancy*, if he did not make good the Treaty, he at last writ a Letter with that token, which was the signal, that now he would be obeyed. So they opened their Gates to the King presently. All his Troops entred the Town, with Pikes levell'd, Ranks closed, Match lighted, and in a perfect posture for fighting, if they had met with any treachery or opposition. We possest our selves of all the Quarters and Fortifications, and then gave orders, that, all the Garrison of *Lorrain* should lay down their Arms. A friend of mine, one *de la Serre*, and one of the principal Officers in the Garrison, when he heard us cry, *Down with your Arms*, was in a rage, and ready to hang himself; and told me, if he had thought they should have been us'd at this rate, the King should never have come in, till he had beat the Walls about their Ears. I softned his indignation a little, and prevailed upon him to bear his misfortune with moderation. Thus the King was absolute Master of *Nancy*, the Government of which place he bestow'd on Monsieur *de Brassac*.

The End of the Second Book.

BOOK

B O O K III.

The Sieur de Pontis *is made Commiſſary General of the* Swiſſes *in* France. *He is out of favour with the King for quitting this Command. He goes into* Holland *with Mareſchal* Brezay. *The Battel of* Avain, *where he takes Count* Feria, *Lieutenant-General of the* Spaniſh *Army, Priſoner. The taking of* Tillemont, *and the Barbarities of the* Dutch *Souldiers.* Louvain *is beſieg'd. The Sieur* de Pontis *attempts the Caſtle of* Arſcot *with four hundred Muſqueteers. The Quarrel he had with an Officer of the Army upon this occaſion.*

I. **I**N the Year 1634, ſome months after *Nancy* was reduc'd, the King was pleas'd to do me the honour, to make me Commiſſary General of all the *Swiſſes* in *France.* He underſtood that many of the *Swiſſes* had a good opinion of, and confidence in me, and that having deſired me very earneſtly to teach them their exerciſes, I could not decline it ; upon which account they came oftentimes to my Quarters, where I endeavour'd to inſtruct them according to their deſire. Knowing therefore, that theſe honeſt Fellows had a particular eſteem for me, he ſuppos'd that this kindneſs of theirs would make it an eaſy matter for me to manage them as I pleas'd. So that asking me one day at *Verſailles,* whether the *Swiſſes* continu'd their viſits to me ſtill, as they us'd to do, and if they improv'd at all ? and I replying, that they came to me conſtantly ſtill, and that they were a little ſlow, but very good men to the beſt of their capacity ; he preſently return'd upon me ; *Well, I muſt make you Commiſſary General over them all within my Kingdom, that you may diſcipline them, as you have already done your own Company.* I embrac'd this propoſal with great ſatisfaction, becauſe it was a very honourable Poſt, and expreſt to the King my grateful acknowledgments for the favour he had done me, in making choice of me for this Command. But not knowing very well how to compaſs it for want of Money, I proceeded no farther at that time, being willing to try whether the King would do me any greater kindneſs, than merely to ſhew his good inclinations toward me.

The perſon at preſent in that Office was one *Ferrary,* whom his Majeſty did not like at all. And this among others, was one reaſon why the King pitch'd upon me for it, that I, who was continually about his perſon, might ſucceed a man for whom he had no kindneſs. Some time after the firſt mention of it, he took occaſion to ſpeak to me again, and told me, he would have me ſell my Command of Lieutenant in the Guards, to help towards the purchaſe of my Commiſſary's place. As a particular mark of his favour, he told me too, that he would undertake to help me to a Chapman for my Lieutenant's place, and make the beſt bargain he could for me. I very readily agreed to all theſe propoſals, which were for my advantage, as well in point of gain, as of honour. But I ſaw plainly the conſequences of being engag'd in a buſineſs, that I knew muſt coſt me three times as much as my Command would bring me in. But yet I let the King go on, not daring to oppoſe his pleaſure, and hoping he would at ſome time or other recollect, that he was richer than I, and what was impoſſible for my circumſtances, to him would be very eaſy. He ſent Monſieur *de Chenoiſe* to me, who had a mind to buy a Lieutenancy in the Guards for his Son, the Baron *de Boucant* ; and the management of my buſineſs lying in the hands of ſo powerful an Agent as his Majeſty, the bargain was ſoon agreed at twelve thouſand Crowns ; which was more by one third than Lieutenants of the Guards Commands uſed then to go at. The King then urged me to treat with Monſieur *Ferrary* for his Office, and promis'd me a Bill upon the Treaſury, by which the Exchequer ſhould ſtand engag'd to my Creditors, for what Moneys they ſhould advance towards this purchase, if I happened to dye in the service. This put me upon treating in good earnest, and Monsieur *Ferrary* and I drove the bargain for thirty thousand Crowns.

II. My Friends in the mean while coming in very thick to proffer me the Money, I sollicited the King, that he would please to give me the Bill upon the Treasury, which he had done me the favour to promise me, and likewise made my interest with some other persons who might be assisting to me in the procuring it. Going one day to wait on Monsieur *de Bullion* for this purpose, and meeting Monsieur *de Bellievre* upon the stairs, who was afterwards first President of the Parliament of *Paris*, I was very importunate with him, that he would give himself the trouble of recommending my business to the Superintendant. He went up with me again at first word, and did what I requested of him with that usual civility and good grace, that hath got him the respect of all mankind. Though Monsieur *Bullion* was a perfect Creature of Cardinal *Richelieu*'s, who had no kindness for me, yet he made me this civil answer, That he should be very glad to serve me, but if the King granted me this peculiar priviledge above the rest of his Officers, he would bring them all upon him ; that they would expect the same favour, which the King could neither give them without dipping his Exchequer in vast summs, nor deny them without creating me as many Enemies, as there were Officers in the Army : But however, that I might present my Petition to the Council, and that they would debate the matter in his Majesty's presence.

I do not question but he discoursed the thing with the Cardinal, and receiv'd positive orders to oppose it. For, notwithstanding the King was fully determined to grant me this favour, notwithstanding he had acquainted the Cardinal with his intention, who pretended to like it well enough ; notwithstanding by a particular act of condescension, he had undertaken to put in my Petition himself ; yet for all that I was baulkt of my expectation. Insomuch that the King, at his coming out from Council, gave himself the trouble of speaking to me in these remarkable expressions, *We have been taken short, we have lost our cause ; but trouble not your self, I will make you a-mends, I will give you something that shall be better for you.* I confess it was some astonishment to me, that a Prince should thus lose his cause in his own Council, and in a business that depended entirely upon his own free bounty ; and that, when he had an inclination to grant a favour, and reward the services of one of his Officers, it should not be in his power to effect it. But it is no hard matter to see from what cause this want of power grew.

But still, tho the King had made me this promise, to assist, and make me amends some other way, I did not much care to depend upon a promise, which I saw so plainly, when it came to the push, might possibly not be in his power to make good. I should have been better pleased with ready Money ; and finding my self thus engaged, upon the confidence the King had given me at first, fearing now that my Creditors might be in danger of losing by me, I had enough of my Command already, before ever I got possession of it. However, the King was so urgent upon the thing, that I found my self constrain'd, whether I would or no, to get over all difficulties, and enter upon my Office.

III. At my taking the usual Oath, it was required I should appear in a *Swisse* habit which was a Coat of Black Velvet, with a border round it. I had a very rich Cap, which the King had given me, upon which was wrought, a fine large Heron, a Bird of Paradice, and some other Ornamental devices. I sent for a good many Officers, some three or fourscore, and coming at the head of them into the Hall, where the King was, I addrest my self to him, after the *Swisse* fashion. The King receiv'd me, as he us'd to do Ambassadours, standing at the side of his Couch, and taking off his Hat to me ; he gave me his Hand to kiss, and then said by way of Gallantry, *Come Swisse, now speak.* I answer'd, That his Majesty had not allow'd me time enough to learn the language. After I had taken the customary Oath, I was placed by the King ; and as each of the *Swisse* Officers advanced to pay him their respects, I presented them to him, intimating their qualifications and excellencies, and giving a short Character of every one of them ; to inform the King of their several tempers, which I was throughly acquainted with, which was a sort of a little Farce, that the King and Lords who were by, thought a good pleasant entertainment. For I strove in my

speech,

speech, and all my motions, to mimick thefe honeft fellows as naturally as I could; affecting to appear a true *Swiffe*, while I was habited like one.

IV. The King was pleas'd to difcourfe me very largely about my Office, and told me he intended to make it one of the moft honourable Commands about the Court to me. And fo he really did. He annexed feveral very confiderable priviledges to it, and himfelf gave me directions, how to behave my felf with regard to the other Officers in the Army, telling me where I ought to give the precedence, and where not. There was but one *Swiffe* Officer above me, which was the Marefchal *de Baffompier*, our Collonel; and as to the Commanding part, I was firft both of the Regiment of *Swiffe* Guards, and all the reft of them that were in *France*, to the number of feven or eight thoufand: all which was agreeable to their primitive inftitution. It was like-wife the Kings pleafure, that in Marefchal *Baffompier's* abfence, I fhould command in chief, as well in time of action, as in matters of ordinary difcipline: And I muft needs fay, this to me was the moft defirable Office that I could poffibly have thought of.

About a week or a fortnight after I was actually in my Office, and had taken the Oaths before his Majefty, I exercis'd the Regiment, before a great deal of company, and a great many perfons of Quality. I began with the Oath which the Lieutenant Collonel is oblig'd to take, the Ceremony whereof is this: The Commiffary General, reprefenting the Kings perfon, fits with his Hat on; the Lieutenant Collonel, and all the Regiment ftand bare. Then the Commiffary General, directing him-felf to the Lieutenant Collonel, requires him to take the Oath in thefe words: *Do you fwear, as you hope for Salvation, to be faithful to the King as long as you live; and rather to dye, than do any thing contrary to his Intereft; to difcover, or caufe to be difcovered to his Majefty, whatever you fhall know may turn to the prejudice of him, or his Kingdom, &c.* After the Lieutenant Collonel hath taken this Oath, as I have defcribed it, the Commiffary General orders him to give the whole Regiment the fame, and then they pro-ceed to their Exercife.

V. But tho this Office, which I enjoy'd with all its ancient priviledges, had nothing but what was great and honourable belonging to it, yet I found feveral reafons to be quickly weary of it. The King was every day giving me frefh orders for the regula-tion of all the *Swiffe* Souldiers, and would have me bring them to a difcipline, as ftrict as the fevereft Monaftery was under: So that I was cruelly perplext with the trou-ble he laid upon me, and the accounts he expected to be given him of them. His Majefty talkt of nothing elfe but new reformations, and I found my felf a thoufand times more a Slave, than I was formerly. *To what purpofe then (faid I to my felf) is all this honour, that only enflaves, and makes me wretched? and why fhould I fell my liberty, and all the enjoyment of my life, for a little breath, and empty vanity?* Befides all this, I faw my friends run a great rifque in the Money they had lent me for the purchafe; for when the King expreft never fo much inclination to do me good, he was not fuffer'd to bring it to any effect; and the favours he intended me were conftantly oppofed. Some of my friends too laid before me the unhappy confequences of the employment I was now engag'd in, very feelingly; and tho my own fenfe and experience taught me all that, better than they could; yet thefe confiderations laid all together, pro-duced in me a ftrong refolution to throw up this Command, where I found the ho-nour did by no means anfwer the burden; for tho that was great, yet this was not to be endured.

The great difficulty was, which way to bring the King to confent to it; and but to mention fuch a thing to him, I faw plainly was utterly to lofe his favour: But yet I found my felf ready to undergo the worft that could happen; and waiting upon him one day, I told him, that I was reduced to a very fad extremity, that having bought my place upon the credit of his word, that the Exchequer fhould be accoun-table to my Creditors, they were very importunate with me now to give them fecu-rity: *Your Majefty* (faid I) *if you pleafe, may fee what becomes me to do in this cafe; and whether it be fair, that I fhould impofe upon my friends, I had much rather, Sir, give my Command back into your Majefties hands, and refign it with your approbation, than bring my felf into a neceffity of applying to you fo often for a matter of this nature.* The King, tho much offended at the requeft I made to him, yet conceal'd his refentments at that time. He told me, that he had indeed promis'd to turn over my debt to his Treafury, but that his Council for feveral reafons were againft it: And as for any other objection, fince

I was

I was so very uneasie in my Employment, I should think of some good man, that he might approve, to succeed me.

VI. Having obtain'd the Kings leave thus far, I came to terms with one Sr. *Denys*, who made me lose two thousand Crowns by my Office ; for of the thirty thousand I had bought it at, I could bring him no higher than eight and twenty. When I had come off thus by the loss, he desir'd me however to do him one favour, which was, to speak to the King in his behalf, that this Command might be continu'd to him, with the same priviledges that his Majesty in favour to me had grac'd it with. I recompenc'd him good for evil, and promis'd to use all my interest for the obtaining this advantage, but told him at the same time, I was afraid it would not be done ; for I pretty well knew the Kings temper, who allow'd me those priviledges, only in consideration of the long tryal he had had of my faithful services, and that in a season, when very few were found to have devoted themselves so entirely to him. And so it happen'd, for when I presented him to the King, and took the boldness to beg the continuation of the same priviledges, that his Majesty had beed pleas'd to honour me withal; all that I could say to raise an esteem for this Officers good qualifications, and faithful services, was to no manner of purpose. He downright refus'd my request, and sent us away without having patience to hear me out. So that he was to take it as a great favour, that his Majesty permitted him to hold the Office with its common priviledges, before it fell into my hands.

The King in the mean while who was exceeding angry to find me so vehemently set upon throwing up my place, tho he had conceal'd it at first, yet could not forbear within a few days to declare his displeasure so warmly, that I had reason to think my best way would be to absent my self from Court for some time. That which gave the King the greatest offence of all, was, that he fancy'd I was now grown weary of his service. He had observ'd for many years, what methods were taken to draw off his most faithful Servants affections from him ; and the experience of that made him apt to suspect the same of me; which made him say upon my account to the Chancellour, who was pleas'd afterwards to tell it me again ; *Is not this a prodigious thing, that I can no sooner get a good servant, but he is presently corrupted?* But really the King was not so just to me in this, as he was afterwards; and tho I had the honour of being about his person so long, yet it seems I was not sufficiently known ; for no consideration could have taken me off from the Duty I ow'd to my Prince; nor could I ever have serv'd any other person with the same zealous affection that I did him. But I was not long out of favour, for his Majesty shortly after sent me his commands to wait on him, when he went to *St. Geneviere of the Wood.* I staid some days at Court without any employ except that of attending upon the Kings person.

VII. About the end of *May* 1635, when the War was declar'd with *Spain*, a great many Troops were rais'd, and several Armies composed out of them ; one of which was to enter into the *Low Countries* by *Picardy.* So, being out of Office, I begg'd a Command of his Majesty, and that he would give me leave to go with Mareschal *Brezay* into *Holland*; telling him, that I was quite sick of an idle, and useless way of living, and long'd to be doing him some service. The Kings reply was a little surprizing, and who very graciously askt me, Whether I was not content to be near him ? how I could be sick for want of service, when I was actually serving, and attending his person? I answer'd, with pretty good presence of thought, That this indeed was a greater honour than I deserved ; but that my desire of going into *Holland*, was only to make my self more worthy of his service; and to learn in a foreign Nation, and the most accomplisht School of War, several things, that might qualifie me much better for the employments he honour'd me with. The pretence I used was fair and plausible enough, and the posture of my affairs at that time as favourable. But the King, who saw the Servants, in whom he confided most, fall off from him every day, made some difficulty at first of granting my request, fearing, that when I was at so great a distance from him, I should be so much the less zealous for him, and easier to receive any bad impressions, that men might be apt to insinuate into me. For indeed the coldness he discover'd in most of those that were about him, inclined him to a very particular regard for the most inconsiderable of his Servants, where he found a contrary temper ; and therefore it ought to seem less strange, if he stoopt so low sometimes, as to express a kindness for a poor mean Officer, as I was,

to

to fix me faster to him ; since the unhappy circumstances of his Government made such condescensions necessary to him, as would otherwise have very ill become the Majesty of so great a Prince. But how averse soever he was to my making this Campaign in *Holland*, he yielded at last to the sollicitation of several friends of mine, who knew that I was then quite out of my Element, while staying at Coert without any considerable employ; and therefore they followed my business so close, as to get me the Kings leave, tho not without some degree of loathness and reluctancy.

VIII. Mareschal *Brezay* had a particular kindness, I may say indeed, the care and affection of a Father for me ; and as a testimony of the sincere friendship he honour'd me with, presented me with a very fine Gold Medal, with a Sword engraven on one side, and a Purse on the other ; designing to assure me by this, that both his Sword and his Purse were at my service. Which no doubt ought to be esteemed a very singular favour, especially from a Gentleman of his quality and temper; who kept himself pretty much upon the reserve, and was intimately acquainted with very few people. He entrusted me with the raising his Regiment, and made me eldest Captain and Major of it, and as it were his *Aid de Camp* besides. The Army for *Picardy*, which he and the Mareschal *de Chatillon* commanded between them by turns, consisted of at least twenty thousand Foot, and six or seven thousand Horse.

IX. The Generals design'd to besiege *Namur*, a Town scituate upon the *Meuse*. In order to it, when the Army was come within four or five leagues of it, Mareschal *Brezay* sent Monsieur *de Vientais*, Monsieur *Lansac*, and me, with a detachment of three hundred Horse, to go before, and learn the posture of the Enemy, and the outskirts of the Town. At the Village of *Avain* we took some Prisoners, and understood by them, that the Enemy came on with their whole Army, under the command of Prince *Teemas*, their General ; Count *Feria*, Son to the Count *de Benevent*, Governour of *Anvers*, the Lieutenant General ; and the Count *de Buquoy*, who commanded the Horse. We march'd all night, and when we were got up pretty near to *Namur*, left our Squadron in a Wood, that we might come still closer to the Town, and inform our selves better how matters stood. We heard immediately the Trumpets sound, the Drums beat, and all the noise and clatter of an Army upon the march, with Baggage and Ordnance. It was Moon light, and strait we began to discover the Army coming over the Bridge cross the *Meuse*, and we staid to count as far as forty Troops of Horse.

After we had seen and heard too much to doubt any longer whether it was the Enemy's Army, we made haste back to joyn our detachment, and recover the Village of *Avain* as fast as we could. And indeed it was by no means safe to stop by the way, for the Enemy began immediately to send out parties of Horse to scowr the Country, and make a discovery of our Army. If I would have been perswaded by Monsieur *Vientais* and *Lansac*, we had staid at *Avain*, to refresh our selves after the great fatigue we had undergone; but I made it so plain to them, that by this means they were in danger of having their Throats cut by these Scowrers, (and that a danger too, that could bring them no honour) that we continu'd our march quite back to the Army. We told Mareschal *Brezay* what we had seen, who at first could scarce believe the Enemy was so nigh ; but not being able to give the lye to our Eyes and Ears, he immediately gave orders to prevent our being surpriz'd by the Enemy.

The Mareschal *de Chatillon* with the Rear-Guard was a great way from us ; and tho Mareschal *Brezay* would not have been much concern'd to begin the action without him, yet he sent to desire he would come up with all the speed he could. Mareschal *Chatillon* came himself presently after, and looking upon the Enemy, and how they lay, with his usual coldness, he said very roughly to the Officers that were by; *I am glad to see them so near, it is better having them here, than at* Brussels. The Enemies having possest themselves of *Avain*, we were forc'd to draw out our Army into line of Battel, in a very streight Valley, where it cost our Generals a great deal of trouble, to make amends by their skill and prudence, for the disadvantage of the ground. Mareschal *de Brezay* took the Left Wing, and *Chatillon* the Right. Monsieur *de Brezay*, who did me the honour to shew me a great deal of kindness, (as I said before) thinking I had some experience in War, would needs make me that day execute the Office of Serjeant of the Battel, and marshal all the men, which engag'd me to be up and down in several places, and parts of the action, to see the Generals orders duly obey'd.

In the beginning of the Engagement, the Enemies Forlorn Hope made ours give ground, who fell in upon the Detachment that supported them in great disorder. Their Cannon, which was very advantageously planted, made at the same time such a furious Discharge, that a great part of the Troops of our Left Wing were put into disturbance with it. In that very instant a considerable Officer who rid close to me, and whom I was to come to speak with, immediately fell into such a terrible Fright, that he set Spurs, and rid away as fast as his Horse could go. Some that saw him began to cry out, *Ah! such a one runs.* Tho I had no great intimacy with him, yet I was concerned to see that this single Miscarriage might ruine him for ever; and therefore immediately answer'd as loud as I could speak, *No, No, he does not Run, he is going to the Post I have assigned him.* And then I sent a Gentleman after him, who was near me, and one that I durst trust, to tell him how I had vindicated his Honour, and desire him by all means that he would come back to his Post immediately, and tell me publickly, That he had dispatch'd the Business I had committed to his charge. Accordingly he did return, and spoke to me, as if he was giving an account of something he had done, and he owned himself obliged to me as long as he lived, for this good office, in saving his Reputation at that time.

X. Our Troops taking heart again after this first Terror I mentioned, and recollecting with themselves what a Reproach it would be to them, to have been affrighted with the noise of the Guns, and have given way at the very first; came on again bravely, and fell upon the Enemy with such indignation and rage, that after a stiff resistance on both sides for a very great while, they were at last obliged to draw off, and leave us in possession of the Field. I took particular notice of Prince *Teemat,* who, after having fought very bravely, was one of the last that went off. He was followed very close at the heels, and forced to leap over a little Wall to get away; in the leap he dropt his Hat and Cane, at the end of which his Arms were engraven upon a golden handle. I, being very near him, took up that Cane, and gave it to Marefchal *Brezey,* who some time after made a Present of it to the King. Besides, we followed so hard upon Count *Feria* his Lieutenant-General, that he was forc'd to beg for Quarter of me, crying out, *Spare my Life, Ten thousand Crowns Ransome.* So I made him my Prisoner.

But how great and remarkable soever this Victory was, yet it cost *France* very dear, for we lost a world of gallant Men, who were sacrificed there for the publick good. A vast many Colours and Cornets were taken, and abundance of Prisoners. The chief of them were Count *Feria,* whom I told you of before; *Don Charles* Natural Son to the Archduke *Leopold,* Collonel *Sfondrate* an *Italian,* and Collonel *Bronw* an *English* Man, were likewise taken there. As for Prince *Teemat,* and the Count *de Buquoy,* they saved themselves by flight. After the Battel was over, I had a great quarrel with the Commander of the Forlorn Hope, who would needs have it, that Count *Feria* was his Prisoner, because it was the Party he led on, that prest him and forc'd him to retreat, and therefore he belonged to him as Commander of that Party. I answer'd, That I was the Person of whom Count *Feria* asked Quarter, and into my hands he surrendred himself; and farther, that for the determination of the Controversy, I would refer my self to the Prisoner himself. He was asked then, Whose Prisoner he acknowledged himself? And he immediately made answer, That I had given him Quarter, and he surrendred himself up to me. Thus our Dispute was decided by the Count's own Declaration, who immediately, and as a mark of his kindness, gave me his General's Scarf. He also made me a Present of a Box of Reliques which he had about him, and which I have kept ever since. I was in good hopes to have got Ten thousand Crowns from the King too, which is a Gratuity usually given to them that take a General Prisoner in time of Action. But I had just the same Success on this occasion, that I usually met with in the rest of my Life, where what we commonly call the Fortune of this World, seemed continually to flee from before me. As God would have it, Count *Feria,* after some Months, made his escape, and tho the King frequently promis'd me the same Sum of Ten thousand Crowns, which was but my due Reward, yet never any thing at all came of it.

XI. After this famous Action of the Battel of *Avain,* the Prince of *Orange,* who had been declared Generalissimo of both the *French* and the *Dutch* Armies, and who lay at that time above ten Leagues from us, was very much displeased that our Generals had presumed to engage without him. He was extremely concerned, that he had no hand in so illustrious an Action, and could scarce forbear looking upon this Victory as his own loss. When our Troops therefore were come up, and we drew pretty near his Army, the Mareschals of *France* thought it convenient to send me with their Compliments to him, and acquaint him, That whenever his Excellence saw fit, he should find all our Army in a readiness to receive him, and to pay him all the Respect due to his Character. They order'd me also, that if the Prince were coming on towards them, I should leave him about a League from our Army, and return full speed, to give them notice, that all the Generals and principal Officers might go meet him. Commands were sent out at the same time to all the Soldiers and Officers in the Army, to put themselves in the best condition, and make the gayest and most splendid Appearance they could, as a mark of Honour to the Person whom they owned as their Generalissimo, and then the whole Army was drawn out in form of Battel.

When I came to the Prince of *Orange*, I complimented him in the Name of our Generals, with all the Deference and Respect I could, and told him, how eager they were to submit themselves to him, and to take care that the whole Army should pay him the Honours and Respects due to their Generalissimo. But the Prince, who was much dissatisfied at the Business of *Avain*, was at a stand what Answer to make, or what to resolve upon. Observing him undetermined in himself, I began to grow weary, and told him I waited his Highness's Answer to our Generals. Seeing me a little urgent, he told me he would come to our Army, and at the same time gave Order for a Thousand of his own Horse, or thereabouts, to attend him to the place where we lay. But he presently changed his mind, and by that time he had gone about half a League, he told me, it was something with the latest to join our Army that day, and he would put it off till the next. Then he began to open himself, and express his concern for not being at the Battel; for he said to me, tho in a jesting maning manner, *Your Army has got itself great Renown, and I doubt not, triumphs much at present, for the mole Conquest they have gained. If they had staid, and taken our Assistance, they wou'd have had no cause to repent, or at least they would have tried whether the* Dutch *be good Soldiers or not.* I returned him a very respectful Answer, That our Army was prest so hard by the Enemy, that we could not possibly decline engaging; but that he, as our Generalissimo, had the greatest share both in the Action, and the Honour of the Day; That the *French* did not at all question the *Hollanders* Courage, and this War was like enough to furnish them with a great many opportunities of signalizing themselves. Then I took my leave of his Excellence, and came back to our Generals, who were very sorry the Prince was not pleased to come that day, because each single person, and the whole Army in general, was then the most glorious, and in the best condition to receive him, that ever they had been seen. But the matter was put off only till the morrow, and his Excellence was then entertained with all the Respects that became us, and all the Ceremonies usual upon such occasions.

XII. The two Armies marched afterwards to *Tillemont*, a Town that was made remarkable by the unfortunate manner of its being taken, and the Cruelties and Sacriledges in the sacking of it, such I cannot remember to this day without horror. It was necessary first to possess our selves of the Suburbs, and I, being in the head of the Forlorn Hope, had a great Ruffle with Monsieur *Mottehoudencourt:* For he seeing me in the same Rank with himself, and very warm in pushing my advantage, and scaling the Walls first, cryed out, *Sir, Monsieur* Pontis, *You do not march in Order, I am Maistre de Camp, and ought to go before you.* I answer'd him without any disorder, *Sir, Let every one keep to the Post assigned him, keep you to yours, and I will endeavour to make good mine.* My Answer was so far from satisfying him, that it put him into a mighty Passion. He could not away with that Coldness and Resolution with which I spoke, and beginning to swear a little, called out still louder, *That if I did not stop, he should resent the Affront* I answer'd smiling, *That he would remember it for no other purpose, I believed, than to love me the better for it, when we should both get honourably into the Town, and this was all the Resentment the Honour of his Friendship would allow me to expect.* But he did not take what I said for a Jest, and as each of us were still pressing forward, when I was getting up upon an advanced Work in form of a Bastion, and that he saw me almost at the top and like to rob him of the Honour he pretended to of scaling first, he fell to calling out again, but more violently than before, *That if I did not halt,* he *would fire upon me.* It was really a good pleasant thing, to see us two parlying and contending at this rate, for the credit of the Assault; one with all the indifference of a Man in Raillery, and the other with all the fury of a Man out of his wits with Passion. I was no more confounded at this last Compliment, than any of the former; and told him with the same easiness I had done before, *If I were not very well acquainted with Monsieur* Mottehoudencour, *and his generous temper, there would be some reason to apprehend what he threatned, but I was satisfied this was all in Jest. I am going Sir,* said I again, *to make way for you, and to open a passage.* With that I recover'd the top of the Bastion, and the Enemy seeing themselves straitned on all sides, withdrew into the Town.

When I was up, I perceiv'd my self just over against one of the Gates; and the advantage of this Post put Monsieur *Mottehoudencour* still more out of humor; for he was forc'd to fetch a compass, and at last found himself in a Post not near so advantageous as mine. But I had a prophetick Spirit as it hapned, for our Quarrel that begun with the Action, was very happily composed soon after, and how that was I will now tell you. Mareschal *Brezay* having understood that there were several Tan-fats very convenient to set Guards in, order'd me to go and observe them. Thither I went in the midst of a deal of Fire and Smoke, and Musquet Bullets that whistled about my Ears, but none of them did me any hurt. Having got to one of these Tan-yards, I found it really very convenient for a Guard to be posted in; I informed Mareschal *Brezay* of it, and told him at the same time, that it would not do well to venture very many Men there, because if the Enemy should make a Sally, they would be in great danger of being all knockt o'th' head.

Monsieur *Mottehoudencour* hapned to be by, and being a little better humor'd, began now to take his turn of laughing, and said pleasantly to me, *I must own I was horribly enraged at thee even now. I thought if I had had thee in my Teeth, I could have crack'd thy Bones like Nuts. But come, to make us Friends, thou shalt carry me to see this Tan-yard;* which was said out of a gallantry, by no means fit for a person of his worth and condition: so guessing pretty well at his meaning, and thinking he would take it ill to be refused, I told him briskly, *That I would not make my peace with him upon such terms, as carrying him to have his brains beat out; That this was a method of reconciliation fit for none but an Enemy, and I did not take him for such; That there was no need for him to destroy himself meerly for a humor.* Mareschal *Brezay,* who was desirous to appear as full of Courage as Monsieur *Mottehoudencour,* told me hereupon, *That he had a mind to go too, and I should carry them both thither.* I was a little ashamed to see a Mareschal of *France* value himself upon these gallantries, and judging all things to be better than an unseasonable Bravado, I answer'd him with the same freedom I had used to Monsieur *Mottehoudencour, That I had forgot the way.* He pretended to be angry, (tho probably he would have had more reason to be so, if I had shew'd him the place we talk'd off;) and told me, he took this really ill, and for one enemy before, I had now got two. I answer'd him, without concerning my self much at his displeasure, that it did by no means become a General, as he was, to cast away his life by way of Gallantry; that young hot fellows only were priviledged to do such things, and that the meanest Souldier in the whole Army had an interest in the safety of his General's person. Thus all our difference was made up; he had his End, and I had mine; and after they had both satisfied the little vanity they had, they thought themselves never the worse, that they had not gratified it at their own cost.

XIII. The Enemy finding themselves reduced to great Extremities, and not in a condition to hold out against two such mighty Armies, chose not to stand the shock of a general Assault, but sallied out of a Back-gate that was not invested, and so made their Escape. Notice of this was brought to Mareschal *Brezay,* who order'd that they should suffer the Garison to go off, and so make themselves Masters of the Town. I drew his Regiment up against the Gate, having first with great difficulty beaten down the Draw-bridge. But finding this Gate barricado'd on the inside, and that there was no way to clear it, but by going in, I order'd the Soldiers next the Gate to stand very close together, and getting up upon their shoulders, with a Soldier that had a Hatchet, I put him in through one of the Holes where the Beams that supported the Draw-bridge came through. I had a mind to go in after him, but it hapned that just then the Souldiers stood a little wider, so that I fell down among them, and had like to have been stifled. I got up again however, as nimbly as I could, but not being

ing able to draw my Shoes after me, I went in by the same Hole without them, and got the Gate broke open, so that all our Regiment, and the whole Army came in at it.

It was agreed upon with the Prince of *Orange* before, that the *Hollanders* should not enter the Town, because of the violence and outrage that Hereticks use to be guilty of. And the Mareschal *de Brezay*, designing to prevent any disorder, dispatcht me immediately with about twenty Souldiers, to secure a Convent of Nuns. Here I found a great deal of Scarlet Cloath, and other commodities of great value, which had been brought and laid up there, as in a place of security; but knowing very well how rude and undistinguishing Souldiers are in War, I told the good Nuns, that they took the ready course to have their Convent plundered; That I advis'd them not to stay there any longer, and if the Troops came that way, it might not be in my power to prevent their being ransackt. They answer'd me, in great terror and distraction, *Ah Sir! save our Lives, and our Honour; alas! we know not whither to go, nor what to do.* I promis'd them to do the best I could; but own'd to them freely at the same time, that I saw no great safety for them there.

In the mean time the Prince of *Orange's* Souldiers, upon some discontent for a summ of Money due, from the Town of *Tillemont*, broke in among the rest, contrary to the agreement. These wretches spread themselves in an instant through all parts of the Town, plundered, and murdered Priests and Monks with the greatest cruelty imaginable. And the Nunnery that I guarded being a large one, there presently swarmed thither some *Hollanders*, some *Cravats*, some *French*, all as mad as Devils, and grown void of all sence of God, Religion, or Reason. I opposed them as long as I could with the few Souldiers I had, and bore up against this crowd of Madmen, till at last having burst the Gates, they throng'd in, and fell upon our Guard, some of whom were wounded, and the rest fled. For my own part, as I was defending my self still with my Sword, resolving to dye upon the spot, rather than expose so many poor Virgins to their rudeness and violence; one of the Officers, a greater brute than the common Souldiers, endeavoured to cleave me down the middle with his Sable, and let fly a blow at me with his full strength, and he had infallibly done it, if I had not broke the force of the blow with my Sword, which was broke short in two by it. Then, finding that I was defenceless, they threw themselves upon me, snatcht that piece of my Sword that I had left out of my hand, cut off my Belt, and away they carried it. I threatned to complain of them to his Excellency, which gave them some little check; and so giving me my life, they satisfy'd themselves with thrusting me out of the Convent. Then finding no opposition, they broke all the Gates, spoil'd all that came near them, massacred all the Nuns they met, stole all the rich goods I spoke of, and made such a confusion as is not possible for me to describe. It was an unspeakable grief to me, to see one of these poor Nuns, that ran about distracted, with a Knife stuck in her head, and wept, and cry'd out, *Ah Gentlemen, pray save my Life.* I could with all my heart have ventur'd my own life to save hers, but I was disarm'd, and at distance, or if I had not I could never have done any good against so great a multitude.

Meeting the Collonel afterwards, with whom I was acquainted, I began to call out to him in a great passion, *Oh Sir, is this the order you observe in War? After I had by our Generals order brought a guard hither to defend this place, do you allow these Rascals to come fall upon us, and knock us o'th' head as if we were Enemies; to disarm me by violence, and plunder and tear all to pieces in a Religious house, which the Generals have taken into their protection? What would you have me do?* said he, *They are these devilish* Cravats, *that are worse than so many wild Beasts. Pray go yonder,* said I, *and lay about you with your Cane: Scatter these Villains, that have taken away my arms, and had like to have kill'd me.* He answer'd me, That being flesht as they were now, they would kill him too, if he should go amongst them; and that he could not imagine how I got out of their hands without being cut to pieces. This was no satisfaction to me however, and I was enraged to see my self so ill us'd, and that a Collonel could not make his Souldiers obey him. I went then immediately to look Mareschal *Brezay*, being quite out of my wits, and my very Eyes sparkling with anger. There I make my complaint, That his authority was slighted, that I had like to have had my brains beat out at the Convent he sent me to secure; that they had plunder'd all with the extremest rage and rapine; and there was no more perswading these Robbers to reason, than mad hungry Wolves. The Mareschal was very angry at this baseness, and drew a part of the Army behind the Convent, and securing this place, gave six or seven Nuns opportunity to escape, who fled to him for refuge, being got away by the back door.   Some

Some two or three days after, being among some of the Officers of my acquaintance, and going to the Kings quarter, I happen'd to meet with that Rogue of an Officer that used me so scurvily. I quickly knew my Gentleman, for my concern for such base usage had given me a very lively Idea of his face, and I could not possibly forget him : So I went up to him, and in a rage said, *Ob you pitiful Rascal, you are the Rogue that abused me so the other day*; *give me my Sword and Belt.* Upon this, he went to lay his hand upon his Sword, but I presently leapt to him, and caught him by the Collar, and holding the butt-end of my Pistol to his head, I told him, that if he did not give me my Sword and Belt immediately, I would break his head. He had no mind to try me, because he saw I was in a passion, and being confounded, he was forc'd to give me what I required. Then I took him by the Arm, and with the same resolution and authority that I would have spoken to a Common Souldier, said to him, *Thou art no better than a Villain, and I will have thee hang'd instantly, for the outrage thou hast committed, contrary to the Generals express orders.* The poor fellow stood so confounded at my talking so boldly to him, that he thought he came off well with asking my pardon, and promising me to restore my own Sword and Belt, which he had not then about him, but had instead of it given me his own. He made me a present besides, of a Silver Powder-box gilt, and a string of Gold twist, that tyed like a Bandelier, to appease me. He richly deserv'd hanging indeed, for the ravage and horrible barbarities, which both he committed himself, and his Souldiers by his order. But considering he was not under my jurisdiction, and besides, that he belong'd to the Prince of *Orange*'s Army, I was content for my part to take up with the satisfaction he made me, besides my Sword and Belt, which he sent me home afterwards. But his Excellence being complained to by Mareschal *Brezay*, threatned him in my hearing to hang him and his Companions, as they very well deserv'd. But whether he was as good as his word to him, I cannot tell.

XIV. The two Armies parted at their drawing off from *Tillemont*; the Prince of *Orange*'s went toward *Brussels*, as if intending to sit down before that place; and the *French* Army to *Louvain*. They made a halt for some time in the Country between *Tillemont*, *Louvain*, and *Brussels*. But as the *French* went off for *Louvain*, the *Spaniards* shew'd themselves in the Rear of them. Mareschal *Brezay*, surpriz'd to see them so nigh, order'd me to draw three Regiments into an enclosure, to stop the Enemies march. I did it presently, and posted our men very conveniently, both to cover our Army, and defend our selves from any that should attack us. In this encounter I had like to have left part of my Baggage, by the breaking of a Waggon-wheel, when the Enemy were within six or seven hundred paces of us. But running strait to the Ordnance, I bought another for forty Livres, and brought it to supply the place of the broken one; so that I gain'd time enough to get this Waggon off. Our three Regiments being posted in the enclosure I mention'd, the Enemy fell in upon us, and there was a sharp skirmish on both sides. The whole Army in the mean while retreated fighting, being too weak to stand a pitcht Battel, and they marcht at a great rate, which made our Regiments begin to grumble, who cry'd out, that I brought them thither to be murder'd. I answer'd, that I look'd for the Generals orders every minute; that I could not quit that post of my own head; and if the danger was great for them, it was no less for me too.

We had not been long in this perplexity, before Mareschal *Brezay* sent me commands to bring my men off, and join him as quick as I could. The Enemy skirmisht upon us in the Rear, and when we and the whole Army were come up to a little Village, they made a very brisk push upon us, and oblig'd us to leave the Village, and retreat still fighting; till at last, having recover'd a very narrow pass, we fac'd about, and fought upon equal terms. The Enemies having now lost all the advantage, which their numbers gave them before, thought it the wisest course to wheel off, and go charge the Prince of *Orange*'s Rear. But they could not recover him, for he had march'd all night, and put his Troops under covert.

XV. Then the two Confederate Armies join'd again, and went to form the Siege of *Louvain* with united force. It was my fortune to stay at this Siege but ten or twelve days, for a reason that I shall give presently, and therefore I can give no very particular account of it. Only I happen'd, by way of Gallantry, to quarrel with two of our Generals, meerly for bringing them off from a danger they expos'd themselves to, to, out of a pure bravado, and where they would have thrown away their lives very foolishly. Mareschal *Brezay*, and the Great Master *de la Melleray*, being gone up to the top of a Retrenchment in a meer brag, I came behind Monsieur *Melleray*, took him up in my arms about the waste, and carried him quite to the bottom of the Retrenchment; the same I did to Mareschal *Brezay*, and both so quick, that they neither of them had time to think where they were, and then told them with the freedom they allowed me to use with them; *These are pleasant Gallantries indeed, that must cost us all our lives; If the Generals be taken off, who must command the Army? and what will become of the inferiour Officers and common Souldiers?* The two Gentlemen, in the greatest surprize imaginable, lookt upon one another, and laying their hands upon their Swords, began to run after me to revenge this affront. But I, who had no mind to give them any occasion of doing any thing out of season, and which they would have been sorry for, after I had done them so good service, set to running as fast as I could, for fear the jest should be carried too far. I was satisfy'd that in their hearts they were well enough pleased to see themselves brought off from a danger, which nothing but a vain emulation had put them upon tempting. And when they saw me run away at that rate, they were well contented to be out-run, and stood still. However I did not care to come into their presence quickly, to make the matter look better, and in shew, at least to return their pretences of offering to do me a mischief.

A little while after I received a Musquet-shot in the Trenches, it was in the Arm, and did me no great hurt; but when Mareschal *Brezay* heard I was wounded, he pretended to be very angry at me, and said, it was no great matter if I were kill'd. I am sure he did not think so, for presently after he sent his own Chyrurgeon to take care of me, and when I went with my Arm in a Scarf to return him thanks for it, I could not forbear owning to him again, that I was so far from being sorry for what I had done to them, that I thought it was the best course I could take of expressing my honour and value for them, to prevent such desperate venturesome actions, as might very well lose the whole Army. I am amazed indeed, that such great men should be guilty of these follies, as if a General had no other way to shew his courage but by these kind of tricks, fitter for young fool-hardy Souldiers than for Officers, even those of the least quality or consideration; whose lives the King hath a greater interest in than the person himself, and therefore they ought to be made the best of, for his service, and the safety of those under their command, and not lavishly squandered away upon every ridiculous vanity, and for meer ostentation.

XVI. I told you I continued but a little while before *Louvain*. For Mareschal *Brezay* being in some distress for want of Hay and Forrage for his Horse, gave me in command to go force the Castle of *Arscot*, about eight or nine leagues distant from *Louvain*: where there was a great quantity of provisions of all sorts, both for man and beast. For this undertaking he appointed me twenty Waggons, and about four hundred Musqueteers; and with these I marched by night up to this Castle, which was hemm'd in on all sides with very wide Ditches, and defended by a strong Garrison. I found means to bring my men up to the Gate, some by Boats, and some by wading up to the middle upon the rubbish of the Bridge that was broken down. Then with great Levers I forc'd the Gate, and when we had made our way in, after two or three hours dispute, the Garrison were constrained to retire into a Tower, and from thence they capitulated with us. I immediately loaded the Waggons that came with me with Hay and Oats, and sent them to Mareschal *Brezay* with a message, that if he would send me the Carriages of the Ordnance, there was store enough to load five hundred of them, with Wheat and Hay, and Oats, and Barley, and other provisions: For there were vast Granaries in this Castle, and all full, because the whole wealth of all the Country thereabouts had been brought in, and laid up there. Then I began to contrive how I should fortify and barricado my self up, for the defence of my self and our Corn; and Monsieur *Brezay* having sent a fresh supply of Waggons to a very great number, I return'd them back to him all laden as before, which was a very seasonable refreshment to our Generals, and their Attendants.

XVII. At this time there happened a warm dispute between the Marquis of *S.* who is now Mareschal of *France*, and me. He had a mind to share with me, when he saw what quantity of forrage and provisions I sent to the Army, and coming with his Company to the Castle where I was, would fain have been at dividing the spoil.

There

There had been no good understanding between us before; because once, when I was to appoint quarters, I had ordered a house for him, where he had room enough, and a great deal of forrage, but little convenience of Kitchin or Cellar, because the Master of the house was not at home. This put him in a passion, and provok'd him to reproach me, by saying, That I took very good care to assign him a dry lodging. When he was come then near the Castle of *Arsex*, which, as I said, was begirt round with large Moats full of water, he sent to speak with me. I went out to him, but kept a barrier between us, and five and twenty, or thirty Musqueteers, who were to give fire if he had offered the least violence. Then the Marquis began to give me joy of my succesful attempt; and told me very civilly, that he was come to be reconcil'd to me, and that he acknowledg'd the difference between us to have proceeded from a fault in him, and a little heat of youth. I perceiving very well that these compliments were strain'd, and designed to serve a turn, answer'd him with some indifference, That I was very glad for his sake, he own'd himself in the wrong. Tho my answer was not very agreeable to him, yet he past that by, and at last fell upon the matter, that was the true bottom of all his compliments: He desired to come in, and have some loading of forrage. I told him, I could dispose of nothing in that Castle without an order from the Generals, for they had sent me thither, and all that was there belong'd to them; nor could I suffer him and his Company to come in, without their positive command; but if he pleas'd to come in single, the Gate should be open'd to him alone.

He presently began to change his note, and told me, with an Oath, I spoke like a Prince, and a King. Then he threatned me to enter the place by strength of arms, and make himself way with his Sword. The hotter he grew, the more coldness I put on; and without any concern I told him, I would not advise him to that method, for if he stirr'd, I would order my men to fire upon him without delay. The evenness of temper with which I answered his blustering, surpriz'd him, and he reply'd, *Thou art as cold as a Well-rope, and yet thou threatnest to kill me.* I told him, I did my duty without passion. At last he took the safest course, and withdrew, tho still talking big, which I was not in the least disturb'd at. But apprehending however, that he might complain to Mareschal *Brezay*, and prepossess him against me, I immediately writ to him, and gave an exact account of all that had past between us. So when the Marquis went to make his complaints to him, and among other things to my disadvantage, told him, that I guarded the Castle so ill, that he could easily have surpriz'd it, if he had had any such design. The Mareschal, who understood my management, and the true reason of his complaint, by my Letter, told him freely, that he gave no great credit to what he said, and thought me more careful than that came to. He writ back to me by the same Messenger, and in his Letter was pleas'd to commend what I had done, in refusing to admit the Marquis, and denying him forrage. With this he sent me a positive order in the Kings name, to receive no person whatsoever into the Castle, nor give out any forrage, except the party brought an order, either under the Prince of *Orange*'s hand, or Mareschal *Chatillon*'s, or his own.

The Marquis, who knew nothing of Mareschal *Brezay*'s answer, nor this fresh order, came a second time to the Castle, and told me, that he had spoke with Mareschal *Brezay*, and that he was displeased at my carriage to him; he told me moreover, that unless I would rebel against the General's order, I must open to him instantly. This last was what I expected, and therefore presently taking the Letter out of my pocket, I shewed it him at a distance. and said aloud; *Here's one can tell me Mareschal* Brezay's *mind better than the Marquis of* S. *Here you may see how he commands me to open the Gate, for he commends me for not opening to you the other day, and forbids me in the King's name to admit any body, without shewing a particular order from our Generals. Therefore, Sir,* said I, *let me see your order, and every Gate here shall be opened to you.* The Marquis was in a strange confusion to see himself so shamefully disproved, by the very person whose Authority he pretended to; and went away in a rage, without any other satisfaction, than that of saying several rude things against Mareschal *Brezay* and me.

XVIII. I was not so fortunate however afterwards, as I promis'd my self from being possest of this Castle. But, according to my old fate, what would in all probability have made another man's fortunes, to me turned to no manner of account. The misunderstanding there was between the Prince of *Orange* and our Generals, hindered our success against *Louvain*, and it was agreed to raise the Siege. Mareschal *Brezay* sent

sent me about twenty Waggons, with a detachment of some Companies commanded by the Lieutenants, and told me, that the Siege being now upon raising, he would have me load those Waggons with Wheat, and Hay, and Oats, and leave those Officers that brought those Companies in the Castle, and return to the Camp with the Troops under my command. This news I confess was a great surprize to me, for I took it for granted *Louvain* would be taken, and then the Castle of *Arscot*, that I had taken such pains to keep, would fall to my share, with a good part of the moveables that were brought in thither, and lay in Chests, which I had been very tender of all along, looking upon them as my own, and not caring to break them open till all was over. But I reckon'd without my host; and all my diligence in preserving them was these Officers gain, who as soon as ever they got my place, broke open all, and furnisht themselves at the expence of them to whom these goods belonged. I went away much dissatisfy'd, after having loaded the Waggons Mareschal *Brezay* sent with all the speed I could, and put them under a Convoy of the four hundred Musqueteers, whom I carried back to the Army.

Some leagues from thence we discover'd a party of four or five hundred of the Enemies Horse, that seem'd at some distance from us, and came cross us to cut off our passage. At first we gave our selves for lost, and took it for granted, considering that we were in a plain, which gave the Horse a great advantage against us, that there was no remedy but we must be cut to pieces. But the Guide put me a little into heart, for he told me, that a little further there was a narrow pass upon a rising ground, where we might put our selves under cover of some Woods; and that if we made the best of our way, we were time enough to recover the place, before the Enemy got up to us, who must of necessity fetch a compass by reason of a Ditch that lay in their way. I immediately drew my men into form of battel, and as I us'd to do, hemm'd them in with the Waggons, ordering some of them to get up into the Carriages. Then we whipt on the Horses, and putting on apace, came up to the place I spoke of, and there were met and attackt by the Enemies Horse. I ordered our men to halt, and exhorted them to behave themselves well, and make a general fire upon the first that came up. I must own, I never was better observ'd in my life, and that Enemies were never more briskly entertained. For immediately they discharged so bravely upon the first Assailants, that a great many of them were laid dead upon the spot, and so cool'd their courage for a second attempt: So the rest that were wiser went off, though much fewer than they came, and left us to keep on our way without more danger or disturbance.

By this time Mareschal *Brezay* had intimation, that some Squadrons of Horse had met with me, and concluding we were all destroyed, he began to be very angry at me, and laid all at my door, supposing I came out too late, and had spent time unseasonably, in staying to enrich my self with the booty of the Castle. In this ill humour I found him at my arrival, but when he understood we had sustained no loss, and all was safe, he chang'd presently from a deep malancholy, into an extreme good humour, and told me with some degree of amazement, that he could not imagine which way we could bring our selves off. I gave him a relation of the whole matter, but at the same time exprest my dissatisfaction, that the King's men should be expos'd to such hazards, and all for a little forrage.

XIX. The Siege was rais'd quickly after, and the Army was sent for good quarters towards *Ruremond*, but indeed we fell into very bad ones. This being a sandy Country, there happened so violent a storm, and such mighty hurricanes, that for five or six days together we breathed nothing but Sand, instead of pure Air. Five or six thousand men were presently choak'd with it, or else died in a little while by distempers that this corruption of the Air bred among them. For, besides what they suckt in by breathing at the Nose, that which was eaten with our meat, which was all tainted continually, infected their bodies to that degree, that they were quickly overrun with it. This weakned our Army, and reduc'd them to such a wretched condition, that they were more like an Hospital of sick men, than a Camp of Souldiers, that made fighting their business. Upon which several begg'd to be dismist, and long'd for a little of their own native air to recover their health and strength, which this malignant air had almost quite consumed.

Among these many sick poor wretches, I saw one day a man habited like a Beggar, who ask'd an Alms, and was almost eaten up with vermin, and all over Scabs. After
having

having viewed him well, I knew him, and found he was a Gentleman, that had spent his estate, and was brought to these wretched circumstances by his own extravagance. I took pity on his condition, and giving my servant Money to buy him necessaries, I bad him go along with him. We clothed him, and then he exprest to me a great desire to go back into *France*, for he was sure he should dye of want and sickness in that Country. With much ado I got him dismist, for he belong'd to our Army, and Mareschal *Brezay* had orders to let no body return into *France*. The sickness, and wretched condition he was in, having forc'd him to leave the service, I was very importunate with the Mareschal that he might go home, who did not know how to deny me for this man, what he granted scarce to any body; so I sent him away, and let him have fifty Crowns to bear his charges. But tho he hath recovered himself since, and lives very well, yet he made it appear, that the greatest kindnesses are but little acknowledged; and that a false notion of honour tempts men wilfully to forget obligations, which they are asham'd to remember. For he never came near me, so muchas to thank me, for six whole years, nay he took all occasions of avoiding my company; and it was above nine years before he paid me what I had lent him, to redeem him out of his misfortunes.

XX. While our Army lay sick in *Holland*, I lost and found again a very valuable Horse, and the best I was then Master of, after a very odd manner. Some body having taken occasion to steal him from me in the very Camp, some days after he was gone I met a Gentleman mounted upon a Horse exactly like mine. I presently told him without more ado, that the Horse was mine, and enquir'd whom he had bought him of. He answer'd me very frankly, That might very well be, for he had him dog-cheap of a Souldier, that sold him for three Pistoles, and that for the same Money he was at my service. I gave him the Money accordingly, and took the Horse which I thought mine, but really was not so. Some time after, as I was speaking very loud, and calling to some body in the Camp, my true Horse, that was thereabouts, and having been long used to me, knew my voice, began presently to neigh and whinny exceedingly, as if he had a mind to let people know, that he heard his Master's voice. I was as well acquainted with his whinny too; and sent a Servant to the place where I heard him, to see if I was not mistaken. He knew my Horse again, and came back to give me an account of it. Whereupon enquiring out the man that had him in keeping, I forced him, tho with some difficulty, to restore him to me. So after a little while I had got both my own Horse, and his likeness. But it was not long neither before this latter, by a good pleasant adventure, found his own Master too. For the Officer whose really he was, meeting me one day upon his Horse, challenged him, and made me the very same compliment, that I should have done in his circumstances, That that Horse belonged to him: And to confirm it, he gave me an undeniable token, which was, that we should find at the bottom of one of his feet a piece of green cloth in the shape of a Plaister, which was laid there for a hurt he had got on that foot. We found the matter even so. He gave me a Case of Pistols, and I let him have his again. And thus by these two odd accidents, those that possest what they had no right to, were dispossest again, and the two Horses were both return'd to their true owners.

The End of the Third Book.

BOOK

BOOK IV.

The Sieur de Pontis is in the Prince of Orange's particular Favour, who invites him to his Service, but he declines it. The King makes him a Captain of the Guards. The Trick that was play'd him, to deprive him of this Favour. A great Consternation in the French Army, when Piccolomini and John of Werth were the Spanish Generals. The Sieur de Pontis is sent to relieve Abbeville with the Regiment of Brezay. His Behaviour to the Person that got the Command given him by the King out of his hands. They create him trouble at Court, upon occasion of his Garrison at Abbeville. He is taken Prisoner in a Fight. The Siege of la Cappelle. The Sieur de Pontis prevents the Swisse's Rising. Arras besieged and reduced.

I. DUring the time our Army endured such hardship in Quarters, the *Spaniards* had besieged *Schink*, a Fort lying upon the *Rhine* some fifteen or sixteen Leagues from *Ruremond*, and carried the place. The Prince of *Orange* was resolved to retake it, and to this purpose marched both the Armies toward that Fort. Then it was that I began to have very free access to the Prince, and (if it be not too much presumption to call it so) a particular intimacy with his Excellence; for with such he was pleased to honour me, and that hapned upon this occasion. He was desirous to know the Officers of our Army, and their Names, and therefore contrived that they should come in order into a Hall where he was. I, as the rest, went in my turn, and Mareschal *Brezay* having been so kind to mention me to him formerly much to my advantage; and having likewise the honour to be known to him, by my being deputed from our Generals, to express the Army's zeal to receive him as their Generalissimo, he did me the favour to discourse with me something more particularly than the rest, when I came to make my reverence to him. He asked me several Questions about the War, in which I gave him the best satisfaction I could; and at last put it to me, whether, if he should have occasion to use them, I could furnish him with three or fourscore stout Musqueteers that had their Arms in good case. I answer'd, because I knew I could make my word good, that I could supply him not only with fourscore, but a hundred, or two, or three hundred, if he pleased to command them. That I durst be very confident, there was never a Regiment in the whole Army that kept their Arms so well, and so bright as ours, (which was Mareschal *Brezay's*) and that it was made up of very gallant Fellows. The Prince then asked me, what course I took with our Souldiers to make them keep their Arms clean, and in so good case, even when the Army was upon the march; and I told him, that whenever we came to any Village where there dwelt a Gunsmith, I always took care to have all the Arms of the Regiment well scowr'd.

This Conference with the Prince, in which he did me the honour to discourse me upon several Subjects, brought me so far into his favour, that he exprest an extraordinary kindness for me; insomuch that at my going away, as I was taking leave to make room for another, he had me give him my hand. I in respect refused that, and offer'd to kiss the Prince's; but he would have no denial, but took my hand, and laid his own upon it, with this familiar expression, *I have a mind to be your Friend, and would have you be mine. You have given me better satisfaction than any body, I am very well pleased with you, for I love People that talk to me freely, as you I perceive have done.*

Ggg   Ever

Ever after that time, whenever the Prince saw me, he would call me to him, and seem'd industrious to give me publick marks of his Favor, sometimes honouring me so highly, as to walk with me a good while together. I soon imagin'd, that all this was meant to draw me over to his service, for Princes do not use to be so extremely obliging for nothing. And afterwards he told me, *That if I would stay with him in* Holland, *he would use me like a Friend.* This was something extraordinary for a Prince to say; and I suppose the thing he chiefly expected from me, was my fidelity to the person I served. And this was the very thing too, that kept me from refusing this offer, though in truth long experience at Court had taught me, how little such friendships of great Men are to be depended upon. Therefore I exprest my self with all manner of gratitude and submission, but at the same time told him, *I was engaged in* the French *Service, and not inclined to quit that.*

However this particular grace of the Prince created me great envy, every one gave his judgment of it as he pleased, and it gave great offence, that his Excellency frequently took delight to prefer me above others. Which, to speak freely, I cannot like in a person of that character, who, methinks, should be tender of them whom he honours with his Favour, and not expose them to the ill will of their acquaintance, by extravagant Commendations. But on the other hand, it is very injurious to fall foul upon them that are innocent, for such a miscarriage. For if a Prince be either prepossest in one's Favor, or think one Man really deserve to be valued more than others, when the person so valued does nothing but his duty, he is not to be blamed. And those that are less regarded, do very unjustly, if they take occasion from hence to hate him. Even Mareschal *Brezay* telling me, *He could not tell how I had got the* Prince *of* Orange's *Affections.* I answer'd him roundly, but fully, *I have done nothing to* him, *Sir, but what I do to you every day; that is, endeavouring by the discharge of my duty, to give you both satisfaction; and if he honour me with his Favour, this is an Argument of his generous Nature, which inclines him to love them that are zealous in his Service.* He returned upon me, *Well, be sure you keep firm to your duty, for I my self would snatch you out of the* Prince *of* Orange's *Arms.* Whereupon I made him this hearty, but respectful Answer, *Sir, you are my General, and my particular Patron, and, next to the King, you shall always command me. I have too just a sense of your Favours, to return them with Ingratitude, and that is a thing I can never do.*

I was much surprized afterwards, to see a great Carriage and six Horses brought me, as a Present from the States, to convey my Baggage. The Prince had procur'd it for me, as a mark of his Favour, and it was maintained at the States charge, without costing me a Penny. It came indeed very seasonably, for two of my Horses were shoulder-slipt, and my Carriage was left behind. And again, when we were come to the Fort at *Schinck*, the States provided me a Boat at their own expence, all the time I continued there.

II. The Siege was formed against this Fort about the beginning of *September*, in the same year 1635; and at this Siege it was, that the Prince of *Orange* had a mind to try whether I was a Man of my word. For, having laid a secret design against the place, he desired of me that I would supply him out of hand with two hundred Musqueteers, such as he had ask'd me for, and I did so. His Attempt was discovered and prevented, but he profest himself as well satisfied, as if it had taken effect. I cannot recollect any thing very remarkable that happen'd in this Siege. Only the Cardinal Infant was bravely repuls'd, who came with his Army to the Relief of the Besieged; for there was an Agreement before, between the *French* and *Dutch*, that they should carry on the Siege, and the *French* should only concern themselves with keeping off the Enemy; which they acquitted themselves of very bravely, and forced them to retire, without doing any thing to purpose. When Winter came on, the *French* Army went into Quarters in the Canton assign'd them, and the Prince of *Orange* left Count *William* of *Nassau* to carry on the Siege, who took the Fort by Capitulation, about the end of *April* the next Spring, that is, after about some eight Months Siege in all. Our Regiment was distributed among four several Towns, and in each of those I had Quarters; but I spent most part of the Winter with the Prince of *Orange* at the *Hague*.

III. The King mean while was graciously pleased to think of me, though I was at a distance from him, and gave me a Command of Captain in the Guards. The truth is, after having been so long in his service, I had some title to expect such a reward. I saw abundance of other people less faithful than I had been, who yet made very great fortunes by it. And I for my own part stuck just where I was; the unalterable devotion I had ever shewn for the King's person and service, being in truth so far from helping, that it hindred my advancement. I do not speak this so much to complain of ill usage, as to shew what lamentable circumstances my Prince was in, who, tho he was possest of a great Kingdom, had it yet infinitely less in his power, to make those whom he took for his faithfullest servants some tolerable amends, than his Minister had to make his creatures great. The King straight dispatcht a Mandate under his Privy Seal to me, to return into *France*. Monsieur *Boulogne* my particular good friend, whom I have had occasion to mention several times before, writ to me at the same time to make all the haste I could to *Paris*, but took no notice what the particular business was that requir'd it, only in general terms, that it was a matter that might be of some importance to me.

Monsieur *de Ch.* the Kings Embassadour in *Holland*, having receiv'd the Pacquet from Court, and (as he us'd to do) open'd the Letters; when he saw the King had bestow'd this Command upon me, dealt very unfaithfully with me. He was desirous to take this opportunity of advancing his own Nephew, and to keep me in *Holland*, upon pretence of some great design against *Guelderland*; so he very basely kept the Kings Letter for me, to himself, and dispatcht his Nephew to Court, that he might discourse Cardinal *Richelieu* upon those designs of his, and get the Command, the King had laid out for me, for his pains. But his Nephew lost his labour, for the King answer'd them with more resolution than was common to him, that he had dispos'd of that Command before. Still I labour'd hard to be dismist, for Monsieur *Boulogne's* Letter made me very eager of returning to *France*; and besides all that, Money began to grow low with me. But, whether through some private opposition from the Cardinal, or some underhand correspondence between the Ambassadour and our Generals, to obstruct my return, I could never get leave to go, and was forc'd, sore against my will, and contrary to the Kings express command, to stay in that Country all winter. So the King not having (if I may so say) authority enough to procure my return, tho he heartily desir'd it, dispos'd of that Command to another person, after having staid for me several months.

IV. About the beginning of Spring the next year 1636, we took Shipping, and when I waited on the Prince of *Orange*, to take my leave of him, he exprest some concern, that I refus'd to stay with him, after so many kind offers as he had made me. But knowing that that very constancy he esteem'd me for, was the thing that hindred it, he profest himself well pleas'd with my conduct. *And if you would have me,* (said he) *I will write to the King in your behalf, and signifie your good services to him.* I answer'd him great respect, That being the *French* Kings natural Subject, I was engag'd to attend his service; but nothing could ever make me forget the many marks of grace and kindness that I had receiv'd from his Highness: that I had a more grateful sense of the honour he had done me in approving my service, than was possible for me to express; and that if he would condescend to honour me yet more with his recommendation to the King, this would be an exceeding addition to all his former favours.

V. When we were come into *France*, our Army quartered for some time in *Normandy*; but shortly we received fresh orders to joyn the Count *de Soissons*, and Mareschal *Brezay* at *la Fere*. Thither I went with our Regiment, and being extremely harrass'd, I went into a Granary, and there laid me down to sleep; which happened very luckily upon a double account, for by that means I not only refresht my self, but escap'd a great danger. The Enemies lying in that Country with a powerful Army of forty thousand men, under the Command of Prince *Thomas*, and the two famous Generals *Piccolomini* and *John of Werth*, plunder'd and seiz'd several Towns, and all fell before them. There had not been known so general a consternation in *France* of a long time; and the power of *Spain* had then got such a mighty ascendant over us, that it lookt like fool-hardiness to pretend to oppose it. We apprehended they had a design to besiege *Catelet*, and the Count *de Soissons* intending to send me thither, made great enquiry after me. Mareschal *Brezay*, who knew well enough where I was, shew'd great tenderness for my safety upon this occasion; and being of opinion,
that

that to fend me to a place which could not poffibly hold out againſt ſo great a force, was manifeſtly to expoſe me, he would not own that he knew any thing of me. And there in all probability I muſt have been loſt, for not being of a temper to ſurrender tamely, I ſhould have been likely enough to expoſe the place to have been taken by ſtorm. When great ſearch had been made for me to no purpoſe, another was ſent thither in my ſtead. And the Enemy ſitting down before the place in *July* 1636, quickly made themſelves Maſters of it.

VI. From *la Fere* our Army moved to *Bray*, to prevent the Enemies croſſing the River. Every one fortify'd himſelf in his poſt the beſt he could : For my own part, throwing off my Doublet, I workt ſo hard with the reſt of the Officers and Souldiers of our Regiment, that in four hours time we entrencht our ſelves ſo conveniently in a meadow on this ſide the River, and over againſt a hill, which the Enemies muſt come down, that we lay quite under their Cannon. I had alſo contriv'd to have a great many Stakes driven down in the River, to hinder their Horſe from getting over. Afterwards I diſcover'd a man at ſome diſtance trying the Ford, and went preſently to tell the perſon who commanded the Regiment of *Champagne*, that he ſhould put himſelf in a readineſs, and might expect a ſharp bout quickly ; becauſe their poſt was leſs convenient, and lay more open than ours. At the ſame time I ran to Mareſchal *Brezay* to inform him, and receive his commands : But he was in ſuch a perplexity, that he knew not what orders to give. I was a little ſurpriz'd to hear him ſay, *Make good your own poſt as well as you can* ; for they were all at their wits end ; and I am ſure this coufnſion in the Generals, was likely to diſcourage the Souldiers, as much as their dread of the *Spaniſh* forces. The Enemies began to ſhew themſelves, and having planted fourteen pieces of Cannon upon the hill, play'd them upon our Regiment, but it was all noiſe and ſmoak, without any great matter of execution. For we lying intrench'd at the foot of the Hill, and as it were ſtuck down into the ground, the Bullets flew over our heads, and could do us no miſchief. Whereas we on the other ſide had opportunity to fire upon them without being ſeen, and gall'd them terribly. So not being able to force this quarter, they remov'd their Cannon to fall upon the Regiment of *Champagne*, which indeed they tore horribly, becauſe they lay a great deal more expoſed.

Our Generals, ſeeing themſelves preſt in this part, gave order for the Army to march, and retreat to *Noſle* ; for there was no likelihood of ſtanding it out, and beſides the Enemies had a ſtrange advantage over us, by I know not what terror that had ſeiz'd all our men. It was their intent to repoſe the Army in this Village, but I told the Count *de Soiſſons*, I had been informed that there was a great Morais behind it, and if the Enemy ſhould follow hard upon us, we might endanger part of our Troops by ſo long a defile. Upon this advice, tho they had begun to work upon the Trenches, yet it was reſolv'd the Army ſhould make no ſtop, till we were got beyond this Morais. As the Count of *Soiſſons* was ſet at Table, where he did me the honour to ſet me with him, we had all on a ſudden news brought, that the Enemy were come up a great way towards us, that our Out-guards were beaten from their Poſt, and the Forlorn-hope in danger to be all cut in pieces. They were about two thouſand Horſe detach'd from their Army, and bore forward to charge ours in the Flank. Then every one hurrying to Horſe ran to the attack ; but we found our men broken. So we were forc'd to retreat fighting, and try to ſecure our Army at *Noyon*. The Enemies were much exalted with ſo much good ſucceſs, and our mens hearts fail'd them ſadly, who had only juſt ſo much ſtrength left, as would ſerve them to make off. The *Spaniſh* Generals ſeeing the Count *de Soiſſons* too weak to ſtand againſt them, and withdrawn with the Army to *Noyon*, went to lay ſiege to *Corbie*, reſolv'd to force a paſſage farther into *France*, and to follow their blow as far as they could.

VII. Some time after this, the King being at *Chantilly*, ſent me his commands to wait upon him as ſoon as I could. His Majeſty having never ſeen me ſince my Journey into *Holland*, asked me a great many queſtions, and enquired after the news of that Country ; and, after I had told him the principal matters, he diſcours'd me particularly about the Prince of *Orange*, and gave me ſufficient intimation, that either the Prince had writ, or ſome body from him had ſpoke in my favour. For he asked what charms I had uſed to inſinuate my ſelf ſo far into his affections. Whereupon,

upon, being well aware of the King's jealous temper, and that this might incline him to suspect this mighty confidence, I answer'd him with the same freedom I had done Mareschal *Brezay*, That I had used no other arts but the faithful performance of my duty, and that I was much beholden to his Excellence for valuing my services that his Majesty had commanded me to pay him. At last the King asked me, why I did not come sooner, after that Letter he had sent me? I told him I never received any such Letter from him, and that when I ask'd leave it was denied me, upon pretence that my presence there was necessary. His Majesty not caring to open his meaning any farther, nor to tell me his design of making me Captain in his Regiment of Guards, only reply'd, that I was certainly the unluckiest fellow in the world, and never had any fortune. I, knowing nothing of the matter, could not make him any answer, tho it were easy to have replyed, that my fortune was in his disposal, and he might make me happy whenever he pleased. Just then I happen'd to take notice of a Half-moon that they had made before the Castle gate, and could not forbear smiling. The King perceiv'd it, and ask'd me what I laught at? I told him, That it was my humble request to his Majesty, that that Half-moon might be taken down, and not stand there for a reproach to *France*; as if the person of so great a Prince could not be safe, without such a Fortification as that was.

The King then ordered me to hasten with my Regiment to *Abbeville*, to carry the *Swisses* their pay, and put succours into the Town before the Enemy besieged it. He ordered at the same time a *Valet de Chambre* to be sent for, who in the presence of his Majesty, Cardinal *Richelieu*, and Monsieur *de Chavigny*, quilted sixteen hundred Pistoles into my Wastecoat. With this order away I went, and making the best of my way to joyn Mareschal *Brezay*'s Regiment, we marched day and night, and made so good haste, that we came time enough to save the Town. We got into it about two in the morning, to the exceeding joy both of the Inhabitants and the Garrison, who waited most impatiently for this reinforcement, expecting to be surpriz'd every hour, and either forc'd to give up the place, or have it carry'd by storm. We found the Town illuminated with Candles and Torches in all the Windows, as if it had been all of a flame, and nothing could be heard but shouts of men, women and children, crying, *God save the King*. They had indeed great reason to rejoyce, for the Garrison was much too weak to defend the place, and if we had come one half day later, there had been small hopes of saving the Town.

VIII. The next day, about ten in the morning, we saw seven and fifty Squadrons of Horse, who came up in full expectation to carry the place. At the same time Monsieur *d'Alais*, who had withdrawn thither, and had a small Squadron of Horse with him, sallied out, and I followed him with our whole Regiment, divided into several Battalions. The rest of the Garrison were posted upon the Ramparts, and as many Inhabitants as were in a condition to bear arms, were ordered to shew themselves there too, so that nothing was seen but Souldiers, resolv'd to hold it out to the last. Several Vollies of Cannon and Musquet shot were given from the Town, rather to make the Enemy believe that they wanted no Ammunition, than out of any prospect of doing them any hurt. The Enemy debated for two hours what course they should take, and in the mean while ten or twelve of the Count *d'Alais* Trumpets sounded several Alarms, to signify that if they came on, we were ready to receive them. At last, thinking this might put a stop to their conquests, if they attempted a City so well garrison'd, they went off, to carry their victorious arms another way.

IX. I staid at *Abbeville* with Mareschal *Brezay*'s Regiment about a year, for we were under continual apprehensions of some attempt upon us, because the Enemy had Garrisons in several Towns near us. Some days after my coming thither, the Officer that would have got my command from me, which the King intended me in the Guards, came thither too with the Marquis of *Brezay*'s Regiment, of which he was Major. Monsieur *de P.* one of the stoutest men of his time, followed him close, having a quarrel against him, upon the account of a Box on the Ear, which this Officer was said to have given him. All their acquaintance on both sides were concern'd to make up the business. Monsieur *M.* protested he never give the blow, but Monsieur *de P.* not brooking, that the world should think he had received it, resolv'd to revenge it whatever came out. Monsieur *M.* who pretended great kindness to

me,

me, notwithstanding the dirty Trick he had play'd me, which I then knew nothing of, beg'd that I would interpose in the Case, and proffer'd to refer himself to the judgment of any persons they would chuse, and make any satisfaction they thought fit for him. I was desirous to reconcile the Quarrel by fair means, and used my utmost endeavour to persuade Monsieur *de P.* to it. I walked with him several times to this purpose, and told him, I neither knew the ground of their difference, nor desir'd to know it. But, let the Affront be what it would, it could not be so great, as not to admit of an honourable Accommodation, without coming to the Extremities he aimed at. I advis'd to put it to the judgment of Friends, and told him all that long Experience had qualify'd me to say upon such an occasion, to incline him to terms of Reconciliation, and undeceive him of his Notion, that no way but fighting could save his Honour. He continued deaf to all I said, or if he gave me the hearing, yet (which was as bad) he was still inflexible, and resolv'd to pursue his design. And about ten or twelve days after he did so, and fought Monsieur *M.* without the Town, whom he wounded mortally in five places, and was wounded in two places himself.

X. Monsieur *M.* being thus hurt, I had him brought to my Lodging, and took all imaginable care of him till his death, which happen'd about three Weeks after. I spared neither trouble nor charge to do him service, and had as tender a regard to his Soul as his Body, keeping a Monk constantly in my house all the time of his illness, who never stirred from him. The most surprizing Circumstance was, that Providence should so order the matter, that I should ignorantly oblige a Man so highly, who had disobliged me extremely, and utterly ruined my Fortunes, by designing to get the Command designed me by the King out of my hands, and being the principal occasion of his Majesty's giving it away to another person. This poor Man feeling his Conscience burden'd with this Fault, and the more so, in proportion as he receiv'd fresh kindnesses from the person to whom he had done such ill offices, resolv'd at last to be plain with me upon the business. Some days before he died, I observ'd him all in reary, and after a great struggle with himself, he spoke to me after this manner: *Ah! Sir, my dear Friend, I can no longer conceal my greatest pain from you, I must, I must at last own to you the Remorse I feel, for having injur'd you in a matter, of which you could never have the least Jealousie. I have sought a thousand opportunities to mention it to you, and ask you as many Pardons for it. I conjure you therefore, dear Sir, to forgive a Man, who needs nothing else to make him unhappy, than having been instrumental in ruining your Fortunes.* I, in perfect amazement at this Discourse, and not able to guess what all this meant, answer'd him with an innocent sincerity, *That I believed he loved me too well to be guilty of what he accus'd himself.* But my Answer adding more to his Sighs and Tears, he reply'd, *Alas! that is the very Consideration that cuts me to the heart, that I who had so much reason to love you, should yet suffer my self to endeavour my own Advancement at your Expence. But if you do not forgive me before I tell you the Story, I shall run mad; since the wrong I have done you is so great, that if you do not forgive me, now I am going to give an account to God, I shall have reason to fear he will not forgive me neither.* There was little room for deliberation in the sad circumstances and great disorder he then lay, so that I told him instantly with great compassion, *That I assur'd him, and solemnly protested, I would never resent the thing; and that if he had really done me any Injury, I forgave it him with all my Soul.* Upon this assurance, which I gave after the best manner I could, he discover'd the whole Matter in these words: *It was I* (said he) *dear Sir, that obstructed your Preferment. It was I that hindred you from being now Captain in the Guards. It was I that contrived you should be detained in* Holland, *and by my Uncles means kept the King's Letter from your hands, which order'd you to come to Court, and take possession of that Command.*

I must own this astonisht me strangely. But my Concern to see him in this condition stifled my Passion, and I again assur'd him, *That I forgave him heartily, and instead of loving him less upon this account, should love him more for declaring himself so freely to me, because this was an Argument he knew me, and entertained the opinion of me that I could wish he should.* And I can say with great truth, that I still retain'd the same affection for him, and after his death buried him with all the decency and solemnity of a General; the two Regiments marching with their Pikes trailing, and all the other Ceremonies of great Commanders Funerals. He was at that time deserted by all his Friends and Relations, and Providence so contriv'd it, that the only relief he had came from that

very

very Man, who, according to the false Notions of Honour in the World, ought to have been his greatest Enemy. His Father was not wanting indeed to express his thanks to me, and paid me exactly all that I had laid out upon his Son's account.

XI. While I stay'd in Garison at *Abbeville*, I happen'd to have a great Ruffle with the Officers of the Customs for Salt. Our Souldiers, who were but indifferently paid, had got into a little way of trading, much for the convenience both of the Citizens, and themselves. They went and bought Salt at St. *Vallery*, and then sold it again to the Townsmen at good Rates, so both Parties had an advantage by it, only the Custom-Officers were enraged, that they could not hinder that which turn'd to their prejudice. These Gentlemen therefore made their complaint to the Duke of *Angoulesme*, who, for some private considerations, took their part. For my part, not having wherewithal to pay the Regiment, I let them go on, seeing no great harm in the thing, and thinking this as well for the King's advantage, who had such a method for his Troops to subsist, without either the expence of his own Pocket, or the burdening his Subjects. I gave them no express Orders indeed for what they did, but only connived at it.

Coming about this time to *Paris*, to give his Majesty an account of the Garison, he discourst me upon several Matters, and kept me with him till almost One a clock at night. I told him what Monsieur *M.* had declar'd to me upon his death-bed, concerning the Command he was pleas'd to intend for me, and from thence took occasion to present him with my most humble thanks, telling him, *That this at least was out of my Enemies power, to take away from me my Gratitude to his Majesty.* Speaking afterwards of the Garison, I told the King I was driven to great straits for want of Money to pay the Souldiers. And his Majesty enquiring what course the Garison took to subsist then ? I answer'd him with the freedom he gave me leave to use, that they had found out a way to pay themselves. *They go Sir,* said I, *and buy Salt cheap, and make a little Money of selling it again, till your Majesty have a convenience of sending them their Pay.* The King laught, and told me, *Hark you, I will not hinder them from playing the Knave thus, but if they are caught by the Magistrates, I will not hinder them from being hang'd too.* I answer'd merrily, *That they were stout Fellows, and I was much mistaken if they would be caught.* And so this went off thus in Merriment.

Not getting to Bed till Three that night, I took it out next day, and slept till Eight in the Morning, which prevented my waiting early upon the King ; and it was my very good Fortune, that I had an opportunity of discoursing him the night before. For the Duke of *Angoulesme* came to the Louvre in the Morning, and told the King a dismal Story of the Disorders of the Garison at *Abbeville.* I came in this very nick of time, and met some of my Friends, who said, *I'le assure they are talking finely of you above.* I went up however, not much dismay'd, because I had discours'd the King about it already. When I was at the Chamber-door the King saw me, and because he had a mind the Duke of *Angoulesme* should talk over the Matter while I was by, he gave me a Sign, that I should not discover my self. I presently understood his Majesties meaning, and slipping behind the Company, got just behind my Lord *Angoulesme,* who railed at our Garison very warmly. Then the King seeming surprized, and having a mind to draw him in still deeper, said, *But what ! Is not Pontis at Abbeville? And does not he restrain these Disorders? Yes Sir,* said the Duke, *he is there, but he is as bad as the rest, though they say he does take some little Care. Be cautious what you say,* said the King, *for there is one hears you.* With that I shew'd my self to the Duke of *Angoulesme,* and told him smiling, *In earnest, Sir, I am much obliged to you, for the good office you have done me to his Majesty.* He being extremely surprized to see one that he never dreamt had been so near, began to recant, and in some disorder said, *Oh ! Sir, Monsieur* Pontis, *I have been informed thus of you, but, for my part, I never believed it.* The King and all the Company could not hold laughing at this sudden come-off, and I as readily reply'd, *Oh ! Sir, I am the more obliged to you then, for endeavouring to make the King believe what you never believed your self.* He shuffled the thing as well as he could, and all went off with a Jest, and Monsieur *Angoulesme* complimented me with the assurance of his Favour, and any service he could do me.

At my return to the Garison, I found the Bustle greater than before. For the Souldiers taking confidence from their not being forbidden their Trade, acted barefac'd, and carry'd on the Matter with a high hand, never regarding either the Officers, or the Archers of the *Gabelle,* because they were not strong enough to encounter them.

them. They went one day to the number of three or fourscore well armed, and all in a body to *St. Vallery*. The Officers of the Customs sent as many Archers out after them, with orders to fall upon the Souldiers, and bring them in bound hand and foot. This was sooner said than done. They met with one another, and fought furiously. Several Archers were killed, and several Souldiers wounded, but the Souldiers had the better of it. When they were come back to *Abbeville*, two of the wounded came to shelter themselves at my house, as in a Sanctuary. I began to scold at them, and call'd them a hundred Rascals, that their Rogueries would ruine me, and turn'd them out at a back-door, but yet lodged them in a poor Cottage, where they were privately lookt after. The Officers enraged at the loss and the disgrace of their Archers, came to me immediately with open mouths, and told me, My Souldiers had put the whole City in confusion, threatning that the King should know it. I pretended to be very angry at the Souldiers my self, and proffer'd, if they could apprehend any of the Criminals, I would see Justice done upon them immediately. I my self went upon the search with them, and tho no discovery could be made, yet these Officers were so well satisfy'd with me, and so cruelly harrassed with the scuffles they met with, and where they generally came off with the worst of it, that a day or two after they came to my lodging to propose an accommodation. They told me they saw I was a man of honour, and heartily devoted to the King's service and interest, and therefore the best method they could think of to put a stop to all these disturbances, was, to make their application to me, and offer me an expedient which they had found out; which was, That the Souldiers should be allowed to go buy Salt at *St. Vallery*, only instead of selling it again to the Inhabitants of *Abbeville*, they should bring it into the King's Granaries, where it should be taken off their hands, at the same price the Citizens used to give. I quickly saw how fair a proposal this was for our men, but having a mind to be little intreated upon the point, I answered these Officers, That they were very honest civil Gentlemen, but the Garrison had not deserved so much favour, and I was resolv'd to hang all that I could find had been faulty. But whether they made a favourable judgment of my intention, or whether from some other cause, they importun'd and conjur'd me so vehemently, that at last I was forc'd to grant, what I wish'd a great deal more than they. I proposed the matter to the Souldiers, who embrac'd it most willingly, and afterwards sold their Salt to the King's Stores, and drove underhand bargains with the Townsmen besides, so keeping both up to a good round rate. Thus I got both the King's approbation and the Peoples hearts, but especially the Inhabitants, who thought themselves infinitely obliged to me, for both exercising so good discipline, that the Garrison did them no injury; and allowing them so considerable an advantage by their means. I had also one particular piece of respect paid me during my stay at *Abbeville*, which was to have a voice allowed me in the Council of Monsieur *le Seve*, then Intendant of Justice, and since Provost of the Merchants at *Paris*; who, as a particular favour, would have my Vote in his determinations, and by this confidence express the friendship he did me the honour to have for me.

XII. In *May* 1637, Mareschal *Brezay*'s Regiment, which I commanded, was ordered to joyn Cardinal *de la Vallette*'s Forces, who was attempting to enter the *Low-Countries* with a considerable Army. The King would have constituted me his Lieutenant at *Abbeville*, but I had no inclination to that Post; for tho it were honourable, yet it oblig'd me to a private and peaceable life, and robb'd me of the only pleasure I had, which was to follow the Army, and fight for my Country. But I was much urged to it, and verily believe the City had a great hand in the importunities used to perswade me to this Office. But my constant answer was, that I would readily take it, provided the Regiment I then commanded might always continue at *Abbeville*; and I would never hearken to it upon any other condition. The Inhabitants, who seem'd so well satisfy'd with my Government, seem'd as much concern'd at my leaving them: and the chief of them desired however to make merry with me before I went; and entertain'd me three or four days as well as they could. The Gentlemen of the *Gabelle*, I suppose, were not so very loth to part with me. But it is a hard task to please all the world.

I went to joyn our Army commanded by Cardinal *de la Vallette*, and the Duke of *Candale*, and was not long before I paid for the civil usage, and all the good fortune I had met with for a year and a half in the Town, where every thing conspir'd to ease and to divert me. Our Army being come to *Castle-Cambray* in the *Low-Countries*, I with two hundred men at the head of the Army, was order'd to set a guard farther on, and the Horse had orders to support us. But this order being suddenly changed, and the Horse sent off to another Post, we soon found our selves hemm'd in with some Squadrons of the Enemies Horse, and at first took them for our own. But we were soon undeceiv'd, and finding our selves thus surpriz'd, threw our selves into a place full of Hedges, where we made a good defence a great while. Seeing at last, that our Enemies grew upon us continually, I thought it a madness to pretend to hold out against more than 1000 Horse, that were all upon us and we without any prospect of being reliev'd. So I cry'd out, *Quarter, Gentlemen, Quarter: We have given you proof enough of our Valour, and it is meer fool-hardiness to stand it out any longer.* Seeing them charge us still, I cry'd again, *Quarter, Gentlemen; If you deny it us, we will make work with you ; and you may chance to repent it, for we will sell our lives dear, and fight it out to the last man.* Then they stopt, knowing what it is to deal with men when they are desperate; and gave us the Quarter we askt. The Officers and I were detain'd, the Souldiers were sent back, and they carry'd us to *Cambray.* As soon as ever the King heard I was taken Prisoner, he had the goodness to send Monsieur *de la Sabloniere*, Groom of the Wardrobe, with my Ransom, and as much Money as I needed for my charges, and to recruit me for the loss I had sustain'd in the fight. So I continu'd under confinement not above six weeks or two months at most.

XIII. At my return in *August* or *September* 1637. I went to joyn Mareschal *de la Melleray's* Army, about the time when he designed to besiege *La Cappelle.* He was then under the Kings displeasure, and Cardinal *Richelieu*, who had a great kindness for him, was in some perplexity upon the Kings ill opinion of him. The Mareschal in the mean while, desirous to make himself considerable by some extraordinary action, thought himself obliged to undertake the Siege of *La Cappelle.* The Cardinal was of another opinion ; he thought that if this attempt should prove unsuccessful, it would quite lose him with the King, and therefore he endeavoured to divert him from that design, and writ him word, that he should consider there was danger in the undertaking, and the place strong enough to bring a disgrace upon him. The Mareschal was not thus prevailed upon, and answered his Eminence, That tho the Garrison were a good one, yet he saw well enough it might be taken, for several reasons which he gave him. And when he had writ this Letter, he laid Siege to the place. The Cardinal being exceeding fearful for a person he lov'd, writ him word again, That he advis'd him to let that Siege alone, and gave him some reasons that intimated plain enough, his Eminence did not then stand so fast himself, as to secure him against the King's displeasure, if he should miscarry. For the great advances the Enemy had made upon us for some years past, had given a shock to the interest of this great Statesman, all whose wit was little enough, to bear him up against the insults and complaints of a whole Kingdom ; and so was all his policy too, to get loose from all the new intrigues form'd against him, as I shall shew in some measure hereafter. Mareschal *Melleray*, still unmov'd with all the Cardinal had said, sent back word, that the place was actually invested, and he did not question but to give a good account of it. And after several other things said upon this occasion, he added at the bottom of his Letter, as himself was pleased to tell me, that noted sentence of the Poet, *Audaces fortuna juvat.*

At this Siege God preserved me after such a manner, as I can never sufficiently admire, by snatching me on the sudden from a Post where I was oblig'd to be, and where if I had been, my death had been unavoidable. One day, when my Regiment was to come on upon the Guard in the evening, having heard that Monsieur *de Rambures* my particular friend, was indisposed the night before, I went to visit him. When I came to his Tent, they told me he was at the head of the Trenches. I went thither to him, and found him shivering, like a man in an Ague-fit, and told him with great tenderness, that he plaid the Fool to be there, when he scarce could go or stand. *You*, said I, *had more need be in your Bed. Are the Trenches a fit place for a sick man? If the Enemy should make a sally, what can you do in this condition?* He told me his illness was nothing, and for the Enemy, they were not likely to make any sallies ; that they had been very quiet all the night before, and did not seem to design any great matters. I told him, that according to the little experience I had, I was of a quite contrary opinion, and I thought there was the greater ground to fear them, for the very

reason

reason why he thought there was none at all. That the Enemies being so quiet lookt to me very suspiciously, and could portend no good; and that skilful Seamen are always jealous of a great calm. While I was talking at this rate very seriously, the Count *de Bussy Lamet* interrupted me, taking me aside with a whisper, which was to tell me, that he had a Pasty of Red Deer sent him of a Present, and desired my company at the opening of it, which was to be that morning to breakfast.

In the mean while came the Mareschal *de Melleray*, to whom I said with the freedom he allowed me to take, *Do not you make a conscience, Sir, of letting a sick man, as Monsieur* Rambures *is, that had an Ague all night, and hath it still upon him, stay here at the head of the Trenches? Pray, Sir, command him to go to bed, for he has at present a worse Enemy than the Spaniard to encounter.* Monsieur *Rambures* took me up, and pretending to slight his distemper, when he thought himself concern'd to be upon duty, turned what I said into raillery, and told us he was very well. Monsieur *Melleray* urged him to withdraw, but he would not be prevailed upon to leave his Post, and, by not taking our advice, he became quickly after the cause of his own death. Then Monsieur *Melleray*, who had laid his design upon the Town, told me I must needs oblige him in one small piece of service, which was to go immediately from him to the Lieutenant of the Ordnance, and bid him get four thousand Baskets of Earth ready, by six in the evening exactly, for he had absolute occasion for them. I promis'd him to go, and as he turned about to speak to some body else, Monsieur *Bussy Lamet* told me again in my Ear, that I should stay till the Mareschal was gone, and then we might go and breakfast together, before I executed my Commission. But Monsieur *Melleray*, who would have had me gone instantly, seeing me again, cryed, *What are not you gone yet? I thought you would have flown for my sake.* I told him I durst not go before him, and only waited his motions. Whereupon he answered, That since I was not gone, we would walk both together as far as the end of the Trench, and then take Horse and go both about our business. Thus I lost my Breakfast, of which I had need enough, but by a particular good providence; I miss'd an accident too, which must undoubtedly have cost me my life, as you will see presently.

As soon as I had parted with Mareschal *Melleray*, who went to overlook the Works, I made haste to the Lieutenant of the Ordinance's Quarter. By that time I was got six or seven hundred paces, I heard a great noise of abundance of Guns. I turn'd about, and saw all the Trench and the Curtain on fire, and fancied it was a great skirmish, and that the Enemy had charged us in our Trenches. Just then was I in greater confusion than can be exprest. On one side my friendship for Monsieur *Rambures* call'd me to the Trenches; on the other, the fear of offending Mareschal *Melleray*, put me upon obeying his orders. At last I resolv'd, if it were possible, to satisfy both obligations: Then riding full speed, as soon as ever I met with the Lieutenant, I told him without more ado, that Monsieur *Melleray* had sent me to order in his name, four thousand Baskets of Earth, to be ready at half an hour after five in the evening; and for fear he should not understand me right, I repeated it over again to him. He made answer, that the Mareschal commanded an impossibility. I repeated it a third time, without staying to reason the case with him, that he must do what he could, but my orders were to bespeak four thousand at half an hour past five in the evening; and so I left him, galloping back again full speed to the Trench: But all was over. All was broke and in disorder, and by the way I met poor Monsieur *Rambures* with his Thigh broke, and carrying back to his Tent. The first words he said were, *Ah, Sir, poor* Bussy *is killed, and so are all the rest that you saw with me at the head of the Trenches. The Guards let themselves be surprized, and that hath lost us all. What you told me is come upon me; and I had been wiser if I had believed you.* I was then quite transported with grief, seeing one of my friends lost, another so dangerously wounded, and so terrible a slaughter in so very short a time. But this was no time to talk; and Monsieur *Rambures* himself begg'd me to run to the Trench, and see if they did not want me, and whether it was not necessary to draw down my Regiment to beat back the Enemy. I ran immediately to put them into a posture of fighting, and Mareschal *Melleray* meeting me there, said in great concern, *What Monsieur* Pontis *have not you been where I sent you?* I told him the thing was done, and I had told the Lieutenant, and repeated it thrice over; that the Lieutenant thought it could hardly be done, but he would endeavour to satisfy him the best he could. Then he told me there was no occasion for my Regiment, for the Enemies were repuls'd already; and then, speaking to me, with great goodness and affection, said, *We have had strange work here in the little time you have been away. You are beholding to me for your Life, for if you had stay'd at the Trenches one quarter of an hour longer, you had had no better Fortune than poor* Buſſy *and* Rambures, *who are both kill'd.* Sir, ſaid I, *I muſt confeſs I am obliged to you, you have loſt one of the beſt Friends and Servants you had in Monſieur* Buſſy, *for he was really a very gallant Man : For Monſieur* Rambures, *he is only wounded.* Monſieur *Melleray* lamented the loſs of Monſieur *Buſſy* very much, ſaying, *That he had indeed loſt one of his deareſt Friends, and the Cardinal one of his moſt faithful Servants.* Then he order'd me to get my Regiment in a readineſs for the Attempt in the Evening, and that he was going juſt then to learn the neareſt way. I had a mind to go with him, and ask'd whether he would not pleaſe to take me with him, that I might receive his Commands. He told me at firſt, there was no need for that. But thinking again upon the matter, he gave me leave to attend him. And after we had taken due notice of the place, and made all neceſſary obſervations, he carried on a Lodgment there in the Evening above a hundred and fifty paces towards the Town, by the help of the Baskets he had or-der'd, to make a paſſage over a Canal. I ſhall give no farther account of this Siege, not remembring any particulars very conſiderable concerning it, but will now proceed to what befel me the year after, when I was ſent into *Franche-Comte.*

XIV. In the year 1638, about the Month of *June*, I was commanded by the King at *Paris* to go to the Army, under the Duke of *Longueville's* Command, which beſieg-ed *Poligny* in *Franche-Comte* ; and the Commiſſion I had given me, was to obſerve what condition the Army was in, and give his Majeſty an account of it. Some time after my coming thither, having no Employ, but what my Eyes were taken up in, the Victualler of the Army, who pretended to confide in me, deſir'd I would bear him company to the Mountains, whither he was then going for Proviſions. I was very glad of the opportunity, being weary of living idle ; and what then ſeem'd on-ly an accidental undeſigning Journey, prov'd of mighty importance to the Kingdom, as I ſhall now ſhew you.

As we travelled through theſe Mountains, it was our Fortune to meet with an ho-neſt old *Swiſſe* who carry'd Letters. I preſently knew his Face, having ſeen him in the Army a great while ago ; and being very deſirous, by reaſon of the diſorders and confuſions of the War, to get his Letters from him cunningly, that I might know whether they contained any thing that might be of uſe to the King, I preſently rubb'd up my old acquaintance, and accoſted him very friendly. *How now honeſt Friend,* ſaid I, *how far are you travelling through theſe Mountains all alone ?* I am going to ſuch a place Sir, ſaid he, to carry ſome Letters. *I fancy* (ſaid I again) *I have ſeen you a good while ago in the* French *King's Guards ; Did not you carry Arms there about ſuch a time ?* Yes, Sir, (ſaid he) I was there about that time, and ſerv'd in them ſo many years. *I thought I was not miſtaken,* (reply'd I) *I perceive my memory hath not quite forſaken me. Well my old Friend, and how is it ? Have you your health well ſtill ? Are you ſtrong and luſty ?* Ah! Maſter, (ſaid he) yes truly, thank God, I am as well as a Man at my Age can expect to be. *Look you Fellow-Souldier* (ſaid I) *we have both of us one com-fort, that if we cannot expect to live as long as other People, we have the leſs time to live in fear of death. For my part I find the beſt thing an old Man can do, is to cheriſh himſelf a little, and not give way to melancholy. Tell me therefore prithee, Is there any thing good to be had hereabouts ? What Price does Wine bear among you ?* The very hearing of that word Wine clear'd up his countenance, and made him look gay, as the temper of that Country is, and telling me, that there were good Proviſions and Wine to be had at tolerable eaſy Rates *Well,* ſaid I, *we will drink one Glaſs together then, and renew our old Acquaintance ; Come on, let us drink a Health to old Age.* Then I brought him to an Inn hard by, and there, after he had drunk ſome Bumpers, I took his Pacquet , and open'd the Letters, and found the *Swiſſes* were upon Riſing, to defend their Rights and Priviledges, which they thought the King of *France* intended to take from them, be-cauſe the Duke of *Longueville* was at that time beſieging *Poligny*, where there are ſome Saltpits, from whence they were priviledg'd to fetch Salt. Theſe poor Fellows are wonderful jealous, and tender of their Liberties , and thought the King deſign'd to incroach upon them by degrees ; and therefore they ſollicited one another by Letters, to take up Arms, and ſend Souldiers into ſeveral parts of the Country to maintain their Priviledges.

Conſidering what might be the conſequences of ſuch an Inſurrection, I left the honeſt Fellow faſt aſleep, and went preſently back to wait upon Monſieur *Longue-*
ville,

ville, to whom I made no particular mention of what had paft, but only told him, that being now of no ufe to the Army, after I had fulfill'd the King's Command, I begg'd he would pleafe to difmifs me, that I might give his Majefty an account of the bufinefs he had intrufted me with. From the Camp at *Poligny* I made all the hafte I could to *Paris*, and went immediately to wait upon the King; to whom, after having given him an account of the Army, I prefented the Pacquet of Letters which I took from the old *Swiffe*, and told his Majefty how I got them into my hands. The King, much furprized at the News, and as much pleas'd with the Service I had done him, writ away to the Duke of *Longueville*, and the *Swiffe Cantons*, to fatisfy them he had no defign at all upon their Priviledges; that there was no real ground for their Jealoufies; that he ever did, and ever would love and protect them againft all Men living. And this quieted the difturbances which were upon the very point of breaking out in their Countries.

This fingle Accident would have been enough, perhaps, to have made any Man's Fortunes but mine, but a higher hand order'd things fo, that what would have been of great fervice to other people, never did me any at all. And really I could fit and reflect for ever, and with much wonder as well as delight, upon the different Providences of my life. For, though I was then wonderfully ftupid, and had no fenfe of better things, yet now I can plainly obferve in a thoufand inftances, the care Almighty God took of me, when I had little or no regard for him. He preferv'd my life again the year after this, which was 1639, when I was manifeftly expos'd to extreme danger; and he made the melancholy and difcontent which I fell into upon an occafion I am now going to relate, to be the inftrument of keeping me out of that danger.

XV. A Friend of mine one day entertaining Monfieur *de Feuquieres*, and another acquaintance at dinner, I, who had a defign to go along with Monfieur *Feuquieres* into the next Campagne, he being a Man of excellent experience, and I defiring above all things ftill to improve my knowledge in military difcipline, invited my felf to dine there too, that I might have an opportunity of breaking my mind to him. One of the Company, a particular Friend of Monfieur *de Feuquieres*, did nothing all dinner long but whifper firft with me, and then with another, which Monfieur *Feuquieres*, that loved people fhould always talk aloud, was much offended at. When dinner was done, the fame Gentleman took Monfieur and Madam..........into a corner of the Room to difcourfe them privately; fo another Gentleman and I were left all alone, much difpleafed at this way of Converfation. For I, who talkt freely to people of the beft Quality, and had the honour to be frequently admitted into the confidence of Princes, was not acquainted with fuch ufage. This Gentleman and I therefore rofe up, and would needs be gone. And though Madam *de*............endeavour'd to ftop us, perceiving that I was, and might very well be diffatisfy'd, yet I took my leave in a pett, without mentioning any thing of my intentions to Monfieur *Feuquieres*. This Refentment of mine put a ftop to my Journey, and by not waiting on Monfieur *Feuquieres*, as I defir'd to do in that Campagne, I efcap'd being at the famous Battel of *Thionville*, where I fhould have found it a hard matter to efcape with life; becaufe I fhould certainly have kept conftantly near the perfon of that excellent Man, who was loft there.

XVI. Upon this I went another way, and for fome time this Campagne ferv'd in the Army that lay at *Vervins*, under the command of Cardinal *de la Vallette*, and the Duke of *Candale*. There I was in quality of Major of Brigades, that is, Major of four or five Regiments, whofe office it is to receive the General's Orders, and fee them duly executed by the Troops under his command. We had befides another Army at *Maubenge*, which the Enemy had blockt up, being encamped between us and them. It being therefore our great concern to join in thefe two Armies, there was a Council of War call'd by Cardinal *Vallette*, to advife how we might get to the Relief of that at *Maubenge*. Monfieur *Gaftion*, the Marquis *de Preflin*, and two other Gentlemen came and offer'd their fervice to our Generals, to get through the Enemy, and carry intelligence to the Town that we were come up, and ready to relieve them, that fo they might be ready upon a day appointed, and the Enemy be attackt on both fides at once. The Generals accepted this offer, as very advantageous for both Armies; and they being well mounted, fpurred on ftrait upon the Enemy. The Centinel perceiv'd them, and gave notice to the Guard, who mov'd to cut off their paffage. The

Marquis of *Praslin*, and two others, by the help of a rare good Horse, got through them. But Collonel *Gassion*, whom the Enemies had inclosed, was as bold an attempt as the other. For throwing himself with Cloaths, Boots and Spurs on into the River, with his Bridle round his Arm, he swum over to the other side, and so came round another way to our Army.

The other Army at *Maubenge*, understanding our motions by Monsieur *Praslin*, and the day we designed to attack the Enemy, put themselves in readiness, and stood to their arms, in expectation of our falling on. As we drew up near the Enemy, there rose such a terrible fog, that one could not see ones way ten yards before them. The whole Army was much disturbed at this, fearing they might fall into an Ambuscade before they were aware. The Regiments under my command were very troublesome, tearing my head to pieces with shouts and questions, not knowing where they were. And, which made it still worse, the Generals were a great way off, for we went at the head of the Army, and marched first. At last, wearied with their bawling, I had a mind to try if I could make any discovery, and went about some forty paces before the Troops, and streight I began to descry some of the Enemies Troops very near me. Then I call'd out to my men, *Forward, forward, To me, to me.* I ordered them to sound a charge, and we laid on so briskly upon them that met us, that they made small resistance, and went off in the mist, so opening a passage for us. For the Troops at *Maubenge* attacking them behind at the same time, they durst not venture to engage two Armies at once.

XVII. This Campagne of the year 1639, about the month of *July*, the Mareschal *de Chatillon* after Monsieur *Feuquiere's* Army was defeated, had orders from the King to besiege *Yvois* in *Luxemburgh*. I was at that Siege, and wounded there by a Musquet bullet in my Leg. But my wound was not so bad, as to disable me from executing the King's Commission of razing that place to the ground. I interceeded however for the sparing the Portal of a Church, where I was not a little surpriz'd to find the Arms of our Family, plac'd there by one of my Relations, that built it, having been a Canon of that Church. The King, who came to *Yvois* after it was taken, would not grant my request till he had seen the Portal. And he being of a good humour, as he was pleasing himself with walking over the ruines of the Town, I took the liberty to tell him, that tho no place could refuse access to his Arms, yet such walks as those ought not to be allowed his person; and I should deserve to be punisht, if, having the honour to be his guide, I led him over ruines and precipices. The King reply'd very pleasantly, *It is but reasonable Princes should follow those whom they have chose for their guides.* When the King had viewed what places he had a mind to, and this Portal among the rest, he granted my desire. But the fatigue and heat of working about the demolishing of this Town, which I never favour'd my self in, threw a sudden swelling, and great inflamation into my Leg. So Monsieur *de Seve*, with whom I had contracted an intimate acquaintance at *Abbeville*, lent me his Coach, and I went to *Sedan*; whither the Count *de Soissons*, Duke of *Guise*, and some other persons of honour retir'd, during their disgrace at Court. I was particularly known to all the company about the Count, and received so many visits, that I had not time to keep my bed. The Count was pleas'd to visit me himself, and no question had an end to serve in it, for this honour was not without a design at the bottom. I, who was pretty well acquainted with the blind side of great men, fell into discourse of his Highnesses great exploits, and enlarg'd much upon the action of *Bray*, and several other things, which I thought most likely to please him. But I knew well enough how to distinguish between my respects and gratitude for his kindness to me, and my main duty, and natural obligations. Therefore when he sent me a purse full of Pistoles next day, telling me, that I might possibly have occasion for Money, in the condition I was in, I would not take it: But sent it back again with this Compliment, That since it did not become a private man, as I was, to refuse a present from one of his Quality, I begg'd him, not wanting Money at this time, to do me the favour to keep that Purse for me, till I had more occasion for it. And it was very happy I behav'd my self thus to him: For Mareschal *Chatillon* did me the favour to write me word as a friend presently after, that my stay at *Sedan* made a great noise at Court, and the King took it ill my Lodging should be the rendezvous of the Count's Family. This news confounded me, and made it necessary for me to be gone next morning for *Paris*, desiring only a Gentleman to make my excuse to the Count *de*

Soissons,

Soiſſons, and acquaint him, that an order from the King occaſioned my ſo ſudden leaving of the place.

XVIII. The next year, which was 1640, I went to the Siege of *Arras,* which was inveſted about *June* by Mareſchal *Chatillon,* and Mareſchal *Metelleray.* The two Generals intending to ſurprize the Town, parted their Forces, and made a ſhew of beſieging ſome other place. So a good part of the Garriſon within this ſtrong Town drew off to reinforce ſome other Garriſons which they were in fear for. But *Arras* was much ſurprized to ſee themſelves inveſted all on a ſudden at the ſame inſtant of time with two Armies in two different parts, ſo that it was impoſſible to put in any ſuccours to them. They preſently drew the Lines of Circumvallation, and Trenches for the Camp. Imagining this Siege might be a work of time, I built me a wooden houſe glazed, and two pretty lodging rooms in it, into one of which Monſieur *Chatillon* uſed to withdraw ſometimes, and there ſteal a Nap to be free from diſturbance.

The Count of *Iſembourg,* Governour of *Arras,* having ſallied out before we inveſted it, to reinforce the Garriſon of *Bethune,* which he apprehended we had a deſign upon; was terribly inraged to ſee *Arras* thus blocked up, and reſolved to put ſome relief into it ; but all the paſſes were ſo ſtrongly kept, that he could find no way of doing it with ſafety. Therefore he ſollicited the Count *de Lamboy,* Commander of the *Spaniſh* Army in the *Low Countries,* to come and raiſe the Siege. The Count accordingly came and encamped ſome leagues from *Arras,* and detached ſome Troops to charge our Trenches. We were at a Council of War in Mareſchal *Melleray's* Tent, when this alarm was given. As ſoon as ever I heard the noiſe, I thought of getting to Horſe, and repairing to my Poſt. Monſieur *de Comminges Guitaut,* my very good friend, ſeeing the riſque I ran of falling into the Enemies hands, who would cut off my paſſage, cryed out, that I ought not be ſuffered to run ſo upon certain death. So the Generals proffer'd me a Convoy of Horſe to ſee me ſafe at my Quarter: But I depended upon the goodneſs of my Horſe, and deſired they would let me go alone, aſſuring them, that I thought this method the leſs dangerous of the two; and ſo away I went immediately. I had a moſt excellent Pad under me, for which I have ſince refus'd fourſcore Piſtoles, and I had reaſon to value him at more, for he ſaved my life upon this occaſion. For as I galloped to recover my Quarter, a Squadron of Horſe ſoy'd me, and rid up full ſpeed to ſtop me, preſenting their Piſtols, and crying, *Stand, ſtand.* I did not care for obeying thoſe orders, ſo long as there were any hopes of eſcaping left, and therefore ſpur'd on with my Piſtol in my hand, and without regarding them, paſt by. There was a little beyond this a very ſteep Hill, which I muſt of neceſſity get up to ſave my ſelf; for the Horſemen ſtill purſued after me, and had blockt up the common road. Finding my ſelf thus ſtreightned, I put my Horſe to it, for his own and his Maſters life: And the poor creature, as if he had been ſenſible of our danger, ſcrambled up this ſharp aſcent ſo faſt, that he had like to have burſt for want of breath. The Enemies were amazed to ſee me get up at this rate, and not daring to follow me this ſteep way, they went up another part of the Hill, to try if they could ſtop me once more. But I getting up a great while before them, gave my Horſe a little breath, and made much of him for the good ſervice he had done me, and then put on again; ſo that I got the heels of them quite, and at laſt reach'd my quarter.

Our Generals, hearing I was purſued by a Squadron of Horſe, were concern'd to know what was become of me. But Mareſchal *Melleray* coming to my quarter a little after, found me at the head of my Regiment, which I had drawn out, and put into a readineſs to do their duty. But there was no occaſion for it at that time, for the Enemy only ſhewed themſelves, and percieving our Camp was in a poſture to recieve them, they wheel'd off again.

XIX. In this Siege I loſt ſeveral things, contrary to my cuſtom, for I us'd to have the good fortune of keeping what I had. One day I ſent out my Servants to get forrage for my Horſes, which were in all about eighteen or twenty. I charg'd them not to carry out above two or three, that if any unlucky accident ſhould happen, I might not hazard the loſs of them all at a time. My Servants for all that, greedy of bringing home more booty, took out ſeven or eight. Some Troops of the Enemy came upon them, and my ſtout blades took no further care but to ſave themſelves, and left my Horſes for pawns. Among the reſt there was one draught Horſe, the

beſt

best of that fort in the world; he was naturally stout and fierce enough for a War Horse, and only wanted tail and shape to make him fit for a General. This Horse not being us'd to the *Spanish* Dialect, and percieving he was got into Enemies hands, began to fall on with his feet and teeth, upon every body that came near him, and grew so mad all of a sudden, that those who had taken him not being able to rule him, let him go again, and said they were sure it was the Devil in the shape of a Horse. He was tyed to another, and so brought him off too; and they were seen come full tilt into the Camp, and streight to my Stable, which they were very well acquainted with the way to. I was much pleased with the stoutness of the Beast, and bad a Servant go see if the rest had taken the same freak, and got away too; but we heard no news of them.

Another time, as I was one night upon the Guard in the Trenches, I lost all my belly-timber. My men had made ready my dinner over night, against next day; and I us'd always when I was upon the Guard my self, to invite all the Officers that went upon duty, with me to dinner. Next day expecting my dinner with some impatience, I had news brought me, that all my provisions were stoln. They took from me above forty Hams, a Powdring-tub full of Salt Meats, and a great many other things, to a considerable value. However I had some good luck with my bad; for our Generals, and some of the principal Officers, hearing my misfortune, sent me in a sufficient recruit for my loss: and I found it was for my Interest to be robb'd, when there was more got than lost by it.

XX. The Besieged one day design'd a considerable Sally, and expected the shifting of the Guards, as the properest time, because then there is always some little confusion. They came out of the City with about eight hundred men, and made up directly to the quarter where we lay. Seeing them come on so briskly, I cry'd out to our *Mareschal de Camp; Sir, these honest fellows hope to have a good bargain of us, and intend to beat us soundly, if we will but let them; I will go meet them* (said I) *and make them a Compliment:* And directing my self to the Officers of our Regiment, *Come Gentlemen,* (said I) *let us go back into the Town with them.* With that I went out of the Trench, and most of the Officers and common Souldiers follow'd me. The Enemies seeing us come on, as brisk to the full as they, were satisfy'd with the civility we intended them, and turn'd short to another part of the Camp, where they were not so well prepar'd for them. There, to give them their due, they fell very foul upon the Regiment of Guards, who gave way, till at last those that supported them beat them back into their Trenches. I had observ'd two or three Officers of my Regiment take no notice, when I call'd to go out of the Trenches, and yet when no danger was nigh, none talkt so big as these men. I thought it became me to make them know their duty; and when I came back, said in some heat, as you may imagine; That since it was a rule the Regiment should obey him, whose place it was to command them, I pretended a right to see this discipline duty observ'd; and I would have that man shot, that did not march when I gave the word. *If you will not observe commands* (said I) *take my place, and I will take yours.* This reproof, given with some passion, because indeed I had always a strict regard for discipline, created me several Enemies: and they said among themselves, *He could but talk thus if he were our General.* I told one of these Officers too, to move him the more, that it was in my power to ruine his honour; and that he was very stout when there was no danger, and shrunk back when there was. He, being conscious in himself that what I said was true, excus'd the thing, and begg'd me to spare him.

XXI. Besides this, I had a great dispute with Monsieur *de P.* the Lieutenant Colonel of my Regiment, upon an occasion that ought not to have bred any quarrel. The Souldiers made perpetually complaints to me for want of their pay, and I thought of an expedient to get some Money, and desir'd the Lieutenant Collonel that he would motion it to the Treasurers of the Army. He, perhaps by the Treasurers, instead of seconding me in the thing, took me up, and askt me very briskly, What I had to do with that? telling me farther, that it was always my custome, not to content my self with my own business, but to concern my self in other people's. I answer'd him with much the same air, That it was my business to take care of the Regiment's good; and since the Souldiers had complain'd to me, I was concern'd to see it remedy'd; and if others did not what they should do, it became

came me to put them in mind of it. He still went on with provoking language; and told me I ought to keep my own Office, for other people knew well enough how to discharge theirs, and had no need of my advice. Seeing him thus unreasonably averse to the common interest of the Regiment, and without any manner of provocation, I thought it was my turn to be sharp too, and told him, that, no disparagement to his quality, there were persons of great honour that thought it no diminution to ask my advice; *And you your self,* said I, *Sir, can do it sometimes, without supposing it any reflection upon you.* Upon this we both grew warm, and there was reason enough to apprehend some mischief would have come of it, but that the Generals, having notice of the thing, reconcil'd us again; and we have been very good friends ever since.

XXII. But the Bishop of *Auxerre,* who was his Relation, hearing of our quarrel, took so violent a picque against me, and to unbecoming his Character, that he resolv'd to do my business effectually with Cardinal *Richelieu,* who hated me already, as much as he lov'd this Bishop. His Brothers, with whom I was intimately acquainted, gave me notice of it, and told me several times, that I must look to my self, for he would ruine me; and he was a terrible man, when he was set upon mischief; which I thought a most extraordinary qualification in a Bishop. I desir'd them to do me good offices to him, and am sure they would have done it with all their hearts, if it had been in their power; but they told me, they had no manner of influence upon him; that he was of a fierce inflexible temper, and like enough to ruine them too, if they should give him any offence. You may well imagine how easie I was with the thoughts of such an Enemy, whom I could call to no account for his injuries neither, because his Robe was his protection. The only way left then was to try what submissions would do; and I can truly say, it is incredible how many of those I made him, and how many several engines I set to work to soften this barbarous man; fearing him especially upon Cardinal *Richelieu*'s account, whose power I had reason to dread: Nay, I went once to his house, with Monsieur d'*Orgeval,* to proffer him any satisfaction he could desire. I protested, that what past between his kinsman and me, was without any the least intention to affront him; but I was come to wait on him, and express my very great concern, that he thought himself injur'd in it. He pretended to be surpriz'd, and told me, I had not injur'd him at all; but as I was arguing the matter with him, and came closer to the point, he very rudely turn'd his back to me all on the sudden, and went away into his Chamber. Thus I lost all my labour upon him, and what his Brothers had told me was true to a tittle, That he would be my ruine; for he occasion'd my being in disgrace, as I shall shew after the taking of *Arras.*

But the true reason why this Bishop would never be reconcil'd to me, was an unhappy necessity he had brought himself under of hating me immortally, by the discourse he had with the Cardinal upon my account, to ingratiate himself there the more effectually. For among other things he told him, I was so absolutely devoted to the King, that whatever he commanded I was ready to do it. This was the very worst thing that could have been said of me to his Eminence, who was fearful and jealous, and apprehended nothing more in any body about the King, than this readiness to serving him, which was laid to my charge. I explain my self no further upon this point now, but you will see hereafter, he shewed me how he understood it, by reducing me to those circumstances which I shall shortly describe, and making me as unhappy as it was possible for me to be; and depriving me as much as he could of my last refuge, his Majesty's protection and assistance. The most remarkable circumstance in all this passage was, that when a Cavalier and an Officer of the Army, as Monsieur de P. his Relation was, could so soon lay aside all his resentments against me; a Bishop, whose character should inspire him with dispositions to Charity and Peace, should hate a man that only fancied had injur'd him, beyond all reconciliation, and value himself upon revenging it to his utter ruine. This so very distant behaviour of a Gentleman of the Sword, and one of the Gown, might be Theme enough for reflection, to a man that understands better than I, how far the wisdom and vertue of a Bishop ought to extend.

XXII. The King having sent out a very large Convoy one day for recruiting the Camp with provisions, and a Squadron of above five thousand Horse along with
them:

them. Mareschal *Melleray* went likewise out of the Camp to meet them, with three thousand Horse more. The Enemies Army snatch'd this opportunity to charge our Trenches. As soon as they were discovered at some distance, the Marquis of *Grammont* who commanded the Horse, said to Mareschal *Chatillon*, with whom I then was waiting for orders. *Sir, Yonder is the Enemy coming, we should go meet them with some Squadrons of Horse to break their first push, and prevent their forcing our Trenches.* The Mareschal *de Chatillon*, who all the world knows was of a strange cold stiff temper, answered without any concern, *Sir, our business now is not to engage the Enemies Army, but to defend our Lines. But, Sir,* said Monsieur *Grammont* again, *it is with a design to defend them that I would march out against them ; the first aggressor is commonly the better man. Say you so, Sir,* reply'd Monsieur *Chatillon, and if you be repuls'd, who shall defend the Trenches then ? Look you,* said he, pointing to *Arras, That Town is our Mistress, and our business is to take that; win it we must at any rate, though it should cost us the last drop of blood in our bodies. We have nothing to do to go seek out Enemies, our work must be to stand still till they come, and see what they have to say to us. Ah, Sir,* said Monsieur *Grammont* in a great passion, *this is perfect Envy. You injure me in stopping me upon this occasion. I will assure you I will complain to the King of it. Well, Sir, I am content you should complain,* reply'd the Mareschal, *but I beg I may know when you do it, and be by : But in the mean while, Sir, upon my honour, I command you to your post, and stir not.* Monsieur *Grammont* withdrew much displeased, and said, he must obey the General, but he would complain, and that loudly.

By this time the Enemies fell on about Monsieur *Ramtzau*'s quarter, and charg'd so furiously, that they cut several Regiments to pieces, plundered all that quarter, and prepared to advance still farther, to try if they could put any succours into the place. The Fort of *Ramtzay* was taken and retaken several times, but at last we continued Masters of it. I attended Monsieur *Chatillon* all the time of the engagement, which lasted about five hours, and had the satisfaction of seeing the whole action without being concerned in it, because our quarter was not attackt, lying a league off. Some of them came to Monsieur *Chatillon*, crying, all was lost, and that the Enemies were coming on to force us ? he reply'd with great indifference, *Stay, stay till they have done ;* and presently after he ordered a body of Reserve, consisting of four thousand Horse, to charge the Enemies all at once. The thing was no sooner said than done. They charged immediately so briskly, that they cleared the Trenches of them, recover'd some Cannon that were lost, and drove them a great way beyond the Camp. Then we saw plainly, and Monsieur *Grammont* himself confest, that it was an instance of Mareschal *Chatillon*'s wisdom to oppose the Horse going out of the Camp, for their stay was the very thing that saved all from being lost.

XXIII. At last when we had sprung a Mine, and made a large breach, and had two more ready to spring, our Generals summon'd the Town to surrender, declaring to them, that if they were able to hold out after two Mines more, they had some reason not to comply; and if they doubted the truth of what they said, they would give them safe conduct, and an opportunity of convincing themselves. Some persons came therefore from the City, and took a particular view of all. And then being satisfied it was impossible for them to hold out any longer, they agreed to a Capitulation, presently after they had made their report; for they allowed them no more than an hours time to consider of it, for fear a longer delay should give them opportunity to defeat the success we expected from those two Mines. So after they were come to a perfect agreement on both sides, and the Articles drawn, the City was delivered into the King's possession again, in the month of *August*, 1640. Cardinal *Richelieu* had promised the Government of it, if it were taken, to Monsieur *St. Preuil*, and he kept his word with him, and put him into it presently after it was reduc'd. Monsieur *St. Preuil*, who as I have said before, was my very particular friend, had given me intimation of it before, and urged me mightily to ask the King for the Lieutenancy of the Town. This was what I could have been well enough pleased with, upon the account of the friendship between us; but not prevailing with my self to beg it, I desir'd him to ask it for me, telling him, he who had so easily secured the Government for himself, might very well obtain the Lieutenancy for me. He that knew well enough how the Cardinal stood affected to me, durst not engage in such a request upon my account; and so, after the reduction of *Arras*, the Lieutenancy under the King was dispos'd of to Monsieur *du Plessis Belliere*; and I staid there for some time in Garrison with my Regiment, which was still that of Mareschal *Brezay*.

The End of the Fourth Book. L l l BOOK

BOOK V.

The Sieur de Pontis is in disgrace. An account of his Confe-
rence with a ghostly Father, upon occasion of a great Fault,
which he and the Sieur de St. Preuil designed to commit. The
cunning management of a Minister's Son, who over-reaches
Cardinal Richelieu, and a great many other persons in France.
Monsieur St. Preuil is in disfavour, and several considerable
particulars related, that were the cause of his Ruine. Monsieur
le Grand invites the Sieur de Pontis to make one in that
Party that was forming against Cardinal Richelieu. Upon
this Occasion the Sieur de Pontis writes a most bitter Letter,
which the Cardinal gets into his possession. The King's Jour-
ney to Roussillon. The Cardinal's tottering Fortune, and his
Victory over his Enemies at last. A long Conference between
him and the Sieur de Pontis, whom he tries once more to draw
over to his Service and Interest. The Cardinal's death, and
shortly after that the King's.

I. IT was not long after the reducing of *Arras*, before I felt the mischievous Effects of that Prelate's Malice, mention'd in the former Book. He set Cardinal *Richelieu* so violently against me, that I found my self in a moment stript
of all, and not allow'd to see the King, any more than the Cardinal, that hated me.
Who, by a piece of confidence that a Man could scarce believe, did not scruple to
flie so high, as to make use of his Authority against one of his own Officers, and one
for whom he knew very well his Majesty had a particular Favour and Esteem. Being
one day come to *Paris* by the King's express Command, to make large Recruits, and
carry them to *Arras*, I employ'd some time in executing this Commission; and some
few days before my return to *Arras* with my new Levies, had a mind to entertain the
Treasurers of the Army at *Aubrieres*, a League out of *Paris*. I treated them as nobly
as I could, sparing no cost to welcome Persons, whose Favour and Friendship it was
my interest to secure; and little thinking, God knows, of the Misfortune that was
then coming upon me; and which made it but too necessary to have husbanded that
Money more prudently. This day of jollity and pleasure, was succeeded by another
very black one to me: For while I was set at Table with my Friends, and my
thoughts wholly bent upon mirth and diversion, there came a Messenger to the house
to speak with me from Monsieur *de Noyers*. I rose immediately, and enquired what
his business was; and he deliver'd me an Order under Monsieur *de Noyers* his own
hand, the substance whereof was, That the Cardinal sent to tell me in the King's
Name, that I need not trouble my self to carry the new Recruits I had raised to *Ar-*
ras; and bade me take notice, that I must be sure not to go out of *Paris*, without the
King's particular leave to do so.

This Message struck me like a Clap of Thunder, and I stood perfectly stupid and
confounded at it. At last, when I was come to my self a little, I told the Messenger
I would not fail to obey the Order he had brought me; and then striving to overcome my self as well as I could, that I might not break good company, I sat down
with my Friends again, without expressing any concern. But in spight of all my
endeavours to the contrary, they perceiv'd it in my countenance; and presently
told me, they saw plain enough by me, I had heard some ill News: But I
put it off as well as I could, and would not discover any thing of the matter to them.
About

About the same time that this Order was brought me, the Cardinal had dispatched Billets to the Exchequer, to forbid them paying me my common Assignments. So I saw my self all at a push brought as low again as I was when I first came young to *Paris*; and not daring to make my appearance at the *Louvre*, was dismal melancholy to see my Fortunes utterly broken in a moment of time. The King, however, still retain'd the same kind inclinations towards me, and sought all opportunities to assure me that he did so. But he stood in such awe of the Cardinal, who had presum'd to shock him so boldly upon my account, that he found it necessary to act a little underhand upon this occasion, and durst not own his kindness for me publickly. So that having a mind to speak with me, he sent me a private intimation, and appointed me a convenient time and place to meet him at; that he might, by all means, conceal it from the Author of my disgrace. One would very hardly believe, that a King should be reduc'd to all these little Contrivances, for fear of one of his Ministers: But the absolute Authority this Cardinal had got over the whole Kingdom, and the Pride he took to make the King himself sensible of it sometimes, is well enough known to justifie the truth of what I say.

II. One day particularly his Majesty desir'd to speak with me, and sent me Orders by *Archambaut*, the first Groom of his Bedchamber, (a person whom he lov'd, and had a particular confidence in) to be in such a Gallery at *St. Germains*, an hour before day. I was punctual to my time, and when I came near the Centinel, desir'd he would have no suspition of me, telling him it was by the King's command, that I came thither at so unseasonable an hour. The Centinel, upon hearing my Name, told me he had directions to let me pass, but entreated me to walk at some distance, because the Rules of the Guard admit no Man to come near a Centinel. So I walk'd in expectation of the King's coming out, who came out suddenly, and took two or three turns with me, as it were by stealth; and after some other discourse told me, He intended to carry me with him to *Versailles*, but that Night had alter'd his resolution, and therefore bade me go to his Privy-Purse, who would furnish me with some Money. The condition I was in, made me diligent to observe such an Order as that was; and accordingly I receiv'd 500 Crowns. Which I lookt upon as a plain demonstration, that he did me the honour to have kind remembrances of me still; and that if it was not in his power to prevent my Misfortune, yet he had a very tender sense of my Sufferings.

And here by the way, I cannot forbear mentioning a Visit I made to Monsieur *Noyers*, who was not my Enemy at the bottom; and therefore I was so free with him, to ask the Reason of my being us'd at this rate. His Reply was like what the Fathers of the Inquisition at *Rome* usually make: *You must needs think* (said he) *the King hath some ground for what he does.* But Sir, said I, I am not conscious to my self that I have done any thing to deserve this. *O look again* (said he) *examine your self, and recollect better. It is not a likely thing all this should come upon you without some very great provocation.* He quarrell'd with Mareschal *Brezay* upon my account, because he, who lov'd me very well, thought Monsieur *Noyers* was my Enemy, and did ill offices; though really I dare be bold to say, that he never hated me in his heart.

III. *Idleness*, they say, *is the Mother of Evils*; and so I found, by experience, in the time of my disgrace. For having then no manner of employment, there happen'd a very unlucky business, which yet Providence so dispos'd, as to make it the occasion of great good to me. There was a certain Lady of quality, both rich and beautiful, with whom Monsieur *St. Preuil* was in love, and would fain have married. A Cousin of *St. Preuil*, and a very pretty Gentleman, was in love with her too, and made the same pretensions to her. Their Passions thus meeting in the same Object, created, as it generally does indeed, a mortal hatred and jealousy between the two Rivals. And Monsieur *St. Preuil*, impatient of any other Pretender, resolv'd to fight him, and determine their difference this hellish way. It is you know one of the common testimonies of the friendship of the world, to engage ones best Friends in this kind of wickedness; and accordingly he chose me for his Second, upon this bloody occasion. But before the design was put in execution, we spent two Months in an employment, that I cannot without horror so much as mention now; which was to fence every day together, that we might learn some extraordinary Pass, by which each of us might quickly dispatch our Man. There was nothing but horrible consequences to be expected

pected from so devilish and mischievous an exercise, if God by a mercy, which I can never adore sufficiently, had not prevented our putting it into practice at last; and how that was brought about I will now inform you.

About this time he put it into my mind to go to Confession, and ask the advice of some good grave Father with regard to our design. I went to the *Feuillans* of *St. Honorius* Street in *Paris*, and desired the first Monk I met, that he would do me the favour to bring me to the speech of the most pious and most learned person of their Monastery, because I had a matter of great consequence to impart to him; as indeed I had felt several pangs of conscience about the matter. Accordingly he sent a very reverend Father to me, and, as the story will shew you, a very honest man. He was an old Gentleman, one *Boromeo*, whose very aspect was able of it self to strike terror into such an old Sinner as I was. After our first salutation, I begg'd the favour of him to hear my Confession, to which he consented. After having revealed to him among other matters, the present engagements I was under, and what wicked industry had been used to prepare my self for a Duel; the good Father, full of horror and amazement to see me in so wretched a condition, said with much vehemence, and great indignation; *With what face have you dared to come before the Tribunal of Jesus Christ, while you continue under this wicked thought of committing so detestable a fault, and exercise and set your self every day to destroy both the body and soul of one of your Brethren? You are in a worse condition than the Devil himself. For that accursed Spirit desires the ruine of others, because he is ruin'd beyond all redemption himself. But you are within the bosom of the Church, and a Member of Christ, and yet you, notwithstanding all this, are contriving to damn one of your own Brothers, and one of your own Members. If this had been some rencounter, which could not have been foreseen nor prevented, and you had lain under an absolute necessity of defending your self; or if it had been any sudden transport of passion, your crime had been much less; and the guilt, tho great even so, had yet made you with such mitigations more capable of mercy. But to sit and prepare your self for such a cursed action in cold blood, and for a long time together to use art and exercise, that you may stab your Brother to the heart with greater sureness and dexterity; Is this to act like a man? Is this agreeable to the Character of a Christian? I cannot give you any Absolution, while you continue under such Circumstances: No, God forbid: I should draw your guilt upon my own head if I did; and my Absolution would be to the full as wicked as your action.*

At the hearing of these words, pronounced with great zeal and emphasis, I was perfectly thunder-struck, so amaz'd and confounded, that I scarce knew where I was. But God was pleased to assist me: And I was so far from opposing any thing the good Father had said to me, that I told him with great temper; He had oblig'd me very highly in the sharpness he had used; that I was now convinced the design I had was what both God and Man must needs abhor; and that now all the hopes I could pretend to, were from the great Mercy of God, and the benefit of his Prayers. The good Father seeing me so sensibly affected with his reproofs, began to speak to me in a milder tone, and with great compassion said, *Your fault, Sir, is must be confest is so great, that it seems to be above all forgiveness; but nothing is impossible with God. You must implore his Mercy, you must have recourse to Prayers and Tears. And yet, alas! which way can you ask his Mercy? With what confidence can you pray, or come into his presence, with so black a guilt about you?* Perceiving my self moved with the affectionate behaviour of this good Father, and the prevailing power of Truth, I rose up, and he rising at the same time, I embraced him with most sincere kindness, and told him, That I found no reason to hope from any thing in my self, but I reposed great confidence in his Prayers, and I begg'd them of him most heartily. He embrac'd me again, and with the compassion of a true Father answered, *Well, Sir, I promise to remember you in the holy Sacrifice of the Mass. It is to be hoped that God, for the sake of that blood which Christ hath shed for Sinners, will hear my Prayers.* I begg'd to know his name, that I might have the happiness of visiting him sometimes. He told it me, and withal, that he should be exceeding glad to serve me, and so I went home, very much mov'd with what had past.

IV. Monsieur *St. Preuil* came, according to his custom, to practice with me as before, and was much surprized to hear me say, I intended to trouble my self no farther about that matter; that I had discoursed a man who had dealt plainly with me, and being very well satisfied with one Lecture upon the subject, I had no inclination to provoke another. *St. Preuil*, whom all the world knew to be an obstinate man, and who

who very feldom troubled himfelf with going to Confeffion, anfwered me merrily ; *Nay, now we are come to a fine pafs, what new fit of devotion hath poffeft thee now, man ? Thefe art grown mighty confcientious. But prithee where is this man? I would fain fpeak with him too. Would you?* faid I, *well, and you fhall if you will. I am pretty confident he will ftun you as well as me, though you were ten times as wicked as you are. But who is it,* faid he again ; I promifed to carry him to him, and then told him who it was, and withal, that this good Father had not fpared me, and I was very fure would be no more tender of him. *I proteft,* faid St. Preuil, *thou art bravely hoodwinkt with thy Monks, this was the only qualification wanting to compleat thee.* Hark you, faid I, *do not think to put it off with a jeft. I am much miftaken if he do not difarm you prefently, as much as he has done me. Put on all your Courage, and keep as much as you pleafe, you muft do it to purpofe, if you are able to ftand before this Monk. Well,* faid he, *that's as time fhall try.*

I carried him to the Monaftery, and Father *Borromeo* coming into the Garden to us, *Father,* faid I, *I have brought you here a wickeder wretch than my felf ; though I own that before God I may have more to anfwer for than he. Pray try if you can convert him.* And then I went into another walk, leaving them to talk freely together. St. Preuil having opened his cafe to the good Father, he took him up fo roundly, and gave him fo lively a reprefentation of the horrible wickednefs of that crime in particular, and his whole converfation in general, and the dreadful judgments that threatned him for them, that as ftout as he was he brought him down ; and he that came thither with a defign to ridicule the Monk, was confounded above what can be expreft. Infomuch that after we had taken our leave of the Father, he faid to me in our way home ; *I have it up to the hilts. He hath talkt to me at fuch a rate, that if I would be fure of my Salvation, I fhould think the only thing I need do, were to turn Capuchin.* I was aftonifh'd to find this Monks difcourfe had made fo deep an impreffion upon his mind. For, befides that from that inftant he laid afide all thoughts of this Duel, it made fome confiderable alteration in him; for till then he had been a rank Atheift, and ufed his utmoft endeavours to corrupt me. I went feveral times afterwards to vifit Father *Borromeo,* and was always very much edified by his converfation. But ftill both Monfieur St. *Preuil* and I were grievoufly out of the way, which, as I perceive fince, we ought to have taken, if we would have lived like Chriftians indeed. And we fhall fee prefently the tragical end of this unfortunate man, whom I always lookt upon as my friend, and who falling afterwards into Cardinal *Richelieu*'s disfavour, as I was at prefent, came at laft to a moft unhappy death.

V. I formerly took notice of fome Horfes that I loft, while we were befieging *Arras :* But now, while I was out of favour, I loft a moft extraordinary one, which I call'd *Millefleurs,* becaufe he was curioufly fpotted, and mark'd with all forts of Colours. The manner how he was loft, and return'd to me again, giving an occafion to fpeak of the perfon that ftole him, obliges me to give a fmall account, which I dare fay will be entertaining enough, concerning the man who had not the fortune to cheat me, till he had exercis'd his faculty firft upon almoft all *France.* He was the Son of one *Regis,* a Minifter in the City of *Orange.* He had lifted himfelf in the Emperours fervice, againft his own natural Prince, the King of *France.* At the battel of *Wolfenbuttel* our men took him Prifoner, and he was to have been beheaded, which is the punifhment ufed to Subjects that bear arms againft their own King. But this young man, who had abundance of wit, made ufe of it in this extremity, and pretended he was a Relation of Monfieur *Lefdiguieres,* calling himfelf the Baron of *Champoleon.* The Count *de Guebriant,* hearing he was related to Monfieur *Lefdiguieres,* faid, He was too much obliged to Monfieur *de Lefdiguieres,* not to fpare the life of any Kinfman of his. So he committed him to the care of Monfieur *de Choify de Caan,* Chancellour to Monfieur the Duke of *Orleans,* and Intendant of the Army at that time, that he might conduct him to *Paris.* When they came to the laft Inn near *Paris,* Monfieur *Choify de Caen* excus'd himfelf to the young Gentleman, that he had no convenience of lodging with him at his quarters, becaufe he had a Family there, a Wife and Children of his own, and it was the cuftom of *Paris* for every man to lodge at his own houfe ; but that he fhould be glad to fee him as often as he pleafed ; and fo gave him at parting ten Piftoles to fupply his prefent occafions.

VI. Our young Baron, being a perfon of a great deal of wit, and a moft prodigious memory, one that talkt pertinently upon all forts of fubjects, and knew all the

Mmm   Princes

Princes of *Germany*, and understood all the different Interests of their several Governments, resolv'd to put a trick upon the Court of *France*, which he did with wonderful dexterity and address. He found means, by some friends, that he quickly got at *Paris*, to gain access to Cardinal *Richelieu*: With him he discoursed over all the concerns, and most private Intrigues of *Germany*, and that with so much ingenuity, such solidity, and in so taking a manner, that he perfectly imposed upon him : And made him believe that he was an exceeding fit person for his purpose ; that he was acquainted with most of the Princes of the Empire ; that he could for a word speaking procure five or six thousand Horse, that this Duke, that Count, and the other Prince, were ready to furnish him with. The Cardinal had a mind to be satisfy'd in the truth of what he said, and to that purpose he conferr'd with some of his Confidents, who were perfectly well acquainted with all the affairs of *Germany*, about it. He read over besides several Memoirs that he had by him, concerning all these several Princes ; and at last finding all agree with what this young Baron had told him, he grew very confident and secure, and therefore having no manner of jealousy about him, he spoke thus to a person of his own Court ; *This young man hath an exact knowledge of all these matters, we must employ him, and he may be of great use to us.* To put him into a good disposition for his service, he gave order to Monsieur *des Noyers* to draw a bill for four thousand Livres for him. He finding the jest turn to so good account (and being a most extraordinary dextrous person at every thing) presently counterfeited Monsieur *des Noyers* his Letter, and instead of four, put in twelve thousand Livres, and subscribed it *Noyers* as well as Monsieur *des Noyers* himself. For in truth he could do whatever he had a mind to, his wit his fingers, his whole body was entirely at his disposal, he counterfeited all sorts of hands to a miracle, plaid extreme finely upon all kinds of Musick ; and in short he was out at nothing, but did all with a natural easiness, a gracefulness and exactness peculiar to him.

He was not content to over-reach the King's Treasury only, but cheated several private men at the same rate, under pretence of being sent by the Cardinal to transact some important affairs in *Germany*. Among others he attempted to catch the Duke of *Bouillon*, but this bout he was caught himself, and fell very pleasantly into his own Net. He went to wait on Monsieur *Bouillon*, and made him a very handsome and elaborate compliment to incline him to grant his request, which was to give him a Letter of recommendation to *Sedan*, whither he said the Cardinal sent him, to take that place in his way to *Germany*, and there negotiate some affairs which the Court had intrusted him with. The favour he desired of Monsieur *Bouillon* was, that when he came to *Sedan*, he might have a good Convoy to secure his passage forward. The Duke *de Bouillon* could not refuse him, because of the Cardinal, whom he durst not offend, and therefore writ to his Lieutenant at *Sedan*, and commanded him to furnish that Gentleman the Bearer with a good Convoy, because he was sent into *Germany* upon business of great consequence. Our Baron had no sooner got this Letter, but he counterfeited another extreme like it, and in that wrote to the Lieutenant ; That the Bearer was a Gentleman of great quality, one for whom the Cardinal had a particular affection and esteem, and was sent by him to dispatch some very important business in *Germany* ; therefore it was his order, that he would furnish him with what Convoy he should desire himself to secure his passage thither, and deny him nothing he wanted ; for he thought it very fortunate, that such an occasion as this offered it self, whereby he might shew the Cardinal how ready he was to serve him. But he could not tell how to counterfeit the Seal, so conveniently as the writing ; and therefore was at the trouble of having one made on purpose, from the impression upon Monsieur *Bouillon*'s original Letter.

After this was done away he went to *Sedan*, where when he had delivered the forged Letter to the Lieutenant, he upon reading it promised to see his Master's commands duely obeyed. The young Baron was in great haste to be gone that night, but the Lieutenant told him that was impossible, for their best Horsemen were abroad in the Country, and would not come back till the evening, and besides the remaining part of that day was time little enough to get all things ready ; but he promised him all should be at his service next morning early, and so should three hundred Pistoles, which was the summ he desired to be furnished with. The young Baron was very uneasy under this delay, fearing that before next day his trick might some way or other happen to be discovered. But there was no remedy, and therefore making a vertue of necessity, and endeavouring to keep up his character, he went to wait

on

on the Dutchess of *Bouillon*, who was then at *Sedan*, and received him with great civility and respect.

In the mean while, as ill luck would have it, the Duke of *Bouillon*'s Secretary came that very night from *Paris* to *Sedan*, about some business of his Master's. He presently understood, that a Gentleman was come from *Paris* a little before, with a Letter from Monsieur *Bouillon*, and orders in it to his Lieutenant to send a good Convoy with the Bearer, and supply him with two or three hundred Pistoles, if he desir'd it. He was much surpriz'd that his Master had mentioned nothing of the matter to him, and said immediately, that he by no means understood the meaning of this being made a secret to him, that he knew Monsieur *Bouillon*'s temper pretty well, and that he did not use to scatter his Pistoles so liberally, and that he had a great mind, for his own satisfaction, to see this Letter. They shewed it him, and upon sight of it, *Well,* says he, *I cannot deny this Writing and Seal to be my Master's, but still I am mightily mistaken if this be not a forged Letter; for though it be my Master's hand, I am sure it is not his sense.* Then he went to wait on the Dutchess of *Bouillon*, and told her his thoughts freely. But this Lady who was cruelly afraid of the Cardinal, was very urgent, that the Gentleman might have what he wanted. *We do not stand very well with the Cardinal already,* says she, *and this unhappy accident will quite ruine us. We had better run the risque on't, and pray let them give him whatever he would have.* The Secretary answered very resolutely, that he did not question but the fellow was a Cheat, and he desired to see him before they parted with any thing.

Next day, when the Baron came to enquire if all was ready, the Lieutenant told him, he had given orders for every thing, and that he might be going as soon as he pleas'd; but Monsieur *Bouillon*'s Secretary came thither the last night, and desired to speak with him before he went. This news a little disordered him, but setting a good face upon the matter, he reply'd very briskly, That was very well, and he should be exceeding glad to see him. They brought them together, and when the Secretary had viewed him well, he said before all the Company; *Sir, I came from Paris since you did, and am a little surpriz'd my Master should never take any notice to me of the Letter you have brought. I am pretty well acquainted with his temper, and must own, I can very hardly believe he would have kept this from me. And besides, I never saw you at our house, though I were there at that time.* The young Baron in great wrath to find the trick discovered, answered him, *What it seems you take me for a Cheat then? I would have you to know I am a Gentleman. I will complain of this usage to the Cardinal.* *Sir,* said the Secretary, *I will venture what you please, that this Letter was never written by my Master, tho both the Seal and the Hand are very like his. You are very rude to me* (said the Gentleman) *and this affront you shall pay dearly for. Well, Sir,* (said the Secretary) *though it should cost me my life, you shall not go till I have first written to my Master, and in the mean while you and I will be Prisoners together.*

Still Madam *Bouillon* cry'd, *Pray let him go, give him all he wants; this man will be our undoing:* But the Secretary was so obstinate, that both were put under confinement, as he desired, till they could hear farther from the Duke of *Bouillon.* Some time after, there came a Minister to make Madam *Bouillon* a visit, who being in great grief about this business, communicated to him the occasion of all her fear and trouble; and begg'd he would take the pains to go see this man that they had secur'd. This Minister was well acquainted with the young Baron's Father at *Orange*, and had been formerly acquainted with him himself. So when he was come into the room, and had lookt a little earnestly upon him, he recollected his face, and told him he desir'd a word with him in private. When they were alone, *Ho Sir* (said he) *are not you such a mans Son? Are not you asham'd to bring a scandal upon your family, by such a pittiful action?* The young man was much confounded, and confest the whole matter to him; begging him to excuse the necessity that had driven him to these courses; and assist him in his present condition, by getting him free of the ill circumstances he lay under. He told him too, tho the Letter now under examination was, he must confess, a forg'd one, yet the Duke of *Bouillon* did really give him one much to the same purpose; and that Cardinal *Richelieu* did indeed make use of him for some business in *Germany*, the affairs of which Country he understood perfectly well, and had received from the Cardinal a considerable summ of Money to carry on this design. The Minister promised to get him his liberty. And having informed the Dutchess of *Bouillon*, and the Secretary in the truth of the whole story, it was thought the best way to dismiss him quietly,

quietly, and make as little noise of the thing as they could, for fear of disobliging the Cardinal.

VII. Upon this he hired him a place in the Coach to go back for *Paris*. But growing no wiser by his late misfortune, he cheated the Master of the Coach, as well as he had done other people. For seeing the Book-keeper much perplexed in telling the Money, because people had paid in several sorts of coin, and odd pieces, he, who was exceeding ready at every thing, pretended great civility, and told the man, the tale of that Money was very easy. He took all the Money, and having sorted it out into several parcels, according to the several kinds of Money, made all the summ come right presently. Afterwards taking it all in both his hands, and powring it into the Bag, he contrived to slip some of it up into his sleeves, which was never found out till they came to *Paris*; and then emptying the Bag, they found a great deal wanting. But he for his part was got off by another wile in this Journey.

There was an honest old burly *Swisse* rode by the Coach side, and our Baron in great civility and compassion told him, he saw that travelling on Horseback was very inconvenient to him, and if he pleased to accept his place in the Coach they would ease one another, and ride in the Coach by turns. The *Swisse*, who was a good plain man, at first excused himself from accepting the offer; but at last the Baron was so obliging, and so importunately civil, that there was no refusing him. So he alighted and came into the Coach, and the Baron took his Horse. When they came to pay at the Inn, he called to the *Swisse*, *Do not trouble your self, Sir, I will lay down for you, and we will reckon by and by.* Thus he did several times, till at last this honest fellow, with the true simplicity of a *Swisse*, gave him his Purse, and told him he would have him take as much as he was out of pocket already, and what he might be more till their Journeys end. But the young man, when he had got the *Swisse*'s Horse and Purse both, which was the very thing he would be at, took no farther care than to make off, and so he left the Company, and galloped before quite to *Paris*.

Then it was, that he found an opportunity of trapping me, as well as other people. He took lodgings in a Taylor's house, and had a room well furnished, making his Landlord believe, he was a person of great Significance, that he had orders from the Cardinal to go into *Germany*, upon a Commission of consequence; that he was to have the command of seven or eight thousand Horse there, and if he pleased would make him his Intendant; he promised him mighty matters, and puff'd him up with wonderful expectations, till by degrees he had hookt him in to provide him a noble Equipage, a great many fine Cloathes, and abundance of Plate. This generous Taylor, promis'd himself to raise his fortunes this way, and never thought his Money in any danger, with a person that past for so great a Favourite and Confident of the Cardinal's, He had a mind to provide him better Lodgings, and brought him to a very well furnish'd House, where I then lay, and so plac'd him still more conveniently for the acting his part. He was of so pleasant a Wit, so happy a Memory, so well vers'd in History, and had such an excellent faculty of setting off all he had a mind to say, that all that heard him talk were charm'd with his conversation: Every body strove who should enjoy him most, his company and friendship was courted, as a person of the best quality and reputation; and he manag'd himself so well as always to be thought such a one. In short, he had an art of bewitching all the world to that degree, that the most nice and ingenious persons were ready to serve him, and thought it an honour to do it even with their Purse, as well as any thing else. I was as deep in as other people, and as absolutely charm'd with his company, and professions of friendship to me. Then he went constantly to wait upon Cardinal *Richelieu*, and some other great people at Court, and put upon them as cunningly as upon any of the little ones.

At last, when he had got a good quantity of Plate and Cloathes together, and sent them away before him, and provided a handsome Equipage, he set his heart upon my Horse *Millefleurs*, which was really one of the best and beautifullest Pads that ever went upon a Road. He borrowed this Horse to go wait upon his Eminence at *Ruel*, and had ordered his Equipage to stay for him at a place he had appointed them. No body could suspect any thing from a man that behav'd himself so genteely, and I, was as easie as others, never scrupled the lending him my Pad, but thought it an honour to oblige him. And I paid for my honour: For, instead of going to *Ruel*, he made directly for *Flanders*, and troopt off with all that he had borrow'd. But by

good

good Fortune the Knave was taken Prifoner by a Party out of *Aire*, or *Bethune*, and my Horfe was afterwards retaken by another Party from *Arras*; and there fell into the hands of an Officer, for whom I had procur'd the Command of a Company.

In the mean while, hearing no news of my Horfe, and knowing how the poor Taylor, and fome others that had been concern'd with him, were left in the lurch, I began to be fatisfy'd that I was robb'd as well as they. I wrote away into *Catalonia*, *Provence*, *Flanders*, *Germany*, and every place where I had any acquaintance, that if they could light of my Horfe, (for he was very remarkable, and generally known) they fhould feize him, and fend him back to me, for he had been ftolen away from me. Shortly after Monfieur *Bourgailles*, who fucceeded me as Major of the Regiment of *Brezay*, and to whom I had given my Command of firft Captain freely, being then at *Arras*, wrote me word, that the Officer I had fpoke of, had my Horfe. I fent away to him prefently, and thought he had more honour, and more friendfhip for me, than to keep my Horfe, which I valu'd fo much, from me. But truly his anfwer was, He had fwapp'd another for him, and there was no reafon he fhould lofe by the bargain. A little after, this Officer's occafions call'd him to *Paris*, and the Major fent me word he came upon my Horfe. I went ftrait to his Lodgings, as foon as I had this notice, and not finding him within, examined the Stable. There I found my own Horfe, and bade the Groom faddle him, and when his Mafter came in, tell him I had taken him out to go to fuch a place, and he would not be angry. So I went home with my *Milleſteurs*, but never heard any more of my Captain, who did not think fit to come and make his demands, for what he knew well enough he had no right to. I loft this fine Horfe afterwards, when I was taken Prifoner, and carry'd into *Germany*, an account whereof you will find in the fequel of thefe *Memoirs*.

VIII. The particular friendfhip that had been all along between Monfieur *St. Preuil* and me, ever fince my being Lieutenant in his Company of Guards, obliges me to give an account of his difgrace, and his death, which happen'd at this time, while I my felf was out of favour. I imagine that a Relation of the whole matter will not be thought tedious or impertinent, and fhall therefore lay down the feveral heads of Accufation brought againft him, becaufe the great intimacy between us, gave me an opportunity of knowing the whole truth of the Cafe, and as well what might be faid in his juftification, as what he was really guilty in.

You muft know then, that Monfieur *St. Preuil* was grown ôdious, and at laft loft his Head upon four or five Articles; and all this by the judgment of God, who thought fit to make an Example of the moft obftinate Man that perhaps ever was in the Army. Though the greateft part of the matters alledg'd againft him, and which brought him to ruine, were not, in truth, fo much to his difadvantage, as the World generally believ'd. The firft Article was this: A Monk of the famous Abby of *St. Vaſt* at *Arras*, bearing a grudge to his Prior, and refolving to be reveng'd on him, came to fee, or fome other way gave information to Monfieur *St. Preuil*, that there were a great many Arms in that Abby which had lay'n conceal'd there, ever fince the *Spaniards* had been in poffeffion of the Town. To confirm this, he left a Note with him, that fignify'd the feveral places exactly where thefe Arms were to be found; and he affur'd him, that there were a great many more befides, conceal'd in a Nunnery of the fame Town. Upon this News, Monfieur *St. Preuil* made a Vifit to the Prior of that Abby, and told him, *He was much furpriz'd at an Information that had been brought him, concerning fome Arms that lay hid in his Monaſtery; and that he muſt deliver all thoſe Arms to him, becauſe they were the King's Right.* The Prior would own nothing of the matter, and Monfieur *St. Preuil* told him at laft, *He knew well enough where to find them*, and went away in a paffion. But prefently after he came again with his Guards, and ordering fearch to be made according to the Monk's inftructions, he found, and carried them away, and gave the Prior very rough and threatning language, telling him, *That he would lay all the Monks Monaſteries in the Town flat to the ground; and that they were only a Neſt of Rogniſh Monks that were Traytors to the King, and held Correſpondence with the* Spaniard. Still this Prior ftood it out, that he knew nothing of the matter, and poffibly he might fay true; for it is a very common thing for fuch Religious Houfes to change their Superiors frequently, and fometimes to keep the new comers in ignorance of many things done the time of their Predeceffors.

From

From this Abby, Monſieur *St. Preuil* went to the Lady Abbeſs of the Nunnery which the ſame Monk had told him of, and ſaid, *He was much concerned to hear that they ſhould offer to conceal a great many Arms that belonged to the King, and that he was come in his Majeſties Name to demand them.* The Lady anſwer'd, *That truly ſhe had been but a Year Abbeſs, and for her part was privy to nothing of that kind ; That ſhe believed her Nuns knew nothing of it neither, but if he would pleaſe to come, and ſatisfy himſelf, the Gates ſhould be opened, and no oppoſition made there to the Service and Intereſts of his Majeſty.* Monſieur *St. Preuil* took the liberty they offer'd him, and coming at mid-day with a great deal of company, he went into the Monaſtery, and took all the Arms away, which were found exactly in the place he had been directed to. But this created Monſieur *St. Preuil* a world of Enemies, and rais'd a mighty Clamor againſt him. The Nuns Relations gave out, That he broke into the Monaſtery by Force ; that he abuſed the Nuns, and expos'd them to be abuſed by vile profligate Fellows. There was indeed one Nun in that Monaſtery exceeding handſom, and all the Town knew it well enough ; and this was it that gave ground to that part of the Accuſation. But I, who knew Monſieur *St. Preuil* throughly, dare engage for him, that he could never have been guilty of ſo brutiſh an Action. 'Tis poſſible he might throw out ſome reproachful words againſt the Nuns, in the paſſion he was in, to find Arms conceal'd in their Monaſtery. But this was excuſable in a perſon of his haſty temper, and upon ſuch an occaſion as the Service of his Majeſty was concern'd in ; and this was ſo far countenanc'd above, that when this buſineſs came to be known at Court, the King immediately ſent his Mandate to depoſe the Prior.

IX. He was more to blame in the ſecond Article alledg'd againſt him. There was a Mealman of *Arras*, who, under pretence of going to buy up Corn in the Enemy's Frontier Towns, us'd privately to carry them intelligence concerning the condition of the Town and the Garriſon. Monſieur *St. Preuil*, upon information given of this, ſecur'd him, and would have had the Law took its courſe. But the Man's Wife, who was one of the prettieſt Women in all that Country, fell at his Feet in tears, and begg'd him, for her ſake, to ſpare her Husband's life. Monſieur *St. Preuil*, vanquiſhe with her tears, ſaid, *Look you Miſtreſs, I do pardon your Husband for your ſake, but let it be your care that he be guilty of this no more, for I won't pardon him again.* It was ſaid, that he was too familiar with this Woman, and that her Husband was ſenſible of it ; nay more, that he kept on his former correſpondence with the Enemies, and was adviſed by them, to ſuffer his Wife to be thus abuſed, and pretend ignorance, that ſo by her means he might gain a more perfect underſtanding of the Governour's deſigns, and be more capable of doing them ſervice, for which they promis'd to reward him abundantly.

This poor Fellow however was caught a ſecond time, and put in Priſon. But for all Monſieur *St. Preuil's* brave Reſolutions to puniſh him, if he were found faulty any more, he pardon'd him then too, not being proof againſt the entreaties and tears of his Wife, whom he lov'd. But he threatned him however, *That nothing ſhould ſave him from the Gallows, if he did ſo any more.* Three or four Months after, the Mealman, depending ſtill upon the Governour's kindneſs for his Wife, ſet the old Trade on foot again, and carry'd on the ſame correſpondence as before. But then he found himſelf miſtaken in his Meaſures ; for he that was content to diſpenſe with his Wife's fidelity to her Husband, only to ſecure him in the breach of his own to his King, in hopes of a great Reward from the Kingdom's Enemies, was at laſt rewarded with a Halter for all the good ſervices he had done them. A Spy, that was taken at *Arras*, diſcover'd him, and depos'd that he came thither upon this Rogue's perſwaſion, and upon the confronting of them, the Mealman was convicted of Treaſon againſt the State, and as ſuch by the Intendant of Juſtice and Preſident of the Place, was ſentenced to be hang'd.

The condemnation of this Man, as well as he deſerv'd it, yet ſet People bitterly againſt Monſieur *St. Preuil* ; and every body ſaid, he had hang'd the Husband, that he might have a freer enjoyment of the Wife. Which was very far from true : For though he carry'd himſelf very ill upon her account, as was notorious from the Preſents he made her, yet he did not hang her Husband for any other reaſon , than his own manifeſt guilt. Nay, in truth, he had no hand in condemning him, for all that was done by the Intendant of Juſtice, and the Preſident. But Providence brought on Monſieur *St. Preuil* inſenſibly to his ruine, becauſe of his impiety , and great ex-

travagances. And I muſt own it as a particular mercy, which I can never be ſufficiently thankful for, that having great reaſon to love him, and being extremely obliged by him, I was yet in no degree a partaker in his Follies, notwithſtanding the mighty intimacy between us. It was not long of him that I was not engag'd in his Faults,
for during my diſgrace I ſtole down to *Arras* to ſee him, and he then took great pains
to draw me into the ſame diſorderly courſes with himſelf. But my ſenſe of Honour,
and the conſtant regard I had for Juſtice, made me abhor the Crime I ſaw him engag'd in; and I diſcourſt him with ſo much earneſtneſs, and gave him ſo lively a re-
preſentation of the conſequence he had reaſon to apprehend from his vicious exceſſes,
that we had like to have quarrell'd downright. *I have no mind* (ſaid I at laſt) *to loſe
my Head with you. And if you do not take heed, ſome end will come of this, that cannot turn
either to your Honour, or your Advantage, and really I could find in my heart to have no more
to do with you.* What then, *reply'd he with ſome concern*, have you a mind in good ear-
neſt to make an eternal Quarrel, and renounce all Friendſhip with me for the future?
No, ſaid I, *it is not poſſible for me to hate you; and I am ſo far from doing ſo, that I
ſhould be wanting to one of the greateſt duties of a Friend, if I ſhould forbear reproving you
upon theſe occaſions. But then I cannot be ſo complaiſant neither, to ſhew my friendſhip, by engaging in things that I am very fearful will turn to your diſhonour.* 'Tis ſtrange to me, ſaid
I again, that *you ſhould not conſider how every body's mouth is open'd againſt you. They are
eternally complaining of many things which you ought to redreſs. All this muſt be naught at laſt.*
Theſe words made ſome impreſſion upon him, but not ſo much as I could have wiſht
for his ſake they had done. For if he had conſider'd what I ſaid as he ought, inſtead of being angry, and taking it ill from me, he ſhould rather have turned his paſſion againſt himſelf, and have taken care to mend.

X. The third Article was grounded upon nothing but meerly a misfortune, and *St.
Preuil* was in no fault at all about it. The Mareſchal of *Melleray* having taken *Bapaume* upon Capitulation, it was agreed, that the Garriſon ſhould next morning at
eight of the Clock draw off, and go to *Doway*. There was notice given at the ſame
time to the Governours of the frontier Towns to ſtop the Couriers, and ſend out no
Parties, becauſe this Garriſon was to go from *Bapaume* at the hour aforeſaid, and
would be at *Doway* by three in the Aftereoon. But ſome hinderances happening, the
Garriſon could not move till three or four in the Afternoon, and ſo was forc'd to lye
abroad all night about a league ſhort of *Doway*. The Convoy allowed them by Mareſchal *Melleray*, being ordered only to ſee them ſafe within a league of *Doway*, was
gone back. That evening a Spy brought Monſieur *St. Preuil* word, that four hundred of the Garriſon at *Bethune* were making a Sally upon ſome deſign; whereupon
a Council was called, at which I my ſelf was preſent, being then at *Arras* upon a viſit
to the Governour, and we were all of opinion, that they might make ſome attempt
upon the place, and that it was the ſafeſt way to put the men all in a readineſs, and
command that they ſhould ſtand to their arms:

About midnight came another Spy, and he ſaid there were four hundred men
and ſome Horſe ſally'd at the Gate over againſt *Arras*. So, after calling the Captains together, it was reſolv'd to go out, and face the Enemy. I went along with
Monſieur *St. Preuil*; and we were about ſix hundred Foot, and three hundred Horſe.
When we were at ſome diſtance from the place where the Garriſon of *Bapaume* was
encamp'd, Monſieur *St. Preuil* and I rid on before with a detachment of Horſe, and
when Monſieur *St. Preuil* ſaw the fires of their Camp, he ſaid, *Theſe are certainly Enemies, we muſt charge them briskly before they are aware of us.* I was not altogether ſo eager
as he, and therefore enquir'd of him, whether the Road between *Bapaume* and *Doway*
did not lye thereabouts, for poſſibly it might (I told him) be the Garriſon from *Bapaume*. He ſaid, that was impoſſible, for his Letters ſaid they march'd out at eight
in the morning, and were to be at *Doway* by three in the afternoon the day before. Then
we joyn'd our Troops again, and made ready for fight.

The Garriſon of *Bapaume* ſeeing us come on to charge them, put themſelves in a
poſture to receive us, and march'd forward with an intent to defend themſelves; but
however they firſt ſent a Trumpet that belong'd to Mareſchal *Melleray*. The Trumpet ſeeing our men come on hotly, durſt not come up to them, but wheel'd about to
recover the Rear of our Troops. So at firſt there were ſeveral ſhot made on both
ſides. Thoſe of *Bapaume* ſeeing the action come ſo warmly on, and ſuſpecting we
did not know who they were, call'd out, *Bapaume, Bapaume.* Aſſoon as ever Monſieur

fieur *St. Preuil* heard this word, he founded a Retreat ; but the Souldiers were so elevated, and hot, that there was no keeping them from plundering the Baggage. At laſt, when we began to cool a little, we conſulted what was fit to be done in this caſe. For my part, I told Monſieur *St. Preuil*, that it lookt to me like a very ugly buſineſs ; that Mareſchal *Melleray's* honour was at ſtake, and the miſchievous conſequences of injuring that, ought to be prevented by any ſort of ſatisfaction. Monſieur *St. Preuil* was much of the ſame opinion, for he ſaw the dangerous effects of it as well as I.

He went therefore immediately to wait on the Governour of *Bapaume*, and ſpoke to him in theſe very ſubmiſſive terms ; *Sir, I am extremely concern'd at this misfortune that hath happen'd : I heartily ask your pardon, but I ſolemnly proteſt there was no malicious deſign on our ſide. I had notice ſent me yeſterday, that you would be at* Doway *yeſterday by three in the afternoon without fail, and it is now ſix in the morning. Who could have imagin'd that you ſhould be in the field all this while ? Beſides, I had intelligence that there was a party ſally'd out of* Bethune. *We thought you had been that party, and the rather, becauſe you drew up againſt us, without ever ſending a Trumpet. You had all the probability in the world againſt you. As for what is paſt, Sir, I aſſure you, that neither you nor any of your Souldiers ſhall be loſers by it : For I will order reſtitution to be made you immediately. You know your ſelf one cannot govern men always, when they are in the firſt heat of action : This put it out of my power to contain mine now, ſo ſoon as I deſir'd to have done it.*

The Governour, who was a man of honour, made a very civil return. That he was very well ſatisfy'd it was purely a misfortune ; that the Trumpet they ſent was afraid and ſo did not deliver his meſſage ; and that he thought himſelf much oblig'd to him for his civility. Monſieur *St. Preuil* order'd all that was taken from them to be reſtor'd, and paid ſome of the Souldiers out of his own Money for what they had loſt ; which the Governour reſented ſo kindly, as publickly to acknowledge his generoſity. Monſieur *St. Preuil* however was aware what advantage his Enemies might take of this unhappy accident, to run him down at Court for it, and therefore he entreated the Governour of *Bapaume* to give him in writing what he had ſaid by word of mouth, and ſign it with his own hand, that if there ſhould ever be need of any ſuch thing, he might produce it in juſtification of himſelf. Which he immediately did, with great expreſſions of kindneſs ; and did not only ſign it himſelf, but took care that all the Captains with him ſhould ſubſcribe it too.

But, tho the innocence of Monſieur *St. Preuil* was ſo clear in this particular, yet his Enemies made uſe of his misfortune to bring a malicious accuſation againſt him : And, which happen'd very unluckily for him, he was upon no good terms with Monſieur *Melleray* before. For the Mareſchal going to take a view of a City in *Flanders*, went through *Arras*, depending upon *St. Preuil*, who was much his friend, for ſeven or eight hundred Horſe, to attend him to the place whither he was going. But he was much concern'd at *St. Preuil's* refuſal, who told him, he could not poſſibly let him have them ; for if the Enemy ſhould attempt the place, when the Garriſon was ſo much weakned, he might hazard the loſs both of the Town, and himſelf. This denyal gall'd the Mareſchal much, and the more, becauſe he had told Cardinal *Richelieu* at his coming away, That as for Horſe, he was ſecure of them from the Garriſon of *Arras*.

XI. The fourth Article was really the ſtrongeſt and moſt conſiderable of them all ; and I was a witneſs of that too, being at *Arras* when the thing which gave foundation to it hapned, upon an occaſion that I ſhall now relate, tho I hinted ſomething toward it before. I was ſaying, that Monſieur *St. Preuil* and I had no very good underſtanding between us, and I came almoſt to downright breaking with him for his extravagances. Some little time after my return to *Paris*, Monſieur *St. Preuil* writ to Mareſchal *Brezay*, that we had had ſome little ruffle, and he would be glad to be reconcil'd to me, and to make his peace by procuring me the Lieutenancy of *Arras*, which Monſieur *de Pleſſis Belliere* was content to lay down for my ſake, provided he might be conſidered for it, which he would undertake to do ; therefore he deſir'd him to diſpoſe me for the accepting of this Command ; and knowing what an abſolute power he had over me, there was no queſtion but I would do whatever he would have me. Mareſchal *Brezay* did me the honour to make the motion, without taking any notice of Monſieur *St. Preuil's* having written to him about it : And he urg'd it ſo far, that I reſolv'd upon a Journey to *Arras* for this purpoſe. Monſieur

St. Preuil

St. Preuil receiv'd me as he us'd to do, that is, with great civility and respect, and we supp'd together in very good company. As we were at Supper he spoke to Monsieur *de Aubray*, Commissary of War, who was at Table with us, and desired him to muster speedily, because the Captains complain'd mightily; and Monsieur d' *Aubray* reply'd very civilly, He would do it whenever he pleased.

Next day very early all the Officers in the Garrison beset Monsieur *Aubray*'s lodging, making a clamour, and demanding the Money that was due to them. He, inraged in all likelihood to see himself so importun'd, answered them pretty roughly, That he had his orders, and it was not their business to correct his Commission, that he would take his own time to prevent false musters, and do it when they least expected it. The Officers, as much provoked with his answer, as he was with their demand, came streight to Monsieur *St. Preuil*, and complained to him of Monsieur *Aubray*, that he would not pay them; that he always cheated them, and put them off, &c. Monsieur *St. Preuil* went presently to Monsieur *Aubray*'s lodging, and desir'd me to go along with him, which both I and the Officers did. He told him at first, that he was come to see if he would please to appoint a muster that day. Monsieur *Aubray* made answer that his order was his direction, and he should take his own time. How! said Monsieur *St. Preuil*, *you gave me your word, it should be done when I pleased. Sir*, said the Commissary, *I must not depart from the King's orders, I must look after my own business, and you to yours. I will make you do it*, said *St. Preuil*. So from compliments they fell to sharp words, and at last from words they fell to blows. For Monsieur *St. Preuil* being extremely passionate, was transported so far as to Cane him; and if I had not immediately stept between to part them, this scuffle had gone a great deal further. I was the only man indeed that was for it, or took Monsieur *Aubray*'s part at all, for all the Officers were exceeding glad to see him so ill used. I foreseeing what scurvy consequences this unhappy business might have, and that this single action was enough to ruine Monsieur *St. Preuil*, did all that ever I could to make it up, before Monsieur *Aubray*, who was related to Monsieur *Noyers*, writ any thing of the matter to Court; and I brought Monsieur *St. Preuil* so far, as to agree to make him any satisfaction. But he would accept of none, threatning continually to complain to the Cardinal, and the King. At last, finding it was not in my power to bring this business to any good conclusion, I went my way back to *Paris*, without troubling my self any farther about the affair that brought me to *Arras*, where I could plainly foresee, there would in a little time be great changes and confusion.

XII. Going one day to wait on Monsieur *des Noyers*, as I was coming in at the Chamber, I saw him in discourse with the Count *de Charost*, and therefore stood still at the door. They happened just then to be talking of Monsieur *St. Preuil*, and Monsieur *Noyers* in a great heat, said so loud that I could hear him, That he made mad work in the Garrison at *Arras*; that he had raised several imposts upon the City; that he broke into a Monastery by force, and abused some of the Nuns; that he first debauch'd a Mealman's Wife, and then hang'd her Husband to have her more absolutely at his command; and that he had abus'd a Commissary of the Army. The Count *de Charost* seeing me as this discourse past, said, *Yonder is one hears you, who can inform you of him, for he was his Lieutenant*. Monsieur *des Noyers* answered, *Ho, I know Monsieur* Pontis *was St. Preuil's Lieutenant, and therefore he will be sure to excuse him*. Then I went up to them, and said to Monsieur *Noyers*, *I must confess I had been particularly obliged to Monsieur* St. Preuil, *but yet I should be very far from excusing any thing he had done ill in, because I was sensible, whatever I was indebted to him, I owed the King a great deal more*. Well then (said he) *is not it true that he broke into a Monastery, and forc'd some of the Nuns ? Sir*, said I, *I dare give you my Oath, nay I will forfeit my hand if he ever did. I know very well he went thither to take away some Arms that lay concealed in their Monastery; but the King himself declared his approbation of that, by the Mandate he sent to remove the Prior from the Abby of* St. Vast, *and the Abbess from her Nunnary*.

Upon this Monsieur *Noyers* grew warm, and maintain'd that he said nothing but what he certainly knew to be true; and he had it from very good hands, that he hang'd the Mealman on purpose to enjoy his Wife. I answered, he did not hang him, till he had been caught three times, and plainly convicted of holding correspondence with the Enemies. I kept my self still to those things I was well assured of, and said not a word of the rest, to shew him, that I was concern'd to justify the innocence

only,

only, and not the real faults of Monfieur *St. Preuil*. But Monfieur *Noyers*, who was violently prejudiced against him, inveigh'd against him ſtill warmly, infomuch that at our going out the Count *de Charoſt* told me, It would become me as *St. Preuil*'s friend, to deſire him, that he would take ſome courſe to compoſe this buſineſs, and loſe no time in making his peace. I went preſently, and told Mareſchal *Brezay* all I had heard Monfieur *Noyers* ſay against *St. Preuil*. He told me I had beſt go to him as faſt as I could, and let him know from him, that it was abſolutely neceſſary he ſhould come to *Paris*, and reconcile himſelf with Mareſchal *Melleray* and Monfieur *Noyers*, whatever came on't; that all his friends would uſe their intereſt for him, and that if he himſelf, that was the Cardinal's Brother-in-law, h.d thoſe two Enemies, they would have it in their power to ruine him. I entreated him to write a Note, that Monfieur *St. Preuil* might be more inclin'd to believe me. But he utterly refuſed that, and ſaid, *No, not I; for though I ſay thus to thee now, if thou ſhouldſt tell any one that I ſaid it, I ſhould give thee the lye.* I told him, I hoped there would be no occaſion for that, for I ſhould be ſure to tell no body.

Immediately then away went I poſt to *Arras*, and after diſcourſing Monfieur *St. Preuil* till three a clock in the morning, I brought him at laſt to reſolve for *Paris* next day. We took Horſe and travelled together accordingly. but after a little while he changed his mind. For by that time he had gone ſix or ſeven leagues, he turn'd his Horſe head all on a ſudden, and told me, He would not ſtir from *Arras*, for when once they had him at *Paris*, they would take his Government away from him. All that ever I could ſay would not perſwade him otherwiſe. For in truth he was ſtruck from Heaven, and condemned already by a decree of the divine Juſtice. So we both went back to *Arras*; and I finding it was impoſſible for me to prevail with him, or do him any good, was loth to ſtay and partake in his miſery, and therefore return'd to *Paris*.

XIII. In the mean while his Enemies made it their buſineſs to poſſeſs the King, and Carninal *Richelieu* against him, eſpecially Mareſchal *Melleray* (who was grievouſly offended with him, for the accident to the Garriſon of *Bapaume*; and ſtill remembred his being denied the Convoy of Horſe he requeſted of him) gave this Stateſman ſo ill an opinion of him, that it was an eaſy matter for Monfieur *Noyers*, when he backt all the reſt with a freſh charge, to ruine him compleatly. The King and Cardinal being thus diſpleaſed with him, Mareſchal *Melleray* had orders to ſecure him as he went into *Flanders*, to have an eye upon *Liſle*.

When the Mareſchal was come near *Arras*, he ſent to Monfieur *St. Preuil* to order quarters for the Army. Every body then thought him loſt, and ſome of his friends adviſed him to ſhut the Gates, telling him, that ſince he muſt dye, he had better do it with his Sword in his hand, than by the ſtroke of an Executioner. But he very bravely reply'd, he would never be guilty of taking up arms against his King; that he knew Mareſchal *Melleray* was a man of generoſity, and he would go meet him himſelf. Accordingly he did with fourſcore or a hundred Horſe, and when he alighted to compliment him, the Mareſchal diſmounted too; and after thoſe compliments were over, they rode on together. Monfieur *Melleray* told him, he was order'd to lodge part of the Troops in *Arras*, and ask'd him if he had made any preparation for it. Monfieur *St. Preuil* anſwered, that he had taken care for every thing. He asked him again what Regiments he ſhould bring into the Town. *St. Preuil* reply'd, that his own ſhould lodge there by all means, and that he had drawn all the Souldiers of the Garriſon into a corner of the Town to make room for them.

When they were come to the *High-ſtreet* of *Arras*, the Troops were diſtributed on all ſides, and when all was ſecured, Monfieur *Melleray* immediately told Monfieur *St. Preuil*, that he was ſorry his duty obliged him to tell him, that he had the King's order to ſecure his perſon. So poor *St. Preuil* was apprehended, and afterwards carried to *Amiens*, where he continued Priſoner ſeveral months. I would fain have gone to ſee him in Priſon, and begg'd the King's leave to do it. But his Majeſty referr'd me to the Judges that were to try him, and they denyed me, becauſe no body was ſuffered to come at him. It was certainly a great mercy, that he fell thus into diſgrace with men, when his fortune and advancement had made him proud and haughty, and baniſh'd all thought of his Souls ſafety. And ſuch he acknowledg'd it before his death, telling his Confeſſor in Priſon, that God had ſuffer'd this misfortune to come upon him, to awaken his thoughts and remembrance of him, for he had all along forgotten

ten God, and liv'd in wickednefs. All this happen'd while I was in difgrace. For
tho orders were fent me not to ftir out of *Paris*, yet I very often took journeys privately; but with this caution, that I firft gave notice of it to fome of my friends,
that had the beft intereft, as Marefchal *Brezay*, and the Count *de Charoft*, that if there
was occafion, they might excufe it to the Cardinal.

XIV. About the fame time Marefchal *Brezay*, who (as I have faid before) honoured me with a very particular affection and efteem, would needs undertake one
day to make my peace with the Cardinal, in whom he had a very good intereft. He
bid me meet him one morning very early at the Capuchins in St. *Honorius* ftreet, and
he would take me along with him to *Ruel*. This offer was very welcome, becaufe I
was quite tir'd with the pitiful fort of life I then led at *Paris*. I came exactly to
the time and place appointed, and fo did he, and away we went both together to *Ruel*.
But we found he had undertaken more than he was able to perform: For as we follow'd the Cardinal, who was walking in his Garden, after the firft addrefs, and a
little difcourfe, Marefchal *Brezay* told him, There was one *Pontis* behind his Eminence, who was very defirous to pay his duty to him. The Cardinal, affoon as ever
he turn'd about, and faw me, cry'd *Your humble Servant*; the very compliment with
which he always difmift the people he hated. I underftood that language well enough,
and knew he meant by it, that I had nothing to do but to walk off. Which I did
as faft as I could; and taking Horfe rode a good round rate back to *Paris*, fancying
I heard the Cardinals *Humble Servant* perpetually founding in my Ears. Marefchal
Brezay told me afterwards, I was to blame in going away fo foon; I told him, if the
door had not been open, I would have jumpt over the wall; and that there was no
ftaying for me after fuch a Compliment.

But another worfe bufinefs with his Eminence happen'd to me fhortly after, which
might very well have been my utter ruine, and yet by a ftrange turn of Fortune turn'd
to my advantage, and brought me into favour again. I confefs, whenever I reflect
upon it ftill, I cannot imagine which way it was poffible for me to get clear of fuch a
mifcarriage fo luckily; and how a mighty Minifter of State, who had fought all
occafions to undo me, fhould yet, when he found one fo much for his purpofe, make
no other ufe of it than to exprefs his kindnefs, and try afrefh to win me over to his
fervice. The manner of it was thus:

XV. Monfieur *Cinqmars*, Grand Querry of *France*, was at that time violently bent
againft the Cardinal, and was forming a ftrong Cabal againft him, who ftood then the
common Mark for all the great Men at Court to aim at. He knowing me to be one
that ftuck clofe to the King's fervice, and confequently the Cardinal's Enemy, thought
it might be for his purpofe to engage me in his defign of fupplanting this Man, whom
no body was able to endure. And fuppofing my prefent difgrace might incline me
yet more, fent a Confident of his, one *Fouquerolles*, Lieutenant of a Troop of Light-
Horfe, and told me by him, That fince my Misfortunes were owing to Cardinal
Richelieu, who intended my utter ruine, I fhould come into him, who was able to
fupport me againft this Tyrant, promifing me befides a great many fine things, which
there is no need of mentioning now. This was when the King defign'd his Journy
to *Perpignan*, and fo he pretended to engage me to go thither.

I was much perplex'd what courfe to take upon this occafion. For it was eafie to
forefee Monfieur *Cinqmars* his ruine, and I made no queftion but he muft at laft be
crufht by fo formidable an Enemy. But then I was afraid too, that the Grand Querry
after having open'd himfelf fo freely to me, fhould take fome pique if I refufed him.
However, till I had time to confider better of the matter, I thought the fafeft way
would be to fhelter my felf under the King's command not to ftir from *Paris*. So I
told *Fouquerolles*, that Monfieur *le Grand* had done me a greater honour than I could
deferve, in remembring me at a time, when almoft all my Friends had forgotten me;
that I fhould be fenfible of it as long as I liv'd, and retain all the gratitude that fo
particular a Favour requir'd. But the King having exprefly charged me not to go
from *Paris*, I could not then comply with the offer he made me, but I entreated him
to believe, that if I could undertake that Journey without a breach of duty, I fhould
be entirely at his difpofal, and therefore I defir'd he would give me time to afk my
Friends advice about it.

I then

I then wrote to Monsieur *Vievemont* my particular acquaintance, to desire he would discourse Monsieur *de Vennes*, another of my Friends, upon the business. I would not mention Monsieur *Cinqmars*, but only told them in general, That I was at a great loss what to do upon this juncture of the King's going to *Perpignan*, whether I should attend him, notwithstanding the Order that was sent me, and which, I was satisfy'd, came only from the Cardinal. But the Error I committed was, that writing in a passion, I inveigh'd bitterly against him, and laid him out in his true colours, mentioning him in scurrilous terms, as Hat, and Redcap, and the like. I took all imaginable care that this Letter should be deliver'd into the person's own hand to whom it was directed; but notwithstanding all my caution, the Cardinal got it, who kept a strict eye upon me; and though I had given this fresh provocation, yet by a new and surprizing fetch of Politicks, he turn'd all his Rage to Favour, and an opportunity of persuading me to be a Creature of his, as I shall shew presently.

XVI. The King was then at *Fontainbleau*, and intended to set out from thence for *Perpignan*. He did me the Favour to send his trusty *Archambaut* to me, to bid me make ready to attend him. I askt *Archambaut* whether he had brought me this Order in writing, who told me, No. Then speaking freely to him as a Friend, I said, That having a written Order not to stir from *Paris*, and no written one to go, if the Cardinal should think fit to call me to an account for this, I should soon see my self deserted by the King himself, and left to the mercy of one who was sure never to forgive me, and therefore I could not go from *Paris* without another kind of Order than that he brought me. But I have thought upon a method (said I) to bring my self off in this business, I am satisfy'd thou lov'st me, and therefore prithee tell the King that you found me very ill. And, in truth, I am so much worse than if I had a Fever, and my circumstances were better. And this was my real sense at that time, my heart was set upon nothing but Favour at Court; and while I was out there, I could never think my self tollerably well. So little impression had the inconstancy of such Favour made upon me, though I had great and long experience of it, both in the case of several great persons, and in my own. The Sieur *d'Archambaut* promis'd to deliver the King this message, as I desir'd him. So when he came back to *Fontainbleau*, he told the King he found me very much out of order, and yet that I exprest so great inclination to wait upon his Majesty, as soon as I receiv'd the message, that it was very plain I was still the same Man, and as zealous to serve him as ever; but in all probability if I should venture upon this Journey, in the condition I then was, it might endanger my life. All this was exactly true, though not in that sense the King understood it. His Majesty exprest himself very well satisfy'd with my fidelity and good inclinations. But was loth I should hazard my life to so little purpose, and therefore commanded *Archambaut* to write to me in his Name, that he charg'd me not to travel till I was perfectly well again. And this was not till after his return from *Perpignan*; and then there was an end of my disgrace, just where another Man's was most likely to begin.

XVII. The King travelling by way of *Roussillon*, and the Town of *Collioure* being taken from the *Spaniards*, there happen'd a Quarrel between Cardinal *Richelieu*, and the Grand Querry, who both desired the Government of this place for one of their Creatures. Monsieur *le Grand* having made his application first, carried it from the Cardinal, who was answered afterwards by the King, that he had put it out of his power, by promising it to another before. The Cardinal knew well enough that the Grand Querry was that other, and lookt upon himself as extremely affronted, that one, whom he had raised, and was since become his Enemy, should get this Government out of his hands. He thought himself absolute Master of all, and that it was a Condescension to ask what was in his own power, and was much enraged at the King's refusing him: and concluding, that the malice of his Enemies was at the bottom of all this, he began to apprehend a shock in his Fortunes, for he was very sensible that there were strong Cabals against him. For this Reason he resolved shortly after to withdraw into a place of safety, that if any thing should happen, he might secure himself by a retreat. These are great Mysteries, and such as I do not pretend to give an account of here.

All that is pertinent for me to add is, that before he took that last refuge, he contriv'd, by a very cunning fetch, to play me against the Grand Querry, and use my name to

carry

carry his point against an Enemy, whom he could not with any patience see gratify'd before himself. Tho all my disgrace was owing to him, yet knowing that the King had no aversion to me, and that it was uneasie to him to have me kept thus from about him, and all by a constraint in which himself had no hand, he thought he might possibly obtain that in my behalf, which had been deny'd him before: And would not baulk the doing a kindness to an Officer that he hated, if he could but retort the affront and repulse he was afraid of, upon his chief Enemy. He pretended therefore to be concern'd for me, and to have me in his thoughts upon this occasion, and with his usual simplicity, (when the King had refus'd him this Government for his own friend) said, *But pray Sir, does your Majesty never think upon poor* Pontis? *he hath nothing, and wants this; and besides, that his services may give him a title to this Government, for his reward, he will take more care in it, and manage it better than any body else?* The King saw thro this disguise presently, (as himself did me the honour to tell me afterwards) for he knew my present misfortunes were all his work; and this was nothing but his own Interest, under the pretence of compassion, which he put on upon this occasion. The King had no mind to let him know he smelt the design, and therefore seeming to relish the proposal very well, he reply'd very readily; That as for the man (meaning me) he had no objection against him; but he had past his word already, and it was no longer at his disposal. So the Cardinal, that had with so much artifice pretended a kindness for me, and all to serve himself indeed, saw at last this Plot, tho so well laid, fall through; and was forc'd to take other methods for the suppressing his Enemy; as he afterwards did, and as our Histories shew; where you find a long account of the tragical end that the Grand Querry, and his Confident, Monsieur *de Thou,* came to at last, and what occasioned the fall of those great men.

XVIII. When the Cardinal had taken care of their Tryal, he return'd to *Paris,* and went from *Lyons* the very day appointed for their execution. His March from *Lyons* to *Paris* was one of the most remarkable things that ever was heard. He being not well, contriv'd to travel without ever stirring out of his Bed, which was, to be carry'd as he lay, Bed and all, by sixteen men. He went into no House where he lodg'd at the door, but Monsieur *Noyers,* one of his dearest Servants, performing the office of a Harbinger, went always before, and took care to break down the sides of the House, and make a passage by the Windows of the Room where he was to lye. Then they built a Scaffold too in the Street, and steps to go up to it, that so by this passage his Eminence and his Bed of State might be brought into his Chamber.

There were Chains stretcht all along the streets of *Paris,* to hinder the crowd and clutter of people, who came from all parts to gaze at the triumphal Entry of a Cardinal, and Minister of State, laid at ease in his Bed, and returning in pomp after the Conquest of his Enemies. I was there among the rest when he went by, and stood in *La Verrery-street.* He was not so sick, but he could look round about upon the crowd, and seeing me among them, he call'd to the Lieutenant of his Guards, who went close by his Bed; *I saw Monsieur* Pontis *just now, go tell him I would have him come to the Cardinals Palace, at my alighting.* The Officer came, bawling among the people; and enquir'd if I were there. I heard him name me, and shew'd my self, and then he deliver'd me the Message the Cardinal had commanded him. My friends began to blame me, for being so unwise to appear, saying, that some mischief was now coming upon me; That the Cardinal must needs have a bad meaning, that I was too hot, and ought not to have tempted an unnecessary danger. I, on the contrary, who had all the confidence of an innocent man, and never suspected my Letter's being intercepted, told them I was resolved to go, and see what the Cardinal had to say to me; and accordingly went straight to his Palace, at the very time he came thither. There I presented my self among the rest, but there being abundance of company, either I was not discern'd in the crowd, or, if I was, he would not speak to me before so many people, but put it off to some more seasonable time. As he came in, he said with a seeming satisfaction; *Ah, God be blest, there is no pleasure like being at one's own home.* And as the persons, through the midst of whom he past, prostrate themselves with a very profound respect, he only said to them, *Your humble Servant;* but it was with an air very distant from that that he said it to me in, when he chas'd me with this Compliment out of his Garden.

XIX. Wh...

XIX. When I faw he took no notice of me, I defired the Lieutenant of his Guards to let his Eminence know, I had been there in obedience to his command. He promifed he would, and entreated me to come again next day for an anfwer. I came feveral times before I could be admitted to fpeak with the Cardinal, who for feveral days was taken up with vifits from perfons of quality, that came to make their Court to him, after fo long a Journey. At laft, as I was one day with Monfieur Prefident *Mole* in the Antichamber, word was brought, that his Eminence asked for me; fo being introduced, even before the Prefident himfelf, as foon as I came in, they that were near his bed withdrew into a corner of the room, all but two Pages that were in waiting at the beds feet. I came near and kneeled down, and kift his Robe. The firft queftion he asked me was, Why I did not go with the King to *Perpignan?* I told him, that having received an order not to ftir from *Paris*, and not any other afterwards to warrant my going, neither from his Majefty nor his Eminence, I durft not prefume to go. *And is that*, faid he, *the true reafon why you did not go?* I told him, I had no other, but my fear of difobeying the King and his Eminence. *But is there not* (faid he again) *fome private reafon that prevail'd with you to ftay behind? For if the Kings confent was all you wanted, I am fure he is too gracious to have denied you. There muft needs be fome fecret caufe, which you have no mind to difcover. Your Eminence knows very well* (faid I) *that it was by no means fit for fuch a one as I, to defire the King would give me leave to be about him, when I had been forbid his prefence, for fome reafons, which it did not become me to enquire into. I am fure* (reply'd he) *the King would not have taken it ill from you, and you might eafily have found friends, who would have undertook to fpeak for you, without applying to the King in your own perfon. My Lord* (faid I) *that's very true, but I beg leave to tell your Eminence, that I have all along made it my bufinefs, to trouble thofe that honour me with their friendfhip as little as I could, and feldome to make ufe of them upon my own account. I am fenfible the King is very gracious to me, and for that reafon have received his corrections as well as his favours thankfully, becaufe the greater his goodnefs has been to me, the greater I am fatisfied is my fault, when I have offended him. I am very glad* (faid the Cardinal) *to find this is your temper, for no body can have too grateful a fenfe of the King's favours. But methinks for all that, a man is to blame, when he does not fhew a juft value for the happinefs of being near his Majefty; and that it looks too like a flight, when one is fo unconcerned, and it is indifferent to him whether he enjoy his prefence or not. And there is a great deal of difference between being troublefome to ones friends, and defiring them to intercede for him upon fuch occafions: And therefore I cannot believe but you had fome other reafon, which you would not have me know; for in fhort, no Prince is fo far provok'd, but that there may be means found to foften him again.* He did me the honour to talk after this free manner, and we lookt as if there had been a fort of friendly conteft between us, he ftill upon the attack, and I upon the defenfive part. At laft, finding his queftions were fo often repeated to no purpofe, and that I ftood my ground, he faid, Since I would not fatisfy his queftions, he would not fatisfy me why he fent for me. But bids me go from him to Monfieur *Noyers*, and he fhould tell me; commanding one of the Pages of his Chamber, whofe name was *la Grife*, to go with me to Monfieur *Noyers* lodgings.

XX. This mighty earneftnefs of the Cardinal's to know what kept me behind at *Paris*, coft me a great many reflections. I had no intimation yet of my Letter, that I wrote upon this account, being got into his hands, and I fancied all his uneafinefs might proceed from an accident fome time before, which made him very jealous of me. Being one day with the King, his Majefty beckned me after him into the Wardrobe. It was a place where I never had been, and fo did not prefume to follow him. But he ordered the Gentleman Ufher to call me in. Then fitting down very thoughtful upon a Cheft, he began to ask me, What was the meaning, that all the Captains to whom he had given Commiffions had quite forfaken him, and that fcarce any of them gave any attendance about his perfon? I made the beft excufe I could for them, telling the King in general, that the old Officers were quite worn out with hardfhips and wars, and no longer capable of doing the bufinefs of their places; feveral had loft their limbs, and were maimed in the fervice, and fome perhaps might be weary with the fatigue of the Army. The King replyed, and asked me more particularly, What fhould be the reafon that fuch a man (naming him) left his fervice, and was gone off to the Cardinal's. I faid to him freely, and without any hefitation, *He could be no great gainer by the change, that left the Mafter, and put himfelf under the Servant.*

Thefe

Thefe were my own words, and fuch as I am fure the King was well pleafed to hear. This poor Prince then began to reckon upon his fingers the perfons that had deferted him, lamenting in fome meafure his own misfortune. And I muft needs fay, tho I tryed to excufe them as well as I could, yet I was much affected to fee fo great a Monarch abandoned by the greateft part of his own Servants; and could not but be amazed, (confidering the honour and affection I bore him) how any body could betray fo poor a fpirit, as to prefer the fervice of a Subject before his, though that Subject were never fo great. He feem'd to me to be extremely penfive and uneafy, all the time we were together, turning the difcourfe perpetually from one fubject to another, fometimes fitting quite mute, and fometimes asking fome foreign queftions; fo that, knowing that he did not ufe to talk at this loofe rambling rate, I concluded fomething lay heavy upon his mind, which he was loth to declare, though he would have been glad, if I could by degrees have ftumbled upon it. For the King having at that time a great defign in agitation againft Cardinal *Richelieu,* there was reafon to imagine he had a mind to intruft me with fome fecret relating to that matter.

But it happened that our difcourfe was interrupted all on a fudden, by Count *Nogent,* who peep'd either through a crack in the door, or the Key-hole; which the King perceiving, asked if any body were there. Then Count *Nogent* fcratching at the door, the King in a furprize rofe up fo haftily, that he had almoft beat me backward, difcovering by his behaviour, that he was concern'd at our being found together in that place. As foon as Monfieur *Nogent* was come in, he told the King, the Cardinal had fent him to know whither his Majefty intended to ftay within, becaufe his Eminence would wait on him. The King faid, the Cardinal fhould be very welcome. Afterwards this Count asked me privately, what the King was talking of with fo much vehemence and gefture, giving me to underftand, that he fufpected fomething from our difcourfe. I confefs I had a great mind to check his curiofity, and tell him he meddled with what did not concern him: But fearing a man of that intereft with the Cardinal, I only anfwered, That the King, as he ufed to do, talked feveral things about the Armies, the Souldiers, and the Officers. He fufpected this to be no better than a put off; and replyed, That there was fomething elfe in the wind. And when he came back to the Cardinal, he raifed fome jealoufies of me, telling him he found me alone with the King in the Wardrobe, and that his Majefty had committed fome fecret of confequence to me.

XXI. This private and familiar conference with the King it was, that I imagined the Cardinal had a mind by degrees to get out of me, when I waited him upon the occafion before mentioned. When the Cardinal's Page had brought me to Monfieur *Noyers* his lodging, his Eminences Livery made me way through all the crowd, that waited to be admitted. Every one made me room, in refpect to the Page that introduced me. And going with him directly up to Monfieur *Noyers* his Chamber, after our firft compliments, when he underftood the Cardinal had fent me to him, he took me with him into his Clofet. There he began to put the fame queftions the Cardinal had done before, asking me over and over again, Why I did not go with the King to *Perpignan.* I found prefently, that this was a thing agreed between the Cardinal and Monfieur *Noyers,* and that I had reafon to think they had fome private intelligence of the bufinefs. I thought it the idleft thing in nature to ask me fo many times the reafon of a thing, which they knew better than I, and if I durft have been fo bold, could almoft have found in my heart to be downright angry: But I confidered who I fpoke to, and kept within bounds for fear of the Cardinal, and ftuck clofe to the anfwer I had made his Eminence; That having been ferved with an order from the King, figned by Monfieur *Noyers* himfelf, not to ftir out of *Paris,* he muft have been the firft that would have condemned me if I had gone. Still he turn'd and wound me about a hundred feveral ways, in hopes to make fome difcovery from me: But when he faw me proof againft all his crofs queftions, after a great deal of this difcourfe, he reacht a File of papers that lay upon his Table, and drew off that fatal Letter written to Mr. *Vitremont,* concerning the King's Journey, and full of reflections upon the Cardinal; and giving it into my hand, faid, *Look upon that Letter a little, fee if you know your hand and feal again.*

No tongue can exprefs the confufion I was in, when this Letter was produc'd againft me, which I could not think fhould ever fall into thofe hands, without Witchcraft; for I thought my felf fecure, both of the perfon with whom it was entrufted to convey,

vey, and of him to whom it was sent; but the latter hath protested to me several times since, that he never receiv'd it. At last, not being able to deny my hand, nor used to flinch upon these occasions, I rather chose to own the whole thing freely, and said very bluntly, *'Tis true, Sir, I own this Hand and Seal to be mine: This Letter I must confess was written by me, and consequently I am oblig'd to own all the contents of it, tho my Head were to pay for it before night.* Monsieur *Noyers* was well enough pleas'd with this frank acknowledgment, but yet he took me up pretty roundly, and spoke with all the vehemence imaginable: *This is fine* (said he to me) *here you have had the impudence to use the Cardinal at this rate, who is the greatest and best Genius in the World ; one that does good to all mankind ; and one that raises such as are worthy of his favour, out of the dust, and advances them to the highest and most honourable posts ; one that is ever labouring, and makes it his whole business to satisfie all the Kings Subjects ; and obliges his very Enemies ; nay, one that at the very time when you were reviling him after this scandalous manner, try'd to do you service, and begg'd the Government of* Coliovre *of the King for you. And is it possible that little inferiour Officers should fall foul upon the power above them so insolently ; and so far forget themselves, as to reproach and affront those persons, that their Prince thinks fit to trust with the care and management of his Kingdoms ?*

I answer'd him, That I confess my self to blame to use such language of a person, to whom I ow'd all possible respect ; but I begg'd him not to take it ill, if a poor Prisoner as I was, let fall any indiscreet complaints, and cry'd louder than was becoming. That this was the only liberty left the afflicted, to unload their breasts by lamenting their misfortunes. That the world does not think any body the more guilty, nor at all resent it, if they forget respect a little upon these occasions; because then it is not so much the person that speaks, as the passion. *This, Sir,* said I, *is the only ease poor Prisoners have left : Their tongues are not confined, they express themselves freely, and no body thinks the worse of their cause for it. Nature, Sir, puts us upon complaining when we are hurt ; and it looks like stupidity to suffer and stand mute all the while. In short, I own I had not so much temper as I should have had ; but I dare say you your self have so much goodness, as to excuse me in my misfortune, when I was sensible of nothing I had done to deserve it, and yet saw my self struck to the ground on a sudden, and opprest with a load so heavy, as that of my disgrace is to me.*

Monsieur *Noyers* was moved with my way of expressing my self, and besides I do not question had secret instructions to make the best of this occasion to invite me into the Cardinals service ; so he told me, he would speak to the Cardinal in my behalf, and undertook to make my peace most willingly ; to shew me by this instance that he really lov'd, and was not less my friend now, than he had ever been. So I took my leave, and told him I should acknowledge my obligations to him. I went home, and was amazed at the several little fetches, and politick designs of this great Statesman, who hated me for my fidelity to the King, and had long waited for a fair pretence to undo me, and yet chose rather to improve this occasion that offer'd it self to him, into a means of fixing me to himself, than of my utter ruine.

XXII. I went several times to Monsieur *Noyers,* and always found so many people waiting upon business that I could never speak with him. At last, one day I met Mareschal *Brezas* and Mareschal *Melleray,* who both told me, they could not imagine what I had done to gain upon the Cardinal, but he was quite another man with regard to me, and often spoke of me with a great deal of kindness. Monsieur *Brezas* told me, he would introduce me to him ; Monsieur *Melleray* said, No, he would do it. So after a small struggle, they agreed to carry me to wait on him both together. We all went to the Cardinal's Palace, and at our entrance into the Chamber they said to him ; *My Lord, here is Monsieur* de Pontis, *we have brought him to your Eminence, very sorry for having offended you, and ready to make a tender of his service to you. I will be security for his fidelity,* said Mr. Brezay, *And so will I,* said Mr. *de Melleray.* All this while I said not one word, giving them no authority for the engagements they were so ready to make in my behalf, nor confirming them no further than by a respectful silence.

Then the Cardinal, directing himself to me, said in a jeering insulting tone ; *Well, Monsieur* Pontis, *you have stood in your own light all this while. You thought to get more, and raise your fortunes more effectually, from another hand, but you had been no loser by the bargain, if you had applied your self to me.* This compliment, I own, stirr'd a great deal of indignation in me, to see my constant devotions to the Kings service made a jest of, and

that

that they thought me a man to be corrupted. But I must keep in my passion, and therefore answered with all the outward demonstrations of respect, that were due to him; That I was all astonishment at the honour his Eminence had done me, in having such a one as me in his thoughts, that I must acknowledge my self very unworthy his favour; but yet my Conscience did not tax me with having ever been wanting in my obedience to his commands; and that I had endeavoured to pay his Eminence all the service in my little power. But indeed I thought my self obliged not to forsake the King's service, for this would have been the highest ingratitude, since his Eminence himself could not but blame me for that, as knowing, that both my fortune and my life depended upon his royal bounty. The Cardinal pretended not to understand me, and made answer, that what was past should only serve to make us better friends hereafter, and that he would have me come and see him again.

But I, who did not understand his Court, nor the modes of it, resolved to frequent it but very little more for the future, than I had done heretofore. And I thought it convenient to acquaint the King with the whole matter; who would not have been well satisfied, to have had me conceal the particulars of an accident, in which he was so nearly concern'd. Having given him some little hint of it, he took me into his Closet, and there I gave him a full relation, of all that had past between the Cardinal, Monsieur *Noyers*, and me; at which he laught heartily to himself. But when, among other passages, I told him what Monsieur *Noyers* had said concerning the Governours place of *Colioure*, which he assur'd me, the Cardinal had begg'd of his Majesty for me; the King was so full of indignation at this gross dissembling, that he could not forbearing crying out, *Ah, the Knave!* Then I askt him if he would give me leave to go wait upon the Cardinal, as he had urg'd me to do; telling him, that if his Majesty pleased, I would never see his Eminence's face more, except in a Picture. But the King answered, that I had better not scruple that, but go wait on him as others did, to t ke off all jealousie of me, and keep my self at least in that degree of his kindness, which he now profest for me.

XXIII. From that time, which was about the month of *September* 1642, matters went very well with me at Court: For I was constantly about the Kings person, who carry'd me with him several times to Cardinal *Richelieu*'s, when he went to visit him near his death; but he did not use to take me into the Chamber where he lay. The day this great Statesman dy'd, some hours before his death, I was in the Kings Bedchamber, Monsieur *Noyers* came in great joy, and told him, the Cardinal was upon recovery, for he found himself now much better, and had taken a Medicine that did wonders upon him. The King, who was satisfied the Cardinal's distemper was mortal, when he heard this news, continued just the same, without any alteration in his countenance, either of Joy or Grief. Some time after came another, and he told the King, that his Eminence was dead, and he saw him expire. The King did not depend upon this first account, but staid for a second, and a third; and when he heard it confirm'd on all hands, he contented himself with this reflection to some that stood by him, *Then there is a great Politician dead.* Presently after Mareschal *Melleray*, and Mareschal *Brezay*, who had been his creatures, came and threw themselves at the King's feet, and begg'd his protection. The King took them up, and told them, that he had always had an esteem for them, and would always continue to love them, provided they would serve him faithfully. In this he shewed a great deal of goodness, for he never exprest the least resentment of their having been so absolutely at the Cardinal's devotion. And there is no question, but there is a great deal of policy in managing ones Enemies sometimes, when any extraordinary accident obliges them to change their measures, and come over to our party.

XXIV. I was not long happy in the Kings favour after the Cardinal's death. This Prince scarce ever enjoy'd any health afterwards, but wasted away in a kind of Consumption, which at last brought him into a most lamentable condition. He stood one day in the Sun, that shone in at his Chamber Window, to warm himself, and I coming in to wait on him, not observing that, stood directly between him and the Window; whereupon the King said, *Ah* Pontis, *do not take that from me, which thou canst not give me,* I did not understand his Majesty's meaning, and being concern'd I did not, continu'd still in the same place. Then the Count *de Tresmes* told me, it was the Sun I took from the King; and I withdrew immediately. This poor Prince grew so lean, and worn, that he could not forbear bewailing himself; and would

fou.-

sometimes uncover his naked bony Arms, and shew them to those of his Court, that came to visit him.

When he lay upon his Death-bed, Monsieur *Savoray*, first Gentleman of the Bed-Chamber, having given the word one day, that all the company should go out, that the King might take a little rest; and drawing to the Curtain on that side of the Bed where I stood, to signifie that I was to go with the rest; the King immediately drew back the Curtain, and commanded me to stay; for he had no inclination to sleep, but had a mind to be eased of the crowd and clutter of company. Then he began to talk familiarly with me; and seeing from within his Bed, through his Chamber at the Castle of *St. Germain*, *St. Dennis's* Steeple, he askt me what that was? I told him *St. Dennis's* Church; he said, looking death already in the face, *Then there is the place where I must lie.* Then drawing his Arm out of his Bed, he shew'd it me, and said, *Here* Pontis, *see this Hand, and this Arm, what Arms are here for the King of France ?* I observ'd them, but with unspeakable anguish of mind, for he was just like a Skeleton, with skin drawn over the bones, and cover'd with great white spots. After this he shew'd me his stomach, which was so miserably lean, that you might easily tell all his bones. And then, being no longer able to contain, I burst out into a violent passion of sighs and tears; and made his Majesty sensible, at my leaving him, that I was extremely afflicted to see him in that condition, which gave me more pain, if that were possible, than he felt himself.

I say nothing here of the constructions that were put upon his distemper: These are secrets not easie to be known, nor of any great use if they were known. This we are sure of, he dy'd when God saw fit, and in his disposal is the life and death of the greatest, as well as the meanest men. 'Tis to little purpose, that we trouble our selves to know the true causes of the deaths of Kings, when we know that all those causes are subordinate to the will of him, who is the King of Kings. He was very negligently attended in his illness, and scarce ever had any thing given him warm, and in good order. This, I confess, added much to my trouble, to see a King, with so many Officers about him, worse lookt after than the meanest Shop-keeper in *Paris*.

I was not in his Chamber when he dy'd, for all company was kept from him: But I can say with great truth, That death of his afflicted me to such a degree, that for three months together I was almost senseless: For I lov'd this Prince most tenderly, and was always passionately fond of his service; and I will presume to say, I should be exceeding happy, could I bring my self to be so zealously affected for the faithful service of him, where no man ever loses his labour; and who deserves our love infinitely more than all the Princes of the Earth. God, no doubt, intended by this most sensible instance of the zealous and disinterested affection I bore to his Image upon Earth, to teach me how much better I ought to love himself, the great Original. And really, I have often wondred to see what a strange temper I was of toward this Prince: For tho I valu'd my services so high, as to think all the favour he shew'd me but a poor recompence for them; yet still I was so thankful for them, that when some have found fault with him upon my account, I have several times answer'd, *Is it not honour, and reward enough for such a worm as I, that so great a Monarch will admit me near his person ?* Thus, whatever consideration I had for my services, still I lookt more upon his accepting them, and always valu'd that most; and thought all I did was but a discharge of that obligation, which the being born his Subject laid upon me. Thus, without ever attending to it, I practic'd that to an Earthly King, which the Gospel hath taught me since, ought to be practic'd to the Heavenly one; to look upon our selves as unprofitable servants, and infinitely happy to be thought worthy of fighting under his banners, and performing his divine commands.

The End of the Fifth Book.

BOOK

BOOK VI.

The Marefchal of Vitry, *engages the Sieur* de Pontis *to attend his Son, the Marquis of* Vitry, *and undertake the Command of the Queen's Regiment. The Vigor with which he quell'd a* Mutiny *among the Souldiers, and aſſerted the Marquis of* Vitry's *Authority, in oppoſition to all the Officers. The Siege of* Rothcuil *in* Germany. *A part of our Army routed at* Tubinghen. *The other part under the Sieur* de Pontis *his Command, defend themſelves bravely againſt three Armies, and at laſt ſurrender upon Terms. What happened to him while a Priſoner in* Germany. *He is forced to pay his Ranſom twice over.*

I. I Was not long, after the King's death, out of employment. And though, after ſo many years ſpent in the Service to no purpoſe, I had reaſon enough to grow weary of it, yet I was engaged afreſh, without any other deſign, than leading the remainder of this miſerable life as well as I could ; thus going along with the ſtream of the World, which carried me away with it, as it did ſo many other People. Marefchal *Vitry* ſurprized me one morning before I was up, and as, I being aſhamed to be found ſo, threw my ſelf out of the farther ſide of the Bed, telling him, he put me out of countenance, and what a Jeſt it would be, if the World ſhould know how he had caught me, he told me he had a buſineſs of moment to impart to me. Then drawing back the Curtain, and urging me to lie down again, he promiſed he would ſpeak to me unſeen, that he might not make me uneaſie. Then he told me he came to ask a kindneſs, and would not ſtir till I had engaged to gratifie him. I, who only deſired to get quit of him as ſoon as I could, told him, without knowing the buſineſs, that I was his very humble Servant, and would do whatever he pleaſed to command me. So, in ſhort, I forced him to be gone, for having got my word, he went away well ſatisfied, without explaining himſelf any farther at that time.

Shortly after he told me that the thing he deſired, and that I had blindly engaged for, was to be firſt Captain of the Queen's Regiment, of which his Son was to be *Maiſtre de Camp.* And conjured me, by all the friendſhip I had for him, to take upon me the inſtructing of his Son, who being unexperienced, would want to be ſupported and managed by one well skill'd in the profeſſion. This Propoſal, I confeſs, ſtartled me, for though I had paſs'd my word, yet thinking ſuch kind of employments a little below me, I did all that ever I could to get off again. But I could not go back from my promiſe, and the Marefchal took care, by abundance of civility and kind promiſes, to oblige me to acquieſce in it. For he aſſured me, the Regiment ſhould be wholly at my diſpoſal, that his Son ſhould bear the Name only, and I have the Government ; that I ſhould diſpoſe of the Companies as I pleaſed ; and that the accepting this Employment, and inſtructing his Son, would be the greateſt Service I could poſſibly do him. There was at that time a great difference between the Duke of *Angoulefme* and him, for having been Governour of *Provence,* and not beloved by the People of the Country, the Court had taken the Government from him, and put in Monſieur *d' Angoulefme.* This occaſioned ill blood, for the Marefchal of *Vitry* ſaid, the Duke of *Angoulefme* had done him ill offices at Court. He intended to drive this Quarrel higher too : but having no great reaſon to expect Juſtice would be done him, the matter by degrees was dropt, and came to nothing.

II. In the mean time, while the Queen's Regiment was raising, I went to divert my self at a Friend's Country-house, and made a Nephew of my own, Lieutenant of my Company, who was afterwards kill'd in the King's Service by a Musquet-shot. While I was in the Country, Orders came from Court, for me to go to *Sens*, and carry four Regiments, that lay there in Garison, to *Troyes*. I sent the Marquis of *Vitry* word of it, that he might bring his Regiment thither too, and, in obedience to my Order, went to *Sens*. Quartering one day in a Mannor belonging to Monsieur *Bellegarde*, Father to the present Archbishop of *Sens*, this Lord came, and told me, that Mannor was his, and he desired I would not quarter upon it. I answered with all imaginable civility, that these Quarters were assigned us for four days, but upon his account I would endeavour to get the Order changed, and remove the Regiments next morning. Nay, if he pleased, I would try to take them off immediately, but it grew late, and the Men had supped, so that staying that Night could be no great prejudice. He thought himself much obliged by my Answer, not expecting such a Compliment from an Officer that had his Orders, and so many Troops under his Command. For I confess, I have often wondred very much my self at the rough behaviour of some Officers, who think the having power in their hands, gives them a priviledge to be rude and bearish, when they might as well sometimes shew some respect to persons of worth and honour; and, though they cannot go back from their Orders, yet they might at least execute them in a civil and gentle way.

III. While we staid at *Troyes*, there happened a great Mutiny among our Men. A common Souldier of our Regiment, a wicked hardned Rascal, had got drunk, and stabb'd a Woman big with Child into the Belly, which killed both the Woman and the Child she went with. This was too horrid an Action to be excused by the Wine, and so I took the Rogue, and had him tryed at a Council of War. The greatest part of the Officers, that were young and raw, instead of indignation at so black a Crime, openly appeared in favour of the Fellow that committed it, thinking (it may be) their honour concerned, to stand by a Souldier, in opposition to the Townsmen, that demanded Justice upon him. All the Souldiers mutiny'd to save their Comrade; for my part, I had so great a detestation of such Outrages, and was by no means of a humour to bend under a mutinous Souldiery, that I urged to Monsieur *Vitry*, that this was his first Campagne; that if he did not assert the King's Authority, not only the Officers, but the very common Souldiers would despise him; that he would draw the *Odium* of a whole Town upon his head, who might prefer their Complaints at Court, if he let such a Fault go unpunished; that this occasion, in short, was of mighty consequence to him; and that commonly, all one's following management depended upon good beginnings. Monsieur *Vitry* was very much of my mind, and resolved Justice should have its course, notwithstanding all the importunity of the Officers; and that he depended upon me for the compassing this business.

This was, in truth, a good generous and bold Resolution for a young Lord, like him, to undertake the opposing himself against the whole Regiment; but since he did me the honour to repose great confidence in me, and that his Father had directed him to do nothing without my advice, he thought I would not engage him in a matter which did not make for his honour. Accordingly I took the business upon me, and carry'd it on with so resolute and so high a hand, that I had the Malefactor condemned to be hanged and strangled, and made all those Captains that appeared in his favour to sign his Sentence. But seeing these Officers came however to Monsieur *Vitry* for his Pardon, though they could not deny condemning him neither; fearing that those importunities might prevail upon his youth and good nature, I conjured him not to vilifie his Authority upon this occasion, and advised, that he would rather go divert himself at his house near *Brie-Comte Robert*, telling him that possibly there might be some mischief; that I saw People were heated, that most of the Officers were new and unexperienced; and therefore I thought it my duty to urge his going, that if any thing should happen amiss, his Reputation and Authority might not be concern'd in it, but all the ill consequences might fall upon me. I gave him so many good Reasons for what I said, that at last I prevailed with him to go, and leave the whole burden of the thing upon me.

Finding my self left in full power, and not fearing any yielding in any body above me, I set my self to the supporting the King's Authority, as I ought, and mustered up all the courage and resolution I had, fearing nothing so much, as not to be feared as I ought. When the time of Execution was come, I drew up all the Regiments, resolving to dye, rather than submit to the humour of raw Officers, and mutinous Souldiers. The Criminal being brought out, they began to make a great Noise, and the Sedition running high, they made ready for Blows, and putting their Match to the Pan, cryed all together, *Mercy, Mercy.* I stood single against so many Men in Arms, and ready to give Fire, most of the Officers seeming pleased with the Souldiers Revolt, and openly approving it. But having learnt by long experience, that Boldness and Resolution is all in all upon such occasions, and that Authority once exerted presently quells Sedition, seeing one Blade make a greater bustle than the rest, that opened his throat, *Mercy, Mercy*; I broke through the Crowd, and going boldly up to him, seiz'd him by the Collar before them all, and said to him, in a commanding tone, *Say you so Sir? Do you pretend to mutiny? Have you the impudence to rebel against the King's Orders? You shall be hanged immediately, without more ado. Prepare your self to dye.* Then I exalted my voice, and shewing my anger in my eyes, *That Man* (cryed I) *that dares to stir, and does not behave himself quietly, I will shew him that I know how to do Justice upon him, and preserve the King's Authority from being slighted. Who do you think you have to deal with, Gentlemen? It is no less than the King himself that you oppose.* Immediately I had my Man bound, who in great confusion fell at my feet, and had no other concern now, but to beg mercy for himself. I pretended to be inexorable, and leading him toward the Gibbet, told him, there was no mercy to be expected for him, and therefore he should recommend his Soul to God, for hanged he was like to be, and that presently.

When I had seized this Fellow, all the rest were so daunted, that they presently grew quiet and silent, no body daring to open his mouth, except the Man that thought he should be hanged, who beg'd to be spared with tears and cryes. In this interval the Malefactor, upon whose account all the Sedition had been raised, was just going to be turned off, and seeing there was no hopes of life, was desirous to disburden his Conscience, and declared before all the World, That as for the murther upon the big-bellied Woman, drink was the cause of it; but he thought himself obliged to discover several other Crimes besides, to vindicate the innocence of several persons who had been falsly charged with them. There he confest publickly several Murthers he had been guilty of, and then the Executioner did his office.

When the time came for the other to be hanged too. I, seeing the Mutiny composed, thought it better not to be too hasty, nor carry things too far, for fear of exasperating People; besides, that I was really softned with the concern and submission of this Cadet, who had not yet had time to come to himself. So for the present I contented my self with confining him; and told him, that since no formal Tryal had pass'd upon him, I pardon'd him, upon condition he should serve a whole year, and not quit this Regiment; which he most willingly embraced, as a very gentle Pennance upon him. After this so resolute and successful Action, the chief of the City of *Troyes*, the President, Counsellors, Chamberlains, and several others came to my Lodging, to thank me for the seeing Justice done upon so wicked a Wretch, and exprest mighty acknowledgments and gratitude for it; I told them, I had done no more than my duty, and was obliged to see Justice done, as I then did.

IV. Monsieur *de Vitry* came afterwards and joined us again at *Bar*, when our Troops were come thither. And there I told him, That since he had been forbidden by his Father, for the Reason I hinted before, to join the Duke of *Angoulesme*, I had best go wait on the Prince at *Langvic*, and receive his Orders. He was of my opinion, and staid with his Troops at *Bar* till my return. So I waited on Monsieur the Prince, and told him, I came to acquaint his Highness, that our Troops were advancing; that Monsieur *de Vitry* was at *Bar* with the Queen's Regiment; and that he was desirous not to command it himself, but to wait upon him, if he pleased to give him leave. The Prince told me, he should be very glad to see Monsieur *Vitry*, and think it an honour to have him with him. And then gave me a Ticket for our Motions and Quarters.

V. I was not away above seven or eight days upon this Journey; but yet my absence gave occasion to a new sedition in the Queen's Regiment, against Monsieur de *Vitry*. The Officers had a great dispute about precedence, and not satisfied with standing to Monsieur *Vitry's* determination, because he was young, and had not authority enough to regulate them; they, without his knowledge, deputed one *Fortiniere* a Lieutenant among them, to complain to his Majesty. Monsieur *Vitry* being as yet unexperienc'd, knew not what course to take, nor how to manage himself to get clear of this affront, and expected my return with great impatience. In this condition I found things when I came back, and soon was informed of the quarrel by the Officers, who had a mind to possess me in their favour, and came immediately to ask me, if I, who was one of them my self, would not take the part of all the Officers of the body. At first I suspected some quarrel with Monsieur *Vitry*, and not caring to engage my self, *Gentlemen* (said I) *I perceive here hath something happened in my absence, I can give you no positive answer till I have consulted Monsieur de Vitry. You would be the first that should blame me, if I should proceed so rashly. It is strange you can neither give, nor submit to command; and that being appointed by the King to keep up discipline among the Souldiers, you your selves break it every day, and refuse obedience to the person who hath authority to command you.*

I went then to give the Marquis of *Vitry* an account of my Journey, who was very well pleased at the Prince's answer. I expected he should mention this matter to me first, and took no notice of it my self. And so he did, telling me he had met with some difficulty since I left him; That all the Officers of the Regiment had carried it so high, as to send a Deputy to complain at Court, without his knowledge. *How, Sir,* said I, *are not you Maistre de Camp of the Queen's Regiment? Hath not the Kings Commission submitted all the Officers to your command? Are not all their fortunes owing to you? their Commands were in your gift, and it was in your own power, as well to have preferred any other persons as those: Such an affront therefore, Sir, to your authority, which is indeed the Kings Authority, should by no means have been endured. A man must put himself forward, and exert all his power upon such occasions as these. How* (said I) *send a Deputy to Court without ever consulting you! Oh, Sir, you must not put it up; farewel to all respect and authority, if this be suffered. If you keep these people under your first Campagne, they will stand in awe of you hereafter; but if they exceed their duty, and once get the upper hand of you, they will be continually mutineering, and you will never be able to restrain them. There is no middle state in these cases, you must either govern them, or they will govern you.* Monsieur de Vitry answered, *Alas! what would you have me do? I was all alone; no body took my part; and I waited for your return. Oh, Sir,* (said I) *what does your being alone signify, when you had your command to bear you out? What is a single Officer in opposition to so many private Souldiers, and yet must not he be accountable with his life to the King, for the discipline and good order of all the men under his command? Are not all the Officers of your Regiment bound to submit to you, and have not you the Kings Authority to command them? There is no ground for fear Sir, when a man hath right on his side, and the Kings power to back him in it? Mutineers must be reduced by methods of prudence and resolution. But since they have put a slight upon your Youth, I will take a course to make them respect your Person, and repent of their Disobedience.* Then I desired he would send away a Courier to the Mareschal of *Vitry*, and I would do my self the honour of writing to him, and representing the whole matter. *Come* (said I) *for fifty Crowns you shall make these Officers know themselves*; and so Monsieur *Vitry* agreeing to it, I wrote to his Father the Mareschal to this purpose.

My Lord,

BEing obliged to go for a few days to Longvic, and there receive his Highness the Prince's Orders, there happen'd in my absence an unhappy disorder among the Officers of your Sous Regiment: They have shewn themselves so disrespectful to his Authority, so ungrateful to their Benefactor, and so unmindful from what hand they enjoy the benefit of their Commands, as, unknown to him, to depute one Fortiniere, a Lieutenant, to make their Complaints to the King and Queen, concerning their Precedences: Thus casting a slight upon my young Lord your Son, who is the proper judge of such disputes. If this Deputy hath not been to wait on your Lordship, this is still a farther
slight

flight upon your Authority too; for tho they refus'd to be determined by the Son, yet they ought to have demanded Justice from the Father. The concern I have in the Interests of your Family, made me think it my duty to give your Lordship an account of this Insolence; that they may be convinced of your Authority at Court, and what will be the consequences of your and your Son's honour being thus injured. Pray, my Lord, see this Fellow cassier'd, and let all the world know, that if any shall presume to oppose the Authority of a person whom the King hath set over him, he must expect to be punish'd as such insolence and disobedience deserves. I am My Lord,

Your Lordship's most Humble, and most Obedient Servant,
De Pontis.

Upon the receipt of this Letter the Mareschal of *Vitry* went immediately to the Queens Court, and there found that *Fortiniere* had been caballing, and made a mighty bustle. But the powerful arguments on his side, backt with his Quality, and Credit at Court, prevail'd so far upon the Queen, as to undo all that *Fortiniere* had done; and besides that, to obtain leave for confining him, which he did accordingly. After this he gave me the favour of a most kind obliging Letter; much extolling my affection for his Son, in standing by him against all the Officers of the Regiment, and conjur'd me to continue my kindness to him; he told me, there was no danger now from *Fortiniere*; that he had imprison'd him, and undeceiv'd the Queen in several things, of which she had been prepossest. At the same time he writ to his Son upon my account, in such a manner as made me rather full of confusion, than proud; telling him, that till this considerable accident, he did not perfectly understand the person, to whose care he had committed him. That there are but few such friends to be found, who will prefer another mans Honour before their own Interest; that he thought himself more oblig'd to me, than it was possible for him to express; and that he commanded him above all things, to respect, observe, and be directed by me. When I had read this exceeding civil Letter, that the Mareschal did me the honour to send me, I burnt it presently, loving to oblige the persons who do me the favour to love me, but fearing such commendations, as rather expose a man to the envy and hatred, than recommend him to the esteem and affection. of the generality of people. Some time after, the Mareschal sent back *Fortiniere*, whom I reprimanded severely; giving him to understand, that he was more to blame than all the rest of the Officers; first, in that he who was an old Officer was so far from teaching the new ones their duty, that he joyned himself in the revolt with them; and secondly, in that undertaking to carry the complaints of the rest, he made all their guilt his own. He excused himself as well as he could, and would fain have been admitted into favour again, and have had a Company. But neither Monsieur *Vitry*, nor I, would ever give him one. For in truth he deserved to be punished, much more than to be rewarded.

VI. Monsieur *de Vitry* then went (as I said before) to the Prince, and I followed him with all the Regiments; and here I cannot forbear taking notice of one thing, which I saw in my Journey at *Vanderange*, because it is something unusual. This Town lies upon the confines of *Lorrain*, some fifteen leagues from *Metz*. The people of it are pretty equally mixt of Catholicks and *Hugonots*. The same Church serves them both. The Curate of one Congregation, and the Minister of the other live together in very good friendship. On *Sunday* the Catholicks go to Mass from eight in the morning till ten: And at ten the Catholicks leave the place, and make room for the *Hugonots*; and salute one another with great civility as they pass. The Minister preaches to the *Hugonots* in the very same Pulpit which the *Cures* had preach'd to the Catholicks in before, only they have the Body of the Church and no more for their use, and the Quire and Altar is used by none but Catholicks. And again, when the Catholicks have gone to Church at eight a clock one *Sunday*, the next they do not go till ten; and so constantly they change their hours of devotion by turns. In a word, there is so great an equality of behaviour among them, that when I had been entertain'd by the *Cure*, the Minister came, and invited me to dine with him too; and after this sort of vicissitude every thing is done among them.

VII. When

VII. When we had joyn'd the body of the Army then with the Prince, who was to leave the Command of it to the Mareschal of *Guebriant*, the Mareschal entertain'd his Highness, and all the principal Officers of the Army, at *Selbourg*, a Town some ten or twelve leagues from *Longvic*. He did me the honour to invite me, and would needs make me perform the Ceremonies of his house. It was one of the most splendid Dinners that ever was made: There were two Tables with the same Services in two different Rooms. The Prince's Table had about twenty persons at it; for only his Highness, the Mareschals, the Lieutenant Generals, and Mareschals *de Camp* sat there; the other was the Maistres *de Camp*, where Monsieur *Vitry* sat, and I with him, being appointed as I said to welcom the Guests, and conduct them into the Dining-room. For as soon as notice was brought me, I immediately left my Napkin, and went to meet and introduce them. In the Princes Dining-room were several Drums and Trumpets, which all sounded when his Highness drank. And some six and twenty or thirty more were placed without, as were also several Instruments, which answered them within, and all together made a most delightful Musick.

When they were at the dessert, Monsieur *Rantsau* Lieutenant General came into the Court. I knew the Prince had no kindness for him, and therefore as soon as they brought me notice, went and whisper'd Mareschal *Guebriant* in the Ear, that Monsieur *Rantsau* was below: He was much perplexed, and said, *Let him alone, and make as if you did not see him.* So I went and sat down again. Monsieur *Rantsau* was much out of humour, that no body came to receive him. At last he grew weary of waiting, and came briskly up into the room where his Highness was. As soon as Monsieur *Guebriant* perceived him, he and the rest rose, and put on some surprize, and every one offering him a Glass, they told him, He was come a little with the latest, but there was enough left still to dine on. At the same time they set before him Partridge, Pheasant, and all sorts of Wild Fowl, and being one that lov'd to eat well, he was taken very good care of.

VIII. After all this great entertainment all the Troops marched, and when they were come to the Plain of *Benfelt* near the *Rhine*, the Army was drawn out, and every one took his leave of the Prince, who was to go back from thence. Several would have attended him back, but he would suffer none of the Company to do it. My friends however, understanding we were to go into *Germany*, writ to me very earnestly to come back, telling me I had seen *Germany* already, and to go thither again was but loss of time. Monsieur *d'Espenan*, to whom the Prince was very kind, and who was indeed his particular Favourite, said, he would speak to him for me; which he did, and with great difficulty got me leave. But upon second thoughts, considering how ill Mareschal *Vitry* might take it, if I deserted his Son at that rate, I resolved to continue my Journey, and sore against my inclination, to pass the *Rhine*. But, by endeavouring to keep the Mareschals favour, I lost the Prince's, who lookt upon himself to be affronted, and was very much displeased with me. When I came among the rest, to take my leave of his Highness, and kiss his hand, he not knowing my design, said in a low voice, *Do not you go with me, I have granted you a dismission.* I answer'd, His Highness had done me a greater honour than I deserv'd, in granting a favour to me, which had been deny'd to others: But in consideration that my return might create great complaints against his Highness, and much envy to my self I begg'd his leave to stay behind. The Prince, offended, as if I had not a due sense of so very particular a favour, grew downright angry, and said, *You are an ungrateful man, I did that for you, which I would do for no body besides, and now you do not thank me for it;* and presently turning away from me, complain'd to Monsieur *Espenan*, that he had askt a favour for me, which I slighted, as soon as it was granted. And really this prov'd a most unhappy accident to me, tho in truth my fault was not want of gratitude, so much as excess of generosity: For I did not so properly ask my self to be dismist, as give way that another should ask it for me; and when I declined the making use of this grant, I did not consult my own choice or pleasure, but was content to force and forego them, rather than disoblige the Mareschal *de Vitry*, by leaving his Son, and breaking my promise. But it must be confest, I made a very false step, in giving way that his Highness should be apply'd to for a matter of such importance, before the thing and all its consequences were duly weighed; which I cannot but say gave the Prince just occasion to find fault with me, and to tax me with levity at least.

         IX. When

IX. When all the Army had taken leave of his Highneſs, they paſt the *Rhine* at *Offenburg*, ſome leagues diſtance from *Strasburg* : And from thence, under the Command of Mareſchal *Guebriant*, went and ſat down before *Rothenil*. The Marquis of *Narmanſtier*, Brother to Monſieur by the Mothers ſide, and Mareſchal de Camp, ſent me with fifteen hundred men, to paſs the *Black Forreſt*, and oppoſe the Enemy's coming, while all things were putting in a readineſs for the Siege. We had like to have been all loſt in the Snows, and had the greateſt difficulty in the world to get out of them, they lying upon theſe Mountains in ſome places above three foot deep. When we had ſpent ſome little time in this wretched poſt, Mareſchal *Guebriant* ſent to ſeek us out, and ſupport us with ſome freſh Troops ; and we made a very brave Retreat in ſight of the Enemy, who purſued us no farther than the Forreſt. Thus we came to the Siege of *Rothenil*, where nothing conſiderable was done on the Enemies ſide, except one Sally, in which our men were in very great diſorder. I had ordered my Nephew, (whom I mentioned formerly) to go along with me, and view the Guard ; and when we got thither, I found the Regiments that were upon duty, and but now raiſed, extremely negligent, and almoſt as little upon their guard, as if they had been in a peaceable Country. Obſerving this, I cry'd out to them, *Why how now Gentlemen, ſure you have forgotten that you are upon the Guard : The Enemies would make a fine advantage of you, if they ſhould attack you in this condition.* Oh we have Centinels, and Guards lye before us, ſaid they to me. *Ay* (ſaid I) *but your advanced Guards will be beaten, before you can ſtand to your arms.* After that, I took a view of all the advanced Guards, and the places where the Centinels ſtood, and made my Nephew note them down in his Pocket-book ; that ſo when my Regiment ſhould mount the Guard, I might be inſtructed in all the Poſts.

Juſt then my fears came to paſs ; for ſix hundred men or thereabouts made a Sally out of the Town, and came powring in upon that quarter, where I ſtill was ; and having eaſily forc'd the *Corps de Guard*, advanc'd briskly to charge the groſs body. I and my Nephew ſaw our ſelves encompaſt in a moment : For the diſorder was ſo great, and every body ſo unprepar'd, that the Captains, Lieutenants, and private Souldiers, who were but lately come to that trade, all ran together, without hearing one word I ſaid to them, or at all regarding the endeavours I made to rally, and put them into heart again. And really, when I ſaw ſo many men quit their poſt ſo eaſily, who yet at other times made mighty pretenſions to Gallantry and Courage, I could not forbear calling out to them, *Oh rare! Gentlemen, what! I perceive then, the Officers ſet the private Souldiers an example for running away.* I and my Nephew not being capable of ſuſtaining the force of ſo many Enemies upon us, both retreated ; and going through ſome winding ways, we found our ſelves purſu'd, and blockt up by four luſty Rogues, that lookt as if they would fain be cutting our Throats ; and were ſupported by ſome more behind them. Upon this we leapt a hedge juſt by, and recover'd a foot way, narrow and riſing, from whence we might diſcourſe them from the higher ground : And there turning back upon them, we ſtood our ground. Thoſe that dogg'd us ſo cloſe before, did not think it convenient to attack us upon this hill, and ſo went off about their buſineſs.

In the mean while, that Quarter being all loſt, we haſtned to Monſieur *Vitry*, to give him an account, and putting our Regiment into a poſture, made ready to try for our Trenches again. When neceſſary orders were given, we brought on our men to the charge. There was a broad way which we ſhould have gone, but it was directly commanded by a Spur-work, planted with eight or nine pieces of Cannon ; upon the very mouths of which we ſhould put our ſelves, which was not fit for us to do. For the declining this paſs, I wheel'd off the Regiment a half turn, and breaking down a hedge, we went that way, tho all the Officers and Souldiers were not eaſily perſwaded to it, becauſe we lay all open. The Enemy being forc'd to turn their Cannon gave us ſome time to advance in : But however we could not do it ſo quick, but that three of their pieces were levell'd at us, and took off three of our hindmoſt Ranks. Every one preſt forward without ever looking behind him, and ſcarce any body perceiv'd it beſides us ; who went ſmiling to Monſieur *Vitry*, and told him in his Ear, *Three of our Ranks are ſcattered, but pray Sir, make no words of it, for fear the reſt, who knew nothing of the matter, be diſcouraged.* Our paſſage, tho ſo much expoſ'd, was ſucceſsful enough, and we charg'd the Enemies ſo vigorouſly, that what we had loſt was quickly recover'd again, and they beaten back into the Town. This was much for the honour of the Queens Regiment, and for Monſieur *Vitry* in particular, who commanded it.   S ſ f   X. Ma-

X. Marefchal *Guebriant* had a mind one day to go take a view of a poft that lay much expos'd, to place a Battery there, but I conjured him not to go, for fear he fhould come back no more. He yielded to my advice, and I went thither in his ftead. Upon obfervation of the place, I found it very fit for his purpofe : But difcover'd at the fame time, a fort of Window, with a Culverin planted in it, that threatned me. This put me to fome ftand, and I knew not how to get backward or forward, for fear of meeting death either way. At laft I came off without hurt, for it feems that blow was referv'd for a Marefchal of *France*, and not an inferiour Officer. I made my report to Monfieur *Guebriant*, and he refolv'd to go thither himfelf. I oppofed his intention all I could, and reprefented the danger to which he expos'd his life ; for there was no way to get under covert of that piece of Ordnance. But he made anfwer, That his honour lay at ftake for the taking of the Town, and would hearken to nothing I faid to him. So go he did, and there met with the death I had given him warning of : For this Culverin was difcharg'd upon him, and broke his Left Arm all to fhatters. When he was brought back to his lodging, and I went to fee him, he faid to me with great unconcernednefs ; *Well, my Friend, my Life is at an end ; this place was deftin'd for my Death.* He lived fome days after. In the mean while his being hurt was kept very private, and the Enemies, who heard nothing of it, fet a Capitulation on foot from that very day. He lay in his bed, and figned the Articles before them with his Right hand, with fo great refolution and evennefs of temper, that they never difcerned his hurt, but thought only, that he kept his bed for fome flight indifpofition. When the Town was furrendred he was carried into it, and there died a little while after, triumphing in fome fort, both over *Germany* and *France*. For all the other Lieutenant Generals were much difpleafed at his befieging this place, and lookt upon him with a very jealous eye for it.

XI. After Marefchal *Guebriant*'s death, Monfieur R..... fucceeded in the Command of the Army, and upon decamping from *Rothenil*, one part of us went into quarters near *Tubighen*, with Monfieur *de R.*.... and the other, where Monfieur *Vitry* and we were, went to *Meninghen*. In this fatal place it was, that our Army received a terrible blow, which was owing chiefly to the General's ill conduct, whom Wine made too negligent of the duty of his command. For, inftead of watching over his Troops, and fecuring them as he ought to have done, he minded nothing, but flept as it were continually in the midft of the Enemies ; who fell on with a mighty force in his quarter, cut his Troops to pieces, and took him Prifoner. Our quarter was fome four leagues diftant from his ; and we came to be informed of this difafter by the following accident. That very day at four in the morning, I had fent the Serjeants to his quarter for bread for the Camp, with orders to be back by nine or ten a clock at fartheft : They did not keep their time, and I began to be very uneafy, the more fo indeed, becaufe I had heard the noife of Guns. I went to Monfieur *Vitry* and told him, without queftion fomething ill had happened ; that thofe Guns we heard could have no good meaning in them, and my advice was, that a man fhould be difpatcht away upon one of his fleeteft Horfes, to bring us word how matters ftood. Monfieur *Vitry* liked the propofal : But all the other Officers both of ours, and the reft of the Regiments that lay with us, cried, the beft way was to make off, that if the Enemy fhould attack us there, while we were cut off fo from the main body of the Army, there was no remedy, but we muft all be cut to pieces.

I oppofed this advice of theirs ftiffly, and told them on the contrary, that having had orders to continue in their Poft, we could not, without fome affurance of the General's being taken, quit it, without incurring the danger of being punifhed for Cowards, Traytors and Deferters; that therefore the firft thing to be done was to get a knowledge how matters were with him, that fo if the General were afflicted we might move to his relief ; and if he were taken, we might fecure an honourable retreat. At laft, whatever they could urge, did not hinder me from carrying my point ; and fo I difpatcht a man upon one of Monfieur *Vitry*'s Courfers, with a charge to make no ftay, that we might have fpeedy notice what was fit for us to do. This fellow made great hafte to the General's quarter, and greater back to us again, and told us, the Enemy had got all into their hands, and the whole quarter were taken Prifoners.

XII. Our

XII. Our next care then was for a speedy retreat. It grew late, and would require good haste to reach the Forrest, which was three leagues from us. So all things were managed with great hurry ; and, there being a narrow Bridge to pass, near the rise of the *Danube*, the Regiment of *Mazarin*, commanded by *St. German*, whose day it was to march in the Van, made haste to get over the Bridge first, and make room for the rest who were to support them. I went my self to view the ground, where it was to be drawn up as soon as it was got over, and came back to them again. But the Enemies Horse waited for us at the passage, and the Regiment were no sooner got to the other side, but immediately a thousand Horse charged them, and cut them to pieces. Since then there was no hope of passing there, we all thought the best way was to get to *Menighen*, and there barricade our selves up the best we could, to gain either a fair capitulation, or an honourable death. Monsieur *Vitry* commanding all these Troops in chief, and having, as I observed, been ordered by his Father, to do nothing without my intention, I found the Office of a General would devolve upon me, in this important exigence. And besides, it is very usual in such extremities, to resign ones Office freely into the hands of a more experienc'd person, and one in whom the Souldiers repose a greater confidence. I told Monsieur *Vitry* we must provide for the worst, and manage this occasion dextrously, which might chance to be the most honourable action of our whole lives. Then calling out aloud to the Souldiers, *Come friends, and fellow Souldiers,* said I, *we must dye ; but if they will not give us our lives, we must sell them as dear as we can.* Every one then laying a helping hand, in a danger where all were equally concern'd, the Gates and Avenues were all barricado'd, and I went my self, and posted all the Centinels, the Guards, and the Reserves, in the most advantageous and important places. I endeavour'd to encourage them all, by my words, my example, and that extraordinary Courage, which I really felt, and thought it was convenient to shew upon this occasion. And to give Monsieur *Vitry* his due, I must needs say he seconded me in every thing ; for tho he was young, and this the first Campaign he had made, yet he signaliz'd himself above the rest ; and exceeded all the expectation that men could possibly have of him, both by his bravery, and great presence of mind.

XIII. After we had made the best provision we could for securing our little body of the Army, in which there were more sick and wounded than fit for service, for we were not above sixteen or seventeen hundred fighting men at most ; about nine or ten a clock at night, there came one of the Duke of *Lorrain's* Trumpets, to summon us in his Highness's name, that we should surrender at discretion ; and if we refused, to threaten us, that the Army should come upon us next day, and then no quarter was to be expected. When I heard them summon us to a surrender at discretion, I cryed out in a rage, *Yes, I warrant you, we shall surrender at discretion! What ! shall they dispose of our persons and lives as they please? No, no. We were not born Gentlemen, and Frenchmen to yield like Cowards, and be used like Rascals. No. We will dye, dye with our Swords in our hands ; and a dear bargain they shall have of us. Let them come with their whole Army as soon as they please : We'll shew them what it is to attack desperate men, they shall have a taste of our Courage, and perhaps repent that ever they tryed it.* All the Officers and Souldiers, who relisht this sort of discretion no more than I did, and were besides animated by the warmth I exprest my self with, resolved to dye, rather than surrender themselves at this rate, without fighting. So the Trumpet went back, and we put our selves into a posture of defence. Next day three Armies of the Enemies appeared before *Meninghen*, that is the Emperours, the Duke of *Bavaria's*, and the Duke of *Lorrain's*, who was Generalissimo ; and the day after that, fourteen pieces of Cannon came up, which were planted against the Village, and beat all the Walls and Houses about our Ears, in five hours time.

About two hundred paces from the Village there stood a Chappel, where the Enemy had set a guard of fourscore men, and they stood very conveniently to do us mischief. I was not able to endure to see the Enemies insult over us, by coming up so close, and told Monsieur *Vitry* it was a shame, to suffer a guard of theirs so near the Town ; and dangerous too, to let them continue there, and that threescore stout Boys must be sent, either to dislodge them, or dye in the attempt. All the Officers received this advice but coldly, and I suppose every one spoke for himself it would be his fortune to be sent, and therefore urged many reasons to aggra-

difficulty of the undertaking. I saw presently their opinions were more the result of fear than judgment; and being desirous to set them a pattern, *Well, Gentlemen,* said I, *I understand the meaning of all this. It seems I must go my self, and I will shew by the success, that the advice was good.* Immediately I took threescore men, with several Trusses of Straw, and went in the night, with all the boldness that became a man, who had not only his Enemies to encounter, but his own men to encourage too; for their spirits began to sink at the number of their besiegers, and the little hope there appeared to get off from this difficulty honourably. When I came up near the Chappel, I found the guard but carelesly kept, because they were under no apprehension of any sallies out of the Town: So we fell on briskly, and cut them in pieces. Then I set fire to the bundles of Straw, and burnt the House down; shewing both our enemies and friends at once, what advantage we had got, above the expectation of either. All my Comrades were envy'd for the honour of this action, and they who objected most against it before, would have been glad to have had a hand in the attempt.

An action so bold as this, and perform'd by so few, when they were besieged by three Armies at once, gave the Enemy such a damp, that they immediately retir'd three hundred paces, for fear of some great Sally, and not knowing what to think of the valour of men so desperate as we. And indeed in all such cases, where the strength is so unequal, the want of numbers must be made up with Courage; and the exposing one's self to the greatest dangers ought not to be esteemed rashness, because in those Circumstances, this is the only way left for mens preserving themselves, or consulting the safety and honour of all the rest.

Next day (as I said) the Cannon came up, and made such a destruction among the houses of this Village, which were no better than Clay, and Earthen Walls, that nothing was to be seen, but ruines and rubbish. Yet even from hence I took occasion to encourage several, telling them, That these ruinous heaps were now as good to us as so many Ramparts against the Enemy, when they attack us. Monsieur *Vitry* desiring me to go up into a little sort of a Turret over one of the Gates, to observe how the Enemy lay; I, who saw a little better than he did, what danger I should be expos'd to, said, *Sure Sir, you have no mind I should ever come down again. Well then, farewell Sir;* and immediately, that I might encourage others, and shew them this was a time to venture, and fear nothing, I went up. But I was more fortunate than I expected, and receiv'd no hurt; so I plac'd a Centinel there, and then came down again.

A little after, the Centinel told us, the Armies came on, that every thing was ready for the Assault, and the Forlorn-hope already drawn out at the head of them. We put our selves into a posture for receiving them, and a bloody business it must needs have prov'd, considering how resolv'd we were, not to betray the honour of our Prince, nor surrender our selves tamely to our Enemies at discretion. But before the Assault, they sent a second Trumpet, to tell Monsieur *Vitry,* that the Duke of *Lorrain* entreated him not to drive things to the last push; that he might be confident his Highness would use him with all the Honour and Civility he could possibly expect; and several other things, which went no farther than the security of Monsieur *Vitry's* own person. Seeing no terms propos'd, but what concern'd him alone, and no notice at all taken of the rest of the Troops, I askt the Trumpet, whether he brought us the same terms that he brought our General; the Trumpet reply'd, They would use us all like men of honour. This answer made us resolve upon a surrender; with this Condition, That the Officers should pay their Ransome, and the private Souldiers should have their Lives.

The reason why our Enemies chang'd their measures so suddenly, was the mistake our extraordinary Courage led them into; for they thought by our holding out two days and two nights against three Armies, that we could not possibly be less than five or six thousand fighting men; and that the destroying of so many, when reduc'd to despair, and entrencht behind timber and rubbish, must needs cost them abundance of blood. It was agreed then, to confirm our capitulation the better to us, that hostages should be given on both sides. The Duke of *Lorrain* sent us one, and ours being a great while getting ready, he that came from the Enemy was much dissatisfied, and complained of the delay that was made in sending ours in exchange. At last, his patience was quite tired, and growing jealous perhaps of so long a delay, he would fain have been going back again. But I, who foresaw what would be the consequence of this, stopt him, and presented a Pistol to his head with these words: *No, Sir, by your leave,*

;ou shall not go, and you shall stay here upon this very spot. *That would be a pretty thing indeed,* *for you, after you have made your observations here, to go back like a Spy, and tell the Enemy* *our condition. You shall stay, Sir, whether you like it or no.* This put a stop to him, and but for this we should probably have been all lost; for to be sure, if the Enemy had known how few we were, they would never have agreed to the Capitulation. So when our Hostage was sent too, we surrendred. The sick men were left at *Mo-* *ningben*, and all the rest conducted by some Troops of Horse to the Enemy's quarters, and all saluted the Duke of *Lorrain* as they past by him. Five or six of us that were principal Officers were allow'd to ride, and wear our Swords. So we endeavoured in our present misfortune, to make as good a shew, and march as gracefully as though we had not been Prisoners.

XIV. That evening the whole body deputed me to go pay their respects to the Duke of *Lorrain*, and beg that he would see his promise made good to us. His High-ness answered, That he knew how to observe Articles; but I reply'd, That notwith-standing the word he had engaged, several of our Officers had been very much abused; that some had been robb'd, some stript, nay, and others kill'd: And therefore I was come most humbly to beseech his Highness, that such **Violences** might not be suffer'd, contrary to the Law of Nations. The Duke seem'd much amaz'd, and answer'd me in a passion, *What! have they stript them? Have they kill'd them? Do you know who they are* *that have done this? Stay here with me, that if you know any of them, I may punish them for it* *before your face.* His Highness immediately publish'd a prohibition through all the Ar-my, charging that our men should not be touch'd upon pain of Death.

The ill conduct of the Enemy's Generals, and the licentiousness and disorder of their private Souldiers, produc'd a very great confusion among our men: Some lost their Cloaks, some their Hat and Feather, some their Coats, and scarce any body escap'd the outrage of these brutish men; who thought they had a right to plunder us because we had surrendred, tho that was not done, but upon an engagement of being used honourably. The sight of this Injustice provok'd me to undertake the de-fence of my fellows, thinking my self sufficiently secur'd by the fresh assurances his Highness had given me: So seeing some of them abus'd, I went strait to their relief, and as if I had been an Officer on the other side, fell to Caneing the Rogues, with that boldness and authority, that honour and zeal for Justice gave me. Our men too seconded me in the matter, pretending not to know me, that I might be the more capable of serving them. But fearing some treachery behind, because I found my self perpetually encompast with Robbers, I unbuttoned my Cloak for fear of foul play, and lest any one should suddenly catch at it, and drag me down backward. This foresight was very serviceable to me: For as I was going between two high and thick hedges, a Horse-man, that lay conceal'd behind, whipt off my Cloak in an in-stant, and rid away with it by the hedge side. I turn'd back in great wrath, and wish'd I could have leapt the hedge, to correct that Rascal, who had the impudence to lay hands on me, against the Generals express command to the contrary. But not being able to do more, I contented my self with giving him hard words, and put it off as well as I could, with saying, that my Cloak was heavy, and very inconveni-ent to me.

Discovering a Captain of ours abused by a Horse-man, who was taking away his Coat embroider'd with Silver, I ran to him, and after five or six good blows with my Cane, made him quit his prize, and rescu'd my man that had like to have been stript. But, being out of all patience with this disorder and ill usage, I went to the Duke of *Lorrain* again, and told him, That every body slighted his order; that the Capitulation was broke every hour, and no promise they made was kept with us; that I had been robb'd of my Cloak my own self; and that the outrages my fel-low Souldiers endured were such, that I was forc'd to importune his Highness once more, that we might be us'd like men of Honour, as he had engaged we should. The Duke seem'd to be exceeding angry, and said, He would hang them every Mo-thers Son. And in truth, presently after he did justice upon one Trooper, that had the impudence to take away one of our Officers Cloaks, before his very face; for riding after him immediately with his Pistol in his hand, some five or six hundred paces, he got up to him at last, and broke his head; which put a stop to their vio-lence for that day.

XV. The Enemy refolved to retake *Rothenil*, and fo we were all carried thither. But we had like to have been quite famifhed by the way, and had not fo much as one bit of Bread to eat; fo that when we met with any Brambles, or Sloe-trees, by the way, there was fure to be fo many Skirmifhes of People fighting for Sloes, and Black-berries. This unwholfom dyet threw me, and a great many others, into a Flux, which was a great afflicion to us in Prifon. But what I feared moft of all was, left the Duke of *Lorrain* fhould find me out to be the perfon that had banter'd him formerly, and hindred the making his efcape at the Siege of *Nancy*, of which I gave an account before. For this Reafon I took great care to have my Name concealed, and had my felf called, *The Captain of the Crown.* For the fame Reafon I declined being his Highnefs's Prifoner, which was what he did me the honour to make me a proffer of, when *Rothenil* was taken; and they came to debate of cafting Lots for the Prifoners, to divide them into three parcels, that the Emperor, the Duke of *Bavaria*, and the Duke of *Lorrain*, might each of them have their fhare. For though it had been much better for me to have fallen into the hands of a perfon, who had ufed me with all poffible civility, yet fearing I might come to be difcover'd afterwards, and he might refent the ill office I did him at *Nancy*; when he did me the favour to afk me, if I would be his? I took the liberty to anfwer, That his Highnefs did me too much honour; that I pretended to no Priviledge above my Fellows, and defired rather to take my chance, as the reft did. So I fell to the Duke of *Bavaria*'s fhare. And a young Gentleman, a Relation of mine, who was Lieutenant in our Regiment, being the Duke of *Lorrain*'s Prifoner, I, thinking he would be near his perfon, and confequently in lefs danger of being plunder'd, gave him two hundred and fifty Piftoles of mine, and a Jewel worth as much more, defiring he would keep that Money for me, and take care to be near the Prince, to avoid the danger of robbing.

When he had got my Money, and my Jewel, he compounded with the Colonel, whofe Prifoner he was, telling him, he was a poor Cadet; but if he would promife him his liberty, he would try to gratifie him with fifty Piftoles, which he would borrow of Monfieur *Vitry*, for he had the honour of being known to him. The Colonel, who defired nothing fo much as ready Money, and perhaps never thought he fhould find this Man fo good a Chapman, promifed to carry him fafe away, upon condition he would pay him thofe fifty Piftoles. It was eafie for him to find fuch a Sum, and thus he got his liberty. He came back into *France*, and betraying a great indifference for him who was left behind Prifoner in a ftrange Country, minded nothing but his own pleafure, as if the Money would never have an end. Nay, when that was gone, he found another method of getting frefh Supplies for his Expences, and went to the Treafury, and there, in my Name, took up my Penfion. And when his Friends and Relations reproached him, with taking no care to get me my liberty, his conftant Anfwer was, that I had Friends enough to take care of me; and all he could do, would fignifie nothing. Which I take notice of here, to put thofe People out of countenance, who are capable of fuch dirty actions; and to fhew that a true Friend is often more faithful, and more tenderly concerned in fuch cafes, than our own Relations.

XVI. After the taking of *Rothenil* by the Enemy, I and my Companions that fell to the Duke of *Bavaria*'s fhare, were carried to *Aufburg*. As we were upon the Road, though I was almoft at death's door my felf, yet I lent my fine Horfe *Millefleurs*, to one of the company, who pretended to be very fick; but inftead of reftoring him to me, that we might take our eafe by turns, he took no farther care than his own convenience, though at my expence; and went on a good way before, without ever ftaying for me. I was almoft quite fpent, and propofed to five or fix of my Comrades to go reft and refrefh our felves a little, at an Inn hard by. But the refrefhment I went for, coft me very dear. For after we had eat and drank, and came to pay the Reckoning, I took a Crown in gold out of my Pocket, and threw it down upon the Table, as we ufe to do in *France*, and faid to the Landlady, *Pay your felf out of that, and give me the reft again*; and afterwards taking the remainder, and putting it in my Pocket, without ever counting it, five or fix *German* Troopers, who were drinking in the fame place, obferved the indifference I fhew'd about Money; and gueffing by this piece of gold, which they faw me throw down upon the Table, that we might
be

be fome of the *French* Nobility, and had a good many Piftoles, they were refolved to fet upon us, and rob us.

After we were gone a good way, thefe *Germans* came galloping up to us; I had ftaid a little behind, and happened juft then to be all alone. The Troopers as foon as they came near call'd out, *Your Purfe*. I, who was much furprized at fo unexpected a compliment, prefently leapt a Ditch, and drawing my Sword, called to my Comrades, *Here*, *To me*, *Gentlemen*, *to me*, and then began to defend my felf as well as I could, without ever confidering how many were upon me. They fhot twice, but did not hurt me. And for all they could do to get within me, ftill I kept them off, with my own motion, and the management of my Sword. All this while my Comrades, and that very man among the reft whom I had lately refcued from the Trooper that would have ftript him, inftead of making up to my relief, fled into the Marfhes, and left me fingle to the mercy of five drunken *Germans*, armed with Hangers and Mufquetoons, and Piftols. I defended my felf after this manner for half a quarter of an hour, and it may be, at laft, they might have been tired as well as I, if one of them coming behind me, and furprizing me, had not laid at me with his Hanger to cleave me down the middle: I turned about, and received the blow upon my Sword, which was broken with the force of it, and that gave them an opportunity of falling all upon me. They rifled me, and took away feven or eight Piftoles which I had left, and unbuttoning my Breeches fearched me for more, and took from me the Gold Medal given me by Marefchal *Brezay*, which I fpoke of formerly. But ftill they left me that which was moft valuable, my life; being no doubt particularly reftrained by God from killing me, which in all probability they muft needs have done otherwife, confidering the refiftance I made, and that they were drunk when they fought with me. I found fuch heat and refolution in this difpute, that if my Companions had not deferted me as they did, I almoft fancy, we fhould have been at leaft as likely to difmount thefe Horfemen, as to have been robbed by them.

Upon this I went and made my complaints to Lieutenant Colonel *Mirek*, whofe Prifoner I was, and told him how I had been robbed and abufed by fome Troopers, who had taken away my money, and among other things a Gold Medal, which I was more concerned for the lofs of, than for any thing elfe. He told me, I was to blame not to put that into his hand. Search was prefently made for the Rogues, which he ordered more for the fake of the Medal, which he had a mind to, than for any thing elfe; and one of them was taken and hang'd for an example, but I never could get any of my things I had loft any more.

When we came near *Ausburg*, the Prifoners that were on Horfeback had orders to alight and walk, and fo they led us into the Town by four and four, behind our Enemies, who marched thus triumphing over us into the Town. There was no remedy but this bitter Cup muft be drank, as well as all the reft, which I was not at all prepared, or ever lookt for, when I furrendred my felf upon a promife of our being honourably ufed. Afterwards I prefented Colonel *Mirek* with my pretty Horfe. They put us all in Cellars, where we had no Bed but Straw, nor any light but what could come to us through the Chinks and Grates of the Cellars. That is, in plain terms, they threw us into Dungeons, to extort from us a higher ranfome.

In this wretched condition did we live three long months, and had nothing to fubfift upon, but the Alms we fent to beg about the Town for poor Prifoners. For the people are generally charitable in that Country, and there were fome good women, that would bring us Bread, and Beer, or Cyder in their Aprons, and let it down to us through the Grate by Ropes. We fent to ask fome Charity of the Monks, who could do whatever they pleafed in that City. But from them we had nothing but hard-heartednefs; and the *Lutherans* fhewed themfelves much kinder and more compaffionate than thofe Monks, who value themfelves upon acting like great Politicians in thefe cafes. Which enraged me to that degreee, that I and fix or feven more of us were refolved to be revenged on them for it, as you fhall hear fhortly.

XVII. When we had lain in thefe Dungeons two or three months, and fuffered inconveniencies and miferies greater than can be expreft, and all this while none of my friends ever thought of me, or ever made application at Court, either that I might be ranfomed, or exchanged, God alone remembred us, and fent me a man full of Charity, who, as he was vifiting the Prifoners, out of a principle of piety and
compaffion,

Compassion, was moved with the sad condition to which he saw me reduced. He was a Picture-drawer in *Bretagne*, who came to trade in that Country, and took compassion on me, without the least acquaintance in the world. When he saw in what a wretched and poor case we lay, he asked me at first, Whether if he should furnish me with fifty Crowns, I could pay him again at *Paris?* I was surprized, and almost struck dumb at so charitable a Proposal, from a person whom I had no knowledge of. But after a little consideration, I told him honestly and frankly, That if I lived to come back into *France*, I would engage to pay him; but if I should die in this place, his fifty Crowns would be lost. *I will not deceive you, Sir,* (said I) *nor shall my present misery and want tempt me to deal unfairly with you.* The good Man, after pausing with himself a good while, reply'd, *Well, Sir, come, it's no great matter; I am satisfy'd with your promise to see me duely paid, if you live to go back into France; and if you chance to dye, though I should lose fifty Crowns, I shall not think my self one whit the poorer, when they are bestowed in Charity upon one, whose Circumstances need them so much.*

Then he ask'd me, if I had any Friends in any of the Cities in *Germany?* I answer'd, No, not any. He enquired again, if I knew any body at *Amsterdam?* I told him, I had some acquaintance with one Monsieur *de Cumans*, a very civil Gentleman, and a Merchant there. *I am very glad of that,* (said he) *for I know him too, and will write to him about you.* I exprest my thanks for his great Charity as well as I could; and from that minute lookt upon this Man, as one sent by Providence, to comfort me in that great extremity. Next day he was as good as his word, and brought me fifty Crowns, part of which I distributed among my Fellow-Sufferers, thinking my Charity to them, a proper expression of gratitude for that bestowed upon my self. This good Man writ away presently to *Amsterdam*, and told the Merchant, that he had seen one *Pontis* at *Ausburg*, who gave a great character of his generosity, and spoke of him, as one of the best and civillest Gentlemen he had ever met with; and who at present stood in great need of his assistance, being a Prisoner of War, and in a very lamentable condition.

XVIII. And here I will give you an account how the friendship grew between this Merchant of *Amsterdam*, and me. When I went with Mareschal *Brezay* into *Holland*, (as was before related at large) I observed something exceeding generous and desirable in this Man's temper, and contracted a particular acquaintance with him. Little did I think, when I made him my Friend, that I should by so doing, provide my self with a Deliverer one day; and that seven or eight years after, I should be indebted to his liberality, for my freedom from such deplorable circumstances, as I have now been describing. But God, I doubt not, thought of that for me, and gave me in it such an instance of his Providence and Mercy, as I can never shew my self sufficiently thankful for. After my return out of *Holland* to *Paris*, he sent his Son to me, and desired I would take care to have him taught the Art of dying in Scarlet, after the fashion of the *Gobelins*, conjuring me to have an eye upon him, and to satisfie for his Board. I undertook this readily, and was a Father to this young Man, looking after him as my own Child; and omitted no possible care for improving him in his profession, and making him an honest Man. I supply'd him with Money for all his expences, and especially, I attended him like a second self, all the time of a long and dangerous sickness, which he lay ill of at *Paris*, sparing neither for care, nor trouble, nor cost upon him. His Father afterwards desiring me to commit him into the hands of some honest Man, to go along with him to *Calais*, from whence he was to take Ship to return into his own Country; I did not think my self too good for this office, but travelled along with him, and never left him, till I saw him set Sail; and then I writ to his Father, and sent him word, that I thought my self obliged by the mutual friendship between us, to bear his Son company as far as the Ship. It will be no such great wonder, if after all this, the honest Merchant behaved himself so generously, as I am now going to shew you he did, when he understood to what a deplorable condition I was reduced in *Germany*.

XIX. About six weeks after the Limner of *Bretagne* had been so charitable to give me the 50 Crowns I mentioned, in Prison, and so brought us out of the Cellars into a Chamber, under a good Guard; the Merchant's own Nephew came to *Ausburg*, and desired of the Governor the Count *de Fougues*, that he might have leave to speak with me. It was granted; and he came in one evening, as we Prisoners were at Supper

per upon a Beef's Head with very scurvy sawce; of which I could eat none, being at that time very ill; and coming into the Room with a Torch before him, he askt whether Monsieur *de Pontis* was not there: I presently went to him, and convinc'd him I was the person he enquir'd for. After he had saluted me, he told me who he was; and that his Unkle understanding my misfortune, had sent him on purpose to make me a proffer of his Credit, his Help, and his Purse. Finding my self extremely obliged by so unusual a generosity, I answered, That I could in no degree deserve, that he should take so long a journey upon my account; but indeed I had undergone so much hardship since my being a Prisoner, that I was not in a capacity to refuse an offer so much to my advantage; which yet was contrary to my custome, for I had never used to make use of my friends for my own Interest.

After a world of complements on both sides, I told him, that the person who had acquainted his Unkle with my misfortune, had been so charitable to lend me fifty Crowns, tho unknown, and the first favour I would beg, was to see him paid. He did so: And then telling the Count *de Fouques*, that he would be responsible for me, he brought me, and my companions, (whom I furnished with some Money) out of Prison. For upon the credit of Monsieur *Cumans* I received eight or ten thousand Livres, which I made use of to supply our present occasions, and to pay some part of my Ransom, that I might be still more at large; being loth to lay down the whole summ, because I liv'd in continual hopes of being exchang'd for some Prisoner of Quality; and so was content to wait, tho it were something the longer, for the honour of being set free that way.

All this while I was much importun'd to give my *Parole*, that so I might be at perfect liberty, to go about without any Guards; which I could have been very well pleased with, for it was by no means agreeable to my humour, to be always attended, and under restraint. But I could not prevail with my self to give it a great while; for not being so secure of the rest as of my self, and not caring to part with my Comrades neither, I was afraid, if any of them should afterwards make his escape, for want of Money to pay his Ransom, I might be thought to have a hand in it, and their fault be charged upon me.

XX. In this interval, when I had my liberty in some degree only, it was that we laid a design for causing some insurrection in the Duke of *Bavaria*'s Territories, out of our resentments against the Monks I told you of; who had provoked us exceedingly, by denying that relief which we had reason to expect from Catholicks, and Priests, and Monks. For they were not satisfied with lending us nothing themselves, but pretended a mighty zeal for the Duke of *Bavaria*'s Interests, in whose Dominion their power was in a manner absolute: They gave out, when we were taken out of the Cellars into a Chamber, that the Count *de Fouques* had done very ill to allow us any inlargement; and that no methods could be too strict to secure our persons, considering we were *French*, and might occasion disturbances in the State. Of this fresh Charity of theirs our host inform'd me, who had himself a great concern for our miserable condition. And observing with much indignation how far their politick zeal transported them against us, I resolv'd to be reveng'd on them whatever came on't, and thought I might justly make them smart, for their base and barbarous behaviour towards Prisoners and Strangers of their own Religion. Tho it must be confest at the same time, that I had pitcht upon a violent course to bring this about. But in short, if I was to blame in my measures, my zeal for Justice I thought would bear me out; and I think I could say, that I was not so much concern'd to vindicate my own private cause, as that of the publick, of Charity, and of Religion; all which these Monks by their carriage to us, had made so manifest a breach upon.

We were allow'd to walk abroad sometimes with some Guards; and one day, when they happen'd to be at some distance from us, I said to my fellow-prisoners; *I do not know what you think of it Gentlemen, but for my own part, I am fully resolved to be reveng'd upon these Monks of Ausburg, that are a scandal to our Religion, and have not shew'd us half so much Charity as the Lutherans. If you will take my advice, we ought all to combine together, and try if we can do the King a piece of service, by endeavouring to reduce a Town into his Majesty's possession, where these Monks exercise so rigid, and so uncontrouled a power. The greatest mischief that can come upon us is but Death And Death is an honour in such a cause; besides that it will be our advantage too, by putting a period to so much misery. Let us then choose to die, rather than endure so unjust a Tyranny. Let us vindicate Religion and Piety, and serve our King, even in this diftant Country, where we are ftrangers, and prifoners for his quarrel.* I had no sooner said this to them, but they were all of the same mind with me, and expreſt the same inclination for the service of their Prince.

At the same time we contriv'd together to feel the pulse of some *Lutherans*, and try to engage them on our side. To this purpose went up to a *German* Captain, who was walking at some diſtance from us; and having at firſt difcourſt him upon indifferent things, we very luckily difcover'd, that the man whom we had a mind to engage, had the same defign himself, and would fain be founding us upon the matter. When therefore when we had gained an opportunity of talking freely with this Officer, and he had open'd his breaſt as freely to us, he aſſur'd us of his refolution to aſſiſt us, and that nothing in his power ſhould be wanting to that purpoſe. Afterwards I found means to break the ſecret to a Maſter *Echevin*, who was a man of great Gallantry, and had formerly commanded in the Army : For I, knowing that theſe imperious Monks were grown intolerable, and odious to all the world, ventured to ſpeak of it to him, and finding him no leſs violently ſet againſt them, I imparted our reſolution, which he liked of very well, and promis'd to ſecond me to the beſt of his ability, profeſſing himself horribly tir'd with the preſent Government. So being ſecure of some friends in the Town, and pretty ſure beſides, that all the *French* Souldiers, that might happen to be then at *Ansburg*, would readily joyn with us, it was agreed, that our Town-friends ſhould get one of the Gates into their poſſeſſion; that we Priſoners, who were a good many, ſhould ſecure another; and that I ſhould firſt give the Prince notice of the whole deſign, that he might move that way to our relief, and countenance and farther our attempt, by appearing at the time when we were to put it in execution.

All our meaſures were exceeding well taken, and having communicated the deſign to but few perſons, (for fear of some treachery) we had great reaſon to hope for good ſucceſs. In the mean while I contrived a way to ſend a man privately to the Prince to acquaint him with the whole matter, and deſire that he would ſecond our undertaking. But his anſwer was both a ſurprize and an affliction to us, for he ſent us word; that the King's buſineſs would not allow him to come to our aſſiſtance; that his Majeſties Armies were otherwiſe engaged, and harraſſed, and but in an ill condition; that I ſhould conſider therefore very well before I attempted any thing, for fear we ſhould hazard being all loſt. And thus our deſign fell through. And, tho at that time we were extremely diſſatisfied that it did ſo, yet upon cooler and more ſerious reflections upon it ſince, I cannot but acknowledge there was more heat and raſhneſs, than wiſdom in the attempt; and all this occaſioned by paſſionate reſentments at the barbarity of a parcel of hard-hearted Monks: So that the ſucceſs would have been uncertain at the beſt, and our own utter ruine might very probably have been the conſequence of it.

And now, after having refuſed a long time to engage my *Parole*, for the reaſon I mentioned before, I and my Comrades reſolved to do it laſt, not being able to endure the ſlavery and conſtraint of Guards any longer. But before we engaged, I argu'd with them very earneſtly, that they ought rather to dye, than not be true to it; and that it was a moſt unbecoming thing, for men of honour, as we pretended to be, to engage for any thing, except they are fully reſolv'd to make it good. One of them afterwards had a mind to make his eſcape, and it was in my power to do it as well as he; but I oppoſed him in his intentions, and would by no means give way that he ſhould be guilty of ſo much baſeneſs: Nay, as a further diſcouragement, I told him upon this occaſion, a ſtory that I ſhall always remember; which was, that my Maſter the late King caſhier'd an Officer, that made his eſcape after his *Parole* was paſt; and declar'd, a man that had been falſe to his own honour, was not fit for his ſervice.

Aſſoon then as our *Parole* was given, and we at liberty, I began to ſee company, and frequent the Duke of *Bavaria's* Court. I got acquainted with ſeveral great perſons, and particularly the Count *de Cœurſe*, a favourite of the Prince. The Duke of *Bavaria* himself, to whom I was a little known, receiv'd me very graciouſly; and being informed, that I was the man who commanded in the buſineſs of *Meningken*, he would ſeveral times have perſwaded me to ſtay at his Court; telling me often, *You ſee no body thinks of you in* France; *I am confident they will let you dye here, and never exchange you for any Officer of mine. Therefore if you will take my advice, even ſet up your reſt here. I will put you into ſuch an Employ as ſhall pleaſe you; nay, you your ſelf ſhall be your own*
chooſer.

chuses. Nothing could be kinder and more engaging, than my usage from this Prince, and the importunate offers he made me to enter into his service. But whatever resentments I either had, or had cause to have against the Court of *France*, where in truth I was quickly and perfectly forgotten, yet I could not prevail with my self to stick to a Court-life, nor relish any proposal of that nature, how much soever it might turn to my advantage: Besides I lived in hopes still that my friends would do something for me. And it is most certain, if Mareschal *Vitry* had not unfortunately died about the time we were made Prisoners, he would have used his interest very vigorously for me, and would have taken care, that the action of *Meninghen* should have had its due character and value. But my misfortune was, that the Mareschal being dead, Monsieur *R.....* who knew not how to answer it to himself, that he should be so shamefully suprized, when Monsieur *Vitry* and I shewed so much resolution and conduct in holding out against three Armies with a handful of men, did all he could to diminish and stifle this action; and so by robbing others of the honour due to them, hoped in some measure to conceal his own shame.

XXI. At last, finding my self utterly forsaken, and forgotten by all my friends, I resolved to send away a Courier to *France* at my own charge, and write to Monsieur *Servien*, and Monsieur *d' Avaux*, to beg that they would speak to the Queen in my behalf, and contrive to have me exchanged for some other Prisoner. Monsieur *Servien*, I suppose, either because he was taken up with business of greater consequence, or because he had no good news to send me, never answered my Letter. Monsieur *d' Avaux* did me the favour to write back to me, and sent me word, he had written to Court in my favour, but there were so very many Prisoners, and every thing at present in such confusion, that he very much questioned, whether he should be able to do me the service he desired, but however he would endeavour it heartily. Still I lived in expectation, and could not believe it possible, that an Officer who had spent all his life in the Army, and whose services were well known to all the Court, (not to say any thing of this last, which I thought might deserve some sort of reward) should be neglected and forgotten. But the event taught me by sad experience, that I reckoned without my Host; and as much as I had seen of the world, I was not then sufficiently convinc'd, that imprisonment or death, for the honour of one's Prince, and the good of their Country, is too often lookt upon as a recompence sufficient for all the services a man hath done them.

While I lived in hopes of good news from Court, I went to visit several places in *Germany*, particularly *Munich*, where his Highness of *Bavaria* usually makes his residence. I had the honour to discourse with his Highness pretty often, and very freely upon several occasions that offered themselves. Monsieur *de Fouques* and I were talking one day before him of several fine Horses, rare Birds, and many other Curiosities, which the King of *Spain* had presented to the King of *France*; and Monsieur *Fouques* was saying, that though these two Kings made war upon one another, yet there was no hatred between them; and adding afterwards, that he could not believe the King of *France* had any design upon *Germany*. I took him up there, because I thought such discourse was not for the honour of the Kings pretensions; and answer'd him boldly before his Highness; *For my part, Sir*, (said I) *it is my opinion, that the King my Master hath still a great ambition to recover that Throne at one time or other, upon which his Ancestors have sat heretofore.* The Duke of *Bavaria* presently turned this into raillery, and said, He was not at all surpriz'd at my answer, for in truth he expected no other from me; that I was a true *Frenchman* upon all occasions, and continued so still, tho driven into *Germany*; and he perceived I had a mind to take some sort of revenge upon them that had made me Prisoner. And indeed I never stood much upon ceremony, where the honour of *France*, and the Arms of the King were concerned. For how just provocation soever I might have at that time, not to speak any thing to the advantage of the *French* Court, yet I could never devest my self of that natural inclination and tenderness for my Country, which always disposed me to vindicate its honour upon such occasions, where the character of a good *Frenchman* depends upon having a less regard to ones own private interests, than those of ones Prince and Nation.

XXII. At last I grew quite weary of this sort of life in a strange Country, and finding we were no more any body's care in *France*, than if we had been dead; and understanding too, that we were to be sent to the lower end of all *Germany* to bear Arms
there

there, I refolv'd to come to terms for my Ranfome, and perfwaded my fellow Prifoners to do the fame, having lent feven or eight of them Money, by the help of Monfieur *Cumans* correfpondent, who had orders to deny me nothing I defired of him. That very day the Collonel invited us to dinner, and when we had din'd, he bad us take leave of our friends, and come again to his Lodging, telling us we fhould eat a Pafty with him in his Garden, and drink a parting Bottle to the King of *France*, and his Highnefs of *Bavaria*'s health. At the fame time he made great excufes for not ufing us as we deferved ; affuring us, our ill treatment proceeded from no malice or contempt, but was to be imputed to the Cuftom of the Country, and the common right of War, which intitles a man to the getting an honourable Ranfome for his Prifoners : Adding, that if it were his fortune ever to be Prifoner in *France*, he fhould not take it ill to be fo ufed, for the enhancing his Ranfom. I told him, without taking any great notice of his complement, That we had been very hardly ufed indeed, and I durft promife him, if ever he were fo unhappy to be our Prifoner, he would have reafon to commend our ufage, and foon difcern the difference between the cuftoms of *France* and *Germany*. But however, fince it was the cuftome to ufe Prifoners of War thus, I would promife him, we would retain no grudge againft the Country in general, nor himfelf in particular ; nay, that if I met with any opportunity of ferving him, I would do it with all my heart.

Thus we left him, intending to return again when we had taken leave of our friends : But as foon as we were got out of his houfe, there happened a fad misfortune both to him and us : For as he was leading his Wife down ftairs into the Garden, his Spurs threw him down, and he fell quite from the top of the fteps to the bottom, and there ftruck his Head violently againft a little Pillar, and broke his Skull with the blow. He was fpeechlefs prefently, and within four and twenty hours dyed. We came back prefently, and finding the poor man in this lamentable condition, we refolv'd to go off without delay, for we had our Pafs-ports; and were afraid of what happen'd accordingly, that they fhould confine us again. But the Collonels Lady prevail'd upon us to ftay, almoft whether we would or no. And the Officers of the Garrifon in the mean time wrote away to the Duke of *Bavaria*, to defire he would give them leave to ftop us, for now the Collonel was dead, we were going away, without paying our Ranfome,

His Highnefs not being informed, from any other hand, how the cafe really ftood, granted their requeft ; and fo, after all the barbarities we had undergone before, we fuffered at laft the greateft injuftice that could poffibly be done us, and were forced to be ranfomed over again. And I am fure I may fay, the loffes I fuftained this year were greater than my circumftances could poffibly bear ; for after eighteen Horfes (fome of which were very valuable ones) and all my Baggage had been taken from me, I was conftrained to lay down my Ranfom twice over. Nor do I put into this account the Money I lent my Companions, part of which I loft too into the bargain.

The End of the Sixth Book.

BOOK

BOOK VII.

The Sieur de Pontis *returns into* France ; *he expreſſes his Reſentments againſt the Court a little too boldly, and at firſt refuſes to engage any more in the ſervice. He is commanded to go guard the* Mountains *of* Provence *and* Dauphine *during the firſt War of* Paris. *A Generous action of the Chevalier* de Pontis, *his Brother, who had been taken by the* Turks. *An account of what happened upon the Marriage of the Sieur* de Pontis *his Niece, and the troubleſome buſineſs that this Marriage engaged him in.*

I. WHen my Ranſom was paid the ſecond time, I made all the haſte I could out of a Country, that had given me ſo much reaſon to diſlike it. So away we went for *France*, one or two of my fellows and I, leaving Monſieur *Rubentel* who was falling ſick, behind us at *Uberlinghen*. I gave him what Money he was likely to have occaſion for, and left my ſelf only juſt enough to carry me to *Lyons*, depending upon meeting a freſh ſupply there. When we were about a days Journey from *Ausburg*, a *French* Souldier that had made his eſcape overtook us, and ſeeing him on foot and bare of Money, I bought him a Horſe that he might bear us company, and bore his charges the whole Journey. Which accident, and the loſs of one of my Horſes that died upon the Road, drain'd me quite dry by that time I got into *Switzerland*. Not knowing who to apply my ſelf to, I concluded at laſt to go wait on Monſieur *Cumartin*, Embaſſador from the King in that Country ; and told him, Though I had not the honour of his acquaintance, yet neceſſity compell'd me to implore his compaſſion upon poor Priſoners that came out of *Germany*, and wanted Money to finiſh our Journey into *France*. After ſeveral other queſtions had paſt, he asked how much I wanted ; I anſwered him, we ſhould have occaſion for about five hundred Crowns. Tho he ſeem'd to boggle a little at firſt, becauſe I was not known to him, yet he received me after a very obliging manner, and furniſhed me with a thouſand, or twelve hundred Livres, which ſerv'd me till I reacht *Paris*. I went preſently after to wait upon the Queen, who asked me a great many particulars about the Country from whence I came, and hearing all that had happened, promiſed to be mindful of me, and immediately gave me ſix hundred Piſtoles. But alas! this was but like a drop of Water to the Ocean I had loſt, and that I ſtood in need of at that very time to equip me out afreſh, for going into the Army once more, which the Queen would needs engage me to do.

Monſieur *Cumans* in the mean while, who had ſupplied all my wants of Money in *Germany*, according to his uſual generoſity, writ to me, to deſire I would not be uneaſie, nor ſtreighten my ſelf upon his account, but bad me pay him when I could ; and if I were not in a condition to do it, he ſhould reckon himſelf fully paid, in having had it in his power to do me ſervice. And here I cannot forbear obſerving, what a mighty difference there many times is, between that Friendſhip which great men do you the honour to make profeſſions of, and that which plain honeſt men really have ſo you. For at the very ſame time that I lay deſerted, and utterly forgotten of ſome Noblemen, who knew very well, that I had frequently done them ſervice, at the expence of my own life ; even then did a Stranger, a *Dutch-man*, and a Trading man, behave himſelf to me throughout the whole buſineſs, with a largeneſs of Soul more like a Prince, than one of his condition ; and all this in gratitude for the care I took of his Son. But notwithſtanding Monſieur *Cumans* great Civility, I, who could never endure to be outdone by my friends, in the little emulations of generoſity and kindneſs, and was deſirous to pay off my debts faithfully, ſold an Estate which I had in *Beauce*, for fifty thousand Livres, and paid Monsieur *Cumans* his Correspondent at *Paris*, what Money I ow'd him. At the same time I put two of my Nieces that were poor, and had been recommended to my charity, into the Houie, placing one of them in a Convent of *Ursulines* , and the other in St. *Mary*'s Mona- stery, both in *Provence*. Thus when I had most occasion for Money my self, I was de- firous to make some acknowledgment for the charity I had lately received from Strangers, and the eminent protection of God over me.

At my return from *Germany*, I found that the Relation I had trusted with my Mo- ney, had made use of it for his own pleasure , and was extremely enraged to see so base a disposition in him; nor would I ever be reconciled , till he had restor'd me my Jewel, and engaged to give two hundred Pistoles to my Nephews. When this was done, I had a mind to let him see, that this unworthy behaviour had not alter'd my affection for him; and, as a pattern of generosity for him to copy after, gave him the first Company of the Queen's Regiment, which had all this while been reserved for me. For I had no inclination to go abroad with Monsieur *Vitry* the next Cam- pagne, being much offended at what I had heard, that his Mother Madam *de Vitry*, had not spoken so well of me to the Queen, as she might have done; and finding so ill a return made me for the service I had done her Son , at the hazard of my Liberty, my Estate , and my Life. But still I continued to love and honour Monsieur *Vitry*, and he exprest all the Sentiments of a Person of Quality, and a true Friend for me.

I forgot to tell you, that when I came back to *Paris*, my honest Picture-Merchant came to see me, and congratulate my return. I was extremely glad it was in my power to entertain him, and exprefs'd by all the possible civilities how much I thought my self obliged by the charity he shew'd me , when in a strange Country, and un- known to him. Afterwards I bought a Case of Pictures, very curious ones, which cost me four hundred Livres, and made him a Present of them. But this good Man had a generous Soul, and would by no means accept of them, telling me in his honest plain way, *Pray, Sir, do not oblige me to take this ; Come, I am richer still than you are ; and your occasions for money are greater than mine.* So we contested this point of gene- rosity some time, I carried the cause at last, and engaged him, whether he would or no, to take what he could not refuse, without putting a slight upon me.

II. Being to receive one of my Pensions, I went to *Fountainebleau*, where the Court was at that time, to sollicit the Queen for payment. Her Majesty having given me assurance that she would remember me, I was in continual expectation of seeing her promise made good. But after two months stay at *Fountainebleau*, and a great deal of money spent to no purpose, in hopes of receiving my due, I grew weary at last of so tedious a delay; and thinking I had got a fair convenience of putting her Majesty decently enough in mind of her promise, I presented the Ticket for my Pension, and told her, She was graciously pleased to say she would think of me , but since I per- ceived a multitude of other business of greater concern , in which her Majesty was involved, had been the occasion of my being hitherto forgotten; I was come to re- turn the Grant which my Master, the late King, had done me the favour to bestow upon me, that so she might gratifie some other person with it, of more desert than I could pretend to. The Queen was a little surprized, and said to me in some heat, *You are very impatient, wait a little longer.*

I did so, and was resolved to see what would become of this second promise. But at last I grew impatient again , and seeing my self so long put off in the getting so small a sum as five hundred Crowns that were due to me, was resolved to apply my self a third time to the Queen, and contrary to the advice of my Friends , which I ought to have followed, rather than my own opinion, went a little too warmly to of- fer my Grant again. She took it, but in the sudden passion she was in, threw me the Paper back, and full of indignation, to see me so importunate, said, *Oh! the late King hath often told me indeed, that you were hasty and passionate. Madam,* said I, *the late King was my Master, and his taking notice of me, though but to reprove my failings, was an honour greater than I deserved. But, Madam, I dare assure your Majesty, if he found any fault with my humour, he never could find any failing in my fidelity.* The Queen said, She did not speak so with regard to my fidelity, but she blamed my passion. Thus was I paid for my obstinacy, and taught to my cost, to take my Friend's advice another time. And yet methinks there was a great deal to be said in my excuse, and some allowance might

be

be made for a Man that finds himself driven to extremities, and is mad to see such a return made for his Services.

Upon this Reprimand, I kept aloof off; and Monsieur *d'Etampes*, the Master of Requests, coming into the Room some time after, made up towards me, and began to enter into discourse with me. I said to him with a smile, *Have a care what you do, Sir, do you know that you are talking with a Man in disgrace, and one that the Queen hath but just now been in a great passion against?* Say you so? (reply'd he very pleasantly) *Well, I would discourse with you for that very reason, that I may convince you my friendship for you is not the less for all that.*

III. The Queen, who was gone into her Closet, came out in the evening with only one light before her, and was very intent upon reading a Letter. I took her for Madam *Senecay*, because her Majesty did not use to appear so slenderly attended. I could be pretty free with that Lady, and came behind her, as if I would look into the Letter she had in her hand, and said, *Madam, Will not you do me the favour to speak for me to the Queen?* Her Majesty turn'd short at this Compliment, and I stood much confounded, and most humbly begg'd her pardon for my insolence; telling her, that seeing her alone, which was very unusual, I took her for one of the Ladies of her Court. The Queen, who some way or other was grown calm in three or four hours time, and perhaps displeased at her self for having spoken to me in so much passion, said to me in the most civil and obliging way that possibly could be, *This is a Letter come to me just now, and brings me word that my Son Anjou is well, and began to wear Shoes this very day.* It was too great a favour for me to expect, that her Majesty should discourse thus to me after my intemperate heat; but she favour'd me yet farther, and bade me be in the way when she went to the Play, and she would speak to the Cardinal in my behalf.

I was there exactly at the time, and her Majesty having spoken to the Cardinal as she promised, his Eminence called me to him, and told me the Queen had remembred me, and spoke kindly of me to him, and that if I would be at his Levee next morning, he would give order to have me admitted into his Bed-chamber. When I found things go so well on my side, I could not forbear rallying my Friends a little, who had most of them deserted me, telling them briskly, That I perceived their kindness was of more use to others than me; and instead of employing and depending upon my Friends, I had always found it the best course to sollicit my own business my self. Next day I waited upon the Cardinal, who wrote me a Ticket with his own hand, by vertue of which I had my Pension presently paid me.

IV. But still I was much dissatisfi'd and out of humor, to see my self continue no way employed, nor at all considered for my Service, and especially to find that last action of *Meninghen* quite stifled and disparaged, by an envious General; who had no other way to cover his own disgrace, but by detracting from our deserts. I foresaw too, that they intended to engage me in the next Campagne, though my losses by my imprisonment had put me out of a condition to equip my self for the Service. Then I was out of all patience I confess, and full of resentment at this hard usage. I went and made my complaint to a great Minister of State, and with all the strength of reason I could, represented to him the deplorable Circumstances which my Service to the late King had reduced me to. This person, instead of giving me any satisfaction, fell foul upon me for ingratitude, and told me, That since the King designed to employ me in this Campagne, I had nothing to do but to obey. Upon this I reply'd very hotly, and indiscreetly, That all the World took notice how unjustly I had been dealt with; that an old Officer, as I was, ought not to be used at this rate; and as for the next Campagne, I was positively resolved not to be concerned in it; that I had lost all, in losing my Master the late King; and was very little sollicitous now for any thing that could happen to me.

This Answer provoked him to that degree, that he procured a Warrant against me, to clap me up in the *Bastile*. I had notice of the thing, and at first made a Jest of it, thinking this was meant only to fright me. But being afterwards assured by one of my Friends, that it was really true, and if I were found at my own lodging, I should be confined in two hours time, I thought it unseasonable to carry it big any longer, and went privately to a Lord's house that belonged to the Court, who told me, he was very much my Friend, but had not interest enough to protect me, and was afraid I could not be safe with him. Then I went to Monsieur *Harcourt*, and desired I might take Sanctuary with him, who received me with great kindness and generosity, lodged me in a private Room, sent my Dinner and Supper up constantly into my Chamber, and did me the honour to come and sit with me every morning and evening.

Here I continued to play least in sight for several weeks, till Mareschal *Melleray* coming one day to the Count *d'Harcourt's*, and I having the honour to discourse him, he told me he would engage to speak for me, and make my peace with the Queen. Accordingly he carried me to the *Louvre* in his own Coach, and presented me to her Majesty, who did me the favour to tell me, that she had given out no special Order against me in particular, but only a general one, to secure all the Officers that refused to go with the Army. Thus the passion I fell into, though it gave me great apprehensions of being utterly out of favour, yet gave me some comfort at least, to find my self in good graces at Court, and perfectly at liberty again.

V. After this I was order'd to go into *Provence*, and carry over some Troops, consisting of five or six thousand Men, into *Catalonia*. I cannot, at present, recollect any thing very remarkable, that happen'd to me upon this occasion. This was during the first *Paris* War, when every body knows the whole Kingdom was in great disturbance and confusion. I received a Command besides, to guard the Mountains of *Provence* and *Dauphine*. For this Service I raised a Regiment of Foot, and a Troop of Horse: But found a vast difference between these Troops, and those I had commanded under the late King. For then the strict Discipline he kept up, gave me an absolute Authority over my Souldiers, but now I was wearied out with perpetual complaints of these Fellows, who gave themselves up to Rapine and Licentiousness, and thought they were privileged by the disorder these Civil Wars occasioned, to shake off all manner of obedience. I could not endure this insolence, nor was in a condition to keep these Brutes under as formerly, being slenderly supported, and very ill paid, and therefore chose rather to quit the Employment, which I could not honourably discharge. So I delivered up my Regiment to another Officer of a temper something more passive, and less nice in point of Discipline than mine. While I was thus employed in maintaining the King's Rights about *Provence* and *Dauphine*, I married one of my Nieces to a Gentleman very well descended of the Family of *Poligny*. This Niece was Daughter to my eldest Brother's Son. And as I now married the Daughter, so by an accident much of the same nature, I had married the Father several years before. There was something so very observable in both these Matches, that I think they deserve a particular Relation here, and therefore I will give you the Circumstances of both, and begin with that of the Father.

VI. I forgot in these *Memoirs* to tell you, that I had a Brother who was one of the Knights of *Malta*, concerning whom I think my self obliged to relate one very remarkable Story here. He was a Person of great Wit and Learning, could speak several Languages, and among the rest the *Turkish*, as perfectly well as his own Mother-Tongue, the *French*. This inclined him to make some stay at *Constantinople*, where he applied himself to consider that place and state thoroughly, and with great judgment observed the strong and the weak sides of it. I remember he hath often told me, and made a report of the same nature, to the great Master of their Order, that if the Christian Princes would once unite together, it were a very easie matter for them to make themselves Masters of that famous City; and that he always thought the support of the *Ottoman* Empire was owing, not so much to any strength of its own, as to the divisions among its Enemies. He had the reputation at *Malta*, of a Man of bravery and courage; and for my own part, I think in my Conscience I was but a Coward, and a meer Chicken in comparison of him.

In one of his probational Expeditions aboard a Vessel of their Order, he was attacked, and taken by some *Algerines*. He immediately threw his Cross over-board, knowing, that the *Turks* hate the Knights mortally, and either kill them, or set very extravagant Ransoms upon them. He had some good Fortune with his bad, for he fell into the hands of a Master much more generous and civil, than the generality of those barbarous People use to be. The *Turk* asked him, what he could do? he answered, he had skill in Horses, and could manage them, and teach them all that would make them valuable; that he could draw too, and design, and do a great many such

such things. The *Turk* who had travell'd and was well accomplished, was very well satisfied with so dextrous a Slave; and buying up some young Horses, the Knight managed them to his Master's content, and convinced him he had pretended to no more than he was able to perform. Thus three years past on, in which the Knight made several attempts to escape, but could not.

At the end of this term, the *Turk* highly pleased with his Slave's service, said to him, *I am very well satisfied with you, and am ready to give you good proofs of it, if you have any kindness to ask me.* The Knight answered him, That he was infinitely obliged to him, and thought a Slave ought to ask nothing more of his Master, than that his services may be well accepted. *I commend your Modesty* (replyed the *Turk*) *and understand your meaning, tho you dare not speak it out. Serve me one year more, and then you shall see what I will do for you.* One may easily imagine what care and pains this Knight took all that year, to confirm himself in his Master's favour. So when that was expired, his Master sent for him into his Chamber, and said to him, *You have served me not like a Slave, but a man of honour; and now I will use you like such a man, and reward the care and affection you have shewn in my service. Tell me therefore to what place you desire to be conveyed, how you would be habited, and what you have occasion for. Ask every thing freely, and you shall have it as freely of me, as you should from the best friend you have in the world.* Being told, that he was desirous to go to *Marseilles*, he clothed him according to his own mind, and found out a Vessel for him, paid his fraight, and gave him more Money than he asked for. And thus he was sent back, as highly favoured by this *Turk*, as the *Turk* had been satisfied before with the faithful service of the Knight, without ever discovering who, or what he was.

VII. Upon his arrival at *Marseilles*, he writ me word how extremely dissatisfied he was with my elder Brother, who was not so generous and kind to him as he ought to have been, and betrayed a great deal of coldness and indifferency for his sufferings, during the time of his Slavery. The hot disposition which I knew the Knight to be of, and the angry terms in which he exprest himself in his Letter, made me apprehensive some mischief might come of this. So I askt the King (for it was in his life time) that I might take a Journey into *Provence*, and went thither post. When I was once upon the spot, it was no hard matter for me to compose all quarrels: For I furnished the Knight with whatever he desired; and when I had equipped him sufficiently for his return to *Maltha*, I was inclined to oblige my elder Brother too with new proofs of my affection. I begg'd that when his Son was a little grown up, he would send him to *Paris*, and promis'd to see him instructed in Philosophy, and all other exercises of a Gentleman, that were fit to accomplish him for the world. He was very willing to embrace the proposal, and accordingly sent him to me, when he was about thirteen or fourteen. I took all imaginable care of him, and spared nothing for him, but had him educated as my own Son. This happened some months before the Siege of *Rochelle*, of which you have an account in the first part of this Book.

VIII. But before I give a relation how this Nephew of mine was marry'd, I must tell one story more, which tho it be strictly true, yet I am sensible will look something Romantick; and that is, how my Brother, the Knight of *Maltha*, found an opportunity of making the *Turk* whose Slave he had been, a grateful return, by an act of generosity, greater than that had been shewn him before. Five or six years after he had been set at liberty, happening one day to be at *Marseilles*, and walking with a friend of his upon the Key, he saw a Vessel make into Harbour, and some Souldiers coming to shore, with several Slaves that they had taken. There was amongst the rest one *Turk*, who presently awakened in him the Idea of some face he had seen before, but he could not suddenly recollect whether he were the very person he imagin'd him to be or not. At last coming up closer, and taking a nicer view, he found it to be his old Master. Upon this, he threw his arms about his neck, and embracing him in a great rapture of joy, he said; *Providence hath ordered, that you should meet me at Marseilles, because you were so generous to dismiss me from Algiers, and used me with all the kindness and respect of a Friend. And now you shall be convinced that God does not let good works go unrewarded; and that a French-man thinks it a reflection upon him, to be outdone in civility by any forreigner whatsoever.* Then he enquir'd whose this Slave was, and what his Ransome; which when he had paid, he gave him a noble Entertainment, shew'd him all the curiosities of *Marseilles*, and then supply'd all his occasions, gave

Yyy

him

him a great deal more than he had formerly receiv'd from him, and so sent him back safe to *Algiers* again, according to his own desire. The Duke of *Guise*, who was then at *Marseilles*, had a mind to speak with this *Turk* himself; and having several times heard the story from the Knight, was us'd to say, *Well, now I believe you, because I have seen your Turk, and am an Eye-witness of your kindness, and what you desire him in return; but otherwise I should have lookt upon your story as no better than a fiction, and a kind of Romantick adventure.*

IX. The Knight some years after had a considerable Lordship in *Provence*, for several belonging to the Order lye there; and happen'd to engage himself unfortunately in the quarrel of a friend of his, to whom he was Second in a Duel; where though he got the better of his adversary, yet he received a wound, that some days after cost him his life.

I confess I cannot sufficiently express my abhorrence of this custom, or rather of this madness, that puts so many gallant men upon these fatal engagements. I have been told, that within the time of the late Queen Mother, *Ann* of *Austria*'s Regency, there were reckon'd up nine hundred and thirty Gentlemen, that were kill'd in Duels, within the several Provinces of this Kingdom; and no doubt a great many more there were, whose deaths were either conceal'd, or else imputed to other causes. Such a number of men, scattered through the parts of an Army, in several Posts, I fancy were enough to win a considerable Battel. And really, the wisdom and Justice of the present King *Lewis* XIV. is in this particular highly to be commended, who by a severity becoming both a Christian and a Prince, hath resolved never to pardon any Duellists; and so hath found a way to make these Combats now as uncommon, as they us'd to be frequent in the reigns of his Predecessors. And for my own part, I cannot but have an exceeding honour and value, for those many Lords and Gentlemen, whose Courage is out of all danger of being call'd in question, that have made a publick Declaration under their hands, that they could never look upon those men as persons of Valour, who place their honour in playing of prizes, and by a brutish stupidity lavishly throw away those lives that were design'd for the nobler purposes, of serving the Kingdom, and the defence of their Prince.

Let us dye in Gods name, at the mouth of a breach, or in a fair Battel, at the head of a Company, or a Regiment, where our Death is honourable, and our Life a Sacrifice paid to God and our Princes, who have a right to it. But who in his senses would ever expose himself to these bloody encounters, where not only our Life, but our Fortune and Honour are lost with it too; and in which we cannot lose our lives, but we must lose Heaven and our Salvation at the same time.

X. Now I come to speak of the favourable circumstances, which concurred to the matching first of my Nephew, and afterwards of his Daughter to both their advantage; and they are such as were likely enough to be thought no less Romantick, than my account of the Knight of *Malta*, did not that sincerity and strict regard to truth, which I have been known to observe all my life long, secure me from any suspicion of falshood. It happened then, while my elder Brother's Son, who was sent to me out of *Provence* to *Paris*, continued under my care, that a Lady of *Dauphine* came thither with her Daughter, about a great Suit of Law then depending, concerning the Guardianship of this young Lady, which was like to be taken away from her. I had heard some discourse of the thing, and thinking my self obliged to take their part, as being my Country-women, had a mind first to dive into the true reason of the Mother's carrying on the cause so zealously. Making a visit one day, I took the freedom to ask her, if the interest of her Daughter was the only prospect she had in this Suit; she answered me very frankly, that she sought no advantage of her own, and valued nothing comparably to her Daughter, and for her sake alone it was, that she gave her self all this trouble. I believ'd what she said to be true, and answer'd her with as much ingenuity and openness, that since she proceeded upon so generous a principle, I would shew as much generosity to her, and serve her both by my self and my friends, as heartily as if her concern were my own.

Accordingly I began to make my words good, and set all my friends to work in behalf of this Lady. Her adversaries resolv'd to trouble and tire her out, both by delays and expences, which are always very great at *Paris*, especially for such as are not settled inhabitants there; and used all arts to spin out the cause to as great a length as they could. The whole Court removing to the Siege of *Rochelle*, as I shewed formerly, this Lady found it necessary to follow them thither, that she might not seem to desert her Cause, which then lay before the Council. The extravagant charge of this business, and at a time when she wanted Money too, forc'd her one day to confess to me the great concern she was in to see her estate wasted thus to no purpose, and her self reduced to want of Money, to supply her present occasions for this Journey. I encouraged and supported her under it the best I could, assuring her I would do my utmost to bring this troublesome contest to an honourable conclusion. Then I asked her what Money she wanted, and upon her desire that I would lend her five hundred Crowns, I furnished her presently after with two hundred Pistoles. And at last I made so good interest among my friends, that the Lady carried her point.

XI. She esteemed her self extremely obliged by the service I had done her, and resolved upon the most effectual return of my kindness that was possible to be made. For having seen my Nephew several times, who came to me from *Paris* to *Rochelle*, and was then about sixteen years old, she would needs marry her Daughter, who was a great fortune, and for whose interest I had been so sollicitous, to this young Gentleman. The great confidence she had in me made her open her thoughts freely, and she profest her self highly pleased, that she had this way of making an acknowledgment for all the trouble I had been at upon her account, and her Daughters. I confess this proposal was some surprize to me, for it was what I never lookt for, nor had the least design in the world to hook it in, by any service I had endeavoured to do her. I thought this civility very obliging, and told her, she did me a great deal of honour ; and that the young Lady her Daughter deserved a much better match than my Nephew, who was but young yet, and no body could tell what sort of man he might make. She took my complemental answer for a refusal, and told me, She perceived I lookt higher, and thought her Daughter a match not worthy my Nephew. I presently rectified this mistake, and convinced her I spoke sincerely, that it was my real opinion her Daughter deserved much better, and all could be said of my Nephew was, that he was a Youth of good hopes, and one that I durst promise my self might do very well in time. *But Madam,* said I, *since you have done me the favour of so generous an offer, I agree to, and accept it with all the gratitude in the world ; and only beg that in consideration how very young both of them are, you would be satisfied with my Nephews continuing some time longer at Paris to perfect himself in his learning ; and this, Madam, without laying any restraint upon you, so that if in the mean while any other person whom you think better of be proposed, you are at full liberty to entertain him, nor shall I think my self ill dealt with at all.* She protested she was fixed in her choice of my Nephew, and designed her Daughter for no other man, and that nothing could possibly hinder it, except my refusal.

Some time after her return home she sent me word, that great applications were made for her Daughter, and she was under some apprehensions of having her stolen ; therefore intreated for the preventing of so great a misfortune, that the Marriage between her and my Nephew might be concluded. This Letter came to me before the Siege of *Rochelle* was ended, and I resolved upon sending my Nephew into *Dauphine* forthwith. To this purpose I provided him a handsome Equipage, and hastened his Journey all I could, that a match so much for his advantage might not be lost. All necessary preliminaries were put in good readiness before his arrival, and then no time was slipt, but the very next day after his coming they were contracted, and some few days after that were married.

XII. My Nephew and this Lady of *Dauphine* had a Daughter called *Anne de Pontis,* who is indeed the occasion of my relating this extraordinary accident of her Father's Marriage ; for now I am to tell you, that as my protection to a Lady in a Suit of Law brought about the Father's match, during the Siege of *Rochelle* ; so the like protection of another Lady called *Poligny,* while I was sent to guard the Mountains of *Provence* and *Dauphine,* occasioned the Marriage of the Daughter too, for this Lady gave her Son to my Niece, as a reward for my care and kindness upon that account.

The *Poligny*'s are a very good Family in the Province of *Dauphine,* and possest of a considerable Estate called *Vaubonnes,* which is a sort of little Kingdom, being a distinct Royalty consisting of fifteen Villages, all inclosed with precipices and natural

trenches,

trenches, and no paſſage into them, except by three ſeveral Bridges of Stone. Mon
ſieur *Poligny* was then ſome ſixty five years old, and had a Son to whom he gave the
name of his Lordſhip *Vaubonnes* ; but there was in the Family beſides him, a Natural
Son called *Richard*, whom Monſieur *Poligny* made Steward, or Bailiff of this Mannor,
and who managed his buſineſs ſo, as in a few years to be worth above two hundred
thouſand Livres. Monſieur *de Vaubonnes* being yet but very young had a Governour
with him, who took a great deal of care of him, and educated him as was fit for his
quality. When he was grown up to about twelve years old they gave him a Gun,
and his Governour carried him abroad ſometimes to teach him to ſhoot, by practiſing
upon Thruſhes and Black-birds.

One day as they were out upon this ſport, they met Mr. *Richard*, who took the
freedom to come very boldly, and ſhoot all over their grounds. This young Gentleman provoked at his confidence, asked by whoſe leave he came a fowling there,
told him he was diſpleaſed with it, and bad him take care he did not hear that
he did ſo any more. *Richard*, who was an inſolent fellow, and of a converſation as
ſcandalous as his birth, replyed very warmly ; That this was no new thing, for he
had always uſed to fowl there, and wondred he ſhould pretend to find fault with it.
Monſieur *de Vaubonnes* replyed, He could not tell whether he had uſed to do ſo,or no ;
but he adviſed him to come there no more, for if he did, his Gun ſhould be taken
away from him. *Richard* replyed inſolently, That he would break any man's head,
that ſhould offer to take his Gun, let him be who he would. The Governour hearing him talk at this ſawcy rate, told him, Sure he forgot himſelf, and did not con
ſider he was ſpeaking to his Lord, that he was but Bailiff of *Vaubonnes*, and held all
he had under Monſieur *Poligny*, and owed all his fortunes to him. *I know well enough
(ſays Richard) from whom my fortunes come, and do not intend to be taught by you, and you
meddle with that which does not concern you. When young Maſter is grown up, I ſhall ſpeak my
mind to him upon this buſineſs.* The Governour anſwered him, That Monſieur *Vaubonnes*
his concerns were his ; that if he did not intereſt himſelf in them, he did not deſerve
to be about him ; and he adviſed him to behave himſelf as became him, or it would
be the worſe for him. Upon this they came to hot words, and parted for that time
with much anger on both ſides.

XIII. From that moment *Richard* reſolved to be reveng'd upon Monſieur *Vaubonnes*
his Governour, being moſt enraged at him, becauſe he had heated him ; and beſides,
he lookt upon the young Gentleman under his care, as no better than a Child. One
day he came with a deſign to aſſaſſinate him, and had the impudence to come up ſo
far as the very Court before the houſe, and ſeeing him with the young Gentleman
at the door, he diſcharg'd his Gun at him, kill'd him, and fled away. The in
ſolence and blackneſs of this attempt, provok'd Madam *Poligny* extremely. She pro
ſecuted the fellow by all the ordinary courſes of Law, and at laſt had him ſentenc'd
to be hang'd, by the Intendant of the Province. The Murderer ſaw he was gone,
unleſs he could remove the Cauſe out of that Province ; and ſo went to *Fountainebleau*,
there to put in an Appeal before the Council, pretending that Madam *Poligny*'s intereſt was ſo great in the Parliament of *Grenoble*, that he could not expect any fair hearing there. This happened a little before the firſt *Paris* War, and I was then at *Fountaine-bleau*. But not knowing any thing of this wretch, nor his crime, nor having yet the
honour to be related to Madam *Poligny*, he obtain'd the Kings protection, and leave
to bring it before the Council ; and all the while took care never to ſtir without three
or four luſty Foot-men at his heels, and ſome friends beſides, as wicked and deſperate
as himſelf.

Shortly after Madam *Poligny* ſent me a Letter, giving an account of the baſeneſs
and wickedneſs of the action, conjuring me to uſe my intereſt at Court againſt this
Murderer, who had been condemn'd to be hanged at home, and remov'd his Cauſe
to the Council by an Appeal. The aſſaſſination was ſo horrid, and I ſo affected with
it, that I reſolv'd to vindicate this Lady to the utmoſt of my power. Underſtanding
that Monſieur *de Gue*, Maſter of the Requeſts, had the matter referr'd to his examination, and was to be the Reporter of it to the Board, tho every body advis'd me to
object againſt him, and told me *Richard* had been very powerfully recommended to
his favour, yet I would never do it, for I knew him to be a perſon of honour and integrity, and a very good Judge. I went to wait on him, and told him, the Reputation he had for juſtice and honeſty, made me very confident he would do Madam

Poligny right ; that her Adversary was so great a Villain, that he could not pretend to deserve any favour ; and that for my own part, I had no farther concern, than meerly what the justice of the cause gave me ; but after being entreated by that Lady to give her what assistance I could, I did not decline to become the Accuser of so base and bold an invasion upon the House of a Lord in the Country, and his own Feudatory Lord too. *Therefore, Sir,* (said I) *I require justice at your hands, and ask it against a Villain and a Murderer, that is unworthy of all mercy.*

Just as I was pressing the matter thus warmly, *Richard* came into the room where we were, attended as he used to be with a company of fellows as bad as himself. As soon as I set my eyes upon the guilty wretch, I took courage afresh, and raising my voice, *Look you, Sir,* (said I) *I desire you once more to do justice. Here's the very Murderer, that hath the confidence to appear before you with a Sword on, after having made no better use of his arms than basely and cowardly to sacrifice a man of honour to his own revenge. Against this fellow I require justice, who tho he be the King's Prisoner, and convict of an Invasion, hath the insolence to go armed still. Pray, Sir, commend him to behave himself like a Prisoner, and keep that respectful distance that is due to his Majesty's Councel.*

Tho *Richard* had been (as I said) very strongly recommended to this Master of Requests, yet so bold an address from one who had no Sword on at that time himself, made such impression, that both Judge and Criminal stood a while confounded. But at last, as justice will be heard, and the person to whom I spoke being an honest man, he could not forbear telling *Richard*, that I was in the right, and therefore he forbad him the wearing his Sword before him any more. Which made him go away very much down in the mouth, and highly enraged at me, for getting him to be so shame-fully disarmed.

The Reporter then promised me justice should be done. But being desirous still to make more sure of it, I set my friends upon him too, particularly Monsieur *de Lionne* who was then at Court ; and who, after some coldness between the Master of Requests and him, upon a former quarrel, was reconciled to him, upon this application that I engaged him in. I made use of Mareschal *Villeroy* too, who honoured me with his particular friendship, and undertook this business of Madam *Poligny* with the greatest civility imaginable. For having invited me to meet the Reporter at dinner next day at his House, when we rose from table to wash, the Mareschal said to Monsieur *du Gue, Well, Sir, you must needs rid me of the importunate solicitations of this man* (meaning me.) *He makes me believe I have some interest in you. Does he say true? And may I depend upon not being denied by you? You do me honour and justice in thinking so, Sir,* said the Master of Requests; *I can no more deny any thing you ask, than you can ask any thing fit for me to deny. Very well, Sir,* said the Mareschal, *all I desire is, that you would for my sake take care of Madam* Poligny's *business, and see that she hath Justice done her. They say the fact she prosecutes for is so horrid, that the Rascal is not fit to have any mercy shewn him.*

To make my story short, I will only add, that this Reporter, who was a very good Judge in his own disposition, saw himself so warmly plyed for justice, that *Richard's* appeal was thrown out, and the cause dismist to the Parliament of *Grenoble,* there to be re-heard, and he to stand and fall by that Tryal. This news confounded him so, that finding he had no other evasion left, and that he was lost to all intents and purposes, he resolved to submit himself, and come ask my pardon. Accordingly he did, and took all the humblest submissive ways to prevail upon me. He conjured me not to cast away all pity for him, but to write to Madam *Poligny* in his behalf, assuring her from him, that he was very ready to make her what satisfaction she pleased ; that he acknowledged his fault with great remorse, and confest the Devil had put him upon committing it.

I asked him with some indifference, whether he considered what he said, and if he spoke heartily. *For* (said I) *if you engage me in any promises for you, and do not see my word made good, I shall then turn your Adversary my self, and you will make but a bad business of it.* He protested he spoke sincerely, and was resolved to be true to his promise. Upon this assurance I proffer'd to write to Madam *Poligny,* being really moved with compassion at the forlorn condition I saw him in, and desiring to put a good end to a Tryal of so horrid a nature. Accordingly I acquainted the Lady how I found Mr. *Richard* disposed, and desired her rather to proceed gently, and think of some accommodation, and do an act of mercy to a wretch that profest a hearty repentance for his fault, and a great inclination to make her any manner of satisfaction.

Z z z　　　　　　　　　XIV. Some

XIV. Some time after this it was, that the King sent to me to pass some Troops over into *Catalonia*, and *Italy*. In the mean while *Richard* had sent my Letter to Madam *Poligny*, who easily granting his request, said, They would try whether this man would behave himself any better, and keep the promise he had made to me. To this purpose they chose four Referees, and the Duke of *Lesdiguieres* for Umpire over them, to make an end of this difference. But he, thinking the summ in which they amerced him too great, evaded this arbitration, and found a trick to get an Inhibition, and appeal, without their knowledge; pretending to the Kings Councel, that he had since found several Papers for his justication, which never had been produced in any Court before. And growing insolent upon the success of this underhand dealing, he dwelt boldly in his own house, within three Musquet-shot of *Vaubonnes*; and walk'd every where unconcern'd; but still taking care to be attended with six or seven of his friends, as fit for a halter as himself.

The good old Gentleman Monsieur *Poligny*, who was still alive, of a peaceable disposition, and one that hated Quarrels or Law-suits, was much perplexed; and was for three days together blockt up as it were in his own house, by this Rascal; who scowred the Country, and was in perpetual readiness to do mischief. I was then in *Provence*, near *Marseilles*, taken up in executing the Orders, which I was saying the King had given me. Madam *Poligny* seeing all *Richard's* fair promises come to nothing, and that her self, her Husband, and her Son, were exposed to his insolences and his outrages perpetually, came to me, and acquainted me how very ill a posture her affairs were in; conjuring me, by all the ties of the relation between us, as well as those of friendship, to assist her all I could in rescuing her from the violences of this Tyrant.

I told her, She knew me too well to question the zeal, with which I was ready to serve her as long as I lived, and that her interest was as dear to me as my own, and therefore I would do all that possibly I could for her upon this occasion; but finding my self at that time engaged in the Kings business, and indispensably oblig'd to conduct his Majesty's Troops, and be faithful to his Orders; in obedience to which I had foregone even my own Interest; all I could do at present, was to serve her with my friends; and do that by writing, which if I were at my own disposal, I would have done by word of mouth. I told her farther, I durst depend so entirely upon my friends kindness, as to promise my self, that my sollicitations by way of Letter, would be as successful to her, and as effectual with them, as if I were there to move them in person.

XV. But the Lady I discourst with was too well acquainted with *Richard's* insolence, and passionate disposition, and the necessity of my presence, to satisfie herself with my offer of managing her business by Letter. And tho she could not draw me off from the Kings Commission, and saw it impossible to gain what she desired just at that present time; yet she took a course shortly after, to fix me to her family by closer obligations, and engage me in the defence of all her interests. She came to see me, and said, She must needs impart to me a design, which I should have no great cause to dislike: That she considered, her Son at this age was not in a condition to resist the violence of so furious a man as *Richard*; that she found she wanted such a one as me, to put a check upon his insolence; that she had thought upon a way to bring us closer together than ever we were before, and that was to marry her Son to my Niece *Anne de Poutis*, (Daughter to the Nephew you heard of) that both of them were much of an age; and this new relation would make the concerns of their family become mine. I thought the proposal very obliging, and advantageous, and told her, my Niece did not deserve so great an honour; but if I refused it for her, it was only because I durst not accept it. She presently understood the consent I gave, and seem'd much pleased with it; so that taking me at my word, she urg'd the concluding of the match speedily, which we did without any great matter of formality, being very well satisfy'd in one anothers integrity, and fair dealing. I told her, I hoped she would not find herself mistaken in the good opinion she had of me; and I durst be bold to promise, that as soon as ever I had discharg'd my duty to his Majesty's Commission, I would employ my self heartily in her business, and would rather dye, than not bring her off with honour.

The

The Marriage being thus concluded, and all the Ceremonies over, young Monsieur *Vanbonnes* and my great Niece, who had about sixty thousand Livres to her portion, were marry'd with a great deal of state of solemnity. And when I had performed the Kings commands, in conveying over the Troops, I resolv'd to see my Nephew and his new Wife put into possession of their Estate. I carry'd him to *Vanbonnes*, and took ten or twelve of my friends, and all our men, well armed and well mounted, along with me. Mr. *Richard*, upon the news of our coming, shut himself and his Bullies up in his own house, and thinking that no time to appear, he went away privately the night after, to avoid any mischief, that he apprehended might come to him upon our account.

But understanding shortly after, that my friends were gone, and I left alone at *Vanbonnes*, he took courage, and return'd to his house again. Next day he had the impudence to desire he might visit me, and that I would give him leave to walk abroad. I told the man that brought the message, that I would not advise Mr. *Richard* to come where I was; and that if he took the confidence to do so, he might chance to repent it. He began to swear at this answer, and rail at me lustily, saying, I was a very pretty fellow to forbid him stirring abroad; and that, when time should serve, he would see which of us two was the better man. This however was more boasting than true Courage; and it appeared afterwards, that he was brisk only then, when he thought his the stronger side.

One Holiday, he sent to tell me, he supposed I would not be against his going to Church at *Vanbonnes*; I answered, it was my advice, that he should go to Mass somewhere else, for I would never endure that a Murderer, who had cowardly assassinated a man of honour in the Castle of *Vanbonnes*, should appear in that Church, to beard the Lord of the Mannor, whom he had affronted by that violence. I commanded my Souldiers, who were stout fellows, to be upon their good behaviour, and led Madam *Poligny* and my Niece to Church, resolving to dye rather than suffer this Villain to come there. When I was in the Church, word was brought me, that *Richard* was coming. I answer'd the fellow that told me, *Go tell him I expect him, and he shall find me here.* At the same time I dispatcht a bold fellow, and my *Valet de Chambre*, to a narrow street, through which *Richard* was to pass, and ordered them to secure that post immediately. *If Richard come there* (said I) *tell him I have ordered you to keep that Pass, and that you desire he would go no farther. If he retire, let him go, and do not pursue him, but if he pretends to advance forward, or any way abuse or affront you, fall on vigorously, and we will bear you out.*

Our two Souldiers being gone to their Post, *Richard* got intelligence of it, and durst not venture forward, for fear of being forc'd to make a shameful retreat. He satisfy'd himself with railing after his usual way, and giving me a great many hard words; and I could easily bear what I did not hear. Seeing himself driven to extremity, he grew raging mad; and that which made him worse was, that some Officers of *Lesdiguieres* Regiment, hearing what had past, came to see me, and offer me their service against this Brute of a fellow. So he was forc'd to hide again, and durst appear abroad no more.

XVI. One day they had made an agreement to go all together and breakfast at a Village about a league off from *Vanbonnes*: I was against it at first, apprehending some mischievous attempt from so enraged and desperate a man, and being loth to be drawn into any troublesome brangling business, that might create a suit at Law: At last I agreed, because I could not stand out against all the rest, who were very eager upon the frolick. But we trifled away so much time in walking up and down, and discoursing by the way, that when we came to the place, it was a fitter hour for dinner than breakfast. Monsieur *Poligny* and I perswaded them to return home, for we should be sure to meet with better provision there, and immediately we two moved back again. But young Monsieur *Vanbonnes*, concern'd for the loss of his breakfast, without taking any notice of it to us, told the Officers, it was not fair to go back again without drinking one Glass; that breakfast was ready, and they might eat a bit while we went on before. So they staid to bait, and let Monsieur *Poligny* and me go all alone, who imagin'd they would have follow'd us immediately.

When we came over against *Richard's* house, which overlooks the high-way, he got sight of us, and discovering no body else that follow'd for above a quarter of a league, resolv'd to come and attack us. With this intent he and five or six of his

friends

friends made a Sally, and ftood in the high-way at a turning, where we were to pafs. They were all on foot, but well arm'd with Swords and Piftols, and one of them had catcht up a Halbert. Seeing the place and pofture they had fix'd themfelves in, I prefently concluded, there would be the Devil to do, for there lay our way, and I was not of a humour cut out for retreating. Poor Monfieur *Poligny*, whofe years requir'd nothing more than peace and quiet, was much diftatisfy'd that our friends had forfaken us, and fo, to fpeak the truth, was I too. But this was no time for confideration, and all we had to do was to make amends for their abfence by our own refolution and courage. When we came up within fome forty paces of *Richard*, the Rogue pull'd his hat down over his face, and then cocking up the brim, walk'd in the middle of the Road, with an air of more fiercenefs than was natural to him, and cafting a malicious ftare upon me, as if he could have torn me in pieces: and his inclination I am fure was good to have done it, but I was more than ordinarily fortify'd upon this occafion. We came on our ufual pace ftrait towards him, and at laft he drew a Piftol all on a fudden, and came up with it to me, fwearing and curfing like a mad man. Seeing my felf in fome extremity, I clapt both my Spurs to my Horfe, who was exceeding nimble, and underftanding his Mafters pleafure by that fignal, threw himfelf with incredible force and fwiftnefs into the middle of the armed men, overturning fome, frighting away others, and driving them to creep away as well as they could, and hide themfelves under the hedges.

But I kept clofe to *Richard*, who was the caufe of all this quarrel, and braved it more than any of the reft; and taking him by the Collar of his Doublet, I gave him fuch a turn with all my ftrength, that his heels went over his head, and flat upon the ground I laid him; then I rid my Horfe over his body feveral times, and could have been well enough pleafed to have broken a Leg or an Arm of him, but had no defign upon his Life. But it was otherwife ordered, for my Horfe always leapt over him, without ever treading upon his body at all. My Cloak was twice fhot through, and my Horfe much wounded. I had alfo one thruft with the Halbert, which had like to have gone through my Neck, but providence directed the ftroke, and it only pierc'd the top of my Doubler. Indeed my Horfe was never more ferviceable to me than now, for he turn'd and wheel'd like an Ape; and I manag'd him at will, to run down firft one, then another, before they could recover themfelves, juft as if he had been a reafonable creature.

But yet in the midft of all this hurry and danger, there was one thing very Comical; which was, to fee the good old Gentleman Monfieur *Poligny*, who, as foon as ever he faw me make up to thefe fellows, and lay about me with my Sword and my Horfe, regarding the trouble that this action might bring upon him, more than the prefent fervice I did him, cry'd out with all his might to *Richard* and the reft, *Gentlemen, you fee I am no way concern'd in this fquabble; Bear witnefs it is Monfieur* Pontis *that does all.* And then directing himfelf to me, *Ah Sir,* (faid he) *you fpoil all, you have utterly undone me; I had the Law on my fide before, and now they will profecute me.* I anfwer'd him without any great difturbance, *Well, well, Sir, be fatisfy'd, they fee you are not concern'd; the fault is wholly mine, if it be a fault, I take all upon my felf very willingly; I am the perfon from whom they are to look for fatisfaction, and I am content to anfwer it all for your fake.*

At laft our friends who had ftaid behind came up, and ran to the noife, juft as the fcuffle was over, and the affaffinates got off. They were aftonifh'd at our good fortune, and very forry that they had mift this only occafion, in which they could have been ferviceable to us. But honeft Monfieur *Poligny* could not be quiet, nor forbear telling all the world how much this quarrel went againft him, and reproach'd me feveral times with having been the ruine of him, for that this fellow would now take the Law upon him, and be reveng'd for all by a frefh profecution. Madam *Poligny*, who was a Lady of a mafculine and generous Soul, when fhe had an account of the whole action, commended and thankt me very heartily, for having thus repreft the infolence and rage of this Villain.

XVII. *Richard*, who was very good at taking all advantages of Law, loft no time, but went away the very next night to *Grenoble*. There he clamoured againft me, for affaffinating his perfon, and put in a Petition to the Parliament, who, without any farther information, granted him a *Habeas Corpus* againft me, unlefs I put in my Appearance for fuch a day. I had feveral friends and relations at *Grenoble*, and particularly

larly Monſieur *Calignon* a Councellor, who immediately gave me notice of all the proceeding, and that an Uſher (whom he had managed) would come to ſerve this Decree upon me, at ſuch a time. I immediately ſent away two or three men ſome leagues from *Vaubonnes*, (for ſo he had adviſed me to do in his Letter) to pretend the taking away this Inſtrument by force from the Uſher, that came to ſerve it. All our deſign in this was only to gain time, that ſo we might not be brought to a hearing, before the Judges could be informed of the true ſtate of the Caſe. The Uſher, who was privately in correſpondence with us, when the men ſent by me met him, cryed out, that they offered violence to a man in his Office; and, the better to carry on the jeſt, very formally made a verbal Summons upon the place. This however deferred the proceedings a while, which was all we propos'd to our ſelves by it. And *Richard* fill'd the Country with his noiſe and railing at this violence, and our being guilty of ſo great a contempt and affront (as he call'd it) to the authority of the Parliament.

Monſieur *Leſdiguieres* had receiv'd a very partial and falſe account of our firſt quarrel, and writ me word, he was extremely ſurpriz'd to hear ſuch reports of me; that the violences I had committed in the Country were in every bodies mouth, and all the world cry'd ſhame of them; that he indeed could ſcarce believe them, becauſe he had always had a good opinion of me: But if thoſe rumours were true, and I went on at that rate, he ſhould be forced to make uſe of that power the King had given him, as Governeur of the Province. It is eaſie to conceive, how much I was aſtoniſhed to find ſo juſt, ſo innocent an action, warranted by all the Laws of Nature and Nations, (for indeed it was no more than my own neceſſary defence, when my life was attempted) ſo much run down by all the world, as if I had done ſome very heinous thing.

But to diſabuſe Monſieur *Leſdiguieres*, and prevent the ill conſequences thas *Richard*'s caballing and unjuſt ſollicitations might bring upon me, I wrote a very reſpectful, but at the ſame time a very vehement anſwer in my own defence, acquainting him, That I perceived my Enemies had traduced me to him, and inſtead of giving him a true relation of the matter, had diſguiſed it with lyes, and poſſeſt him againſt me by ſeveral falſe inſinuations; That I had the confidence to hope, a perſon of ſo much honour and juſtice as I knew him to be, would be ſo far from condemning, that he would commend me for what I had done, when he was more truly informed. Then I related the fact with all its circumſtances at large, and all that had paſt between us before this encounter, and cloſed my Letter with expreſſions to this purpoſe. *And now, my Lord, I beg your leave to ſay, that I muſt have behaved my ſelf juſt thus upon ſuch circumſtances, and ſuch provocations to the beſt Nobleman in the Land, and never a man in the Kingdom could have forced me to take other meaſures. The King is my Maſter: And it is my duty to preſerve my honour and my life for his ſervice. If I had acted any otherwiſe, than as I did upon this occaſion, I ſhould deſerve to be uſed like a Coward and a pitiful Fellow, both by the King, and by your ſelf (My Lord) to whom I have the honour to be the moſt humble of all your Servants,* &c.

My Letter was as ſucceſsful as I could wiſh, for it undeceived Monſieur *Leſdiguieres* perfectly, ſo that he ſent me a very kind and civil anſwer, telling me, he was very well pleaſed to know the truth of the matter; and, now he did ſo, he aſſured me, that this accident would only contribute to the increaſing that regard and good opinion which he had always had of me and my conduct.

XVIII. This I thought was my time to drive *Richard* to his laſt ſhifts, and take him down in the midſt of all his triumphs, and therefore I entered my action againſt him, and knowing he had been guilty of great ravage in the Country, I brought all them in whom he had oppreſſed, or any way wronged. After all their complaints had been atteſted, and informations publickly given in according to form of Law, I had them all preſented to the Parliament, and the witneſſes to them.

In the mean time Monſieur *Calignon*, Madam *Poligny*, and ſeveral other friends of ours, employed themſelves very vigorouſly and ſucceſsfully in my behalf, and brought the Cauſe into a readineſs for being heard. Then the wretch ſeeing no hopes of eluding the matter, and that all his applications and ſhifts could not ſignify any thing in arreſt of judgment, but the Gallows muſt be the reward of his wickedneſs, thought the wiſeſt part he had left to play, was once more to throw himſelf at my feet, and ask forgiveneſs; and ſubmit to any other conditions, though never ſo hard, provided I would but ſpare his life.

As

At first I was extremely provoked because of his falshood and baseness, in breaking his promise to me before, and the insupportable insolence of his behaviour since, I could not prevail with my self to hearken to any terms of accommodation whatsoever, and thought that both a regard to justice, and the quiet of the Country, made the hanging of such a fellow absolutely necessary. But at last his continued importunities, and the desperate condition he was in, giving me some little grounds to hope still, that this would be a warning, and mend him for the future, I began to be softned, and think of taking some milder course, and shew him some mercy. I told him therefore, that though he had lost all his credit by the breach of those promises he made, when he came to me at *Paris*, upon this very account of saving him once before, I was yet content to grant, what he could have no just pretence to expect ; but in the first place he must resolve upon three things : First, That he would absolutely, and for ever quit that Country. Secondly, That his Estate should be sold ; and then in the third place, That all the fees, and other charges of the Tryal, should be paid out of the money that rose upon that sale.

Richard, who though he was hard put to it, yet thought however, he had better buy his life at the expence of his estate, than be hanged with a Purse about his neck, told me, He was resolved to submit, and ready to do all this, upon condition his life might be saved. And this was the full and final conclusion of all this troublesom business. His Lands were all sold, the Charges of Suit were paid with part of the money. He asked Madam *Peligny*'s pardon, left the Country presently, and hath never been seen there since. And in truth, considering what a wretch I had to deal with, I stood in need of a great deal of good management, resolution and perseverance, to bring him to, and get a head over that insolence of his, that nothing was able to daunt or subdue. His rage, his heat of temper, and his despair working upon a busy and designing head, made him fit for all sorts of wickedness and extravagance. And it was a signal instance of the Divine Justice, that this haughty, this bloody-minded wretch, should at last be brought to stoop, and glad to submit to the pleasure of that very man, whom he would have been best pleased to destroy, and whom of all the world he hated most.

The End of the Seventh Book.

BOOK

BOOK VIII.

The Sieur de Pontis *comes to* Paris. *The sudden death of one of his Friends, puts him upon retiring from the business of the world. He goes into the Country to a Friend's House. He defends that House from some Troops of Monsieur* Turenne*s Army, who made an attempt to plunder it. He withdraws wholly from the world. His Piety during that retreat. A Letter written by him to a Governour of two young Noblemen at Court, containing directions for educating Persons of Quality. His Death.*

I. AFter all this trouble that I had run through upon occasion of my Neice's Marriage, I returned to *Paris* again, and carried young Monsieur *Vaubonnes* thither with me, to learn his exercises. But he fell into a most unhappy business there, and was very innocently engag'd in an accident, that had very near cost him his life. There lodged a Gentleman in the same house with him, that had a great quarrel depending. He desired my Nephew one day to lend him his Pistols, and without mentioning one word of this quarrel, prevailed with him to bear him company. My Nephew, who was young, and ignorant of the world, lent him the Pistols, and thinking no hurt, nor knowing whither he was going, went along with him, attended by a *Valet de Chambre*, that I had recommended to his service, who was a very stout young fellow. When all three were come to the house, this Gentleman desired my Nephew would go in with him, because he said, he had some business there. When they were come in, and unhappily had met the person against whom the quarrel was, he presently fell into a passion, and talked like a mad man, in a most provoking manner. From words they came to blows, and he setting one of his Pistols to his head, shot him stone dead. This was all done in an instant, but seeing the noise bring in a great deal of company, my Nephew, in great confusion at so sudden, and fatal an accident, was for recovering the door. He and his man drew immediately, and standing close by one another, they made their way out through all the people, that came crowding in to see what the matter was: They made the best of their way to my Lodging, and the Gentleman that had done the thing got off, and made his escape another way.

My Nephew, though he was very little to blame, yet durst not say any thing of the matter to me: But the dejection and disorder that shewed it self in his countenance, presently gave me some uneasie suspicions. At length, the *Valet de Chambre* seeing the importance, and the ill consequences of such a business as this, related the whole matter as it past; and then my Nephew discovered his part in it, and vow'd he was in no fault at all; that he was not in the least acquainted with the Gentlemans design, who had committed the Murder, till they were come all together, and the very time of action; and his going along with him was intended for no more than a walk, or making an indifferent visit. I was much surpriz'd at this ill news, and knew not what course to take: At last I resolv'd to go wait on the Abbot *Servien*, who was a relation of my Nephew, and who was the great inducement to us, to bring him out of *Dauphine* to *Paris*. After I had told him the business, and we had consulted with some friends what was best to be done, it was thought the safest way for this young Gentleman to make all the haste he could into *Dauphine* again: For tho he were never so innocent, yet considering how far he had been unhappily engag'd to appear in the thing, it would have been very difficult for him to justifie himself, and convince the Judges that he had no share in the crime.

II. Now as this tragical accident drove my Nephew from *Paris* home again, so another which, though the death were natural, yet appeared to me more terrible, prevailed with me shortly after to withdraw wholly from the world. It pleased God at last to bring me out of the wretched condition in which I had lived so long, without any other notions of goodness, than what proceeded meerly from honour and natural generosity, and a virtue meerly moral and humane. And to this purpose he made use of the surprizing death of a friend, for whom I had a tender affection and particular honour, to put me into some saving terrors, and make me reflect upon my self. The infinite deaths of my friends, which I had been an Eye-witness of in the Army all along, made no deeper impression upon my mind, than just what served to lament the loss of the men I loved; but this pierced me to the very heart, and made me think of bewailing my self and my own circumstances, and to entertain my mind with very serious considerations of what, for ought I knew, was as likely to be my own fate, as any other man's.

Going one day to visit this friend at his Country-house, with no other design, than to enjoy a little diversion and good company, I spent some time with him and his Lady, as pleasantly as I could. When I design'd to return for *Paris*, I was providentially stopt by the very person, who had the chief part in the dismal tragedy I am going to relate, and by that means became the first instrument of my Conversion. For fancying me to grow weary, and suspecting I might steal away in the morning without taking a formal leave, he order'd my Bridles and Saddles to be hid, and used his utmost endeavour to divert and make me easie. He told me, his Brother was to draw a Pond the next day, and engag'd me to go along with him, and see them fish. I had the honour to be intimately acquainted with his Sister-in-law, and as we were taking a turn together in the Garden, and talking very freely upon several subjects, she told me all on the sudden, that she observ'd some very odd look about her Brothers Face and Eyes, and askt me if I did not discern it too. I told her, I had but very small skill in Physiognomy, but I had not discovered any thing unusual in him. Still she carry'd the discourse on farther, and said, She thought he had death in his face. I took a more nice view of him when we met again, and told her, that all the dismal looks she saw, were more in her own imagination, than her Brothers face.

The event however convinced me, that she was a great deal more critical than I, whether she spoke thus through some unaccountable natural instinct, or whether being more used to him, she discovered something extraordinary, which I could not find out: As we two were going back alone in his Coach after dinner, he was seized with a kind of convulsion, and a trembling all over his body, which lasted about as long as a *Miserere*. What his Sister had said came fresh into my mind, but trying to turn it off with a jest, that I might not fright him, I cryed merrily, *Why how now, Sir, what's the matter? You mutter and make faces like a Jugler shewing his tricks. Come, come, let's divert our selves, and do not be melancholly. Let us alight and walk to get us a heat.* So the thing went off, and made no great impression upon him: But I began to be under some apprehensions, and had sad presages of this unhappy accident.

III. Next day, as we were sitting by the fire after dinner, he, his Lady, and I, having all of us received Letters from *Paris*; Come (says he) *Monsieur* Pontis *shall read us this news first.* I needed no great entreaty, and read my Letters, which had nothing of any consequence in them. Then he read his own, where there was no great matter neither. As his Lady was beginning hers, in which she had all the Court-news, he had a mind to make himself merry, and turning to me, *Look you here* (says he) *you see how old Age is despised; no body regards us now, we are no sooner out of sight, but out of mind too. There's none of us, but my Wife in favour.* The Lady who was very reserved, seem'd offended at a discourse that reflected upon her modesty, and clapt her Letter together again; *Nay, Sir* (said she) *if you talk thus, I will read you no news of mine I promise you: This to me is very fine.* He seeing her take it in earnest, turn'd the discourse, and engaging to hold his tongue, prevail'd with her to read her Letters. Then he said, he must go write to his Brother, and she having Letters to write too to some friends of hers, went with me out of his Chamber, and there we left him to write all alone.

Thus no doubt Providence order'd it, to save a Lady so very affectionate and vertuous as she was, the being present at an accident, enough to have kill'd her too. I

was

was no sooner gone down stairs, but meeting a Foot-boy, I bad him go into his Masters Chamber, and see if he wanted any thing. He went up presently, and the first thing he saw when he came in at the door, was his Master stretcht all along upon the floor, lying upon his back before the fire, with his hands cross his stomach, and dead, as if he had lain there four and twenty hours. So surprizing a sight frighted him extremely, and instead of going in, he ran away, and came to me in a perfect distraction, crying, *Sir, Sir, my Master is dead. Come quickly, for God's sake, come quickly.* *What sayst thou Child?* (cryed I) *How! dead!* And running strait to the Chamber as fast as I could, I came in, and found the body in the posture described just before. *Ah Lord God!* (said I) *what a sight's here?* Presently the news flew round the house, and all the family came running in; nothing but sighs, and groans, and tears to be seen or heard, and every one almost out of their senses with the suddenness of the accident.

But one thing surpriz'd me above all the rest, when I took a particular view of the body, which was, that exactly upon his two Ancle-bones there was a little burn, about the bigness of a Half-Crown, and as round as if it had been drawn with a pair of Compasses: His Shoes and Stockings on both Feet had a hole quite through them in this place, and the burn went into his Skin as deep as the thickness of a Six-pence. That which made it still more amazing was, that his Feet lay a great distance from the fire, and I could not possibly devise how they should come to be burnt that way. You may imagine what a consternation the whole house was in: They ran about like people out of their wits: They brought Drugs upon Drugs, Cordial Waters, and all sorts of Medicines, to make him take them. They heated Napkins, and rubb'd his Stomach with them, to try if there was any bringing him to himself, as if it had been a swooning fit. But all they could do was to no manner of purpose, for he was stark dead, and mov'd no more than a log.

By this time his Lady, who could not be kept long in ignorance, ran in an extreme passion into the chamber where the dead body lay. But I put my self between, took her in my arms, and laid her upon the bed in her own room, with these words: *By your favour, Madam, this is no place for you, you can do no good here now, pray to God for his soul, he needs that most, and it is the greatest kindness you can shew him.* The very same day, a little after this, the Chamber where the dead man lay took fire, in a beam under the Chimney. And the next day, which was that of his Funeral, the Chimney was on fire again, so that we were perpetually pursued with misfortunes, one upon the neck of another. I ordered all matters as well as I could, and so as to express my respect due to the memory of the deceased person, taking care to bury him decently, though without any great solemnity.

IV. But such an amazing death as this sat close upon my Spirits, and made strange impressions upon me; it put me upon making very grave reflections upon the uncertainty of the present life, and how unstable all things here below are. Thus I used to argue often with my self: Why! this man was lusty and well but a quarter of an hour ago, and yet he is dead in an instant. What hinders but I may dye in as little a time as he? I then who am alive and well just now, perhaps may be gone a quarter of an hour hence. Ah poor wretch, what will become of thee then! What indeed can become of thee in this condition, so unprovided, so void of all thoughts of death? It is high time now to think of it to purpose. Perhaps Almighty God intends this death as a particular call and warning to thee. One thing I had from his Confessor's own mouth, which added to my wonder and astonishment still more. For he told me, that one day as he was confessing, they both heard three loud knocks at the Chamber door. He rose immediately to see who it was, but opening the door, found no body. When he was come back, and had put himself in a posture to go on with his confession, he heard a knocking again, still louder than before. This made him rise again to see who knockt so very violently, and finding no body the second time, he cryed to his Confessor, *Ah, Father, this doth not concern you.* And accordingly he took it as sent to him for a warning, and notice of his dying shortly after.

V. A very particular friend of his and mine, coming thither some few days after, I related to him all the circumstances and manner of his death; and he, who was a person of great piety, took occasion from thence, to discourse me concerning the vanity of the world, and how perfect a nothing the most flourishing fortunes of it are; he

repre-

represented to me very lively, the frailty of mans life; how very quickly he is changed from a state of vigour and perfect health, to a dead Carcass, and a cold Grave. To this purpose he discoursed with me above an hour together, and finding my mind already softned and prepared by that surprizing accident, this conference affected me still a great deal more, and I began to resolve every day more and more, to disengage my self from the world for all together.

In order to it, I applied my self to a person of great Piety and Learning for advice; who told me first of all, that a man who had spent all his days in a Camp and a Court, as I had done, ought to think very well before he attempt any such thing. I answered, That my Conversation it was true had been very much to blame, but they were such old Sinners as I, that stood in greatest need of assistance. He in his great wisdom replyed, That Jesus Christ was come to call Sinners indeed, but it was highly necessary that I should examine very thoroughly, whether this intention of withdrawing came from God; and whether I did not rather forsake the world in revenge, or in a peevish humour, because the world had before begun to forsake me. That besides, one who had taken some liberties, and conversed with people of quality, and great variety of company, would find it extremely difficult, if not absolutely impossible, to undergo so great a change all on the sudden, as that solitude I pretended to retire into would prove; that the best way would be to try to wean my self by degrees, first live as privately as I could at my own house, keep home, and break off the custom of making visits, and going into company, and then spend some months in the Country, at some friends house. This advice I could not but allow was very prudent: And though I felt my self very eager and impatient to take my leave of the world once for all, yet I took other measures, and followed his counsel.

I began to look back upon my past life, and could not without amazement reflect upon the six and fifty years which with so much eagerness I had spent in the Camp and Court, and all this to raise a trifling and transitory fortune, without taking any manner of care for another life; or having any effectual impressions made upon me by death, which I was so frequently put in mind of, by instances set before my Eyes in the Army every hour. I took a view of the many hazards and apparent dangers to which my life had been exposed in all that time, some of which you have seen in these *Memoirs*; and then looking up to the infinite mercy of God, which had preserved me from death a thousand and a thousand times, to give me an opportunity at last of working out my salvation, I felt my self perfectly lost in thought, and my mind opprest with the mighty, the many mercies of God to me, many as the moments of my life, for each moment I saw plainly might very well have been that of my death and utter ruine. Then I proceeded very seriously to compute, what benefit I had reaped of all my labours and long hardships, of all that service which with so much fidelity and diligence I had paid, and especially to my Master the late King. And here was a goodly account indeed. For I had devoted my self entirely to a Prince, who I knew must dye, and when he did so, all I had left me was the sorrow for his death, and the sad consideration of having lost him for ever. This sorrow then however gave me a clearer sight, how good and merciful a Providence it was, that I should out-live this Prince, for I am sure the chains that tied me fastest to the Court, were broken at his death. And I found my self much more at liberty, much better disposed now to attend to the call of God in that surprizing death of my friend, which he made use of as a means to disengage me perfectly from the world: The world which I had loved so passionately before, though it had made me so ill returns for my kindness.

VI. Being some months after upon a Journey from *Paris*, to spend some time in the Country, there happened an accident at *Melun*, just as I had done Supper, which gave me very great disorder. I had sent my Servant to look after my Horses, and take care they wanted nothing, and as soon as he was gone out, a general weakness seized me all over, and such a sinking of my Spirits, that I thought I should have dy'd immediately: Not being able to cry out, or call any body, I said to my self, *What! shall I be so miserable to dye without any help? Perfect, O my God, the mercy thou hast begun in me, and take me not away in this condition.* I was very strong, considering my age, and so put my self forth to rise from my Chair, and staggered along to the Bed-side, threw my Arms round one of the Bed-posts, and there with bustling about, and keeping my body in motion, with the blessing of God, I scattered the Vapours, that rose and had

like

like to have choak'd me. I took no notice of this to my Servant when he came in again, but only order'd my Bed to be warm'd, and went into it, and next morning went on my Journey, towards the place I intended for.

After some months spent in the Countrey, where, by reason of the frequent visits of my friends, I found my way of living less private than in the Town; I came back to *Paris*, and address my self again to the same person I had consulted before; and begg'd him to help. and take some care of me; assuring him, that my way of life was as yet nothing different in effect from what it had been formerly; and that in short I found it necessary to take up still more strictly, and live after another kind of rate than I had hitherto done. After some discourse together upon the matter, he advised me to take more time, and consider of it a little longer still. And thus he put me off from time to time, till at last the second *Paris* War came on.

VII. Madam *Saint-Angel* had desired me (being a relation) to go do a little business for her at her Estate of *Saint-Angel*; and there I presently found my self perplexed again with troubles that I never thought to be concerned in any more. For Mareschal *Turenne's* Army, who were guilty of very great disorders in their way from *Bourdeaux*, surpriz'd me here so suddenly, that I had scarce any time to provide for my own defence. All the Court of *Saint-Angel* was immediately full of Cattel, and the Granaries fill'd with the wealth of all the Inhabitants thereabours. Apprehending the House was in danger of being plundered, I went to meet the Troops upon their march, and to try if I could find any of their Generals of my acquaintance at the head of them. The first I met was Mareschal *Hoquincourt*, whom I went and paid my respects to, and told him, that being accidentally in the Country at Monsieur *Saint-Ange's* house, who had the honour to be known to him, having succeeded his Father in the office of First *Maitre de Hotel* to the Queen; I came most humbly to intreat the favour of him, to take that house into his protection. and secure it from being plundered. Monsieur *Hoquincourt* reply'd with an Oath, *How should I secure Monsieur St. Ange's house, when I could not secure one of my own, and above twenty more of my friends and relations that have been all rifled? There's no such thing as discipline in this Army: The Souldiers are mad with perfect hunger, and are but so many Robbers. Sir,* said I, *since they are Robbers, and hungry Wolves, you will not take it ill I hope, if we defend our selves, and kill as many of them as we can.* He answer'd me, *Do your best, in Gods name, defend your selves from their violence and rapine; and if you can keep them from plundering of* St. Ange *do.*

But I quickly saw what a folly it would be, to pretend to hold out with thirty or forty Souldiers, against so many Troops that might powr in upon the House, and therefore resolv'd to try some other way for securing the Castle. I went to Monsieur *Vaubecourt*, *Mareschal de Camp*, who was a friend of mine, and desir'd his assistance in this difficult point; but he gave me no better satisfaction than Monsieur *Hoquincourt* had done before; For he told me, he was very sorry to see me so unluckily engag'd; and assur'd me, there was never an Officer in the Army could secure me from plundering. However (said he) *I will give you some of my Guards if you please; tho I must tell you beforehand too, that I gave a Gentleman, who made the same request, two of them yesterday, and yet his house was pillaged, and both my Guards knockt on the head.*

Just then Monsieur *Turenne* went by about forty paces off, and knowing me at that distance, call'd me to him, and askt me what made me there; raillying me for my paltry equipage, for in truth I had a rascally Horse under me, and not so much as a Bridle on him, for I could not come at my own, it being lockt up in the Castle, the Draw-bridge to which I had ordered to be broken down. I answered Monsieur *Turenne*, that I happen'd to be at Monsieur *St. Ange's* house, and was much distressed for the passage of his Army. He had shew'd me great kindness all along, ever since I had the honour to be acquainted with him, and his Brother Monsieur *Boniston*, at the Prince of *Orange's* Court, who was their Unkle, and who (as I observed formerly) was exceeding gracious to me. So he offer'd me his service immediately, and askt what he could do for me. I told him, if he would favour me with three Regiments, I would post them at three Mills hard by, and by that means I should at once save the Castle, and do the Army service, by taking care that they should have a good quantity of Meal and Bread. Monsieur *Turenne* embraced my proposal presently, and told me he was very glad of it, for provisions were scarce with them; and entreated me, that since I was well acquainted with the Country, I would set the Guards of the Army in the most convenient places. I did so very

willingly,

willingly, but firft took the Regiments of *Turenne*, *Uxelles*, and the *Marine*, and fee them about five hundred paces from the Caftle, to block up the avenues. I chofe to keep them at this diftance, for fear the very men I fet to guard the houfe, fhould be the firft to rob it. Then I went to fet the *Corps de Garde* for the Army, in the places where the Enemy might advance; and having appointed five hundred *German* Horfe a very forward poft, the Commander began to fwear in his own tongue, and faid, They perceived I knew where to fet them to be knockt on the head. Tho I did not underftand the language he fpoke, yet I eafily gueft his meaning, and without taking any notice, ordered a thoufand Foot to fuftain thofe five hundred Horfe, and three hundred Horfe more to fupport them again, with the fame number upon both Wings; which prefently won me the Collonels favour, infomuch that he came and gave me his hand, and proffer'd to do me any fervice.

VIII. When I had difcharged my truft, and fet all the Guards and Centinels upon a little River juft by, I went back to the Caftle with an Officer, whom with fome others I invited to fupper. But was told to my great furprize, that the Souldiers were come on the backfide of the houfe, and had made a breach already in the Wall of the Bafe-Court, which they were upon entring at. I was enraged to fee that all my meafures were broken, and all my care to no purpofe, and that the three Regiments had not begirt the Caftle quite round, as I gave order they fhould. In this paffion, not knowing what to refolve, I took this courfe at laft. I told the Officer with me, it was to no purpofe to undertake the beating off thofe men, with a few Firelocks in the Caftle; and therefore if any thing could, Authority, and not Oppofition muft do the work. *I know a little back door* (faid I) *which we muft go through, and fo go ftrait into the breach. Pray be fo kind to follow me, and be pleafed to do as you fee me do.*

So through this door we went, and directly to the place where the Souldiers had made a large paffage, and running upon them with my Cane in my hand; *How Rafcals* (cryed I) *what do you think to play the Rogue here, while the Enemy are forcing the Quarter?* And fo laying on as hard as I could about their pates, and then pufhing them with the flat of my Sword, we alarm'd them fo effectually, that they never attempted to defend themfelves, but to make their efcape, and recover their Quarter. This was the only way that could have been taken to manage thefe Rake-hells; and while their principal Officers acknowledged their own felves, that they could not mafter them; and by their want of Authority fuffered the greateft diforders, and outrages to pafs without controul; I found out a means to fhew them by this inftance, how they ought to preferve their Authority upon fuch like occafions. Some of them telling me, they wondred how I durft ufe fuch an arbitrary method over Troops which were not under my command; I told them again very freely, That I had commanded long enough to make Souldiers obey me; and had at any time rather quit my Commiffion, than endure to fee my felf maftered by thofe that ought to fubmit to me. That feeing no other way to get clear of the difficulty I was in, I had without any great confideration pitch'd upon this; and that at fuch times a man muft venture all, and reduce all that experience hath taught him into practice. Afterwards I fent Monfieur *Turenne* nine Veals for his own Table, and made him fome other prefents in acknowledgment of his civility to me. I took care likewife to provide the Army with Meal and Bread, according to my promife. And the Troops decamping from thence two days after, I went back to *Paris* fhortly after, not caring to engage any more in troubles of this kind, but purfuing my defign of retiring from the world.

IX. This was in the time of the fecond *Paris* War, when it was reported that the Prince intended to attack it with his Army, and to come in at one of the Suburbs. Being then at a houfe in that part of the Suburbs, I faw every body in a terrible confternation. I told them, provided they would keep clofe in their own houfes, there could be no danger; for the Gates were too ftrong to be eafily forced, and all they had to do was to defend their own dwellings. But when the Enemy fhould enter the place, they fhould fatisfy themfelves as the Souldiers made any hole in the Gates to clap in a Plank, as their way is at Sea, when a Gun hath made a breach in a Ship. For as there, all their care is to keep out the water, and prevent the Veffels finking; fo, when an Army powrs in upon any place, the main bufinefs is to hinder the Souldiers

diers from getting into their houses, for so long as they are in the streets, the Officers allow them no leisure to do mischief, because it is necessary to advance as fast as they can.

At last, after a great many hindrances, I was happy in an opportunity of shaking off business and the world, and withdrawing into a religious solitude; where I recollect all the accidents of my life, the hazards and dangers I have got over, and bless and thank God every day, for the signal and unusual favour of preserving these little remains of life, for the bewailing and atoning for my former miscarriages. One of the greatest advantages of my retreat was, the more free enjoyment of Monsieur *d'Andilly's* conversation, and the particular friendship he honoured me with. He was the fittest person that could be to take off all relish of worldly pleasure from me, for no body better knew the vanity of it. He was there at the same time, but after a very different manner. For in the midst of all that vast esteem due to his great worth, he had kept a mind lifted above ambition, such as would never suffer him to devote himself to any Master less than God, and always shewed a generous contempt of the world, even when most loved and courted by it. But for my part, I must own, I had been a Slave to it all along, had undergone real evils in hopes of an imaginary happiness; had pursued a false and treacherous fortune that always fled from me, and the vain satisfaction which I sought, would have made me but more unhappy still in the possession of it.

This single pattern of Monsieur *Andilly's* life both past and present was a continual lesson to me. I often admired his management of himself at Court; and knew, that having several times discoursed the King in private upon very nice points, and once particularly concerning Duels, he delivered his opinion to him with so much freedom, and at the same time with so much prudence and caution too; that his Majesty heard him with great satisfaction. And, after telling him that he did so, commanded, that when ever he had any advice of that kind to offer, he should desire a private and particular audience, and should be sure to have it.

It is with great pleasure that I call to mind so wise and good a temper in my Master; the late King, which though very necessary, is not yet very common in Princes. For they are beset with a company of people, who generally make it their business only to please and flatter them. And if some one by chance, out of a sincere zeal and respect, hath the boldness to tell honest truth, it is very seldom that this advantage is made use of, or the person esteemed, as he really deserves.

I have frequently discoursed Monsieur *Andilly*, about the excellent qualities of this Prince, which he was a witness of as well as I, and among others, of one piece of good nature peculiar to him; and that was, when any Mother applyed to him in behalf of her Son, or any Wife for her Husband, though their passion sometimes shewed it self in their expressions, and carryed them beyond the respect due to him, he never took notice of it, but received all they said with great sweetness and compassion. And if any of those about him were offended at such disrespectful behaviour, he would presently say, *Alas! You must consider, it is a Mother or a Wife that speaks, and the concern of a Husband or a Child is so tender, that if we cannot relieve them, yet the least we can do, is to hear and to pity them.*

I am obliged to Monsieur *Andilly* for one thing particularly, which I cannot omit mentioning in this place, and I value it the more, because I hope to find it a great comfort at my last hour, and an earnest of Gods mercy to me in another world.

I had the Government of a small place in *Dauphine*, which I had a mind to quit, and could get but a very small consideration for it. But a *Hugonot* Gentleman having advised with some of his own perswasion, and considering, that in case of any Civil War, if they were Masters of this Town, they might by vertue of that, command all the Valley in which it stood, (which would be of great consequence too, in regard of all the Country thereabouts) he desired me to part with this Government to no body but him, promising to give me my own price for it. I should have thought seven or eight thousand Livres a pretty good bargain, but upon discourse he told me at last, that rather than go without it, he would give fifty thousand.

I confess this was some temptation to me: The remembrance of my past losses, the years I was now grown into; an age, when a man is always too fond of what he hath, and too fearful of losing it, and too greedy of what one hath not, made me of opinion, that nothing could be more natural, than to accept such a proposal, especially when it offered it self without my seeking, and was so very convenient for me.

As

As to any case of Conscience in it, I was satisfy'd, that if I were disposed to consult those who give rules in such matters, I should find enough who would determine it in favour of my own opinion; and tell me, that as long as there was no present visible inconvenience in the Sale, and that I lookt at nothing farther than a good valuable consideration, which was freely offer'd to me, I need only take care of the Money, and leave the event to God, without troubling my self with scruples about things, which perhaps might never come to pass.

But upon conferring with Monsieur *Audilly* upon the matter, I was so affected with the generous and Christian notions, that his pious discourse infused into me, as to make me inflexible by any other considerations. For he convinced me plainly, that the chief rule for deciding Cases of Conscience, is to consult the integrity of a mans own heart above any thing else, and do nothing but what one can fairly answer to one's own Conscience. And if I aim'd at this only, I should easily see, that since the *Regents* proffer'd more for this place by forty thousand Livres than it was really worth, this must be done upon a prospect, that at one time or other it might be of some use to them against the Catholick party; and then it was plain, I could not put it into their hands, without betraying the interest of my Religion, and the Crown, for the sake of my own private advantage. And that, if I would shew my self as true to God, as I had done to the late King, I should express my fidelity upon this occasion, and take a pleasure in preferring his glory before any thing else.

I yielded presently to these reasons, which I found agreeable to the sense of several very learned persons besides: Possibly the infinite mercy of God may remember me one day for this action. Tho' I look upon it as meer chaff and nothing, in comparison of the misdemeanours of six and fifty years spent in the Wars, and at Court, which I ought to dread, as vast Mountains capable of overwhelming me at the day of Judgment; and should do so, if he had not given us his own word, that when we have sincerely endeavoured to give him satisfaction in this Life, his Mercy shall set us above his Justice in the next.

In this solitude I feel daily the pleasure of living in a holy quiet, and remote from the clutter and vanity of the world, without any other business than to prepare for death, to make satisfaction to God for my sins, and in some measure make up the loss of so many past years. Now my own experience hath taught me, how much more easie and gentle the yoke of my Saviour is, than that of the World; how many charms Retirement hath more than Busiuess; and how much even that bitterness and hardship undergone by me, in the different employments of a laborious life, contributes to the recommending the several exercises of a solitary and religious life. And now, when I compare the service I have paid to several Kings, with that which I endeavour to pay at present to the King of Kings; and consider the infinite distance between Him and the greatest Princes; and the inestimable happiness, which beyond all humane appearance, I have attained, to know the greatness and Glory of God, I could employ my self continually in repeating that Hymn in the daily Prayers of the Church; *Now to the King Eternal, the immortal, invisible, and only wise God, be honour and glory for ever and ever, Amen.* And since (as I said) the thoughts of death at present wholly entertain my thoughts, I have taken for my Motto in this retirement, the following Verses, given me by a friend of mine.

> *From Courts and Camps, to peaceful shades retire,*
> *My Soul; scorn vain, and to true Joys aspire:*
> *Hence to thy Heaven, wing'd with devotion, fly;*
> *Who would for ever live, must learn betimes to dye.*

This gallant Souldier after his retirement liv'd with wonderful simplicity, and renounc'd all the notions of his own judgment, tho that were very great; submitting himself entirely to the directions of a person, whom he chose to guide him in the methods of this new life, upon which he had now entred. He was sensible what difference there is between God and the World; and wisely concluded, that his experience of the one might be a prejudice and hinderance to him in the service of the other. Therefore looking upon himself as one that stood in need of a Governour, he shew'd himself so easie and so tractable, as plainly proved, he had brought his mind into a perfect and absolute subjection to God.

After

After his retreat, he had several trials, and particularly in point of losses, as himself hinted, which did but teach him better to disengage his affections from the riches of this world. Particularly the loss of fourscore thousand Livres at once, by the breaking of one, who had his Money in his hands. This must needs be the more sensible affliction, because it was the greatest part of what he had drudged for six and fifty years together : And all the world values that more, that is of their own getting, than that which cost them no pains, or descends to them by inheritance. And besides, his generous nature always made him dread the being burdensome to his friends, (as several passages in his *Memoirs* shew) and this very temper it was, that kept him back from the highest preferments. But, which is a further commendation of his worth in this respect, this very fear, which this loss, and some others that threatned him, gave so just occasion for, could not prevail with him to accept a considerable summ for his Government in *Dauphine*, when he was told it could not be taken without injuring his Conscience. From whence we may well conclude, that tho he exprest some dissatisfaction upon occasions concerning his Estate, and the wants he was reduced to, yet he at last submitted all that worldly Wisdom, to the strictest rules of Religion, and disinterested Piety.

In the beginning of his retreat, he happen'd into a very dangerous business; by which Providence sure intended to shew what he was, to such as did not yet know him throughly; that after having been Eye-witnesses of his great courage, presence of mind, and wise conduct, they might be the more edified by that great change, which they saw had brought down so great a Soul, and prevailed with so much Wisdom to be govern'd by the directions of another. A person of quality being upon a Journey into the Country, in the time of the second *Paris* War, desir'd him and some other friends to bear him company, because the Countrey was full of Troops, and parties of Souldiers. One of the company, with more heat than discretion , and utterly unskilful in all matters relating to War, seeing some Horse-men upon the Road a good way off, spurr'd on, and without saying one word to any of his own company, rode full speed up to them, crying, *Who are you for? Who are you for?* A Cornet of Horse that was there, who understood the trade a great deal better, presented his Musquetoon, and cry'd, *Nay, who are you for? Come on, alight, and down with your arms.* The Gentleman, much confounded, that he had advanc'd too far, and left those at a distance that should have born him out, and not used to fire and fighting, was lighting from his Horse; but both being in a passion, the quarrel grew so hot, that the Cornet was just going to let fly his Musquetoon at him.

The Sieur *de Pontis*, who assoon as ever he saw this Gentleman ride off from his company so madly, guest what would happen, and said to a person of quality that rode near him, *Yonder is one going to make both us and himself more trouble than he is aware of.* And immediately he, and the person to whom he spoke spurred on. He found the Cornet just ready to shoot, and bore up so briskly to him, that before he could discover him, or defend himself, with fire in his eyes he cryed out all on the sudden, *Down with your arms, you Sir.* This Cornet, as much surprized then, as the Gentleman was before, presently lower'd his Musquetoon, and said, *Ay Sir, with all my heart; I see you understand your business; but this Gentleman thinks to swagger, and knows nothing of the matter.* All this was over in an instant, by reason of the mighty haste the Sieur *de Pontis* made, who by this means sav'd the lives of several persons; for if the Cornet had shot, no doubt a great deal of mischief had follow'd; whereas now, all the disorder was quieted, and presently the Sieur *de Pontis* found a friend of his, among those that were in company with the Cornet, and went and embrac'd him, asking a thousand pardons for the Gentleman, that had begun the quarrel so indiscreetly. And the two acquaintance, after several compliments and expressions of kindness on both sides, drew off their company, and went each his own way , and had after this a very quiet and prosperous Journey.

From this single action, when he was threescore and ten or twelve years old, worn with the hardships of War, and full of wounds and scars, one may make a judgment how vigorous he was in the youth and flower of his age; and what reason Cardinal *Richelieu* had to court so gallant a man over to his party, considering the continual fears he had of his Enemies, which all the world knows were very many, and very powerful.

Besides, the Sieur *de Pontis* had so great a reputation in the world, not only for Courage, but for Wisdom and Experience in all matters, and punctilio's relating to

War,

War, that several years after his retirement, there happening a great quarrel to arise in the Regiment of Guards, between the Lieutenants and the Captains, upon some dispute concerning their particular Commands, the former came in a body, and begg'd Monsieur *Pontis*, as a man whose great knowledge and experience they were content to abide by, to mediate, and decide the Controversie between them. And tho the retired life he had now engaged in, made him a stranger at present to all business of this nature, yet the posture of their affairs would not allow him to refuse it, and he applyed himself to this accommodation with so much greater success, in regard that his integrity, and religious life, and his great age and experience, added weight to all his determinations, and procured him more authority and esteem. So after a prudent management of this dispute, and frequent conferences with the Officers principally concerned, he inclined both sides to agree upon reasonable terms, and settled a very good correspondence between them all again.

Whoever hath read these *Memoirs*, no doubt will be very well satisfied, that the Sieur *de Pontis* was not only a person of great valour and conduct, and capable of taking up quarrels by his prudence, but also of fitting young Gentlemen for the world, and giving them good instructions for the behaving themselves wisely and honourably, which people of quality commonly learn too late, at their own cost, and after having made abundance of false steps. Nor can it seem strange, if after a long experience of the hardships and pleasures of the world, and both by his own, and a great many other peoples example, having discerned the excellencies and the defects of the different ages of man, the vices most peculiar to their several conditions, and the dangers incident to their several stations both in Courts and Camps, he was able to teach others, who had seen less of the world than himself had done. This induced a Gentleman of his acquaintance, who had the care of two young Noblemen at Court, to consult him in his retirement, and beg the assistance of his advice for the discharge of that employment. And though his modesty made him think himself less qualified to gratify this request, especially when he was now in a manner quite out of the world, and above fourscore years old, and being a man, that had made arms more his business, than writing or study; yet there appear several excellent strokes in his answer, many very useful and wise observations, which I suppose the Reader would be well pleased to see in his own words, and therefore I have thought fit here to insert this Letter at large, as he wrote it to his Friend.

The Sieur *de Pontis* his Letter to a Governour of two young Noblemen at Court.

S I R,

IF I were in any degree less your Servant, than I really am, it were very easy to have excused my self, from that proof of being so, which you now desire of me; for I should have made no scruple to own to so good a friend as you, that my great age hath put it out of my power to give you satisfaction, since even my Experience is almost quite lost and gone, and all that is left of that, is only the few Ideas of what hath past over most frequently, and made the deepest impression upon my memory. This is all I am able to present you with, and shall think my self very happy, if any part of it may be of use to you; Tho it were too great a presumption to hope this, in me, who knows with what wisdom and discretion you educate the young Gentlemen committed to your care; and therefore I have great reason to look upon your desires of my advice, rather as a complement, and an effect of your great civility to me, than any argument that you really stand in need of any such thing.

However, in obedience to your commands, I shall take my usual freedom in declaring my opinion sincerely, since you profess some want of directions, how to carry your self to these Gentlemen, with regard to the age they are growing into, in an easy and gentle way, according as you find their temper and inclinations; to moderate their passions and desires, without rigorous and rough

rough methods; *so as that you may keep up a fair character and continue acceptable, both with them, and my* Lord *their Father, and all their Relations of quality, that are but too fond, and seem to adore them. In good earnest, I do not only lament, but bear a part my self in your difficulty and trouble; for indeed you have a great many people to satisfy, a great many faults and defects to amend, and a great many different parts to act, in order to the discharging this trust with credit and success.*

And first of all, I must freely confess to you, that I never could approve the opinion of those people, that are against their Childrens *having any more Learning, than just so much as is necessary for a* Gentleman *(as they are pleased to express it) For since* Knowledge *is the best finisher of humane nature, that which teaches men to reason right, and to speak gracefully in publick; what can be necessary, if this be not, to those persons whose* Birth *and* Employments, *and* Station *in the world put them in such circumstances, as have most frequent occasions to exert these accomplishments?*

I know some are of opinion too, that the conversation of vertuous and witty Ladies, *pollishes the mind of a young* Gentleman, *and gives it a finer turn, than the company of a* Man of Learning. *But I must beg leave to dissent in this particular too, and dare not advise to such conversation, for fear of the many mischievous consequences that often attend it, and that* Youth *finds it self insensibly engaged in.*

Not but that there ought a great difference to be made, betwixt one who is designed to make the Gown *his profession, and one that is to be educated to make a* Gentleman *and a* Souldier. *The former ought to make study the business of his whole* Life; *the other need only follow it, till some fifteen or sixteen years old, so as to get some knowledge of* Philosophy, *of ancient and modern* History, *and the main rules of* Politicks, *and so as to manage himself regularly, and converse with people of several qualities, as becomes him.*

When this is over, it were fit he went into the Academy *to learn to ride, and shoot, and vault, and dance; these exercises will give him a genteel and good behaviour, they will teach him to carry his body straight, to walk gracefully, with a manly and noble mein; to hold up his head, have a steady look, a pleasing countenance, full of civility, always obliging, but without any affectation or constraint. There too he will learn* Mathematicks, *so far as may serve to qualify him for* Fortification, *the attacking or defending of* Towns, *the discovering where* Works *are defective, and how they may be amended; all which (with the addition of your help) may be learnt sufficiently in two or three years time. In my opinion, their failings in these exercises that are of less consequence, should be left to the correction of the* Master, *whose business it is to teach them. But if they contract any ill habit besides, you will do well to make them sensible of it in private. For by dealing thus tenderly with them, their love and respect for you will be the better preserved and increased.*

After they leave the Academy, *I should advise their going abroad into forreign Kingdoms to learn their* Languages, *observe their different Customs and Governments, and entertain themselves with a sight of the most remarkable Curiosities to be met with abroad; and, as a help to their memory in all these things, it were fit they made a Diary of their Travels. But pray be sure you never entertain them with any thing, but what is becoming a man of honour and a* Christian; *that you may excite in them strong desires to practice and imitate such actions as these, and may create an irreconcileable aversion to every thing that is base and low, and dishonourable. But the main point of all, is to make them sensible, that the truest and best way of securing honour to one's self, is the paying Almighty* God *the honour due to him; who always distributes his mercies largely, to those that live in his fear and love. To preserve this opinion in them, you must use great dexterity, in keeping them from all kinds of bad company, but especially from the conversation of lewd and profane wretches, who are the bane of young men, that are setting up for some credit in the world. But this is a very nice and tender, and will require a great deal of good management, so as at once to gain your point, and yet to lose no ground in their kindness and esteem for you.*

You must take special care never to check their passions by authority, and too magisterial a way, nor by correcting them too sharply; but be sure to shew the reasons why you reprove them, chide them with modesty and civility, and satisfie your self with soft methods to bring them into temper. For you are to consider, that some passions are not faulty, nay some are convenient for a man of Quality; such is Ambition in particular, when it puts them forward to follow the Example of my Lord Mareschal their Grand-father; a person that signalized himself upon so many eminent occasions and brave exploits, while he was General to the Kings Armies for many years both at home and abroad; that the King had so high a value for him, and the world so great an opinion of his Courage, that he hath at this very time among most forreigners, the general reputation of one of the greatest and best Commanders of this age.

Some other passions there are so furious and violent, that it is impossible to compose them in a trice, as we see in the case of Anger, and sudden sallies of the Soul. But these are a sort of madness for the time, too strong to last long; and all that can be done in such cases, is to calm and cool them by degrees: For opposition does not abate, but increase their fury, and inclines men to be peremptory and restiff; which by degrees would lessen your credit with them, and lose all the regard they have for you.

You must find a mean for them between a bold indifference, and a timorous bashfulness; and teach them the just differences both between persons and things; what respects are due to persons of quality, and worth, and how they ought to be addressed to; a formal excessive Complement being no less ridiculous an extreme on the one hand, than a Clownish roughness is offensive on the other.

If any sudden misfortune bring them into the inconveniences and hazards so common to Gentlemen now adays, your wisdom must shew it self in taking up the quarrel speedily, by endeavouring to reconcile them through the mediation of Friends, and fetching them honourably off from the ill consequences that attend such quarrels. Your care and good management upon such occasions as these, will above any thing in the world secure you a great deal of honour and reputation, both from my Lord their Father, and all the Families to whom they are related.

Sir, I could enlarge yet more, were I not sensible, that by this time I must needs have convinced you, by what I have taken the liberty to say already, that it is not possible for me to advise any thing, which you do not know much better your self. However, I beg you would look upon this Letter, as a proof of the inclination I have to serve you; and my wishes, that I were capable of doing it; and of my readiness to express to you, that I am most sincerely

                     Yours, &c.

I do not pretend here to any Encomium of the Sieur *de Pontis* his piety, who was so modest after his leaving the world, as never to account himself any better than an old soldier, to whom silence, and solitude, and a life that shut him up from Conversation, were given as his portion; and therefore I shall so far comply with his disposition in this particular, as to add only one thing, which he would often say to an intimate friend of his: That the thing he most dreaded in the service he endeavoured to pay Almighty God, was lest he should insensibly grow fond, and take up with this life,

life, and not sufficiently contemplate the greatness of Him he had the honour to serve. And these apprehensions were the more reasonable in him, because upon continual remembrances of that extraordinary zeal, shewn in all his long hard service to his Master the late King, he might find some ground to suspect himself less zealous, where yet the service was infinitely better, and the Master incomparably greater. He lived about eighteen or twenty years after his Retirement, and at last fell into a very weak and languishing condition; and Nature was so far decayed, that after his first voluntary retreat from the Court and company, he fell into a more strict one the two last years of his life, being lost to all conversation with men, by his extreme deafness; and so finding himself under some necessity of entertaining himself chiefly with Almighty God.

He dyed in the year of our Lord 1670, and of his own age the ninety second; when Nature could last no longer, but was forced to sink under so many years, and so many hardships and shocks, which he had undergone in several Wars, for a long time together. I cannot suffer my self to doubt, but upon the perusal of these *Memoirs*, and considering the many dangers, the cross accidents, and uncommon events, which he was exercised with, every body will be of opinion, that there are some things very surprizing and wonderful, and the marks of a particular providence with regard to him; and that the publishing this account may be of great use, since so many things are contained in it, capable of doing good to those that are about engaging in the affairs of the world, to them that are already engaged, and to them too who have disengaged themselves from it. For all these may learn from this Example of a Souldier, one that had long experience of all the different conditions that could happen to him, both in the Court, and in the Camp, that nothing was ever more true than that observation of the wisest Prince that ever lived; *Vanity of vanities, all is vanity, except the fear of God, and the keeping of his Commandments.*

FINIS.

BOOKS Sold by *James Knapton* at the *Crown* in *St. Paul's* Church-yard.

THE Memoirs of Monsieur *de Pontis*, who served in the *French* Army 56 years, under *Henry* IV. *Lewis* XIII. and *Lewis* XIV. Kings of *France*, containing many remarkable Passages relating to the War, the Court, and the Government of those Princes. Faithfully englished at the Request of his Grace the Duke of *Ormond*. By *Charles Cotton* Esq; Fol.

Lord *Bacon*'s Essays. Octavo.

Scrivener's Directions to a holy Life. Oct.

Dr. *Barrow* of Contentment, &c. Oct.

Sir *William Temple*'s Memoirs of what past in *Christendom* from the War in 1672. to the Peace concluded 1679. Octavo, Second Edition.

———His Observations upon *Holland.*

———His Miscellanies. Two Parts.

Dr. *Tillotson*'s Sermons. Three Volumes.

——— Four Sermons against the Socinians.

The Unreasonableness of Mens Contentions for the present Enjoyments, in a Poem on *Ecclesiastes.*

The History of the Inquisition, as it is exercis'd at Goa. Written by Mr. *Dellon*, who labour'd five years under its Severities, with an account of his deliverance.

Quadrænium Jacobi, or the History of the Reign of King *James* II. from his coming to the Crown, to his Desertion The Second Edition. Twelves.

Plutarch's Lives. Translated by several Hands. 5 Vol.

———His Morals. 5 Vol.

The Life of the Emperour *Theodosius*. Done into *English*, from the *French* of Monsieur *Flechier*, by Fr. *Manning*. Octav.

Kilburn's Presidents. Twelves.

Seneca's Morals. By Sir R. *L'Estrange.*

Norris's Discourses. 3 Vol.

Reform'd Devotions.

Cæsar in usum Delphini.

Processus integri in Morbis fere omnibus curandis a Do. Tho. Sydenham *conscripti.*

A learned Treatise of the Situation of the Terrestrial Paradise. Written in *French* by *Huetius*, and translated into *English* by direction of Dr. *Gale.*

Cole's *English* and *Latin* Dictionary

Robertson's, or the *Cambridge* Phrase, being the best and largest Phrase-Book extant.

Scarron's Novels.

The Governour of *Cyprus.*

The wanton Fryar. Two Parts.

Victoria Anglicana, or an Account of several Victories obtain'd by the *English* against the *French.*

POETRY

POETRY and PLAYS.

BEN *Johnson*'s Works newly reprinted.
Sir *Robert Howard*'s Plays.
Milton's Paradise loft, with Cuts.
Dryden's Juvenal.
—— Miſcellany Poems. *Three Parts.*
Ovid's Epiſtles. By ſeveral Hands.
Waller's Poems. *Oldham*'s Poems.
Cleveland's Poems. *Dennis*'s Poems.
Hudibras, Three Parts, compleat.

Mr. *Dryden*'s Plays bound or ſingle, *viz.*

1 Dramatick Eſſay	14 State of Innocen.
2 Wild Gallant	15 *Aurang-Zebe*
3 Rival Ladies	16 All for Love
4 *Indian* Emperour	17 *Limberham*
5 Maiden Queen	18 *Oedipus*
6 Sir *Martin Marr-all*	19 *Troilus* and *Creſſida*
7 Tempeſt.	20 *Spaniſh* Fryar
8 Mock-Aſtrologer	21 Duke of *Guiſe*
9 Tyrannick Love	22 *Albion* & *Albanius*
10 Conq. of *Granada*	23 *Don Sebaſtian*
11 Marriage Alam-	24 *Amphytrion*
12 Love in a Nunn-	25 King *Arthur*
13 *Amboyna*	26 *Cleomenes*

Mr. *Shadwell*'s Plays bound or ſingle, *viz.*

1 Sullen Lovers	11 *Lancaſhire* Witch.
2 Humouriſt	12 Woman Captain
3 Royal Shepherdeſs	13 Squire of *Alſatia*
4 *Virtuoſo*	14 *Bury* Fair
5 *Pſycho*	15 Amorous Biggot
6 Libertine	16 Scowrers
7 *Epſom* Wells	17 Voluntiers
8 *Timon* of *Athens*	
9 Miſer	Alſo his Odes to
10 True Widow	the King and Queen.

Mr. *Lee*'s Tragedies bound or ſingle, *viz.*

1 *Sophoniſba*	8 *Lucius Junius Bru-*
2 *Nero*	*tus*
3 *Gloriana*	9 *Conſtantine*
4 *Alexand.* the Great	10 *Oedipus*
5 *Mithridates*	11 Duke of *Guiſe*
6 *Theodoſius*	12 Maſſacre of *Paris*
7 *Caſar Borgia*	13 Princeſs of *Cleve*

Mr. *Otways* Plays bound or ſingle, *viz.*

1 *Alcibiades*	6 *Titus* and *Berenice*
2 Friendſh. in faſh.	7 *Venice* preſer'vd
3 Orphan	8 *Don Carlos*
4 Souldiers Fortune	9 *Caius Marius*
5 Second Part of the	10 *Windſor* Caſtle, a
Souldiers Fortune	Poem.

Alſo theſe, and moſt other
Modern Plays.

Mr. *Anthony*	King *Lear*
Abdelazer	Love in a Tub
Bellamira	*London* Cuckolds
Country Wit	Love for Money
Circe	Man of Mode
Chances	*Mulberry* Garden
Cambyſes	*Macbeth*
Country Wife	Madam Fickle
Cheats	Maids Tragedy
City Politiques	Marriage-Hater
Deſtruct. of *Jeruſalem*	Maids laſt Prayer
Duke and no Duke	*Othello*
Devil of a Wife	Old Batchelor
Diſtreſſed Innocence	Plain-Dealer
Empreſs of *Morocco*	*Philaſter*
Earl of *Eſſex*	Pope *Joan*
Engliſh Monarch	*Regulus*
Engliſh Fryar	Rehearſal
Edward the third	*Richmond* Heireſs
Emper. of the Moon	Scornful Lady
Fond Husband	She woud if ſhe coud
Feign'd Courtizans	Siege of *Babylon*
Force't Marriage	*Sir Solomon*
Female *Virtuoſo*	Squire Oldſap
Gentlem. danc.Maſt.	Succeſsful Strangers
Henry V. and *Muſtaph.*	Sir Courtly Nice
Heir of *Morocco*	Sir Patient Fancy
Fortune Hunters	Triumphant Widow
Ibrahim	*Titus Andronicus*
Iſland Princeſs	Treacherous Broth.
Ingratit. of a Com-	Traytor
monwealth.	Vertuous Wife
Julius Caſar	Very good Wife
Injur'd Lovers	Widow Ranter
Innocent Impoſtor	Woman's Conqueſt
Innocent Uſurper	Woman Bully
King and No King	Wife's Excuſe.

FINIS.